WILD IN DEADWOOD

WILD DEADWOOD READS ANTHOLOGY VOLUME 1

LIZANNE AXTEL

CHARLES LEMAR BROWN

ELISE GEDICKE   BRITT JONES

RICO LAMOUREUX   A.L. LONG

VIA MARI   K.O. NEWMAN

AMANDA SPEIGHTS

TINA SUSEDIK

TWISTED TEACUP PUBLISHING

TAKE A WALK ON THE WILD
SIDE OF DEADWOOD...

Listen My Love by LizAnne Axtel

Piper Howard is obsessed with the sultry voice of her favorite audiobook narrator, Ross-C, and jumps at the chance to meet him in person at a book fair. Her plans to discreetly stalk him are derailed when she literally crashes into a brooding stranger—who turns out to be Ross-C himself. As sparks fly, Piper must decide if the real man behind the voice can live up to the fantasy she's dreamed of for so long.

Nowhere in Deadwood by Charles Lemar Brown

With one shot, Violet Daniels starts a string of events that may ruin her world. She must now find a way to save Jack Abbott, the man she shot. The problem is there is nowhere in Deadwood that is safe for Jack Abbott.

Caught in the Cat's Clause by Elise Gedicke

The law states all True Mate bonds are sacred and are not to be denied. I never expected my True Mate to be any type of shifter other than a wolf. Why would I? There was even a law that states shifters can't crossbreed. To my knowledge, there had never been an interspecies True Mate pair before. Until now. My Keegan was a jaguar. So, what do you do when two laws contradict each other?

Every Storm by Britt Jones

After years of serving his country, Morgan Creed returns to his secluded ranch, only to find his life shattered. His wife has run the ranch into the ground, stolen his prized stud stallion and disappeared, leaving him with a 7-

month-old child. Morgan's caught in an unending storm until Harper Emerson blows in bringing a sliver of light and hope.

Deadwood Bound by Rico Lamoureux

Riker, a private investigator out of Los Angeles, arrives in South Dakota to learn more about his family history. While searching his grandparents' cellar, he comes upon a hidden journal dating back to the Old Wild West. What he learns about his great-great-great grandfather's dark past will shake Riker to the core and have him questioning just how thick the blood runs through this side of his family.

Until I Met You by A.L. Long

As one door closes, another opens; this was the case for Dixie Coleman. She never would have believed that she could find love again after losing her husband. But when Bridger Lange steps in to lend a hand, it's like magic.

Furious Protector by Via Mari

When trouble comes to Deadwood, and a certain skill set is needed, I'm the one they call.

I have one thing on my mind when I get to town, and it's certainly not a relationship of any kind.

Until the blue-eyed blonde catches my eye.

She is a force to be reckoned with on a good day, and the job isn't as easy as I thought it would be.

When Jules gets caught in the crossfire, she's going to learn the only protection she will ever need is me.

Killian by K.O. Newman

In the shadow of change, one must find the light, often not in the places first looked. Killian had put Bear Foot Ranch in his rear view the day that he patched in with the Lords of Khaos in Denver. Putting down roots and joining forces with the most unlikely allies will change everything for the new Lords of Khaos: Deadwood.

Love's Beginning by Amanda Speights

In 1879 Deadwood, South Dakota, Laura Miller has built her brothel from the ground up, swearing never to answer to any man—until Jack Bristow comes into her life, forcing her to question everything. Can she hold onto her hard-won independence, or will love lead her down a new path? *Love's Beginning* is a tale of love, loss, and the unexpected choices that shape her future—will Laura find the courage to embrace it?

The Librarian by Tina Susedik

A confirmed spinster, Victoria Forry and her father create a traveling library in the Dakotas. Set up with a wagon complete with books of all genres, with only her mastiff, Salty, at her side, she heads to Deadwood, stopping at gold camps and small towns along the way.

Dr. Zebulon Greer is an undercover agent trying to find the person or persons making counterfeit money. Word has it is someone traveling in a wooden, covered wagon has the plates.

Is Victoria this person or is she as innocent as she appears? Can Zeb overcome his attraction to her and find out the truth?

LISTEN MY LOVE

LIZANNE AXTEL

1

Piper

Once I've checked in to the Lodge, I stand next to my Jeep under the wide, timber framed portico, take a deep breath, and stare back at the grand entrance. Even while driving to South Dakota from my home in western Nebraska I had a difficult time believing I was actually coming to Wild Deadwood Reads.

Bouncing on my toes, I clasp my hands together. I'm really finally here. As an avid reader I've wanted to attend this premier book signing since the very first one. Now eight years later, the crap life's been tossing at me has finally eased and I was able to get away.

Surrounding the building, the pine covered Black Hills stand out in front of a brilliant blue sky. I haven't been back in the area for a good fifteen years. Deadwood has grown and changed since then.

My family vacationed here almost every summer when I was a kid, often coming up for Wild Bill Days. Those are happy memories that ended when my parents both died after a tornado slammed through the hotel where they were celebrating their twenty-fifth anniversary.

I had to grow up fast and take over the management of our family land.

I didn't do a good job.

After a mental shake, I climb into my Jeep. I've found my way since then and now I'm helping other women discover their ideal life paths. While I'm using all my energy to guide and take care of others, I tend to forget about me.

On an emotional level I know the importance of caring for and about myself. I'm really great at 'do as I say, not as I do'. The women currently in residence and employed on my property sat me down a week ago for an intervention. When I agreed to take time off, they actually cheered. Then my forewoman handed me the hotel reservation, a ticket to join the signing authors for breakfast, and orders not to come home without at least one tote bag full of signed books.

The book signing is tomorrow, so today I'm going to go explore Deadwood. I have another assignment from my forewoman's nine year old son. He'd written a report on Wild Bill Hickok and discovered there's this thing called 'Wild Bill Me' where you take selfies with any likeness of Wild Bill you discover around town.

I promised him I'd do my best to find as many as possible and send the photos to his mom. If I find enough and win the big prize we'll share the chocolate coins. That's enough of a reward for me.

Once I make it to the downtown area, I understand why the desk clerk suggested I consider taking the trolley. The race to find a parking spot is like a pack of sharks circling their prey—we're all waiting for someone to leave so we can fight off the others for that empty space.

By some good fortune I'm the only searcher present when an overly full SUV leaves the perfect spot. Grinning to myself, I lock my vehicle. So far everything on this trip is working out great.

I join the flow of tourists exploring the businesses along main street. I grab some pamphlets and cards about the different historical buildings and the opportunities to take a variety of tours. I'm not sure why I bother with all the information. I have to leave on Sunday and most of my time until then will be taken up stalking a few of my favorite authors.

I grab a cold drink and make my way to a huge water tank set up for doggie dock-diving. There's no competition right now so it's a good place to sit, relax, and plan what I want to do with the rest of the day and tomorrow.

Because it's not only authors I hope to meet in person.

I love audio books and frequently have a story going while I work and definitely when I drive. The stories help me focus and the voices of my favorite narrators are like friends keeping me company when I'm alone. Which is, honestly, far too often.

Then there's my all-time favorite narrator. A man who calls himself Ross-C.

The man is an enigma. I've searched online, and asked for help with that from my nine year old friend since I'm not the best with electronic devices. At least I know how to take pictures and send messages on my phone. Even with his help, we still didn't find any information about the man. No photo, no hint where he lives, nothing personal at all. Only listings of the books he's narrated and a couple social media accounts where he reads some really spicy stuff.

I hate to admit I have a subscription for one site and I'm a frequent listener. My guilty pleasure.

Ah, the man's voice... voices... his varied accents sound like he's a native speaker of each place. His tones can go from light and flirty, to deeply sexy in a moment. The thing I like the best? He's got this rumbling purr that's so low it vibrates through my earbuds and settles into my chest. Lower, too. His voice is my ultimate fantasy. The one thing I can count on to relax and bring me pleasure after a long day.

The man must be magical. Some fey being created to excite and thrill with only his voice. I try to imagine what he looks like, but my internal vision changes with each character he portrays. Maybe that's why his identity is so shrouded in mystery. Knowing what he looks like might ruin the illusion.

Not for me. At least I don't think so. I've learned the hard way how to see through the false personas and public faces verses private demeanors. A past so-called business partner was great in public. Everyone loved him. Even me. Until he disappeared with the small profits from our endeavor. Leaving me stuck facing legal issues for contracts and tax documents he'd forged my signature on.

I take a long sip from my soda. I've been lucky. I found a good attorney who guided me through all the bullshit until I was absolved of any responsibility. The lessons I learned—both what to do and what not to do—helped me establish a cottage business and enables me to take in other women who have nowhere else to go.

All I require of the woman I give sanctuary to is the determination to turn their lives around. To do better for themselves, their families, and for the world around us. It's hard work. Emotionally and physically. My spread is tiny compared to the huge ranches surrounding me... partially because I was forced to sell off land to keep what I could. We don't raise cattle, or beautiful horses like our neighbors. I raise bees.

The sun is chasing away the patch of shade I'm sitting in and I'm not ready to move on yet. It just feels good to be relaxing. Using my hip, I scoot my purse along the bench until I'm fully under the awning again. By the time my paper cup is empty, more people are finding seats around me.

I glance at my watch. I've been sitting here doing nothing but thinking and daydreaming for almost an hour? I never take that much time to relax. I'm always doing something.

Taking a deep breath, I smile. I'm not going to berate myself for not having busy hands. Daydreaming about how I'm going to finally meet my voice-only crush was a darn good way to pass the time. Before long there will be dogs leaping through the air, splashing into the long pool in front of me. The spot where I'm sitting is perfect for viewing both the leap and the splash down. I think I'll stick around a bit longer.

2

Charleston

If I ever figure out how I let myself get talked into this weekend, at least I'll be able to come up with some defense for next time. There's a reason I guard my privacy so diligently. Don't allow my face to show in the rare videos I'm forced to make for the book app publicist. If fans knew how to find me, there's a chance they'd overrun my small hometown. If the people in my hometown knew what I actually do for a living, I don't doubt I'd be ostracized or run out of town.

The joys of living in an ultra-conservative small town.

When I suggested a few ways I could attend this book lovers' event and still retain my anonymity—curtains, masks—my ideas were summarily shot down. As were my requests to skip the weekend. Attending is a condition of my continued employment I was told.

Not that I can't record audiobooks anywhere, but my equipment belongs to the app owners and there's no way I can afford to recreate the elaborate and costly setup. I have enough pride in my work to know I wouldn't be satisfied with substandard recordings. Especially without the enhanced bass that augments my trademark sexual purr. If I suddenly disappeared my fans might be disappointed. For a short while. Now when everyone and their chickens have social media accounts, I'd soon be lost in the algorithms. Besides, there's always someone waiting to be the next breakout social media star.

Maybe ending this career isn't a bad thing. Perhaps my time as a premier voice actor is over. I can always go back to doing animation and voice overs. Pays the bills but isn't really fulfilling. Or stimulating. Because, yes, sometimes the books I read are a turn on for me, too. Not all the pauses, gasps, and vocal cues are acting.

I checked into the Lodge a day early and thankfully avoid the small groups of women hovering around the huge lobby seating areas this morning. Hiding out in my suite was already driving me crazy so I'm taking a chance going out in public. Most of the women aren't subtle in their stalking, loudly telling each other what they're going to do once they find me.

Thank god none of them know what I look like. Right now I'm just some guy getting on the trolley. Once seated in the rear of the vehicle I close my eyes and take a few deep breaths. Finally my shoulders relax and the building anxiety backs off. I can do this.

There are crowds everywhere celebrating Wild Bill. Despite all the people, I enjoy the day exploring the Deadwood sites. There's a lot of history packed into this small town and the surrounding Black Hills. I appreciate how the town has incorporated signage for the multitude of historical places and happenings. I had no idea how much history this one area of the country contains. Here in Deadwood they really embrace and celebrate that history.

The gambling doesn't appeal to me. Too many people. Too much noise. I much prefer the solitude and silence of a recording booth. Someday I plan to find a place to live that embodies the quiet and allows me to be who I might be.

With that enigmatic thought shoved to the back of my brain, the scent of food draws me across the street. It's the middle of the afternoon and I'm not really hungry so I settle for an Arnold Palmer and continue toward my final destination for the day. After only turning the wrong way down a street once, I make it to the parking lot where there's a scheduled diving dog competition.

The area is filling up and there's only a few empty spaces on the low, portable bleachers. I watch one spot for a long minute and when no one claims the prime location I move in, hoping the woman next to the space isn't holding it for someone.

Not that I need to sit. I spend a lot of time walking. It's my thinking time, when I make plans, decisions. When I dream. It's just that when I'm in a crowd, I feel less anxious when I'm sitting down. Which I know doesn't make sense. That should feel more confining, less... escapable. When standing, even the imagined press of bodies from a crowd tightens my chest. Makes my stomach clench. I sweat.

It's a control thing. I can't control the movement of others around me but when I'm seated there's a small comfort from the sense of containment. What's to either side or in back of me doesn't constantly change.

I have no idea where my odd enochlophobia comes from. A fear of crowds. I give a soft snort. Just one of those things I was blessed with. My mother's anxiety issues probably had something to do with it. Through study and a few therapy sessions, I've learned to control the physical symptoms most of the time. My solitary walks go a long way to soothe my anxiety. If I can just make it through the next couple of days...

I stand in front of the woman and indicate the empty seat. I mentally clear my throat and speak with an average, low tenor, non-threatening, midwestern voice. "Is this seat taken?"

Shading her eyes when she looks up, she frowns a moment then smiles. "Nope, go ahead and sit. I can't wait for the dogs to start diving."

Making the narrow spot a bit wider, she inches to the side. When I'm seated she leans back a bit and I feel her gaze on me. I glance at her and she says, "That's better. I really couldn't see you with the sun right behind you. Hi. I'm Piper."

"Sorry, I didn't think about the sun." I push the brim of my cap back so she can see my face. I give her a common, ordinary version of my name. "I'm Chuck. Thanks for sharing the space with me."

"Here for the Wild Bill Days?" she asks.

I hesitate before replying. "No. The Wild Deadwood Reads event."

She brightens and her smile outshines the sun. There's sparkles in her brown eyes and tiny lines at the corners like she laughs often. If she has makeup on, it's subtle and minimal. Her mouth, god, her mouth begs for my kisses. Shit, now I'm thinking like the books I narrate. Still, she's beautiful. Possibly the most beautiful woman...

"Me, too. Are you an author?"

"No, I'm, uhh, there in another capacity." Please let that be enough of an explanation.

"Cool. Maybe we'll see each other there."

"What about you?"

"Me? I'm just a book lover. There's a few of my favorite authors going to be here, and I've got a list of others I want to get books from to try. And there's other people I'd like to meet."

"Ah, I see. The cover models, perhaps?" A knot similar to my anxiety forms in my chest. What does this reaction have to do with her meeting cover models? Male models. Ripped male models. The knot spins.

She only shrugs so I'm not sure if I'd guessed correctly or not. Doesn't matter. We might see each other in passing tomorrow, we might not. This is probably our one encounter. It doesn't matter to me what she does.

The agonized squeal of microphone feedback makes me wince. One glance at the tiny platform stage shows me what I already knew. The mic is too close to the speakers. Amateurs.

Piper covers her ears. "Yikes. Too loud."

The announcer gets the feedback under control in a few seconds then glares at someone behind him. I'm guessing that particular someone messed with the equipment. Without further incident, the dock dives begin.

Piper and I chat during the exhibition, mostly comparing the abilities of different dog breeds—which I have no clue about. She's open and tells me about the area of Nebraska she's from. I'd heard of something called the Sand-hills. But from what she says, the land is much different than what I imagined.

She gives me a funny look when I admit to being born and raised in a small town close to the tourist area of Love Beach in South Carolina. We laugh over the differences in the 'sand' of the two areas then she narrows her gaze. "You don't sound like you come from the south. There's not a bit of an accent."

Without thinking, my next words take a distinctly southern turn. "Ah assure y'all, ah do call the south mah home."

"There it is." She touches my arm and electricity jolts from the contact. Her fingers twitch against my skin before she draws back her hand.

Returning to the neutral accent of the Midwest, I say, "I once needed people to understand me and while that accent serves me well in South Carolina, in other parts of the country, not so much. In other words, 'Ah don' get much respect' when I come off too Southern."

She chuckles. "I don't see it, but who am I to judge. Oh look. What are those doxies doing?"

A line up of dachshunds, two regular sized and one a tiny little thing stand at the edge of the dock. Their handlers hold them back with handles on the top of their life vests. The announcer says, "Dogs don't have to be large... or have long legs in order to have fun dock diving. Today we have with us three champions showing off their best dives. First, Max."

One of the handlers moves back, drawing their doxie to a much closer starting line than the large dogs are using. A second handler catches the dog's interest with a brightly colored toy. Bouncing on its front legs, the dog pulls at the restraint. Then the dog runs toward the dock edge, the lure floats through the air, and the pup splashes into the water with the prize tight in its jaws.

The crowd erupts with cheers. Once the noise dies down, the second doxie performs, landing four inches further than the first. Then it's the miniature's turn.

The anticipation surrounding this one little dog's jump feels like everyone in the crowd is holding their breath. This doxie is the feistiest of the three, barking and lunging toward its lure. When released the dog bursts into action, its short legs pumping to propel it from the dock. Success!

We all clap and cheer as the doxie ignores its handlers and swims a victory lap around the tank.

The finals of the competition are exciting but not as much fun as watching the little guys. I remain seated while the crowd disperses, telling myself it's so I don't have to deal with the people. I know the truth. It's because Piper hasn't risen yet either.

"It was nice to meet you, Chuck," she says as she pulls the strap of her bag up to her shoulder. "You made watching the dogs even more fun."

"You, too." I really don't want her to walk away. We'll be in the same location tomorrow, but there's no guarantee I'll see her in the crowd. I want to see her tomorrow. Probably the next day. The day after that.

I always thought when the hero of one of the romances I narrate says or thinks 'mine' about a woman the author was merely using poetic license. Or fulfilling personal dreams. Now, I'm not so sure it's fiction.

Because all I can think of when I look at Piper, is *mine*.

3

Piper

Chuck looks like he wants to say more but isn't really sure what that might be. I've enjoyed just talking with him, watching the dogs show off, and I'm reluctant to leave. I know I should though. Because of those scary tingles when I touched his skin. Of how I feel all jittery inside. How I need... something...

I'm old enough to know what all that means, even if I've only experienced those emotional feelings through books. And listening to Ross-C. I'm also old enough to realize I've got at least ten years of life experience on Chuck. Doesn't fate just suck when I meet someone who I could possibly care for, and he's too young?

Before I think better of it, I ask, "Any plans for the evening?"

His brows draw together and I gnaw on my bottom lip. Have I crossed a line? Misread his expression? Then his face clears. "Sorry," he says. "You surprised me. I was just thinking about asking you the same thing."

"So?" we say in unison then laugh.

He holds up one hand and I nod for him to speak first. "I'm not here with anyone, in case you were wondering."

"Nope, wasn't." I am such a liar.

He rubs his palm along his jawline and my fingers curl. Is his short beard soft? Or bristly?

"You?" he asks. "I mean, friends or anyone you have plans with?"

"Nope again." The truth this time. "I figured on just heading back to the lodge whenever I got tired. Grabbing something to eat somewhere. Hmm, yeah, no. I've got no plans."

"Join me for dinner then? Nothing fancy. I heard good things about Mustang Sally's from the Lodge concierge."

I glance around at the now nearly empty parking lot then point in what I hope is the right direction. "It's that way, isn't it?"

"Yes. I think so. I get turned around in the mountains."

"Aren't there mountains in South Carolina?"

"Some. Nothing like these though. If I remember right, there's a trolley stop right in front of the restaurant that could take us back to the Lodge when we're done."

I pause a moment before saying anything and realize I feel perfectly safe with Chuck. "I drove today, so I'll get us back to the Lodge."

"Don't feel obligated."

"I wouldn't offer if I did. Come on, with all the people in town for the Wild Bill days, who knows how crowded the restaurant might be. Oh, and if you see anything that looks like Wild Bill, let me know. Picture, statue, a guy on the street, whatever."

"Uh, okay. Why?"

"I'm on orders from the son of a... a friend of mine to do the Wild Bill Me challenge of taking a selfie with every rendition of Wild Bill I see. I could use more since I want to win us the biggest prize."

Chuck laughs and that damn tendril of delight curls through my chest, around my heart and tickles down to my belly. And lower. This young man is dangerous to my middle aged libido.

It's not just his voice, or how easy he is to talk with. I like how he looks, too. I've discovered an interesting fact about myself is while I drool over book boyfriends who are ripped and muscular, all angles and hard planes, powerful and sometimes harsh, in real life I've always been attracted to a different type. Give me a lean man with soft edges. Maybe even a bit of what some call a dad-bod, fit but maybe with a bit of a belly. Even better if there's some hair on his chest.

I wonder what Chuck looks like without a shirt.

"Sure, I can do that."

Oh god, how many of my thoughts did I say out loud? "Uh..."

"Help you find more Wild Bills. Sounds like fun."

Now is not the time to lose focus. I'm having dinner with a new friend. That's it. After tomorrow, we'll go our separate ways. I need to remember why I'm here in Deadwood. My goal isn't to hook up with some young guy. My one and only goal is to meet Ross-C.

Dinner is delicious and it's difficult to stick to one glass of wine. The vintage is good, but not as flavorful as the wines being developed across the road from my place at the Turquoise Creek Ranch. Of course I'm partial to their local fruit and honey meads since they use my honey.

Spending time with Chuck is a delight. He makes me laugh with stories about being a child living so close to a touristy beach town, although I sense there's some sadness underlying his happy memories. I'm able to steer the conversation away from me and my past fairly easily. He's trying to impress me so follows my lead. He doesn't have to do that but after I'd attempted dating again a couple years ago, it's refreshing to not have to listen to a guy make everything about himself and then mansplain what I already know.

After eating we stroll to my Jeep. I have the insane urge to grab Chuck's hand and just hang on tight. There's something about this man—this younger man, I remind myself. He's an old soul. That young body though, could never really be interested in someone like me. He may have that sexy dad bod. That doesn't mean he wants a woman on the wide hipped, slightly droopy downside of her thirties.

Fighting back a sigh, I discover another Wild Bill, this time on a sign in a store window. "There's a Bill. Time for another selfie."

"Let me take it," he offers and I hand him my phone.

I arrange myself into a 'vogue' pose with the poster. The song came out the year I was born and was one of my mother's favorites. I grew up dancing with her in the living room. If Chuck understands the visual reference it might make him realize the age difference between us. I don't even want to think about that. He takes the picture, then pulls out his phone and takes another.

At my expression, he grins. "To remember today."

"Well then you need to be in the picture, too. Get over here." I point to the sidewalk at my side.

He moves closer and wraps one arm around my shoulders. Holding his phone at arm's length, he takes a couple of shots then steps away. After checking the pictures he holds out his phone to show me.

"Aw. I'd love copies of those."

"What's your number, I'll send them to you."

I pause my wild thoughts. Do I dare give him a way to contact me?

"I promise I'm not a stalker or anything like that. It's just the easiest way to share. I can... I'll erase your number right after if you want."

Damn it. And he's sensitive and considerate, too. He'll make a wonderful husband for someone. A lucky woman who's more appropriate. Closer to his own age. And why the hell am I thinking about him as a husband? That one glass of wine was obviously one too many.

"No, don't be silly. It's fine. I appreciate that you're understanding about how the world works now. Women need to be careful."

"They do. So, we're okay?"

"Yes, of course."

When we're back at the Lodge, he stares at the entrance for a long time before exiting the vehicle and tugging the brim of his cap down low over his eyes. Almost like he wants to enter the building without being noticed. Then I see groups of women milling around the lobby. There had been women there when I checked in, too.

I circle the Jeep and slip my arm through his. His gaze jerks to me. I shrug and indicate the full lobby with my free hand. "Looks like an obstacle course in there that a handsome guy like you doesn't want to tackle right now. I think I can help you through this. They might not pay so much attention..."

"If I already have a beautiful woman on my arm," he finishes.

"I don't know about beautiful..."

He turns to face me. "You're very beautiful, Piper. Whoever made you believe otherwise..." He shakes his head. "Let's get this over with."

Casual is how we look on the outside. Inside I'm a jumble of emotions. Besides my hand around his elbow and our upper arms aligned, our bodies brush together as we walk. For once I'm happy with my wide hips. From what I can tell we don't attract much attention. Not that I can say for sure, I'm a bit distracted.

When we're out of sight, Chuck takes a deep breath. "We did it."

"How about that?"

"May I escort you to your room? No motives other than making sure you're safe."

What could it hurt? I'm not ready to let him go either. Once my door closes, this night and whatever fantasies are floating in my mind will be over. This isn't one of those 'I just met you but I love you' stories. Today was simply a fun day. "That would be nice."

He waits until the lock clicks open at the press of my keycard then takes a step back. "Good night, Piper. I hope... we run into each other tomorrow. Maybe after... The signing's over at five. Would you join me for supper again? Or breakfast on Sunday before you have to head home?"

Yes, my mind shouts. Both would be fabulous. Reining in my thoughts I nod. "I'd like that. You've got my number. Until tomorrow then?"

"Until then. Good night."

"Night."

We stand there like a couple idiots staring at each other until the noise created by a yet another group of women heading toward their rooms breaks whatever spell we're under. I finish backing through my door. "Sweet dreams."

4

Charleston

I had a rough night. Between my rising anxiety about today's exposure and the hard, throbbing need I experienced every time Piper entered my thoughts, I didn't get much sleep. Luckily the physical need was easy enough to deal with, although in an entirely unsatisfying manner. Those releases thankfully also eased some of my anxiety. At least moaning Piper's name made me forget about showing my face to my fans.

Including Piper. I don't even know if she listens to audio books. Which would be better? If she has no idea who I am and how popular my voice is? Or if she knows and is already a fan? There's also the chance once she discovers how those ladies in the hotel lobby were waiting for me she won't want to have anything to do with me.

Fame isn't comfortable for everyone who stands in the spotlight. I suspect Piper isn't happy to be the center of attention in a group either. Nothing specific tells me this. It's just a feeling. So many feelings have taken residence in my chest over the past—I glance at my watch—twenty hours. Every damn one has Piper at its heart.

Until this weekend I've kept my face and my private life separate from my narrator gig. Despite all the techniques and knowledge I've acquired over the years, I have no idea how I'm going to handle being shoved into the spotlight in a few hours. I don't know. I might be fine. I fucking hope I don't dissolve into an anxious mess. Or run away. Either would be a disaster.

If the worst happens—if Piper witnesses the phobia-induced downfall of the popular Ross-C—what will she do? When my phobia hits hard, I can't always find my way back without someone noticing there's something off. I don't always choose the best method of regaining control. That's when I find a way to escape the situation.

How can I expect someone else to accept or deal with all this?

The best course of action would be to tell the people who brought me here, who insist I become a 'public' personality, just tell them I won't do it. I won't be put on display. Even if that means losing my job, I'll maintain my dignity.

That's what I should do.

But I won't.

Leaving the safety of my room, I monitor my breathing as I make my way to the conference center and the Wild Deadwood Reads book signing. There's a technique I used years ago when I was in high school of slowly building up a sort of tolerance to being in a crowd. Arrive early. Move around the space as much as possible, partially to discover escape routes. Knowing how to get out of the crowded area sometimes lessens the actual need to escape. Seems silly when I think about it now.

Even though I left my cap in the room, out of habit I still lift my hand to lower the visor to cover my eyes. Maybe I shouldn't have tried this without that minimal protective disguise. Leaning against the wall across the hall from the entrance to the conference room I study the flow of people. There's almost a pattern to how they move from one author's table to the next. An instinctive dance I wish I could learn.

Where's Piper? Does she follow the same pattern or make her own way? She'd make her own way. I chuckle at my mental image of her moving against the tide of attendees. Then I alter my thoughts. She wouldn't disrupt the flow, but she would make it her own. Shit, I have no clue what all this means.

Except that I want to see Piper. Even if our paths in the crowded room don't cross, I need to see her. The compulsion is so strong it calls for action. I push off from the wall and ignoring the flash of panic, step through the doorway and into the cacophony.

I'm surrounded by conversations, with the joyous squeals of friends meeting friends, the higher pitched voices of children, the low rumble of the men in the room. There's more of us than I imagined there might be outside of the cover models. Picking out individual conversations and attempting to match the person's speech patterns and tempo in my head to create new characters for myself helps me focus.

As does keeping to the center of the walkways between rows of tables. Most of the attendees seem to bounce from table to table only crossing through the center. Or they use the less traveled space to stop and check their table maps and plan which author to visit next. I keep my pace slow and concentrate on the movement around me. This enables me to avoid many of the accidental contacts.

Stretching to look over the heads of the people near me, I scan what I can see of the room. Damn it. Where's Piper?

5

Piper

Recalling my dreams isn't one of my talents. Usually there's just an odd feeling that I know I've dreamed but no clue as to the content of those dreams. So when I woke up this morning with my mind full of possibilities... With Chuck. I stare at myself in the mirror watching how my brush glides through my hair.

Like his fingers had in my dreams.

Disgusted with myself, I toss the brush to the counter and roughly divide the length of my unruly hair into three sections. I create a braid that will fall over one shoulder instead of down the middle of my back. It's only a little fancier than my regular style. I want to look as good as possible when I finally meet Ross-C later today. I end the braid with a unique scrunchie I've been saving for this special occasion. A plain dark purple elastic with book charms hanging from short ribbons.

Since the organizers are doing a special event to introduce my favorite narrator later this afternoon, I'll have plenty of time to visit with the authors and fill my large book bag. Mentally reviewing my list, I chuckle. Maybe two bags.

The breakfast buffet with the authors is fabulous and gives me—and the other readers—an extra opportunity to meet and talk with our favorite authors. As a bonus, a few authors have special swag to give away just for breakfast attendees. The slight weight in my tote bag makes me happy. It's more fun items I can share with the women under my care.

Some of the models also join us for breakfast, delighting their fans. Echoing my thoughts, I overhear others wishing Ross-C would show up. Then the object of my wishes changes. I wish Chuck was here to share this breakfast time with me. I need to head home early tomorrow so all we really have is today. I want every minute with him that I can squeeze into the day.

He said he'd be at the signing but I don't know in what capacity. Will he be busy with...whatever? Or will he be able to actually spend time with me? Mentally, I shake my finger at myself. He has his life. I have mine. We just happened to cross paths here in Deadwood. There's mutual attraction.

A mutual attraction I really don't know what to do with. As the 'older woman' I need to be the responsible one and nip this in the bud.

I'm damn tired of being responsible.

Maybe I should just see where this desire takes us. There's no reason why our chance meeting can't lead to the more my dreams hinted at. What I think I recognized in Chuck's expression last night. Some naked fun. A one night stand. At least there's a definitive ending point we'll know in advance. We can spend the night with no expectations for the future hanging over our heads. And when the sun rises tomorrow, I'll hopefully have sensual memories to take home with me.

The thought should make me happy. But no, I already feel a miserable sense of loss. This whole situation is crazy. Maybe being around so many romance authors and readers has infused my imagination with possibilities that have no base in reality. There's no guarantee Chuck thinks about me in *that* way. I'm too old for him, too set in my life to have room for a man. Book boyfriends and Ross-C's smooth voice in my ear are all I need.

The authors gather at one end of the room for a group photo. The photographer is efficient in arranging the large group so everyone will be seen. I join many of the other readers in pulling out my phone and taking a few photos of my own. As the authors drift away to find their tables in the big event room, a guy dressed like Wild Bill directs the rest of us toward the hall.

A Wild Bill? I need one more selfie to reach the highest prize level for Leo. Obviously I'm not the only one on a Wild Bill Me quest and laughing, Wild Bill poses with anyone who wants a selfie. Now all I need to do is stop off at the visitor's center in the morning as I leave town...

A foolish wave of sorrow washes over me at the thought of driving away—not from Deadwood, but from Chuck. Squaring my shoulders, I tell myself that's the only way this weekend can end. I may luck out and spend some quality time with him this evening. Or maybe we'll just have supper together. There's even a chance that after a night's reflection, he'll have realized the differences between us are too great and he won't want anything to do with me.

Overwhelmed by so many options, I join the line of readers waiting outside the closed doors of the ballroom. Chatting with the women around me helps me find my center and brings me back to a realistic present. As an impatient group, we pass the few minute until the organizers finally open the double doors. The line behind me has lengthened and disappears around a corner. That makes me happy. Wild Deadwood Reads has been a successful event for many years and with this turnout that's not going to change. Now that I've finally gotten here, I'm already planning to return next year.

Those at the front of the line disburse quickly, some rushing toward specific tables, others beginning a more orderly circuit of the room. Last night as I studied the booth diagram, I decided that an orderly path is the way to go. That way I won't inadvertently miss what might end up being a new favorite author or a fabulous book.

But I don't feel like following the crowd so I move quickly toward the far corner of the room and the last table on the chart. This author writes children's books and I choose a couple for the library I set up in the bunkhouse. Some of the women come to me with their kids and I try to make their transition as easy and comfortable as possible. Books go a long way to help everyone feel at home.

Stopping at every table takes time but I don't want to skip any of the authors or vendors. It has to be damn hard to smile and invite people to interact. Doubly difficult I'm sure for newer authors and first time signers. Hopefully my short visits are encouraging. Eye contact and a smile always seems to brighten an author's expression.

As I move along the row of tables I scan the room looking for Chuck.

With the constant stream of people down each row and adding the tall banners many of the authors use, I can barely keep one person in sight and focus for more than a few seconds. Women are in the majority here, so that helps my search. Recognizing him won't take that long, even at a distance.

I wish we'd planned on a time to meet. At least that way I'd know if there was still hope or if I've been ghosted.

My bag gets heavy and the weight is satisfying. Time to pull out my second tote. I smile as I even out the load between the two totes. Books make me happy.

Not as happy as finding Chuck would be though.

As I get closer to the side room designated for the Ross-C meet and greet I keep my eye on the slowly forming line. I need to make sure I get a seat. It's why I came to Deadwood after all.

A soft, wistful voice in my head claims that if I had to choose between the narrator and the young man who's captured my interest, Chuck would win.

The voice is unfortunately correct. If I only have one possible night with him, I don't want to waste a moment of that opportunity. I'm probably setting myself up for some level of emotional pain. Odd that I don't care. Even odder is that the lack of concern doesn't bother me.

No time to think about all that now. Since I haven't seen Chuck yet, I need to hurry through the rest of the tables and get in the line for Ross-C. Missing his introduction would make two disappointments. Not gonna happen today.

I'd set my heavy bags down while I studied my table diagram. There's a couple vendors of book related items and the cover model area that I don't absolutely have to visit. I don't need to pretend I'm the heroine on a book cover with one of the handsome men who are a huge draw for many of the women here. Probably some of the male readers, too.

Plan made, I bend to grab my bags then back into the main walkway.

"Oof. Hey, careful..."

Shit, I wasn't watching where I was going and I've backed into a solid body. Hands land on my shoulders, keeping me upright when I stumble forward. Dropping the bags that overbalanced me, I turn to find Chuck's grin focused on me.

"When I said we'd run into each other today, this wasn't exactly what I meant." His fingers flex before he releases me.

"Chuck. Finally. I was beginning to think..."

"I wasn't going to show up?"

He's jostled from behind and steps closer to me. Oh, that's much better. "Yeah, maybe."

A faint ruddy color rises from under his beard to tint his cheeks. "I have a confession."

My heart drops to the soles of my feet. I don't want to hear this but for my own sanity, I do need to listen. "Okay?"

He leans a little closer and speaks softly. I strain to hear over the low rumble of conversations around us. "This is, um, well not many people know this. I have an officially diagnosed phobia of crowds."

Drawing my brows together I lean back to study his face. His shadowed expression is wary and when laughter erupts from a group nearby, his gaze skitters that way then returns to me with a hint of fear. I've seen that reaction before in some of the women I've helped. The causes of the fear may be different but the effect is the same.

I take his hand. "I understand. You should have said something sooner. I would have met you somewhere quieter, less... populated."

Relief eases the tightness around his eyes and a bit of a smile returns. "I appreciate that. Thank you. But I need to be here."

He's never said why and I'm about to ask when there's a commotion at the head of the line forming to see the narrator. We both turn and while excitement fills me, he seems to shrink in on himself. Like he doesn't want any attention focused on him.

I offer what I hope will be an acceptable option for us. "I really want to attend that presentation to meet my favorite audio book narrator. From the look of that line, there's probably going to be a lot of people just like me."

Chuck flinches and my concern grows.

"I want to spend time with you after that. And I don't want you stressing or anything by thinking you need to go with me. We can meet somewhere quiet in maybe an hour? With less people? Would that work for you?"

He's staring at the women pressing close to the closed door of the smaller conference room. Now his expression is flat and shut down. Probably a defense mechanism. Once he's no longer surrounded by his phobia, I wonder how long it takes for him to decompress. How can I help bring him back to the man I met yesterday?

Is a strong, clearly debilitating phobia like this a deal breaker for me? Hell, no. I'm a fixer. I help people. And I know everyone has something—a fear, phobia, anger—some baggage we carry with us wherever we go. It's far better for us to have this in the open than for him to try to hide it and his reactions anytime there's a lot of people around.

He would probably find comfort in the wide, open spaces of the Nebraska Sandhills. The quiet of my land. How even crowds like at the county fair or high school sports tend to be more spread out. A woman with an armload of books bumps into me and moves on without even a murmured 'sorry' or 'excuse me'. At home there's more respect for personal space.

The desire to take him there takes root and as I fight the temptation to offer an invitation right this second, I know it's too soon. That would add to his feelings of being overwhelmed rather than comforting him.

He slowly returns his focus to me. "After the presentation? Yes. I'd like that."

A cheer and applause rise as the door to the room opens. After a moment's hesitation I rest my palm over Chuck's rapidly beating heart. "I need to go so I can get a good seat. Will you be okay?"

He blinks a few times. "Okay?" A deep breath lifts his chest and he darts a quick glance at the doorway. "Yeah, I'm okay. I, um, need to be somewhere in a few minutes, too."

"Can I text you when I'm back in my room? We can make plans from there?"

Covering my hand with his, he nods. "Please. I'd like that."

With our gazes locked, time feels like it stops around us. This would be the perfect time to kiss him. Instead, his lips form a sweet, natural smile. "Get going. I'll see you soon."

Then he just turns and walks away.

6

Charleston

How does Piper reach past my fear and uncertainty to offer me a calm such as I've never experienced before? She didn't balk at my confession—although just saying the words didn't explain how it affects me. How it affects my ability to function around people and in uncomfortable situations.

Like this one.

I should have said more rather than just walking away from her. That had to raise even more questions. But not as many as she's going to have in less than three minutes.

I'm counting on Piper understanding why I haven't told her who I really am. She seems to be okay with my phobia so maybe she'll see my lack of honesty as part of that. Shit. Have I been dishonest with her by not coming clean on why I'm at this event? Especially when she claimed I'm her favorite narrator. I've dug myself into a deep hole and now I need to find a way to climb out.

I sneak into the small conference room from the utility hallway and now I'm hiding behind a curtain, lines from the *Wizard of Oz* circling through my brain. *Pay no attention to the man behind the curtain.* Within the next three minutes, though, the attention of everyone in the room will be on me.

The publicist straightens my shirt and circles me with an appraising eye—making me feel like I'm on an auction block. I really wish I'd worn my cap. I'd feel less exposed. That thought makes me realize how much I use tugging a cap brim down over my eyes makes me feel less exposed. Another something to work on.

Finally the dour woman deems me ready to meet my public.

I'm honored so many listeners are fans and may be touched by how I present the words someone else wrote. I know I'd be unknown and still doing commercial voice overs and radio work if not for them. Honestly, there's part of me that's excited to meet them.

Just not all at once.

Most of all, I'm worried I'm going to be a disappointment. From fan emails and even some snail mail forwarded from the AlphaReads app, I'm fairly certain they expect me to look like one of their heroes. Like one of the muscular, physically perfect cover models. Can these women look past the physical me and simply focus on my voice?

Focus. What's the old advice for speaking to a group? Imagine them all naked. Yeah. No. Not appropriate in this situation. Pick out one person and speak only to them. That I can do, as long as that person is Piper. I'm tempted to peek through the curtain to see if I can find where she's sitting but the publicist is guarding that split in the curtain. With my requests for privacy and the room set up here, she already thinks I'm a diva, I'm not giving her any more ammunition.

After a glance at her expensive watch, she arches her brows. "It's time. Ready, Ross?"

No. I'm not. But I nod and take a deep breath. I reach to adjust my non-existent cap and let my hand fall back to my side. I'll find Piper. This is for her. I'll be okay. We'll be okay. Please let her understand.

"Thank you all for being here." The publicist's voice is muffled slightly by the thick curtain. "We're pleased so many of you are sharing this exciting moment with the AlphaReads app. If you're standing at the back of the room, don't worry. I'll have vouchers like everyone found on their chairs available for you. Three months free access to AlphaReads."

There's people standing? They filled all the chairs? Shit. Panic beats against the wall of my chest and I slow my breathing. Again. But the image of the crowded doorway hovers in my brain. No way out. Too many bodies. Breathe.

Wiping my sweaty palms against my thighs, I drag my imagination away from the crowds and visualize Piper's smile waiting for me. There's encouragement in her expression. And something more. Desire. Am I only imagining this, or have I seen her heart and not realized it until now?

"... introduce to you for the first time in person, our number one requested narrator, Ross-C."

I straighten as the curtain is pulled to one side. It's just me. And a room filled with expectant faces. Where's Piper?

The applause and cheers fade. Restless whispers fill the room filled with doubt and disbelief. I knew I'd be a disappointment.

"Say something," the publicist hisses at me.

I lift the microphone but remain silently scanning the crowd. Where?

There. Second row, way at the end. She's leaning forward, her eyes wide with what I hope is only surprise. When our gazes meet she dip her head, hiding her reaction. My heart sinks. I've lost her.

Then she straightens and holds my gaze. I wish I was closer so I could clearly read her expression. She smiles softly, gives a sharp nod then mouths, 'You're okay. You can do this."

When all I do is stare, she jerks her head toward the room and taps her finger at the base of her throat. 'Talk to me. They'll listen."

Her belief in me gives the mental shove I need. Keeping my eyes on her, I hold the mic close to my lips and a sexual purr rumbles into the room. This is the place for my deepest, sexiest voice, the one authors of dark romance choose most often. The purr turns to a growl. "You honor me, my lovelies. I... hmmm... your interest... hmm, oh yes, it is oh, so stimulating. I would return... the favor." Another purr.

The room erupts with sighs and soft moans. Piper's lips twitch and she leans back in her chair. 'See,' she says silently. 'Keep going.'

I move to the small table set on a riser and sit next to it, facing my fans. The anxiety is still buzzing along my nerve endings but I'm under control. I find my normal voice and say, "Thank you for being here. I appreciate your interest in my work."

"Do MacArthur," someone shouts from the back of the room.

"I've voiced more characters than I've kept count of. I'm not sure I remember every single one of them by name." Thank god the crowd laughs. Another layer of anxiety fades. My tone remains a clear tenor but I add a faint Scottish accent. "However, I do remember Mac and how he... hmm... seduced his woman with little more than a fierce kiss... ah, yes... and a swat to her backside."

The room explodes with more character requests and I spend the next ten minutes in an odd combination of this public space and my own private world. Luckily that helps keep me calm and less of a flight risk. And it's a good test of my memory. I had to ask a couple of times for a little more information to focus in on a single character. Maybe when I get home, I'll actually figure out how many sexual fantasies I've brought to life.

Piper won't care. The number won't impress her.

Piper's voice rises above more character requests. "Probably like most of us here in the room, I'm your biggest fan."

Laughter stops the other requests and she continues, "I have a question instead of a request. I'd like to know how you got started doing audio book narrations."

The idea of her as my biggest fan makes me smile as I answer. "I was a theater nerd in high school and loved taking the character roles." I indicate myself from head to toe. "Never was built to be the hero. Always the sidekick or an occasional bad guy along the way. That's when I started experimenting with different voices and vocal techniques."

After that the questions focus more on process and ability rather than me performing actual voices. I become more comfortable and relaxed and the hour speeds by. I'm scheduled for another half an hour to be available for autographs and the dreaded fan photos. I thought that would be more than enough time when the event coordinators contacted me. With the number of women lining up while I shift behind the table it might not be long enough.

The publicist smirks and places a stack of five by seven photographs on the table followed by a few markers.

"Where did you get this?" I ask as I pick a picture up to study my own face. The photo is a couple years old but other than my hair being shorter, I haven't changed much.

"We've had it on file. You don't remember having to submit a photo as part of your application, do you? Have fun." With another twist of her lips, she walks away. I really dislike her.

My feelings are totally opposite for the first visitor to my signing table. "Piper. Thank you." I hope she understands the depth of my appreciation for what she did for me this afternoon.

"I'm glad I helped. We can talk later." She glances over her shoulder at the long line. "You've got some work to do, Ross-C. I'll be in the lobby by the fire-place whenever you're done."

"I'll be there as soon as I can."

"Start your signing with one for me, please." Her grin is infectious and after signing a simple *Love, Ross-C* while wishing I could express more, I hand the photo to her. Then I turn my smile to the young woman next in line and get into character.

"What's your name, love," I purr.

7

Piper

It's probably going to take longer than the organizers planned for Ross to sign autographs, so I have a little time to myself. I head to my room to drop off my heavy bags. I got a great haul that will keep me in reading material for a few months.

I hold my emotions in check until I reach the elevator. Thankfully I'm the only passenger because... oh my god. I drop my bags and slump against the wall. Chuck is Ross-C? "Holy shit. Chuck is Ross-C."

Fantasy and reality have just slammed into each other and I'm not sure what to think. Or what to do. I like Chuck. A lot. He may be a momentary distraction but he's still a real person. Ross-C has always only been fantasy. A voice that elicits the deepest desires. Now, the two are one in the same.

How am I going to handle this situation and my scattered emotions?

The elevator doors whisper open on my floor. In my room I set my tote bags on the desk and sit on the end of the bed to revisit the past couple of hours. Maybe that will help me clear my head.

I'm so proud of how Chuck—or should I call him Ross-C now? —handled his reactions to the crowd. At the end of his Q and A he appeared reasonably relaxed. I don't know if the number of time he looked at me while he spoke made any difference but it sure made me feel good.

Especially when he showed off so many voices and each accompanying deep rumble. His trademark purr. Sometimes though, it was more of a growl that settled in my chest. It's as if the rumbling is created just for me.

Does everyone who listens to Ross-C feel that way, too? Does his purr affect them in the same way? I sure as hell hope not. I want that just for me. I want him, just for me. At least for tonight.

Or is it Chuck I want to be with tonight?

Giving up on trying to find answers, I decide to change out of my rumpled shirt. On impulse I'd packed a sundress and this evening is the perfect time to ditch the jeans and be a little feminine. I don't wear makeup so creating a French braid is enough to complete my new style. After glancing at the few items in my non-makeup makeup bag, I slip my toothbrush into my purse.

Just in case.

Sitting in my room isn't going to answer any of my questions so I go back downstairs. After peeking into the conference room I guesstimate it will be another half hour at least until Ross is able to escape. I find a comfy chair near the fireplace in the lobby and settle in to wait.

It's been a long day and my breakfast wore off a long time ago. Taking a chance I discover there is a DoorDash in Deadwood so I order some Mexican food for Chuck—Ross—and I. That should be safe since we'd discussed our mutual love of soft tacos while at the steak house yesterday. Chuckling to myself at the memory, I complete the order and settle in. Hopefully the timing will work out and we'll have warm food for supper.

I should have brought one of my new books down with me to keep my mind from wandering. Although I'd probably be imagining Ross reading it which would defeat the purpose. I stare into the cold fireplace instead and lose myself in daydreams of Chuck's handsome face combined with Ross's compelling voice.

"I don't know how celebrities deal with all the signing." Ross plops down in the chair next to mine and flexes his fingers. "I have permanent writer's cramp."

"Poor baby. The price of fame."

"Ugh." He sits forward with his hands clasped between his knees. "I'm sorry, Piper. I should have told you. I can't imagine what you must have felt to suddenly see me when the curtain opened. Or what you're feeling now."

"You for sure surprised me."

"Are you angry? Hurt?"

I pause for a moment to categorize my scattered thoughts. "No. Never angry. Maybe a little hurt. Because you didn't trust me, I guess. Or that you didn't really care enough for me to know." Pain and regret fill his eyes. Reaching out I rest my palm over his clasped hands. "That was just momentary. I know you had reasons for not saying more about yourself. Besides, I'm just someone you met by chance at a weekend event."

"No. Not just someone."

"In any case I'm good with moving on from that point."

"Piper, I promise you—"

My phone chirps. I grab it from the side table and grin at the message. "Supper's on the way."

"Piper..."

"We can talk later if we need to. I'm okay. I told you about the women I work with. I've dealt with my own past and trust issues—stories for another time. As much as I can, I understand why you kept Ross a secret. In fact, I bet you hoped to get out of this afternoon somehow so nobody would ever know Ross-C was even here."

"How? How did you figure that out?"

"I've learned to watch people, to see what their words and actions mean. Because it's not always the same as what they say."

"You're a wise woman."

"Don't know about that. I've learned from experience, I guess." This would be a good time to bring up our age difference. But, thank god, my notification tone goes off announcing the arrival of our take-away.

"I've got it," Ross says as he rises to meet the delivery driver. I'm not surprised when he hands the girl an extra tip. It's just one of those little thing that show him to be a kind and caring person.

"So where shall we dine?" he asks.

"The patio area?"

His nose crinkles as he thinks and glances around the lobby. "Know where that is?"

"Follow me, mister gets turned around in the mountains." I take the bulging sack and wince at the weight. I may have over ordered.

"Lead on, MacDuff." Lifting the cardboard drink carrier, he peers at the large cups. "Four drinks?"

"Not intentionally. The poor kid who took my order didn't understand what an Arnold Palmer is and got really flustered. Even when I described how to make one. So I ended up ordering a lemonade along with a tea. And a cup of ice to mix them in."

"You went through all that for me?" He stops and when I realize he's not at my side, I turn back. Tipping the drink carrier, he spreads his hands. "Piper, I don't deserve your kindness."

"Being deserving has absolutely nothing to do with me, or anyone else for that matter, being kind. Get over yourself, Ross."

He hangs his head. "Sorry."

Being so contrite is adorable and all I want to do is wrap him in my arms for a long hug. Well, maybe that's not all. Here in the hallway isn't the place for any of it. I settle for taking his free hand.

I'm pleasantly surprised there's only one family enjoying the early evening on the patio. Ross and I sit at a small table and spread out our Mexican feast.

Long after we've finished eating we've moved our chairs closer and sit shoulder to shoulder watching the evening fade to twilight. The earliest stars twinkle as we talk. Mostly unimportant topics yet the words seem to bind us together. I have never been so comfortable around a man before.

I'm not sure how to handle this feeling. I know what it's like to have the threat of disapproval hanging over my head. Of being afraid to disappoint in some way. There's none of that with Ross. In just a couple of days I met a man, a younger man, and damn it, I've fallen in love with him.

I glance sideways at him. His head's resting on the tall back of his chair, his eyes are on the sky. The epitome of relaxation and calm. But he's not calm. He's still flexing his fingers against his thigh although I'm not certain his hand is still cramping. Then there's that bulge behind his zipper.

He wants what I do. So why doesn't he make a move? At least say something. Aw, hell. I'm tired of waiting. If I'm wrong about his condition then I'm wrong. It won't be the first time. "Ross, give me your hand."

He jerks slightly and turns his face toward me, his brows low in question. "Huh?"

I tap his shoulder. "Your hand. The one that you wore out signing your autograph."

His low chuckle is encouraging.

"I'll massage it for you," I say, letting my eyes drop to his groin for a brief moment.

The chuckle cuts off suddenly. "Piper?"

I arch my brows. "Hand, please."

Holding my gaze he lifts his hand and presses his palm to mine. I turn my attention to stroking his fingers and applying pressure to the tight tendons and muscles.

"That's good. So good." He closes his eyes and purrs.

8

Charleston

I'm not sure how long Piper strokes and manipulates my hand before releasing me, but feeling her hands on me wasn't long enough. My hand is relaxed, my dick however is about as far from relaxed as it can be. This can't be the end of the evening.

Attempting to ease the discomfort of my tight jeans, I angle onto one hip and reach again for her hand. After pressing my lips to her palm, I slip easily into one of my favorite characters, my accent a soft Cajun drawl. "Come back to my room, *cher*."

She sighs. "Ross, you don't need one of your voices. The real you is who I want to know. Not a voice. Not a character someone else wrote. You."

I spent long enough this afternoon talking to fans while using my entire repertoire of voices. Honestly, it's difficult to focus on not performing. Clearing my throat and taking a deep breath helps to a certain degree. "I'm going to need your help."

Surprise lights her dark eyes. "My help? I don't understand."

Admitting this isn't easy. Neither is being myself. When around women, it's often simpler to assume another identity. Then if I'm rejected, I can tell myself it's the character who hasn't succeeded. Not me. I'd noticed the quickly hidden disappointment in some of my fans when they met the real, physical me. They were hoping for a body that matches a voice.

But what voice goes with a dad bod with no visible abs? There's no sharply chiseled jaw under my beard. I'm comfortable with myself. I just don't want to disappoint Piper. "If you wish to know the real me, then you'll need to stop calling me Ross. Use my real first name."

"Chuck?"

A good, boring name, but it's not me. Until I heard it from her lips, I never liked it. I wait a long moment before shaking my head. "Charleston."

She gives me a doubtful look, mirroring my feelings about the pretentious name. "That's a bit much, isn't it? What about a nickname? Do you have a favorite?"

"My name is either great for nicknames, or a real pain. I can't think of any I've particularly cared for. Dad used to call me Charlie. Mom still uses my full name. I'll never be anyone but Charleston to her. And she won't even tell me why she chose that name."

Piper clasps her hands at the base of her throat and sighs dramatically. "Maybe a long lost love."

I shudder. "That's creepy."

Her teasing grin fills me with hope. "Or a character in a book."

"That makes more sense. Hell, maybe she named me after the city. We did vacation there quite a bit when I was a kid. I suppose the why doesn't matter."

Tapping her finger against the table, Piper makes a few suggestions. "You used Chuck yesterday. We could stay with that."

I frown my opinion and she makes shooing motions with one hand. "Okay, so not that. Maybe take the end of your name and be Easton. Or just Ton. No, that's silly. Give me a minute."

Fascinated at how her open expression draws me closer, instead of leaning in to kiss her, I force myself to ease back in my chair and watch her think.

"Let's see, Charleston. Charles. I've heard Carl used for that." She wrinkles her nose and shakes her head. "No, you don't look like a Carl. Chip? Chase? No, none of those either."

"Maybe a nickname is a hopeless cause." It doesn't really matter to me. I want to hear my name—whatever version she chooses—in her soft voice, how she modulates the syllables as her moods change. How she whispers it in satisfaction, screams it in release.

Fuck. I shift but the movement does little to calm my insistent dick. Time to rethink my invitation. Maybe Piper in my room, alone, is not a good idea.

Or maybe it's the best idea in the universe.

"I know," she says and I watch as a faint blush rises to cover her cheeks. "When I was a teenager my favorite book was a fantasy called *When The Eagle Screams*. I had a book boyfriend crush on the hero. His name was Chaz. I could, if you don't mind..." She lowers her gaze then looks up at me through her long lashes. "I could call you Chaz?"

Chaz. A book boyfriend name seems somehow appropriate. "For you, sweet Piper, I am Chaz."

"Good. Now about that invitation..."

Without another word we rise together, gather our trash and leave the patio. The elevator is crowded with readers. Piper stands slightly in front of me, shielding my... condition from the women who eagerly ply me with questions and requests. Many of them have obviously been enjoying the hotel bar.

Their giggles and overly loud goodbyes follow us down the hall until the doors close on the continuing party. Pausing outside my door, I look into Piper's eyes and silently ask a question I can barely find the words for. In answer, she rests one hand on my shoulder and touches her lips to mine. The briefest, lightest kiss.

Once the door closes and I turn on a light I'm surprised at the condition of my room. Now I'm thankful I'd forgotten to put the no service tag on the door. The bedding on the king mattress is smooth and wrinkle free, so my restless night isn't exposed. The pile of towels next to the tub is gone with clean linen folded on the rack. Even that pristine fold in the toilet paper is perfect.

A faint pink highlight's Piper's cheeks and she jerks her thumb at the bathroom. "Mind if I...?"

While she's in the bathroom I turn one bedside lamp to its lowest brightness then darken the rest of the room. The small circle of light is enough to provide illumination without the stark light from the other fixtures.

Piper pauses with her hand on the doorframe but I've made the room dim enough I can't read her expression. Finally she crosses the room. "Mind if I open the drapes? Your room is higher than mine. I'd like to check out the view."

I join her at the window. After a quick glance at how the final light of the day catches on the pines covering the Black Hills, I watch her reflection in the glass.

"I know you're looking at me," she says before pulling out the desk chair. "Chaz, we need to talk."

Uh oh. Not a good sign. Talking is one of the furthest things from my mind right now. And I know when a woman says 'we need to talk' in this situation, it's not looking hopeful for me. Even my dick knows and some of the blood flows back to my brain. I sit on the corner of the bed closest to her and have to clear my throat before I say, "Okay?"

"Chaz, I like you..."

Great, she's moving me into the friend zone.

"Probably more than I should. Because there's a big difference in our ages. I'm not sure... How old are you?"

She's hung up on age? A short wall of hope stops my downward 'only friends' spiral. I could add a few years to myself, but I won't. I've already used up my quotient of misdirection and half-truths. "Twenty-six. And you?"

She squints one eye at me. "I thought you were younger, with at least ten years between us. Thirty-five."

"Only nine years then. I don't understand. How does that make a difference?"

Her expression is sad and resigned. "You should be with someone closer to your own age."

What a bunch of bullshit. "Piper, you're a reader. You listen to the books I've narrated. Isn't one of the most popular tropes an age gap?"

She shrugs one shoulder. "Yes. But it's the man who's older."

"And that's okay with you?"

At her nod, I slip to my knees in front of her chair so I can gather both of her shaking hands in mine. "Why are we any different? There's plenty of cougar romances."

"Oh, so I'm a cougar now?" The spark of desire returns to her eyes.

Lifting one of her hands, I press her palm to my cheek. "And you make me purr." Putting action to my words, the sound rumbles in my throat.

"Chaz, I..."

"Don't you want me to purr for you? Isn't that what this evening has been leading up to?" I nuzzle her palm, rubbing my beard against her skin. She rewards the action with a gasp. "Piper, you could be a hundred years older and I would still want you."

She chuckles. "You're being ridiculous."

"Nine years doesn't sound so crazy now, does it?"

Silent, she watches me and catches her lower lip between her teeth. I'm barely able to contain my groan and press another kiss to her palm. "Not so crazy. Not for one night," she mumbles.

No, not for one night. I want forever. She is my future. My love. Mine. If I say any of this now, she won't believe me. Think it's just a trick to get into her pants. Probably figures I have a harem of fans. Those thoughts couldn't be further from the truth. It's too soon to expose the depths of my feelings. Sex is great but tonight I will be making love with her.

I move my lips to the inside of her wrist then trail soft kisses up her arm. Her flowy dress has short sleeves and once I meet the barrier of fabric, I move my nibbles to her shoulder, following the low, round neckline.

Her breath comes in short pants and her fingers tangle in my hair. "Chaz, I have a confession."

"Another one?" I murmur against her warm skin.

Moving her fingers under my chin, she lifts my head. "I did a little snooping."

There's enough desire fogging my brain I lower my brows and tilt my head in question. I've got no clue what she's talking about.

She digs in a pocket then pulls out her closed fist. "I shouldn't have, but I peeked into your grooming kit. Thought—hoped we'd need these."

I hold my hand under hers and she drops a few crumpled condom packages onto my palm. The hopeful run I made to the store this morning is paying off. I toss them over my shoulder on to the bed. "Yeah, baby, you know we will."

9

Piper

Chaz—oh, how this name feels right to me. Chuck never seemed to fit. Charleston is too proper. Ross-C belongs to his fans. Chaz belongs to me. I wish. For tonight he is my wish come true.

He rises to his feet and pulls me out of the chair and into his arms. He's warm and solid and my arms slide around him like they belong there. His palms against my back mold me closer. I rest my cheek against his chest and sigh.

"Piper, I want you to know... need to tell you..."

Reluctant to move I lean back only enough to see his face. "Do you have a confession, too?"

He blinks in confusion then his chuckles spark delightful shivers wherever our bodies touch. "I suppose this could be. It's been a long time. A really long time since I've been with someone. Even wanted to be with a woman."

His statement doesn't surprise me. From what little I really know about him, he's not the kind who's into casual relationships. That thought does surprise me and my breath catches. So what is he doing with me? We can't be anything more than casual. We won't be together once the morning comes. The only real outcome is that I'll go home with memories.

I'm damn sure going to make sure they're good memories.

"I have to admit my sex life has been just as lackluster." I rise to my toes to kiss him. "How about we change all that tonight, Chaz?"

"How about we start right now?" Skimming my hips with his palms, he gathers the cotton fabric of my sundress and pulls it over my head.

"Careful, Chaz. I'll need to wear that back to my room."

"Who said you're going back to your room?" Then he lifts me in his arms. After a quick kiss, he turns and tosses me to the bed. Holding my gaze, he strips off his shirt and kicks off his shoes. Then he stretches out beside me and props his head on one hand, his gaze roving over my body.

I don't try to cover myself. He's got to know what he's getting with an older woman. My hips are wide, my belly soft and a little poochy. I'm not sure I'm ready to lose my underwear yet though.

"Piper, you're beautiful, baby." He arches one brow and drops his voice. "Don't you dare try to tell me otherwise." Then Chaz returns. "You are perfect as you are."

Tentative, stroke my fingers through the soft hair covering his chest and trailing lower down his belly. "So are you."

"Now that we've got that settled," he says before he pulls me closer for a much more satisfying kiss. This is the one I'm going to count as our first kiss. He teases and tempts, nipping at my lips then soothing with the slow dance of his tongue. At last when our tongues meet, he sighs and, god help me, purrs. This isn't a character. Isn't him playing a part.

I don't know how I'll be able to leave this—him—behind.

It feel like I'm drowning in him, in our kiss. I don't need air, only this. Then he skims his hand down the front of my body to my navel then back to my lace covered breasts. He thumbs my nipples to tight peaks then takes each into his mouth. The scrape of his teeth shoots pleasure and need straight to my core and with a moan, I arch my hips in invitation.

Chaz lifts his head and grins, then returns to his ministrations. His mouth distracts me so I don't realize his hand has moved under the elastic of my panties and curved over my mound. Then he returns to possess my mouth and capture my sighs with his kiss. He repeatedly draws one finger along the seam of my sex, each pass going lower and deeper.

"Ah, there it is," he groans as he touches the evidence of my arousal. When he draws the slick heat up and circles my clit, I'm embarrassed by my whine. Somehow he senses my discomfort and nips my earlobe before whispering, "Don't hold back, baby. I need to hear every sound, every desire. Tell me, show me. So I please you."

"You do. Oh. Oh."

"That good, baby?"

"You know it is."

"Not unless you let me know." Drawing his lips lightly over my skin, he moves down my body. My panties disappear. He cups one hand under the small of my back. "Lift your hips."

Planting my feet against the mattress, I do and he slips a pillow under my butt. There's a vague question running through my fuzzy brain. Where, when did he grab a pillow?

Using his fingers, he spreads my folds. "Beautiful, baby. Glistening." Then his mouth is on me and who the hell cares where a pillow comes from. He takes a long slow lick. "Delicious."

He hums his delight as he uses his mouth, his tongue, his fingers to wind my body tight. Different than his purr, the hum vibrates through me but just before I'm ready to fly over the edge, he slows. Stops. Damn it.

I lift my head to find him watching me. "Chaz?"

I can't see his mouth but his eyes seem to sparkle in the dim light. "Yeah, baby?" he says and the movement of his lips trigger my orgasm.

Twisting my fingers in his hair, I hold him in place as I cry out my release. Before the orgasm fades, he begins again, his fingers and mouth more insistent than exploring. My muscles tighten. Every cell of my body focuses on the renewed pleasure, demanding more.

"That's it, baby. Come for me again." I don't know if he says the words, or if I imagine them but when his lips tighten around my clit and he hums...

A silent scream vibrates my throat as my hips arch, begging for more. Despite how I writhe with the pleasure, Chaz stays with me, not allowing my body to calm, driving me to a third orgasm.

I've never come this hard before. Before the tremors ease, I burst into tears.

He crawls up the bed beside me and gathers me into his arms, shifting me so I'm sitting in the cradle of his crossed legs. "Shh, baby. It's okay. Did I hurt you?"

"No... no, of course not." I attempt to wipe my face with my palms and he catches my fingers then reaches over me before pressing a corner of the sheet into my hand. "I can't... not this..."

"I don't have a shirt on for you to dampen with your tears."

I sniff again then give in and wipe my nose with the sheet. "You read too many romances."

He chuckles. "Enough to know that tears are also a release of tension and emotion. It's okay, baby. Cry if you need to."

Fresh tears threaten. What the hell is wrong with me?

He presses a kiss to my forehead and removes the elastic band at the end of my braid. Tender fingers move through my hair, releasing the braid. He continues to stroke over my scalp. Now I feel like purring. "I love... your hair, Piper."

I sense he was going to say something else. I don't care. Right now he could recite the dictionary and I'd be happy. As long as he uses his real voice.

Finally I feel in control again, although Chaz's attentions are building an undeniable need for him. When I toss the sheet behind me my hand lands on a crinkly square. Ah.

"I want something, Chaz."

"What, baby?"

I don't say anything, just hold out the condom.

"You sure?"

I give an eyeroll worthy of a moody teenager and he gives a soft snort. "I want this too, Piper."

His erection is hard against my hip and must be uncomfortable. My wiggle makes him groan. "Then what are we waiting for?"

Before he moves, I capture his bearded jaw in my hands and kiss him hard. I don't want there to be any doubt, any questions between us. Then I move from his lap and while he strips out of his jeans I kick the bedding to the end of the mattress.

"Take off the bra." His voice is raspy and filled with wanting.

Holding the condom package between my teeth, I watch him watching me. The intimacy of the moment wraps me in comfort. Almost like we've been together like this for years. Maybe lifetimes. The idea is silly of course but I hold tight to the feeling. This will be something to cherish in the coming years.

Once we're both naked he joins me on the bed. I hold out the condom but he shakes his head. "You do it, baby. Please. I need your hands on me."

I push on his shoulders until he lays back then curl against his side and wrap one leg over his. He lifts my hair and lets it drift down like a waterfall. "I want to feel your hair everywhere. But not this time, Piper. I'm too ready."

His voice deepens but this time I don't mind when the character comes out. "I... hmm, I'm hard for you... so hard... you... ah, Piper... fuck, yes."

With one hand wrapped around his cock, I use my teeth to open the condom. After a few light strokes that bring out a growl, I roll on the protection then lay back, pulling him half on top of me.

Braced on his elbows, he lifts his body and adjusts his position. With the head of his cock teasing me, he freezes. "Need to make sure you're ready."

"Chaz, sweetie, I am so ready. Don't make me wait."

He leans in for a long, possessive kiss. "Help me in."

I wrap my hand over his and guide him... home. The only word expressing how I feel at this singular moment. He's home.

"Move," I complain and pinch his earlobe.

"Hey, woman. That hurt." Despite the whine, his smile is softly irreverent and damn sexy. The best part, he begins a slow, smooth thrust and retreat.

Our hands are everywhere, learning each other's body, discovering the depths of pleasure and climbing to the heights of ecstasy. Our kisses are both sweet and demanding, passionate and caring. There are no words, only the sounds of delight and longing.

Until his cock hits just the right spots. "Ah, there. Like that... Chaz..."

A faint voice in the back of my head says I'm a fool for acknowledging the perfect stroke. Past partners have always taken that as a sign to go faster or harder. Or both. But Chaz keeps the same easy pace, building on the constant pressure until I'm gasping.

Then he slips his hand between us and presses on my lower belly. Sparks ignite. He takes my mouth in a wild, fierce kiss, capturing my cries as I explode. Then with a deep groan he straightens his arms and arches his back. His hips jerk and his strokes are short, hard, furious.

He throws his head back and pistons into me. I wrap one leg over his butt and press him tighter. A deep growl sounds in his chest and he drops his head, eyes wide as he holds my gaze. "Pi...per. You're mine. Say it."

I won't fight my emotions and will only speak truth to him. "Chaz, yes. Yours. I'm yours."

He presses my hips deep into the mattress and it feels like he's grown thicker, harder inside me, filling me until... I keen his name as another orgasm cascades over me.

"God, yes... fuck..." I swear I feel each pulse of his release, imagine how it would feel without the latex barrier. His arms shake. I wrap him in my embrace and pull him down, gladly bearing his weight in the long moments as his release calms.

"I'm heavy," he says.

I tighten my hold. "Oh my god, yes. You are. But I love the feel of you on me. In me."

He yawns then give me an abashed look. "Sorry, baby."

"Don't be. I didn't sleep well last night. I could use a little rest. Maybe a short nap."

"Stay with me?"

"I'm not going anywhere tonight, sweetie." I'll deal with leaving in the morning. I'm not going to do anything to spoil what's happened, or what may happen the rest of the night.

"Good." He kisses the tip of my nose and rolls off me. "Wait here. I'll get us cleaned up then I'll hold you in my arms while we rest up for round two."

The play of his butt and thigh muscles as he walks to the bathroom make my mouth water. I hear his soft moan, probably as he removes the condom and bite back a grin. Even that's a sexy turn on. I have got it bad for this man.

He stops at the mini fridge on the way back to bed and hands me a bottle of water. "Hydrate, baby. And let me clean you up."

Once he's satisfied with his aftercare, and that I've finished the water, he crawls back into bed and pulls up the covers. Tucking me against his side and encouraging me to rest my head on his shoulder, he asks me which of his narrator voices is my favorite.

"I like your Chaz voice best," I reply.

"Not what I asked."

"Fine. I think I like the one with the very slight Russian accent. But if you ask me tomorrow, that might change."

"Then I will ask tomorrow," he says slipping into that voice. "Now, my Piper." He purrs sending awareness speeding along my spine. "Shall I tell you what we are going to do after our rest period? Or make you wait? Ah... baby...I think waiting is best. You will rest now. Sleep. Imagine what I may do when you wake. The anticipation, you know, is... hmm... purrrrrrfect."

10

Charleston

Early morning light is pouring in through the open curtains when I wake. I'm wrapped around Piper, my morning wood trapped against the soft globes of her ass. I don't know how I'm managing to sport a hard on after last night. I should be worn out and limp as a wet dishrag. But I'm not and she feels so good, I snuggle closer.

"Again," she mutters. I'm not sure if it's a question of frequency or a request. I'm not even sure she's awake. Then she wiggles and turns to her back, a lazy smile on her kiss swollen lips. "Hi, sweetie."

"Morning, baby."

I'm about to start our day with another round of lovemaking when a harsh claxon sounds. She jerks and her muscles tense. "My phone."

"What the fuck's wrong with it?"

She scoots from the bed and trips over the fallen bedding as she stumbles toward the desk and her purse. "Phone's fine. The ringtone... oof."

"That's not a tone, Piper. That is one hell of an obnoxious noise."

"I know. It's an emergency." She retrieves the phone and answers with a panicked, "What's wrong?"

While listening to the caller, she gnaws on her lower lip. Her eyes widen. "How close?"

Emotions rise and fall in her expression. Fear, anxiety, relief, determination. This morning isn't going to go the way I hoped. Even my dick knows that's true, making it a little more comfortable to roll out of bed. I find her dress and drop in on the desk chair. It takes me a little longer to find her panties and lacey bra. Then I head to the bathroom to allow her some privacy.

When I emerge she's dressed and staring at her phone. Her eyes are sad when she looks at me. "I have to go."

"What's going on?" When she remains silent, I press for answers. "Piper, tell me. What happened? Why do you need to leave?"

She draws a shuddering breath. "There was a storm early this morning. It's been so dry lately. Lightning. Lightning strikes started a number of small wildfires. There's one too close to my place. I have to get home. I have to make sure the women are safe. That my bees are okay."

I'd learned about her bees, her small business selling honey, and her dreams of expansion during the quiet times of the night. She's as passionate about her business as she is responsive to my touch. The alluring combination makes me ache to experience every moment of life with her.

Now she's standing in the middle of the room, turning one way, then another, lost in not knowing what to do. She's strong and independent. Right now, though, she needs someone to take care of her. "Piper?" I wait until she stops fidgeting and looks at me. "Didn't whoever called you say everything is okay now?"

She nods. "Chris, my forewoman. Yes, okay. That could change at any moment. What if the wind switches? The fire moves in a new direction? Spreads? What if—"

"Piper, baby, take a deep breath. We'll get you home. Give me two minutes and I'll be ready to leave. We'll grab your stuff then head out."

"You don't need to do anything."

Rolling my gaze to the ceiling, I shake my head. "I don't have to, but I'm going to. I'm going with you. In fact, I'm going to drive. You're in no condition."

She crosses her arms. "It's not like I've been drinking. I'm fine, Chaz. You don't need to worry about me. I'll take care of this." Her shoulders droop. "I didn't want our time together to end like this. I... umm..."

"Do not say goodbye. This is not the end for us. Piper, let me help. Even if all that help is simply being with you. To offer comfort. A little peace." Because it has to be said, I take the chance. "Love."

Her eyes go wide, then narrow. "Help is good. Comfort too. We all need that. But love? Don't say things you don't mean."

I take a step closer, invading her personal space. "I mean what I say. I love you, Piper. I've fallen hard for you. I can't let you go. I'm asking for a chance. A chance to prove my love for you."

"But I'm—"

"If you bring up our age difference again I'll have to..." I slip into a dark character voice. "Have to chase the argument from your brain. Perhaps with kisses. Maybe something more... strenuous." I return to Chaz. "I'm telling you the truth, Piper. I am in love with you. I am going with you to check on your bees. I hope to use every second of our time together to prove what I say. You don't have to love me right now. That may come later. It may not. I can't make you love me. I hope to be around though when you do."

"Chaz, it's too much. I can't think about us right now. I have to get home."

I rest my hands on her shoulders and kiss her cheek. Then I encourage her to sit. "Two minutes, I'll be ready. Here." I hand her my watch. "Time me."

"Don't be silly."

"Check the time. I'm starting now."

I manage to finish dressing, throw everything into my single duffle, and with her hand in mine, leave the room in a minute forty-five. It takes her a little longer once we reach her room, but within fifteen minutes I'm stowing the last of her books in the back of her Jeep.

I hold out my hand. "Keys."

She clasps them against her chest. "Why?"

"I told you I'm driving. You're still upset. That's not being safe. Especially on mountain roads. Give."

With a dramatic sigh, she hands the keys to me. "Fine." Her phone pings and she glances at a message.

"Everything okay?" I ask.

"Just a reminder I set for myself. So I'd stop at the visitor center to pick up the Wild Bill Me prizes. Oh, I hate to disappoint Leo. But we don't have time."

"Not if we stand here talking about it. I can't imagine it would take more than a few minutes to check your selfies. Is five or ten minutes really going to make a difference? Now get in."

I park in front of the visitor center and check my watch. "You go in. There's a coffee shop just down the street. We'll meet back here in ten minutes tops."

Thankfully she doesn't argue and my plan works perfectly. I hand her a large coffee with cream only. After I take a fortifying sip of my double shot latte, she gives me directions out of town and we're on our way. She's got satellite radio and asks what I'd like to listen to. I defer to her choice and she turns on an oldies channel.

This better not be some sly reference to her age. But she seems to relax and sings softly along with the music. We travel with little conversation for a couple hours then take a short break at a fast food place for lunch. She places a couple calls, making sure there's no immediate fire danger to her livelihood. Relieved with the good news, she offers to drive the rest of the way and I hand her the keys.

The rolling hills, which she says are really just plant stabilized sand dunes, fascinate me. The landscape is open under the clear blue sky although in the distance there's a gray smudge overlying the blue. Smoke from the fires? I don't ask because I don't want to increase her worry.

This part of Nebraska is so different from where I grew up yet I feel oddly at home here. Perhaps that has a lot to do with Piper. The feeling is soul deep though. This could be the *where I belong* I've been searching for.

The closer we get to her land, the more Piper leans forward over the steering wheel to peer into the distance and up into the sky. I offer an uninformed opinion. "It doesn't look too bad. Does it?"

"No, but out here, especially when we're under drought conditions, it only takes a puff of wind to change everything."

Probably to keep us both focused on something other than a destructive wildfire, Piper tells me about different points of interest as we pass and more about her home. So I easily recognize the two story white farmhouse with a thick columned front porch when we pull into the drive.

A group of women rush to greet her when she exits the vehicle. I remain seated, enjoying the outpouring of emotions. The reactions show me so much about Piper.

One woman breaks away from the others and circles to the passenger side of the Jeep. A young boy follows her. She leans on the open window. "So, you're Ross-C."

"Umm, yeah?"

She grins. "Not what I expected. No worries. Piper said to call ya Chuck. And that you've got something for my son. Leo, come say hi to Chuck."

"Hi, Leo." I say as his mom steps to the side and he approaches the Jeep. "So, you're the one who knows all about Wild Bill."

"Yes, sir. Did a report for school. Got an A."

"Good job. Now, hang on a second..." I reach into the rear seat for the bag from the Deadwood visitor center. "Piper worked really hard to get those selfies with Wild Bill for you. I even helped. Guess how many."

"She sent some to Mom. I hope there's more. I can't wait to see them." He screws up his face and squints one eye. "I'm guessing she got enough for the grand prize. That's at least twenty-five."

"She did. And here's your prize." I hand him the bag.

His huge smile is my reward. I wish Piper was here to see it. He backs up a few steps then turns to dash away.

"Leo?" His mother's voice stops him dead in his tracks. "What do you say?"

"Sorry. Thank you, mister Chuck." He glances at his mother. "I'll go tell Piper thank you, too." At her nod, he runs off.

She opens the passenger door. "Welcome to Honey Hills, Chuck. Grab your stuff and I'll show you where you'll be staying."

My hopes faulter. Of course Piper might not want to advertise our new relationship.

With a smirk, she continues, "Which just so happens to be Piper's room."

11

Piper

Once I hear the bees are in no danger from the fires and the fact is confirmed by every woman on the ranch, I finally relax. I've been so tense and on edge all day, my muscles ache. Maybe I can get Chaz to give me a massage later.

I feel bad about leaving him in the Jeep. I just needed to know everything right away and he would have been a distraction. To me and possibly to the other women. I sent my forewoman, Chris, to welcome him. I told her he's Ross-C but I'll introduce him to the other women as Chuck. I've encouraged many of them to listen to audio books, so they know who Ross-C is. With that moniker, there's no way he wouldn't be a distraction.

Once all the fire related threats are taken care of, with his permission, I'll let them know who he is.

When Leo pulls on my sleeve to thank me for the Wild Bill Me prize, I'm thankful Chaz made me stop at the visitor center. The kid has an adorable, gap-tooth grin that's a more than perfect reward for taking a few selfies. I make a mental note to send the rest of the photos to his mom.

The rest of the day I spend taking Chaz on a tour of my property. We take the UTV loaded with a couple of shovels, buckets and a large tub of water. Just in case. Thank god we don't find any flames or smoldering embers.

I have hives in three different locations to take advantage of the natural wild flowers and clover I've planted. Each of my little hive cities is also near a creek or natural spring. He didn't say anything, but I'm fairly sure I impressed Chaz.

He impresses me as well by asking intelligent questions. I can tell he loves to learn. He's so much more at ease here than he was at the signing. Other than during special gatherings, the only real crowds out here are the neighbor's cattle. The largest area spread—Turquoise Creek Ranch—raises horses is small herds, so no crowds.

With his arm around my shoulders we stand on the crest of a hill and watch the distant smoke. The nearly constant breeze caresses my skin, tosses the hair I didn't control with a braid this morning. Chaz faces me, tucks strands of my hair behind my ears, then kisses me.

"Thank you for bringing me here. Showing me why you love this land so much. I understand, baby. I really do understand. I feel it, too."

In the evening we share a meal with the women and kids in the bunkhouse kitchen then head to the main house. The Honey Hills office and a storeroom are on the main level with access through a side door. I'm okay with the women entering without informing me when they need something. That keeps life easier.

The second floor is off limits. This is my private space. I've allowed very few people up here and I wait for my chest to tighten or knots to form in my belly when I lead Chaz up the stairs and give him the nickel tour. Nothing. Except for a rush of happiness when he praises my simple decorating. And the rise of desire when he places his leather grooming kit on the vanity in my bathroom.

Like he belongs right here.

This morning he said he loves me. How can I tell if his words are honest and forever, or simply because we shared a remarkable night together? Then I wonder if love is a contributing factor to the pleasure our bodies experienced.

Now that I know my livelihood is safe from the fires, I should open my heart and tell Chaz that I'm in love with him, too. I'm not sure how it happened. I certainly wasn't expecting to ever feel this way about another person. Not after my heart was stomped on... I refuse to think about that time. To relive the moments of pain and betrayal. I can't believe I thought I loved that bastard.

How could I have been so blind? Simple. Because I hadn't yet met anyone like Chaz. He gives as much to the building of our relationship as I do. Sometimes so much more. My past pseudo love affair was my education. I had to learn what not to simply tolerate and accept as my fate in order to find the one I can truly love. To the depths of my soul until the end of time.

Except he's only here with me temporarily. I don't know how long he can stay before he has to return to his life, his job, his home. Even for love, I won't leave this land. I can't. Not the women who depend on me. Or the tiny bees that mean so much to the life of this planet. Can Chaz and I make a long distance relationship work?

There's too many variables. Too many questions. Too little time and hope. And he doesn't know how I feel. We can't make any decisions until he knows I love him.

Once we crawl into bed, he tends to my sore, tired muscles, both relaxing and rejuvenating me. I'm about to return the favor when the downstairs door slams and footsteps pound up the hall. I slip from the bed and jerk on a long tee. There's a knock at the door.

"Piper, sorry, but I got a call from Micah at Turquoise Creek."

I glance at Chaz. He's pulled on his jeans and nods.

I open the door. Chris focuses on my face and I'm thankful for her discretion. "What's going on?"

"They've got a small blaze that looks like it might be shifting toward the road. Across from the south west corner of your land."

"Call him back and tell him we'll be there to help. Organize a couple crews and get them on the way."

"Already done." She grins. "I'm staying here in case we need coordination and sending Jane out to watch over the hives closest to that location. We'll be on the walkies."

"Excellent. I'm heading over to TCR."

"Me, too," Chaz says from right behind me.

Chris hands me a walkie talkie and backs away. "I'll get your Jeep fitted out. You should be good to go in under five."

"She's efficient," Chaz says.

"She is. I'm not sure I could run this place without her."

We drive toward a soft glow in the dark night. From a mile away, it looks like nothing more than a campfire, but when I park on the side of the road, I see sparks and flame rising at least seven feet into the air. I take Chaz's hand. "It may not look like much, but it only take a few seconds for a blaze to explode. As long as we can contain this here, make sure no sparks escape and that the embers are smothered, we should be fine. There will be someone watching this area for a few days. Fire is sneaky."

Like the other vehicles parked here, I leave my lights on to illuminate the darkness. I hook my walkie to my belt while Chaz grabs our shovels then I lead him toward the cowboys working to establish a fire line. "The road will act as a natural fire line, but it's better if the blaze can be contained before it reaches a road. Out here it doesn't take much wind to carry fire a good distance."

Chaz squares his shoulders. He glances sideways at me and winks. This time his voice is soft with a Texan drawl. "Well then ma'am. Let's be puttin' this fire out. So we can get back to startin' the one this fire so rudely interrupted." Then, damn the man, he leans close and purrs in my ear. "That fire we were working on isn't going to go cold anytime soon."

He speaks with one of the cowboys who gets him started clearing vegetation along a line they'd already determined. I'm about to join them when Micah stops beside me. "Who's the new guy?"

"Name's Chuck. I met him in Deadwood this weekend. He, uh, was curious about the Sandhills."

The owner of the Turquoise Creek Ranch gives me a knowing look. "He's probably getting more than he bargained for. Baptism by fire, so to speak. Come help me start a second line of defense."

Even though I'd prefer to work beside Chaz, I won't risk any fire getting through and start at one end of the line Micah draws in the sandy soil while he begins clearing the other end.

The work is hard—I'm always amazed at how the shallow plant roots are so difficult to dig from the loose soil.

Micah's sister arrives with their small water tanker. "Sorry that took so long. The pump's acting up."

She hands out cold bottled water and I stand next to her while the men attach hoses to the side nozzles on the tank and aim the flow at the base of the blaze and over the area around the fire. She points with her bottle. "Who's the new guy?"

I chuckle then cough as smoke blows over us. "You sound just like Micah. I met him in Deadwood."

"How was the event? I really wanted to attend this year. Promote my latest release."

Although not many people realize it, Alice is a best-selling romance author, as well as co-owner of the ranch and the driving force behind recent new businesses based on their property. Their new winery uses my honey for their mead which has helped my business grow. I owe her a great deal.

"It was great. I have plenty of reading material for a while. And I found some kid and mid-grade books for my little library."

"What I really want to know..." She falls silent until the cowboy adjusting the waterflow walks away. "Did you get to meet Ross-C?"

I try to keep my expression neutral but she sees through my attempt. "You did. What's he like? What does he look like? I'm so envious."

"Can I tell you a secret?"

She makes a motion like she's zipping her lips.

"I met him. He's nothing like I imagined. We... uh..." I know I'm blushing so I duck my head.

"You didn't. Girl, you're living in a romance novel. Now tell me... no, you don't need to tell me that, I can imagine. So what now? He just a weekend fling?"

As though he knows we're talking about him, Chaz joins us and grabs a water. "I haven't worked this hard in a long time."

Alice's eyes go wide. "That's him, isn't it?"

I move my mouth but no sound comes out. Chaz pauses only a moment then holds out his dirt covered hand. "I'm Charleston Ross."

Alice takes his hand. "Charleston Ross? Ross-C? It *is* you."

"Please, just call me Chuck. And you are?"

"Oh, sorry. I'm Alice. My brother and I own this land. Thank you for helping out. Looks like we're well on the way to having this blaze under control."

Chaz clears his throat. "Look, Alice, I'd appreciate it if you'd—"

"Not out you? No problem, Chuck. Although..." She glances at me and waggles her eyebrows before grinning at Chaz. "I've always wanted to put my books on audio. Maybe we can make a deal."

He bends closer to both of us. I know what's coming and watch Alice's face. He purrs but somehow it's different than when he purrs for me. That tiny thing makes me love him even more. "Ah, Alice. How could I not...hmm...desire... a deal with you. I am at your... hmm...your command."

Alice presses her water bottle to her cheek. "Oh my lord. Now I have to have you." At his smirk, she waves one hand. "To narrate my books, I mean. I'll leave that other having to Piper. Now, I need to cool off. I mean, check in with Micah."

I poke Chaz in the chest. "You are an incorrigible flirt, mister Ross-C."

"I know. Chaz, on the other hand, is all yours. Only yours."

After three days of containing small fires on the neighboring lands, the ranchers declare the emergency over and the fires completely out. So of course Alice plans a party for the following weekend.

The faint aroma from their smoker has floated over to my place raising everyone's anticipation. The ladies in my bunkhouse have been baking and making salads for a couple days to add to the feast. I'm happy to let them provide our share, and I add a variety of honeys to go with the biscuits and cornbread.

Spirits are high when we pile into our vehicles. The welcomes when we pull up close to the pool area make Chaz grin. "The people here are unlike any I've met. I've never felt like I belonged before. Only a week and the Sandhills are in my blood. They're now home to me."

He circles the Jeep to open my door. "Mostly because you're here, Piper." Once he closes the door, he traps me against the vehicle with his body. "I love you, Piper. Since the first time I told you, the only thing that's changed is that somehow, I love you even more. Deeper. Unshakable. I want to stay in Nebraska. With you."

"Chaz, I should have told you how much you mean to me. A week ago I knew I loved you. I was afraid your declaration was only because our first night together was so spectacular. I didn't know what I could offer you for the future. That doesn't matter. I should have said I love you."

He rests his forehead against mine. "I'll never let another day go by without telling you, showing you. No matter where I am, together or apart, I'll find the way. You'll never need to doubt. Never worry. I love you now, this moment. I will in the next and the next. Forever, baby, I love you."

"I'll never get tired of hearing that. Never tire of returning those words to you from the depths of my heart. I love you, too, Charleston Ross. More than I ever believed possible."

"Just call me Chaz." He curls his finger under my chin and lifts my head. His kiss is soft, reverent, and promises a lifetime of desire and delight.

We break apart to the sound of clapping and cheers. My face burns but I don't care. I won't hide my love for this man.

Alice strolls by, pausing to pat Chaz's chest. "Welcome to the Sandhills, Chuck."

EPILOGUE

One year later~ Deadwood
  Charleston

This year's Wild Deadwood Reads is even larger than last year and I'm actually having a good time. Now that I don't have an audiobook app publicist overseeing my every move, it's easier to relax and meet my fans. Since I've completed the narration for most of her books, I'm sharing a table with Alice to promote the audiobooks and my availability. My personal client list is growing.

When I decided to move to the Sandhills to be with my woman, I had no idea how I might be able to continue my craft at the level I expect of myself. Alice came to the rescue. Her vintner is married to a songwriter whose brother is a rock star. He built a state of the art recording studio at the Turquoise Creek Ranch that I'm allowed to use. The recording quality is top notch and the reverb has upped the impact of my purr.

This year Piper has a vendor table right next to Alice's. They've created book swag featuring the cover of Alice's latest book attached to a small straw-shaped container of Honey Hills honey. Piper's almost sold out of the small jars we brought along. A successful conference for everyone.

I was able to rent the same suite as last year and I've arranged a surprise for Piper. I know romantic gestures like wine and flower petals and chocolate in a hotel room is trite, a common trope, and nothing special. So I didn't do that.

Okay, I did order chocolates. Watching her enjoy a sweet milk chocolate truffle filled with coconut turns me on. So the candy is for me as well.

Finally the ballroom doors close. We pack up our tables and since there's not much left, Alice puts everything into one huge rolling tote, and we head toward the elevators.

"What shall we do for supper?" Piper asks.

Alice casts me a quick glance then yawns. "You know, I'm worn out. I'm going to pass on food tonight."

"You okay?" Piper asks. "Can we bring you something?"

"Nope, I'm good. I'll see you at breakfast." She turns her face so Piper can't see and winks. "Maybe," she whispers.

After she gets off on her floor, Piper and I are alone in the elevator. She presses against me and dances her fingers along the skin at the edge of my beard. "Maybe we should just order in a delivery like we did last year. Eat in our room."

"I plan on it," I growl in her ear.

"Promises, promises."

She turns away before I can capture her lips and the doors open. I take her hand and we stroll to the room. My nerves are jittery as I anticipate her reaction to the surprise. If I don't do this right I don't know how I'll ever make it up to her.

I stand behind her at the door and disengage the lock then shove the door open.

"Oh my... Chaz, what is this?"

I encourage her to enter and shut the door behind us. She takes a few more steps forward.

A layer of red paper covers the window and surrounding wall. Red heart shaped balloons fill the entire surface floor to ceiling. The light from the room's lamps sparkle off the shiny mylar.

"This is... what did you do, sweetie?"

"I wanted to surprise you, baby."

"Surprise is an understatement. When did you do this?"

"The hotel staff is very helpful. Go on, take a closer look." It's difficult to breathe. The future depends on what happens in the next two minutes.

A small table is centered in front of the balloons, a layered display of chocolate surround a heart shaped card. She glances back at me before picking it up and reading the interior.

"Chaz?" Holding the card against her chest, she faces me.

I drop to my knee and hold out the ring I've hidden from her for the past five months. "Piper, I love you. I will stay with you forever, no matter how you answer now. But I want the world to know you're mine. Always mine. Marry me. Please?"

The card flutters to the floor. "Stand up and kiss me, husband to be. I want the world to know that you're mine, too. I love you. Of course I'll marry you."

ABOUT THE AUTHOR

Happy endings with a spicy twist!
A writer once wanted to write different things
Like short little tales of the joy loving brings,
True lovers who struggle with all of life's stings.
Instalove magic to tug your heartstrings.
A little bit hot, a little more steamy,
And always, you know, with heroes so dreamy
With a promise the endings happy will be.
Her brain is a library with stories to tell,
She writes and she hopes you'll like them as well.

LizAnne lives in the capital of Husker Nation, sharing a home with her two siblings and way more multiple fandom collectables than should be allowed.

LizAnne website: www.lizanneaxtel.com
　　~~LizAnne also writes romance and fantasy *with a sparkling twist* as *Lizzie Starr

NOWHERE IN DEADWOOD

CHARLES LEMAR BROWN

1

"Last warning!" Voilet Daniels slowly squeezed the trigger of the Colt .45 as she shouted. The revolver bucked hard in her hands as the hammer fell. The sound filled the room and all but deafened her. The glass in the lower corner of her back door shattered as the bullet passed through it. As loud as the shot sounded in her small kitchen, she knew it would draw no attention in this town. Since she had arrived in Deadwood, she could not recall a single night when there had not been gunfire after the sun went down.

Instinctively, she thumbed back the hammer and readied the pistol for another shot. The smell of gunpowder filled the room. The dull thump of a body hitting the wooden planks of her back porch told her there would be no need to fire again. With care, she removed the spent cartridge and replaced it with a fresh bullet. Carrying the gun with her, she navigated through the darkness toward the front door of the house.

She had chosen the location of her house carefully. Not too far from the crowded storefronts and gambling houses, but far enough away to allow for a bit of privacy, if not quiet. She paused briefly in the entryway, pushed a strand of her long red hair away from her face, then opened the door and stepped out onto the porch. Gun pressed into a fold in her long skirt, she scanned the street, allowing her eyes time to adjust to the semi-darkness.

The evening air felt thick and stagnant to Violet. She found herself wondering if it was truly so, or if the fact that she had just killed another man had her feeling contrary. Stepping down from the porch, she decided the air quality had nothing to do with her mood. Hell, it wasn't like this was the first man she'd shot. Not even close. She tried to remember how many men she had sent to the grave as she made her way along the edge of what passed for a street.

"Where ya headed this time o' night?" a woman's gruff voice questioned from the shadows.

"That you, Jane?" Voilet was already bringing her revolver to bear as she spoke.

"Hell, yeah, it's me," Jane answered roughly, "Now how 'bout you answer my question?"

"Just shot a man through my back door," Violet lowered the gun as she spoke, "Headed to get Sheriff Bullock."

"He done went home for the night," Jane announced, and stepped away from the wall she had been leaning on, "I reckon I could go get him, if'n ya want me to."

"I'd appreciate that," Violet nodded, "Please be quick."

"As you wish," Jane offered a mock bow then took a pull from the bottle she was holding. At six feet tall, Jane was an imposing figure, and Violet was glad she was her friend. As Jane stumbled off down the street, Violet wondered what people thought when they saw her and Jane walking around town together. At five foot four, Violet's head scarcely reached the underside of Jane's breast. Adding to their height difference, Jane's lanky frame and Violet's curves and folks must find them quite amusing.

Violet decided she did not give a damn what people thought as she watched Jane weave and sway down the street. When she was satisfied that Jane was indeed sober enough to reach Sheriff Bullock's house, she turned and started back toward her own home. Loneliness, like the night's darkness, surrounded her, and she felt herself shiver.

The short trip back gave her time to think, perhaps too much time. Had she become so calloused that the killing of another human did not even elevate her heartbeat? She ran through the events that led to the shot. The sound of a horse on the trail behind her house had caught her attention first. Nothing unusual about that, since it was a well-traveled route out of town. Many nights she drifted off to sleep listening to the click of horse hooves passing by, however, this particular horse had left the trail.

Through her bedroom window on the second floor, she had watched as the horse and rider made their way toward the back of her home. Who he was and what he wanted was of no concern to her. That he was approaching her back-door under cover of darkness had her dander up even before she reached for the gun on her nightstand.

By the time she made it downstairs to the kitchen, the unwelcome guest was already pounding on the door. The shadow of his body was as wide as the door in the darkness, and he had muttered something Voilet could not understand.

"Move along or I'll shoot!" she had shouted.

"I warned him," Violet muttered to herself as she stepped back up on her porch and opened the door.

Carefully, she made her way down the foyer and into what she called the parlor. From the shelf above the woodburning stove, she retrieved a small box of matches and a candle. She lit the candle, placed it in a tarnished brass candle holder, and made her way to the kitchen. For a split second, she considered opening the back door to see if she recognized the body but then reminded herself of what curiosity could do to a cat. The thought brought a smile to her face as she spoke aloud, "I haven't met too many cats that have shot as many men as I have."

Her bravado waned, the smile faded, and what she considered good sense prevailed. She set the candle on the table, pulled out a chair, and sat down to wait. The pistol she laid next to the candle and smiled at the eerie way the light played along the barrel, making it almost seem like a living thing.

Within minutes, her patience had worn thin. She rose to her feet and took the gun from the table. As she reached for the candle, the sound of a hard rap on the front door made her jump. Aggravated by her own skittishness, she twirled, the gun in one hand and the candle in the other, she made her way back to the entryway.

"Who's there?" Violet raised the gun as she spoke. She had not lived this long by being careless.

From the other side of the door, Jane's voice registered irritation. "Who the hell ya think it is? Good Lord, ain't been fifteen whole minutes since ya sent me to fetch the Sheriff here and..."

"That's enough, Jane," Sheriff Bullock's voice interrupted Jane's rant.

Violet stepped forward, unlocked the door, and opened it. The sheriff stepped back and allow Jane to enter first, then as he followed her inside, he said, "Jane tells me you've shot another man, Violet."

"That is correct, Sheriff," Violet did not miss the irony in his voice. Holding the candle up so he would not miss her smile, she nodded then added, "Right this way. folks."

"Don't suppose this one was cheatin' at cards?" Bullock offered as he followed the two women through the house.

"No, sir, he was not," Violet answered over her shoulder. "And before you ask, he did not accuse me of cheating either."

"Ah, then an unwanted suitor?" Bullock taunted as they entered the kitchen.

"Unwanted, yes. Suitor, no," Violet responded and pointed at the door.

Violet stood back as the sheriff reached for the door. Before he could pull it open, Jane spoke up, "What if'n he ain't dead?"

Bullock laughed. Violet knew him well enough to know it wasn't amusement, but rather the thought that he had perhaps been careless, that brought about the sound. As if to prove his point, he drew the revolver from its holster before reaching for the door once more.

As he swung the door wide, the light from the candle illuminated the scuffed, worn soles of a man's boots. Violet moved closer. More of the man became visible. He was tall, at least six feet Violet guessed, but not nearly as wide as she thought he would be. The darkness had played a trick on her. She blamed the long black duster he wore for part of the illusion. In her mind, she had shot a rather pudgy fellow, but this man was solid muscle. The tied-down holsters on each of his legs were no illusion, and neither were the walnut-handled revolvers in them. Both still had their retention straps in place.

Sheriff Bullock reached back, took the brass candle holder from Violet, and leaned closer to the body. Violet watched as Jane stepped past him, circled the man's body, and squatted across from the sheriff.

"Lord have mercy," Jane exclaimed as she looked up at Violet and asked, "How many times did ya shoot him?"

"Just once," Violet answered as she moved closer herself.

The sheriff reached out and gave the man's shirt a hard tug, sending buttons flying. As he passed the candle across the man's torso again, Violet counted at least three exit wounds before she saw what she knew was the entry wound her .45 had caused.

"Don't think you can count this one," Bullock half-chuckled as he pointed at the entry wound. "You might have grazed a rib, but you definitely shot wide left, Violet."

"It isn't like I keep count anyway," Violet was glad it was too dark for either of them to see the blush on her cheeks. The idea that she had missed a shot that badly bothered her.

"Jane let's roll him over and have a look at his back," Bullock instructed as he reached across and took firm hold of the edge of the man's duster.

As Jane positioned herself to assist the sheriff, the man's right hand shot out lightning-fast and grasped her wrist. Wide-eyed, she looked at Bullock, and in a hushed voice, said, "Sheriff, he ain't dead yet."

"It would seem not," Bullock responded as the man's grip loosened and his hand fell back to land on the porch once again. "Help me get him inside, and then you can fetch Doc Babcock. Violet, how about a bit more light?"

Violet understood Bullock's request was not merely a question or even a suggestion, it was an order. Without hesitation, she turned and busied herself gathering matches and candles.

"Doc's out of town," she heard Jane tell Bullock as they half-carried, half-dragged the big man into her kitchen.

"Not sure Doc could do much anyway," Bullock responded to Jane's announcement.

"Table?" Jane asked Bullock as Violet turned from lighting the last candle.

"Ain't big enough," Bullock answered, then asked Violet, "Where do you want him?"

Violet felt the heat spread across her face. Where did she want him? She didn't want him. Didn't want him in her house. Didn't want him in her life. Didn't want him at all.

"Preferably, out of my house," she answered, trying to sound dignified but feeling like a failure even as the words left her lips.

Sheriff Bullock turned to face her. "You shot him, until he dies, he's your responsibility." His tone let her know there would be no negotiation. "When he dies, send for the undertaker, but until then he's all yours."

"You mean if he dies," Jane corrected him.

"Pretty sure, it's when he dies," the sheriff stated flatly, then asked again, "Violet, where do you want him?"

With a huff and an eye roll, she pointed as she spoke, "I guess the parlor for now."

She led the way, holding a candle in front of her as she went. Two thoughts entered her head simultaneously as she entered the parlor. The first was that she was thankful for the wounded man's sake that she had swept the parlor rug earlier in the day. The second was that there would be no way to get the blood out of the rug, and it would be ruined. She was really beginning to regret that she had missed her shot so badly.

"Put him down there on the rug," Violet ordered as she crossed to the room, carefully raised the chimney of an oil lamp, and used the candle to light the wick.

Once she had it lit, she set the candle on the potbellied stove she used for heat in the winter and turned with the lamp in her hand. She glared at Bullock and asked, "Would it be too much to ask of you to help me get his coat and shirt off before you go?"

Before he could answer, Jane chimed in, "I can help her. I've done my share of doctorin', ya know."

"Thank you, Jane," Bullock smiled at Violet as he spoke. With a nod, he touched the tip of his Stetson hat, then stepped out of the parlor and disappeared. Violet heard the front door open and close as he let himself out.

"Well, I'll be damned," Jane, who had already started to remove the man's clothing, paused and looked up at Violet with a toothy grin as she spoke, "he's kinda purty in a hard kinda way."

Violet shook her head as she looked down at the man's rugged face. It was a bit weathered with a couple days of scruff, but Jane wasn't wrong. With dark hair streaked with grey and chiseled features, he was definitely easy on the eyes, but then Violet reminded herself there was no sense in admiring a dead man. "Don't reckon purty is going to keep him from dying," she stated, her voice cold and harsh, "guess we better get to it."

2

Jack Abbott slowly opened his eyes and choked back the scream that threatened to escape from his throat. He figured if he was dead, then old Saint Peter must have turned him away at Heaven's gate, because every preacher he had ever heard assured him that no one who reached Paradise would ever feel pain again, and every inch of his body hurt like hell.

For a long time, he lay still, staring up at the ceiling. His thoughts were jumbled something awful, and the harder he tried to concentrate on just one, the worse it got. He told himself that they didn't have ceilings in hell, so he must be alive. Many times in his life, he had felt pain, but this was a whole new level of torture. He inhaled and exhaled in steady, shallow breaths. Not because he wanted to, but because anything deeper brought about sharp shooting agony that threatened to take away his consciousness.

Slowly, he turned his head to the right. Two chairs with a small table between them. Something was not right. Suddenly, through the fog, he realized he was at eye-level with the legs of the chair. He was on the floor. Why? Why was he on the floor?

He pushed down hard on his elbows, expecting to feel wood beneath them as he sat up. For a split second, it registered somewhere in his brain that he was not lying on the floor but on a mattress. Then the pain hit, and he heard someone scream just before his world went black.

～

An angel with the most beautiful green eyes floated through Jack's dreams. At least, he thought she was an angel. The way her long red hair perfectly framed her face gave him pause. He had never considered the possibility of angels having red hair.

The angel's mouth moved. She was speaking to him, he thought. The voice was sweet, gentle to the ear, but he could not understand her. She looked away and then back at him. Again, she spoke, but not to him this time it seemed. Suddenly, her face disappeared, and another angel's face appeared. Jack felt himself wince.

The new angel was a harsh contrast to the first. Her hair, thinner, unwashed, and stringy was a darker shade of red, closer to the color of dried blood on sunbaked earth. It framed an almost masculine face with eyes set too far apart and a mouth that turned down at the corners in a perpetual frown. This angel seemed much taller than the first one.

"I think he's awake," the second angel's voice was harsh and deep when she spoke.

Nope, just dreaming, Jack thought to himself. From the depths of his memories, he recalled his mother telling him that he could control his dreams. She said that if there was something or someone in the dream he did not wish there, he could simply tell it to leave, after all, it was his dream.

"Go away," he told the second angel.

"I think he's tryin' to talk," she looked away as she spoke and then back at him.

"Go away," he repeated.

"Cain't understand him. Give him some water," she ordered before her face disappeared, and the first angel's face floated back into his vision.

This dream was beginning to irritate him. He willed himself to wake up as the beautiful, green-eyed angel lifted his head and gently poured water into his mouth.

When she laid his head back, he muttered, "Guess Momma was right."

His vision widened, but the dream continued.

"He called you Momma," the second angel was back, and she was laughing, at least he thought it was laughter. "He called you Momma, Violet," she repeated, then laughed so hard she began to choke.

"Dammit, Jane," the pretty angel chided, "he's delirious. He does not know what he's saying."

So, the angels had names, Violet and Jane. Not the names he would have picked. Wow, wait a minute. Was this really a dream? And if so, why didn't he get to choose the names of the women in it?

"Delirious but awake," Jane pointed out when she finally got control of herself.

"Yes, awake," Violet nodded her agreement. "How about you go get Doc?"

Jack vision cleared. Like smoke dissipating, the dream faded, and the room slowly came into view. Violet leaned closer. She smelled of soap and perfume. He was convinced that no angel in Heaven had ever smelled as lovely.

"So, you've decided to live after all," Violet's statement had a certain callousness that he found adorable.

"How long?" He managed, though each word took effort.

"If you're asking how long you've been here," Violet raised one eyebrow as she spoke, "the answer is five days."

Five days. The cogs in Jack's mind whirled. If Sam McKinney found him like this, he was as good as dead. Where was his horse? His saddlebags? He reached for his guns and realized that he was naked except for the thin sheet that covered his body. Panic set in, and he tried to push himself up. Pain, sharp and excruciating, overtook him and he had to fight not to lose consciousness again.

"Easy!" Violet placed a hand on his chest. "Lie still, damn you."

Jack did as he was told. Violet's hand on his chest felt good, too good, perhaps, but there was comfort in the weight of it there near his heart. The pain slowly abated, and he felt like he could breathe once more.

"Sorry," he apologized, even though he wasn't quite sure why.

Violet removed her hand and tucked a stray strand of hair behind her ear. Jack tried to read her face but could not. She looked away, and his heart panicked. *What the hell is wrong with you?* he thought, even as he mentally begged her to turn back toward him.

"Should be me apologizing," Violet told him as she turned back and offered him another drink of water. "I shot you."

Jack's eyes widened.

"Mind you, it was an accident," Violet continued as she helped him take a swallow and then wiped away the water that spilled from the edge of his mouth. "I thought you were trying to break into my house."

Jack tried to remember her shooting him. He could not. He tried to recall coming to her house, and once again the memory simply was not there. He closed his eyes and forced himself to concentrate on his last memory.

The sound of running water and the odor of his own sweat mixed with dirt surfaced. A chunk of gold dropped into a leather bag. Washing sand from a miner's pan. The rustle of feet approaching. Sam McKinney had appeared not forty yards away. Jack knew why he was there even as he raised the rifle in his hand. The first bullet struck him just above the hip in his lower back as he turned to run. The second hit a bit higher as he grabbed his gun belt and scrambled into the trees where his horse was hidden. He remembered feeling the sting of a third as he pulled himself into the saddle.

"He's upstream!" Sam McKinney's scream was the last thing he remembered.

Four times, he had been shot four times, counting the bullet Voilet had put in him. He was glad he could not remember that one. Damn, he was a lucky man. Had Sam taken the right trail, he would have come out right behind Jack instead of forty yards downstream and downhill. At that range, Jack knew he would have died right there in the creek.

"Sam McKinney," Jack looked into Violet's eyes as he spoke the name. If he died, he wanted her to know who was responsible.

"Nice to make your acquaintance, Sam," Violet smiled. "I'm Voilet Daniels."

Jack squeezed his eyes shut tightly, fighting back frustration. When he opened them again, he nodded at the glass of water in Violet's hand. Once again, she helped him take a swallow.

As Violet set the water glass on the table beside them, Jack, his voice hoarse and cracked, said, "I'm Jack Abbott. Sam McKinney shot me. Unarmed." It was all he could muster.

Violet nodded, she understood but did not reply. Without asking for permission, she folded the sheet back to his waist and began to check his bandages. Her touch was firm yet tender. More than once, he grimaced. She either did not notice or did not care because she did not react but simply carried on with her examination.

When she was finished, she pulled the sheet far enough up to cover his chest but left his arms free. Seemingly satisfied, she rose.

"Too bad he didn't shoot me in the leg," Jack's grin was as weak as his voice when he spoke.

Violet calmly reached past the water glass on the table and picked up the gun that had been hidden from his view. "If you would like, I can remedy that," she said with a smile of her own.

Jack's grin widened, and he chuckled, then winched in pain. A quick flash of what Jack thought might be sympathy spread across Violet's face, then just as quickly disappeared. Stone-faced, she turned to leave the room.

Maybe, it's the close call with death, but I think I may be in love, Jack thought to himself.

Violet Daniels. The name was familiar to him. He tried to remember why but could not. He searched through his memory bank and hoped it wasn't a name he had seen on a wanted poster. Surely, not.

Someone knocking on a door broke his train of thought. Three voices grew louder as he watched the doorway Violet had left through. Violet and Jane's voices he recognized, but the gruff male voice he did not know. *Must be the doctor,* he thought to himself.

"Right this way, Doc," Jane's voice instructed, and a moment later, she appeared with a man carrying a large black satchel worn from much use.

The doctor looked haggard. His scruffy beard needed a trim, and his hair looked like it had been a short eternity since it had seen a comb. He looked down at Jack with a smile. "So, they tell me you went and got yourself shot."

Normally, Jack was not fond of doctors but decided instantly that he liked this one. "Wasn't tryin' exactly," he smiled back.

"A bit hoarse, I see." The doctor knelt beside him and opened his bag. "I've got something here that will help with that."

"Jack Abbott," Jack said in way of introduction and raised his hand. The motion caused him to flinch.

"Lyman Babcock," the doctor took the hand in his but instead of shaking it, he eased it back to where it had been resting at Jack's side. "That's quite an accent you have there, Jack. Where might you hail from?"

"Texas," Jack answered.

Doctor Babcock nodded and then began his examination. With meticulous care, he uncovered each wound and examined it. He pressed gently around each before applying fresh bandages and moving on to the next. Voilet's shot he inspected last.

"You're one lucky fella," Babcock grinned as he placed a foul-smelling salve on the entry wound.

"Don't feel so lucky," Jack told him as his nose turned up at the smell of the ointment.

"Jane, help me turn him over," Babcock instructed.

Jack's eyes widened, and he could feel the sweat beading up on his forehead. Babcock shook his head as he spoke, "Sorry, partner, but I've got to take a look. If any one of those wounds get infected, you're done for. Jane here did a good job of stitching you back together, but I need to take a look."

Jack clenched his teeth and nodded.

3

Violet concentrated on the cards in front of her. It felt good to be out of the house and sitting at a poker table again. Six long days of watching over Jack had been hell, but now she was back where she belonged: the Bella Union Theatre.

She closed her eyes and breathed in the atmosphere. It seemed strange to her sometimes that a woman who grew up as she did in a well-respected family in the heart of London, England, was so very comfortable at a poker table in a saloon in the middle of the wilderness. Oh, but the scent of fine cigars mixed with whiskey and the musky odor of men who knew what an honest day's work was, yes, this was something she had come to love. The buzz of conversation and the clinking of coins were like music to her ears. It had been a long time since she had thought of any other possible life for herself.

"Miz Violet, I believe it's to you," E.W. Adam spoke softly over her shoulder. Since E.W. usually spent his time as a lookout at the Faro table, Violet was not prepared for him to be behind her, and his voice, so close, gave her a start.

Mud Rogers, who sat to her left, chuckled, "First time I've seen her react to anything all evening."

Mr. Dakota Smith on her left twirled the edge of his handlebar mustache and smiled, "Got a face like a statue and nerves of steel. Careful, Mud, she'll take your money and make you like it."

Violet liked Mr. Dakota. He was an older gentleman. He kept his gray hair cut short and was as likely to show up to the poker table in bibbed work overalls as anything else. Most nights he broke even, but now and again she had seen him leave with a decent amount of winnings. She was fairly certain that he was a much better poker player than he let show, and even more certain that Dakota Smith was not the name he was given at birth, but then in a town like Deadwood, there were many men who had taken on new names for one reason or another. She had picked up his tell the first night they played together. Violet wondered how many times he had lost a pot because he twirled that damn mustache at the wrong time.

Mud Rogers, she did not like, and it took a lot for her to dislike someone. She had never caught him cheating, but she had heard that he was very good at it. That, and the way he looked at her like an old coyote stalking a rabbit, made her wary every time he showed up at the table.

"Not tonight, old man," Mud grinned, then ran his finger along the top of his right ear. Violet had a hard time keeping her face emotionless. Inside, she chuckled to herself. If Mud touched an ear, you could safely bet, he had nothing short of two pair.

"I fold," Violet said as she slid her cards towards the dealer.

"Likewise," Mr. Dakota shook his head as he spoke.

"Well then," Mud stared past both of them and declared, "Looks like it's just you and me, Jim."

Jim, also known around town as Grasshopper Jim, was quite the character. The story behind how he got his name varied depending on whom you asked. Hell, even the stories Grasshopper told sometimes contradicted one another. Violet had heard someone say once that the only person in town who could spin a yarn better than Grasshopper Jim was Jane herself. However Grasshopper got the nickname, it was the white hat he often wore to the poker table and the big white horse he rode that set him apart.

"Well, hell," Jim shrugged and tossed chips into the growing pile as he said, "I reckon I might as well call ya."

Mud fanned his cards out on the table: two queens, two nines, and an ace. He was in the process of reaching for the pot when Grasshopper Jim made a clicking sound that brought Mud up short. Without saying a word, Jim turned his cards over: three twos, a jack, and a seven.

As Grasshopper pulled the pot to his end of the table, Mud shook his head and whined, "I guess lady luck just ain't with me. Think I'll call it a night."

Violet watched as he cashed in his few chips and left.

"I see you allow ladies to participate," a female voice spoke from over Violet's shoulder. "Mind if I have a try?"

Grasshopper Jim nodded at the seat Mud had vacated and, with a wiry grin, said, "The last fella that sat there claimed lady luck was the reason he wasn't winning; maybe she'll be kinder to you."

"I'm Alice Ivers, and he can have lady luck; I won't be needing her," the woman who belonged to the voice eased into the chair and nodded at Violet as she spoke. "Gentlemen and Miss, y'all ante up and make your bets, and I'll take your money with no regrets."

"Well, I'll be damned," Mr. Dakota grinned. "Poker Alice right here in Deadwood."

Violet managed to rein in the emotions that threatened to betray her. Of course, she had heard of Poker Alice; it wasn't like there was a multitude of professional woman poker players. Violet looked at the young woman and tried to recall what she had heard about her.

"Looks like y'all've gotta empty chair here," a big barrel-chested man with an unkempt beard and narrow-set eyes pulled the chair out, and as he sat down, asked, "Mind if I sit in?"

"Not at all," Mr. Dakota answered, and then made introductions around the table.

The new arrival made eye contact with each of the players as Mr. Dakota offered up their names, and when Mr. Dakota was finished, the man smiled, "Nice to meet y'all. I'm Sam McKinney."

For a fraction of a second, Violet's face registered shock. Immediately, she composed herself. Thankfully, Sam McKinney had turned to Grasshopper Jim as he spoke and had not seen her reaction; however, Alice had, and when Violet looked her way, she gave her a knowing smile.

Violet kicked herself mentally for letting her guard down. She had not gotten to where she was today by acting like a greenhorn at the table. She blamed her lack of mental control on Jack and the five days she had spent pampering him back to life. Once again, she cursed herself for shooting poorly on that fateful night.

Her mind whirled. Should she excuse herself from the table, hurry home, and tell Jack that Sam McKinney was in town? She decided that the notion was foolish. First, it would look suspicious if she left just when two new players arrived. Second, she was not far enough ahead to call it a night, and the five days she had been away had really taken a chunk out of her stash. And, finally, she told herself, what do you really know about Jack Abbott? He could be a dangerous man who deserved to be shot.

As the next hand of cards was dealt, she considered that final thought. Somehow, it did not ring true, and she decided that on her return, she and Jack were going to have a long talk.

"What brings you to Deadwood?" Alice directed her question at Sam, as she picked up her cards.

"I could ask you the same question," Sam's brow furrowed as he looked up from his cards and met her gaze.

Alice smiled. It was a sweet smile, but something in it told Violet it held more danger than Sam McKinney could handle. With care, Alice laid her cards face down, nodded, and said, "I was simply following the gold, and it led me here. But you sir, well, you don't look like a professional gambler, and you sure as hell don't look like a miner. The accent, if I'm not mistaken, is from the southern region. My guess would be Texas."

"Very observant of you, ma'am," Sam grinned as he spoke. Violet noticed that the grin softened his features slightly, but the softness did not reach his eyes. There was something dark and cruel behind them.

Grasshopper Jim bet two dollars. Alice raised two dollars. Violet looked at her hand once more, folded, and passed her cards to the dealer. Mr. Dakota stacked his cards in front of him and eased five dollars to the edge of the pot in the center of the table. "I'll see your two dollars and raise ya another." He grinned and winked at Alice as he spoke. Violet noticed that Mr. Dakota had yet to touch his mustache. Sam tossed five dollars into the pot and turned to Grasshopper Jim.

"Reckon I'll let you three settle this one," he smiled, "I'm with Miz Violet."

When the hand was over, Alice pulled the pot across the table to where she sat. It was not a big win, but it was a win. Violet figured it would not be the last pot that ended up in front of Alice before the night was through.

"So, Mr. McKinney," Alice arranged the winnings in front of her as she spoke, "you still haven't told me what brought you to Deadwood."

Sam McKinney's jaw tightened. Violet watched from the corner of her eye as he picked up a pair of coins and rubbed them together in a circular motion. At first, she thought he was going to simply ignore Alice altogether, then his face relaxed, and he said, "I'm lookin' for a fella."

"Well, aren't we all," Alice chuckled at her own joke, then as the cards were dealt, she asked, "Does this fella you're lookin' for have a name?"

Violet stilled herself. She tried to recall who, if anyone, knew Jack Abbott was the name of the man she had shot. She had spoken to no one. As far as she knew, Sheriff Bullock did not know the name unless, of course, Doc Babcock had passed it on after his examination. So, those who knew Jack was at her house were herself, the doctor, possibly the sheriff, and Jane. *Well, shit,* she thought, *if Jane knows, then half the town knows, and what half a town knows, the other half already knows or will know shortly.*

Sam continued to rub the coins between his thumb and fingers as he snarled, "His name is Jack Abbott."

Alice shook her head as she picked up her cards. "Never heard of him myself," she stated flatly.

Violet pulled her cards to the edge of the table, but before she picked them up, she looked over at Alice. Alice was watching her with a great deal of interest, and Violet got the feeling it had nothing to do with the poker game they were playing.

"So, Sam," Alice's eyes shifted from Violet to Sam, "I hope it's okay if I call you Sam, Mr. McKinney."

Mr. McKinney laid the coins aside, picked up his cards, and shrugged. "Don't bother me none one way or the other."

"Wonderful," Alice smiled. "Then Sam, can I ask you one more question?"

Mr. McKinney looked across the table at Alice, and Violet could see the hate in his eyes. It was obvious that he was not used to being questioned. She wondered if it was because Alice was a woman that he was so agitated. The more she considered it, the more she thought it had nothing to do with gender.

"Ma'am, I sat down here for a friendly game of poker," irritation was etched on his face and evident in his voice as he spoke. "But since you seem bent on interrogation, I'll answer one more question, if'n you promise it will be the last."

The mood at the table shifted instantly, and the tension in the air threatened to replace the haze from the cigarette smoke that hung above them. All eyes turned to Alice. The sweet, kind face of the young woman who had sat down beside Voilet was now an unreadable blank mask. Violet suppressed a shiver and wondered if the hand Alice held beneath the table contained a weapon.

"Apologies for the questions," Alice stated, straight-faced, "but if I have too much on my mind, it affects my ability to concentrate on the game."

Mr. McKinney blinked and raised an eyebrow as if to indicate he was waiting. Alice took a breath and then let it out slowly, "I was just wondering why it is that you are looking for this Jack Abbott fella?"

Mr. McKinney looked around the table and then back at Alice before answering, "Jack Abbott killed my youngest brother. When I find him, I'm gonna kill him."

4

Jack Abbott's eyes narrowed at the name he had just heard come from Violet's mouth. He looked from her to Jane and back again before he spoke, "I think it best if I find other lodgin'."

"Have you lost your mind completely?" Violet's eyes narrowed, and her lips pursed. "Sam McKinney is in Deadwood. He is looking for you and is planning on killing you when he finds you. Actually, I believe his words were that he would shoot you on sight. It is only a matter of time before he finds out you are alive. There is nowhere in Deadwood you can hide."

Jack smiled as he pushed himself up from the chair he had been seated in and, in a long Texas drawl, said, "Ain't plannin' on hiding from anyone. Just don't want to put you fine ladies in harm's way."

He nodded first at Jane, who blushed red. Jack figured it was due to his calling her a lady. When he turned to nod at Violet, her face too had reddened, but he was fairly certain it had more to do with frustration or aggravation than with embarrassment.

"You know what, Jack Abbott," Violet spat the words out as if they tasted bad, "You just go on and get yourself killed, and don't you think for one measly second that I'm gonna give a rat's ass."

Jack thought about sitting back down but decided if he was going to be dressed down by this beautiful woman who had both shot and saved him, then he would take it standing up like a man. In the softest voice he could muster, he said, "Well, now, Miz Violet, I had no idea that you cared so much for me."

The words were barely out of his mouth when Violet erupted, "Care for you! Care for you! What in the hell makes you think I care for you? I just told you I would not give a rat's ass if you went and got yourself killed."

Jane chuckled from her side of the room. A steel-eyed squint from Violet silenced her, and she quickly turned her face away. Jack allowed Violet to fume for several seconds before answering her question in the same slow soft tone, "I've been around some in my lifetime, Miz Violet, and one thing I've learned is that women don't get all riled up about a man they don't give a rat's ass about. And Ma'am, I don't believe I've ever seen a woman in my life as riled up over old Jack Abbott as you are right now."

As Jack watched, Violet's face went from a light pinkish blush to a dark red that would make the most beautiful rose jealous. Her mouth opened and then closed tightly. Her brow furrowed. Her eyes narrowed, and for a long moment, she simply glared at him.

When she finally managed to compose herself enough to speak, she asked, "Did you really kill Sam McKinney's youngest brother?"

"I did," Jack nodded.

"Why?" Violet's next question came on the heels of his answer.

Jack stared hard into Violet's eyes for a long second before he answered, "Because he was tryin' to kill me."

"Explain." The single word from Violet was not a suggestion but an order.

Jack saw it for what it was and decided that now would be a good time to return to the seat he had vacated. Slowly, he eased himself into it and then looked up at Violet. In all his life, he had never cared what anyone thought of him as long as he knew he was on the side of right. Maintaining his honor and self-respect had always been more important to him than other folks' opinions. And while that had not changed, there was a part of him that needed Violet to understand who he was and a hope in him that when she did, she would like him.

"The McKinneys own a great deal of land in Texas. They run cattle on it and are quite well-known, not only as cattlemen but also as those who don't mind bendin' the rules to their favor when need be. Sam McKinney had three brothers and more cousins than one could count running around Kaufman County where I was the sheriff." The surprise on Violet's face caused Jack to pause. He waited, wanting that bit of information to sink in, before beginning again, "Sam was the oldest, then there was Frank, Thad, and John. Frank caught some folks passin' through McKinney land and hung them. Claimed they had rustled some cattle. Normally, he would have gotten away with it, but one of the men was kin to someone high up back in Washington, and so when word came down, I arrested Frank. There was a trial, the jury found Frank guilty, and they hung him. I reckon that was the start of the bad blood between me and the McKinneys."

"Because you arrested him?" Jane interrupted with a question.

Jack nodded at Jane and then turned his attention back to Violet. Her features suggested that some of her frustration had abated, but the squint of her eyes indicated that there was still enough aggravation to get him in serious trouble if he did not step lightly.

"All of this happened while Sam and Thad were driving cattle north to

Dodge City," Jack continued. "I'm not sure if John even tried to contact them before he decided to brace me, but I'm sure glad they didn't all come for me at once."

"Why's that?" Jane asked, once again interrupting Jack. This time, she received a stern look from Violet. Jack raised an eyebrow Jane's way and worked hard to suppress a grin.

"Because, Miz Jane," Jack answered her, but his eyes were locked on Violet, "Sam, Thad, and John, all fancied themselves gunfighters. They all had reputations and had all killed men. By all accounts, Sam was the fastest, but rumor had it John wasn't but a split second behind him on a draw."

Jack pushed himself forward until he was sitting on the edge of the chair, and his eyes narrowed a bit. "When John caught up to me, I was in Elmo, Texas lookin' for a man who had stabbed a fella in the back and robbed him. A witness had identified him, and we got word of where he was, so I went to get him. I rode into town, stepped down off my horse, and heard someone holler at me. When I stepped around my horse to see who it was, John McKinney was standin' in the middle of the street."

"So, you killed him in a gunfight?" Violet asked. "And it was fair?"

"I did," Jack nodded. "And it was fair. Turned out John wasn't quite as fast as he thought he was."

"Well, I did not spend the last five days nursing you back to health just to see you step out in the street and get yourself killed," Violet stood hands on both hips and informed him.

"If you were the sheriff and it was a fair fight, why are you in Deadwood?" Jane asked, ignoring Violet's glare this time.

Jack smiled. "Politics. That's the short answer."

"What's the long answer?" Violet's features had softened a bit, but Jack could tell she still had her dander up.

"In the commotion following the gunfight, the fella I was lookin' for got away," Jack explained. "By the time I got back to Kaufman, those in power had already decided that my services would no longer be needed. When I asked why, they told me they did not feel it was a good idea to have a gunslinger as a sheriff. They said it would draw a lot of unsavory men that were tryin' to make a reputation for themselves. I tried to reason with them. Tried to tell them I was no gunslinger, but they had already made up their minds. Then they told me they wanted me out of town. Even suggested it would be best for all if I left Texas."

"And so, you did," Jane smiled.

Jack shook his head. "No, Jane. Not at first. I hated the thought of running, so I stuck around for a few days and kinda mulled over my options. It's funny how folks treat you differently once the powers that be decide you're not wanted. By the end of the fourth day, I decided there was no reason for me to stick around a place where I wasn't needed, so I saddled up and started ridin'. I meandered 'round for a while, then one night I overheard two old fellas talkin' in a saloon in Dodge City, Kansas. One of them said they'd found gold in the Black Hills of the Dakota Territory. The other one said if he was younger, he would love to give it a try. As I listened to them talk about what they would do with all that gold, I thought to myself, here is an opportunity."

"An opportunity for what?" Violet seemed to relax as she asked her questions. "To get rich?"

Jack pushed himself up out of the chair. He was still stiff and mighty sore, but he knew that if he was going to face Sam McKinney, sitting on his ass any longer than he already had was not going to be helpful.

"Comfortable," he said, and rolled his shoulders trying to loosen them up. "Not rich, just comfortable. You see, I figured if I could pan or dig enough gold for a stake, I'd head west. I got this dream of a little valley somewhere in Wyoming territory, or maybe Montana territory, either one as long as it's west of here. A little valley with a small cabin set up against the base of a mountain. Maybe even a wife and some kids someday."

"So, you'd hang up your guns and be a farmer?" Violet smirked.

Jack grinned at her. "Ain't nothin' wrong with bein' a farmer. My father was a farmer and a cowhand, but I was thinkin' more along the lines of a rancher. I know cattle, and with enough gold to buy a herd and enough land, I believe I would make a right fine cattleman."

"At the rate you're going, I would say it is more likely you're going to make a right fine dead man," Violet shook her head, and her eyes widened as the words left her lips.

Still grinning, Jack crossed the room until he stood in front of her before he spoke. "Miz Violet, you may well be right, and if you are, then I would hate to meet my Maker with any regrets." Before she could react, he leaned down, wrapped his arms around her waist, pulled her in close, and kissed her soundly.

5

Violet stared at the cards in her hand. It had been two days since Jack's kiss had left her breathless. In those two days, she had closed her eyes at least a hundred times and mentally relived the kiss. Whether by instinct or desire, when he had wrapped his arms around her and pulled her close, she had looked up at him. When his lips met hers, her body melted into his, and she kissed him back with a passion she thought had died long ago.

When it ended, he had walked out with a smile on his face. Across the room, Jane grinned and raised an eyebrow. Violet had stood right where he left her, trying to decide if she wanted to kiss or shoot him again. As she looked at her cards and the growing pot on the table, she still was not sure if kissing him again would be the wisest move, but at least she had lost the desire to shoot him.

"Seem kinda lost tonight," Alice leaned close and whispered.

Violet shrugged. "Lot on my mind," she half-whispered back.

When the bet reached Violet, she folded. As the hand played out, she looked around the Bella Union Saloon. For reasons unknown to her, she found the hum of conversation and the clink of glasses coming from the bar rather irritating. Even the smell of Poker Alice's cigar aggravated her. Violet watched as Alice pulled yet another pot towards her ever-growing pile.

"I believe I'll call it a night," Violet nodded across the table at Grasshopper Jim and then smiled at Mr. Dakota.

"I reckon it's time for me to head to home as well," Alice announced as she stuck her cigar between her teeth and gathered in her winnings.

Both men shrugged as if to say guess they might as well call it a night too, but neither actually spoke the words aloud. Each player cleared their money from the table, and the two men headed for one last drink at the bar.

As Violet turned to leave, Alice stepped to her side. "I think I'll walk along with you partway," she said.

Not sure how to respond, Violet smiled and started for the front door, with Alice trailing along behind her. Violet's gut told her that Alice was not merely being polite. Several times throughout the evening, Violet had caught her looking her way as if she was studying her. It had been more than a little unnerving, and had Alice been a man, Violet would have said something about it, but since she was most definitely a woman, Violet figured she was probably just trying to figure out her tell.

"Was watchin' you at the table tonight," Alice announced as they made their way along the edge of the street.

"Saw that," Violet turned her head far enough toward Alice to see she was looking her way again, "I don't have a tell, if that is what you were wondering."

Alice laughed, "Actually, you do, but that's not why I was studyin' you."

"Is that right?" Violet stopped and faced Alice. She could feel herself reddening and was glad it was too dark for Alice to see her face.

"That's right," Alice answered, and tossed what remained of her cigar into the street. "As for the tell, when you have a good hand, those green eyes of yours are a shade darker than usual. It is a very subtle difference, but I assure you it happens."

Violet did not have a response, and the more she thought about it, the more frustrated she got with herself. She was just about to turn and walk on when Alice continued, "The reason I was studyin' you and the reason I decided to walk with you for a bit was because I figured you could use some female company."

"Really? And why is that?" Violet knew she had in no way hidden the confusion in her voice as soon as she spoke.

Alice laughed, "Well, darlin', being a woman poker player is hard enough in and of itself, but bein' a woman poker player who has fallen in love and is fightin' it... well now that's a whole 'nother animal altogether."

"What the hell are you talking about?" Violet managed to keep the volume of her voice down, but she could not hide the anger in her tone. "And who the hell are you to..."

Alice held up a hand as she interrupted her, "Listen, I've been where you are. Had folks whisperin' behind my back and talkin' out the side of their mouths when they saw me. Right or wrong, it happens, but I can promise you I ain't that kinda person. If I have something to say to you, I'm gonna come right to you and we're gonna have us a talk."

"Is that so?" Violet felt like her head was spinning.

"Yes, ma'am," Alice assured her. "That's why I figured maybe we'd have us a little talk. You could tell me how you're feelin' or not feelin' about that kiss old Jack Abbott laid on you a couple of days ago."

In the dark, Violet could not tell for sure, but all of her senses told her Alice was grinning from ear to ear. "Who told you Jack Abbott kissed me?" she snarled, unsure why it mattered.

"Who do you think?" Alice asked in return.

Violet inhaled deeply, then let it out slowly as she thought, and said, "Jane. Damn, her."

Alice chuckled. The sound was strange as it echoed off the surrounding buildings. "She does talk a good bit when she's had a few, and I reckon if you traced the grapevine back far enough, you'd find her with a bottle in hand, spinnin' quite a yarn. But no, I heard it from the Mary Farnum."

"The mayor's wife?" Violet chided herself as soon as she asked the question. Of course, it was the mayor's wife, she was the only Mary Farnum in town.

"Listen," "Alice reached out, looped an arm over Violet's shoulder, and softly said, "Us women have to stick together darlin'. How 'bout we traipse on up to your house and find us a drink?"

Whether it was the sisterly way Alice's arm felt or the shock of knowing everyone in town was talking about Jack kissing her, Violet did not know. What she did know was that, for the first time in a long time, she did not want to sit alone in her house tonight.

"Maybe just one drink," she said. Then, as the two started up the street with Alice's arm still draped around Violet, she added, "And I do not for one minute believe my eyes are a darker shade of green when I have a good hand."

"Believe what you want," Alice laughed, "Tonight we're gonna talk about love, perhaps tomorrow we'll argue about poker."

~

Violet eased herself down into the warm water. One of the reasons she had purchased this particular house was this little room. Billed by the seller as a small guest room that could be rented out if she ever found herself in need of additional funds, she knew the instant she saw it that it would be her bathing room.

Like so many men, the seller had doubted her card-playing skills as well as her ability to bluff, and it had cost him dearly. She had known the instant she saw the house and its location that she wanted to buy it and would have willingly paid the asking price, but after the crack about her finding herself in need of funds, she had faked a smile and said, "It's a nice place, but I think I'd like to look around a bit."

"Look 'round, look 'round," he had stammered. "Ma'am, if you ain't noticed, there ain't a lot of options in this town right now, and I cain't promise you I'll hold this while you have a look 'round."

"I understand," she had turned and started for the front door as she spoke, "and I would not for one second ask you to hold onto it, but a woman in my position must watch her funds, and this might be more than I can afford at the moment."

That was a lie, of course, at that precise second, she had enough to buy the house three times over, thanks to several good nights on her way to Deadwood. Even now, the thought that the man had used her gender to judge her poker skills irked her. She smiled as she looked around her little oasis in the middle of the wilderness, for that was what she considered her bathing room. It had taken the man less than five minutes to fold under her bluff, and she had taken possession of the property for just over half of what he had originally asked for it. He had walked away mumbling something under his breath, and she had moved in that very day.

The brass tub she now relaxed in had been among her first purchases, and she had not regretted it one iota. She had purposely kept the furnishings in the room to a minimum. Of course, she had bought an additional wood-burning stove just for her bathing room. Some might have questioned the necessity of having a second stove, but Violet did not like the idea of having to haul water through the house. In her mind, the extra work would make the bath less enjoyable, and since she had the funds, she figured, why not?

Besides the tub and stove, three other items completed the furnishings in the room. The first was a small wooden table which held soap, clean rags, and a small bottle of perfume she had carried with her when she had started west. This she used sparingly, unsure when she would find another bottle whose floral scent she liked as well. The second was a large rug laid out beside the tub, and the final item was an old mirror. It had originally hung behind the bar of the Nuttal and Mann's saloon, where Violet had first met Jane. The memory saddened her, not because of the memory of their meeting but because of what the death of Jane's good friend, Bill Hickok, had done to Jane.

Violet shook the thought of Hickok's death from her mind and stared across the room at her face in the mirror. *Did she really have a tell*, she wondered. She concentrated on her eyes, but the distance was too far for her to really tell much. She had never gotten the chance to play cards with Wild Bill, but now she found herself wondering if she had, if he would have spotted her tell. She shook her head. Damn, Alice had really gotten into her head. Well, tell or no tell, she was sure glad she had been there when they brought in a new mirror. It had not taken much to convince Tom Nuttal to sell the old one to her.

Her thoughts turned to last night's conversation with Alice. She smiled at the memory of how one drink had turned into several and how she had nearly choked to death when Alice talked her into trying her cigar. *I believe Alice and I could become really good friends if I wasn't going to leave with Jack*, she thought.

The thought sprang from seemingly nowhere and shocked Violet through and through. *Even if he gets out of Deadwood alive, I have no intention of going anywhere with him*, she argued with herself, and decided drinking with Alice again was not a good idea.

"So, tell me about the kiss," Alice had ordered after their second drink.

Violet thought she remembered giggling as she told Alice, "It was nothing all that memorable."

"You are an awful liar," Alice had accused.

"What makes you think I'm lying?" Violet had asked.

"Same thing that makes me think you got a good hand at poker," Alice had answered, "your eyes brighten up a bit."

Whether or not her eyes had brightened or not, Violet could not confirm, but that she was lying about the kiss being memorable, of that Violet was certain. She had not been able to get that kiss out of her mind since Jack had walked away. No one had ever kissed her and made her feel the way that Jack's kiss had, not even her late husband.

She had long since given up on love, and the thought of love at first sight, or first kiss, for that matter, was not something she had ever really believed in. Hell, she was nearly thirty years old and far too old to be fawning over any man like some... *Goodness gracious*, she interrupted her own thought, *what is the matter with you?*

And before she could stop herself, the answer arrived: *You're falling for Jack Abbott.*

6

"And just what is it you would like for me to do?" Sheriff Bullock asked.

Violet inhaled deeply, trying to maintain her composure. "I want you to run the McKinney brothers out of Deadwood."

Violet watched as the sheriff used his index finger and thumb to massage his forehead. To her, it was obvious that he was stalling. She had been in too many poker games to allow such a tactic to succeed. "You aren't afraid to them, are you?" she asked.

Violet had asked the question hoping to elicit an outburst of masculine ego. She did not get it. Instead, Sheriff Bullock, looked up at her with a half-smile and said, "Now, Violet, if I didn't know better, I would think you were suggesting I was a coward."

Violet felt the blood rush from beneath her collar. In frustration, she clenched her teeth and narrowed her eyes, "So, what are you going to do?" she asked.

"Everything that I possibly can do within the restraints of the law," Bullock answered. "Which is, at this time, nothing."

"Nothing!" Violet half-stood as she shouted. The volume of her own voice shocked her, and she quickly returned to her seat and repeated in a more appropriate tone, "Nothing?"

"That is correct. Nothing," Bullock nodded. "After talking to Jack, I spoke with the McKinney brothers. They claim they have no idea what Jack is playing at and swear they weren't even in the area when he was shot. Without witnesses, it's their word against Jack's, so all I can do is wait and see what happens."

Voilet's frustration boiled over, and she could feel the tears welling. "What happens, huh?" She stood as she spoke. "What happens is that the two of them will confront Jack, and Jack will die. That's what happens." She turned and started to leave, afraid that if she stayed any longer, the dam of waterworks she was fighting to hold back would break, and the sheriff would be the first man in many years to see her cry.

"Miz Violet," the sheriff's voice stopped her in her tracks.

"What?" she asked, but did not turn to face him.

"If there is a shootout between any of the parties we just discussed," his voice was calm, but Violet could sense the seriousness in his tone, "anyone who lives through it will not be welcome in this town. We cannot have law and order if we allow such activities to continue here. So, if you have any sway over Jack Abbott, I suggest you have a visit with him."

～

Violet knocked on the door to Jack's room, stepped back, and ran her hands down the front of her blouse. It had taken her most of the last two hours to formulate the speech she planned to use to get what she wanted, but as she stood waiting for Jack to answer the door, she found herself wondering if a life with Jack was truly what she desired.

"Two seconds," Violet heard Jack say from the other side of the door.

Violet felt her pulse quicken and cursed inwardly. The way this man, whom she barely knew, was able to affect her she found infuriating. The thought occurred to her that if she turned and walked away quickly, Jack would never know she had come to visit him. She shook her head. She would have her say.

The door swung open, and Violet stood speechless. The rehearsed speech that she had planned disappeared like smoke in the wind. They say time and distance makes the heart grow fonder, but this was ridiculous. It had only been two days, and he had been just across the street and down the way a bit, yet here she was, unable to get a word out.

"Well, hello, Miz Violet," Jack smiled and raised an eyebrow as if he had been expecting her to stop by.

Violet could feel the moisture in the palms of her hands. She squared her shoulders and wiped them along the edge of her skirt. "We need to talk," she finally managed.

"Do we now?" Jack's smile widened. He stepped back, half-bowed, and waved his arm, indicating she should enter.

"Yes, we do," she answered, and brushed past him.

She heard the door close behind her as she surveyed the room. It was small but neat. A bed took up the largest area, but there was also a chair and a small chest of drawers on which was a pitcher of water and a basin. Behind those, hung on the wall, was a small mirror with a chipped corner.

"Do you have a chosen topic for the conversation we need to have?" Jack asked as she turned back to him. After closing the door, he had leaned back on it, as if to bar her escape.

Any desire or thought Violet might have had of escape vanished. She simply wanted to step into him and feel his arms wrapped around her again, instead, she said, "Your kiss the other night indicated to me that you have feelings for me."

"Is that so?" Jack smirked.

"Are you saying, I'm wrong?" Violet asked.

"I think I will wait to confirm or deny such accusations until I have additional information," the smile left Jack's face but not his eyes.

Violet felt her jaws clench. "Do you always have to be such an ass?" she nearly spat the words.

"Not always," Jack pushed himself away from the door, "but there is a big difference in bein' shot and havin' a beautiful woman break your heart into little pieces."

"And what would you know of broken hearts?" Violet asked.

"More than I care to admit," Jack answered, "but I think we're strayin' from the original topic."

"Indeed, we are," Violet agreed. "The kiss. As I said, I believe it indicated you had feelings for me. And since you have chosen to withhold... well, since you won't verify those feelings, you leave me no choice but to move forward. I came here to tell you that I believe I feel something for you as well."

"Oh, so you love me now?" Along with his question, the smile returned to Jack's face.

Violet felt herself wince at the word love. "I don't know that I would go so far as to say love," she admitted, as much to herself as to Jack, "but there is something there, something special. Something I haven't felt in a long time, maybe never."

"So not love, but not mere infatuation either?" Jack queried.

Violet felt herself flush. "Damn you, Jack Abbott, for being an infuriating ass! No, it is not mere infatuation either. I don't know what it is, but I would like the opportunity to explore it, and for your information, I'm no stranger to heartbreaks myself."

The features of Jack's face softened, and he pointed to the chair in the corner. Violet was not sure she wanted to sit down but did so anyway. Jack crossed to the bed and eased himself down onto it. For a long minute, he simply looked at her. When she started to speak, he raised a finger to his lips as if to say no. Without understanding why, she obeyed.

After what seemed like an eternity of silence, Violet began to hear her own heartbeat thumping beneath her breasts. As she watched Jack's eyes studying her, Violet began to fear she had made a grave error in coming. She was sure he was mulling things over in his mind. She could appreciate a man who did not jump to quick decisions, but the anticipation of the outcome of his pondering left her feeling nearly breathless.

When she thought she could take no more, he finally said, "Miz Violet, you are correct in thinkin' that the kiss meant I had... have feelin's for you, but here is the problem as I see it. First, I am leavin' town in the mornin' and headed west. Second, I am a hunted man. If the McKinneys don't shoot me down in the street on my way out of town, then they will surely follow along and hound me until either I or they are dead. I do not think that is the kind of relationship you want."

Violet felt as if her heart was about to deflate, but she refused to give in. "So, you would just leave town empty-handed? I thought you planned to find gold and gather a stake."

The smile returned to Jack's face. "Thanks to Miz Jane, I won't be leavin' empty-handed. You see, Miz Violet, I already had plenty of gold for a stake when Sam McKinney tried to shoot me down. As a matter of fact, I was in the process of cleaning my tools and heading to town when he came on me. I had the gold in my saddle bags, and I guess Miz Jane found it when she stabled my horse for me. She looked after it and my guns until I moved in over here."

Jack reached down and pulled a pair of saddlebags from the floor and patted them. Violet noticed for the first time that Jack was wearing his gun belt. The walnut handles of both guns visible in the holsters tied down to each of his legs. So, she had failed. He was going to die in the streets or be driven out of town for killing the McKinneys. In that instant, she was angrier than she had been in a long time. This man had disrupted her life. The desire to win at cards, which had kept her soul breathing when she had lost her husband, seemed to have disappeared, and Jack Abbott was to blame. She had just offered her heart, or at least a chance at it, and now she felt foolish, and Jack Abbott was to blame. Had she not saved his life? Had she not nursed him back from death's door itself? Housed him. Saved him. The thought hit her like a shot of whiskey on a dry throat. She had an ace in the hole, she had saved him.

"You owe me." The words were out before she had a chance to consider their ramifications, "I saved your life. You owe me."

Jack laughed. The sound startled Violet, and she flinched. She felt heat as redness flash across her face when Jack said, "How 'bout we do a little arithmetic, Miz Violet? First, you shot me. That is one. Then you saved me. That is also one. But one cancels out the other, and so that makes us even."

Violet had heard enough and started to rise from the chair she was seated in, but before she could, Jack stood himself, "Now just a second, Miz Violet. I can see you're a mite riled, and I'm sorry for my part in that, but good sense tells me - and I'm sure when you stop to think this through, it will tell you too - that havin' feelin's for a man like me ain't all that smart. Now, as for owin' you, I reckon I do owe you something for puttin' me up and tendin' me while I was mendin'. If you'll allow, I'd like to give you..."

Violet cut him off before he could finish the sentence. "Oh, no, you don't," she said as she rose from the chair. "You can keep your damn gold, Jack Abbott." And without another word, she pushed past him and out the door.

7

"The McKinneys have been tellin' it 'round town that you're leavin' because you're scared," Jane told Jack as he gathered his saddlebags and duster off the floor of the lobby.

"That so?" He smiled at her.

"It sure is, Jack," she answered. "You want I should tag along with you for a while just in case they was to try shootin' you in the back again?"

Jack looked at the woman standing in front of him. The faint smell of whiskey on her buckskin outfit might fool some folks, but Jack was not one of them. That Jane was very capable with the pistol she wore, he had no doubt, but putting her in danger on his part was something he was not willing to do.

"Thanks for the offer, Miz Jane," Jack felt the ire rise in him as he spoke. The thought of the way he had been hunted was beginning to eat at him. "You know I was raised poor," Jack was not sure why he felt the need to explain himself to Jane, but he did. "My Pa worked on a cattle ranch. He was a good hand, and when he met my Ma, the rancher made him foreman and gave him a little house to live in. Now I'm not sayin' we ever went hungry. We always had food, but except for a few furnishings and some personal items, my folks never owned a darn thing." Jack paused and looked around the room before continuing, "Crazy thing is they were both as happy as larks just livin' there on another man's land. Trouble was, I was not. I wanted a place of my own."

"Ain't nothin' wrong with that," Jane said.

"No, I reckon there ain't, Jane," Jack agreed, "but there ain't nothin' wrong with bein' satisfied with what you have either, and Pa told me that often. He also told me that there was no shame in walkin' away when there was no profit in stayin', so in case you're wonderin' if I'm scared, I am. Anyone who walks into a gunfight without at least a bit of fear is a fool, and believe me, I am a lot of things, but a fool ain't one of them. I want you to know that I'm not leavin' because I'm scared. I am leavin' because there is nothin' to be gained by shootin' it out with the McKinneys."

"I ain't so sure about that," Jane interjected. "As I see it, Sam McKinney is a bad hombre, and if'n you don't kill him now, you're gonna have to keep one eye over your shoulder for the rest of your life."

Jack considered what Jane had said and could see the wisdom in it, but even as he pondered on it, his mother's words rang in his ears: violence begets violence. In that instant, Jack felt tired, tired clear through. He was tired of shooting people, tired of being shot and being shot at, but mostly he was tired of feeling like his dream of having a place of his own would never become reality.

"Miz Jane, words cannot express how grateful I am for all you have done for me," Jack threw the duster over his shoulder and offered Jane his hand as he spoke, "If you ever decide to venture west, look me up. I believe I'll find me a bit of breakfast and then be on my way."

As Jane shook his hand, she said, "If I ever get out that way, I'll sure 'nuff look ya up."

She released his hand, and Jack held the door for her. Before walking through the door, Jack took one last look around and wondered how long it would be before he slept in an actual bed again.

~

Jack finished his breakfast and laid two coins on the table. As he rose from his seat, the thought crossed his mind that in the days since he had left Violet's house, he had not seen either of the McKinneys. He had not tried to hide his presence from them. A visit to Banner Grocery for an order of supplies should have been enough to let anyone who cared to know that he planned on leaving town. He had not gone into details about his travel plans with the owner of the Montana Corral when he had gone to check on his horse and purchase a pack mule, but Jack had told him he would be around in the morning to pick the animals up and would settle his account then.

The more he thought about it, the more the fire in his chest began to burn. So be it, if they wanted trouble, then let them come. If not, he would saddle up and ride out, leaving trouble behind him, and with any luck, the McKinneys as well. He crossed the room to the door, opened it, and stepped out onto the wooden planks of the boardwalk. Stepping to one side of the door, he studied the street. His duster thrown over his shoulder, he held his saddle bags in his left hand. His right hand floated just above the pistol in his right holster.

The street was busy. Folks hustling here and there about their daily business, but none of them were Sam or Thad McKinney. Jack released the breath he had been holding but refused to let himself relax. He turned and headed toward the livery.

With long, steady strides, he made his way down the street. His horse was saddled and ready, along with a pack mule. He paid his bill, mounted his horse, and rode to the Banner Grocery.

He dismounted, checked the street for any sign of the McKinney brothers, and stepped inside. James, who was behind the front counter, looked up as Jack shut the door. There was something about the store owner's demeanor that caused Jack to pause.

"Got your order all ready to go," James announced.

"Somethin' botherin' you?" Jack asked as he approached the counter.

James shrugged. "Gunplay, even the possibility of gunplay, bothers me, and from what I've heard, where you are, the possibility of gunplay increases drastically."

Jack thought about trying to explain that he was a peaceable man but decided, since he was in the process of leaving town, it was not necessary, so instead he nodded and said, "How much do I owe ya?"

James handed Jack a piece of paper with everything he had asked for written on it. Alongside each item was the price, and at the bottom the tally. Jack paid, picked up the supplies, and made his way to the door.

At the door, he paused long enough to say, "Just so you know, I never shot anyone who wasn't shootin' at me."

Opening the door, he stepped out onto the boardwalk with the supplies. Across the street, he spotted Jane watching him. So, she had decided to play the part of his guardian angel after all. He smiled and nodded.

Stepping down into the street, he began to load the supplies into the panniers on the mule's back. His thoughts turned to the trail. He was looking forward to the smell of clean air and the sounds of the mountains.

As he pulled the canvas top of the pannier closed and secured it, Jack saw a man step quickly through the door of the Banner Grocery. He could hear folks running and doors slamming shut as he turned slowly around and started out into the street. What had been a busy thoroughfare was now deathly quiet. Somewhere down the street, a piano played, unaware of what was happening.

Jack spotted Sam as he stepped down off the boardwalk on the far side of the street. Thad was already in a position off to Jack's right. In Jack's mind, the world slowly faded away until there was nothing but the stretch of dirt between him and the two McKinney brothers.

"You shouldn't have killed John," Sam snarled as he squared himself.

Jack saw no reason to respond but simply waited. He sensed movement to his left and realized Jane was still on the boardwalk. "Jane, you stay out of this," he shouted, "this is between me and them."

He did not look to see if she had obeyed. He stood with both hands ready above the holsters at his sides. Noise no longer existed. It was as if the air itself had vanished, and there was simply nothing between Jack and the McKinneys but space. He had never faced two people at once. His mind worked out the logistics. He was sure Sam would be the faster of the two. Could he draw and shoot in both directions at the same time? It was something he had never practiced, and he found himself wishing he had.

He could feel beads of sweat forming along the edge of his mouth. Was he fast enough? *We'll know soon enough, Jack*, he told himself. And then Thad dropped his hand to his gun.

Both of Jack's guns cleared as Thad's gun started up. Jack knew before he pulled the trigger on the gun in his left hand that Thad was too slow. As his eyes shifted to Sam, Jack knew Sam had beaten him. Sam was faster than Jack, if only by a split second. Jack fired anyway, and as the gun in his right hand bucked, Jack felt the bite of Sam's bullet as it grazed his left shoulder. Sam had not taken enough time to aim.

Jack worked the hammer and pulled the trigger of both guns once more, watching as both McKinney brothers staggered backwards. Jack's aim had been true. Each of the brothers had taken two bullets to the chest, and as they tumbled backward into the dirt, Jack had no doubt that both were dead.

Jack dropped both guns back into their holsters and turned to see if Jane was still on the boardwalk across the street. She was there, and as his eyes met hers, her eyes went wide with fear, and she grabbed for her gun.

Jack spun, drawing as he turned. The sound of a single gunshot rang out as he completed the turn. He watched as a man's body toppled from the boardwalk into the street in front of him. Both guns followed the body to the ground as Violet stepped out into the street, the gun in her hand still trained on the man she had just shot.

Jack holstered his pistols once more and then turned to look at Jane. Jane smiled and shrugged before sliding her own gun back into its holster. When Jack turned back to Violet, Sheriff Bullock was moving quickly along the boardwalk in their direction. By the time he reached them, people had begun to fill the streets.

"It was a fair fight," Jack heard someone say, "I saw it all from the window. Those McKinney brothers braced him both at the same time, and then the third fella tried to shoot him in the back."

The sheriff met Jack and Violet on the street beside the third man. "Any chance you know him?" Bullock asked.

Jack looked down and nodded, "Yep, that's Clem McKinney. He was a cousin of the other two."

"Well, I reckon there's enough witnesses, so a trial won't be necessary," Bullock looked around at the crowd as he spoke, "but we can't have gunfights if we are to have law and order, so I'm afraid..."

"I was on my way out of town when they braced me," Jack cut him off, "I reckon I'll be on my way, if that's okay with you."

"It is," Bullock nodded.

"What about me?" Violet asked.

Both Jack and the sheriff turned to her with confused looks on their faces.

She looked from one to the other and then asked Bullock, "Am I in the clear here?"

Bullock looked down at Clem McKinney and back at Violet, "Was he about to shoot Jack in the back?"

"He was," Violet answered.

"Then I reckon you're in the clear," Bullock said.

"In that case," Violet smiled as she spoke, "how would you feel about buying my house?"

"Well, now, I..." Bullock started to answer before Jack cut him off.

"Wait just a darn minute," Jack said.

"No, you wait just a darn minute, Jack," Violet turned and pointed up at him as she spoke, "I just saved your sorry hide, so shall you do the arithmetic or shall I?"

With a chuckle, Jack pulled her close and kissed her. When he released her, he shook his head at Bullock and then said to Violet, "You finish your business with the sheriff and pack your things, I'll go find you a horse."

ABOUT THE AUTHOR

One Pen – Endless Possibilities. I cannot think of a better way to describe my writing. Born and raised in Southern Oklahoma by a high school English teacher and a newspaper columnist, there was little doubt that at some point I would turn to words for comfort. Surrounded on all sides of my family by spinners of yarns and tellers of tales, there was little hope that I myself would not become a storyteller.

CAUGHT IN THE CAT'S CLAUSE

ELISE GEDICKE

PROLOGUE

I've always appreciated the male physique, but not as much as I have since meeting my True Mate, Keegan Rowe. He was sculpted from the finest mold. Pure muscle, tanned skin, and the dreamiest eyes. He was sex on legs.

We met four months and twelve days ago. We've been on the run from my pack for four months and eleven days.

Here's the thing about shifters: they find human authority laughable but hold their laws so sacred that lawbreakers end up dead. There are no shifter jails, just a whole lot of unmarked graves. Keegan is a shifter too. He knows the law as well as I and, technically, we did break it. But we also followed it. So, what do you do when two laws contradict each other?

The law states that the bond between fated True Mates is sacred. Finding one's True Mate is rare. Like humans, shifters fall in love, get married, have kids, get divorced... But a True Mate? That's different. If two shifters are married and one spouse finds their True Mate, it's the law that the other must step aside. A True Matehood is celebrated, even by the abandoned spouse. That's how sacred the bond is. Most shifters don't find their True Mate. They'll find a lovemate or a companion. True Mates go beyond love and physical attraction. The bond links their souls and forms a mental connection that love-mates don't possess. It's believed by some that most shifters don't have them, and a True Mating only occurs when two shifters are so perfect for each other that the bond can't help but be formed.

There are many different kinds of shifters and each species has their own set of laws, but the one law we all agree on is that shifter species don't mix.

I'm a wolf shifter. I never expected my True Mate to be any shifter other than a wolf. Why would I? There was even a law that states shifters can't crossbreed. Why would there be a law that stated that when there was a chance that mates could be from different species? Except, to my knowledge, there had never before been a cross-species True Mate pair.

Until now.

My Keegan was a jaguar.

1

I moaned, ignoring the hard rock below me and concentrating all of my energy on the hard body above me. Keegan, my True Mate, was worshiping my body as if we didn't have a care in the world. In truth, in these fleeting, precious moments when we felt safe enough to rekindle our bond, we didn't have any cares beyond the feel of each other.

I loved how gentle he could be. Loved when he took his time and cherished every inch of my body. But not now. I needed him like I needed air. I locked my arms tightly around his broad back and yanked him closer to me.

Keegan latched onto my neck, sinking his long canines into my flesh at the same time that he drove his hard cock into me. I silently screamed in rapture.

I refused to allow myself to feel regret for the need for silence. I longed to scream to the world that this perfect man on top of me was *mine*. The possessive need was very difficult to ignore, but I had to. For now, we were safe in a cave in the northern part of Canada. We didn't know where exactly, as it had been a long while since we had dared to enter human civilization. North was our goal, but the trackers on our trail were making our journey slow and treacherous.

Our shifter senses were great, but so were our trackers'.

If I had screamed at the top of my lungs as I so desperately wanted to, I could lead the trackers on our trail directly to us.

I felt his sweet caress inside my head. He knew what I was thinking, what I was feeling. Keegan was a very passionate lover and despised the need for silence.

I could feel my orgasm rising as he pounded into me. Keegan wasn't being gentle, and I didn't want gentle. The cold stone beneath me was biting into my back as he pushed me harder, faster, higher. I reveled in it. His strength, his power, his love... It was all Keegan, every part of him. And I loved it all. From the tips of his blonde hair all the way down to his fuzz-covered toes. He wasn't just Keegan anymore, as I wasn't just Sasha. We were one.

True Mates.

Keegan and I had met by pure chance. If I hadn't gotten a flat tire, and if he hadn't pulled over to see if he could assist a stranded car, we would have driven right past each other on that dirt road outside my home in Deadwood and never have known our other half was in that passing vehicle.

I had never been the exhibitionist type, but damn if I didn't let him claim me right there on the side of the road on the hood of my car where anyone who passed us could see. I had worn my True Mate's mark before I even knew his name.

Others might say I'd been too rash in allowing Keegan to claim me because, if I had realized Keegan was a jaguar, I would have never sealed the deal. In truth, it had never mattered to me what Keegan was. I'd known as he'd taken me that this man, this beautiful, wonderful man, was feline. He could have been fully human or a fluffy bunny. It didn't matter. He was *mine*.

I had brought him to my home, believing that the Law of True Mates was stronger than the law to keep shifter species separate.

I was wrong.

Once we'd stated that we were True Mates, the doubting and the shouting started. How could I be so naïve as to believe this *feline* was my True Mate? I was a silly girl with hopeless romantic dreams... None of them would listen.

Our shouting brought the attention of our neighbors, who were also part of my pack. It wasn't long before our Alpha showed up at our door. Drake hadn't even given Keegan and me a chance to explain or prove that our bond was real. The moment he saw Keegan, he'd declared our bonding nonexistent and sentenced Keegan to death. I could either die with him or I could kill him.

I chose Option C. We fought our way out of my father's house, escaping into the wilderness. My pack had been chasing us ever since. I was fairly certain my brothers were leading the hunt.

Keegan and I hadn't even left with the clothes on our backs or the supplies in our cars. We'd shifted mid-fight. Everything we owned had been left behind. On the rare occasion when we had to enter society, we'd had to steal clothes and money. We weren't proud of it, but desperate times called for desperate measures. As an unmated, unmarried female, I had still been living in my father's house with my pack in Deadwood. Keegan's house was in the outskirts of Phoenix, Arizona. His car and mine had been left in my father's driveway. We had nothing but each other.

Keegan increased the pressure of his bite on my neck as his right hand reached up to roughly pinch my left nipple. My orgasm exploded around him. My nails dug into his back, drawing blood. He didn't care. I could feel through our bond how much he loved it.

Reflected on his neck was the same mate-mark he'd placed on mine. The need to mark each other had been irresistible the first time our eyes met. Though the mark of a True Mate would never fade, Keegan liked to reaffirm his claim on me. Often. I didn't mind in the least.

Keegan pulled out of me and then a moment later I felt the spurts of his release land on my belly. Condoms were not an option for us, and not just because we were in the middle of nowhere without a supply. As True Mates, we couldn't stand the feel of something between us. Even something as thin as a condom. Problem was, unprotected sex tended to have reproductive consequences. We both understood that we couldn't risk pregnancy. So as much as I hated him releasing his seed outside my body, it was a necessary evil.

Keegan, my beautiful cat, lapped up his spill, cleaning my body. It was a ritual he performed following making love to me and one that I enjoyed greatly.

After licking his seed from my belly, Keegan continued down and latched his mouth between my legs. I was in Keegan-ecstasy. I loved Keegan's tongue. Maybe it was a feline thing, but damn the man was talented.

I was on the verge of orgasming again when I felt him stiffen. The alarm going through him snapped me from my blissful haze. His eyes widened and he was crouched in a protective stance in front of me a heartbeat later.

If I hadn't been distracted by the sensations of Keegan, I would have smelled what his weaker nose had only just picked up on.

Our cave was no longer safe. My pack was closing in.

~

Stupid, selfish, arrogant... I could feel Keegan's terror as he scolded himself for being so distracted. He believed that he'd selfishly put his need to make love to me above my safety.

I rolled my eyes and stood up. I was not some helpless damsel who needed her mate to protect her. As much as it warmed my heart to see and feel Keegan's protectiveness and possessiveness, I was just as motivated to do the same for him.

Keegan's thoughts relaxed at my touch on his shoulder. Our eyes met, my dark brown to his bright green, and our bodies shouted in that moment our love for each other. I'd only known him for four of those months. That was less than one percent of my life spent in his arms.

But I'd take it. If I died today, I had no regrets. Less than one percent was still more than zero.

We shifted at the same time. Keegan's jaguar was large, bigger than my gray wolf. Though I had never compared the two side-by-side, I was fairly certain he was larger than Drake, my Alpha. I loved his spots. I'd never counted them all, but I longed to. Maybe some lazy morning in the near future, I would lie next to him and count them. Run my fingers through his fur and thank the gods our running days were over.

He brushed up against me. *Someday soon, I promise.*

We walked out of the cave, shoulder to shoulder. The cave wasn't big enough for a fight. We were too easily pinned. We needed space, a chance to run.

I could smell them clearly, my pack. Their scents were so familiar to me and I was ashamed at how much they brought me comfort. To a wolf shifter, their pack wasn't just friends and family. They were warmth, support, and connection.

I smelled my brothers first. Both of them. I hated that they were part of the hunting party sent to kill us. Had they volunteered or had they been ordered to come? Unlike me, they wouldn't refuse their Alpha's command. They were leading the pack to us.

My oldest brother, Dan, had also found his True Mate. All of his life, Dan had believed himself to be straight. Then Colin, a male wolf shifter, had visited our pack and *bam!* my brother was suddenly gay.

Okay, so it didn't really work like that. Dan explained that he wasn't into men. He was just into Colin. And that didn't matter. There was no law that stated two men couldn't be True Mates, as long as both men were of the same species. It was rare to have a gay mating but not unheard of.

Not like a wolf mating a jaguar.

I felt it was pretty shitty of Dan to be hunting me for my choice of life partner. Dan was a stickler for the rules, though. And the law was very clear: don't mate outside your species.

Keegan shivered beside me. I knew it had nothing to do with the impending force coming straight for us and everything to do with the Canadian winter. My fur coat was built to survive this weather. Keegan's wasn't. Jaguars were southern creatures.

I pressed my warmth into Keegan's side. My thoughts were of a warm, tropical beach and the promise of sex, sand, and sunshine.

An image came to the forefront of my mind as Keegan pushed aside my sunny daydream. I saw myself through Keegan's eyes. My human form was a mess, leaf and dirt covered. I was above him, riding him. We were together, one in mind, body, and soul.

I understood what Keegan was showing me. He didn't need warmth. He didn't care that we were surrounded by snow and not sand. He just needed me. It was all he wanted. No matter where life took us, it was all he ever wanted.

I love you, I told him, pouring all my thoughts and feelings into the declaration so there was no room for doubt.

A grin appeared on his feline face, along with a look of pure smugness. *I know.*

I nipped at his shoulder but couldn't help my laugh from escaping. It died the moment my brothers stepped into view.

I knew their wolves as much as they knew mine. We'd grown up together, played together. They'd taught me to fight, track, and hunt. I loved them.

And I would kill them if they tried to hurt Keegan.

Keegan and I pressed our animal heads together, and then I stepped forward. He hated this, watching me walk away from him. We'd discussed many times what to do if my pack caught up to us. As much as we were prepared to fight, neither of us wanted to hurt my pack. They were strangers to him, but Keegan understood that hurting my pack would hurt me. And Keegan would do anything to prevent that.

When I was halfway between Keegan and my brothers, I shifted. Nudity was unavoidable as a shifter. We'd been taught young not to look or objectify our fellows.

Dan stepped forward too and shifted.

My brother was taller than me but shorter than Keegan. Like me, he had dark hair and eyes that we inherited from our late mother. There wasn't much that could kill a shifter, but an eighteen-wheeler truck was one of them. I had been eight. Dan had carried me out of the funeral when I couldn't stop crying.

"Sasha."

I flinched at my name. Not because it was the first time in months since I'd heard anyone but Keegan say it, but because it was *Dan* who said it. My brother, my protector, my friend.

My killer?

"Dan." I struggled to keep my emotions in check. "Are you here to see if I'll abandon my True Mate?"

It was Dan's turn to flinch. "That creature isn't your True Mate."

"We share a bond, just as you and Colin do." I hoped my mention of Colin would make Dan think twice about what he was here to do.

"Sasha, we don't breed outside our species. You've lain with a," he crinkled his nose in disgust, "a *cat.*"

I touched my neck where Keegan's bite shone. Shifters healed quickly and our bodies didn't leave scars unless the wounds were salted prior to healing. But a bite made by a True Mate was different. That mark never faded. I couldn't call it a scar, because it wasn't. It was almost like a birthmark that had finally been revealed. It marked me as Keegan's, as my mark did for him.

Dan's mate-mark on his throat was just as clear as mine. Lovers could bite and mark each other, but those faded like any other wound. It was the mark of a True Mate when they didn't fade.

I hoped it was proof enough.

"Please, brother," I pleaded with him. "I had no more choice in who my True Mate was than you did."

"The law—"

"And laws can't be wrong?" I asked. "The laws were made centuries ago. I understand them, I abide by them. I always have. But Keegan is my True Mate, no matter what the law states." I could see the calculation behind Dan's gaze. I took a step toward him, the cold snow crunching beneath my bare feet. "Why should the law of species be more important than the law of mates?"

As Dan let out a long, frustrated sigh, our brother, Elias, shifted. Elias took after our father. He was shorter than Dan with a broad body of pure muscle. Elias worked for the pack as one of Drake's enforcers.

I turned my gaze to him now. He was the current threat. Dan might be older, but Elias was stronger.

"Feline slut."

I flinched. Keegan yowled behind me. I could feel his hatred toward my second oldest brother. Knowing that if Keegan attacked, Dan would defend our brother and I would lose any progress I had just gained with him, I sent comforting thoughts to Keegan. I needed him to calm down. I could take any verbal jabs my brother had to say.

From Elias' perspective, I'd torn our family apart. I'd shamed our father and Alpha. I deserved what was coming.

But it wasn't Elias' choice whether to attack. It was Dan's.

Dan was more levelheaded than Elias. Drake would have only sent Dan if he believed there was hope of saving me. What Drake didn't understand, what none of them did, was that there was no saving me without saving Keegan. If Keegan died today, so would I. If my pack wouldn't do it, I'd find someone who would. Or a really tall cliff.

You will not die today. I have not had nearly enough time devouring your delectable body.

I felt my cheeks redden at Keegan's thoughts in my head and hoped my brothers believed it was from the cold.

Dan's eyes, though, narrowed. His gaze jumped from me to Keegan and back again. Lovers could mark each other and, depending on how deep the wound was, it could take some time to heal. My mate-mark wasn't good enough proof that I was Keegan's True Mate because it was fresh, but our mental link was. Dan, the only other True Mate present, had been the only one to catch what had just passed between Keegan and me.

He held up his hand to stop whatever snide comment our brother was about to say next. Elias grudgingly obeyed. Dan took a cautious step toward me. He had a calculating look on his face. "If I asked you to close your eyes, would you do it?"

It was my turn to narrow my eyes. "Why?"

"Please, little sister."

Keegan and I debated this silently for a moment and then I nodded. Keegan came forward until he was at my side. I saw how uncomfortable Dan was with the giant feline so close. I put my hand on Keegan's spotted back.

I closed my eyelids, but I was far from blind. Through Keegan's eyes, I could still see my brothers and packmates. His sense of smell might not be as good as mine, but his eyesight and hearing trumped any wolf's. Behind my brothers, there were four other pack members, Garret, Colby, Chris, and Evan. They were formidable trackers and fighters, but they weren't the best. Drake either underestimated Keegan's ability to fight or overestimated Dan's ability to separate me from my mate.

Elias was the only true muscle in this group. If Drake wanted us dead, he would have sent a different hunting party. What was the Alpha playing at?

Dan held up his hand with two fingers raised. "How many?" he asked.

Without hesitation, I answered, "Two." He was obviously talking to me because Keegan couldn't speak out loud in his shifted form. He held up his other hand without lowering the first and I said, "Seven."

Elias stepped forward, clearly pissed off. "What the hell are you doing?"

Dan lowered his hands. "They're bonded." There was a hint of relief in his sad voice.

Elias snarled, "Impossible."

"Think about it, brother," Dan snapped at him. "This isn't some girly fantasy. She doesn't wear his mark because they just fucked." My cheeks burned with embarrassment. There was no way my brothers couldn't smell what Keegan and I had been doing when they'd come upon us. "She wears it because she's his. Their minds are linked. If we kill him," Dan's eyes landed on Keegan, "we kill her too."

I understood then why it was *this* hunting party the Alpha had sent. They didn't believe that the law of species was more important than the law of mates because they didn't believe the law of mates applied. They believed I believed I was in love or perhaps just infatuated with a jaguar. Despite our insistence, it had never occurred to him that we could actually be True Mates.

Elias's eyes narrowed. "She's faking it."

"If we separated them by miles, it wouldn't matter," Dan snapped at our brother. "They're connected. He," Dan indicated to Keegan beside me, "would still be with her just as assuredly as Colin is with me now. Distance won't separate these two."

The look in Dan's dark eyes was pure pity. It was clear he didn't know how to help me.

"We'll leave," I told Dan, anxiously. I hated to admit it, but I was terrified of what would happen now that they knew the truth. "You'll never hear or see from me again. I only ask that you stop hunting us. Just let us go."

It was the best outcome I could see. If Dan backed off, we would never return. Maybe we'd continue west to Alaska or jump onto a boat and head for Asia or Australia. I'd miss my home. I'd miss my father, my friends, and my pack.

But I would have Keegan. He was all I needed. I just wanted us to be able to live our lives without the fear of death looming over us.

I honestly thought my brother might agree to my terms...until he shook his head. "I'm sorry, Sasha. My orders are to bring you home."

Keegan let out a low hiss. I tensed too.

Dan quickly put up his hands. "Easy," he encouraged us. "Here's my proposal. We will escort you, both of you," he indicated to Keegan too, "back to the States. We then will bring you," his eyes landed back on me, "to Drake. He—"

"Keegan," I informed my brother. It only then occurred to me that Dan wouldn't know his name as introductions had never been made the day I had brought Keegan home to my family. "His name is Keegan Rowe."

Dan seemed to struggle for a moment and then said, "Keegan. He will have to wait outside the pack terr—"

"No," I said, which was echoed in my head by Keegan. "We won't be separated."

Dan gave me a look like he was scolding a child. "Sasha, be reasonable. We can't bring him onto pack lands."

"We can and we will," I told him. "If I am going onto pack lands, so is he. The law of mates says you cannot deny one True Mate access. Where one True Mate goes, the other is allowed to follow."

"Drake—"

"Dan, if we can prove to Drake that we're True Mates, just as we did for you, he won't be able to deny Keegan either."

"And he might decide to kill you both!" Dan shouted, his voice full of fear.

Keegan shifted forms. He wrapped his arm around my naked waist and kissed my filthy hair. I leaned into him, unable to help myself.

Keegan's voice was a smooth baritone. "Where she goes, I go."

"Be reasonable—" Dan pleaded again.

"We are," I told him. "If this is our only option, then we face it together." I crossed my right arm over my middle to link my hand with his at my left hip. "Could you allow Colin to walk into a potentially deadly situation without you?"

Dan's silence was answer enough.

"Ask Colin to go to Drake," I told Dan. "Tell him that we will come back, peacefully, if *both* of us have permission to be on pack lands. Make sure Colin tells him what you've discovered too. Whatever Drake decides is our fate, we will abide by. Be it banishment or death."

We waited and watched. Keegan and I slowly moved back, giving the party their space as Dan communicated with his mate.

Keegan and I had shifted back into our animals to protect our human bodies from the cold. I was lying over him like a large fur blanket. Elias would see Keegan's lack of protection against the elements as a weakness. I saw it only as strength. He'd journeyed where no jaguar would dare go in an effort to keep me safe. He'd risked everything, including his own comfort, to safeguard me.

Keegan was anything but weak. Even knowing that my brother had a good amount of muscle on Keegan, there was no doubt in my mind that Keegan would win if a fight ensued between them. Keegan was too focused, too disciplined. Like the cat he was, he always landed on his feet. My brother was too rash. He used his strength as the advantage it was. Unless he was facing an opponent like Keegan, who knew how to turn his strength against him.

Dan finally nodded, but it wasn't to the others. Had Colin been in front of him, I knew that he and Dan would have been holding hands. Even now, Dan's hand twitched as if he was craving the touch of his mate. Sometimes the mental link just wasn't enough.

Dan approached us cautiously.

I stood up and rose as a human. Keegan remained where he was. He could fight as a human, but his advantage was his sheer size against the number of wolves surrounding us.

I put my hand behind me to touch the coarse fur on his head, silently conveying my hope. Dan didn't smell nervous as he approached us. Keegan's responding purr was full of contentment.

I saw the disgust on Elias's face and I flipped him off. I would not allow my brother to make me feel ashamed for touching my mate.

"Colin was able to reach Drake. While our Alpha is still uncertain about the bond I have assured him you have, he has granted you and," he hesitated before saying my mate's name, "Keegan a twenty-four-hour reprieve to return to pack lands and state your case. He'll decide your fate once he has heard you out."

Keegan and I didn't respond to my brother right away. As much as I wanted to go home, it was a risk. We could run now. If we were fast enough, and my brother's pursuit wasn't wholehearted, we could make it. Escape would mean never seeing my pack again.

But we'd be free. Free of prejudices and ignorance. Free to live our lives. All I needed was Keegan.

To my surprise, Keegan brought forward my memories of growing up in my pack. He knew how much being a pack animal meant to me. Keegan was a solitary creature by nature. The idea of leaving home was not as heartbreaking for him as it was for me.

His main concern was if Drake would believe us. Would we be killed if we returned to my pack? Was the risk of death worth the idea of getting my home and pack back?

Keegan nudged me forward. His mind was set, even though mine wasn't.

I sighed and faced my brother. "We'll return with you with the understanding that, if there are any signs of hostility, we're gone and you'll never see us again."

Dan let out a long sigh of relief and finally smiled. He held out his arms to me. "Can I?"

I rushed into his embrace. He was so warm. Gods, how I missed his scent. He was still my Dan.

A low growl rumbled behind us and I looked over my shoulder at my mate. Through our link, I saw what he saw: me, naked, in the arms of another man, who was also naked.

"Ew," I crinkled my nose. "Relax, babe, he's my brother."

Dan let out a low chuckle.

2

We traveled with the pack. Dan was the only one who risked coming near Keegan, but he always walked with me between them.

I felt reassured, having Dan wholly on our side. We had a really good chance of coming out of this alive and safe. Drake and Dan weren't just pack-mates, they were best friends. They'd grown up together. Drake had wanted Dan as a Beta when he took command of the pack from his father. Though Dan had declined the honored position, he remained at Drake's side as his trusted advisor. The pack heavily respected him.

I couldn't get Elias to look at me. Every time I went near him, he would start to growl. And it wasn't a *go away, sister* kind of growl. It was mean and threatening. It made me wonder, *would* Elias hurt me? Was I in danger from my own brother?

Elias and I had never been particularly close. Although Elias and I were closer in age, it had been Dan I had connected with. But Elias was still my brother. I loved him, the stubborn asshole. The idea that he might not love me anymore hurt. Was I *soiled* in his mind, having been touched by a cat?

Keegan made me stronger, not weaker. Loving him made me whole, not damaged.

We would have to cross back into the States in our animal forms. None of us had clothing or passports to get back in legally. We certainly hadn't crossed into Canada using traditional, human means.

It was decided we were going to swim.

Keegan was less than pleased by this route. I wondered if that was why Elias had chosen it. He was issuing a challenge to Keegan, daring my mate to object. Keegan, though, had no intention of backing down. He could swim.

Unlike other cats, jaguars actually enjoyed swimming. Keegan's dislike was the temperature of the water.

I stayed by him. Unlike his, my fur would insulate me from the frigid temperature. I waited patiently for him to enter the water on his own.

Dan stayed behind with us. I wasn't sure if it was to help or to make sure we didn't bolt. Elias and the others had jumped right in and were already halfway across the river.

Keegan slowly sauntered in, his golden fur shining against the winter water.

Dan looked at me, indicating for me to go first. But I had other plans. I leapt onto his back and rolled the two of us into the chilly water. When Dan surfaced, he nipped at me playfully. I barked back a laugh and then hurried after my mate.

I rolled my eyes at his slow paddle. Summer would be here before we made it to land if we crossed on at his pace. He heard my silent snide thought and glared daggers at me. After all, it was *my* stupid brother who had set this path. This was *my* fault.

I easily pushed ahead of him. When Dan and I were a good thirty feet in front of him, I started sending Keegan thoughts of all the naughty things I wanted to do to his body once we made it to land.

His speed increased dramatically.

I could barely contain my laughter as Keegan exited the water at the same time as Dan and me. He shook the cold beads of water off his fur as Dan and I did. As a result, we got each other wet again. Keegan and my eyes met with silent laughter. Despite the cold and wetness, he was enjoying himself.

The others were waiting with an air of impatience about them. I didn't care if they thought we were slow. They're not the ones who had to coax an irritable jaguar to cross an icy river. I had a feeling Keegan was going to have me follow through on every sexy thought I had sent to him in the water.

My canine mouth lifted in a smile. I didn't mind that at all.

Now that we were in the States, we started to scout for faster transportation. My pack lived in Deadwood, South Dakota. We were presently in northern New York by Black Lake. It would take us over a day in a car if we were driving straight. But since none of us had any money, clothing, or transportation shoved up our rears, we were going to have to steal everything.

Every pup in the pack was taught from early on how to pick locks, hotwire a car, and break into human homes unseen. I used to joke with my friends that the pack was raising a den of thieves. As in, a *den* of thieves. Because we're wolves...

I crack myself up sometimes.

A low snicker brought my attention to my mate. He'd picked up on my memory and was laughing at me. I glared, because it was a laugh *at*, not a laugh *with*.

He gave me a look that was pure sex and my loins clenched. We hadn't made love since the day my brothers had tracked us down. That was almost two weeks ago. Both of us were craving each other something fierce. I couldn't fathom how Dan had been able to stay away from Colin for so long. Keegan was right beside me and I felt like I hadn't touched him in ages.

Elias snapped in my direction. There was no doubt he'd been able to smell my desire for my mate and he clearly wasn't happy about it.

I growled low at him.

Ignore him, Keegan told me.

I huffed, indignant, and rubbed my head along his. Keegan knew I was doing it to piss off my brother, but he still took the opportunity to return the touch.

We found a small town a few miles into the States. There was icy snow on the ground, but we covered our tracks well. We couldn't risk our tracks being spotted by humans and any local wolves tracked and killed for coming too close to town.

It was Keegan who spotted the empty residence. It was a three-story house with no smoke coming from either chimney and the lights were off. A quick sniff confirmed his findings. The house was empty of humans and pets.

I shifted, so did Keegan. Without hesitation, he locked his fingers together and I leapt onto them with my right foot. He threw me up in the air with ease. My hands latched onto the edge of the roof and I hoisted myself up to the window ledge. After a quick examination, I verified that there were no alarms or sensors on the window. I didn't even have to use a claw to unlock it: it was already unlocked.

I smiled, loving trusting humans.

Of course, in their defense, what human would believe that their third story attic could be breached from the outside without a ladder?

Slipping easily into the small window, I made sure to destroy any signs of my foot- or handprints in the snow. I journeyed downstairs to let my pack and True Mate in.

It was a good thing the house was dark and it was after midnight. Any human looking out their window would have died of a heart attack after seeing seven, naked, hot-as-fuck men standing outside their neighbor's house.

Sensing where my thoughts were, Keegan rushed first through the door and took me into his arms. His mouth went over his mark on my throat, but he didn't bite down.

I smiled, getting a kick out of this new jealous streak of his. Of course, once we were back home and I saw the females of my pack looking at him, I was going to be just as possessive and jealous.

Keegan took me upstairs to the master bedroom. He pressed me back against the wall of the bedroom, crowding me. I touched the hard flesh of his arms. It was so tempting to just—

Dan cleared his throat from the doorway. I glared at him over Keegan's shoulder. We both sighed, stepping away from each other.

The master bedroom had a walk-in closet. As the other rooms in the house clearly hosted children, all eight of us came to the master to dress. The humans who lived here were going to come home to quite the surprise.

After dressing, we looked around for any valuables or a safe.

Colby hit the jackpot with a floor safe in the den that housed some money and a set of car keys. We went to the garage and found a red truck sitting there. The eight of us squeezed into the crew cab with Elias in the driver's seat.

The drive out of New York was slow and quiet. Given that we were in a stolen vehicle, Elias drove the speed limit. Any tolls or traffic lights with cameras, we all ducked down to avoid our pictures being taken. Elias put on a pair of sunglasses that had been clipped on the visor and he'd taken a baseball cap from the house.

Hours later, when we ran out of gas, we pulled off the road and hid the stolen truck. Then we journeyed on foot across Ohio. Keegan and I ran hand-in-hand. Garret trailed behind the group to cover our bare footprints.

Around the Michigan border, Chris walked onto a junk yard and purchased a rundown beater for a couple hundred dollars. We used the rest of our stolen cash to fill the tank and grab some food at the station.

Keegan lowered me back onto his chest and tucked my head under his chin. Content against my mate, I slept.

I dreamed of blood and terror. I couldn't find Keegan, even through our mental link. I called for him and called, but he never answered. I ran. Elias was suddenly there, crimson liquid drooling from his razor-sharp canines.

I jumped awake.

Keegan tightened his arms around me. *I'm here, I'm right here.*

I clenched my arms tight around his, trying to catch my breath. I inhaled his scent and clung to his warmth, but the terror wouldn't leave my thoughts. What if we were making a mistake returning to my pack?

3

My pack owned a large, gated compound outside of Deadwood. The Alpha resided in a massive building the pack called the Manor. Many of us, like my family, lived in a separate house on pack property.

Routinely, there was a single guard at the gatehouse with sentries posted around the gate at various intervals. Dan must have warned the pack through Colin that we were arriving because there were a number of guards waiting for us at the gate.

My hackles rose. We were *not* going in if we were going to be treated like prisoners.

Dan reached over and patted my knee. "Easy. Drake's just being cautious."

"Keegan's not going to hurt anyone!" I shot back at him. "This is ridiculous."

"With pups on property, can you really blame him?"

A growl was my only response. Yes, there were pups on property. My pack was home to three hundred-plus wolves. What did Drake think Keegan would do? Go on a rampage and start eating the pups? Rape the women? Kill all the men?

I understood that Drake had a responsibility to protect the pack. He was the Alpha. But it rubbed me the wrong way that my Alpha, my family, could believe that *I* would love someone who was capable of their concerns. What did that say about their opinion of me?

Keegan nuzzled my cheek with his human nose. *Let them have their guards, if it makes them feel more comfortable.*

We don't have to be here. We can go. We can leave—

He cut me off with a shake of his head. *This is your home, Sasha. I love you too much to take you away from that. If there is a chance you can get your pack back, it's a chance worth taking.*

I touched his face. *Not at the expense of your life and safety.*

He gave me a wicked smile. *I can take care of myself.*

I knew that, but I still didn't like risking him. I had a sinking feeling in the pit of my stomach that I was sacrificing Keegan for my pack.

Dan parked the car outside the gates and opened the door. Two guards stepped forward to take the keys from him. They would dispose of the car.

I followed Keegan out of the passenger side door. Chris, Evan, Garret, Elias, and Colby immediately surrounded us. Did they doubt our word? Did they think we would run?

While tempted, I held my head up high, took Keegan's hand, and started toward the compound's gate. There were seven guards waiting for us. My father also waited at the entrance, behind the guards. I tried to meet his eyes, but he wasn't looking at me.

I hadn't noticed Colin until he was running forward. The guards parted, allowing Colin to leap up into Dan's waiting arms. Their kiss was passionate and so intimate that I had to look away out of respect.

My grip on Keegan's hand tightened. *That* was what I wanted. To be able to come home to my pack with my True Mate. To kiss him openly in public without shame or fear of retribution. Even if Drake allowed us to stay, would I get that? Would my pack forever shun me for who fate chose to be my True Mate?

When they broke apart, Colin and Dan rested their foreheads against each other. It was obvious they were communicating silently. Dan was tall with some bulk. Colin was of average height for a human male but was considered short for a shifter. He had curly blonde hair he kept cropped around his ears and the brightest blue eyes I'd ever seen. On multiple occasions, I had heard Dan refer to them as his favorite sapphires.

Colin finally pulled away from his mate and turned to hug me. "Look at the trouble you've gotten yourself in."

I let out a short laugh. "Life was getting a little boring for my tastes."

He chuckled too and turned to kiss my cheek. "Come. Drake's waiting for you."

My nerves, subsided momentarily by Colin's acceptance, immediately returned. I stepped back from my brother-in-law.

Colin glanced back and forth between Keegan and me. I brought Keegan closer to my side. "Keegan, this is Dan's True Mate, Colin. Colin, this is my True Mate, Keegan."

The men seemed to size the other up for a moment and then Colin extended his hand. In a graceful swap, Keegan shifted me to his other side with his left hand and reached his right hand forward to Colin.

I heard many gasps, growls, and curses as Colin, a wolf, and Keegan, a jaguar, clasped hands in full view of everyone. My heart nearly shattered at Colin's open acceptance of my mate. Even Dan hadn't offered me this. Without words, Colin was publicly stating that he believed Keegan was my True Mate.

"You treat her right," he said to Keegan, meeting the bigger man's eyes without any sign of submission. "She deserves the best and I hope for her sake that you're it."

I was nearly in tears.

Keegan nodded once. "I strive to be everything she needs and more every day."

"Good." Colin stepped back, taking Dan's hand. "I guess we should head in then."

~

What disturbed me more than being paraded through the compound was my father's distance. He walked at the head of the procession and had yet to look at me. He had greeted Elias and Dan, but not me.

I remembered the day that Dan had brought Colin home. It was nearly two years ago. Colin had been so shy meeting the rest of us. Dan, who had never hinted before that he'd been interested in men, was so open and honest that it sealed the presence of their bond. Our father had sniffed Colin once, taking in their combined scent, and then had hugged Colin, welcoming him into the family.

My father wasn't an overly affectionate person. The death of our mother, despite that she wasn't his True Mate, had devastated him. My mother had been a kind and passionate person. She always joked that she was too much of an open book to have a poker face. I missed her every second of every day. It was like a part of my soul died the day the drunk driver had run that red light.

For my father, it was like his entire soul had died. It had taken the involvement of both sets of grandparents and one of my uncles to get him to remember he had pups he was still responsible for raising. Gradually, my father returned to the land of the living.

I couldn't imagine the pain he'd gone through. My mother hadn't been his True Mate, but that didn't mean their love hadn't been real.

My father had accepted Colin into the family unconditionally. To my knowledge, he'd never treated Dan any differently even though Colin was a male.

To have him turn his back on me... That was devastating.

Did my father really think I would run from my pack, family, and home for a passing romance?

There was no hesitation in Keegan's stride as we were led through the compound. Even when *pussy* slurs were made in his direction, Keegan never flinched. I was called *whore*, *tramp*, *slut*, and even *traitor*. It was easier for Keegan to ignore the pack's comments. They were strangers to him. I certainly couldn't have done it if I hadn't been holding Keegan's hand and feeling his support.

The scene from *Game of Thrones* where Cersei was forced to walk naked through the streets with the monks chanting "shame" behind her came to mind. Given other circumstances, I might have found the reference funny. Not today.

Keegan, however, did. He let out a loud laugh, resulting in many startled stares. Whatever they'd thought of him before, they likely were adding *insane* to the list now too.

I saw Drake waiting for us outside the Manor at the bottom of the stairs.

Drake's grandfather had built the community, gating us off from the rest of the world after the Deadwood Forest Fire of 1959. When Drake had taken the mantle of Alpha, he'd changed little about our way of life.

Drake held himself tall, his hands clasped behind his back. As a wolf, Drake was huge. He was strong, confident, and merciless. Since becoming Alpha, he'd had three challenges for the position. Drake had beaten them into submission with ease. I'd always looked up to him. He was the center of our pack, our blood, our strength.

Right now, he was also my judge, jury, and possible executioner.

I was no match for my Alpha. To even consider fighting him was laughable. Glancing at my mate, though, I realized that Keegan and Drake might be more evenly matched than I thought.

Keegan raised the back of my hand to his lips. *It won't come to that.* Then he nodded toward Drake, releasing my hand. *Go on.*

I didn't understand what he meant at first. I looked back at my Alpha and the loneliness from being separated from my pack slammed into me. Drake seemed to sense it too, coming forward. The guards moved out of his way without question. I saw some of them lean forward, ready to protect their Alpha, but none dared to warn him against approaching us.

A couple of feet away, Drake stopped. I saw the concern on his face. The last time I had seen him, Drake had been in a rage. He'd burst through our house's front door, splintering it to pieces and had demanded I kill Keegan or die with him. Did he regret those words and the hastiness of his ultimatum now? Even if he did, would he admit it?

No longer holding Keegan's hand, I approached my Alpha cautiously.

It was the small smile on his lips that did it. I ran into his arms. Drake picked me up, holding me close and tight.

Multiple emotions from different sources hit me at once. I felt my own pain from being separated from my pack and reassurance for being back with them. I could feel Keegan's uncertainty and dislike of me being in another man's arms, but I also felt his acceptance that I needed this bond between my Alpha and me as much as I needed the one between him and me. From the bond I shared with my Alpha, I felt Drake's kinship with me and concern for me. But mostly, I felt like I was home.

I know I could have made a home with Keegan and been happy wherever we'd ended up if we'd kept running. It had never even crossed my mind that I couldn't have been content with just him and me.

But the feel of the pack was like nothing else and was something every wolf needed. It was why most lone wolves eventually went insane. We were pack animals. It wasn't just in our blood; it was in our souls.

My heart burst with love for my mate. *This* was why Keegan had risked stepping into a pack of wolves. He'd understood what I'd needed when I hadn't.

I had to protect him. I had to make his risk worthwhile.

Though it was difficult, I stepped back from my Alpha, wiping my tears off my cheeks.

"He's mine," I told Drake. "I don't understand it and I can't explain it, but he's mine. We're bonded."

Doubt and pity were plain on his face. "Sasha, sweetling, he *can't* be yours."

I had trouble meeting his eyes. "I don't know why he is. I don't know what joke the gods are playing right now, but this is real, Drake. If you kill him, you kill me too. I *need* him. I *love* him."

"Needing and loving someone is far different than being bonded to them."

I pointed to Dan. "We proved it to my brother. He understands that I'm bonded to Keegan. He doesn't like it, but he can see it."

I looked pleadingly at my brother. Dan sighed, kissed Colin's hair, and then stepped forward to stand at my side. "She's right, Drake. I've seen it, I've smelled it. They *are* bonded." Drake's lip curled up, but no growl escaped him. Dan wasn't challenging him, but he was contradicting him. "Smell her, Drake. Her scent has changed, just as his has." Dan indicated to Keegan behind us. I noticed he didn't use Keegan's name.

"I can prove it," I offered when Drake said nothing. "Dan had me close my eyes and see through Keegan's eyes. I did it for him and I can do it for you too."

For the first time, Drake's eyes landed on my mate. I wondered what he saw. We were dirty and hungry. Keegan was barefoot in clothes that were too small for his large build. I was also still in my stolen clothes.

"Come here."

I glanced behind me to see Keegan's only response to the Alpha's command was a raised eyebrow. Then the staring contest started. I hated it but I understood it. Keegan was not pack. Drake wasn't *his* Alpha and therefore he didn't need to obey him. But he was on pack land, which Drake ruled.

My heart beat loudly in my chest. Drake couldn't back down. Not unless he wanted to lose the respect of the entire pack. He couldn't submit to a *cat*. But I knew how stubborn Keegan could be. He was just as unwilling to submit to a *dog*. What if the staring contest turned physical? What if it turned deadly?

Fear gripped me. I didn't want to see either man hurt. Drake was my Alpha. He was my protector and guide, my friend and guardian. He was pack. And Keegan... Well, Keegan was my everything.

It was my anxiety that saved the day. Though it hurt his pride, Keegan looked away first, his eyes landing on me. Through our bond, I could feel that he did this to ease my worry. He could have held out. He could have forced the challenge, but he didn't. For me.

Shame filled me. What else was Keegan willing to sacrifice for me?

Everything, he vowed as he stepped forward to my other side. I now stood with Keegan on my right and Dan on my left. I could feel the eyes of the pack behind us, the tension of the guards around us. They did not like having this unknown stranger so close to their Alpha.

Keegan might have lost the staring contest for my benefit, but he was not unwilling to meet Drake's eyes. I felt just as nervous as the guards, but for completely different reasons. Both males could do serious damage to the other.

I wondered if their individual loves for me were enough to keep them from doing so.

Drake stepped forward. Keegan held very still as Drake brought his nose right up to Keegan's shoulder and then neck. He never touched Keegan, but he was very close. I was tempted to reach for Keegan's hand. I held back, knowing the action might be perceived as weakness on Keegan's part.

Instead, I sent him reassuring thoughts. I knew he could sense my fear and doubt, though.

Finally, Drake stepped back, wrinkling his nose. He clearly did not like Keegan's scent. Weird, because I loved it. If I was a cat, he would be my catnip.

A snort escaped me at my own joke, drawing everyone's attention to me.

Keegan raised an eyebrow in my direction. He was the only one who knew the thought behind my snort.

Early on in our relationship, I had asked Keegan if he regretted that I wasn't a cat. Even if I wasn't a jaguar, would he have preferred me to be feline?

Without answering my question, Keegan had made slow, passionate love to me. To this day, my cheeks redden at the memory of that night. It was only afterward that Keegan had said, "*I love everything about you and would never change a single thing. If you were a feline, you wouldn't be my Sasha and I love my Sasha. So, the answer to your question is a simple and emphatic no.*"

I wondered if he did now, seeing as he was currently standing in the center of a giant wolf pack being judged by my Alpha.

Keegan met my eyes. *My answer remains the same.*

I smiled. *Good.*

Drake's eyes narrowed. Like with Dan, I could see the cogs working in his brain. I knew he was fighting with the evidence before him and the entire history of shifters. Was it possible we were the first True Mate pair of different species? Or had there been others who had been killed or terrorized into hiding? Had their mating survived?

Could ours?

'til death and beyond, Keegan sent me.

Still won't be long enough, I replied. Gods, how I loved this man.

Finally, Drake let out a long sigh. My hope rose tenfold. Dan had had a very similar reaction.

"I can't deny that the two of you are bonded." He spoke loud enough so the pack could hear too. There were many murmurs of doubt following their Alpha's announcement. Quieter to me, Drake said, "Unfortunately, I am not sure what that means for you. I can't see a future here."

I reached for Keegan's hand. He gave it quickly and willingly. "Can we at least stay the night? We're both tired and hungry. We can figure out our future in the morning." I added because I had to, "But we will have a future, Drake. Even if it's not here."

He met my eyes, his full of sadness and pity. "I hope so, little one. I truly do." Louder, he said, "You have my permission to stay the night." To Keegan, he stated pointedly, "I highly recommend you do not wander about without Sasha or Dan with you. The pack will physically leave you be and I expect the same behavior from you."

Drake's words were clear: he couldn't stop the pack from verbally attacking Keegan. I wondered how they would react to me. They'd been so cruel when we'd first entered.

Drake turned to my left, looking beyond Dan. "Are your daughter and her True Mate welcome in your house, Xavier?"

It took me a moment to gather up my courage to look at my father. I didn't know if my things were still at his house or where our cars were for that matter. We'd left with no possessions, no thoughts other than survival.

My father's face was stone-cold as he shook his head once. "No."

My heart sank. I felt my knees give out. Keegan quickly caught me, wrapping an arm around my waist while supporting my weight fully.

Dan stepped forward. "They can stay with Colin and me."

Soon after their mating, Colin and Dan had started construction on a house of their own. They'd remained in my father's house, completely welcomed, until theirs was complete. It was a quaint house on the outskirts of the compound. I loved their house, but it wasn't *my* home.

After a nod from Drake, my father turned and walked away. Elias followed him, looking smug and victorious. Tears ran freely down my cheeks and suddenly I was angry.

I found my footing and stomped after my father. "Mom would have accepted Keegan." It was a low blow. I wasn't ashamed by my words, though. My father stopped but didn't turn back around. "As soon as she knew Keegan was my True Mate, Mom would have welcomed him with open arms."

My father squared his shoulders and said, still facing away from me, "The day you brought that *thing* home to us was the first day I was grateful your mother wasn't alive." I flinched—his blow was lower. "You haven't just shamed yourself and our family. You've shamed her memory."

He continued walking, the pack separating to allow him to pass. Many reached out with a supporting hand.

Strong arms wrapped themselves around me, drawing me back onto a hard chest. I hung my head, defeated.

Colin touched my shoulder. He still was the only one who willingly came near Keegan. "Come," he said, "let's get you home."

4

There was no containing my sorrow.

I barely made it to Colin and Dan's home before my knees gave out and my vision blurred. As soon as we were through the threshold, Keegan picked me up, cradling me to his chest. I barely registered him asking directions to a bathroom. Colin and Dan's house only had one and it was in the master bedroom. Colin led us in, told Keegan he would leave us clothes and we could take the bed tonight.

In the privacy of the bathroom, Keegan held me against him one-handed as he bent to turn on the bathtub. Then Keegan stripped me bare. He leaned me up against the counter as he removed his own clothing, always keeping a hand on me.

Before the water was halfway full, he stepped over the edge and sat. He placed me between his legs and cradled me to him.

I don't know how long we stayed there. I was beyond exhausted and cried out. Keegan didn't seem to mind. He kept his thoughts to himself, only sending me feelings of love and reassurance. I was too emotional to offer him the same courtesy. He was front and center for all my pain, fear, and grief.

I probably should have bought him some popcorn to my pity party.

The closest event in my life that I could compare it to was the loss of my mother. The difference, and probably the cause of the greater pain, was the fact that my father was *choosing* to abandon me.

Drake, *our Alpha*, had verified that Keegan and I were bonded. My father was still *choosing* not to accept me or my True Mate.

Through my haze of grief, I realized Keegan was lifting me out of the tub. Keegan must have washed me and my hair. I don't remember him doing so, but

I was now clean. He dried me off and even brushed my hair. I couldn't remember the last time I'd brushed my hair.

I'm not sure if I slept. I know I eventually relaxed into my exhaustion, but I did not rest. Keegan gripped me tight under him, practically resting his entire body on top of me. I didn't feel squashed or constricted. I needed his weight to remind me what it was I was gaining. Otherwise, the sorrow of my losses would have crushed me.

At some point during the night, I reached for him. He was not asleep either and responded immediately. His touches and caresses were so soft and sweet that it nearly brought me back to tears. But these tears were good tears.

No matter what tomorrow brought, I had Keegan.

～

I could feel Keegan's eyes on me as I woke. He was lying on his side, arm propped up to support his head. I didn't remember him leaving me last night, but he must have to shave. I reached forward and touched his bare skin.

Human needs had taken second place when we'd run. Shaving, showering, clothing... We hadn't bothered with any of it. That hadn't stopped our human bodies from producing hair. My armpits and legs were nearly as hairy as Keegan's. His once clean shaven face had come to support a full beard and mustache.

Now Keegan once more resembled the Good Samaritan who'd stopped to aid me on the side of the road. I regarded myself grudgingly. I might be clean, but I certainly didn't look like myself. I was going to need a good while in the bathroom with a hacksaw to get off all my extra fuzz. No Shave November has started a bit early for me...like in January.

Though the thick down comforter was still pulled up to our chests, I knew he was as naked as I. I liked naked Keegan. I could look at naked Keegan all day and all night. I would never grow tired of naked Keegan.

His nostrils flared and his eyes shifted. In a blink, they went from bright green ovals to long slit pupils. I had never feared or disliked his feline eyes. I hadn't needed time to get used to them anymore than I had his scent. They were as much a part of him as his muscles and hair were. His cat eyes were beautiful.

It was the scent of my arousal that caused him to lose control over his eyes. His cat liked the smell of me. Slowly, sensually, I moved my thighs against each other. To our advanced ears, this created a sound like rubbing silk.

His fangs protruded.

I smiled wickedly at him.

He pounced. One moment I was lying on my side facing him and the next I was lying on my back horizontally on the bed with the covers thrown off and Keegan holding himself over me. I reached up and linked my arms around his neck.

As he lowered his head to kiss me, his right hand brushed down my side to my sex. He rubbed my clit for just a moment before dipping a finger inside, checking to make sure I was wet enough to take him.

He needn't have bothered; I was always wet enough for him. For me, Keegan's very presence was all the foreplay I needed. I was never turned *off* around him.

I felt his smile against my lips. He'd picked up on my thoughts. There was an aura of male satisfaction about him now. Great, as if Keegan wasn't cocky enough.

A low rumble quaked through him as he laughed. He rubbed his stiff cock over my slit, dragging a moan from me. *Just cocky enough*, he said as he broke our kiss to lift himself up.

My legs automatically widened, trembling. I loved the sweet anticipation of penetration that flowed through me like a drug.

Similar thoughts and feelings from Keegan echoed my own. He'd often say or hint that being inside me was the most wonderful feeling in the world. But it was these moments beforehand, when our bodies were preparing to connect that I felt our minds were most in sync. We were one before our bodies were.

The tip of his cock grazed my opening. I moaned and couldn't look away from him. His cat eyes and fangs weren't the only parts of him that had shifted. His ears were now pointed on top of his head and his tanned skin appeared spotted in some places. He was a sight to behold.

I knew my body was also starting to resemble my animal-counterpart. My vision kept skipping from seeing colors to seeing in shades of gray. My nails had lengthened and sharpened into claws. It was a good thing Keegan liked the scratches I left on his body. A little pleasure-pain was good for the soul.

My fangs were also protruding from my mouth.

As he seated himself fully inside me, I tipped my hips upward. I needed just a little bit more of him. Always more.

His name chanted reverently in my head.

Suddenly, my hands were pinned above my head, fingers laced with his. The bed didn't so much as jostle.

There was a wicked gleam in his eyes. I knew then what he was about.

I could feel his love for me, the contentment he felt only when he was inside me. But I also felt his worry. His memories of caring for me during the night were a dark shadow on his mind, followed by his deep desire to ensure that I never felt unloved, never felt lonely, never felt unwanted.

As a woman, I was used to multiple orgasms. While I felt there were down-falls to either gender, that was definitely one of the pros.

But Keegan only let me have one this morning. Slowly, purposefully, he brought me to the very edge of pleasure. Then he would back off until my body was once again under control. Again and again, he brought me right up to the brink of orgasm without letting me tip over the edge.

It was torture. It was pleasure. It was frustrating. It was wonderful.

I was beyond begging, understanding, want, or desire. All I could feel was Keegan. Every touch, every kiss, every stroke was like a fiery caress to my soul.

When he finally let me peak, I was lying flat on my stomach with Keegan spread over me. His weight was heavy without crushing me. It was his bite that caused my release. As his canines sank into my neck, I cried out as my pleasure finally ripped through me.

I felt his body shudder on top of me. I was in such a haze of euphoria that I didn't realize he was still inside me. We'd agreed months ago that he would not release inside me for fear of pregnancy. We weren't running now, but we also weren't necessarily safe.

I wondered if this was his way of saying he was done running. No matter what happened, we would stand tall and face it together.

As I came back to myself, I started to feel uncomfortable. I couldn't figure out the cause. Keegan had just made unbearably slow love to me. I was still riding my high of long-awaited release. Why was I feeling discomfort?

Picking up on my distress, Keegan started to lift himself off of me.

I cried out in pain.

He froze. For several moments, we both laid there unmoving. Even our minds were still, as if afraid any motion would cause me more pain. Carefully, I tested moving by slowly shifting my hips side to side.

I didn't even get to the other side.

What is this? We both echoed through our bond. I could feel his fear and uncertainty and I'm sure he could feel mine.

If I didn't know any better, I'd say he was stuck inside me. Oh gods, I could just see the faces of my packmates now. Not only was my True Mate a feline, but we were so unfit for each other that his penis got stuck inside me during sex. The imagined humiliation was nearly as bad as my current pain.

I couldn't understand it. We'd had sex before. A lot of sex. Despite being on the run, we'd always managed to make time for us, to reconnect and strengthen our bond. How could he possibly be *stuck* inside me? What sort of fucked up cosmic joke was this?

We remained frozen for perhaps ten minutes before we felt the immediate difference. His cock started to shrink back down to its flaccid state. As it did, whatever was gripping itself inside me also released its hold.

As soon as he was free from my body, Keegan threw himself off of me and was across the room. I turned on the bed to stare at him. Our minds were so confused, neither of us could make sense of the other's thoughts.

I looked down at his cock and my jaw dropped. Small, curved spikes were retracting back into the skin of his appendage. *Spikes?* No wonder I was in pain. I saw blood on his penis and winced. That was my blood.

My hand went between my legs and we both watched as I lifted it up. It wasn't a lot of blood, but there was definitely crimson on my hand mixed with the evidence of his orgasm.

"What the fuck was that?" I might have been the one to voice the question out loud, but we were both thinking it.

The look in his eyes, now completely human, was one of disbelief and horror. I could both see and feel his mind whirling, not understanding. I got off the bed and he stepped back from me.

I glared at him. "Your cock isn't going to jump out and start attacking me. Stop being stupid. We need to figure this out."

Keegan was pressed into the wall by the door as far as he could go. I closed in on him. Though he knew the blood was there, I still held up my hand to show him. "What is this?" I demanded.

He shook his head. "It's a myth. It's not possible."

"Are you kidding me?" I reached down and gripped his flaccid cock in my fist. "You had *barbs* coming out of your penis! You were *stuck* inside me. And your response to it is that it couldn't have happened because it's a myth? What the fuck, Keegan?!"

I fought back the urge to shove him. I wasn't angry at *him*. Not really. I was scared. Whatever this was, what if it kept us apart?

"Jaguars don't have lovemates," he said slowly, his head hung in shame. "We fuck, we procreate, and we move on. Most shifter felines are the same. We keep to our territories and only journey out for sex. Wolves are most famous for finding lovemates and True Mates. I always thought it was a silly practice... until I met you," he added quickly. "Feline males have barbed penises. As far as I know, shifter felines have never resembled our animal-counterparts in that way."

"Then what myth are you referring to?"

He shook his head. "It's just a story. It's not—"

"If you say 'it's not real', I am going to go out into the desert, find a cactus, bring it back here, and shove it up your ass to see how *you* like it. After that, you can tell me what's real or not."

Despite the seriousness of the situation, Keegan cracked a smile at my threat. He knew me well enough to know I'd follow through if he didn't comply. "It's a story my mother told me when I was younger."

My entire body sagged in sympathy. Keegan didn't talk about his mother. Like most feline shifters, Keegan didn't know who his father was. Felines copulated to procreate but they didn't raise their young like wolves did. It had saddened me greatly when Keegan had told me he'd been on his own since he was twelve years old. He'd woken up one day and his mother was just gone. She'd taught him what she felt he needed to know and had vanished from his life. It was expected of feline shifters. The human foster system was flooded with their kits.

As a wolf, a pack animal, I couldn't imagine it. No pups of ours were going to be abandoned. Ever.

"She said that in the wild feline males have barbed penises to hold the female in place to guarantee pregnancy."

I swallowed nervously. "You're not a wild jaguar."

He shook his head slowly. "No, but upon finding their True Mate, jaguar shifters more resemble our animal-counterparts."

My jaw dropped. "Are you telling me that you've had barbs coming out of your penis this whole time and you haven't told me?"

"What?" he gasped. "*No!* This is the first time it's happened."

"But this isn't the first time we've had sex."

He paled. "It's the first time I've come inside you."

I shook my head. "No, it's not. The first time we made love, on the side of the road, you came inside me."

Keegan's brows furrowed in concentration. I let him have his thoughts, not wanting to intrude or distract him. Finally, he looked at me guardedly. He took a step forward, careful as if he was trying not to scare me.

I rolled my eyes at his ridiculousness. His penis might have barbs, but I wasn't scared of *him*. Keegan would never deliberately hurt me.

He leaned in and sniffed. Then he backed away again. "You're in heat."

My eyebrows shot up and I let out a very unladylike snort. "No, I'm no—" The look on his face stopped my contradiction.

Like our animal-counterparts, female wolf shifters had an annual mating cycle. We could get pregnant in our human forms anytime during the year, but it was during the six-week period in the spring that we were guaranteed to get pregnant. Most of us either abstained, which was difficult as hell given how horny we were *before* we went into heat or we used protection. Human birth-control didn't work on us because of our advanced metabolism but a condom was a physical barrier that worked just as well for shifters as it did for humans.

It had been December when Keegan and I had met. We'd been on the run for over four months, plus the long trip with my brothers to get us back here.

My jaw dropped. Oh gods! I was in heat!

My hands flew to my navel. Was I pregnant? The idea of pregnancy had crossed my thoughts when he'd come inside me just now, but the chances had been slim in my mind then. I hadn't realized I was in heat.

Keegan's hands gently rested over mine. The remorse was clear on his face and through our bond. "I am so sorry, I hadn't realized. I wasn't thinking when I—"

My glare stopped his apology. "Don't you dare. If we made a pup, or a kitten," I added for him, "then we did. I'm not ashamed. *Any* child of ours will be loved so much by me they'll need therapy as an adult." He cracked a smile. I raised a hand to his cheek. "Do you think it's possible?" I asked with heavy excitement. "Do you think we made a baby?"

I could still sense his nervousness. "Well, my body certainly tried."

I let out a long breath, unable to keep the smile from my face. "A baby."

There was a taste of panic in his mind. "Is there a way to know for sure?"

I shook my head. "It's too soon. Wolf shifters have about two weeks into the pregnancy to decide if we're going to carry to term as a wolf or as a human."

"What's the difference?"

"Length of the gestation period and what form the pups are when they're born."

"*They?*" he gasped out.

I nodded. "With True Mate pairs, wolves usually have multiples at birth. But there's a chance it's just one baby, because you're, you know, *you.*"

Keegan, big, strong Keegan, had to lean against the wall for support. If I was being honest, he looked a little green too. "What happens if you stay human?"

"I carry to term as a human would in nine to ten months." I added before he could ask, "If I carry as a wolf, it will only take about sixty days."

"Is there a test we need to go get?" His voice was very dry, and his eyes wouldn't focus.

My eyes narrowed suspiciously at his behavior. "No, it's too soon. In about a week or so, we'll be able to smell if I'm pregnant."

He nodded once and proceeded to faint.

I cringed to think of the sounds Dan and Colin had heard from their bedroom throughout the night. From my crying to our lovemaking, I couldn't imagine they had a decent night sleep.

They came bursting through the door at the sound of my scream at Keegan's head hitting the hardwood floor.

"What happened?" Dan demanded.

"He fainted!" was my obvious answer. I was crouched by my mate, trying to rouse him both physically and mentally.

"Why?" Colin asked as Dan repeated his question of, "What happened?"

"He—" I cringed. Even if I was pregnant, I didn't want to say it to my brother until Keegan and I had a chance to celebrate ourselves. This was personal and private. "I don't know," I said instead. "He just went down."

Dan came closer. His nostrils flared and his eyes landed on Keegan's nudity...and my blood still coated there. I felt my cheeks heat, but I met Dan's accusing gaze.

"He could no more hurt me than you could Colin," I said fiercely. At the same time, I called silently to my mate, *Wake up!* I did not want to face my brother alone. *Are you fucking kidding me?* I shouted at Keegan. *You'll face an entire pack on the off-chance I would be accepted back in, but you faint at the possibility of a baby. What the fuck?* He stirred but didn't regain consciousness. I sat up straighter and slapped him, hard, across the face. *Get up, you coward! I am not telling my brother about your barbed penis without you!*

His eyes flew open.

I bowed my head over his chest, letting out a breath of gratitude. His thoughts came flowing back into me. Concern for me and the baby mixed with embarrassment for his fainting.

I reached up and kissed him. "You stupid, stupid man."

He held me close and then I felt him stiffen as he realized we had an audience. The next moment I was shielded behind him with Keegan crouched between me and Dan. His growl to my family was low and menacing.

Dan stood up carefully, backing away with his hands raised. The look in his eyes though was a mixture of amusement and disgust. "Seriously, cat, she's my sister."

Colin let out a small laugh, eyeing the two of us on the floor meaningfully. "I'm gay, honey. Trust me when I say you're the one I'd rather be seeing anyway."

Dan closed his eyes and let out a low groan. I made a similar noise and thumped my head against Keegan's hard, muscled back.

"We'll let you two be," Dan said, urging Colin from the room. "We're headed out anyway to speak with Drake."

I didn't look up and only nodded into Keegan's back.

Keegan and I were silent for a long time following Dan and Colin's departure. For a while, the only sounds I picked up on were our heartbeats. Eventually he moved. Keegan stood up, extended a hand to me. I took it without hesitation.

I had to break the ice and I wasn't exactly known for being tactful in awkward situations. "So, the idea of a baby makes you faint?"

His cheeks flamed with embarrassment.

I let out a light chuckle and pressed myself against him. I cupped his face in my hands, pecking his skin with gentle kisses. "Don't worry. I'll protect you from the big, bad baby."

5

It was odd, waking up alone. For months, Keegan and I had slept wrapped around each other, never separating out of want, need, desire, and necessity.

Keegan had tackled me to the bed after my sassy remark and had proceeded to prove—or perhaps reaffirm—that he was all man. His strength and libido inevitably became too much for my sleep-deprived body and I had finally succumbed, completely sated.

Despite my multiple, earthshattering orgasms, Keegan had not penetrated me with his cock while making love to me. I could pick up on his worry and fear of hurting me again. While a part of me also wondered the same things, I refused to never not have intercourse with my mate again. Pain and freaky penis barbs bedamned.

That seemed to spur Keegan's determination further to providing me alternative avenues to achieving the pleasure. While I couldn't argue that he'd certainly succeeded in pleasing me, I also had not changed my mind.

I knew right away that he knew I was awake. I had the sense that he had hoped I would sleep longer and never know he had left my side.

Wondering where he was, I closed my eyes and concentrated on seeing through our bond. Shock filled me as I recognized the street where I'd grown up. He was a single house away from my father's. Fear gripped me. What was Keegan doing?

Through his eyes, I saw him walk up the driveway, cross the brick path, climb the three steps, and wait. It was unnecessary to knock on a wolf shifter's door. With our sense of smell and hearing, we always knew when someone was there.

My father opened the door. Like Elias, my father was a stocky man. He'd served Drake's father as Beta when he'd had been Alpha.

What are you doing? I shouted through our bond. I couldn't sense malice in Keegan's motives, but I also couldn't detect why he would wander, alone, through a wolf pack compound to my father's house.

Keegan did not answer my question directly.

"What the fuck do you want?" I flinched at my father's hostility. His eyes were narrow and he crossed his arms over his wide chest.

"I only came to talk." Keegan stood relaxed. "I understand why you wouldn't accept me, but how could you turn Sasha away? She's done nothing wrong."

My father's upper lip raised to bare his elongated canines. "She fucked you, didn't she?"

I could feel Keegan pushing aside his need to defend me from such cruel words. "She cried herself to sleep last night."

Had I just imagined the twitch in my father's sinister glare? Why would he care if I had cried last night? My pain and suffering had been his doing.

Keegan didn't wait for my father's response. He boldly continued on, "I love her with everything I have and everything I am. For whatever reason that fate put us together and despite the hardships we have both endured, I can't help but be grateful for this fluke of craziness. At the end of the day, I get the best gift of all: her.

"I don't know why you pulled away from her or feel the need to punish her. I didn't come here to rub your face in her pain or even our relationship. I just wanted you to know that I love her and I will protect her with my life. You raised an amazing, smart, wonderful, funny, and beautiful woman. Of all things, you should be proud of that."

I could feel the tears sliding down my cheeks as Keegan turned away from my father.

"If you love her, you'll leave."

Keegan paused and turned back. "I can't do that."

My father's nostrils flared. "Then you don't love her. She'll only be safe when she's away from you and you're too selfish to do it."

I could feel the thoughts whirling around in Keegan's head and couldn't help but feel a pang of fear. What if Keegan decided my father was right? Would he choose to leave me? I had trouble catching my breath and had to follow along with Keegan's steady inhales and exhales to calm down.

Though he could feel my panic, Keegan ignored me to address my father. I was so shocked by his next words that my jaw dropped. "Sasha told me your late wife was your lovemate but not your True Mate."

My father's visibly stiffened. "Your point?"

"My point is only this, you were nearly rendered incapacitated by your grief at her loss. I have seen Sasha's memories from that time, and I know and can empathize with your pain." Keegan quickly hurried to speak when my father opened his mouth to interrupt. "Now take your pain from losing your lovemate and multiply it by ten, a hundred, a thousand..." He shook his head.

"It'll never be enough. She's my *True Mate*," Keegan emphasized. "I couldn't leave her any more than she could me. It would not only ruin her, but it would destroy her. In your mind, I don't love her enough to leave, but to me? I love her enough to stay."

Keegan let out a long sigh when my father didn't reply. "For her sake, as well as any future grandchildren, I hope you find it in your heart to accept her. She has such a big heart and it pains me greatly to see her grief over losing you. Speaking as an orphan, no child should have to know the pain of abandonment."

With that, Keegan walked away.

$\sim$

"Are you fucking nuts?!"

Surprisingly, the question didn't come out of my mouth upon Keegan entering the house, but Dan's. Colin and he had come home during Keegan's return walk and had been as happy as I was to discover where my mate had journeyed off to.

Despite my brother's tempered question, Colin's concerned expression, and my annoyed one, Keegan sauntered into the house, closed the door, and walked right up to me. He cupped my face in his big hands and kissed me.

I was dressed now in one of Dan's shirts and Colin's sweatpants. The shirt was too big for me and flowed down to my knees, but the pants fit pretty nicely. I had never considered that Colin's lean frame was so similar to my own before.

Keegan was dressed in a pair of jeans and black t-shirt that smelled like Elias. My nose flared, wondering where he had gotten them from. My brother certainly wouldn't have given those over willingly.

Keegan lifted his head from mine. He tucked my long hair behind my ears. "Good morning," he mused as if we were alone on a deserted island. "I'm sorry I wasn't here when you woke up."

Turning me in his arms, Keegan encircled my waist and pulled me tight against his hard chest. He looked at my brother, who still looked pissed, expectedly.

"You could have been killed."

Keegan leaned his chin on my shoulder and snorted. "The only shifter in this place that is anywhere near my power level is your Alpha. I made sure to steer clear of him."

"That's beside the point. There are over three hundred wolves in this pack. You're outnumbered, despite your power." While I felt Dan could have said it more nicely, his statement was true.

Keegan let out a small sigh.

Without warning, a pulse of power radiated through the room. When it hit me, it felt almost like a caress, a blanket of security. In contrast, Colin and Dan struggled to remain upright. Both looked like a huge weight was bearing down on them. It was affecting Colin a lot more than it was Dan, though my brother was clearly struggling. Colin's neck was completely bared to my mate in submission and he was nearly down on his knees. My brother was stubbornly gritting his teeth and forcing his neck to remain rigid. Despite that, he was unable to meet Keegan's eyes or keep his back straight.

And then it was gone.

Colin and Dan straightened with relief. They reached for each other, needing to physically reassure the other was well. No doubt both were thinking *what the fuck* like I was.

Keegan allowed Dan and Colin a few moments to collect themselves before saying, "That was barely a fraction of my power, pups. Believe me, I was in no danger in walking around your little sanctuary."

"We will circle back to that little display in a moment," Dan said. "Why did you go see our father in the first place?"

I felt Keegan shrug behind me. "My only sense of Xavier is from Sasha's memories. I wanted to get my own feel of the man without the blinders of a daughter's love."

Dan surprised me by nodding to this statement in understanding. "And?" he prompted.

"Xavier's terrified. My nose isn't as strong as yours and even I could sense it. To you guys, it must be pungent."

I tilted my head in confusion. My father? Terrified? That didn't make sense. I'd seen many emotions from my father over the years from happiness and joy at pack hunts to the heart wrenching grief following my mother's death. My father was many things, but he was not a coward.

Keegan's lips pressed against my hair. "Baby, he's not terrified for himself. He's terrified for you."

That was like a knife in the gut. "But he—"

"Sasha." My gaze flew up to meet my brother's. "Losing Mom nearly destroyed him. Can't you see that he feels your mating will destroy you? He can't bear it."

I shook in Keegan's arms. "Then why would he push me away? Why wouldn't he keep me close, help protect me?"

Dan shook his head. "I don't know, honey. Maybe in some twisted way he feels like this will lessen the pain of either your departure or your..." Dan's voice trailed off. He couldn't vocalize the words *your death*. "He's hurting, Sasha. Just as much as you."

I flinched, turning further into Keegan's hold. "We haven't decided if we're leaving yet."

I resisted the urge to put a hand on my navel. With the possibility of a pregnancy, I didn't know if leaving was the better or worse option. On one hand, the pack was the best protection for my pup—or kitten, I couldn't help but add with a small smile. On the other hand, what if the pack rejected my baby because he or she had a jaguar father?

Gods, I loved the idea of Keegan being a father. I knew without a doubt that if I wasn't pregnant, I would do everything in my power to be some day. Keegan deserved the joy of holding his baby in his arms. I was just selfish enough to want that for him.

"Regardless, Sasha, I think you need to give him time." Dan steeled himself and then finally looked at my mate. "You let yourself be brought here," he accused. "There were only six of us in the hunting party. You could have easily overpowered us and continued on with Sasha. Why didn't you?"

I was confused. I knew Keegan was powerful. I'd even measured him up to Drake. But the kind of power Dan was referring to, that Keegan had just demonstrated... That puzzled me. Keegan wasn't an Alpha. Felines didn't have Alphas, not like wolves did. There were some who lived in prides, but they were small groups and rarely matched any wolf pack in numbers.

"The same reason you didn't attack me right away," Keegan replied evenly. I felt his gentle nod toward me. "Hurting you would have hurt Sasha. If you had left me no other alternative, I would have taken you out in a heartbeat."

Dan gave us a wry smile. "I believe you."

"Keegan." When my mate's attention turned to Colin, I didn't miss the way Dan stiffened as if he no longer wanted Keegan and Colin in the same room together. "What I felt, that was impressive. I didn't know felines could be that strong."

"Wolves gain strength from each other. Lone wolves are weaker, but felines thrive in solitude. However, even for a cat, I am unusually strong. I also feel like my power has grown since mating with Sasha." He shrugged. "Perhaps I'm somehow feeding off of the pack through her."

An odd look crossed Dan's face. "You submitted to Drake last night."

I felt Keegan stiffen behind me and knew his eyes narrowed at my brother. "No, I conceded to his will. We're on his land and under his protection. For Sasha's sake and sanity, I did not push the issue further."

"But you could have," Dan said. "And there's a chance you could have won."

Keegan nodded once. "Perhaps. So long as Drake allows us to live here peacefully, I pray we never have to find out."

I stepped away from my mate, needing to see his emerald eyes. "Why didn't I know how powerful you are? I've never felt it."

Keegan's lips twitched before he bent to lower them to mine. "Love, you aren't a threat to me. I doubt you'll ever be able to feel my power the way any other shifter would."

I recalled how I had felt safe and secure at Keegan's demonstration while Dan and Colin were in obvious distress. I wasn't sure I liked their reactions to Keegan's power, but I did take a moment to bask in the fact that I was the one exception to his strength.

Keegan picked up on my train of thought. He took a single step forward and knelt at my feet. Taking my hands, he kissed each palm and finger pad before placing them on his face, so I was cupping him around the ears. From that position he kissed each wrist and then bared his throat to me.

It was an act of submission, pure and simple. He was kneeling at my feet with his throat and stomach exposed to me.

I wasn't anywhere of significant rank in the pack hierarchy. Like Colin, I could fight but I wasn't strong like Drake, Elias, or Dan. I'd seen submission ceremonies before. They were most popular when someone new was joining the pack and vowing their loyalty to Drake. On occasion, when challenged, Drake would bring the wolf to heel, who would then have to publicly submit to him. However, I had never been on the receiving end of it.

For Keegan, strong and powerful as he was, to submit to me, it was overwhelming. His message was clear: no matter how powerful he was, it was I to whom he was loyal. His strength was my strength. His power was my power. I had only to order and he would obey. His display brought tears to my eyes. I felt protected, loved, cherished, humbled, indestructible... I wondered if this was how Bruce Banner felt just before the Hulk burst free.

A smile broke free of Keegan's serious and sincere face and he burst to his feet. "Gods, I love you, woman. Only you would think a comment like that when I'm trying to be all mushy and romantic."

My laugh was cut off by his fierce kiss.

~

After learning the true strength of Keegan's power, I wondered if Drake knew too. My Alpha wasn't stupid, and he knew more about that side of shifters than most because he had been born to such power.

It still amazed me that I'd been so blinded to Keegan's power. No wonder he'd felt so sure of himself striding into a pack of wolves as the lone feline. Despite our superior numbers, he was probably strong enough to hold all of us at bay just long enough to get away.

I paused in my walk and blinked.

Was *that* how we'd gotten away the first time? Had Keegan unleashed his power enough for us to escape the compound? While I would never consider our fight to freedom the day I'd brought Keegan home to have been easy on our part, it could have also been so much worse. Had he gotten us away safely?

When my mental quandary remained unanswered, I figured that to be confirmation enough. Wow, I'd been so blind.

To everyone else, the strength of his power had probably been obvious. Being his one exception, maybe I shouldn't be kicking myself so hard for not having recognized the signs before now. After all, I'd had other things on my mind too.

I was on my way to the Manor without Keegan. As much as I wanted him at my side, Dan, Colin, and I had persuaded him to remain behind. I was less likely to cause an uproar of stepping into the Alpha's home without Keegan than I was with. That irked me.

As I walked, I ignored the stares of my packmates. Whether they were in human or wolf form, they stared. Did they think I had some contagious feline plague? It broke my heart to see shifters whom I'd known my whole life look at me as if I was a stranger. One pulled her three-year-old daughter away from me as I passed them on the sidewalk.

I tried not to let my pain show on my face.

The compound was set up similar to Deadwood's historic Main Street. We had paved roads, sidewalks, shops, and businesses. Within the compound, there were no money exchanges. I could walk into Nan's bakery and walk out with fifty pies and never be charged a dime. The pack also kept an organic farm that was profitable. Though everything worked on a barter system, you never turned away a packmate in need.

Sadly, I wondered if the same still applied to me.

As I walked toward the steps of the Manor, I bore the glares of the guards in wolf form at the entrance. While Drake openly stated he hated having guards at his home, he understood the old tradition.

The Manor itself was set up much as I envisioned a medieval castle might be. There was the main hall with rows and rows of tables and chairs. The Alpha hosted three meals a day with an open-door policy to all pack members. Though some chose to eat in the seclusion of their homes, it was rare. Wolves were social creatures.

Melancholy pierced my heart because I knew I would not join in on any pack meals until I felt Keegan would be welcome too. Even if we had to sit at our own table with perhaps just Colin and Dan as company, I didn't think I could handle the stares, glares, and glowers from my packmates at breaking bread with a *cat*.

To the right of the main hall was the pack meeting room. It was massive with a ceremonial dais at the forefront for the Alpha. Most of the time, we met outside, but the indoor meeting room had come in handy during some nasty storms or long winter days. It was mainly used as a hang out center. Drake had had televisions and video game consoles hooked up some years before. Many teens went there after school to work on homework or socialize.

For the most part, the pack didn't have *crime*. Not in the way humans thought of it anyway. There was no such thing as theft. With our heightened senses, none could get away with taking something that wasn't theirs.

Some of the most heinous human crimes, like assault, rape, and murder, were rare but unfortunately happened in our society too. However, the human concept of *innocent until proven guilty* didn't exist for us because the guilty party was scented almost immediately.

The Alpha would then pass judgement. It was tradition for the Alpha to take the victim's request for punishment under account, but not a requirement.

In the end, it was always the Alpha's decision. If death was owed, the Alpha would deliver the final strike himself.

A shaming or cast-out was a far worse punishment than death. A wolf who was shamed was considered forgiven in the Alpha's eyes, but he would bear the scars from his Alpha's claws for the rest of his days. Everyone, whether from their own pack or not, would know he'd done something that resulted in his Alpha slashing him with his claws and then pouring salt over the wound so it would never heal. No one would trust the wolf again.

To be cast-out was to be exiled from the pack. Lone wolves don't survive. I'd lasted as long as I had because of my bond with Keegan. If I'd been on my own, I would have gone mad from loneliness. It's said that some lone wolves are driven so mad by the isolation that they commit suicide just to end the pain. While some packs will take in a lone wolf, most won't. Without the scent of a pack, a lone wolf's scent is...*off*.

Some lone wolves are driven to insanity and turn feral, unable to ever take human form again. Feral wolves can create packs on their own. Some acclimate into the wild while others were known to be vicious and attack pack dens.

"Hey, Sasha!"

I stopped on the stairs leading up to the Manor's front door. Bradley McMillian was running down the stairs toward me.

"Um, hi, Brad." I couldn't remember the last time I'd talked to my high school boyfriend. Still feeling the need to be polite, I asked, "How are you?"

"A bit better than you, I think." He gave me a crooked smile that used to make my heart fly that now my pulse didn't even register. "I heard about your ordeal. I'm sorry." I cocked my head in confusion. Ordeal? Was that what the pack was calling my mating a jaguar? Funny, I called it a miracle. "You look good, but you're far too thin."

Startled, I looked down my tall figure. I had lost weight while on the run, but I didn't think it was *that* noticeable. I was just grateful I'd been able to finally take a razor to my legs, pits, and pubes. There was nothing like a silky, bare labia to make a girl feel like herself again.

Before I could figure out how to respond to that bold assessment, Brad continued. "So, where's the kitty cat?" I let out a low growl so sharp that his eyes shot open in surprise. "Whoa, easy," he called truce. "I was just kidding."

I shook my head to clear it. "No, I'm sorry. I'm just...a bit touchy."

Brad nodded as if in understanding. "I can see that." He cleared his throat, "I'd still like to meet him. I gotta ask, though, did he really challenge the Alpha yesterday?"

My back stiffened at the question. "What? No." Well, there'd been a bit of a challenge, but I wasn't about to feed the rumor mill more with that acknowledgement. "Their meeting was a bit...tense," I decided, "but they worked it out."

"So, where is he then?" Brad asked, looking around in obvious curiosity. "He's not afraid to come to the Alpha's home, is he?"

I heard Keegan's snort in the background of my mind.

"No," I answered evenly. "He's still with Dan and Colin at their house. We're going to be staying with them until we can figure some things out."

"That's nice of them. Still, it's too bad about your dad."

Pain shot through me at the too-casual statement. Soothing caresses entered my mind and I swore I could feel ghostly lips on the nape of my neck. I suppressed the groan I felt rising in my chest. I couldn't help but tilt my head to the side and lean into the feel of him, even though he wasn't anywhere near me.

"Holy shit." I jumped at the sudden exclamation, but it was Brad's closeness that had me feeling uncomfortable. "I can't believe you let that thing bite you."

Before I could stop him, he raised a hand and touched a finger to my mate-mark.

The fierce and possessive growl echoed not just through my head but the entire compound. I knew I wasn't the only one who heard it when heads and shouts of fear turned in the direction of Dan's cabin.

Then I felt the rush of the wind and the heat of asphalt underneath my paws.

I glanced down at my human hands and suddenly I understood. "Brad, step back!" I jumped down to the base of the stairs just in time to see the giant jaguar running full throttle toward us.

But my ex did the worst possible thing in this situation and shifted. A gray wolf, nowhere near the jaguar's height and weight, leapt in front of me. Fuck me, was Brad trying to protect *me*?

Keegan, stop! I shouted, but my mate was too furious.

It wasn't a law but an unspoken rule that Brad had broken. Mate-marks were sacred and no one touched yours but your True Mate. It was beyond rude, it was insulting. The only scent on a True Mate should be the bond between them. Having another touch your mark would be like me walking up to Brad's house and peeing on it. His action had unintentionally challenged Keegan's position as my mate.

Then the stupid, chivalrous fool stepped *between* us. Brad was going to get himself killed and Keegan was going to be blamed for it.

The two males ran at each other head-on, but before they could collide, a large black wolf slammed into Keegan. The impact rang out like thunder. Brad went rushing past, unable to turn in time to continue his attack on Keegan.

I ran forward as Keegan turned on the black wolf, whom I recognized as Drake's Beta, Camryn. Ignoring Brad, I put myself between the two giant animals and placed a hand on each of their snarling snouts.

Keegan immediately calmed under my touch and I could tell he was no longer seeing red. He still wasn't happy, but he was under control again. Camryn, recognizing me as pack, also calmed but he didn't let down his guard as Keegan did.

I was about to say something to both of them about apologizing to each other when Brad the Idiot came to stand by me. In that moment, I wished for lightning to just strike me down. What was *wrong* with him? Didn't he see that Keegan was the last person I needed protection from? I was so frustrated I couldn't even find his desire to protect me sweet. It was just plain annoying.

Keegan's eyes landed on Brad, who raised his hackles in response.

"ENOUGH!" The ground shook with the booming voice. All of us at the base of the stairs, except Keegan, bared our throats as Drake came storming outside in human form. Drake was a powerful Alpha. He didn't need to be in wolf form to assert his authority. "Brad, shift."

My ex cowered and whimpered as he heeded his Alpha. Having ripped from his clothes upon shifting, Brad stood naked before his Alpha. His shoulders were hunched and he couldn't look up from the ground.

I quickly stepped away from him and over to Keegan. I wrapped my hands around my mate's thick neck, burying my face in his spotted pelt.

"Apologize to Keegan." I wasn't the only one who was shocked at the Alpha's order. In fact, mine probably seemed stronger because I was also feeling Keegan's. When Brad seemed to stumble for words, Drake stated in a stern voice, "You touched a True Mate's mark. You owe Keegan an apology as well as everyone here for disturbing their peaceful afternoon. Now, Bradley!"

"I'm sorry!" It came out nothing more than a squeak.

"Go home." Brad shifted and ran, not looking back at us, with his tail tucked between his legs. Drake walked up to Camryn and placed a hand on the wolf's head. "Thank you, my friend. You probably saved the fool's life."

Camryn nodded once then stepped forward. I was surprised when the large wolf paused before me and inclined his head again. I'd known of Camryn, everyone did, but I wasn't close to him like either of my brothers. For Camryn to acknowledge me so, and in public, was as good as him throwing me a bridal shower and offering to walk me down the aisle.

I sent him a quavering smile before he walked off.

Drake rested his hands on his hips and let out a long sigh. "Sasha, Sasha, Sasha. What am I going to do with you? Relax," he waved off Keegan's irritation at his words. "I'm just pointing out that this is your first day here and already the two of you are causing trouble."

I buried my heated face in Keegan's shoulder. He was right about that, though in this case it wasn't either of our faults. Brad should have never touched my mark and Keegan was within his rights to defend me and our bond.

"I'm going to touch her. Don't bite my hand off." I smiled against Keegan at Drake's warning. Then I felt the hand on my shoulder. I turned toward my Alpha and threw myself into his arms as he squatted by me. "Shhh," he encouraged, placing a kiss on the top of my hair. "This whole thing is going to take some getting used to. For everyone. Perhaps you should take your mate home, Sasha."

I nodded into my Alpha's hold. Lifting my head, I quickly wiped my tears. "I'm sorry."

He pinched my chin. "Don't be. From what I saw, you seemed to have everything well in hand before I came out."

Yeah, before Brad had tried to protect me again.

Drake helped me rise. He lifted my hand and kissed the back, then he placed that hand on my mate's broad shoulders. I noticed that he was careful not to touch Keegan himself. "Go home, Sasha." He nodded once to Keegan. "Cat."

My mate just rolled his eyes and then started home. I walked beside him, my hand still on the flat of his back. The gathered audience parted like the Red Sea to let us pass.

～

I knew what was coming as soon as the cabin came into sight. I was grateful Dan and Colin were out. No sooner did we step through the threshold, did Keegan shift back into human form and slam me up against the closed door. In one swift movement, he had ripped open my pants and thrust inside me. My pants hung ruined from my waist and thighs, but I could care less. Keegan bit down on my mark.

It took me several minutes to come down from my orgasmic high to realize that Keegan was still inside me, completely hard. He was kissing me lightly up and down my neck, nibbling on my ear too. Despite the pleasure that act caused, I found myself suddenly very irritated with my mate. He'd seen to my pleasure, but not his own. He'd held himself back from me under the guise of protecting me.

I knew he could sense my irritation, but he continued to try to coax me back to blissful happiness rather than acknowledge the cause behind it.

I pushed at his shoulders. He was too big and strong for me to force him back from this position under my will alone. I was truly pinned by him, which I normally craved, but not now. I felt his sigh as he took a step back. My annoyance with him kept me from releasing my groan as his hard cock slipped from inside me.

Before he could pick up on my intentions, I tackled him. I felt his surprise through our bond. Still, he made sure that it was his body that took the impact of the floor, securing me to his chest. I batted away his arms, taking his hands and pinning them to the hardwood by his head. His green eyes were amused. Both of us knew that I wasn't actually pinning him. He was allowing me to manhandle him as I was.

"Stop," I snarled. "Stop trying to protect me."

He shook his head. "I would do anything for you, my love, but I cannot do that."

A growl escaped me. "I'm not fragile!"

Suddenly, I was flipped with the hardwood under me and his body draped over mine. My ripped pants were still dangling from my legs and my shirt was intact. He was completely naked from his shift, which, despite my annoyance with him, I didn't mind in the least. Naked Keegan was my favorite Keegan.

His bright green eyes bore into mine with an intensity that shook me to my core. "You will listen to me very carefully, Sasha Rowe. I. Love. You. Not because of some stupid bond that was forced upon us or because I had no choice in choosing you. I love you because you are strong, smart, and independent. You're also far too stubborn for your own good. You care for those who don't deserve your kindness."

I felt tears gather up in my eyes and I frantically blinked them away, not wanting to miss a second of his beautiful face. It also didn't pass my notice that he'd put *his* last name at the end of my first. I'd circle back to that later. He was on a roll and I was enjoying it.

"Baby, your pack means more to you than I can comprehend. Maybe it's the jaguar in me or my own need for isolation. It kills me to see you craving their acceptance and only receive their ire and hate. You deserve so much better. Watching you struggle to walk to the Manor this morning was like a knife in my heart. I can't protect you from what I don't understand.

"But this?" He rubbed his still hard cock between the folds of my damp labia. I could not suppress my groan this time. "I can protect you from *me*."

I highly doubt my flash of anger was the reaction he'd been expecting following his heart-filled speech but, damn, if his last sentence didn't light a fire inside me. I bucked my hips, lifting his body just enough to get my feet between us and then kicked him back.

He flew up, landing as gracefully on his feet as any self-respecting cat. I crouched before him, growling.

He wanted to protect me from *himself*? Oh, that just pissed me off. Everyone thought I needed to be protected from him. My father, my brother, Brad... But for Keegan to say it too? Fuck that shit! Keegan was the *last* person I needed protecting from.

I thought he understood that. I thought we were a team. I thought he believed that we protected each other. I was not some fucking damsel who needed to be safeguarded. I might not be as strong as him, but I was still strong. Our bond didn't decrease who I was. Our bond had released me, finally allowing me to be who I *am*. If he couldn't understand or see that then he wasn't the man I thought he was.

Barbed penis be damned. I was getting his cock back inside me and I was going to *make* him understand that he was mine, dammit. Every fucking piece of him belonged to me and I was just selfish enough to want it all.

"Sasha," he warned, picking up on the thoughts in my head and his face clearly expressed his unhappiness about it.

But I didn't attack. Instead, I stood up slowly. With extra wriggles of my hips and breasts, I slipped from the confines of my clothing. First my shirt, because I knew how much he loved my breasts. I made sure to brush over my nipples, completely unabashed, and made sure he sensed the pleasure I felt at my own hands.

Trailing my hands down my sides, I let out a soft sigh. The band of my pants was still around my waist. Keegan had only ripped a hole into the legs to gain access to my pussy.

A memory flashed in front of my eyes and I knew it was Keegan's, not mine.

His body rumbled with his chuckle. He lifted his head from his meal of my sweet juices. "It wounds my masculine ego when you giggle every time I go down on you."

"I'm sorry," I said, even though I wasn't. "I just can't help it."

His tongue scraped up the sensitive skin from my knee to my folds. "And what, pray tell, is so funny every time you think the word pussy?"

My grin was wide as I admitted, "I keep thinking that you like pussy."

"I do like pussy." He emphasized his point by tracing through my folds with a single finger. He was so close to inside but refused to enter. Frustration mixed with my amusement. "I was hoping I was making that point clear enough but perhaps I need to work on my oral skills."

"I will never deny you practice," was my gasped response.

"Just answers?"

I shook my head. "It's silly!" I groaned when he took my clit between his teeth but purposely didn't do more. "Fine!" I cried out. "I can't call my vagina a pussy around you because I keep thinking you're a pussycat who likes pussy, which makes you a lesbian!"

A snort escaped him, and he let go of my clit. I let out a groan of pure sexual frustration. "Gods, I love you, woman." Our eyes met. "Now, lay back, shut up, and watch me enjoy your pussy like the dog you are."

From anyone else, I would have tensed at being called a dog, but from him, in that silky voice with his breath so close to my most intimate of places, I could do nothing but obey.

While that was one of my favorite memories of us, I pushed it aside now. Keegan was not going to distract me from what I wanted. Not this time.

6

I turned my back to him as I slithered out of my ripped pants. I'd been going commando because I had no idea where any of my underwear was, like the rest of my possessions. Bending at the waist, I took my time getting each leg out of the pants while giving him a complete, unveiled view of my ass and wet folds. The evidence of my orgasms was still there, dripping and waiting for his tongue.

Naked, I stood, keeping my back to him. I knew Keegan's eyes were following my bare ass as I walked. I enjoyed the fact that, even though he felt he should, he couldn't look away.

I entered the bedroom and went straight for the large king mattress. Neither Keegan nor I had bothered to make the bed this morning, and the sheets and comforter were still scattered from our lovemaking earlier.

But I didn't want to make love right now. I wanted a down-and-dirty fucking where Keegan couldn't hold back from me. I wanted him, all of him, between my legs, in my mouth, in my heart, and under my skin. I was going to prove to him that he was *mine* and I was not in need of protection from him.

Lying in the center of the large bed, I propped my head up on two pillows. He hadn't followed me into the room, but that didn't matter. My mind was completely open to him.

I let out a long sigh, settling myself.

I started high. With featherlight touches, I ran my hands across the nape of my neck and across the base of my throat. I purposely avoided my mate-mark, knowing that touching that would end this too quickly and for the wrong reasons.

I'd never felt my breasts were anything to write home about. I was tall for a woman and, though my boobs were small, I knew Keegan loved my breasts. He loved how reactive they were to his touches and teases.

I took my time, encircling each areola with a single finger. I slowly spiraled my way closer to my nipples, allowing the nail of each pointer finger to just barely scrape over the sensitive points. The moment I made contact with my nipples, I heard his low, radiating growl from the other room.

I know what you're doing.

I ignored his anger and replied back, *I know what I'm doing too—oh!*

He hissed as I pinched my nipples. It was a hard and quick pull, but effective. I could feel the war in his head. His need to protect me was battling with his desire to claim me. He kept envisioning my pained face from this morning when we'd discovered he was stuck inside me. It was that image that was currently winning the battle.

So, I gave him something else to think about. Gripping my both breasts with my hands, I placed my right nipple between my thumb and pointer finger and *squeezed*.

The intense pain-pleasure went straight to my core. I let out a long moan. I was so wet, dripping with his favorite juice. He loved the taste of me. Maybe it was a cat thing, but what did I care? I enjoyed his tongue inside me almost as much as I enjoyed his cock.

Rolling the nub between my fingers, I drew out the sensation. I also didn't hold back my moans. His hands would have done a better job, but I was no stranger to touching my body. My thighs squeezed together, trying to increase the feeling. But I wanted to draw this out longer, make him suffer and want as much as I did.

I was close too, both to orgasm and winning this battle. The fight in him was waning and we each knew it. Soon, I would have what I wanted.

Giving my left nipple some much-needed attention, I took my right hand and trailed it down from the valley of my breasts to my navel and back up again. I did this several times, each pass getting closer to my mound.

The moment my finger just barely grazed against the top of my slit, an echoing yowl sounded from the other room, followed by pounding footsteps. I ignored his entrance into the bedroom, keeping my eyes closed. This time, when my hand approached my folds, I placed two fingers between them and parted them for his viewing pleasure.

Wood cracked. I could feel through our bond that his hands were gripping the doorframe too hard. The war was lost, but he was still battling. I had to admire his tenacity. He certainly didn't go down without a fight. But I would reign victorious.

Keeping my folds spread with my pointer and ring fingers, I made small circles over my aroused clitoris. Wood splintered as my middle finger snaked down just a little further and dipped into my entrance.

I was going to owe Dan a new doorframe.

Slow and deliberate, I brought my middle finger up to my lips and paused. I could feel his heart pounding in his chest, his cock pulsing and begging, the wood digging into his flesh, but most of all I could feel me through him. We were connected by more than just flesh when we made love. Our minds weren't just on the same wavelength but two halves of a single whole.

I opened my eyes as I dipped my middle finger coated with my own pussy juices between my lips and brought my left hand up to touch my mate-mark.

He pounced with such force, the headboard cracked the wall behind it and the upper right leg of the bedframe broke. The bed dropped at an angle, but the mattress held.

He pulled my hands from my mouth and neck, bracing my wrists in a single grip of one of his above my head. The war was lost, we both knew it. He ducked his head, lapping at my mark. Pleasure coursed through my veins at his tongue's touch.

I have only ever wanted to protect you.

I smiled, turning my face to grip his ear between my teeth. *I know, and I love you for it. But don't ever hold yourself back from me. That hurts more than anything else anyone, including you, could possibly do to me.*

I think he understood what I meant. It was all or nothing. *We* were all or nothing.

Keegan dragged out the foreplay. A part of him was paying me back for the torture I'd put him through. But then finally, *finally*, he was back home inside me.

I cried out, my body shaking with euphoria. I didn't know if Heaven or Hell existed, I didn't know if there was a god or multiple, I didn't know if humans would ever discover shifters, and I didn't know what tomorrow would bring. But none of it mattered.

Keegan was with me, inside me, and I was all his. More importantly, he was all mine.

Later, we found ourselves sprawled out on the floor of the bedroom. Not only did I owe Dan a new doorframe, but I also owed him a new bedframe, mattress, and lamp. There were also claw marks in various places on the hardwood floor and walls, as well as the hole the headboard had created.

Hell, I just owed him a new bedroom.

I didn't care. Keegan and I were sated, whole, and happy. He was lying on my belly, practically purring. One finger was circling my belly button and I could feel him wondering if a baby was growing there.

If there hadn't been before, there was no doubt in my mind that there was now. We'd learned, following his orgasms, that the barbs didn't hurt unless he tried to pull out while they were still attached to my inner walls. It had taken several tries, but I felt we had the postcoital cuddle routine down by now.

A smile crept onto my face at the thought. I couldn't remember ever having a sex marathon, nor could I remember a time when Keegan and I were so relaxed.

Now, it was just us. No pending doom, no panicked worries, no hunting party on our trail... Just him and me. In a very battered, well-used bedroom.

My eyes landed on the punctures and tears in the mattress. "I don't think I'm going to be able to face my brother after this."

He chuckled. "It was well worth it." I was so happy he was over his aversions. Of course, he picked up on my thought, because he turned his head on my belly to face me. "I was never averse to you or even sex with you, Sasha. It killed me before not to come inside you, with you, but my need to protect you overruled. I couldn't cause you harm. I just couldn't."

I dragged my fingers through his hair. "I know, baby, but you needed this as much as I did."

A snort suddenly escaped him. "You certainly have a way of getting what you want."

I smacked him lightly upside the head. "Only way I could think of getting through your thick head."

He grinned wickedly. "Next time you pull a stunt like that, I'll drape you over my knee and tan your backside."

Heat rushed to my cheeks at the thought of him spanking me. *Oh damn.*

Before Keegan could reply, the front door opened and closed. We heard the footsteps come down the hall and then looked in unison at the stunned expressions of my brother and his mate as they saw the state of their once immaculate bedroom.

Keegan's head and shoulders blocked my breasts from their view. He casually draped his arm over my bare sex, causing me to roll my eyes. I didn't even point out that, not only were they family, but they were more interested in his naked butt than mine. Again.

"You're buying us a new bedroom," Dan deadpanned before walking away.

There was a single heartbeat before Keegan and I exchanged a wicked grin and I said, "Worth it."

"I heard that!" my brother shouted back at us.

～

Since we'd already destroyed it, it was agreed that Keegan and I could keep the bedroom until we figured something else out. Colin and Dan had spent the afternoon at my father's, trying to persuade him to come talk to me. They didn't seem to have any more luck with that than Keegan had. However, they were able to pack up some of my things and bring them over to me.

Colin and I unpacked the clothes they'd brought me from my father's house. I was trying not to eavesdrop on Dan and Keegan's conversation from the kitchen, but I couldn't help it. I could both hear them with my ears as well as through my bond. It was hard to block out.

"There are some empty houses we could talk to Drake about for the two of you."

"I'd like that. Your way of life is certainly going to take some getting used to. I'm used to having to blend in more with humans."

"The pack protects and takes care of its own. The moment Drake acknowledged your bond with Sasha, you became part of the pack, Keegan. It might take a while for some to come around and you still have to pledge yourself to the pack, but eventually the others will accept you."

"You certainly seem to have...come around."

There was a slight pause. "I'll admit I didn't like you when we first met, and not just because of what you were doing to my sister when we came upon you." My cheeks reddened at that statement. I grabbed a pair of sneakers Colin handed me, hoping he didn't catch onto my embarrassment. "The two of you... It was hard to accept at first for me. I want to protect my sister and I can't stand anything that is or could be a threat to her. Your relationship puts her in danger, Keegan. Whether the Alpha accepted it or not, there will always be those who dislike and disapprove of it. That threatens both you and her."

"It's one of the reasons I brought her back here. I knew the longer we ran, the less safe we were. I was trying to figure out where we could go, who would accept us. My culture is different than yours. I was used to being on my own. But the toll it took on Sasha?" I could feel Keegan shake his head. "I would do anything to make her happy and being here, even with the lack of reception we received, it is what makes her happy."

"I got to say, you've got balls. You literally walked into the wolf's den for her."

"I would do anything for her."

"Well, I don't doubt you'll have many opportunities to prove that in the coming days and weeks." There was a sound like Dan had slapped Keegan on the back.

I hadn't realized I'd stopped working with Colin and was just standing there listening until the two had stopped talking. Colin gave me a knowing look and my blush returned.

He nudged me with his shoulder. "I like him. He's got guts."

I smiled at him. "It's one of his better attributes."

Colin gestured to the broken bedframe. "I see you're taking full advantage of his other attributes too."

My smile turned wicked. "As often as I can."

He laughed. "Hell, if I wasn't happily mated, I would too. Your man is *hung*."

A loud growl radiated from the kitchen, making Colin and I burst out laughing. Gods, I loved being home.

~

A few days later, Colin and I decided it was time to quit hiding. The only way to make the pack accept Keegan was to smack them in their stubborn faces with his presence. He wasn't going anywhere and neither was I. Drake had given us permission to stay—with the understanding that we would not cause trouble.

Though Keegan and I would wander outside for fresh air, we never journeyed into the main areas of the compound. Dan called it being cautious, I called it hiding.

Keegan was also done wearing Elias's hand-me-downs. I'd found out that Dan had taken Elias's clothes without our brother's permission. Elias, out of sheer stubbornness, was not going to want them back, regardless of how many times we washed them.

So, the goal for today was just to walk around the compound and let my pack get used to seeing Keegan and me together. Colin was going with us because he was amazing at getting people to calm down and see reason. Also, Drake had been very clear that we couldn't cause trouble or be the cause of trouble. Dan couldn't be with us constantly, so Colin volunteered.

Plus, he wanted to take Keegan shopping for clothes and who better to do that with than my amazing brother-in-law with terrific fashion sense. Keegan was going to bitch and moan about shopping, so Colin was there to keep me company as much as help us win over the pack.

Everyone loved Colin. He might still be new to our pack and acclimating to life in Deadwood, but he was an outright sweetheart and didn't have a mean bone in his body.

That was how a week after our return to the pack, we found ourselves walking down the main street of the compound that housed most of the shops and businesses. Colin and I were walking arm-in-arm, chatting, while Keegan trailed behind us. I'd originally wanted to walk with Keegan at my side, but he was being a party pooper about our shopping excursion. His version of shopping was the Walmart clearance rack for simple jeans and t-shirts.

Avery was the pack seamstress. She made everything from scratch. We did keep a supply of department store clothing, but Avery's family had been making the pack's clothing since we'd settled in this area centuries ago. Most went to her or her daughter for their clothing needs.

I planned on asking Avery for a new wardrobe for Keegan. He might be fine in jeans and a t-shirt, but I liked the idea of getting some alternative items too.

We passed Nan's bakery and wandered in for a coffee and danish. While she didn't openly say that Keegan wasn't allowed in her store, she also never asked him what he wanted and only acknowledged Colin and me. I really wanted to refuse to do business with her, but she was the only bakery in the compound. Plus, it wasn't like my refusal would hurt her bottom line because I wasn't giving her any money.

Keegan had to send me soothing thoughts as Nan handed me the three coffees and Colin the bag of goodies. Keegan held the door open for us and even had the good graces to thank Nan before exiting the store behind us. He handled the entire encounter far better than I.

I ran into Patty outside Nan's store. She had been the pack's teacher since I was a pup myself. We chatted and she even went as far as to shake Keegan's hand in introduction. She didn't go out of her way to talk to him but also didn't exclude him either. But I also realized, she acted the same with Colin. Perhaps she really did only want to talk to me. Regardless, once she was on her way again, we headed to Avery's to get Keegan some clothes.

I was nervous that Avery would refuse to make Keegan's clothing, but my worries fell aside the moment Avery's eyes lit up upon our entrance. She hugged me, then Colin, and then Keegan. She had him strip down to his birthday suit so she could take his measurements.

Colin and I both stood back and admired my mate's body as she did.

Keegan sent us both a glare over his shoulder and sent thoughts of vengeance to me.

When Avery was done taking his measurements, she instructed him to dress again. She gave me a knowing smile, "I might be happily mated, but damn, they just don't make them like that anymore, do they?"

Colin and I laughed. I loved Avery's wicked sense of humor. Keegan was less than amused to be the butt of our jokes.

Thankfully, Avery caught on and let the matter drop. She had some things already premade that would fit him. She put them in a couple of bags for us and promised to have more next week. I thanked her, hugged her, and made to leave.

Avery stopped me with a hand on my wrist. "It'll be all right, dear. The pack isn't used to changes and you've brought a massive one to our doorstep. Just give them time."

I hugged her again, so grateful for her acceptance. "Thank you."

She squeezed me tight. "Go on then. I need to get to work." Then she winked at me, "And thank you for the eye candy." To Keegan, she added, "Come back any time."

Colin's and my good mood lasted well into the afternoon until we were walking toward Sam's. Sam made the pack furniture, and I owed Colin a new bedframe. I figured since we were out and about, I might as well order him one. It wasn't like it would be coming out of my wallet versus Colin's. It was the point that I had to be the one to ask for the new frame.

As soon as I had placed the order for the new bed, I made a comment about stopping by the Manor to see what houses were unoccupied. Keegan and I couldn't stay at Colin and Dan's forever. Their home had been built for two people. Plus, it wasn't fair that we were taking up their bedroom. It made more sense to move out before the new bed and mattress were delivered.

No point in ruining *two* beds.

That thought brought out a snort from me and a light chuckle from Keegan.

Colin glanced between the two of us and rolled his eyes, knowing he'd missed something private between mates.

"Dan's at the Manor," he said excitedly. "I wouldn't mind stopping by to see him anyway."

"What is he doing up there?" I asked.

"The pack has had some problems with ferals recently," Colin explained. "It's why we've upped the outside guards."

To be honest, I'd assumed the additional guards had been because of Keegan. "Any attacks?" I inquired as Keegan asked, "Ferals?"

Colin answered Keegan's question first. "Feral wolves. It's rare but we do get the occasional pack in our area. They have a tendency to attack, sensing our pack as a threat. They're too wild to understand that we would only harm them if they harm us. They just sense a pack of our size and can't help themselves." To me, he said, "A few weeks before you returned, they tried to breach the north gate. They were not successful and there were no deaths on either side."

Keegan's brows furrowed. "Jaguars have ferals just like any other shifter species, but they tend to fade into the jungles." His eyes landed on me in obvious concern. "Your ferals attack you?"

Colin and I nodded. I was the one who said, "A lone wolf has a tendency to go mad, commit suicide. Despite that they're feral, wolves still crave the pack life. The word 'pack' is used loosely though as they rarely have an Alpha and tend to attack each other as much as us."

"How big of a pack? How strong?" His eyes glanced around us, as if he was assessing the weak points of the compound's borders.

I stepped forward, dropping my hold on Colin's arm to touch Keegan's cheek. "Baby, there's no need to worry. The pack is used to this. It's why we have guards. Feral packs tend to only have a few members. We're safe in here." I knew it wasn't the pack's safety that concerned Keegan, but mine. I lifted myself up on my toes to kiss him. He kissed me back automatically, though his mind was elsewhere. "I'm safe," I added with emphasis.

Keegan looked over my head to Colin. "Dan is at the Manor discussing the threat with your Alpha?"

I turned in time to see Colin nod his head. "Yes, the guards scented them in the area again this morning."

"Take me to your Alpha," Keegan ordered. At my displeasure for his rudeness, he added, "Please."

Colin nodded again and I took Keegan's hand instead of linking arms with Colin. Keegan was carrying his two bags of clothes. I had a feeling he would have dropped them in the middle of the street and left them it if wouldn't upset me. He didn't like feeling like his hands were full when he might need them.

Calm, I encouraged as we approached the Manor. I did not want Keegan to create an uproar when the guards sensed his mood without knowing the reason behind it.

It took several deep breaths before Keegan was able to get himself under control. I could tell he was torn between keeping me here within the safety of the pack or taking me away from here again. As much as it irritated him, he couldn't deny there was safety in numbers, but his instincts were also telling him to leave the territory and protect his mate.

I squeezed his hand. *We're safe here. This is not the first time ferals have been in the area or attacked us, and they might just be passing through. We don't know until we talk to Drake.*

I don't like it, was the only thing he said back to me.

I pressed my lips to his shoulder, gripping his forearm.

We didn't have to scent out Dan once we entered the Manor. Colin led us to him without fail and walked right into Dan's arms, fitting there as perfectly as two puzzle pieces.

Drake, Camryn, and several guards looked up at our entrance. I had never been in this room before and assumed it was some sort of meeting or conference room. A long table sat in the middle with paperwork and laptops on it. Maps were tacked on the walls, along with several large white boards with writing on them.

Maybe this was a war room, I thought, intrigued.

At a familiar scent, I looked to my left to find Elias sitting in the corner. His gaze narrowed on us, but he didn't speak. I wanted to walk up to him and tell him to grow up. Keegan held me back, reminding me that that wasn't why we were here.

Colin and Dan were conversing silently. Drake gave Keegan and me a look that clearly said we had interrupted something.

Keegan ignored the hint and stepped further into the room, dragging me along with him. "How can I help?"

Drake and I both looked at my mate in surprise. The closer Keegan got to Drake, the closer the guards got also. It took a verbal order from Drake for them to back off. I appreciated Drake's willingness to try to trust Keegan. He didn't know him, but Drake knew me. He was relying on my trust of Keegan, not his own. I felt that said a lot about Drake's personality as a leader. While there was no doubt in my mind that if his own instincts said not to trust Keegan, Keegan would not be standing here, Drake was willing to allow my trust to guide him for now. I appreciated that.

Drake looked inquiringly at Keegan. "Do you have experience with ferals?"

Keegan shook his head. "Jaguars are solitary. We rarely hear or see if one of us goes feral."

"Then how can you help us?"

"I can fight, help guard your borders."

I flinched. I didn't like the idea of Keegan putting himself purposely in danger. I also couldn't deny that Keegan was the strongest shifter here, barring perhaps Drake.

I wasn't sure if I was grateful or disappointed by Drake's reply. "I'm sorry,

Keegan, but I can't use you. My wolves don't trust you and I can't risk having them distracted by your presence. That's how accidents happen."

"Then you make them trust me," Keegan snarled. Many of the guards in the room let out low growls. I swallowed nervously but Keegan didn't seem to notice.

Drake didn't look annoyed at Keegan's attitude, but he also clearly wasn't happy. "Watch yourself, Cat. I will never order my wolves to do something they are not comfortable with. Besides that, it is not worth the hassle of trying to get them to trust you." Drake tapped the tablet in front of him with a map of the area on the screen. "At last count, there were only eight of them. It's big for a pack of ferals, but nothing we can't easily handle."

My hand still in his, Keegan leaned forward on the table with both fists. "You're sure she's safe? That you can keep her safe here?"

Drake's eyes did narrow at that. "*All* my wolves are safe here."

Though clearly frustrated, Keegan stood up quickly and let out a huff of air. "Fine." Keegan started to pull me toward the door when Drake called his name.

"I appreciate your concern for your mate. She is one of mine and therefore my concern too. But the next time you come barging into my office with such demands, you will not be leaving with all your limbs."

I did not like the arrogance in Keegan's smile. "Duly noted."

Colin caught up to us in the hallway. He jumped in front of us, stopping Keegan's long strides. "Dan doesn't think the ferals will attack. He said they were running in the opposite direction. Doesn't mean they can't circle back around, but they weren't headed our way."

That did seem to relax the tension in Keegan's mind.

I turned my mate's head toward me with a hand on his chin. I kissed him. "Let's go home. You have some clothes to try on."

Colin and I laughed at Keegan's defeated groan.

7

Avery's open acceptance of Keegan encouraged others to meet him. Keegan's mind was reeling from all the new faces and names he had to remember. He made a point to shake any hand offered to him and repeat their name back to them. I occasionally had to silently remind him of a name later on. But it was the fact that he was *trying* that I loved.

I never wanted him to do anything that made him uncomfortable. He had pointed out to me that he wasn't *uncomfortable*; it was just a new experience for him that he would have to *get* comfortable with. I supposed there was a fine line there. I just hoped he wasn't pushing himself too quickly.

Unfortunately, I'd made no headway with my father. Elias wasn't much better. Dan had told us one night that Drake had to order Elias to shut up when Elias kept going on about how Keegan had disrespected the Alpha in the conference room. While I couldn't say I was happy about Keegan's attitude in there, he had not been openly disrespectful. Dan felt we needed to know that Elias wasn't calling me by name anymore. He only referred to me as *the feline slut*.

And, yeah, that hurt, but there wasn't anything I could do about it. Elias was free to call me anything he wanted. Just like I was free to call him a stupid, pigheaded, fart-mouth. I just had enough tact to only think the name.

Didn't stop Keegan from hearing it, though. He liked Elias's new nickname.

So, despite my father and Elias, I was flying high the past two days. My pack was coming around. I should have known my euphoria wouldn't last.

Two mornings after our visit to the Manor, we were woken up to the alarm bells of a feral attack. For the compound to ring the alarm, it meant there was plausible danger to those inside. All pack members were to head to the Manor for safety until the attack was over. Even if the compound was breached, it would take a true army to break into the Manor once it was closed up.

At the sound of the alarms, Keegan and I rushed to dress. We met Colin and Dan in the living room. Dan had a possessive grip on Colin's hand, like Keegan did on mine. Dan stood naked, likely planning on shifting.

"I have to get to the gates." Dan was looking directly at Keegan. "Would you please take Colin with you to the Manor?"

While Colin was more than capable of seeing himself to the Manor, I understood Dan's fear. Keegan was strong. He was the best protection Dan could provide for his mate.

Keegan nodded once. I held out my hand to Colin. We would be moving fast and I didn't want us to risk being separated from him. If the threat was great enough for the alarm to go off, we couldn't waste time getting to the Manor.

Dan bent to kiss Colin. Though quick, it was full of love and passion. Dan pushed Colin toward my outstretched hand. With a nod and thank you to Keegan, Dan shifted and ran out the door.

The worry on Colin's face was plain. I gripped his hand tightly. "Dan is strong and experienced. It will also take a hell of a lot more than a couple of ferals to keep him from you."

A shiver ran through Colin. "I know and I appreciate you saying it. I just can't help it. I hate it when we're separated."

I winced, remembering that it was my mating that had kept them separated for five months while Dan hunted Keegan and me.

"Let's go."

We ran quickly toward the Manor. Like many families around us, we kept a tight grip on each other. The sounds of howls and the clashing of claws and fangs outside the compound could be heard through the hustle of the pack members running toward the Manor.

Just outside the entrance, Keegan stopped. I paused in confusion before I understood. I dropped Colin's hand and turned to face Keegan. "No."

"I have to."

I gripped his chin. "No, you don't."

"What's wrong?" Colin asked.

"The idiot plans to leave us here and go fight the ferals."

Colin's face paled. "You can't. You heard what Drake said the other day. Our guards don't trust you."

"I have to try!" Keegan snapped. I could sense his determination. "Something changed from the other day when the ferals were no big deal to today when the entire pack is running for shelter. I can't sit on my ass and do nothing!"

I turned to Colin. "Where's Dan? Does he know what's going on?" Perhaps Dan could send us reassurances through Colin, making Keegan's need to fight moot.

Before Colin could answer, there was a loud howl that shook all of us to our core. Keegan only picked up on the significance of it through his connection to me. The howl wasn't pack. Not my pack. And it had been made by an Alpha.

I shuddered. Wherever Drake was, he was going to have a fight on his hands. Like any pack member, Alphas could go feral. It wasn't unheard of, just rare.

My thoughts cemented Keegan's determination. He kissed me quickly and ran, ordering me inside through our bond. I screamed after him. Colin's tight grab of my arms prevented me following Keegan.

I rounded on him with my fist raised to strike my brother-in-law. Colin was far from a coward, but he also wasn't a strong wolf. For him to stand his ground against me, that was what stayed my punch. I ducked my head in shame at my overreaction. "I'm sorry."

He gave me a quick hug before dragging me inside.

I allowed myself to be blindly pulled. Quickly, I concentrated, watching through Keegan's eyes as he bolted through the streets. He skirted easily around the members racing toward the Manor. Many of them moved automatically out of his way.

As Keegan rounded the corner to the main gates, he skidded to a halt. His eyes landed on the guards in wolf form. The large gates were currently open, allowing the pack wolves to charge through. I saw him searching for Drake or Dan but couldn't locate them. His nose wasn't as good as mine to sniff them out and he wasn't familiar enough with their wolf forms to know them on sight. I also didn't see them, so I couldn't point them out to him. Noticing the gates were closing as the last of the wolves made their way through, Keegan rushed forward and squeezed through at the last second.

Many of the wolves spotted Keegan at their backs and, as Drake had predicted, turned their attention to him instead of the approaching threat. Keegan ignored them because he'd spotted the ferals.

Like all shifters, ferals resembled their animal counterparts exactly. A human would never be able to tell the difference between a real wolf, a feral wolf, and a shifter wolf. But to us, the differences were obvious. The most being their putrid smell. There was just something *off* about them. It made my hackles stand on end and I was the one safe within the compound.

There were a lot more than eight. At quick glance, I could see fifteen to twenty wolves running head-on toward the pack guards. None, however, were big enough to be the Alpha and we could still hear fighting taking place elsewhere.

As was protocol, the pack guards created two half circle barriers between the enemy and the gates. The gates were the weak points of the compound. The walls were too tall for most shifters to climb and too thick for a shifter to barrel through. Keegan and I had been able to escape because the compound was designed to keep an enemy out, not keep members in. We didn't live in a prison.

Keegan didn't join the line of wolves though. Staying behind them, which pleased me greatly, he shifted forms and unleashed the full force of his power.

I watched, my jaw dropping, as the approaching ferals fell over themselves almost immediately. It was like they'd run into an invisible wall. Some crumpled into themselves, whimpering, while others fell to their bellies and, despite the obvious pain they were in, continued to drag themselves toward the gate, inch by agonizing inch.

My feeling of triumph, echoed by Keegan, was short-lived as we realized that his power had also incapacitated the pack members before him.

Cursing, Keegan reined his power back in. While this freed the pack members in front of him, it also freed the ferals.

Movement beside him turned Keegan's attention to Drake as a wolf. I was right: the two were evenly sized. It was an eerie realization. I was raised to believe there was no one stronger than my Alpha. To know my mate paralleled him in size, strength, and power was mind boggling.

It was my assessment of Drake that Keegan took under advisement. He was not familiar enough with wolves and our habits to understand what Drake wanted and meant. The only reason he understood me so well in wolf form was because of our mental link. Otherwise, he might as well be trying to have a conversation with a real wolf.

Various barks and growls from Drake had the pack members breaking formation to allow Drake to pass. I encouraged Keegan to follow my Alpha. Once the pack was safely behind them, Drake and Keegan unleashed their dual power on the ferals.

The ferals once again fell, struggling under the weight of an Alpha wolf and an extremely powerful jaguar. The ferals were likely too far out of their minds to understand the significance of that, but I wasn't.

The feral Alpha's howl echoed again, startling me from my concentration. I blinked my eyes open to find myself inside the Manor. Like the other True Mates, I was sitting in the center of the meeting room. Colin was next to me with his eyes closed. The others too were concentrating through their bonds. Some were relaying what was happening outside to the rest of the pack.

"By the gods," I heard, drawing my concentration to one of the True Mates. Tommy's mate, Sabrina, was a guard outside the gates. Tommy's eyes flew open and met mine. "Keegan's advancing on the feral Alpha."

Fear gripped me. If I reconnected with Keegan now, I could distract him. Next to me, Colin reached forward and took my hand. His eyes were still closed. "Dan can see him," he told me. "Keegan's fine."

I knew Keegan was fine. I would feel instantly if he wasn't. But that didn't mean I didn't fear him not being fine. I wanted to close my eyes and shout at him to be careful, but I dared not. Keegan would turn his attention to me, and I couldn't risk that.

While we were on the run, we relied solely on the other. I never had to wonder if he was okay because he'd been at my side the entire time. I'd been his partner, his protector, as he had been mine. Now, I was stuck within the safety of my pack while he was outside risking his life. I knew he was doing it for me, but in protecting me, he was also protecting the pack.

A series of gasps and shouts came from the mates surrounding me in the center of the room. I couldn't help it. I needed to know. I went back in.

But it wasn't Keegan I should have been worried about.

Through Keegan's eyes, I saw his battle with the feral Alpha. The wolf was *huge* and frothing at the mouth. His coal black eyes were wild, unable to focus. Keegan could sense that the wolf did not understand why he was fighting a jaguar. It confused him enough to give Keegan a better chance. Despite his confusion, the wolf was still dangerous. His uncertainty toward Keegan made his moves hesitant, but no less powerful.

When a giant paw connected with Keegan's flank, buckling his leg under him, I shouted. I knew the others were watching me too, unable to see the raging battle for themselves. I didn't care. Keegan was my only priority.

I felt arms on me but didn't disconnect from Keegan to find out who they belonged to. I assumed it was Colin. What I didn't feel right away was being lifted and carried away. I was so intent on my connection with Keegan and his battle with the feral Alpha that I didn't realize I was back outside until the cool morning air hit my face.

The moment I realized I wasn't inside with Colin anymore, my eyes flew open. I was hanging upside-down over a broad shoulder. "What the—" I turned and gasped out, "Brad? What the hell are you doing?"

Pain raked through me and I knew without a doubt that Keegan had been distracted by my current situation.

No! I shouted, instantly reconnecting with my mate. I could feel his blood oozing down his side by his right ribs. *I'm fine*, I assured him, not knowing if it was a lie. He was in much more danger than I was.

I could feel Keegan's rebuff. He didn't want to be fighting the feral Alpha. He wanted to be with me. He was filled with doubt and regret, knowing he'd left my side. All he'd wanted was to protect me and he'd been in the wrong place.

I knew in that instant what I had to do the moment the feral Alpha's ferocious teeth narrowly missed my mate's throat. Keegan couldn't concentrate and win his battle if he was distracted by me. *I love you*, I told him and closed off my mind to him as something hard connected with the back of my head.

A loud feline yowl echoed through the air just as my world went black.

～

I woke up with a shout. Immediately, I reached for Keegan next to me, but he wasn't there. I felt...hollow. Memories came flooding back to me as fear gripped my insides. Where was Keegan? Was he okay? Did he win his fight with the Alpha?

Despite the empty feeling inside me, I couldn't risk reconnecting with him. I didn't know when it was or where I was. What if he was still battling the feral Alpha and my reaching out to him got him hurt again, or worse, killed? I couldn't risk it. Whatever I had gotten myself mixed up in, I was on my own.

I was on a small bed in a rustic cabin. I didn't smell anything familiar about it, other than Brad's scent. It smelled sterile, like he'd taken the time to clean someone else's scents away. Why would he bring me here? And for that matter, where *was* Brad?

I touched the back of my head and flinched. The bastard had knocked me out. Well, fuck him, I wasn't staying here.

I threw off the covers and gaped. I was chained to the bed. Fucking chained, like some sadistic kidnap scenario in movies. My human ankle couldn't fit through the manacle to break free. Problem was, this chain had a spike attached to it. Right now, in human form, the spike just barely grazed my skin. It was irritating but not painful. If I shifted so I could fit my ankle through as a wolf, the spike would pierce directly through my leg to the bone. This was a shifter's chain. We might not have jails, but we still had to have ways to restrain criminals until punishment was dealt out.

Fucking Brad. I was so pissed, I didn't even hear him approach the cabin until the door opened.

Brad walked in like he was on a fucking family camping trip and just went out to bring in the firewood. He dumped the logs unceremoniously next to the unlit grate and turned to me with a large scowl. "You're awake."

He came over to the bed and had the balls to sit down next to my legs. If it wasn't for the chain, I would have killed him right then and there. I needed to find the key before I could make a move.

I growled at him. "What the fuck, Brad?"

He jumped up and backhanded me across the face. "Watch your mouth, bitch."

The side of my face burned but not as much as my fury. I gritted my teeth. I forced myself to sit up slowly, taking in his angry scent to his stern gaze to his snarling lips. He was acting like *he* was the one here against his will. What the fuck was going on? It took everything in me not to repeat my question in just that manner.

"Brad," I asked more gently, "why am I here?"

Brad gave me a placating look. "I understand you're afraid and, to be honest, you should be. You allowed yourself to be soiled by that *thing*." He stood up, shaking his head. "How could you? It sickens me, to think that I once held you in my arms. That I degraded myself by caring for you."

I blinked. "Degraded yourself?" The words flew out of me before I could stop them. Okay, so, hindsight, maybe insulting the keykeeper wasn't the brightest idea. Even though our bond was currently closed off, I was not going to betray my mate. No fucking way. "Keegan is my True Mate. *Fate* chose him for me. Regardless of that, I love him. With all my heart, body, and soul. You will *never* be able to change that. No one can."

Brad was so furious his hands were shaking. "You are so delusional you can't see your illness for what it is. Wolves should be with wolves, Sasha. Purity above all else."

I wanted to vomit. This was more than just some sick, twisted kidnapping. Brad thought Keegan's and my pairing to be unnatural.

"Drake acknowledged our pairing," I pointed out to Brad. It was drilled into wolves from birth to believe in their Alphas.

Brad winced, but it was like he was remorseful. "I know. Our Alpha's... weak. He doesn't understand as I do. To allow that...*thing* into the compound. To allow that *creature* to walk free... It's disgusting. We are *wolves*. We should not be *subjected* to having a cat walking amongst us."

"But if our Alpha—"

"The Alpha doesn't understand!" Brad shouted. He fisted his hands to his forehead. "No one does! I tried!" He dropped his hands with a small sniffle. Then he squared his shoulders. "I tried so many times, but no one understands. I'm the only one willing to do what needs to be done."

My heart plummeted into my stomach, but I had to know. "Do what?"

He reached forward and touched my mate-mark, just as he had done last week. I cringed as his skin touched mine but, unlike before, I couldn't feel Keegan's response to the touch. My skin turned clammy as my body went cold. I needed to figure out what was happening back at the pack with the feral attack. I needed to know if it was safe to open my mind back up to him.

If Brad registered my reaction, he ignored it. Apparently, he was ignoring a lot of things. "Look what that *thing* did to your beautiful neck." He shook his head. "It's a damn shame... Such a damn shame."

He walked over to one of the kitchen cabinets. Fear paralyzed me when I saw him place a bag of salt on the counter. Brad bowed his head over the bag, like he was praying for forgiveness. "Your mating is unnatural, Sasha. I plan to mark you myself so that you will forever be marked by a wolf, to redeem you for your unfaithfulness to this pack."

He turned toward me, holding the salt in his hand. "This will hurt."

Fifteen years ago, the day before Valentine's Day, Brad had dumped me because I wasn't his True Mate. His brother Walter had just found his True Mate and the jealousy practically radiated off of Brad. I don't think I'd said ten words to him before last week.

Now he was planning on biting me over my mate-mark and salting the wound so it would scar.

The sight of his fangs as he stepped up to the bed broke through my fear. I would not allow him to mate-mark me. I wasn't his mate and I was never going to be his mate. I had to figure out a way back to mine. Even if I reconnected with Keegan right now, he might not get to me in time. I didn't think it was worth the risk, not knowing what was happening at the compound with the feral battle.

Awkwardly with my foot chained, I squatted on the bed. "If you think for one second, I'm going to let you bite me, you're fucking delusional."

"I'm not giving you a choice."

My fangs and claws elongated. The growl that came from me rattled the windows and door. "I have the right to be with my True Mate, same as any other shifter!"

"You have the right to be with your True Mate as long as they are of the same species!" he shot back at me.

I lunged, knocking the salt out of his hand. It spilled open on the floor. While it made a mess, it wasn't going to prevent him from using some of it in a wound if he was successful in putting one on me.

He slapped me again. I landed on my back on the bed. Brad leapt on top of me, but I was able to get my unchained leg between us to kick him off. I shouted out my fear and frustration. I was not about to let this bastard bite me over my mate-mark and then salt the wound!

"Feline slut!" Brad stood up, his claws and fangs bared, but it was a clatter of metal on the wooden floor that held my attention. He hadn't noticed the key at his feet. This time when Brad came at me again, I met his attack. I lunged for him, ramming my fist into his gut and then locking him in a choke hold. And just like at school when we'd been training to fight, Brad flailed helplessly until he sank into unconsciousness.

I dropped him unceremoniously to the floor. And then kicked him in the balls, because I could. "You deserve a lot worse, you racist jerk."

Careful to stand only on my left foot, I grabbed the key that had fallen onto the floor next to him. Once free of that sadistic piece of metal, I placed it around his ankle. *See how you like it!* Then I went to the door and threw it open.

I let out a loud laugh. We were in a hunting cabin on the edge of the pack lands. I recognized where we were immediately. Unfortunately, it was approaching dusk, which meant I'd been unconscious for some time. Dammit.

I opened my mind back up to Keegan and was slammed with immediate, gut-wrenching pain. I turned, vomited, and had no choice but to close our link again. My gods, what was that? Fear gripped me. Keegan was alive, but he was hurt. The pain... Oh gods, that pain...

I stomped back to Brad, furious with him and myself. How had I gotten myself into this mess?

I could shift, I debated. It would definitely get me back faster. I looked down at Brad. Could I just leave him here? I'd send guards to come collect him once I was back.

Keegan was my main concern. What was he going through that he'd been in such pain? How badly had he been injured? In the second I'd opened up our bond, I'd only felt pain.

I hadn't gotten a sense about the battle with the ferals. What if they were still out there? I couldn't leave Brad here undefended. If a feral came upon him while he was chained to the bed, unable to shift, he was dead.

Fucking A. I let out a long, frustrated groan. Brad was a racist son of a bitch, but he didn't deserve to die like that.

Not knowing what else to do, I unchained Brad from the bed. I left the manacle with the spike around his ankle and gathered up the chain. Then I lifted him over my shoulders in a fireman's hold and set out toward home.

8

The compound was in an uproar with signs of the battle everywhere. The closer I got to the main gate, the more pungent the scents from the foulness of the ferals' distinct odor to the blood and bile scattered around the battlefield got.

Dan spotted me first. He was standing amongst a group of wolves, the only one in human form. I could tell they were a search party. I breathed a sigh of relief. My brother wouldn't have let me stay in that cabin much longer anyway, even if I hadn't escaped on my own.

Dan let out a loud curse and ran to me. I tossed the still-unconscious Brad on the ground. I honestly did not care if he broke anything upon impact. There was also a satisfying *chunk* of the chain length falling on his head.

Dan grabbed me in a tight hold. I didn't like the pained look that crossed his face. My gut told me it didn't have anything to do with my ordeal. "Holy hell, Sasha, what happened to you?"

As good as it felt to hug my brother, I needed answers and I needed my mate. I stepped back and gave Brad a swift kick. "Where's Keegan?" I demanded, my gut clenching. "For that matter, where's Drake?"

My Alpha needed to know what happened here. It would be up to him to punish Brad. A part of me was looking forward to that. While Brad had only slapped me a few times, he'd had the intention to hurt me.

Dan's face fell even more and he wouldn't look me in the eyes.

"Where the fuck is my mate?"

After signaling to the guards to take Brad in hand, Dan led me toward the Manor. I saw many of the pack looking at me with wary gazes and I could feel my heart sinking further with each step. I wanted to open the link back up again between Keegan and me, but feared what I would find.

"How bad is he?" Gods, I didn't even recognize my own voice. I couldn't keep the dread from seeping into my soul at what I was about to find. I stared at the entrance to the Manor in trepidation, but I had to see Keegan, no matter what.

"Physically, Keegan is fine." Dan took hold of my hand. "In fact, we wouldn't have survived if it hadn't been for him."

My chin quaked too much to speak.

Dan continued, "Keegan and Drake kept the feral pack at bay. They worked together to overpower them. It was honestly a sight to behold. But they had an Alpha. We didn't expect that, but it explains why the pack was so uncharacteristically large. They would have been drawn to him. Anyway, when he showed up, Keegan battled him solo. Drake was going to, but he was better keeping the feral wolves back. They responded better to an Alpha wolf than they had a jaguar.

"Keegan was winning and so was Drake. It seemed we had the battle well in hand." Dan's face fell. "And then, something happened. Keegan, he... faltered. It was like his mind was no longer there. He was in pain before the Alpha wounded him."

I flinched. That must have been when I'd cut off our connection.

"Drake went to assist him, but the feral Alpha got his mouth around Drake's throat." My stomach fell. Oh gods, no! "Keegan got himself back under control and took out the Alpha, but Drake, he was hurt. The bite, it's harder to heal because it's from an Alpha." Dan squeezed my hand. "He's going to be fine, Sasha."

I nodded once, tears streaming down my cheeks. "Keegan?"

"Our guards got Drake inside the walls, but Keegan refused to go. It was like he was unable to stop himself from fighting. He attacked the ferals, despite being outnumbered."

Nausea rose again. I was unable to keep the bile down. Thankfully, we were still on the stairs of the Manor and I was able to aim the vomit over the side of the rail into the bushes below.

Dan waited until I emptied my stomach—again—before continuing. "After losing their Alpha, the ferals were out of control. It was like he'd been keeping them contained. They were...too wild, untamable." Dan's face grimaced as he added, "Drake wasn't the only one hurt."

I wanted to ask but I knew my stomach couldn't take it.

"Keegan, he...killed most of them. I didn't understand at first. I thought he was protecting us and, on some level, I think he was. But we captured six ferals who submitted and Keegan didn't seem to understand. He attacked them too."

I felt my stomach churn again.

"It wasn't until I reached out to Colin that I realized you'd been taken. Sasha, I'm so sorry. We had to contain him. He was...out of control."

"Where is he?" I managed to get out.

"We had to lock him up. He won't shift back—"

"Where is he?" I demanded.

Dan paused and then nodded into the Manor. "This way."

I would never understand my emotions as I followed Dan into the Manor. In many ways, I was thrilled to hear that Keegan was alive. Had that pain I'd experienced when I'd tried to reconnect with him been *mental* anguish from when I'd separated from him?

Then there were the fears about Drake and the others who'd been hurt. What happened to the ferals Dan had captured? Where were Colin, Elias, and my father? Was the pack safe now?

I could hear him before I could see him. His yowls of pain broke my heart and I sprinted past Dan down a flight of stairs I hadn't even known existed. At the bottom of the stairs was a basement of sorts. In the far back was a large wall-to-wall cage.

Inside was a very large, very agitated jaguar.

Keegan was pacing the cell width, constantly twitching and jumping. He was shaking his head like he had an earache and his tail was curled down between his legs.

I ran to the cage bars. As soon as Keegan spotted me, he stopped his pacing. I reached through the bars, but he didn't come closer. His large green eyes stared at me as if I was a stranger. I rested my head against the bars. "Baby, please."

I didn't realize Colin had been sitting against the far wall until he stood to approach me. As soon as Colin put a hand on me, Keegan rushed forward and threw himself against the bars of the cage.

Colin and I ended up sprawled on the floor from the force of the impact. Keegan hobbled away to resume his pacing. Dan rushed forward to help Colin and I off the floor. He was careful not to touch me.

Keegan must have hurt himself because he only paced as far as the back corner, where he curled himself up on top of what I recognized as the comforter and sheets from the bed we'd been using at Colin and Dan's house.

"It's the only thing I could think of," Colin explained. "I tried not to touch them. I just needed something with your scent on it."

Not knowing what else to do, I opened our mental link back up. The pain was there—oh gods, was it there. Tears filled my eyes and I gritted my teeth to keep from shouting out. I had to concentrate. Beyond the pain, beyond the agony, was my mate. He was somewhere in there, buried underneath all that turmoil.

I don't know how long I sat there, watching him, trying to reach him. Every once in a while, I would feel something akin to relief, but it would quickly vanish. A pillow and blanket were brought for me and food and water. I refused it all. I would take no comforts until my Keegan was back in my arms.

I'm not sure which one of us passed out first. I woke up leaning against the cage, my hand stretched out through the bars. He was still curled in the corner, twitching.

Baby, please, I pleaded with him. *I'm so sorry I did this to you.* My guilt was the only thing that overruled the pain currently coursing through our bond.

I think Dan or Colin remained with me. None of it registered until the last voice I'd expected to hear spoke.

"Sasha?"

Turning my head, still leaning against the bars that caged my wild, unhinged mate, I saw my father squatting down next to me. "Dad?" I croaked out, not completely sure I was seeing things correctly.

"It's me, baby." He reached forward to touch me, only for a growl to echo from the confines of the cell. I looked over to see my mate. He hadn't moved, but I could see his eye just barely peeked open.

Relief swept through me. Keegan might not recognize me, but his possessiveness hadn't changed. First with Colin and now with my dad.

I pressed my hand against my mate-mark, hoping he could somehow feel that.

I turned my attention back to my dad, my hand still on my throat. "He doesn't like it when people touch me."

Dad nodded once. "Understood." He handed me the unopened water bottle. "Will you please drink this?"

I shook my head, looking back into the cage at my mate. "Not until he does."

"Baby, you can't help him if you don't take care of yourself."

He had a point, but I was too stubborn to listen. "What are you doing here?"

My father sat back. I could just barely see him out of the corner of my eye as I kept vigil on my mate. "Dan came to find me. There have been rumors about what happened with the ferals, with Keegan and with Drake. If even half of them are true, the pack owes your mate a debt of gratitude. And I owe you an apology."

At those words, I turned my head against the bars again to face him. I realized then that my father's eyes were red and puffy. Had he been crying?

"Sasha, baby, I love you. But, gods forgive me, when you brought home that..." His voice trailed off as his eyes landed on Keegan in the corner of the cell. He looked back at me. "When you brought Keegan home that first day, I snapped. To claim that a *jaguar* was your True Mate seemed like insanity. I sent Dan after you because I knew that if there was anyone in this world who could get you to see reason, it was him. But then Colin came knocking on my door to tell me that Dan was bringing you home *with your mate.* I couldn't believe it." A tear escaped my father's right eye. "Then you came home. I swear I wanted to see you, to hold you and talk to you. I needed to know you were okay with my own eyes. But you were clutching that man's hand so tight and leaning on him for support..."

Shame laced his voice. "I still didn't understand. How could you believe that that *cat* was your True Mate? I was so sure that the Alpha was going to disprove your claim. When Drake announced that you were in fact bonded, I lost it. I didn't know the lengths your mate would go to protect you. At the time, all I could think of were the *dangers* he would bring to you."

He let out a long sigh. "Dan laid into me the next day. I have never seen him so furious. Dan is my levelheaded child and for him to be so angry with me... I considered for the first time that perhaps I had made a mistake. But it's difficult to admit when you're wrong. I waited, thinking that time would bring some perspective."

My father's cheeks reddened and his nostrils flared as he admitted, "Then Brad came to see me." *That* announcement narrowed my gaze. "He said he was concerned for you. Everything he said made sense to me. He was so certain that you were in danger from your mate...and I am ashamed to say I believed him."

"Did you help him kidnap me?" I hated to ask but I had to know.

My father's head shot up. "Gods, no!" He reached for me, only to jerk his hand back at the sharp yowl that came from the cell. "But I also didn't dissuade him. I had...a feeling his motives were more personal than the generic concerns he'd hinted at. I selfishly ignored them and didn't warn you or Dan what I believed he might do." He dropped his face into his hands.

I believed him. I reached forward to comfort my father but then pulled back at that last second. I paused, because the yowl hadn't come. Keeping an eye on my mate, I reached for my father again. Keegan's eyes narrowed, zeroing in on my hands and arms, but he didn't make a sound to keep me from touching my father. So, apparently, I was the one who had to do the touching. Good to know.

I wrapped my arms around my dad, clutching him to my chest. His rejection had caused me pain and his inaction had resulted in Keegan's current state. Maybe I was too tired to hold a grudge or maybe I was just so relieved my father was talking to me again.

In the end, I decided it didn't matter. I pressed my lips into my father's graying hair. "I forgive you, Dad."

A shudder went through him and a sob escaped his lips.

After a while, my father sat up. Clearing his throat, he turned his attention toward my mate. I let him, not wanting to embarrass him by mentioning his emotional outburst. "So, how are we going to help him?"

I resumed my seat by the cell, resting my forehead once again against the cold metal. "I don't know. I can feel him, but it's like there's a film between us now. He's in so much pain, I don't think he recognizes me."

My dad reached a hand toward me, drawing another yowl from the cell. As he took his hand away, I realized that had been his intention. "Oh, I think he recognizes you. I just don't think he understands why."

"I've been talking to him, trying to send him images and memories of us together, but it's not working."

My father was quiet for a bit. When he spoke, there was obvious hesitation in his voice. "How much do you trust your mate, Sasha?"

"I trust him with my life." My response was immediate.

"Even in this state?" he asked, indicating the cell.

I turned my head slowly toward him, unsure what he was getting at. "Yes."

My father let out a sigh and stood. "You better stand up. I don't think your Keegan would appreciate me giving you a hand."

I stood, marveling at the fact that my father had just called my mate *your Keegan*. I loved the sound of that. I had every intention of getting *my Keegan* back.

My father went over to the wall, retrieving a set of keys I hadn't noticed were there. "Baby, I don't think you're going to be able to reach him from out here." He nodded toward the cell door. "I think you need to reach him from in there. Distance is what caused this rift between you two. I think a lack of distance is what's going to solve it."

My heart leapt at the possibility of hope. Was my father right? That would mean I would have to step into the cell. My eyes landed on my caged mate. No wonder my father asked if I trusted him. He meant to lock me inside with him.

I looked back at my father. "Do it."

"Are you sure—"

"Do it."

"We need to do this quickly. We can't risk him escaping." I nodded my understanding. "I'm going to leave the two of you alone once you're inside," he announced. "I think you two need time to fix your bond and you certainly don't need an audience."

I leaned over and kissed my father's rough cheek. "Thank you."

He gave me a sweet smile, his eyes wrinkling with emotion. "I'll leave the key on the floor outside the cell just in case."

That made sense. If I was alone, I needed a way to get out. And, if I was successful, *we* needed a way to get out. I knew right then that I had no intention of leaving this cage without my mate.

My father inserted the key and waited for my nod to open it. He turned the key and opened the cage just enough for me to slip through. The door clanked shut behind me. I tried not to flinch at the sound.

Keegan's head lifted and his tail twitched.

"Be careful," my father warned before placing the keys on the floor within reach of the cell.

I nodded to him but didn't look behind me. My attention was wholly on my mate.

I took several slow and deliberate steps toward him. The giant jaguar eyed me suspiciously but didn't move. I wondered if he'd hurt himself more than I thought he had when he'd rammed the cell bars.

Carefully, I took a seat in front of him. His eyes narrowed as much as his feline face allowed. His lip twitched like he wanted to bare his fangs at me, but he couldn't make himself do it. *That* made me smile.

"Will you let me touch you?" I asked him cautiously. I tried to send reassurances through our bond, but all I could feel was that gut-retching pain. Thankfully, my stomach was empty from my vomiting.

I didn't get an answer from him.

He stiffened as I reached for him. His head pulled back just slightly, but he wasn't growling. Eventually, my hand connected with his spotted fur and I felt it. The instant recognition in his eyes. He knew who I was. He knew *exactly* who I was.

A laugh of relief escaped me. I flung my arms around his wide feline shoulders, burying my face in his fur.

Sasha.

My name broke through the pain, shattering the fog between us into a million pieces. There was so much love and joy from him, it overwhelmed me. He pushed himself up and cradled me to his warm cat body. I didn't know why he didn't shift back and I didn't care. My Keegan was back, no matter what form he was in.

Exhaustion hit us both hard. We curled together on that hard cell floor, reminding me of the woods and caves we'd slept in for months while on the run. Just like then, I draped myself over his feline form to help keep him warm.

$\approx$

I awoke to two human arms around my waist. Sometime during our rest, he'd shifted back. I felt the smile on his lips as they pressed against mine. I knew right then that everything would be okay. My Keegan was back and we were going to be just fine.

Wrong, mate. My eyes flew open at Keegan's contradiction. *You and I,* he continued, *we are going to be much more than fine.* He kissed my lips again, then my mate-mark, the space between my breasts, my belly button, and finally the top of my mound.

My eyes narrowed. *Did you undress me?*

He looked up the length of my body with a wicked gleam in his eyes a second before his tongue was inside me. *Of course.*

Oh gods! My thighs splayed open on their own accord. *Keegan!* My mate's wickedly talented tongue dipped and probed inside me. And, as if that wasn't wonderfully torturous enough, he pinched my clit. My cry reverberated and I was never more grateful for my father's suggestion for privacy.

More! I pleaded. I needed to reassure myself that Keegan was okay and back with me.

Keegan slithered his way up my body, trailing licks, nips, and kisses along the way. He hovered over me, his green eyes burrowing themselves into mine. "I'm here, Sasha," he said. "I'm right here." He inched his hot length slowly inside me, drawing out the pleasure of his penetration. Keegan lowered himself down, touching his lips to my mate-mark. "And I'm never leaving again."

He bit down and I threw my head back from the force of my shout. My claws dug deep into his skin. He turned his head and I knew exactly what he wanted. My own canines struck in one quick motion.

Pain and pleasure whirled between us, each feeding the other. I wrapped my legs around his hips and held on for dear life as Keegan took me to heights as only he could.

9

It was our rumbling stomachs that eventually forced us to exit the privacy of the cage. I slipped my hand through the bars to grab the key. Rising, Keegan slapped my ass. Hard. I let out a yelp and rounded on him.

"What the hell was that for?"

Keegan stepped forward, raising his hands to grip the bars on either side of my head as he crowded me. The intensity of his gaze shook me to the core. "Don't you *ever* endanger your life again for me. I don't remember much, but I do know that I wasn't the one in control. You entered this cell not knowing if my jaguar was going to attack you."

I put my hand over his heart. "Your jaguar still recognized me, Keegan. And I wasn't about to abandon you."

"Never. Again," he emphasized before resting his forehead against mine for several silent moments. I basked in them.

We really needed to get a house to ourselves. Of course, a part of me feared we'd never leave it and we'd end up dying in an orgasmic explosion. *Oh well,* my inner voice said with a shrug. *At least I'd die happy. My tombstone will read 'Here lies Sasha Rowe. Man, did she like to fuck.'*

His chuckle rumbled through him and he lifted his head to kiss my temple. "Gods, I love you."

I gripped his head between my hands, bringing his lips down to mine. "I love you too. You and me, Keegan, together. Always and forever."

His mental voice echoed my words.

And then the romantic moment was ruined by our stomachs growling ferociously.

~

Clothes, water bottles, and sandwiches were left for us at the top of the stairs. I was mentally preparing Keegan for the kiss I was going to be giving Colin for his kindness when I spotted my father approaching. The look of relief on his face just about broke my heart. Sandwich forgotten, I ran into his arms.

He caught me up, hugging me tightly to him. "Well done, baby. Your mother would be so proud of you."

My heart clenched at his words and I knew tears would have been streaming down my cheeks if I hadn't been cried out. I felt Keegan approach behind us and I stepped back from my father. I cleared my throat. "Keegan, this is my dad, Xavier. Dad, this is my True Mate, Keegan."

"We've met." My father gave me an amused look before holding out his hand to Keegan. "Welcome, officially, to the family."

Keegan surprised us both by stepping forward and giving my father a strong hug. When he stepped back, he brought me against him. "Thank you for your help."

My father looked confused. "You remember me down there?"

Keegan made a face. "It was like watching a muted movie upside-down without subtitles. I recognized things, like Sasha," he pressed his lips to my hair, "but I couldn't figure out a way to get things right-side-up again."

"I'm glad I could help." My dad looked away as he added, "It was the least I could do after everything I've done wrong since the two of you met."

"I'm new to this whole family-thing, but my understanding is that forgiveness is supposed to be a given. I don't hold grudges, Xavier. It's water under the bridge as far as I'm concerned."

My father gave him a grateful smile. "Thank you." He gestured to the food behind us. "You better eat that quickly. There are many who want to greet you."

"How's Drake?" I asked around the mouthful of sandwich. Extra roast beef, nice. "For that matter, what day is it?"

"It's Thursday." Two days after the morning of the attack. "Drake is healing, but not as quickly as Chelsea was hoping. Dan is working to keep everyone in line and get the repairs done as quickly as possible. Camryn is standing guard at Drake's bedside and refusing to leave. The pack needed a leader, so Dan stepped in."

I nodded. Dan was the obvious choice, though he technically wasn't high in the pack hierarchy. He could have been, but he'd passed up that opportunity when he'd turned down the position as Beta.

"Elias is in charge of keeping the captured ferals in line. Patty is with him." I was surprised by that announcement and my father continued without needing me to voice my question. "She's hoping she can get through to them, bring them back."

I'd never heard of such a thing. "Is that even possible?"

My father shrugged. "I honestly don't know. She makes better progress when Elias or one of the other guards isn't near. But no one is too keen on letting her be alone with them."

I thought back to when my father had locked me in the basement cell with my deranged mate. At least I had known Keegan would never harm me, no matter his mental state. Gods, Patty was putting her life on the line being so close to them.

"How many are there?"

"Five," my father said. He shot Keegan a quick glance before adding, "The sixth didn't make it."

I remembered Dan saying that Keegan had attacked the six ferals who had surrendered. I wasn't sure if I should feel guilty about the loss of life. On one hand, all life was sacred. On the other, surrender or no, the feral had attacked my home and endangered my mate, friends, and family.

Sensing my distress, Keegan brought me close to his chest. "Shhh, baby, the fault is mine, not yours. Let me bear this weight for you."

I shook my head. "It's not either of our weights to bear." I looked over at my father. "And Brad?"

Keegan's arms tightened their hold around me.

My father's eyes narrowed, and a low growl escaped him before he replied, "Under house arrest awaiting our Alpha's judgement."

I nodded once. I was satisfied with that answer.

Our sandwiches done—and damn, I could have eaten another one—we followed my father out into the main area of the Manor. I was expecting to see Dan or Colin waiting of us.

I was not expecting to see most of the pack crowded in the main area or to break out into shouts of joy and applause when we entered. My cheeks reddened with embarrassment. I had done nothing to warrant their praise. This was all Keegan's doing. Even in his madness, he'd saved our Alpha's life and protected the pack. I tried to step away, to allow him his moment in the sun, but he kept a firm grip on me. Used to solitude, this display made him uncomfortable.

We made our way slowly to the stairs that would lead us to the infirmary. The pack all seemed to want to talk to us, to reach out and touch us, and to thank us. Even I was starting to get uncomfortable.

A loud whistle pierced the crowd noise and everyone turned toward the door where Dan stood. "Give them a break. It's not like they're going anywhere."

At his words, the others scattered. I was never so grateful to see my brother in my life.

Drake was sitting on a cot in the infirmary. After two days, he should have been up and healed. Wounds made by an Alpha took longer to heal, everyone knew that, but Keegan's were almost healed. Why weren't Drake's?

Camryn sat at his bedside. There was a rolling table with a started chess game between them.

Drake's lips spread into a smile as we entered. "Come in." His voice was raspy. Seeing as he had long gashes through his throat, I was frankly surprised he was talking at all.

I ran to him on the opposite side of the bed from Camryn. I dropped down, hugging my Alpha fiercely. "Thank you." Keegan might have saved Drake's life, but Drake's life had also been in danger because he'd stepped in to save Keegan's.

Drake's lips touched my hair. "You're very welcome, sweet." I stepped back as my Alpha looked over at Keegan. "It's good to see you human again."

"It's good to be human again."

"I have a favor to ask of you." He indicated for Keegan to come closer. My eyes flicked to Camryn, but the Beta didn't flinch at the jaguar's nearness to his wounded Alpha.

"As long as it won't pull me from Sasha's side, anything." Keegan wrapped an arm around my waist. "I doubt I'll be able to let her out of my sight right now."

Drake's inclined his head in understanding. "I'm going to be laid up for a while. Chelsea doesn't understand why the wounds aren't healing correctly. She thinks there might be something in them that's keeping them open." I winced, not liking that possibility. "In the meantime, Dan has taken over leading the pack. I appreciate his efforts, but he has expressed his dissatisfaction about having to do this multiple times. While we believe we took out all the ferals within the pack, no one knows for sure. There could be another attack and the compound fortifications are currently weak. Dan's overseeing this too. He's being stretched too thin."

Drake paused and then held out his hand to my mate. My jaguar mate. "I would like you to be my Champion."

Keegan, having no idea the significance of this offer, listened as my mind reeled. An Alpha's Champion was an old tradition. As far as I knew, the position hadn't been filled in generations. The idea was that, if the Alpha was away from the pack, his Beta would likely be with him as a guard. Therefore, it was the position of the Alpha's Champion to take control of the pack until the Alpha's return. The Champion could be of any rank within the hierarchy. The ideal Champion was someone who was strong enough to protect the pack but not so ambitious that they would start a mutiny against the current Alpha.

What Drake was asking of Keegan was to become the pack's temporary Alpha. He was certainly strong enough, there was no question about that. It was a huge responsibility, especially since Drake wasn't giving us a time limit for when he felt he'd be healed enough to once again take up the mantle.

While I had my doubts, as well as my awed disbelief at the offer, it was ultimately Keegan's decision. He was the one who would be Champion, not me.

Keegan's arm tightened around my waist before he leaned forward and clasped Drake's hand in acceptance. "I'll need help," Keegan informed the Alpha. "I'm still unfamiliar with some of your ways."

Drake shook his head sternly. "Don't worry." He gave me a wry smile. "I have a feeling you'll have more help than you bargained for."

~

One of Drake's first acts back as Alpha was deciding Brad's punishment. At my request, Brad was publicly shamed. Keegan, as my True Mate as well as Drake's Champion, held Brad down as in front of the whole pack Drake slashed his claws across Brad's face and Keegan poured salt into the deep wounds.

He would forevermore bear the scars of his Alpha's claws. While he wasn't banished from the pack, he was no longer welcome at gatherings, nor were many inclined to invite him out of fear of insulting the Alpha. Brad would be alone within the pack.

Patty was making excellent progress with two of them. A male she estimated to be in his early teens and a female in her mid-twenties. The two were showing less aggression with each day. When I last spoke to her, Patty believed they would soon be ready to be coaxed into shifting into their human forms again. It was unknown how long they'd been wolves, so taking human form would likely be a long and excruciating process. I certainly did not envy Patty's job and wished her all the luck in the world.

Unfortunately, the other three wolves, two males and a female, were becoming more volatile. They'd already injured multiple guards during their captivity and Elias no longer allowed Patty to enter their cages. My father told Keegan and I that Elias was going to recommend terminating them to Drake. I didn't know what Drake's decision would be. It would, after all, be his hand that ended their lives.

Keegan and I also were settling into our new house—and just in time too. We'd soon have a little pup or kit running around. My mate was basking in the idea of his pending fatherhood. Every chance he got, he would touch my navel. I would be showing soon and I couldn't wait to see his face when my baby bump finally appeared. At night, Keegan now fell asleep with his ear to my womb, listening to the heartbeat.

Keegan and I were a first as far as we knew. Would the child be a wolf or a jaguar? Or a mixture of both? Time would answer our questions. I decided to go through the pregnancy as a human to give us extra time to prepare.

Neither of us cared about gender or species. We would love our child regardless. As we had learned the hard way, laws could be rewritten but love was forever.

ABOUT THE AUTHOR

I am a full-time RVer. I travel the country in my motorhome with my dog, Porthos. I enjoy reading, hiking, kayaking, biking, and camping. Follow me @elisegedickeauthor!

EVERY STORM

BRITT JONES

BLURB

After years on the front lines, Army Ranger Morgan Creed returns home expecting peace—but finds chaos instead. His champion stallion stolen, his bank account drained, his wife is gone, and in her place... a seven-month-old baby girl he never knew existed.

Struggling to balance fatherhood with managing his remote South Dakota ranch, Morgan's world is turned upside down again when Harper Emerson arrives. Hiding from a past of her own, she's fierce, compassionate. In exchange for a place to stay and room to train her emotional support dogs for veterans, Harper offers to help care for baby Skye.

Neither of them is looking for love. Both are running from the pain of the past. But in the quiet moments between chaos, something unexpected begins to grow—a fragile trust, a slow-burning desire, and the hope that even the most broken hearts can heal.

Because sometimes, love is the calm after the storm.

Tropes: Military Hero, Alpha Male, Rancher, Single Dad, Slow Burn, Close Proximity

1

Morgan Creed

When the plane lands, I turn on my phone. Finally, there's a message from Arden.

I've been worried that something happened. It's been three days since I sent her the text that I was on my way home for good.

I understood with the ranch she couldn't meet me at base when I returned from my last deployment. But her messages have been terse and almost non-existent.

Waiting until I've deplaned, I step out of the crowd and open her response.

Your truck is in overnight parking, slot D-6, keys in the magnetic box under the driver's wheel well. You need to head straight to the ranch. There's a problem.

I try to call but it immediately goes to voicemail. Damn.

I knew she was tired of being a military wife. The whole time we've been together, I've barely been home. I'd get back from one mission, spend my leave at the ranch, and be deployed again.

As for ranch life, well, she'd never lived it day to day before we married. Fiction, movies and summer camp are pretty far from the reality. She was so into it in the beginning. So excited.

The time we've spent together over the last two and half years hasn't been enough to really bond a relationship. If I'm honest the last time I was home was strained. Hell, she went to stay with her mom the last two weeks. We'd barely had a month together and fought most of it.

I did a lot of thinking during that last mission. When I got back, I checked and found out I could retire early but keep my years if I joined and stayed in the reserves. Not what I wanted but it wasn't just about me anymore. I had a wife.

Who am I shitting? My marriage has problems. I run a hand down my face.

Dad's property butts up to mine at the farthest point, a good twenty miles driving. Less if you're riding a horse. He's been trying to check in with Arden, but it's like she's been avoiding him. Either not home or doesn't answer the door, and she's distant when she does.

He'd started just dropping by at random times to at least check on the horses and livestock. He's been worried about my stud horse, Satan, since she said she'd been loaning him out instead of doing the covering at the ranch. The number of cattle has dropped as well. Top it off, he's not impressed with her new hired hand that's supposedly running the place.

Guess I got a lot of making up to do with Arden, and to dad for putting up with the bullshit while I'm gone. Especially since he's got his own ranch to run. Making my way to the parking garage, it's hard not to keep my temper in check. My truck looks like someone drove it through a mud bath.

Yeah, yeah, boys with toys. But damn, I keep my weapons, my tools, my property and my vehicles clean and in good shape. Ranching or battle, you need to be sure the things that keep you alive and sustain you are in working condition.

It's a clear morning and I push the speed limit and make the hour drive in forty-five. My property line starts at the turn off from the county road, but it's two more miles to reach the house and barns. In the distance I see a cloud of dust on one of the rises on the far side of the ranch. I wonder if that's the new ranch hand who's supposed to be taking care of things. Dad said he likes to ride around on a dirt bike. Never seen him on a horse.

Pulling into the drive, I park near the fence by the barn. Damn, two of the wood slats are missing and another section is sagging. I've only been gone twelve months. What the hell has the new manager been doing?

The field truck is parked in front of the barn, but I don't see Arden's new pickup.

Glancing to the pasture where my prime stud, Satan rules, I don't see him either. My gut clenches. Maybe he's on the other side of the rise.

Grabbing my duffel from the backseat, I head to the ranch house porch. A dust cloud is barreling down the long drive. I pause. It's Dad.

I wait for him to pull in and meet him halfway. He wraps an arm around me, giving me a hug and a slap on the back. "Good to see you home and in one piece, son."

"Good to be home." I think.

"Where's Arden?" He glances over the yard, clearly noticing her pickup isn't here.

"She left my truck for me at the airport. Said there was an issue at home." We take the steps to the door together. Dropping my duffel next to Gram's old rocker, we walk in.

"Arden?" I call out. "Arden, you home?"

The only sound is a squeak-thump coming from the kitchen and dining area. I glance at Dad then turn toward the sound. He follows, reaching for the Glock he always has at the small of his back.

Shock, confusion, fear wash over me all at once. Sitting in the middle of the room is a playpen with a cloud mobile hanging above it. Inside is a small child dressed in pink. Legs kicking and arms flaying, fists clenched, the child lets out a gurgle, shifts its head toward me. She kicks and waves her arms in earnest.

Dad meets my gaze. Pressing a finger to his lips, he pulls his weapon and motions he's going to inspect the rest of the house.

Crossing to the playpen, I lift the now whimpering infant to my chest. The child's clothing is soaked as is the blanket beneath her. Glancing around the room, I see a bag with rubber ducks printed on the outside sitting on the counter next to the refrigerator.

"I've got you, little one. I've got you," I croon, bouncing her in my arm. In the bag are four disposable diapers and two outfits that don't smell that great but at least they're dry. I turn to change her on the table, and it hits me, the brand new, and very expensive table and sideboard Arden insisted I buy her the last time I was home are gone.

There are a few tea towels in a drawer. I dampen one then kneel on the floor, placing another under the now silent baby and begin stripping her soiled clothes.

Dad returns before I finish. He shakes his head. "Nothing. And son, I mean nothing. All that new furniture you bought is gone." He looks around the room. "Kitchen set, master bedroom, living room furniture. The old bed set and dresser your grandma used is still in the spare room. The mattress is gone. Third room has a bunch of empty flower pots."

"Will you see if there's any diaper rash medicine in that bag? Then check for baby food in the refrigerator. The way she's sucking her hand, I think this little one might be hungry."

"No diaper medicine, but I've got Vaseline in the truck."

Returning with the salve, he then goes to the refrigerator. "Two bottles and two little jars of baby food." He opens the cupboard. "Looks like she left the old plates and pans. I'll warm a bottle."

After putting a pan of water on to boil he looks at me as he palms his phone. "I'm calling the Sheriff."

Standing with the baby in my arms I nod, tossing him the pacifier I found hooked to the bag. "Wash it, please." The sweet little girl locks her tiny fingers in my beard and pulls. I buzz my lips. It takes a couple times before she smiles.

Dad hands me the pacifier which she eagerly latches on to suckle. Grabbing the bag, I head to the porch and Gram's rocker.

Content for the moment she kicks and waves her arms as I rock gently and skim the papers I found in the diaper bag. I've read the important stuff and have a pretty good handle on the facts before Dad joins me. I take the bottle, and she immediately reaches for it, sucking hard like she's starved.

"Sheriff's on his way?"

"Yeah. Since he's your brother, he's bringing a deputy with to keep everything above board."

"For the best I reckon." Not sure I want the whole damn town in my business, but hell, Fergus is small anyway and everyone always knows everyone's business.

He glances at me, then at the papers on the table between us. "Go ahead, read 'em."

The good, the bad, the ugly, the Creeds don't keep secrets from each other. It's how we've survived.

Shaking his head as he reads, he finally glances up. "This doesn't add up. You were gon—"

"The name on that birth certificate says Skye Creed and her daddy is Morgan Creed. I'm not the one who left her. You set the standard. Creeds take care of our own. I ain't changing anything."

I see the understanding on his face and his nod of approval.

"I do need to make sure this is all legal and a done deal. You know someone who can help with that? Maybe come out here and meet with us this afternoon? I also need to find her doctor to learn about food and everything else."

"Nothing on these papers gave a doctor name?"

"Nope."

"I'll make some calls. I got a lawyer friend. I'll see if he can come. Maybe he'll know how to find the doctor."

"Do me a favor first. Wi—will you check the barns and the pastures? I got a feeling they took Satan, but I need to be sure."

Silently, he makes his way across the yard and disappears inside the main building. I already know Satan's not here. The best damn stud in a five-state area, maybe more. I raised him from a foal when his momma didn't make it.

After I've been gone, as soon as he catches my scent he'll set up a ruckus until I greet him. He's always been more of a puppy dog for me than a stallion. I know in my gut, he's not here.

I'll find you, big guy. I'll bring you home.

2

Morgan

Having sucked her bottle dry, the little girl in my arms squirms. Putting her over my shoulder I pat her back until I hear her drunkard's belch. I laugh. "Well, that sure sounded like your uncle Maddox. Already trying to keep up with the men of the family."

I kiss the side of her head. "You're safe little one. The Creed's got you now. We don't give in. We don't let go. We don't back down."

Dad comes out of the barn and crosses the yard. "Satan and all his tack are gone. The mares are out in their field and Roper was minding his own business in his pasture. I put him in his stall in the stud barn.

"The new ATV she got for her foreman is missing and obviously Satan's trailer and Arden's truck. Satan's chipped and well known. We'll find him. I'll start putting the word out.

"I checked the loft in the barn. Unci's old kitchen table, chairs and bench are up there. We'll get them down later." He pulls out his phone. "I've started a list of items we'll need. The two of you can stay with me tonight."

"No. This is my home. I have livestock to tend. I won't risk anything else happening. I'm staying."

"Well, we got a hell of a lot to do today. Good thing you took the red eye."

The squawk and flutter of birds fill the air. Glancing toward the road I see the sheriff's vehicle heading down my drive. Marshall climbs from behind the wheel, I meet him halfway to the porch. He gives Skye a curious look then wraps me in a bro hug. "Good to see you, man. Heard it was bad this last time. Glad you're back in one piece."

"Good to see you too, Marsh. Hear from Maddox lately?" He shakes his head.

I glance at the officer who just climbed from the passenger side. "Jess? Jessie Canton?" She smiles and gives me a nod. "When the hell did you grow up? Damn, I have been gone too long."

"Who's this cutie," she asks grinning at Skye, who buries her face in my neck.

Meeting my brother's stare I answer. "Skye Creed. My daughter."

"Fuck," Marshall whispers. "You better start at the beginning."

My gaze skitters to Jessie. Her sister and family did a real number on my brother, Maddox. Screwed him up for a couple years. I wonder if I can trust her.

As if reading my mind, she gives her head a shake. "Morgan, I'm not my sister. Or my family. We disowned each other years ago. I have nothing to do with them. I've earned my own way from the age of sixteen while living with my aunt. I can't make you believe me, but I stood up for Maddox.

"I joined the police force in Sioux Falls and was there for a few years before coming home."

"I trust her, Morga,." Marshall chimes in. "She's my top deputy and going to law school on top of it. If I'm not careful she'll have my job in a few years."

"No way in hell. I can't deal with the BS you have to go through," Jessie snaps.

"Can we go inside and talk?" Marshall asks.

"We'll be more comfortable on the steps. All my furniture is gone."

Marshall raises an eyebrow. "Okay, let's start from the beginning."

Jess takes a seat on the steps, pen and notebook in hand. Marshall leans against the post, placing his recorder on the handrail and hits record. Stating the names of all present, he asks me to start at the beginning.

"My truck was left at the airport with a note to get here as quick as possible. Dad arrived here at the same time, so I have a witness. We found Skye in the kitchen in a playpen. Alone. No one else was here."

I'm kicking myself for not taking a picture when Dad pulls out his phone and shows one he took of how we found Skye.

"Satan's gone and all the new furniture. Right after I pulled off the county road onto the drive, I thought I saw a glint in the distance then a cloud of dust on the back road. I'm wondering if they waited to see me pull in before taking off. Maybe one or both of them at least waited that long to make sure the baby was found."

"Both? Jess questions.

"I can answer that," Dad speaks up.

Jess turns her attention to him. "Mr. Creed."

"Montana or Creed, Jess. Mister makes me feel old."

She smiles. "Montana, what do you know?"

"Arden hired a helper just before Morgan came back from his next to last deployment. Shortly after, she fired Morgan's ranch manager with no cause and promoted the young fella who didn't know his ass from a hole in the ground. I started stopping by more often once Abe was gone. But she, they, didn't listen to me and it got to where they wouldn't answer the door or were flat out gone."

Glancing across the yard he gives his head a shake. "Lot of stuff going to need repairs."

He continues. "Morgan came home on leave and seemed to straighten things out a few months back. But once he left things got worse. I caught 'em coming out of the bedroom once. I asked Abe and he said that was normal from the time she brought the new hand on."

Jessie looks at the baby. "Did you know she was pregnant before your leave was over?"

"No. She did leave the birth certificate."

"Can I see the papers?" Marshall asks.

Dad hands them over.

"Brother, these dates don't add up." He looks up at me over the pages. "I saw you the last time you were home on leave. I took you to the airport. There's no way...."

"My name is on that birth certificate. Skye is mine."

Jess looks from one to the other of us but keeps her mouth shut.

"Marsh, the things that matter are they left my infant daughter alone in a house. For that alone I want to prosecute. They also stole my stud horse, my prime source of income."

"Uhmm, they may have done more," Jess speaks up. "Have you checked your bank accounts? Your savings? Retirement funds?"

"Fuck! I didn't think of that. I was worried about Skye." Pulling my phone I start thumbing through accounts. "My checking and Ranch account are almost drained. She went to the limit that required a second confirmation from my phone. Savings always had the two confirmations."

"Pension, government accounts?" Marshall asks.

"No, those I never added her to because it was a pain in the ass. I was going to do it when I was stateside. She was pushing me to get it done, but I didn't get to it because my last leave was cut short when I was deployed."

"Change all your passwords and Pin numbers right now. Then cancel all her ATM and credit cards. Remove her from any online banking," Jess advises.

"Then call all of your financial institutions including your pension and the military. Tell them you're a victim of fraud and theft and file reports. All of your accounts, no matter how small."

Aw shit. Checking accounts, savings accounts and more places I can even remember. I glance down at the little one and remember what's most important. "I need to get food and diapers. She didn't leave anything. I've got to find out who's Skye's doctor is. She didn't leave me that information either. No eating habits, formula, what food she can have. There were only two bottles already made in the refrigerator, two jars of baby fruit and four diapers."

"We'll file child abandonment reports, too," Jessie adds

"Son, I've got Skye," Dad says. "You get busy on the financial stuff." He turns to Marshall. "It's time to call Maddox, he may be able to help locate Satan with his federal connections."

Marshall nods. "I'm also going to call the state troopers, too. Have them send out an investigation team. See if we can find anything on the back road to track them. They can also pull up road film to look for the horse trailer."

Jessie looks at him. "If she wasn't from around here, she probably saw the doctors at the new women's clinic. I'll call for you. We'll get what you need."

"I want her to be seen for a general checkup."

Jess chews her lip then speaks up. "I've got a friend. She's-ah-not working right now. I could call her and see if she'd be willing to go pick up baby food, diapers and stuff for you right now. You'd have to give her your card or cash and maybe some gas money.

"She's trustworthy. Just in a bad patch herself right now."

"I can transfer money to her if that will help."

"Yeah, it would."

Hours later I'm still trying to wrap my head around all that's happened. The state troopers found trailer tracks on the back side of my property. They believe they were parked there for a while. The dust I witnessed was probably from the ATV that was left behind. Arden got a lot, but not everything. If I get Satan back, I can start over again.

Jessie was able to get the name of Skye's doctor. I was able to talk to her and she's working me in tomorrow since Skye hasn't been seen in months. I'll sign the birth certificate at the courthouse beforehand.

In the meantime, Jess's friend was able to get diapers, formula and the baby food the doctor recommended on the phone, along with a couple outfits. Marshall came back later with a car seat and blankets. His deputies will drive by more often for the next week.

Dad and Marshall are right. Unless Arden carried this child for eleven months, she is not my biological child. But my name is on her birth certificate, and no innocent child deserves to be unwanted.

Kissing Skye on the forehead, I cuddle her to my chest. *You are mine. And you are wanted, little Skye.*

3

Harper Emerson

Stay calm and keep your mouth shut. If I could only text Jess.

"Answer me, bitch, where were you today? I drove by and your car was gone."

"I already told you, Floyd. I helped a friend." Knowing he has spies all over town and probably already knows some of this, I try to keep it simple. "They needed some groceries and couldn't go get them. I agreed to help."

"You refuse to help *ME*, but you can run all over town for someone else? Using my car, my gas, and my money? And you changed the fucking door locks."

"It's not your car. I've had that car since I was sixteen. I pay for the gas out of the money I earn at my job at the hardware store. And you don't live here anymore." Oh shit, why did I add that?

His fist flies across the counter separating us. I try to spin away but he clips me below the left eye. I reel back from the impact, lose my balance and fall to the floor in a heap.

Grabbing my hair, he forces me to look up at him. Spittle flies from his mouth as he screams at me. "You're gonna pay for this bullshit game of kicking me out. I own you, bitch.

"Don't..." He kicks out, catching my hip with his steel-toed boot. "Ever..." He kicks again, connecting with my stomach. Grabbing me by the neck, fingers digging in, he lifts my head. The room is spinning, I can't think or focus. I barely hear the sirens in the distance. Thank god for nosey neighbors.

Digging his fingers deeper into my throat he squeezes harder. "This isn't over. What's yours is mine. You are mine. And you better keep your mouth shut or I'll visit your grandpa and give him the same treatment. Bet that stingy ass old geezer would croak pretty easy."

Tossing me to the floor, he lands one more hard kick to my side and heads to the back of my small house. I gasp for air, my vision tunnels. Maybe I'll die and get this over with.

~

"Harper. Harper can you hear me? It's Jess. Come on, wake up. You're scaring the doctors."

Doctors? What doctors? My eyelids feel like five-pound weights as I try to open them. Blinded by the bright lights, I squeeze them shut. "Where am I?"

"The hospital."

"The hospital? Why?"

"You were attacked. I'm here to get your statement so you can file charges."

Floyd. Again. Oh god, why can't the asshole drink himself to death? Surely, he has no liver left.

"I—I don't remember. What happened?"

"Damn it, Harper. You know damn well who did this. I think the whole fucking town knows. Why won't you press assault charges? What does he have on you? He's going to fucking kill you one of these days."

I grab her hand. "My dogs? Are my dogs okay?"

"Yeah. I moved them to my garage. They aren't happy but they're alive and eating."

"Thank you, Jess. You are the best friend."

"Yeah, I know. I'm having them add that to my file for future promotions purposes."

I try to sit up. Nothing feels broken, but I ache all over.

"Just chill, you have bruised ribs and kidney, as well as a concussion. You're not going anywhere soon."

"What time is it? I need to get home and changed. Is it time to be at work?"

"It's been a couple days. They had to keep you sedated to help the healing." She takes my hand and gives it a squeeze. "Your house caught fire. It's not totally destroyed, but also not livable.

"My, my pictures? Gram and Gramps? Mom and Dad? Pe-Pepper?"

"Sheriff Creed let me grab some of your personal items. I've already taken the photos to a place that does restoration. We'll just have to wait and see if they can salvage them.

"Already? How long have I been here?"

"Three days."

"Three days?!"

"Yeah. He worked you over pretty good this time. That's why you need to file charges."

"I can't."

"Why not? You keep telling me no, but you don't give me a reason."

"I can't, Jess. I just can't."

"Can't what?" Sheriff Marshall Creed asks as he walks into the room.

"She won't file charges."

Marshall shakes his head. "Harper, I don't want to see you dead. What are we gonna do with you? Your house isn't livable."

"I'll find something. Maybe work will let me live in the apartment above the store until I can find something else."

"Your boss called. He got an anonymous call threatening his business if he allows you to come back to work. He's letting you go."

"Why'd he call you?"

"He hoped I'd be able to trace the phone number, but we couldn't. Probably a burner. So he's in a hard spot. He's got a family and other employees."

I nod, tears choking me. "I understand. He's doing the right thing."

Plucking the threads on the blanket I try not to panic. What am I going to do? How will I feed the dogs? Will I lose my training apprenticeship?

"I don't like this, Harper. I don't like that we aren't going after someone we know is guilty. My hands are tied if you won't file a complaint."

I shake my head. I can't. It's too dangerous.

"I can't make you do anything, but maybe I can offer you an alternative that could keep you safe and help someone else."

"What?"

"Where did you go shopping the other day?"

"Spearfish. I figured they'd have everything I needed so it would be quicker."

"So this person who didn't hurt you probably would not have been there to see what you were doing?"

"No. He didn't know where I was. Someone saw me drive out of town and told him, but I don't think they knew where I went. Jess knew because she arranged it."

He nods. "My brother could use some help with his daughter. I know you used to work at the daycare, so you know how to take care of kids. You did great by the way with the things you bought. He thanks you again."

"He knows you're talking to me?"

"Yes. His ranch has been neglected, he's got a shit ton of work to do. And we still haven't found his stud or his wife. He's not in a position to hire ranch hands right now, but he can't do the necessary work himself and watch Skye. He also is not in a trusting mood and doesn't want to bring Skye to town for daycare where she might be taken.

"I explained to him your experience with childcare and what you do with the dogs. He has room in one of the barns for your kennels. And he's not opposed to dogs in the house depending on what you're training. As long as Skye is your first priority and she's safe with the animals.

"You saw the inside of his home. It's not large or real modern, but there's three bedrooms. You can live and eat there for free. Including your dogs. He'll keep track of the hours you work for him and when his accounts are resolved he'll pay you your wages.

"You'd watch Skye while he's working. He'll have her when you're doing your training. The two of you can come up with a schedule that lets both of you do what you need.

"One of the biggest advantages I see for you is that it's unlikely anyone would know you're with him in order to tell Floyd. Also, Morgan has spent the last fifteen years in the military. He can and will protect you. You won't be having any more 'accidents'.

"To make this work, you'll continue to shop in Spearfish, or he'll do the shopping. Also, you shouldn't tell anyone in Deadwood where you are. Is that a problem?"

I shake my head. "Jess is really the only one I hang out with. People may talk to me while I'm helping at the hardware store or notice the dogs training in the park. I'm not real social."

"My job will be to find what I need to put Floyd away. I doubt you're the first person he's attacked. Although, if you would work with me this would be taken care of a lot faster."

I look down at my hands. So many secrets, I just.... "You're sure I won't be endangering anyone else? Skye. He won't know where I am?"

"I'm as sure as anyone can be about anything." Marshall heaves a sigh, then pats my fisted hands where they rest in my lap. "I understand more than you think, Harper. I don't fault you. I know about fear. You need to know that I'm here for you just as much as Jess. If this is a deal, I'll talk to Morgan tonight. We'll come up with an exit strategy for when they release you in the morning."

"Please, yes. I would like to do this. It's perfect for me and the dogs. I miss working at the daycare, so taking care of Skye will be like having all the best things in my life."

"It's about time you get some of those best things in your life," Jess whispers, hugging me. "This is going to be the turning point. I'm sure of it."

4

Harper

The next morning, the patient services clerk checks me out in my room. Thankfully, my insurance is still in effect until the end of the month. My co-pays may be high, but I didn't have to pay for them today. The Sheriff takes me to the ambulance bay and has me lay down in the back of his black SUV patrol car where I'll be hidden by the tinted windows.

"In an hour, the hospital is going to call the sheriff's department and report you've disappeared. Probably snuck out to avoid paying. The department is looking for you."

Once he pulls out onto the road, he explains he's doing his normal morning rounds. He's going to check in with all his officers then take his normal lunch to avoid suspicion. He knows two of the lowlifes that hang with Floyd, but suspects there are more that Floyd pays for information in exchange for drugs.

"How did you get with Floyd in the first place?" he asks from the front seat.

"I started working part time at the bar because it was evening hours. I was working at the animal shelter and taking the dog training classes during the day."

"Jess said something about therapy dogs and shelter work? What got you into that?"

"My dad was in the Army and died when I was little. He had some trauma from his time in the service.

"Mom and I moved in with my grandparents. I was raised by my grandpa after my mom and grandma died in a car accident when I was eight. I got hurt in the accident, too. I limp, but I lived.

"College wasn't right for me, at least not regular college. I had a hard time focusing on stuff for a long time after the accident, which made school difficult. I preferred being home on the farm with my grandpa and the animals."

Staring at the roof of the vehicle I realize it's easier to talk if I don't have to see the reactions on someone's face.

"I volunteered at the shelter and loved working with the animals. They had a person come in to talk to us about a special program for trainers. They were looking for people interested in getting certified to work with therapy dogs. I talked to Gramps and told him that's what I really wanted to do.

"Gramps was winding down on the farm and started renting out some of the land and downsized a lot of the animals. He still had the main house, a barn, and plenty of room for me to train once I was certified.

"With my job, the classes, and working with the animals the long ride back and forth started wearing on me. So Gramps got the little house in town for me.

"It was important to me to show him I was mature enough to do all of this. I wanted to pay my own rent and be responsible. I was working at the shelter which doesn't pay a lot and taking the dog training classes. I needed more available day hours for the online classes and practice.

"So I got a job at the bar for evening and night hours. That's where I met Jessie. She came in late one afternoon all teary eyed because she'd lost her dog that she'd had for eighteen years. That's how old my Pepper was when I lost him. She said I was the first one to understand the pain of losing a pet. Well, they are really best friends.

"One night my grandpa came in. He sat at the bar and we were talking and then Floyd sat next to him. Floyd eventually struck up a conversation with my grandpa. I think he may have recognized Gramps."

"That's possible. Calvin Emerson is a good man. He's done a lot for this town. Haven't seen him for a while."

"After a while it became a Friday night thing. Sometimes during the week Floyd would come in and talk to me. He seemed kind of nice.

"My grandpa came in to see me, not to talk business. He switched the night he came in. Or he'd come earlier and leave soon after Floyd showed up.

"Then one night after leaving the bar Grandpa made a stop at the store in Sturgis. He was attacked and had a head injury. Afterward he couldn't remember what happened. His younger brother was worried, so Gramps has been staying with him in Texas recuperating. He doesn't really remember what happened."

"How long ago was that?" Marshall asks.

"Almost five months. He was lucky he didn't die but... Floyd was the one who saved my grandfather. He saw the attack happen and ran the assailants off then called an ambulance.

"Right after that Floyd started coming to the bar more and more often to make sure I was ok. Then he started pressuring me for a date. I felt sort of obligated since he did save my gramps. It wasn't his fault that Gramps suffered a head injury."

"Floyd kept pushing for more and more. Said he wanted to marry me, but I told him no. I wanted to focus on my career as a dog trainer. It was after I refused that he.... he started getting mean. I quit the bar and started working at the hardware store.

"And now I just try to stay away from him."

"You just stay away from him? Not to be rude, Harper, but how's that 'stay away from him' working for you? When he breaks into your home and beats you up?"

"I'm scared, Sheriff. I'm just really scared. It's been a long time since I've felt...safe. And I'm afraid to report him. He says he has friends. Important friends that could hurt me or Gramps."

He sighs, one of those frustrated sighs people do. But I can't help it. I know how vicious Floyd can be.

If I could just have a safe place to hide out for a few days. Heal a little more, then I could ... Oh hell, I don't even know what to do.

The sheriff doesn't let me sit up until we're on ranch property and he's confirmed with Morgan that no one else is around.

Morgan has a sleeping Skye in one of those front-loading baby harnesses and is carrying a bale of hay when we pull in the yard.

"How's it going? Everything okay at the doctor's?" the sheriff asks.

He drops the hay and places his palm on the baby's butt, checking that the tea towel he's used still covers her head from the sun.

His furious scowl speaks volumes. Clenching his teeth, he works his jaw. "I'm damn glad I went to the courthouse first. The doctor made me prove parental status with the birth certificate and my driver's license. Thankfully, I also had my proof of deployment and military ID. As much as it irked me, I did appreciate that the doctor was thorough since she hadn't seen me before and Arden wasn't with me. She left to make copies of my ID's and I'm pretty sure she tried to call Arden and got the same 'no longer in service' message that we did last time we tried.

"When she returned, I explained that Arden and I were no longer together, and I've filed for sole custody and reported child abandonment. Expect a call from her.

"The doctor saw Skye two months ago and she seemed on target at that time. Now Skye is underweight. On the brink of being harmfully so. She doesn't appear to have been abused, but the doctor questions the amount of stimulation she's had, such as with toys, playtime, even just being talked to and cuddled. And obviously food.

"The fact she didn't cry out for us when we came into the house yesterday could be a symptom of neglect. When she didn't express her hunger until I gave her the bottle might be a sign she spent a lot of time on her own and that her indicators of hunger were not always responded to.

"At this time, the doctor doesn't feel that the neglect has caused lasting damage. We need to be attentive, but go slow so as not to overwhelm her at first. I take her back in a month. She will be reevaluated at that time. And if I read the doctor right, so will I."

I'm stunned at how he's holding it together. His voice is calm and controlled. As he talks, he's rocking the infant in his arms and gently stroking her arm or her leg. Sporadically, he kissed the top of Skye's head. But his jaw is clenched and there's fire in his eyes. This is not a man I'd want to cross.

"Doc said at the next appointment, she'd consider a letter of endorsement for my sole custody appeal." He shrugs. "Time will tell."

He glances my way. This time he really looks at me. The minute his gaze hits my swollen cheek, black eye, then drops to the finger bruises on my neck, his glare goes from almost calm back to a murderous rage.

"Who the hell did this to her and do you have the fucker on ice?" he addresses the Sheriff. The softness of his tone is more terrifying than if he'd yelled.

"Not yet. Still looking for him. But I will," the sheriff replies just as matter of fact.

Morgan looks at me with the same comforting gazes he's been giving the baby. "No one will know you're here. And if they do find you, I'll handle it. I promise."

I'm not sure his words are meant as a comfort or a threat. Maybe both.

5

Dad comes up the driveway pulling one of his trailers while I'm talking to Marshall. He smiles as he climbs out of his truck.

"Well damned if this isn't perfect. You two boys can unload the truck and trailer while Harper and I unload groceries and the other stuff. Give this old man a rest from the hard work.

"Old man my ass," Marshall mutters. "We both know you can still out work all of us.

"What all do you have?" I ask.

"A spare bedroom set from my place for you to use, two new mattresses that I picked up this morning: one for you and the spare room Harper is using. A rocker, a couple living room chairs I never use, two small side tables and lamps." He grins. "And your old crib. New mattress for it as well."

Shocked, I ask, "You kept our cribs? All of them?"

"Unci told me I needed to. Said one day you'd want them. She was always right."

He and I had brought down the kitchen table, chairs and bench from the barn earlier and wiped down the bedroom set in the spare room the day before, but we didn't have mattresses or bedding.

As he continues toward us, I see the tension in his body when he gets a good look at Harper's face and neck. Crossing to her, he leans forward and kisses her forehead. "You're safe here. You have all of us now to watch out for you."

Turning to Marshall, he asks. "You're taking care of this, Sheriff?"

"Yes, sir."

"You tell me if you need back up."

"Yes, sir."

"What else did you bring?" I ask.

"I picked up bedding for all the beds, towels, and few cleaning supplies. The food the doc told you to get for Skye. More food for you and Harper since you're staying close to home." He studies his son. "I see you got one of those front-loading things. Would have been damn handy when I had you boys."

He looks back to Harper. "Jessie told me what you needed for your dogs, so I got that as well. She'll be bringing them later today before dark, so you'll have time to walk them around and let them get used to the place, too."

Dad and Marshall are putting the furniture in my bedroom together, Harper has Skye and is working in the kitchen. I'd just grabbed the bedside table from the trailer when my phone rings.

"Maddox just called," I tell Dad and Marshall, placing the tables I carried in where they belong. "He said he's on his way home. He's going to do some recon in the area first. See what kind of buzz he can get. Although not assigned to this area, he apparently keeps tabs. There's been an increase in criminal activity all around us. Missing women, drug fatalities, attacks on our local Native Americans. Mostly against females."

I look at Marshall. "Heads up. He says if you look at a map, the activity is headed toward Fergus. He'll bring more info with him and review what he knows with you in person.

"He's going to reach out to his counterparts in the agency to find out more and what they've discovered so far. Dad, he wants to know if you still keep the old miners' shack stocked. He wants to crash there in the beginning. He'll let us know if he's coming in undercover. Text him on his private line.

"In the meantime, he's contacted a private investigator in the area who he's worked with before. He's given them the basic info on Arden and the theft of Satan. Dad, he wants you to be point on this since we're trying to keep Harper hidden. Contact name is Hitch. Look for a call or an in person at your ranch."

Marshall helps with the rest of the unloading then explains that he and his deputies are still trying to locate the asshole who hurt Harper. Marsh shoots us photos so we know what he looks like. He asks us to encourage her to press charges before taking off, promising to check in later.

Dad and I head to Harper's room next.

"I reached out to Abe," Dad starts.

I glance up from putting the bed frame together. "Who's he working for?"

"Some big ass guest ranch, east and south. It's driving him crazy." He chuckles. "Abe has no patience with wannabes.

"I asked if he'd be interested in coming back since you're home."

"Dad, I don't have the money. Arden damn near cleaned me out. I'm starting over with my horse training business, my livestock has dwindled, and without Satan for stud I'm not sure what I'm gonna do."

"You're my son. You think I'd leave you high and dry?"

"Da—"

He holds up his hand. "I ain't giving you nothing. I'll make you a loan until you're back on your feet.

"Don't go huffin' and puffin'. Hear me out. Abe's winding down. He just wants a place for his trailer like he had with you before. You throw in three squares. He'll help with chores and repairs, and you pay him when you can.

"Look, you got a baby and a woman to protect. He'd be another set of eyes."

I stand up from seating the last screw in the bed frame. "You got this all figured out, don't ya?"

"Hell, I ain't got that much else to do these days but think."

"I don't believe that for a minute. You're always finding trouble. Tell Abe it's a deal, but I'll be paying him as before. I'll borrow from you on a weekly basis, and I want you to charge me the going interest rate. I ain't taking charity."

He gives his head a shake and mutters, "Damned hardheaded boy."

"You raised me, and I'm not any more stubborn than you.

"Can you finish Skye's room while I try to finish fixing that front fence and get the animals settled. I want to be as free as I can when Harper gets her dogs so she has time to tend to them like she needs."

6

Harper

Montana brought in bag after bag. Pulling bedding from two, he immediately throws all the sheets in the washer.

"I can handle the laundry easily while I take care of Skye," I offer. "I can also put the food stuff away so you men can get the furniture done quicker."

"Thanks." He smiles and disappears.

I know from Jess that Sheriff Creed is in his early thirties, Montana doesn't look that much older than his son.

When Skye wakes, I feed her a bottle and baby food. Then lay the padded baby mat that was in the bags on the living room floor for her while I fold all the bedding and towels. At least with the lamps and two wingback chairs the space feels homier.

Sitting on the floor, I cradle her in a sitting position between my legs and hold out a rattle that has a panda head on a spindle. She's a little clueless in the beginning but once I place the spindle in her palm, she automatically grasps it. Together we shake it. Her eyes go wide with the sound, and she smiles. I keep repeating the game until she kicks both her legs and arms in excitement. "Yes, sweet Skye. Yes. We're playing."

Tears nearly choke me. Did they never show this child attention? Play with her? Talk to her? The way she just waits to be fed, to be changed, makes me wonder if they just ignored her cries. Ignored her.

Once all the furniture is inside the Sheriff comes to say goodbye and Morgan follows to check on us. He gets down on his knees, leans forward and kisses her forehead before lifting her to his chest and cuddling her. All the while talking to her. Telling her how sweet she is, how special.

"When she woke, did she make any noises? Call out to indicate she was awake or wanted food?" he asks.

I think back. "No. In fact, she was awake when I came in to check on her. She turned her head to look at me. But no sound. I automatically picked her up, changed her then fed her."

He exhales a disappointed sigh, then rubs his cheek against hers. Shifting her to the cradle of his arm he takes her little hand in his, teasing his thumb over her palm.

"BA, BA, BA," he chants, making a silly face.

He kisses her nose and repeats. When he buzzes his lips in her palm, she responds by kicking her legs.

"That's my girl, kick it." He glances my way. "First time she's done that. I'm taking it as progress.

"Her doctor wants me to keep a journal of the different things she does. Like holding the rattle, maybe reaching for a toy on her own. Crying.

"It doesn't look like she had a lot of interaction. We need to track everything for a while. I've got a notebook where I started. You should probably add to it, too. I'll put it on the table so we both know where it's located.

"And food intake. We're supposed to keep a record of that. Later I'll show you the articles she sent me to read. You may already know some of this, but it will help us be on the same page. She's a little behind developmentally."

Hugging her against his chest, he sways back and forth. "I need to keep telling myself she's going to be okay. Doc thinks we can get her back on track. We just have to go slow. She warned me not to overstimulate too quickly." He sighs. "It kills me that she doesn't cry for food because those needs were apparently not met."

"She doesn't seem to have had much practice sitting up either," I add. "I've been cushioning her between my legs and putting toys in front of her for stimulation."

He nods. "Like you were doing when I came in."

"Yes."

"Now that all the furniture is inside, and our two rooms are set up, Dad is going to finish in Skye's room. There's work I need to do outside before your dogs arrive. You two, okay?"

"Yes, I've got her. We haven't really had time to talk this all through, but if you're okay with it, I'll take the little playpen into the kitchen and start something for supper when it gets close to time."

"That would be great. We'll get a plan together later tonight. I'll take the playpen to the kitchen for you."

I keep my focus on Skye the next half hour, talking to her and touching her. Getting her to grab my finger. Next, I wiggled her legs by getting her to push her feet against my hands. I sing a few songs and talk the whole time. She seems to enjoy the attention but begins to tire, I assume from the interaction that she's not used to. When she starts to doze off, I lay her in the playpen to sleep.

Finding stew meat in the refrigerator, I decide that would be a good all-purpose meal, along with a side of biscuits. I braise the meat and set it to simmer then chop the vegetables.

Morgan's room as well as the spare room that has been assigned to me are set up except for the bedding. After making both beds, I put away the few things that Jess was able to salvage for me after the fire.

Skye is still sleeping, so I go to see how Montana is doing in the nursery.

He's staring down at the white crib, his fingers skimming lightly over the hand painted *Morgan* on the outside of the headboard.

"He's the oldest. The first to come to me," he says sensing my presence. "I was scared to death. I doubt I would have made it if my mother hadn't still been alive."

"I'm sorry. Did you lose your wife in childbirth?"

He studies me for a minute, then nods as if he's just thought of something. "You aren't from around here, are you?"

"No. I grew up about an hour away. I came here because I like to work with animals and there was an opening at the dog shelter."

"And no one's talked to you about the Creeds? No one's gossiped?"

I shake my head. "I'm a little reserved and there was always a lot of work to do. Wait, there is a sign outside the courthouse. Something about Fergus Creed founding the town of Fergus, South Dakota on his land. The Creeds are big supporters of the animal shelter, too."

"Fergus was my grandfather. He came here from Ireland. Married a Lakota woman. He thought he was in Montana territory when he found gold and used it to buy thousands of acres. In a roundabout way that's how I got my name.

"He and his wife had one son, my father, West Creed. West inherited everything and he's actually the one who donated the land to the town and named it after his father. West's wife was also Lakota. The townspeople appreciated his generous donation, then snubbed him and my mother.

"I was their only child and inherited most of the land surrounding the town. What I don't own is because before he died my father sold a few parcels to other ranchers he respected. I've divided the remaining land and given parcels to each of my three sons. Creeds are still the largest landowners in this area."

He smiles. "A couple main roads cut through our property and that helps keep things civil."

"I think I've heard your name a couple of times. I know Sheriff Creed because I'm friends with Jess. She's one of his deputies. I didn't know you had more children."

"Morgan is the oldest, then Marshall, and Maddox. My mother helped me raise them until she passed when they were six."

"Six? All of them? Oh, triplets. Wow!"

"Morgan is two weeks older than Marshall, and Maddox came a week after him."

"I'm sorry, I don't think I heard you right."

He meets my gaze. "Three sons. Three different women."

"Oooh."

"The women came to volunteer at the local reservation for a few weeks one summer. I think their work was helpful, but the extra tutoring was never quite long enough and cultural differences always interfered.

"Because of family, I did spend time on the reservation and got some of the schooling, but I didn't live there. The women stayed for a long weekend before they headed home. They wanted to sow some wild oats before they left. The three friends were rebelling against their families' control and wanted a wild night with someone forbidden in their high society lives.

I never knew about the pregnancies until the infants showed up on my doorstep. None of them wanted to deal with the results of their actions from that night, or a mixed-race child."

"I was blessed with three sons. I love them all and wouldn't change a thing. I consider myself damn lucky." He glances over my shoulder. "They're each strong, honorable men."

His gaze drops back to mine. "You're in safe hands with Morgan. Trust him."

"Dad, can you stay?" Morgan walks in. "I want to take Harper shopping. She needs clothes since most of her stuff was ruined in the fire and she'll need a burner phone. We also need a highchair. I promise we'll be back before Jess shows up with the dogs. I think we can do it in say an hour and a half, max two. I'm not comfortable leaving the place unattended. Then we'll have an early dinner together. Harper has stuff prepared."

"I can't go shopping!" I gasp.. "Look at my face. My neck. People will think you did this."

"No problem," Montana says. "I've got a lightweight balaclava in the truck that will cover your neck and I'm sure one of us has polarized sunglasses. If anyone stares too long just say car accident. Hold on to his arm while you're shopping and that will help sell it."

7

Morgan

Aware of the doctor's advice to give Skye varied experiences I strap her into the car seat, wondering if she's ever been in a car.

We're halfway to the town and Harper has been noticeably silent. "Ask away. You won't offend me. I've heard it all."

"I keep thinking how hard that had to have been on your father."

"Yeah, it was rough. Especially since he'd just signed up for the army. He needed to get away. The town back then was not— we'll say enlightened. Hell, some folks still aren't. They talked and criticized. He didn't care what they said about him, but god help the person that said anything to or about us boys. That happened once.

"Dad needed to see more of the world than what he'd grown up with. He'd already hired a couple guys he trusted to run the ranch while he was gone. Unci, our grandma, kept us at the ranch throughout boot camp. After that each time Dad was assigned, she'd take us and we'd follow him until his four-year enlistment was over. When he was deployed, we'd come back to the ranch then join him again when he was stateside.

"I think most of the gossip had died down by the time we came back permanently. Not that it went away. As kids my brothers and I had our fair share of fights. Sometimes other kids thought we were triplets, but there was always a know-it-all to set them straight. Truth is, we didn't really give a shit. We had each other.

"Town must be growing up if you hadn't heard about the Creeds," he chuckles.

"I'm not much of a joiner. I had my own issues growing up and always kind of stuck to myself and my pets. Kind of a one friend at a time person."

"And Jess is your friend. You choose a good one. Her sister is a bitch, but Jess is solid. Didn't know she was a deputy. But my home time the last fifteen years has been limited."

"You're career military, right? When do you have to go back?"

I grind my teeth. "I transitioned to army reserves after my last deployment."

"Why? You would have been close to retiring."

"My last leave I realized my marriage was suffering. So when I got back from my last mission, I made the transition. It will take longer for me to reach my full retirement, but I'll still get it."

"Oh Morgan, I— this has to be such a shock for you. What's happened with your....with Arden. You gave up your career. What you'd worked so hard for. Can you go back?"

I glance in the rearview mirror. Skye is still clutching the rattle Harper handed her when we buckled her in. A sweet innocent little girl. Her big blue eyes are studying the panda head.

Too quiet. Too small. Too neglected. Abandoned.

A peace, if you can call it that, washes over me. For fifteen years I've been fighting to protect and defend strangers. I've seen things, learned the truth about inhumanity for a reason. Now it's time to protect and defend my own. I'm right where I'm meant to be.

"It doesn't matter. I have Skye. I'm home now."

"What Dad didn't tell you was his father died that summer, and he was grieving when he hooked up with our mothers. I'm not saying he wasn't a little wild, but he always owned his actions. When I was dropped on Unci's, Dad's, doorstep he had already signed up for the army. He got emergency leave to come home and was there when Marshall and Maddox showed up. He's always put us first. He's been a great dad."

She places a hand on my thigh, then jerks it back realizing what she'd done. "Mor-Morgan," she stutters, "this must be so hard for you."

I glance at Skye again. "Not as much as you'd think. I'm okay with Skye. I'll fix the neglect to my ranch, and I'll bring it back. What I'm not okay with and what I won't let go, is two adults abandoning and neglecting an innocent child."

Shifting my attention to Harper I make my vow, "I won't rest until they're found and prosecuted. I owe that to Skye."

At the superstore, she helps me get Skye securely in the baby carrier on my chest. She's still clutching the rattle.

"Let's start with clothes for you first."

She clears her throat. "I don't have a lot of money. The work I do doesn't pay a lot and the dogs have to come first. You already bought food for them."

"Harper, you're working for me now. I'm paying you to help me with my daughter and home. It would be damn hard to run the ranch and see to Skye without you. What I buy for you is part of your wages. Okay. Let's start with jeans."

She picks out two pair and puts them in the basket. When she goes to check out T-shirts, I check the size on the jeans and add four more. I do the same with the shirts while she grabs a package of plain cotton socks and underwear.

I really wanted to get her the pretty satin panties and bra set that she fingered almost longingly but knew that would have looked bad.

I have a feeling she hasn't had much good in her life, at least not for a while. She's so beautiful. Not made up gaudy beautiful, natural beautiful. The kind of beautiful that will still be gorgeous in fifty years. Honest, gentle, kind. I doubt there's a selfish bone in her body.

Damn, I wish I would have met her years ago. Instead, I got married in a fever. A blaze of passion that fizzled out due to distance and different dreams.

"Okay, I'm done," she says.

"Nope. You still need new tennis shoes, boots for working outside, and slippers. I didn't see anything to sleep in, a robe. I know the lingerie here isn't great but they might have a few bras you could use for every day until we can get you to a better place."

Her gaze drops and her cheeks go bright red. I suddenly wonder how old she is.

"I want a copy of the receipt. I'll pay you back when this is all settled."

"Deal." She won't find the receipts after I toss them in the burn barrel.

I walk her to where she can get her personal items which is right near the baby aisle. Giving her privacy but keeping her in my sight, I grab the highchair and notice a walker that would let Skye roll around and sit up. Remembering she worked in day care I ask, "Harper, what do you think of this?"

Glancing her way, I see an old lady talking to her and shooting daggers at me with her gaze. Harper shakes her head while clutching the scarf to her neck and says, 'car accident'. The woman gives me one more stare but softens when she notices me holding Skye's hand. She says something else and walks away.

Blushing, Harper places the little basket of her personal needs in the bigger one.

She shakes her head. "No, that one isn't sturdy enough. Get the red one two down from it. It's more expensive but safer and sturdier. It will last through a couple kids."

Harper points out a few more things we need and recommends that we do a combo of natural cloth diapers and disposable for cost and comfort.

I noticed her gait has changed. "You're limping. You must be tired. Am I pushing you?"

"It's nothing. I'm fine. Really."

"Did that bastard do that to you, too?"

"No. Not really. It's mostly from an accident when I was young. I—I think he just jarred it when I hit the floor. I'll be fine. Do you mind if I grab a water? I picked up some aspirin to take."

Shaking my head, I tilt her chin to look at me. "You get whatever is going to make you feel better. Anything you need. Do not hold back when you are in pain or can't do something. Ask, I'll help. I'm sorry I pushed you. Do you need to see the doctor?"

"No and you haven't pushed. I always limp, it's not always this noticeable unless you know. You've been very kind and thoughtful."

"Do you need anything else I've forgotten?"

"No."

"Then we're done. Let's get you home so you can rest before the dogs get there."

I text Dad to let him know we're on the way and ask him to have the meal ready.

8

Harper

It's not until we get back to his ranch that I realize how much he bought me. Fingering the baby blue and pink bras similar to the plain white one I picked out, I realize that he at least doubled everything I'd placed in the basket. He'd insisted on a hat and fluffy white robe. He even grabbed hairbrushes, moisturizer and bubble bath.

It's been a long time since someone took care of me and treated me to nice things. It feels wonderful.

Montana has the table set and everything warmed when we get home. Placing the highchair between us, Morgan and I take turns feeding Skye. She eats a whole jar of pureed meat, some sweet potato and another of fruit. Tomorrow I'll be better prepared to cook things for her.

I had boiled some noodles for the stew and after warming them, I place them on her tray, holding one out to her. I'd seen her sucking her hand and hoped if I gave her a noodle that instinct would kick in.

Once she grasps the noodle her hand goes straight to her mouth. She doesn't get it in right away, but she will.

Morgan stares at me in shocked surprise.

Montana offers to stay and help clean up, but Morgan shoos him out of the kitchen. Instead, Montana takes Skye and changes her before going to the porch to rock her, leaving the two of us to clean the kitchen together.

Part of me wonders if these men are for real or if this is just a show so I'll lower my guard. Kind of like Floyd pretended. But their every move seems so genuine.

As we finish up, I hear a car pull up and go to see if it's Jess with my fur babies.

Daylan, my black and white Burmese springs from the car as soon as the door opens and races toward me. Skidding to a stop in front of me, he sits but his tail is working overtime while he waits for me to acknowledge him. "What a good baby you are."

He lays down and puts his face between his paws begging for his cuddles. When I give him permission, he rubs against me and licks my face.

Thor, my Caucasian Shepherd, lumbers from the vehicle, pauses to look one way then the other, sniffing and taking in his new surroundings. Sedately crossing the yard, he pauses by me to get his face loved and ears scratched. Then he moves up the steps, sits, and eyes Montana and Skye. Stretching forward, he checks the baby's scent, lets Montana stroke his head, and promptly takes guard position next to them. Daylan follows.

Montana smirks. "Looks like you aren't gonna have to worry about anything, son. These two got your security handled."

Jess pauses at the front passenger seat, lifts the carrier and puts it on the ground before releasing Bliss. She runs like a mad woman, around me and Morgan, over to the porch to smell Montana's boots, back down and straight to Morgan, circling around his legs twice. Then she puts her paws on his kneecap and begs to be picked up. Once in his arms she rests her front paws on his chest and just stares at him head cocked before snuggling up his body, head under his chin and a paw on each shoulder, hugging him.

His shoulders relax as he cups her little butt with one hand and strokes her soft shih-poo fur body with the other. How did I miss it? Leave it to my little therapy animal to read the situation perfectly.

Morgan needs hugs, too.

Jess takes in the situation and snorts. "Guess you'll be looking for a new dog to train. Don't think you're gonna be able to let any of these go. I've got your crates, and the floor pads you use. You want the crates on the porch so you can decide if you need them later?"

"Morgan, it's your house where do you want them? House or barn?"

"They're all house broke right?" He puts Bliss on the ground and crosses to Jess's SUV. "I'll get the crates and put them in the tack room for now. You take the pads inside."

After everything is unloaded, he turns to her. "Why don't you stay and visit while I take care of the livestock."

"Sounds good. I'm off duty."

Montana stands and hands the baby off to me, giving me a surprise kiss on the cheek. He walks across the yard with Morgan. To my surprise, Thor follows them, patiently waiting until they make their goodbyes. After Montana drives off, Thor follows Morgan into the barn.

I wonder if Thor was on a ranch before. He was tied to the post in front of the shelter when I arrived one day. No one knows where he came from. His size put a lot of the staff off and they were talking about putting him down, so I took him. He really is a gentle giant.

"Want some dinner?" I offer Jess.

"Sounds great. I haven't had a real home cooked meal in...well since the last time I was at your house."

I make coffee for both of us, and Jess holds Skye while I heat up stew and biscuits for her. Daylan is on his sleep pad in the other room and Bliss is curled up under the table. This safe, homey feel is probably too good to last. Laid back, relaxed, normal. Like it was before Floyd.

Placing Skye in her new highchair. I cut small bites of banana and place one on her highchair tray. I wait to see if she'll make a move to take it on her own. She doesn't, so I lift it and feed it to her. I do it again. The next one I put in her hand. It's different than the noodle and takes a while, but she finally gets it to her mouth. Then I do another, and another. She feeds herself three. I want to do a happy dance.

I hear the front door open. "Jess, go get Morgan," I whisper

Jess must have told him something because he walks in the room on stocking feet and stops where he can watch.

Taking another chunk of banana, I put it in Skye's palm and she gets it into her mouth. Morgan's eyes go wide. Taking one more I show it to her and put it on the tray. *Please, please, please let her finally make the connection and do it.*

We all wait for what feels like an hour, and then she makes her move. She isn't coordinated yet, but she manages to mash enough on her fingers that she can suck the sweet fruit off.

Morgan looks at me and I swear this time there are tears glistening in his eyes.

9

Morgan

The last month has been both frustrating and the most content I've been in years.

Ace moved his trailer back behind the barn. We're making headway on the repairs to the fencing and the barns. Hay and corn fields are a mess and I need more livestock. I'm boarding two horses that I'm training and I've got two requests for stud with Roper and more for Satan when I get him back.

This afternoon I go back to the doctor and hope she signs the custody papers to support my claim that Skye was neglected but has improved under my care.

I wipe the sweat from my forehead. And I'm in lust with the woman caring for my child. I'd use the other 'L' word, but I don't trust myself with it. Look how I fucked up with Arden.

Harper's sweet, kind, thoughtful, a natural mother, and she loves the ranch. She's insecure about her limp.

All I want to do is lay her down on my bed and worship her. Show her, tell her, convince her how beautiful she is to me.

Topping off the last hay feeder, I hear tires crunch on the drive outside the barn. Shoving my gloves in my back pocket I go to see who's arrived.

One of Harper's clients, a guy who lost his leg in the military and has a few anxiety issues just arrived. Ernest and his dog, Chester, are scheduled for their test next week. Today is their final run though with Harper. Working with him has been especially important to her.

Everything is really tied to her father who came back from war with PTSD. He ended up taking his own life.

Then she was in a car accident with her grandmother and Mom who had taken to the bottle to ease her own grief. They both died. Harper's hip was broken and her knee damaged. More recently her grandpa was mugged and is in assisted care.

Brushing off, I head to the house. Harper has me acting as one of the distractions for the dog and I'll take care of Skye while they work.

Our arrangement has worked out perfectly. Except I've come to want more. So much more.

Training goes well and Chester agrees to come back and let us know the results. He's looking for a job and I've been trying to help. Right after the baby doctor, I'm checking in with Marshall to see if he has anything. After that, I have a surprise planned for Harper.

I grab a fast shower, then take over Skye so Harper can get ready to go with us. Ace is already on the porch eating the extra dessert that Harper saved for his sweet tooth.

"No work while we're away. Just stay with the dogs and watch the ranch while we're gone. Call if anything comes up or call Marshall direct."

He nods, stroking Thor's head.

Skye's doctor is thrilled with her improvement. Her weight is up, her physical responses are more in line with where she should be, as are her motor skills. We schedule the next appointment, and she takes the name of my lawyer and promises to send a letter immediately documenting the neglect she witnessed before and why I should get sole custody.

Next, we make our way to the sheriff's office. Marshall is open to interviewing Chester for a dispatcher job, since he has one person going on maternity leave in a month or so.

This is the first time we've been to Fergus since Harper's attack, and I see the furtive glances she's shooting as we walk. After what that bastard did to her, I understand. She needs to be watchful. "I'm glad you're being cautious. Marshall says Floyd hasn't been seen in town since the attack. We're hoping he's moved on. But stay alert."

Back in my truck, she seems more relaxed. "I thought we could do lunch in Deadwood."

She looks at me wide eyed. "Oh, it will be crazy busy. This is the Wild Deadwood Readers weekend. And Wild Bill Days."

"I know. I have tickets for you, us, to do the author signing. We have dinner reservations at a restaurant I like before we head home."

"That's why I saw you packing a second bag for Skye and the stroller is in the back of the truck."

"I know how much you like to read. Jess told me how you've always wanted to do this. The rest of the day is all about you. Anything, and I mean anything, you want to do. I'll handle Skye. All I ask is that you keep me in sight."

10

Harper

Parking in the designated area we walk through the crowds. I'm so excited. I can't believe he did this for me. I texted Jess and she sent back a half dozen laughing emojis. She said he swore her to secrecy.

I've never met a man like Morgan. The stuff with my family and my own injuries, well I always felt a bit behind everyone else, like I'd missed something, some learning curve. I was socially awkward. Besides, we lived out of town on a ranch. Working with the animals was where I was comfortable. Jess is my first real girlfriend. She feels like a sister.

I never dated a lot. Then Gramps got hurt, there was the whole thing with Floyd, and I just sort of turned in on myself. Feeling safer if I was alone.

Being on the ranch with Morgan feels like home. Except... I wish he'd look at me differently. Like a woman. Not the screw up he probably thinks I am.

I'm not very experienced. But with every romance book I read, I picture Morgan as the hero. He is a hero to me. He's saved me.

Skye is awake so he has her front facing on his chest and her backpack of supplies on his back. She has one fist wrapped around his little finger. His other hand is on the small of my back or on my waist if the crowds are too tight.

Other women we pass are definitely checking him out. I hear one ask another if he's one of the models. But he doesn't look back. I don't think he even sees them. He's focused only on us and our safety.

Leading me inside he grabs one of the floor maps then scans the crowd. "Okay babe, this is all about you. Tell me which author you want to see first, and I'll get you there."

I didn't hear a word after *babe*. He called me babe. Like...like we're a couple. A family. My heart skips several beats. I'm dreaming. This is my recurring dream, my fantasy life.

He runs a palm down my arm. "You okay?"

I nod. "Just a little overwhelmed. So much to take in. So many people." I glance at the map and point to the first name I recognize. LizAnne Axtel.

He smiles. "I'll get you there. This is a baby free day for you. All you have to worry about is having fun."

I'm still getting my emotions in check, when we stop in front of the smiling author. "Hi, I'm LizAnne. What's your name?"

I buy two of her new books and get them both autographed before moving on so the person behind me can come forward. While I'm getting my next autograph, he stops the security guard who's walking the aisle, and they chat for a moment.

At lunch he excuses himself to change Skye telling me not to leave the table. I see him nod to the security guard he talked to earlier, and the woman moves closer to me.

The rest of the afternoon flies by. Today has been a dream come true. I've been able to meet so many of my favorite authors. We even found books for Skye when she's a little older. I feel doted on, cherished, cared for.

Morgan found an out of the way seating area where we spread out a blanket on the floor so he and Skye can play. An older woman stops and admires Skye then looks at me.

"She sure got mama's big blue eyes. You, missy," she waves a wrinkled hand, "hold on to this one. He's a keeper. I've seen how he looks after his family."

I blush and nod. Morgan just hugs me closer. Trying to be subtle I shift one way then the other trying to get comfortable. He notices my hip is starting to bother me and says it's time we head over to the restaurant.

Dinner is great, but we should have planned better. Skye starts to get fussy. We both agree it's time to head home so we order dessert to go.

At home Morgan insists I rest while he bathes the baby and puts her to sleep. I'm snuggled on a chair with my feet up when he returns.

"What can I get you? Some aspirin? Do you have pain meds?"

"I'm fine Morgan. I'm sorry I ruined the day."

He squats down beside me. "Hush, babe. I didn't think. I pushed you too hard. I didn't realize how much walking there is at these things."

"I didn't either. But I had so much fun. Thank you."

He brushes the hair from my face and leans in like he's going to kiss me. Then jerks back and surges to his feet. One hand on his hip he turns his back to me and runs the other over his head.

"Morgan, did you almost kiss me?"

He sighs and turns back to me. "Yeah. All day I've wanted to kiss you, hold you to me. I've wanted you for weeks now. Hell maybe from the first time I met you. But…"

"But what?"

"What I'm feeling for you is more than a romp. It's why I've been fighting it so hard. I won't make the same mistake twice.

"Frankly, you scare the hell out of me."

"What do you mean?" Why would I scare him? Oh no, has he found out about Floyd?

"Arden was a heat storm. I got caught in the flames and didn't think it through. I believed everything I wanted to hear. Even when I knew better.

"Now I'm scared to trust my judgement where women are concerned. And if you're as innocent as I think, I don't want to screw you up, too. But what if..."

I inhale and gather my own courage. "Because of my injury I missed a lot of school and then had a hard time catching up. I always felt behind. I was already shy. I spent more time with adults than kids my own age. I could never really relate to my classmates. Jess is older and has had issues in her life. I think that's why we get along so well.

"I'm...plain. I'm a ranch girl. I like my animals, the fields and my boots and jeans. Parties give me hives. Give me a good book, a coffee or tea, instead of a bar anytime. I hated working the bar, but it gave me the hours I needed to get my training.

"I'm attracted to you, but never thought you'd see me like that. I'm not very experienced and have no clue how to get a man to look at me as a woman. No idea how to flirt."

He runs a hand over his face and starts to pace. "There are a lot of things in the way."

"Like what?"

"I'm still technically married. I've filed for divorce but because she hasn't been found it's taking longer than normal. It will happen, but there's a set time before they can approve my request. I'm not a cheater, but since she left me for another man....

"My ranch is basically starting over. And I'm still committed to the reserves. Mandatory weeks each year and I can be called up at any time. Being left home with just the ranch and the responsibility, that's something she couldn't deal with.

"I have a daughter now. Her well-being and emotional attachments need to be considered. She needs stability in her life, people she can depend on to be there.

"Then there's the age thing. I'm at least ten, maybe more years older than you."

"Eleven. But like I said, I've always been old for my years." I feel he's trying to talk himself out of any possibility of us becoming closer.

"I've got scars and a sketchy hip and knee. At some point it could get worse, and I may be walking with a cane. I'm a therapy dog trainer which isn't going to make anyone rich. I'm not very experienced with men and nervous that I'm not — sexy enough. I'll be disappointing."

He snorts. "Babe, you are so damn sexy. If you only knew."

He rubs a hand down his face. "It's late. How about we leave the door open. Maybe start with a kiss or two and maybe more together time. We'll just see where this may go."

"Okay." I nod. "Are you worried that she'll come back and try to take Skye from you? I think the doctor would support you."

"No way in hell will she ever take that child from me. Arden proved who she is by her neglect, she won't get another chance with me or my family. That's something else. The Creeds stand together. Always. We will always have each other's backs." He studies me and works his jaw as if he's making a decision.

"Biologically, Skye isn't mine. But my name is on the birth certificate, and I will fight with everything I have to keep her. She will always be my child, wanted and loved."

"I'm not sure what you're saying. But I agree, her needs must come first."

"I'm saying my ex cheated on me, got pregnant, put my name on the birth certificate and then abandoned the child. Left her alone in this house for someone to find, or not. My family knows the truth, but no one else. It stays in this room."

What a bitch! How could you ever... I think of Floyd, what he's done. What he could do. But to a helpless child? I will never understand humans. "I will keep your secret.

"If you want more children, you need to know now that childbirth could be hard for me because of my hip. Not impossible, but it may need to be cesarian. I want children, my own or adopted. I want more than one since I know what it's like being an only child."

"I don't do secrets. I don't do lies," he says

I have both. I study his stance, his gaze. Can I trust him with more than my body and heart?

11

Morgan

I run a hand over my hair. "You must think I'm a scumbag or worse. A perv. But I want you. Not just sexually, but I want you in my life. Our lives.

"I think—I think I love you. But all this other shit has me afraid, too. Realizing how young you are. I'm eleven years older than you. And I'm legally still married. Those aren't little hurdles."

I look up. "I'm trying to be honest, here."

Standing, she crosses to look out the window across the porch toward the barn. She's still for so long, I know she's going to tell me to go to hell.

She turns to look at me, wrapping her arms around her waist. "I lied to you. Floyd, or someone he works for, wants my grandfather's ranch. They used me to get an introduction to Gramps.

"When Gramps refused to deal with Floyd, or whomever he's representing, Floyd attacked Gramps and put him in the hospital.

"I didn't know it was Floyd at that time. He was being attentive and acting all worried about me. Even started sleeping on my couch out of concern that someone would attack me, too.

"Gramps has friends. Important friends and he called them from the hospital. They moved him secretly. Everyone was told Gramps was in a coma and moved to a private assisted living facility, until he regains consciousness. His lawyer is handling the estate and basically freezing everything. I talked to Gramps once. That's when I found out it was Floyd who attacked him.

"I couldn't tell Floyd I knew it was him because it would expose Gramps. I tried to just pull away from him, telling him I was fine now and I could be on my own. I must not have done a very good job. Because that's when Floyd started getting mean. Now, for some reason, Floyd thinks I know where Gramps is. I've been denying it.

"Every couple weeks I get a text message on my phone with an update on Gramps. He did have a head injury but was never out of it mentally. It's why when you bought me the burner, I wanted to know if they could use my old number."

"And if you had a phone with your number, Floyd or his group could possibly find you. You're safer without it," I tell her. "What proof do you have that your grandfather is safe?"

"They said... I guess no real proof. Except Floyd has been getting pushier and meaner which I guess means he doesn't have him."

I nod. "Thank you for telling me the truth, for trusting me. I will not betray you or your gramps. My family can help.

"I'd like to bring the whole family into this. My brother Maddox is an FBI agent. He'll have resources to see if there have been any messages sent to your old number. He should also be able to find out if the people helping your gramps are legit.

"Do you think or know for sure that your gramps' lawyer is honest?"

She shakes her head. "I think so, since he's been with Gramps for years. But I haven't known who I could really trust for months. I've been so afraid. I'm sorry I lied to you. I—if you want me to leave, I'll understand."

"I want you right here with me where I and my family can protect you. You just proved your bravery and loyalty by telling me the truth. We'll get through this together.

"I want you Harper, and right now I really need to hold you. May I?"

She practically flies into my arms. "I've been so afraid and I'm so tired of being scared all the time. If I hadn't had Thor, I don't know if I'd have survived the fear."

"We'll get through this. Speaking of Thor. Can you teach him to protect Skye or is she too young?"

She smiles up at me. "You'd think as big as Thor is, people would notice him more. Follow me."

She takes my hand and leads me to the baby's room. Clicking on the night lamp, I see Thor in the soft glow, laying down by the headboard of the crib. If you didn't know to look or see the sheen of his eyes, he'd take you by surprise. Lifting his massive head, he sniffs the air judging friend or foe. Comfortable with our scents he lays his head between his paws and watches.

"Thor claimed her the first night when she was sitting on your father's lap. He'll always know where she is. Tomorrow I'll work with you and him so we're all on the same page with commands.

"Daylan has been making rounds of the house and front yard. They're both familiarizing themselves with the smells, people. I'll work with them more tomorrow to get a routine started."

I nod. "I like knowing Skye has her own personal defender."

"It would be good if the dogs get introduced to your brothers and have more time with Montana. They need to build trust with them as well."

"We can do that tomorrow if you're feeling up to it."

She nods.

I lean in and kiss Skye's cheek, then walk with Harper to the hall.

"I'm gonna take a shower then have some tea on the porch," she says.

"I'll go after you. Will you make me a cup, too?" I don't want tea. I want more time with her.

Joining her on the porch where she sits in Unci's rocker, I settle my hip on the railing and relax against the post.

Tomorrow I'm going to have Ace move his trailer to the side of the house. I want to be able to watch over him and have him closer to help me watch the house and my girls.

Content for the moment, I let my mind wander as I study the stars in the sky. I joined the military at eighteen to follow in my father's footsteps. Now I realize I was running from this town, from being just another Creed boy.

It hits me that my brothers were fighting the same battle. If one Creed boy did something, we were all painted with the same brush. We were a band of brothers but still wanted to be seen as individuals. That's hard when your best friends are your brothers.

I left for the Army after graduation, Marshall moved to Pierre and joined the South Dakota Highway Patrol. Maddox just moved and moved. Rodeo circuit, singer in a band, pool hustler, and we don't even know what else. Pretty sure he's been with the FBI longer than we think. He holds everything close to the vest.

Now two of us are home. It feels good. Right. Taking a deep breath of the fresh air I exhale slowly and glance toward Harper. Peace washes over me. I ran from this town, looking for something. Now I'm home and I've found her.

"Will you come to bed with me? Just let me hold you tonight?"

Her surprised gaze locks with mine. After a long moment where I almost give up hope, she nods. Standing, I take her hand in mine.

I give her privacy to get settled in the bed then join her. To my delight she's pulled on one of my T-shirts. Rolling to my side, I snuggle up to her back. She sighs.

"I always thought I knew what I wanted. Now I do."

"What's that," she asks softly.

"This. You. Skye. Home. I know it's fast. But I hope you give me a chance."

She squirms in my arms and I release her figuring I'm moving too fast and she's running for the hills.

Shifting, then rolling to her side, she faces me and places a palm on my cheek. "I don't know how this works. How it's supposed to work. I've never been in a relationship. I've had sex once in my life and I'm not good at it. But this, you, feel right to me, too.

"I know we have a lot to get through and I'm adding a whole other mess to the life you're trying to sort out. But I don't want to miss this chance at..."

"Happiness? Love? Real love."

"Yes. All of those," she agrees.

Brushing her hair from her cheek, I cup her face and lean up to capture her lips. Warm, soft, minty from her toothpaste, tentative. She trembles beside me. I feel it all. Fear, self-doubt, excitement.

Deepening the kiss, I slide my tongue over her lower lip before urging them apart. Cautious at first, she learns to dance with mine. Her heart is racing. My pulse is pounding.

Shifting us until her back is on the mattress I gaze down on her. "Your pace. Anything I do that you don't like, tell me. I need to get a condom."

She shakes her head. "I got the shot a few months ago. I was afraid he'd...."

Not wanting her to see the rage I know will be in my gaze, I lean forward and softly kiss her forehead while gently stroking my thumb on her cheek. She'd been afraid he'd rape her. Someday I promise myself, Floyd will pay.

"I'm clean, but I want you to be sure."

"I am."

Taking my time, I kiss a path down her neck as I slowly slide my body to the side and sit up. I help her out of the T-shirt and her underwear before I stand to shuck my lounge pants. She opens her arms to me and just holds me for several moments.

I don't remember ever feeling this kind of wanted by a woman. Wanted for myself and not just the sex. Wanted for the feelings we share.

Her touch on my chest is tentative at first then bolder as she responds to my attention. Cupping and stroking her supple breast, I lower my head and suckle one nipple then the other. Her mewl of delight just reinforces how much I want to please her. To show her how beautiful and perfect she is. I take my time worshiping one then the other before kissing a path down to her cute little belly button and farther.

"Oh my." When I run my tongue between her folds she gasps and her hips arch. Her innocence is its own aphrodisiac. When she said she'd had sex, she clearly meant 'slam bang' sex.

I'm going to teach her about making love. Hopefully for the rest of our lives. She already owns my heart.

I bring her to orgasm with my tongue, then another with my fingers. Holding her snuggled against my side and chest, I stroke her from shoulder to thigh. She tenses momentarily when my thumb brushes over what must be one of her scars, but I keep touching, stroking until she relaxes. I want all of her.

Gradually she starts to stroke my chest then moves lower to where my cock is eagerly waiting for her attention. Slipping her smaller palm and fingers around me, she slowly starts to stroke me. "I want you, Morgan. I want to feel you inside me. Please."

"Are you sure? I can wait. I don't want to rush you into anything."

"I'm very sure."

Conscious of my weight, I roll us until she's under me. Carefully working my way into her, I start to slowly move. The way my cock fits in her tight channel is driving me half mad.

"I'm not going to break, Morgan. Love me right."

I do. Using my fingers, I make sure she comes again before finding my own release.

She dozes on my chest. I stroke her hair, caress her back and cup her butt with my hand.

Born in a scandal, raised on the outskirts of the town's society, years of war, and the cluster-fuck of my marriage, how the hell did I get so lucky to find Harper?

I know we're just starting, but this feels right. I'll do whatever I need to make it work. I'll protect her and my daughter. I'm home now.

Something wakes me. Laying still I wait. What was it? A soft little cry reaches my ear.

"It's her," Harper whispers into my chest. "She's crying. Oh my god, Morgan that's great. She's letting us know she needs us."

We scramble from opposite sides of the bed. I toss her my T-shirt that I took off of her hours ago and pull on my pants. Hand in hand we go down the hall.

I lift Skye to my chest. "My good girl. Daddy's so proud of you for crying. I'll always be there for you. I'll always come."

Harper kisses Skye's hand then my bicep. "You check her diaper; I'll go make a bottle. This is the perfect time to let her know that she can use this response to tell us she wants food."

~

Ace and I move his trailer to the side of the house. Dad's right he is slowing down. I need to keep an eye on him.

Mid afternoon I'm standing on the porch looking out over my land with Skye in my arms. Harper comes up beside me.

"Storms coming," I tell her. My gut tells me it's not just the weather that's barreling down on us. Big changes are coming. The Creeds need to be ready.

Harper wraps her arm around my waist and snuggles to my side. "After a storm everything smells so good. The land, the plants, everything is revived by the rain. Storms don't last forever, just long enough to give us a fresh start."

Kissing Skye on the forehead, I hug Harper against my side, holding on to what means most to me. She's right. Better days are coming. We just need to weather the storm.

AFTER THE BOOK

We Are The Creeds

We don't give in. We don't let go. We don't back down.

Montana, The Patriarch
    Morgan, The War Veteran
    Marshall, The Sheriff
    Maddox, The Wild Card

Finding Home

Deep in my soul I know what being unwanted feels like. So do my brothers. So did Montana Creed, our father. Irish-American Indian, he was raised in a place where he was spurned for his heritage yet coveted for his looks. Desired, not wanted.

The summer his father died, while still grieving, he had a two-day fling with three girlfriends from out of state who were rebelling against their own life restrictions. The women returned to their college homes. He signed up for the military.

He came home on leave to find his mother with a baby and a note from one of the women. Two weeks later there was another child and note, and a week after that the third. He was eighteen, newly enlisted and the father of three. Three abandoned children.

We grew up, survived and flourished because of Montana Creed. A decorated war hero, he fought the battles of acceptance for us. Every day of his life. Giving us the most important gift of all. Love.

Don't miss all our stories coming soon...
Morgan ~ Every Storm
Marshall ~ Thunder & Lightening
Maddox ~ Dark Night, Day Light
Montana ~ Face in the Wind

ABOUT THE AUTHOR

Britt Jones is an author of steamy romance with the occasional dash of danger to keep you on the edge of your seat, and your heart pounding.

My alpha heroes are protective and devoted.
My heroines are strong and independent.
The stories are hot!!

I currently live in the Big Apple, where story inspiration is just a walk out the door. A coffee addict, I love taking my pup on walks as an excuse to stop at the various coffee shops in the neighborhood before strolling to the park.

Be sure to follow me on Goodreads BookBub where I post updates of the books I'm writing, snippets and cover reveals.

DEADWOOD BOUND

RICO LAMOUREUX

1

I didn't realize South Dakota was so humid. Or maybe it's not. Maybe this California boy can't stand any muggy weather, let alone the dry heat of his home state.

Upon touching down in Sioux Falls I rented a car and took the one hour drive out to Mitchell, A/C on high while the prairie landscape gave me thoughts of an old TV show I used to watch.

I was on somewhat of a mini vacation. Between cases as a P.I. working out of Los Angeles, my niece, Jamie, liking to joke it stood for Psycho Investigator. A joke laced with truth, as most of my cases do involve taking down serial killers.

But yeah, this trip was supposed to take me in the opposite direction. Away from the world of methodical mad men and a glimpse into my family tree.

What kind of tree? I was not yet sure, for my mother and her sister Mary were the only relatives I had ever known.

The two moved out to California a few years before I was born, my single mother occasionally telling stories of her South Dakota past.

A strict upbringing and a lack of opportunity drove the two sisters west, neither keeping contact with family back home as moving meant disownment.

I lost my mom to a sociopathic killer back in 2016 when he had rooted himself into my life before I had a chance to take him down.

Aunt Mary reached out to their parents after the murder, but was ignored, making that family tree I sometimes wondered about seeming like a weeping willow.

Were they really so cold hearted? An answer to a question I hadn't found out until recently.

Turns out my grandparents had been killed in a car accident two years prior to my mother's death. News my Aunt Mary and I had just been informed of a few days ago when a distant cousin found us via ancestry.com.

My aunt being in no condition to travel, I accepted the invitation to visit the Great Plains and search my grandparents cellar of boxes so as to get a sense of our family's past.

Turning on to Mitchell's main street, my eyes found a grand palace, much of its majestic exterior walls adorned with corn.

Billing itself as the world's only corn palace, I couldn't help but smile while imagining Jamie.

"If that place caught fire, you think it would be the world's biggest pile of popcorn?"

A few blocks later and I was pulling up to the two story house my mother had grown up in. Right away, it was pleasing to the eye.

Two huge fir trees, one on either side. A quaint porch with two large pillars standing guard for a handcarved front door, the columns also in support of a wide terrace, which looked as though it were a launching pad to the cupola topping the house.

Cousin E.B. greeted me at the door before inviting me in for cornbread and iced tea sweetened with honey, the latter of which he said he learned to make decades ago while passing through the small town of Destiny, Georgia.

E. B. was quite the character. Eager to please, fast to joke, and sincere in hospitality.

After about an hour of getting to know each other, he said it was time for his nap, insisting the house and everything in it was as much mine as it was his, and apologizing for not having the strength to accompany me down to the cellar.

Boxes, crates, dressers as old as the old wild west, I was as curious as an archaeologist and excited to learn of my family's past. I was also hopeful, for I've always wondered if any of my ancestors were like me.

Did any of them look like me? Have the same likes or dislikes as me? Drawn to the same type of profession?

I began to explore.

Two thirds of the way through by day two I hit the jackpot. An elaborately designed photo album, made to endure the test of time. Previous to this I had come across items going back every decade of the past century and a half. Everything from kitchenware to clothes. Books to newspapers. But nothing really telling me who my ancestors were.

With a gentle hand I began taking in the old black and white photos of those who had come before me on my mother's side. Men, women, and children whose blood now ran through my veins.

Most were pictured in the Victorian inspired garb of the day, a few of the still images capturing the forever stillness of corpses.

Careful so as not to damage these priceless relics, I removed then placed back one picture at a time, looking on the backs to see if there might be more clues as to who these forbearers of mine where.

Most were blank, but some did have inscriptions, including one of a family of four that momentarily froze me.

A young husband and his wife with their two children.

I was frozen in time, standing in front of a two horse covered wagon.

I flipped the back of the photo over.

The Derard Family.

No other breadcrumbs as to who this splitting image of me was.

I stood up and walked over to an oval mirror attached to an antique dresser and looked back and forth from my reflection to the man in the photograph.

We could have been twins.

With a hurried hand I went through the rest of the album, but he was nowhere else to be found, so I quickly scurried through the remaining third of the items in the cellar.

Nothing.

Frustrated, my eyes fell over the small space as I contemplated.

Just as I moved for the stairs to go up and ask E.B. if he knew who my doppelganger was, I noticed the paneling on the back of the oval mirror. Its center had a discoloration, as if that section had been replaced rather than time worn.

I ran my fingers over the surface. It was smooth, sanded down as evenly as the rest of it.

When my fingertips found the edge of the panel I inspected further. Could I remove it without damaging this antique? Maybe with the right tool.

Unclipping my Spyderco from my pants pocket I flipped its blade out and slid its tip in between the panel and mirror, and with a little pressure slowly lifted.

It began to separate.

Holding the back with one hand and softly prying with the other. I slowly made my way down the large oval.

As I began to work the other side of it while heading back up something fell out from inside and landed on my shoe.

It was a relatively thin, soft leatherbound book.

My heart began to pound against my chest.

Opening the manuscript to the first page I read the title, which was written in pen, along with the writer's name.

Deadwood Bound

Dirk Derard

I lightly began to flip through it. It seemed to be a diary of sorts.

About three quarters in, there was a sealed envelope.

I took the book on up to E.B.

"Well, I'll be damned," was the sentence E.B. kept repeating when I showed him the diary and told him where I had found it, saying rhe words more to himself than to me.

My cousin agreed I should take the memoir and go on up to Deadwood to read it, following in the footsteps of our long ago relative in the pursuit to find out more about him.

And so I made a few phone calls to extend my trip and was back on the road for another four and a half hours.

2

November 12, 1899

The chill in the air was telling me it was time to head back home to De Smet. I had been on the road for nineteen days with Trixie and Joanie, my two faithful horse companions, as we pulled along our ol' wagon of books.

Heading out on October 25th, we had only been with family a couple weeks due to the last quarter of the year being our busy season.

Folks like buying books come fall, storing them away with essentials to serve as helping past the winter as well as for making a good gift come Christmas time.

It starts every May, the three of us setting out for the three-and-a-half-month trip from South Dakota to New York's Book Row, where we fill the wagon with the latest before getting back on the trails for another several weeks.

By the time we roll back on in to De Smet we have about a third of our inventory sold, spending a week or so with the wife and kids before hitting all the populated areas of surrounding states and all in between.

This of course always depends on weather, with Mother Nature sometimes deciding to slow our roll and therefore our yearly schedule.

But today. Today is the day that changed everything.

It had been a good run, me and the two girls selling over fifty percent of what we had started off with, returning home with some gifts that were sure to put some smiles on some faces.

Trixie and Joanie always knew when we were approaching our humble abode, peps in their steps a mile out signaling the year's end to another long journey.

But this time it wasn't Hester and the two children who came out to greet us. It was my dear friend, Charles, who lived in town with his wife.

The Ingalls were good souls, and I always made it a point to save a few books for them with every haul.

But right away I knew this wasn't a visit of good tidings, the sorrow across Charles's face immediately striking me with concern.

"Charles, what is it? Is everything alright with you and Caroline?"

A tear I had just began to notice dropped down from his left eye.

"It's Hester, Dirk. She's gone."

"What? Where? Where are the kids?"

"Maddie and Henry are safe. They're back at my place. It's Hester, Dirk. She's been taken."

"Taken? Where? By who?"

"Not sure. Some are saying road agents. They hit the general store first. Took what they wanted at gunpoint.

"A few of the townfolk overheard one talking about Deadwood, and the name, Al."

With neither of us wanting to say, we knew what this probably meant, as females taken on up to Deadwood usually means one thing and one thing only.

I immediately started to turn around the horses.

"Now hang on," Charles said. "I'm coming with."

"No, Charles. I need you to stay here and look after the kids. Tell 'em ma and pa will be back soon."

"Here, take this."

He handed me out his shotgun.

"You're probably gonna need something more than Billy to get you through this."

Billy was my father's bayonet from his days in the war, wrapped and tucked away under my seat just in case I needed to defend myself while on the road.

While In my possession, Billy had yet to see the light of day.

I placed Charles' shotgun beneath me, next to the lethal blade.

My old friend and I looked at each other, sharing a moment of understanding between two dear friends.

I then set off to retrieve my wife.

3

Before leaving Mitchell, cousin E.B. and I had figured out Dirk had been our great-great-great grandfather. I could only imagine the turmoil he was going through while bound for Deadwood as I sat in the air conditioned restaurant of the hotel I was staying at.

I had driven up here in comfort with about three hundred horsepower, compared to his two horse powered wooden wagon waddling its way through rough trails day in and day out with thoughts tormenting him as to what condition he would find his wife in.

My stomach was in knots with what little I had read so far, unable to finish my dinner as a result. Yet I just had to take in another entry before going back to my room.

4

November 23, 1899

Today my family and I were supposed to be sitting around
the table with the Ingalls, giving thanks before enjoying our
biggest meal of the year. But instead, I find myself eleven
days out of De Smet, not wanting to push Trixie and Joanie too
hard, but at the same time wanting to shave off at least half a
week from what would normally take three.

I personally have never been to Deadwood, the lawless reputation it holds being of no interest to me and my books.

I don't have that much funds, so I hope to find at least a
few souls there in town who will find some value in the written
word while I figure out my plan of action. For I don't know
how long it will take to find Hester, and what kind of resistance
I'll face once I do.

I can sleep with the books, I always do, but food is a
necessity which can't be ignored.

Skies are becoming more frequently gray, and I can only
pray the snow holds off until I reach the capital of sin.

5

Under different circumstances I'd be enjoying myself, the saloons, horses and carriages, etc. Making me feel as though I stepped back in time But instead I find myself overcome with anxiety as I walk the historical streets of Deadwood.

Am I walking alongside the long ago footfalls of my great-great-great grandfather as he took in this town?

Being a simple bookseller, who so far hasn't shown any signs of violent tendencies, does he really have a chance against brutal men who respect nothing, fear nothing, and are so quick to take a life?

It sounds ridiculous given the fact it's been well over a century, but I still feel myself attempting to send out positive energy to accompany his journey forward.

6

December 9, 1899

It began snowing yesterday, and if the cold cutting its way to my bones is any indication, we're fixing to get hit by a storm before the day retires.

The good news is, we're about a day out from Deadwood, the two girls having held up nicely thus far, as if they know their full charge ahead is indeed to get mama back.

Snowflakes whirl about, angels at play, as my mind drifts to a more innocent time.

It was De Smet's annual Christmas party, the community coming together to decorate the town square's space while enjoying an evening of caroling.

My favorite part of this event has always been decorating the large tree, which serves as the town's centerpiece. And my favorite adornment has always been the shiny shredded silver. The tinsel, like icicles dipped in the starry night sky.

But this particular year, my eyes were far more mesmerized by the beauty of Hester. At fifteen years old, she was two years younger than me, her and her family having moved to town a few months prior to this magnificent night.

The butterflies in my stomach were whirling just as much as the surrounding snowflakes, for this night had been destined following the months mentioned serving as a courtship of sorts.

On the first day of the new school year, when Hester walked into our schoolhouse for the first time I fell, and fell hard.

In love, that is. Having to fight myself so as not to gawk. Not to reach out my hand to her. Not to ask her for her hand in marriage.

For trepidation was the next emotion which struck me. Fear that another fella would get to her heart before me.

And so I set out to earn Hester's affection, balancing on the razor's edge of showing her my own but not overdoing it.

She seemed to like the fact that I had a keen interest in books. The story kind. So that ended up being the common ground we built our foundation on.

It was a rather slow process though, neither of us having the courage to act on the excitement we felt when our hands would brush up against one another on account of me offering to carry her schoolbooks.

This is until a week before the Christmas party, Hester giving me the shock of my young life when she slid her hand into mine instead of those books.

And again, her guts proving more solid than mine a couple days later, pecking me on the cheek with those angel soft lips of hers before turning and running on up to her front porch.

And so I was bound and determined I'd be the one to take things to the next level on this festive night.

Offering my hand I had asked her to dance, and halfway through Silent Night, as snowflakes whirled around the most beautiful girl I've ever known, as candle flames danced in her stunning eyes, I leaned in to those angel soft lips and kissed them.

Beyond the snowflakes two dark images brought me out of my reverie, one on either side of the trail ahead.

Getting closer, I realized they were men on horseback, and by the time I was about ten yards from them they steered their mounts to block the trail.

"You lost, boy?" the taller and scrawnier of the two asked.

"Don't believe so," I replied.

His companion was the next to speak up.

"Well, if this snow gets any worse, you bound to be, with it covering up the trail and all."

"I have a pretty good sense of direction, hitting the trails year round and all."

"Also be quite dangerous though. Indians 'round here still havin' a sore spot for losin' these hills.

"But you in luck, mister. My friend here, they call him Pistol Pete. Ain't never seen anyone quicker on the draw."

The man I now knew to be Pistol Pete opened his coat enough to reveal a nickel-plated six shooter.

"And who might you be?" I asked of his partner.

"Just plain Ned" he answered. "but I know these parts like the back of my hand."

"We can get you where you goin', for a price."

"Appreciate it fellas, but like I said, I have a pretty keen sense of direction.

"And this."

I reached down under my seat and withdrew Charles's shotgun, placing it across my lap.

In a blink of an eye Pete had his pistol out of its holster and pointed towards me.

"Toss the gun down," he said matter-of-factly.

"I didn't mean anything by it. I was just-"

"Not gonna ask again, mister. Throw it down to the snow."

Following his order, I then placed by palms out to him.

Ned asked, "what you haulin' back there in the wagon?"

"Books."

He looked to Pete, disappointed.

"Go on and check," Pete instructed his co-conspirator.

He kept the gun on me as Ned rummaged around the back before returning.

"He's tellin' the truth. Ain't nothin' but a bunch of lousy books."

"Get on down here, boy," was the next order to come out of Pete.

"How much money you got on you?"

"Ten dollars."

"Hand it over."

I reached into my back pocket and did as told.

"Hardly worth stoppin' him, Pete. But I reckon it'll be enough to wet our whistles and have ourselves a couple soiled doves."

"We gonna get a lil' more than that, Ned. Unhitch those horses."

"Now wait a minute," I said while involuntarily stepping forward. "These two horses are all I have. They're my livelihood. Please don't-"

As quick as his draw, Pete shot out the butt of his gun and pistol-whipped the side of my head, the immediate tear of my flesh resulting in blood cascading down the side of my face.

He followed it up with a gut punch, which sent me down to my hands and knees, before splitting open my cheek with a kick from his boot.

Trixie and Joanie fought Ned a bit as they were led away, Pete ripping my sheep-skin coat off me and trying it on for size.

He then walked around to the back of my wagon, retrieved a book, and returned to my side.

Squatting down to make sure I saw what he intended to do, Pete struck a match on the leatherbound cover, fanned the book out, and began to burn its pages.

Tilting his face to the side, he lit a cigarette, then took the large flame over to my wagon's canvas, setting it ablaze.

Without thinking, I shot up to my feet, grabbed a small blanket I kept up front, and began to swat at the flames. This seemed to only aggravate the fire, so I turned to the patches of snow at my feet and started to douse it that way.

All while the two road agents rode off laughing with Charles' shotgun and my last ten dollars, Trixie and Joanie at the sides.

7

December 9, 1899

I'm grateful the bastards left me with my gloves on, my double grip secured around the tongue of my wagon as I pulled the books one frozen step at a time.

Snow began to fall a few hours ago, with wind and hail adding to my already pleasant day soon thereafter.

Being pelted by ice is almost as annoying as the bitter cold itself, but worse are my uncertain steps. Already had a couple spills, the first doing a number on my knee that I'm bound to feel for days to come.

But I reckon half my trembling comes from my fury within, giving me the strength to carry on.

Come late afternoon, the bad weather had tapered off enough to where I wasn't in such misery, but the stinging wind still had my head lowered so the brim of my hat could shelter my eyes.

Such was the case, I didn't see the indian standing before me until my eyes fell upon his moccasins, stopping in my frozen tracks and looking up to find he was as still as a tobacco shop statue, the arrowhead of his full draw mere inches from my throat.

With shaking hands, I withdrew the glove from my left and fished out of my shirt pocket a photograph of my family and I.

He looked from the still image to my battered face, to my determined eyes, then to the wagon at my back.

The arrowhead was lowered as the tension of the bow was relaxed, the indian walking around to my haul and taking a look under what was left of my small burnt blanket I had covering my books.

He came back to face me, looked at my uncontrolled shivering arms, and walked over to his own haul.

It was a sleigh topped with buffalo hides.

Untying 'em long enough to take out two, one small and one large, he then fastened 'em back into place and brought the two pelts over to me, plopping 'em over my right shoulder.

I left him long enough to retrieve two books, both illustrated so as to get past the language barrier.

The Merry Tales of Robin Hood and The Jungle Book.

With a childlike curiosity he flipped through 'em, then looked up with a bright smile, moving his hand over his face, touching his forehead, then down below his chin.

I had a sense it was a sign of gratitude.

Polls to his sleigh in hand, he set off to continue his journey.

I personally needed a break from my own.

I pulled the wagon a few yards off the trail, bringing it to rest alongside some trees.

Stretching out the large buffalo hide, I secured it to the wagon, over the books.

I then wrapped the smaller one around me and snaked my way into the literary den for some much-needed rest, fingers wrapped around Billy as I drifted off to sleep.

8

December 10, 1899

Deadwood wasn't as rowdy as I had imagined. I guess the taming of the wild west had reached these parts after all but obviously stopped at the doorstep of whomever had taken Hester. And so, my first order of business was to find the location of my adversary.

Didn't take long, as an old lady sweeping the porch of her storefront was more than happy to engage in some mid-morning chit-chat.

"Al? You must be talkin' 'bout Swearengen over at the Gem. But if I were you, wouldn't waste my time. Last thing on that man's mind is books. Don't even think the bible could do a lick of good for that scoundrel."

"The Gem? Where would that be?"

"Couple blocks up yonder. But I'm tellin' ya. Might as well be tryin' da sell a plow to a bartender."

"Alright, then. Any men of stature you would recommend? Say a gentleman who might find value in the written word?"

"That'd probably be Mr. Adams."

"And where can I find him?"

"Walk on down yonder to Sherman Street and take a right. Can't miss it. Biggest house in town."

The old lady was right. It was the biggest house I'd ever seen. And the fanciest.

I set my wagon down and went for the one book I had hidden in a secret compartment amongst the others, the literary treasure also concealed in its own pouch.

I took my most valuable possession and walked up to Adams' house, a distinguished gentleman sitting on the porch smoking a pipe while looking at me through intrigued eyes.

"Mr. Adams?"

"Yes? How can I help you?"

"My name is Dirk Derard, and I just got into town. I'm a bookseller, and I believe I might have something of interest to you."

"Well, now. I do consider myself a bit of a bibliophile. But first, I need to ask. Do you not sell enough books to purchase yourself a horse or two? Imagine it'd be awfully hard pulling that haul across this frontier of ours."

"Yes, sir. Hardest labor I've ever had to endure. Was robbed by two men around this time yesterday. Took my horses, my money, and a couple more things they wanted.

"Probably not a good thing, me telling you this and all. Gives you the leverage in talking me down in price with what I'm about to show you."

"No, Mr. Derard. I'm not a man to take advantage of another man when he's down on his luck.

"Now go on and show me what you have."

I handed Mr. Adams the pouch.

"First edition. And signed by the man himself."

He took the book out, his eyes growing in interest.

"Oh, my. My favorite founding father."

Using a careful hand, which I appreciated, Mr. Adams

turned the first few pages.

"And in remarkable condition."

He looked back at me with a slight smile.

"Well, now, Mr. Derard. It appears my inability to hold back my foolish enthusiasm has now put the leverage in your hands.

"What would it take for you to part with this literary gem?"

I had to take a moment. Take a breath. Plant my feet shoulders length apart to stand my ground, for although I had truth on my side, it felt unnatural to state such a sum.

"Given the rarity, and condition, a fair price would be...

"Would be one thousand dollars."

I was prepared to have the book thrown back at me.

"Mr. Derard, I'm a fair man, not a fool. I'm a businessman, not a haggler. I haven't got to where I am today by walking away from a deal without the feeling of having come out on top.

"With that said..."

My stomach sank.

"I'd be willing to offer you nine hundred and ninety-nine dollars."

Breathing out a sigh of relief I couldn't help but smile, graciously accepting and shaking the hand of Mr. Adams.

A few minutes later I had in my hand the fruits of my latest book sale, my pouch, having been handed back to me, filled with gold and silver.

Seated back on his porch and opening the book, Mr. Adams politely dismissed me.

"Now I must kindly ask you take your leave, as Mr. Ben Franklin and I have some acquainting to do."

I turned to leave, but an important thought brought me back around to once again face the man who had got me back on my feet.

"Mr. Adams, do you happen to own any businesses by the Gem Theater?"

"I do. A grocery store. Why do you ask?"

"May I give you back one of these liberty heads in exchange for a week or two of rental space outside your store?"

"I doubt you'll find any potential clientele coming out of that Swearengen hell hold. But yes, you may set up there. Plenty of fine decent folks frequenting my grocery establishment."

He held up the book.

"As Mr. Franklin so eloquently put. 'Reading makes a full man, meditation a profound man, discourse a clear man.'

"Indeed, let us fill Deadwood's residents with some knowledge. You may set up in front of my store at no charge for the remainder of this year."

9

December 10, 1899

Tonight, I entered a world I have only ever heard of. A seedy playground of gambling, whoring, and intoxication. All set to the ragtime soundtrack of a piano player's busy fingers.

All being presided over by a figure atop his throne of dirty deeds, or in this case, the overlooking terrace of the Gem Theater.

Al Swearengen, whose face looked as though it had been etched in the image of Satan himself.

I couldn't just stand in this place with an investigative nature, or else I would have been snuffed out like a spark before having a chance to set ablaze.

And so, I headed over to the bar and took a stool.

"What will it be, mister?"

"Whiskey."

This was the first thing to come to mind. I've never had a drink in my life, but just about everyone knows the preferred liquid poison of the day.

As it was being poured and set before me, I nonchalantly looked over the saloon's female occupants for Hester. All appeared to be women of the night, using their body parts to seductively close in on men they hoped would part with more money in exchange for some fornicating pleasure.

The thought of Hester being forced to do such a thing both sickened and infuriated me.

Could she be upstairs servicing someone right now?

I reached for the whiskey with a trembling hand, hoping to hell this drink would put to rest if not just for a while the turmoil I was going through.

I raised it to my lips.

What a pungent odor.

I downed half of it.

I imagine it's akin to tasting tree bark on fire.

Swallowing a furnace and having my chest coated with the devil's breath.

But it's beginning to take the edge off.

It started loosening the tension in my head. Like that of a tightly clenched fist settling itself into a calm, open palm.

With the downing of the second half of the whiskey my body was more accepting, knowing it would bring about more ease to the hardened situation surrounding me.

And indeed, it did, my mind beginning to expand and therefore planting the seed of formulating a plan of action.

10

I found myself standing on the very spot where the Gem Theater once stood, having checked out of my previous lodgings and into this place now called the Mineral Palace Hotel.

Could Dirk ever have imagined his great-great-great grandson would be standing in the same location some one hundred and twenty-five years later, reaching out from the future to learn of his past?

The town has burned down on more than one occasion, so I find myself asking the locals where the few remaining structures of the last century still stand today, then taking my time as I take them in.

Palm against brick as if walls could indeed talk to me. Show me the past. Provide me with the vision of Dirk walking down these streets.

But the only thing that can really take me back is the journal, and so I return to it with eager anticipation.

11

December 11, 1899

With the books once again adequately sheltered now that I've replaced the bows and canvas of my wagon, I stationed myself in front of Mr. Adams' grocery store and began to pitch the people of Deadwood.

No matter the location, the one thing I've learned is people will just stare until one of 'em is brave enough to actually step up and start flipping through a book. Then a number of 'em will follow.

So, I usually find some lonely soul and give him a coin or two in exchange for coming up to the wagon and having a browse.

But this time around, before I could spot a possible accomplice, a rugged lady dressed like a man came trouncing up to me, pointing out a couple of dime novels I had displayed on the tailgate of my wagon.

"Son of a bitch. That done hardly look like me. Who gave you permission to go writin' some book 'bout me?"

The character on the cover did look like her. At least enough for me to know who was standing right before me in the flesh.

"Well, Miss Jane, I don't write the books, I just sell 'em."

"And probably makin' a damn good pretty penny slingin' these lies 'bout me."

"Actually, they're only ten cents each, Miss Jane. Not a lot of profit to be made."

"You callin' me cheap, cocksucker?"

I couldn't help but smile a little at her brashness.

"No, ma'am. They're quite popular. And quite flattering to your namesake.

"You ever read one?"

"Damn it, you two-bit book boy. I look like some saphead to you?"

"My readin' is just fine."

"Alright, how 'bout this. You sign this copy for me, and I'll give you this other one for free."

"Only lead I carry is strapped to my leg."

I produced my Ruyter fountain pen and offered it to her, along with the book opened to the page she was to sign.

Calamity Jane couldn't help but needle me one more time before applying her chicken scratch to the dime novel.

"A sissy pen for a sissy book boy. Why ain't I surprised."

12

December 11, 1899

By late afternoon, I felt I had made enough sales to where I could call it a day.

It wasn't quite time for the Gem to start filling up, but the whiskey was still calling out to me, so I stopped on in.

Hester was again nowhere in sight. No one was, except for the bartender and a couple of Swearengen's gun hands lazily watching the entrance.

As soon as the bartender put it down, I picked up the shot, its once repulsive stench now sweeter than any flower I've ever had the pleasure of inhaling.

Basking in the devil's breath as I savored the first half, Satan himself called down to me.

"Bookseller."

I looked up and over to meet the eyes of Swearengen.

"How's the business of books treatin' you?"

"Can't complain."

"Good to hear. Say, I just might pick up a few. Keeps some

of the girls entertained, so they can entertain better. You know, grand thoughts of romance and all that bullshit.

"You have a taste of one of my doves, yet bookseller?"

"Not yet. Got any novices up there?"

"Matter of fact, I do. One came in last month, and another last week. Of course, I had to taste the goods for myself first, and they've had a few go rounds with some patrons since. But not yet spoiled."

The fury I felt knowing he was talking about Hester drove me to slam back the second half of my whiskey and demand another.

To Swearengen I replied, "Let's see 'em."

I don't think Hester noticed me at first, her attention appearing to be glazed over.

This one here's from the prairie. Domestic type. Takes a while to warm up, but then she's all in."

"And this delicate flower," the pimp continued with his sales pitch, "was one I had to indeed break in. A bit messy, but tasty, nonetheless.

"Both still hold quite a grip, if you know what I mean. So, which will it be, bookseller?"

I did a slight tilt of the head towards Hester.

"Fine choice. All woman. Tell you the truth, this other one is like skin and bones. Those tits no more than mosquito bites. Goin' to take her some time to fill out."

As soon as we got into Hester's room, I closed the door, grabbed her tightly and began to cry.

"I'm so sorry. I'm so sorry. I should have been there. I should have-"

She broke my embrace and walked over to a vanity table, pouring herself a glass of water and adding a few drops of what I presumed to be laudanum from a small bottle.

"You shouldn't have come."

"What? Hester, I.."

I rushed over to my wife, lowered down to my knees, and took her face into my hands.

"Hester. This is me you're talking to. Your husband.

"Remember. Remember that night amongst the swirling snowflakes. Our night. When we promised ourselves to each other. Forever."

Staring into the eyes that once reflected hundreds of flickering candle lights, tears began to formulate in them before cascading down over my caressing hands.

But just when I thought I had her back, she pierced my heart with an icy assertion.

"I'm ruined, this is my life now. Go back to the children. They need you."

"But they need their mother too. I need you. I can't just leave—"

"But you did," she snapped back. "You left, and this is now who I am.

"Now get out. Leave. And don't ever come back."

I was frozen in place from her coldness. My feet would not move. My mouth would not speak. My eyes would not turn from the toxic water she continued to drink.

Until finally she uttered the words that nearly buckled my knees.

"If you've ever truly loved me, leave now. Tell the children their mother is dead. Leave, Dirk. Just leave."

What more could I do? Could I say?

I left.

13

December 11, 1899

There's a patch of woods overlooking Deadwood. Quiet. Serene. Ironic considering what lies below.

I was up there as the sun sank down into the horizon. Working a piece of sandstone on Billy's four sides and tip to bring the bayonet to a razor's edge.

I had tightly bound the base near the socket with twine so as to provide a solid grip, still giving me a foot of blade for what I need to do.

Al Swearengen is a man of reputation, so I can't just go in there and take him out. It'd be a suicide mission. I'll have to start from the bottom and work my way up.

Being a one-man army with zero experience in actual combat, I only see one way of approaching this.

You see, night brings about a different atmosphere. No place on Earth escapes this fact. And so, it will be my ally.

I have acquired a couple of articles of black clothing and a pair of moccasins, making the purchases at different places of business so as not to arise suspicion once the killing begins.

Amongst the trees is not only where my thoughts run wild but is my training ground as well. For if I can master the movement of stealth here, I should be nothing more than a silent breeze back in town.

The whiskey will help get me through. Just enough of the liquid courage to get me started, not enough to impair my body, nor mind.

14

December 14, 1899

I entered the Gem with my stomach in knots, knowing I'd be taking my first life before the night was over.

To avoid slicing my flesh to shreds I had Billy wrapped in deerskin, concealed in my boot and up my pant leg.

Calming myself with whiskey, I began to look over Swearengen's men, contemplating who would be my first kill. But before long the decision was made for me, a scream not to be mistaken coming from upstairs.

Just as I turned to take flight, Hester came running out onto the terrace, Ned the horse thief snatching her up with a claw hand like a bloodthirsty eagle taking into its possession a fleeing prairie dog.

Before I could hit the first step to the second floor Swearengen came bursting out of another door, instantly reacting to Hester's bloodied face like a grizzly bear, grabbing Ned by the back of the collar and his britches and heaving him over the railing.

The tall man came plopping down to the first floor not three feet from me, one arm twisted like a chicken wing, and a leg bone protruding out of flesh and denim.

Over Ned's howling anguish Swearengen yelled down.

"Never damage another man's property."

As he turned to head back through the door from which he came, he said to Hester, "Get yourself cleaned up. It's a busy night."

Piano man then went back to his ragtime, the dying breed of wild west patrons absorbing this latest act of violence as atmospheric oxygen for their rowdy nature.

Ned was left to fend for himself, laboriously inching his way across the floor and towards the batwing doors of the saloon.

This is until Pistol Pete rose to his feet from one of the poker tables and walked over to him, pulling Ned up to his one working leg and slinging his partner's arm over his shoulders to help lead him out.

"You done did it this time, Ned. I believe your days of buffaloin' are over."

"I need the doc, Pete. I need him in a bad way."

"You outta luck, Ned. Cochran hit the trail a few days ago. And that woman doc, well, you remember what happened last time. I reckon she don't wanna see neither of us ever again."

'No one's gonna see either of you ever again,' I thought as I got up from my barstool. 'At least not alive.'

I let the two get a few yards out before I started following 'em, staying within the concealing shadows since I had yet to change into my full black.

To my delight they were heading to a stable, and when I peeked in and saw Trixie and Joanie, my heart skipped a beat. I believe theirs did too, their level of excitement obvious from my scent.

But neither Ned nor Pete took notice of my two girls stomping their hooves and raising their tails, one in too much pain while spread out over scattered hay, the other standing above him not knowing what to do.

Echoing Swearengen, I waited until I was right behind Pete before uttering, "Never steal another man's property."

Not wanting to give the fast gun time to make contact with his six shooter, I introduced him to Billy right away, opening him up with a horizontal slash to the throat.

His hand shot up to his slit gullet, as if he could stop life from pouring out of him.

I was mesmerized. How the dark red flowed out and down over him. How his shocked eyes locked onto mine, having no choice but to surrender his mortality to me.

This fascinatingly morbid moment almost brought about my own death, for my awareness failed to catch Ned clearing leather on Pete's pistol, the sound of the cocking hammer snapping me back to attention so I could take the fraction of a second to thrust Billy into Ned's heart.

And there it was again.

Intoxication of this life-changing moment.

Knowing I would never be the same again.

Knowing nothing could ever come close to what I was now experiencing.

15

I don't know what to say. I feel sick to my stomach. I feel like burning this memoir, as if by doing so it would stop the inevitable.

Or maybe I'm just jumping to conclusions. Maybe I'm misinterpreting.

But I know better. I've dealt with enough mad men to know what makes one.

It pains me to acknowledge the truth. My great-great-great grandfather was one of America's first serial killers.

16

December 15, 1899

Tonight, I am ready for more. So much more.

It's all I've been able to think about.

The locals found the two horse thieves and don't know what to make of it, given the fact the two horses were not taken.

If I would have done so my guilt would have been obvious.

The town officials will put my girls up for auction, and when they do, I'll be sure to buy 'em back.

I have my black on under my denim and plaid, my moccasins stuffed into my coat.

Billy and I are off to take in the night now.

17

December 15. 1899

The sun is rising, and I'm about to lay my head down following a productive night.

I had arrived at the Gem in the eight o'clock hour, the bartender pouring my whiskey before I took my stool. I guess that makes me a regular now.

Once I had the juice flowing through my veins I went outside and took up position near the outhouse in back, switching my attire around to blend in with the night.

With all the drinking going on inside, it didn't take long for someone to come out to relieve themselves, and by the third use of the privy, I had one of Swearengen's men in my sights.

Midway through his stream, I barged in and plunged Billy into the mid-section of his back.

His head immediately shot up like a howling wolf.

I pulled him out of the confined space as I pulled out Billy and threw him to the ground to land face up.

He wasn't moving, but his tallywacker was still leaking, so I waited.

I then mounted the Swearengen scum's chest, my face just a couple of inches from his. Close enough to lock eyes, far enough to also take in his throat.

I held Billy with gloved hands, by both ends and began to sink my weight down onto the bayonet.

The gurgling was music to my ears, the sight, candy to my eyes. But when I realized he was nearly decapitated, I had to stop. For someone else could have been coming out at any time, one piece faster to lug than two.

I dragged the body into a nearby darkened alley and got ready for more, this time waiting up front.

On through the night they kept coming, me spinning my web throughout the crevices surrounding the Gem as I preyed upon those who were alone, experimenting with my methodology of death by blade.

I found the most satisfying to be those I took my time with, for if the henchmen expired too soon, I felt cheated and desired another immediately.

Not wanting to push my luck, I forced myself to stop at nine, trekking on up to the trees above town and into the creek which snaked throughout, washing my blood-soaked clothes and body until there was no sign of carnage left.

18

I have this sick man's blood running through my veins. His DNA embedded into a large part of who I am.

Like Dirk, do I have madness right under the surface? Just waiting to erupt?

No. I refuse to go down that dark tunnel of thought. True, I have taken lives, but only in defense of my own.

The argument could be made that so is this ancestor of mine, going about eliminating the small army of outlaws so as to have a chance at rescuing his wife.

But the enjoyment he finds in doing so is something I absolutely don't share with him.

Instead of finding fascination in the act of killing, which soon obviously led to obsession for him, my first kill was something I did not enjoy at all.

It hasn't gotten any easier, in the sense that if I was to think on it too long, it would start to affect my energy, my spirit. And so I detach myself when taking another's life.

The kill or be killed instinct. The killer instinct. Perhaps I owe this to 'ole granddad, eternally grateful it does not go beyond that.

19

December 15, 1899

I should add newspapers to my inventory of literature, for when I woke this afternoon, the Black Hills Pioneer was selling like hotcakes, the town abuzz with talk of what was being called The Deadwood Slaughter.

Everyone from the mayor on down to the undertaker was busy up to their elbows, and when I stepped into the Gem, the thirst for vengeance was thick.

"We gonna hunt him down, boys. By the time we done with him, he gonna wish the indians got him instead."

"He's lucky he didn't tryin' get me. I would've had him so filled with lead he would've met his maker before hittin' the ground."

With my hand cradling my shot of whiskey, a booming voice came down from upstairs.

"To the man who brings me this nightcrawler's head, one hundred dollars, plus all the pussy and drink you can handle for a night."

The rowdy crowd cheered, with more boasts of what they were going to do once they found me.

Finishing up my soothing shot, someone shocked the hell out of me by slamming a dime on the bar.

"This cocksucker got me crazier than popcorn on a hot skillet," the dime novel I had given her in hand.

"Go on now. Get me another."

I smiled, scooted Jane's dime over to my empty shot glass, and followed her out to my wagon.

Once she was off to take another adventure with herself, bitching all the while, I began to have an internal dialogue with myself.

For the next few nights, the streets will be full with Swearengen's men and the town's night watchmen, so I have no choice but to lay low.

This will give me time to think on what to do next, for things need to come to an end soon.

20

December 19, 1899

Akin to tasting tree bark on fire.

I remember thinking this when pouring whiskey into me for the first time. Now I'd use actual tree bark, in addition to buffalo chips, to help set ablaze this hellhole that helped unleash my inner demon.

I stared at the flame that would set it all into motion. Is it coincidental that it's shaped like a teardrop?

When I looked into Hester's eyes on that night so long ago were such reflections of the candle flames a foreshadow of this very night?

With tree bark and shit chips hugging the Gem's base I kissed the flame to the kindle before throwing the torch through one of the windows.

A few seconds and screams began to rise, whores pouring out like ants from a mound.

Once I set eyes on Hester I'd grab her, throw her on the back of a horse had earlier thieved, and send her back home to the children.

But first I had one more round of killin' to do.

I needed it. And Al Swearengen would be the grand finale.

Taking advantage of the chaos, I'd step in long enough to strike with deaths' hand, then sink back into the shadows and wait for another.

The last word uttered in shock by most of the men I took down was simply, 'bookseller!' the two or three seconds I had with each of them long enough to expand this dark gift into infinite power.

For I now know I will never fear another man. Their aggression will be my invitation. To feed. To grow.

By the time the fire brigade arrived Billy and I were soaked in blood. They rushed to the hydrants, but I had made sure they wouldn't find the wrenches that were supposed to be attached.

I began to hear Swearengen's voice blaring over the mayhem and started following it, deciding I had had my fill of his lackeys and was ready for the main dish of cold revenge.

But the man was no dummy. He had at least a half dozen gun hands surrounding him.

I no longer cared. About the odds. The outcome. My own life. The lust for his blood was too strong.

I was sure I could get close to him, sending him to hell with probably one or two of his men before I was sent following.

But just as I stepped forward, a hand came down on my wrist.

"Dirk, no. Our children need their father too."

I'm grateful Hester had spoken as she laid her hand on me, for otherwise I probably would have sank Billy deep into her out of reflex.

"I'm the one who's ruined now, Hessie."

Her gaze followed mine down to my blood drenched clothes and hand, Billy glistening in the firelight.

I looked back up to those flame-reflecting eyes.

"I can't go back with you."

There were tears of understanding.

There was one final embrace.

And then she was gone.

I looked back over toward Swearengen, now about twenty yards away with more men around him.

Hester had injected enough sense back into me to know my revenge was a lost cause. At least for the foreseeable future.

As there had been some men who had caught sight of me but escaped my grasp and would now undoubtedly inform Swearengen of 'the bookseller.'

This meant I had to hit the trail, Trixie and Joanie once again tasked with the job of pulling me and the books to some-where new.

On up north we're now headed, leaving at our back the raging Swearengen as I silently promise him there will be another time and place.

As I put distance between us and the last wild hold on the American Frontier.

As I say a silent farewell to the family I no longer have.

As I assure myself there will always be a place for Billy and I throughout our travels.

Men of aggression and greed.

Men who need killin'.

EPILOGUE

It's been a couple of months since I left Deadwood.

Three cases have come into my agency since, and all have been solved and sent to a file cabinet in storage.

One thing has stayed consistent; my intrigue with the past.

Dirk's journal is still in my possession. Not on a bookshelf to easily be discovered by a browsing visitor. Ironically, it's somewhat concealed beneath my mattress.

No matter how close or far it is, it continues to invade my thoughts.

Inside the envelope I had found with the old book was a handful of newspaper clippings. Reports of Dirk's handiwork as he continued to spread his madness.

Among them was a piece from The Denver Post dated just shy of five years from his time in Deadwood.

It stated Swearengen had been killed by an oncoming train while crossing tracks on foot.

So, Dirk finally caught up with him. I can only wonder why he chose to make it look like an accident.

But what really keeps eating at me is the question of what happened to Billy?

Did my great-great-great grandfather change his M.O. at some point?

Did he lose the bayonet?

Is it hidden somewhere like the journal was before I discovered it?

I don't think I'm going to be able to put this nagging question to rest until I find the answer.

And so, I think it's time to head back to South Dakota.

ABOUT THE AUTHOR

Rico Lamoureux and his son Journey Teller currently call South Dakota home. Known for their Riker crime thriller book series under the imprint, Riker Books, they are now slingin' ink towards the Old Wild West, with the character of Riker tying into the first of these new tales of the American frontier.

UNTIL I MET YOU

A.L. LONG

1

ONE

Dixie

"Ethan," I called out, my voice echoing through the empty halls of our ranch house. The sunlight streamed in through the windows, casting long shadows across the hardwood floor. "You need to get up. The horses won't feed themselves"

Downstairs, the smell of freshly brewed coffee mingled with the aroma of sizzling bacon and frying eggs. It had been one year since his father, my husband, had passed away—leaving us with a sprawling ranch, 1000 acres of land, seven majestic horses, and 500 head of cattle to take care of. Every morning, we repeated the same routine—I cooked breakfast while Ethan trudged out to feed the horses, his tall frame silhouetted against the rising sun. Around us, Pegasus Ranch was buzzing with activity as our dedicated ranch hands tended to the needs of our beloved cattle. We were barely surviving on this rugged land, with all the bills that seemed to never end, but I refused to give up. This was our home, our legacy, but I was determined to make it work.

As the sizzling sound of bacon filled the kitchen, Ethan's heavy footsteps echoed down the wooden stairs. The past year had been a weight on his shoulders, and I tried to give him space to grieve his father's death in his own way. Turning my attention away from him, I reached for a steaming mug and poured a cup of coffee for him.

"Thanks, mom." His smile was bittersweet.

He bent down to place a gentle kiss on my head before grabbing a piece of bacon from the tray. I watched him as he strode across the grass towards the

barn, his cowboy boots leaving faint imprints in the dewy ground. Every movement reminded me of his father—from his familiar loping gait to his dark brown
hair and piercing blue eyes. At seventeen years old, he towered over me with
his tall frame inherited from his father. As he disappeared into the barn, I refo-
cused on breakfast. With one last strip of bacon carefully placed onto the metal
tray, I turned on the oven and slid it inside to keep warm while I cooked the
eggs. Soon enough, the hungry ranch hands would be returning from attending
to the cattle in the south pasture.

The past year had put us through the wringer, leaving us weathered and
weary. The harsh winter had brought its worst, claiming 20 of our precious
cattle. Each loss felt like a blow to the gut, knowing these were the steers we
were counting on to bring a good price at the auction. With their average
weight of 800 pounds and a market value of $1.88 per pound, the financial
impact was not something we could easily bounce back from. It was a devastating blow that left us scrambling to make ends meet.

The past was done, so I focused on the future and the present day. Grabbing some plates from the cupboard, I began setting the table for the guys. It
was close to 8:00 a.m. and I knew they would soon finish their morning feed-
ings. Once I had set the table. I poured the pot of the remaining coffee into a
carafe and started making another pot. These guys had no problem drinking
coffee until way past noon. It was what gave them that extra nudge to keep
them going well into the night.

As I prepared another pot of coffee, the rich aroma of freshly ground beans
filling the kitchen, I caught sight of Briggs riding up along the fence that
secured the south pasture. His broad shoulders were hunched over and his
strong arms gripped tightly to the reins as he guided his horse towards the
house. As he approached, he quickly dismounted and expertly tied his horse to
the sturdy hitching rail. Something about his hurried movements and tense
expression told me that something was wrong— very wrong. Throwing the
kitchen towel on the counter I hurried to the front door.

"What's wrong, Briggs?" I asked anxiously as I swung open the front door,
and met him at the edge of the porch.

"Ten dead," he replied, shaking his head in frustration as he looked towards
the south pasture. "Something ain't right, Dixie. We lost twenty head this past
winter and now ten more. It's like something is targeting the cattle."

The weight of his words hung heavy in the air, a sense of foreboding
creeping over me as I joined him at the bottom of the steps, gazing out at the
vast expanse of land that belonged to Pegasus Ranch.

"This can't be happening. Not again." I took a seat on the first step and
wrapped my arms around my knees. "I can't afford to lose any more cattle,
Briggs. I'm already up to my neck in bills."

"I'll call Dr. Montgomery, see if he can determine what's been killing
them."

"Do you think there is a connection between the cattle that died last winter and the 10 that have died now?"

"We have had harsher winters, Dixie. They would have survived," he admitted. "I'll make the call."

Briggs fished his cell phone out of his pocket and brought it to his ear. I could hear the faint noise of buttons being pressed as he navigated through his contacts. Dr. Montgomery's number had been saved for years, a testament to their long-standing relationship as the ranch's veterinarian. The tension in my chest eased slightly, knowing that Briggs was calling someone I trusted implicitly. With a heavy sigh, I pushed away from the porch railing and made my way back inside the house to finish breakfast for the men working on Pegasus Ranch. As I finished setting the table, I couldn't shake off the looming worry of losing more cattle. The thought made my stomach twist into knots, a constant ache that refused to dissipate. Already behind on two payments for Pegasus Ranch, I was forced to dip into Ethan's college fund in order to keep things afloat. His dreams of becoming an attorney were slowly slipping through my fingers, and it tore at my heart to see his understanding, but still affected by my financial struggles. Every day felt like a battle against time as I desperately tried to keep our heads above water.

The group of men filed into the house one by one, their hats in hand and expressions of defeat on their faces. With a heavy sigh, they took their seats at the table, ready for another morning of breakfast after their morning chores.

"Ma'am," Reggie spoke up first, tipping his hat in respect.

Out of all the ranch hands, he was the most well-mannered aside from Briggs. The others—Josh, Whalen, and Vincent were a bit rough around the edges and needed some guidance in proper etiquette. It had taken time, but at least now they no longer scooped their food like they were digging for gold. They knew how to hold a fork and spoon properly, though their manners still needed work.

The tension was high at the breakfast table. I could feel it and so could the guys. The knock at the door was the only thing that relieved the uncomfortable silence.

"I'll get that," Briggs said as he rose from his chair.

All eyes were on him as he walked to the front door. When he pulled it open, I could see a full view of Dr. Montgomery. There was an exchange of words that I couldn't hear, so I decided it best I find out what was going on. Placing my napkin on the table, I too rose from my chair.

"Don't get up," I said, knowing the guys would more than likely follow me.

Briggs turned my way when he saw me approaching. "Dr. Montogomery and I are heading out to the south pasture so he can take a look at the dead cattle. We should be back in an hour."

"You are not leaving without me," I intoned. "I'll ride Reggie's horse. Dr. Montgomery, you can ride Josh's."

Ethan came up behind me with a concern look spread across his face. "What's going on, Mom?"

"I don't want you to worry. All you need to worry about is getting to school on time. You need to leave for school in ten minutes." I kissed him on the cheek. Before placing my hand on his cheek. "This is your last day before spring break. You know what that means."

"Yeah, I know." he grinned, knowing that I promised to take him to Rapid City if he got all 'As' on his report card, and buy him a new saddle for his horse.

"You don't seem to be excited."

"I just don't think the trip to Rapid is going to happen."

"Why?"

"I just have a feeling."

"We really need to go, Dixie," Briggs chimed in.

I gave Ethan one last smile before we headed out. As we rode out to the south pasture, the memory of how me and Trent used to take long rides together, just the two of us, played havoc in my mind. It seemed so long ago that I had been on a horse. I guess it was like riding a bike, you never lose what you learned.

Briggs was the first to stop short of the first Black Angus. It broke my heart to see him lying on his side, bloated like a balloon about ready to burst. Briggs jumped off his horse first, followed by Dr. Mongomery. As I watch them approach the Angus, I also dismount my horse. Dr. Mongomery immediately proceeded with a thorough examination of the Angus by collecting a blood sample and a fecal sample by putting on a long glove and inserting a few fingers into the rectum before putting a sample into a plastic bag.

"This should tell us what killed this steer. I'd like to take another sample of another steer to determine a pattern. We might have an epidemic on our hands," Dr. Mongomery advised.

$\sim$

Three days had crept by with no word from Dr. Montgomery, and a sense of unease lingered in the air. Despite this, there were no further reports of dead cattle, giving a glimmer of hope that it wasn't an epidemic spreading through the town. The mere thought of mad cow disease crossing the ocean from its origins in the UK to reach our small American community was enough to make me worry.

As I finished loading the dishwasher, my eyes were drawn to Ethan's truck pulling up the drive. Anticipation bubbled within me as I wondered if his report card had finally arrived. He stepped out of the vehicle onto the gravel driveway, holding today's mail tightly in his hand. My heart leaped at the sight, but I couldn't be sure if he held his report card or not. Judging by the tense expression on his face, I could only assume he did. For most of the weekend, he had been on edge and retreated to the horse stalls, a rare occurrence for him. It was clear that something was weighing heavily on his mind.

I opened the front door and waited for Ethan to step inside. His deep brown eyes met mine, filled with a mix of emotions. I could tell he was nervous as he handed me the one envelope marked Deadwood High School. Ethan was always a bright kid, never giving me any reason to worry about his grades. But since the loss of his father, his academic performance had started to slip. It seemed like nothing mattered to him anymore except Gus, his father's beloved horse.

Taking the envelope from his hand, my fingers glided under the seal before carefully breaking it open. I gave him a reassuring smile before unfolding the letter that would reveal his grades. My heart fluttered with anticipation as I scanned through every class he had taken. I ignored his first and second quarter grades, knowing that they were not a true reflection of his capabilities. The only thing that mattered to me was his third quarter grades. As I moved down the page, each class revealed an impressive 'A' or 'A-' grade. Feeling overwhelmed with pride, I held the letter in my hand and looked up at my son.

With tears of joy in my eyes, I lifted up onto tiptoes and wrapped my arms tightly around his broad shoulders. "I couldn't be prouder of you," I exclaimed.

Ethan's face lit up with a mix of relief and disbelief. "Does that mean... I got all 'As'?" he asked, with a hint of doubt lingering in his voice.

"See for yourself. You should be very proud. I know you dad would."

Ethan took the letter from my hand and scanned the report card. With every 'A' he came across his smile grew across his face. When his eyes finally met mine, he gave me the biggest hug ever.

As we broke our embrace, a sharp knock echoed through the quiet house. The front door stood open and my heart, began to race as I saw Dr. Montgomery standing on the other side of the screen door. With a trembling hand, I pushed open the screen door and met his gaze, bracing myself for whatever terrible tidings he had to share.

"Good afternoon, Dr. Montgomery. Won't you come in?" I managed to greet him, though my voice quivered with fear. "Can I get you something to drink?"

He shook his head sadly as he stepped inside, removing his hat and holding it in his hand. "I'm afraid I can't stay long, Dixie. I received the results from the samples I sent to the lab in Rapid City."

My heart dropped at his words, already anticipating the worst.

"I'm sorry to say that your steers died from the same cause," he revealed, his expression grim.

My hands began to shake uncontrollably as I brought them up to my face, trying to process this devastating information. "I have to let Briggs know so he can gather the rest of the herd and quarantine them," I muttered, my voice trembling, the tears weighing heavy in my eyes.

"Dixie," Dr. Montgomery's voice was gentle as he took hold of my hands and gave them a reassuring squeeze. "It wasn't any disease that killed your cattle. It was poison—large amounts of cyanide were found in their system."

A surge of anger mixed with grief rose within me at this revelation. *Who would want to harm my livestock?*

"No," I shook my head, unable to believe it. "Who would do such a thing?"

2

TWO

Bridger

The position of sheriff in Lawrence County was just what I needed. After three grueling tours in Iraq, and ten years in Minnehaha County, I was ready for a smaller area to cover and less crime to deal with. When I heard that Sheriff Gibson was retiring, I eagerly jumped at the opportunity to take his place. Luckily, there wasn't anyone else under him vying for the position.

As I entered Sheriff Leroy Gibson's office, I saw him carefully packing up his personal belongings into a file storage box. It seemed almost surreal that thirty years of dedicated service to the state could fit into such a small container. But who was I to judge? Despite have a decade as sheriff under my belt, after returning home from my service, my own accomplishments only amounted to a meager crate worth of possessions. Yet, I was proud of what I had achieved and looked forward to continuing the legacy of this small but mighty county sheriff's department.

"Sheriff Gibson," I addressed him, as I waited by the door before stepping inside his office.

"You must be my replacement, Bridger Lange," he replied with a genuine smile as he rounded his desk and held out his hand.

"I am. It's an honor to meet you. I'll make sure to protect your county as best I can."

"I know you will. I'll introduce you to the staff," he offered. "Most of them are out on patrol, but you will meet them later."

With a nod, I followed him out of the office to the dispatch area where a woman in her thirties sat with a set of headphones perched on her head.

"No problem, Ben. I'll let you know if anything comes up," she said through the microphone positioned two inches from her mouth.

She looked up at us and lowered the microphone from her mouth. "Hi Gail." Sheriff Gibson began. "I'd like you to meet your new boss. This is Sheriff Bridger Lange."

"Hello sir," she replied, holding out her hand. "It's nice to have you on board."

"Thank you," I replied, placing my hand in hers.

The day continued with Leroy introducing me to more of the staff and giving me a tour of the building. As we walked, I couldn't help but notice the impressive maintenance and organization of records and files in the evidence room. Unlike some of the cases in larger counties, Leroy mentioned that they didn't have any unsolved cases hanging around, and he intended to keep it that way.

We eventually made our way back to Leroy's office, where I watched him finish packing up his belongings. Suddenly, a frantic voice echoed through the hallway behind us.

"I need to speak to Sheriff Gibson," a woman's voice cried out.

Turning around, I saw a woman standing with an older man and another man who appeared to be around my age. Gail quickly informed her that Sheriff Gibson had retired and I was now the new sheriff.

Unfazed, the woman insisted on speaking with me immediately. Curiosity getting the better of both Leroy and me, we approached the dispatch desk.

As we got closer, I couldn't help but notice the woman's long strawberry blonde hair cascading down her back. Despite her petite size, she exuded confidence and strength. And when she turned to face us, her green-gray eyes met mine and I couldn't look away—they were the most mesmerizing eyes I had ever seen.

"Is there something I can help you with, Ma'am?" I asked, unable to tear my gaze away from her stunning features.

She shifted slightly, allowing me to take in her outfit—a dark blue denim button-down shirt opened halfway in the front, revealing a white tank top underneath that accentuated her assets in a tasteful manner. Despite the tense situation, I couldn't help but feel captivated by her presence. She was undeniably gorgeous.

I couldn't help but feel the electricity shooting through every vein inside me. She had a pull on me that I couldn't fight. No woman had ever done anything like that to me before. Turning my head, because it was the only way I could break the spell she had put me under. I held out my arm toward my new office. "Have a seat." I gave her a slight glance and pulled a chair up to the desk. "Why don't you tell me what is going on?"

Leroy remained standing at the door like an onlooker while I took a seat at his desk. "Now, tell be what's going on."

"This will explain everything," the older man spoke first as he laid a piece of paper on my desk.

"What am I looking at?" I asked as I picked up the paper and began unfolding it.

"It's a lab test of the cattle on Pegasus Ranch. The ranch manager, Briggs...," he paused for a moment as he looked at the man seated to his right. "...found them dead on her land. There were ten in all. The results showed a high amount of cyanide in their blood," he admitted.

"This is Dr. Donald Montgomery. He is the best veterinarian around," Leroy chimed in.

"Someone poisoned my cattle." The soft voice of the woman who captivated me caused me to look her way.

The pain in her voice was unmistakable. I just didn't know how I could help her, but I knew I had to do something for her.

"Mrs...." I didn't even know her full name.

"It's Coleman, but please call me Dixie," she replied with a half-smile.

"Dixie, do you know of anyone who has a grudge against you?"

"No.... everyone around here is like family."

"Not everyone," the man—Briggs—chimes in.

"What are you taking about, Briggs?" Dixie asked, confused.

"Why don't you tell us, Briggs," I pushed, not sure what to make of this guy.

"There was a man that came by Pegasus Ranch a couple of months ago and then again two weeks ago. He wanted to buy up the land and Pegasus Ranch. I told him both times it wasn't for sale," he admitted. "He looked like a rancher himself, so I didn't think anything of it."

"Did you get his name?" I asked.

"No... I didn't get his name," he responded defensively.

"Well, the next time he comes around, it might be a good idea if you do." I said sarcastically. *Who doesn't ask for a person's name?* "In the meantime, I'll do some checking around. Dixie, I suggest you let you husband know what is going on. Maybe this man has spoken to him as well."

"That's highly unlikely," she choked out. "He passed away a year ago."

How was I supposed to know she was a widow, there was a damn wedding band on her ring finger? "I'm sorry for your loss."

"Thank you," she replied, her voice barely above a whisper. "And thank you for your help."

"I'll let you know as soon as I find anything out." I pushed to my feet and placed my hands on the desk as I watched Dixie rise from her chair and step past Leroy.

As she left, there was so much more I wanted to know about this woman other than she lost her husband, or that she owned Pegasus Ranch and someone was out to get her.

~

After an in-depth conversation with Leroy, I learned every detail about Dixie. I learned the heartbreaking truth about her. A drunk driver had taken her husband's life last year, as he was making his way home from a cattle auction. The accident claimed Trent Coleman and three prized Black Angus steers. The guilty party managed to escape with only a broken arm and a fifteen-year sentence for vehicular homicide. My heart ached for her and the immense loss she had endured. I could feel the weight of her grief and struggle through Leroy's words. He also revealed that she had recently lost 20 more head of cattle during the harsh winter. As if one tragedy wasn't enough, now someone was trying to sabotage her livelihood. It became clear that whoever poisoned her cattle must have a desperate desire to take over her family's ranch. Leroy revealed that Dixie had been struggling since the accident, but always found a way to keep going. I couldn't dismiss the thought that someone might have intentionally killed her cattle to get her land and ranch. As I mulled over this troubling possibility, my determination to help her only grew stronger. It wasn't a coincidence that her cattle died around the same time this man showed up. All I know was, it just became my problem too.

"I'll always be around if you need anything," Leroy stated as he held out his hand.

"I'll remember that," I replied, as I shook his hand with respect.

Giving each other one last nod, I watched him pick up the box of his personal items from the floor and walk out of the office. Instead of making myself familiar with the office, I decided to get a jump on helping Dixie Coleman. *Who was I kidding?* It had been less than an hour since she left and already, I felt the need to see her.

After receiving directions from Gail, instead of taking my personal truck, I climbed into the truck parked in the designated spot for the sheriff and switched on the engine. Shops lined the street, bustling with people as I turned onto Pioneer Way. As I made a left turn, my blinker clicking rhythmically, I couldn't help but think of how different this town would look in a few months when the tourists would be crowding the hotels and casinos.

I followed the winding road up the steep hill, taking in the view of the surrounding mountains before turning off the state highway down a county road. Five miles later, there it was—Pegasus Ranch. The iconic archway welcomed me with its towering stone pillars and an ornate iron emblem of two overlapping letters—P and R.

As I continued down the long driveway, a rustic two-story house emerged from behind a cluster of trees. Its exterior was adorned with the same stone as the archway at the entrance, giving it a regal appearance. Beyond the house were several barns, their peaks proudly displaying the ranch's emblem. In the distance, I could see feeding corrals bustling with activity. It wasn't hard to confirm that I had arrived at Pegasus Ranch—several trucks bearing the same brand and name were parked nearby. Bold letters below the unmistakable emblem read 'Pegasus Ranch.'

There was one vehicle out of place—a sleek, expensive black sedan against the backdrop of the modest house. Its glossy exterior reflected the sunlight, almost blinding me as I approached. Pulling my truck up behind it, I turned off the engine and stepped out, I pullout my cell and took a shot of the license plate before trying to get a look inside through the tinted back window. Unable to see anything, I turned away and took in my surroundings. The peaceful countryside stretched out before me, with rolling hills and lush greenery as far as the eye could see. It was no wonder Dixie loved this place so much. The tranquil beauty was a stark contrast to the chaos of city life. As I walked towards the house, I couldn't help but feel a twinge of jealousy at the thought of raising a family in such a picturesque setting. It was something I never had the chance to do. Sure, I had been in relationships, but once they started getting serious, I always ended them. The thought of leaving a woman I loved behind, burdened with the heartache of burying me, was too much for me to bear. She deserved someone who could give her everything she wanted—children, a future, growing old together. And that person wasn't me. For more than two decades, I dedicated my life to serving my country in one way or another. And while I had no regrets about my choices, there were moments when I wondered what could have been if things had been different.

I was about to walk up the steps to the house when a burly-looking guy stepped out of the car from the driver's side. "Is there something I can help you with?"

I looked him over and even though we were the same built, that last thing I wanted was trouble. "No, I'm just here to see Dixie Coleman."

The man, who I assumed was the driver, got back inside the sedan and closed the door. I shook my head and proceeded up the stairs. When I reached the door, I pulled open the screen door, and rolled my hand into a fist and rapped my knuckles against the wooden door. When the door opened and Dixie's eyes met mine, once again she drew me in. *Why did I have this over-whelming need to touch her?*

3
THREE

Dixie

Bridger Lange's piercing blue eyes held a magnetic intensity that made my heart race. I couldn't help but feel drawn towards him, as if he had some kind of invisible hold on me. Even in the Sheriff's office, I found it difficult to tear my gaze away from his captivating stare. And now, here he was, standing mere inches from me, his presence enveloping me like a warm embrace. *"Get a grip, Dixie,"* I scolded myself internally, trying to ignore the fluttering in my stomach and the way my skin prickled under his intense gaze.

"Sheriff Lange. This is a surprise. What are you doing here?" The sound of my own voice wavered as I spoke to Sheriff Lange, trying to maintain a sense of composure despite the effect he had on me. His mere presence was enough to send my heart racing and my palms sweating.

"Can I come in?" His smooth baritone voice echoed between us.

"Of course."

I stepped aside, allowing him to enter my home. As he walked past me, his woodsy, spicy scent filled my senses, making it hard for me to focus on anything else. I fought the urge to bury my face in his shirt and inhale deeply.

Leading him further inside, I couldn't help but feel a flutter of excitement in my stomach. This man, only a year after my husband's death, was stirring up feelings in me that I didn't quite understand or know how to handle.

But then, the presence of Colton Stetson in my living room interrupted us. The man who had been relentlessly trying to convince me to sell him Pegasus ranch. Bridger's unexpected arrival couldn't have come at a better time.

"Sheriff Lange," I said calmly. "This is Colton Stetson. He's interested in purchasing my ranch." My words hung heavily in the air, the tension between us almost palpable.

As I introduced them, I couldn't shake off the feeling that this could be the same man who had confronted Briggs last winter and two weeks ago. The one potentially responsible for poisoning my cattle. The way Sheriff Lange's eyebrows narrowed; I was sure he was thinking the same thing.

"It's nice to meet you, Sheriff." Colton stood and held out his hand like he actually meant it. "I've got another meeting to attend." His eyes move to me. "Think about what I said, Dixie. It is a great offer. It would get you out from under all your debt and allow you to live a very comfortable life."

When he left through the door and it was only Sheriff Lange and I left in the house, I look at him. "Do you think... he could have had anything to do with poisoning my cattle?"

"I don't know, Dixie, but I sure as hell am going to find out," he replied, stepping closer to me.

He stood at least a 6-inches taller than me and given how close he was to me; I had to look up just to meet his blue eyes. "What are you going to do, Sheriff Lange?"

"I'm going to look into Mr. Stetson and find out why he wants your ranch so bad." He bent his knees slightly so that we were at eye level and my head was no longer stretched upward. "If he killed your cattle, we will prosecute him."

"Thank you, Sheriff Lange." He placed his hands on my arms and gave them a light squeeze.

"Please call me Bridger," he replied with a smile that made his features even more handsome, which I didn't think was possible. "I'd love to see the rest of your ranch since I'm here."

This was the most relaxed I had felt in a long time. I found Bridger was actually very easy to talk to. He was a simple man, born in Grant County, near a small town called Big Stone City. When he was barely out of high school, he joined the Marines. It was shortly after his mom died. She was the only family he had left. His dad died years before from stomach cancer. He ended up serving three tours in Iraq. He never got married. When he was honorably discharged from the military, he went into law enforcement. He had aunts and uncles that he had never met but knew they were scattered across the U.S., primarily in North Dakota and Iowa—and no brothers or sisters.

"Thank you for showing me around, Dixie," Bridger said as we made our way back to the house.

"Would you like to have dinner with us? We usually eat around 7:00 p.m." I wasn't sure what compelled me to ask, but I really wanted to see him again.

"I would be a fool to refuse a dinner invitation from a beautiful woman," he replied with a smile.

"Good. I will see you at seven then."

I felt like a giddy teenager as I watched Bridger drive away. He was actually coming for dinner. Ethan would be home soon from Rapid City. This morning before Briggs and I left to meet Dr. Montgomery so we could all explain what had been going on with my cattle, my son asked me if Reggie could take him to pick out a saddle instead of me. I should have felt heartbroken, but I didn't. Ethan was getting older and having his mom take him shopping for a saddle wasn't exactly the best ego lifter for him. Reggie was the closest to him and I was glad he agreed to take him.

Dinner was almost ready. The only thing left to do was make the salad. As I opened the refrigerator to take out the items I needed, I heard the front door open. Ethan walked through the door with a big smile on his face. His smile told me he and Reggie found him a new saddle.

"I take it you and Reggie had a good day in Rapid City," I said as I looked his way.

"I did. You should see the saddle, Mom. It is so, so...," he paused for a moment, his hands going everywhere. "It's indescribable. You just have to see it."

"How about you show me after supper? Go wash up. And change your shirt. The new sheriff is joining us for dinner."

"New sheriff?" Ethan whipped around, and I thought his head was going to snap off. "What happened to Sheriff Gibson?"

"Sheriff Gibson retired. Sheriff Lange is taking his position. I thought it would be nice to invite him for supper."

"Cool."

That wasn't the only reason I wanted to invite him, but at least Ethan didn't seem to mind. I think the high of finding a new saddle was still taking effect and was part of his cheerful mood. I loved seeing him this way. As Ethan headed up the stairs to clean up and change his shirt, I focused back on the salad. I reverted my attention back to chopping the lettuce, but my mind was on Bridger.

The table was all set with the addition of one extra table setting. In half an hour Bridger would be here and it was time to make myself more presentable. When I opened the closet in my bedroom, I couldn't remember the last time I had worn a dress. I guess I never felt the need. As I fumbled through the dresses that hung together in the back of my closet, I chose to wear a long-sleeved boho dress that gathered around the waist and paired it with my blue denim jacket and suede boots.

I took one last look at myself in the full-length mirror, smiling to myself. I really was an attractive woman. As I headed down the stairs, I could hear the guys talking in the kitchen. When I entered the kitchen, their eyes were on me. It had been a while since they had seen me in a dress as well, the last time being

Trent's funeral. I ignored their stares and expressions and walked past them toward the living room. If I was going to get through dinner, I was going to need some liquid courage.

Briggs stepped up beside me and poured himself a whiskey. "You look nice. What's the occasion?"

"Sheriff Lange is coming for dinner," I answered matter-of-factly.

"Bridger Lange?"

"Yes. I thought it would be nice."

Thank goodness for the knock at the door. I didn't want to have to explain to Briggs why I had invited Bridger to dinner. I tossed the amber liquid back, feeling the burn of the whiskey in the back of my throat as it went down.

I nervously slid my hands down my dress to smooth out the wrinkles that didn't exist. I had never been so nervous in my life. Well, maybe once. My wedding day. When I pulled open the door Bridger was standing on the other side, looking every bit the handsome man I met at the Sheriff's office. The only difference was, he wasn't wearing his uniform. Instead, he was wearing a black Ariat long-sleeved shirt that displayed his broad shoulders perfectly with the top two buttons undone showing a glimpse of chest hair. The dark jeans that he wore hung low on his hips and fit him perfectly. He styled his dark hair back showcasing his well-groomed, but, gorgeous bearded face by using a bit of hair gel. I could smell his masculine scent—musky and spicy—which consumed my body with thoughts I hadn't had in a long time.

"I hope I'm not late," he said, breaking me from googling over him.

"You're right on time." I managed to get out as I moved to the side to allow him to enter.

"Whatever you've cooked smells wonderful."

"Come in. I'll introduce you to everyone."

He placed his black hat on the hat rack near the door before following me to the kitchen. Maybe it was selfish of me, but I wanted to be surrounded by people I knew when we had our first dinner together. It had been a long time since I had been on a date and if Bridger would ask me on one; I wanted to make sure I wouldn't be nervous around him. *And so the fun begins.* Hopefully, this night won't turn into a disaster.

4

FOUR

Bridger

As I followed Dixie into the kitchen, seeing four men and a teenager sitting at a long dining table wasn't at all what I expected. I was under the impression that it would be me and her having dinner tonight.

Briggs entered the dining room carrying a tumbler filled with whiskey. Giving me a nod, he took a seat at the end of the table. It was as if he knew exactly where to sit.

Dixie introduced everyone as she went around the table. "Bridger, I'd like you to meet everyone. This is Ethan, my son. And these are the men that work on the ranch, Vincent, Reggie, Whalen and Josh. Briggs, you have already met. Everyone, this is Sheriff Bridger Lange. He is taking over Sheriff Gibson's position."

"It's nice to meet everyone," I replied, tipping my head.

"You can sit next to me Bridger, if you'd like," Dixie offered

Without hesitation, I eagerly accepted Dixie's invitation to sit beside her. Her son, however, eyed me warily, trying to assess the kind of man I was. I couldn't blame him—he had lost his father and here I was, a stranger entering his home and seemingly enamored by his mother. The tension between us was thick enough to cut with a knife, but thankfully Reggie broke it by standing up from his chair.

"Anyone want a beer?" he asked, breaking the silence.

"I'll take one," the men chimed in simultaneously.

"And you, Sheriff?" Reggie turned to me.

"Sure, thank you," I replied. "Please call me, Bridger."

Ethan added in a request for a Coke, keeping his eyes fixed on me. Without missing a beat, Reggie shot back with a teasing response to draw Ethan's eyes away from me. "Do I look like your mom? Get it yourself."

I almost let out a laugh, but caught myself before making things any more awkward. Clearly this kid had already formed an opinion about me and I didn't want to give him any more reason to dislike me.

Dixie, Reggie, and Ethan returned with platters of food and our drinks. Everything looked amazing, but not as amazing as Dixie herself. When she had opened the door, I felt like I had died and gone to heaven. She was an angel—damn those green-gray eyes. Her beauty surpassed any woman I had ever met before. In the past, I had been with beautiful women, but Dixie was different. There was something truly special about her that I couldn't quite put into words.

As we sat around the table, the conversation remained light-hearted. We talked about the high school's baseball team statistics and how much Ethan enjoyed playing football. No one brought up anything about the cattle or Colton Stetson coming by. If I were to guess, Dixie hadn't told Ethan about the recent events involving the ranch and the poisoning.

As the dinner progressed, my initial apprehension melted away, and I found myself immersed in laughter and childhood stories with Dixie and the others. As we reminisced, I couldn't help but notice how beautiful she looked when she laughed, her eyes crinkling at the corners and her whole face lighting up. It was like watching a radiant sunbeam come to life. And every time she smiled, my heart skipped a beat. Her every movement, from the way she tilted her head back in laughter to the way she covered her mouth when embarrassed, was like a symphony playing out before me. Each gesture was graceful and alluring, drawing me in further and further. *How could I be falling for a woman I had only met eight hours ago?*

"I think I'll go upstairs and watch TV," Ethan announced as he pushed back his chair, its legs scraping against the hardwood floor.

Dixie gracefully rose from her chair and began clearing the table, taking hold of the dirty plates and staking them neatly in front of her. Feeling like I should be helping in some way, I rose from my seat and reached for the platter of leftover roast beef and mashed potatoes.

But Dixie was quick to stop me. "Oh no, you don't," she chided playfully with a warm smile. "Why don't you and the guys go into the living room and visit while I take care of this mess?"

When she placed her hand over mine, a bolt of electricity shot up my arm all the way down to what this good lord gave me. No woman's touch had ever done that before. The gentle pressure of her hand lingered even after she had released it, leaving me feeling strangely breathless and flustered. *Bridger, don't do it. Don't break her heart.*

~

Dixie entered the living room holding a glass of white wine in her hand as I finished telling the guys what I found out about Colton Stetson. I needed to let her know as well. This was her ranch, and she had every right to know.

"Me and the guys are going to check on the herd," Briggs said as he set his glass on the carved wood end table and rose from the leather chair.

"Okay," Dixie replied. "Don't you want some apple pie before you go?"

"Nah. We can have some later," Briggs answered respectfully.

Dixie gracefully settled onto the leather couch; her long legs crossed elegantly as she took a sip from her wineglass. The soft light from the chandelier above crafted from deer horns danced across her features, making her green-gray eyes seem to sparkle with warmth and intrigue. I couldn't take my eyes off of her as she met my gaze and placed her glass on the coffee table. I tried to soften my expression, but I knew soon she would be able to read the concern written on my face.

"Thank you for joining me for dinner," she said, her voice low and captivating as she tried to break the tension in the room.

"Thank you for inviting me," I replied, feeling drawn to her like a magnet as I moved closer to her.

I set my whiskey glass down next to hers before sitting down beside her. Her eyes never left mine, and I was mesmerized by their depth and mystery. If I wasn't trying to be a gentleman, I would have learned in and kissed her right then and there.

Shifting slightly to face her, I felt her hand rest gently on my knee. Despite her beauty, I could sense that she was worried.

"What is it, Bridger?" she asked with a shaky breath.

"I did some research on Colton Stetson. You're not going to like what I found."

"I'm a big girl, Bridger," she replied, removing her hand from my knee and uncrossing her legs. "Whatever it is, I can handle it."

"Colton Stetson is a dangerous man. He's not just interested in Pegasus Ranch—he's been buying up ranches all over the country."

"Whose ranches, Bridger?"

"Not in Deadwood. Most of them are in Texas, Wyoming, Oklahoma, North Dakota...and recently Pennsylvania." My words hung heavy in the air as Dixie's expression turned grave. It was clear that this man posed a danger not only to Pegasus Ranch but to numerous others in different states as well.

Her voice trembled as she spoke, a hint of fear and concern evident in her tone.

"Why would he buy up all those ranches? It seems a little extreme to me." Her eyes searched mine for an explanation.

Taking a deep breath, I reached for her glass of wine and handed it to her.

She needed something to calm her nerves before I dropped the bombshell on her.

"Dixie, I got in touch with the Sheriff's department in Midland County, Texas. They're currently investigating Colton Stetson, and it seems like he's been targeting ranch owners like you."

What I didn't tell her was the banks refused to lend the ranch owners any money until they could get back on their feet. Both the sheriff and I thought it was awful strange and that the banks could be working with Colton. This whole thing stunk to high heaven.

Dixie's hand shook as she brought the wineglass to her lips, downing the rest of its contents in one go. I knew she wouldn't take this news well.

As she set the empty glass down, I saw a tear roll down her cheek. This woman who had been laughing and smiling only moments ago was now crying, and I was the cause of it.

With a heavy heart, I lifted my hand and gently wiped away the tear from her cheek with my thumb.

"I can't lose my ranch," she whispered, her voice breaking.

My heart ached at the sight of her in such distress. Pulling her close, I wrapped my arms around her trembling form. "You won't lose your ranch, Dixie. I promise you that."

I could feel her warm breath against my shirt as she buried her head in my chest. The scent of strawberries and vanilla filled my senses. In that moment, I didn't want to let her go. Our bodies fit perfectly together and when she finally pulled away and our eyes met, something magical passed between us. Despite the difficult situation, there was a strong connection between us that couldn't be ignored.

I knew I would do whatever it took to protect her and her ranch from Colton Stetson's schemes. Her eyes, deep pools of green and gray, flicked down to my lips and then back up to meet my gaze. I couldn't resist any longer and placed my hand gently under her chin, tilting her face toward mine. As I leaned in closer, her warm breath danced across my skin, sending shivers through my body. My heart raced as our lips hovered just inches apart. But before we could seal the moment with a kiss, a familiar voice broke through the tension. *Damn!*

"Mom, can I have a piece of apple pie?" Ethan's voice echoed down the stairs, interrupting our brief moment of shared desire.

"Sure." Dixie's voice shook as she responded to her son's request, her embarrassment evident.

When she pulled away from me, her cheeks were flushed with a rosy hue. I remained calm and collected wanting another chance to savor the taste of her lips without any distractions. But deep down, I knew it wouldn't happen tonight. The last thing I wanted was to make Dixie feel uncomfortable or guilty. Instead, I stood from the couch and followed her to the kitchen. I watched her slice the pie in perfect pieces before dishing Ethan a piece on a small white plate.

"I think there is some vanilla ice cream in the freezer," she said as she placed her thumb against her lips and puckered them to clean the remnants of the pie from it. "Would you like a piece, Bridger?"

"Uh... No thank you," I managed to get out, my eyes still on her lips. "I think I'll take off. Thanks again for the wonderful dinner."

"Let me walk you out," she smiled, placing the pie spatula on the counter.

I wasn't sure if it was a good idea or not, but who was I to refuse?

As Dixie led the way to her front door, I quickly grabbed my black cowboy hat from the shelf above the coat rack. The night air was surprisingly warm for mid-March, but a cool breeze still brushed against my skin as we descended the wooden steps and made our way toward my truck.

The only light guiding us was the soft glow of the moon, casting dancing shadows on the ground beneath us. We were alone, with nothing but the sound of our footsteps crunching on gravel.

Before I could open the truck door, I turned to face Dixie. Looking down at her, I found her beautiful eyes gazing up at me.

"Thank you again for coming to dinner," she said softly, her voice barely above a whisper.

With no one else around, I knew I had to take this chance. Stepping closer to her, I gently cupped her chin in my hand and replied, "It was my pleasure," before lowering my lips to hers.

At that moment, everything around us faded away. It was only me and her. I let her feel the warmth of my breath while I wrapped my arms around her tiny waist. I pulled her closer and gently pressed my lips to hers. I should end it there, but I couldn't. Instead, I dipped inside and explored her further. In the distance, I could hear the cattle shifting restlessly. I didn't think anything of it, but it wasn't until several voices broke through the silence that I realized something was wrong.

"Something has spooked the cattle. I'll get the horses ready," I recognized Brigg's voice calling out.

Dixie pulled away from the kiss and released her hold on me, her eyes wide with worry. "The cattle..."

5
FIVE

Dixie

I ran as fast as I could toward the stable with Bridger on my heels. When I heard Brigg's voice, I knew something was wrong. And after Bridger had told me about Colton Stetson, I wasn't about to take any chances that he was the one who was stirring up the cattle.

When I reached the horse stalls, the horses were already saddled and Briggs and Reggie were leading them outside.

"Let me change clothes, and I'll catch up," I said, seeing that someone had saddled an extra horse.

"You aren't coming, Dixie," Briggs replied. "This horse is for the sheriff."

I looked over my shoulder at Bridger, who was already making his way toward me. Placing his hand on my shoulders, he bent his knees slightly and looked directly into my eyes. "You need to say here, Dixie. I'm not sure what we might find out there."

I wasn't happy about the situation, but I knew he was right. I placed my hands on his shoulders and lifted to the tip of my toes and placed a kiss on his cheek. "Be careful."

Giving my arms a gentle rub, he nodded his head and walked toward the horse Briggs was holding and mounted it with ease. I hadn't noticed it before, but on the side of the saddle was a rifle holstered with only the butt visible.

I stood near the horse stable and watched the guys ride off toward the south pasture. Briggs thought it would be better to keep the cattle closer to the ranch, given what had taken place. Even though there wasn't as much grass or forage to eat and my feed cost would suffer, at least we could keep a better eye on them. It was only when the darkness swallowed them up that I turned and walked back to the house. I gazed over at Bridger's truck and, for just a moment, my mind was on the kiss we shared instead of the cattle. Instinctively, my fingers touched my lips, feeling the gentle caress of Bridger's lips on mine. I felt a tingle in my stomach at the thought of having a man in my life. I felt a sense of excitement and guilt at the same time. It had only been a year since Trent died and I felt like I was betraying what we had—like the years we spent together no longer matter.

I turned my head and headed back to the house. I didn't know what I thought, but before I went inside, I looked over my shoulder toward the south pasture one last time to see if the men were on their way back. Darkness was the only thing I saw. The cattle could still be heard. As I turned the knob, two shots, one right after the other, sounded. My breath hitched, and I ran to the corral fence. Before long, I heard footsteps behind me.

"What's going on, Mom?" Ethan's voice sounded behind me.

"Something has the cattle riled up. The guys went to check on them." It was a half-truth, but I couldn't worry Ethan about what was really going on.

"They probably shot a coyote or something," Ethan replied, the gunshots not phasing him a bit.

"You're probably right," I agreed, as I continued to gaslight him. "Let's go inside."

Ethan and I turned and walked away from the fence and headed toward the house. Once inside, he retreated to his room, and I busied myself in the kitchen, wiping down the counters for the hundredth time. My gaze remained fixed on the south pasture as I wiped the counter. All I was doing was making myself sick with worry. I pushed myself from the counter and poured myself a glass of wine, taking the remaining bottle of wine with me to the living room.

I kicked off my boots and tucked my legs under me. My head was spinning with thoughts of what was happening. I hated not knowing what was going on. I turned my head and looked at the clock on the dining room wall. The guys have been gone for almost two hours. Worry started to build inside me that something terrible had happened. It had been too long.

I downed the rest of my wine and made my way to the stairs. Before heading up the stairs, I heard the front door open. Briggs was the first to enter, followed by Bridger.

"What happened? I heard gunshots," I blurted, my eyes focused only on Bridger.

Bridger placed his hand on my arm and I knew it wasn't good. "Someone got to one of the cattle but we were too late. They shot the steer with a tranquilizer gun."

"We think we know how they've been getting to the cattle," Briggs interrupted. "First, they subdue the cattle, then, while the cattle are unconscious, they inject cyanide into their bodies."

"I'm going to take the dart back to the office and see if we can pull any prints off it. We all have a pretty good idea who is behind this. We just have to prove it," Bridger remarked.

~

Sleep eluded me, my mind racing with thoughts of what Bridger would uncover about the tranquilizer dart used on the steer. My heart raced with anxiety and dread, but thankfully, that was as far as they had gotten. It could have been much worse. The longer I lay in bed, the more the darkness enveloped me. It must have been three, maybe four in the morning—a time when even the birds were asleep. My muscles felt weighted down with exhaustion, but my mind refused to rest, constantly replaying the events of the day.

I lay in bed a little while longer, before my fight to sleep lost. Pushing from the bed, I slipped on my robe and headed downstairs. I paced back and forth as I watched the coffee fall in a steady stream into the glass coffee pot. I had set the time for seven, but never thought I would be up four hours before it actually went off. I could remove the pot and replace it with a mug, but what good would that do other than make a big mess? Watching the coffee pot wouldn't make it finish making coffee any faster, so I turned on my heels and headed back upstairs to take a quick shower and get dressed. There was no way I was going to sleep now. I was wide awake.

By the time I finished and headed back to the kitchen, my coffee finished brewing, and another hour had passed. I grabbed a cup from the cupboard above my head and poured myself some coffee. As soon as the hot coffee hit my lips, I looked out the kitchen window into the darkness. I blinked my eyes shut and held them close for a moment before opening them and taking another look. I thought I was seeing things, but clearly, I wasn't. Bridger's truck was parked in front of the house. Had he stayed here all night? No. He was going to see if he could pull prints off the dart they pulled from the steer.

I placed my mug on the counter and grabbed another one from the cupboard. I wasn't sure why Bridger was out there, but I was certain he would be in need of some coffee. Taking the full mug of coffee with me, I opened the front door and walked down the stairs toward his truck. I placed my hand against his slightly frosted window and lightly tapped on it with my knuckle.

As the window rolled down, I saw Bridger sitting upright in his truck. The soft glow from the moonlight cast shadows on his features, but I could still see the determination in his eyes. How long had he been parked here, watching over me? It didn't matter—his presence was comforting with everything going on.

I handed him a mug of coffee through the open window, and he took it gratefully. But as he sipped from it, I noticed the tense set of his jaw and the furrowed lines on his forehead. There was something wrong.

"How long have you been out here?" I asked, trying to keep my voice steady.

"Since midnight," he replied calmly, but there was an underlying sense of urgency in his tone.

I stepped away from the truck as he opened the door, revealing a firearm holstered at his side. My heart raced with worry—*what was happening?*

But before I could ask him any questions, he gently took hold of my arm and led me towards the house. His touch was both reassuring and forceful—he wasn't going to let me stay out here any longer.

"Why are we going inside?" I turned to face him, searching for answers.

"I can't explain right now, Dixie," he said, placing a hand on my cheek. "Please, just go inside."

The concern in his voice only fueled my own worries. But I knew better than to argue with Bridger when he had that look in his eye. Just as I reached the front porch, the sound of static came through Bridger's radio from inside the truck. He quickly handed me back the full mug of coffee before rushing off to answer it.

Reluctantly, I went inside but kept watch through the window as Bridger spoke into his radio from the open door of his truck with a grave expression. It had been a year since I lost my husband and gained Briggs and the other guys as my protectors. But at that moment, it was Bridger I wanted to protect me. I wasn't sure why since I had only met him yesterday morning, but somehow, he made me feel safe.

6

SIX

Bridger

Dixie's worried gaze bore into me, begging for answers. But I couldn't bring myself to tell her the truth and add any more weight to her already burdened shoulders. I hoped the kiss I left her with was all the reassurance she needed to trust me. The marvels of technology never ceased to amaze me—with a simple fingerprint lifted from the dart lodged in the steer's shoulder, a match appeared in the criminal database—one Troy Jones. When I heard the static coming over my radio, it was the call I was expecting. I swung open the door and pulled the microphone from the radio's transmitter cradle.

"What do you have for me, Gail?" I wasted no time getting straight to the point.

"Not much, Bridger," she responded, using my first name instead of addressing me as sheriff, just like I instructed her. "But I found out that Troy Jones is one of Mr. Stetson's employees." My suspicions were confirmed—Stetson was definitely involved in poisoning Dixie's cattle. "That's all I have for now. Are you still at the Pegasus Ranch?"

That was more than enough. I least I knew where to start. Tomorrow, I needed to make a visit to Colton Stetson. "Yeah," I hesitated before answering. "See if you can find out where Colton Stetson is staying and text me the address."

"You got it."

I placed the microphone back in its cradle and shut the door. When I looked up, I could see two of the ranch's men riding in from the south pasture. I had requested they take turns keeping an eye out in case whoever shot the cattle with the tranquilizer decided to return. They must have made a shift switch. Until it was daylight I wasn't going to take any chances of them returning and doing more than just getting to the cattle. If Troy Jones was on Colton Stenson's payroll, I wouldn't put it past him to hire other felons to do his dirty work.

I stepped out from behind my truck and walked toward the stables where the two men were headed. I wanted to let them know what I had found out and to let them know to keep an eye out for Dixie. I needed to get back to the hotel and shower. Since leaving here after pulling the dart from the steer, all I had been thinking about was making Colton Stetson pay for what he had done.

Reggie and Vincent were already removing the saddles from their horses by the time I reached the stable. They looked exhausted and in need of sleep. I should have called some of the deputies to come out to watch out for any activity, but Dixie's ranch hands knew this land better than them, plus they were already here.

"Hey, guys," I said as I walked up behind them. "I take it there hasn't been any activity."

"I don't think whoever it was is coming back," Vincent said with a southern draw in his voice. "Those two shots you took either hit him or scared him off."

"The fingerprint on the dart belongs to Troy Jones," I disclosed. "He is on Colton Stetson's payroll. Do either of you know him?"

"Never heard of him," Reggie spoke up first, while Vincent just shook his head.

"I hate to ask, but could you two keep an eye on Dixie and Ethan until I get back. I have a feeling this isn't over."

"I'll keep an eye on them. You two get some sleep." Briggs said behind me as his boots echoed off the concrete floor with determination.

I turned my head to face him curious to why he was here instead of out in the pasture with Whalen and Josh. "I take it you heard what I said."

"I did." Briggs stood a couple of feet in front of me and I could feel the anger dripping from his words.

He was the last person I wanted an altercation with, so I tipped my hat to him and walked around his solid frame. He was built like a bus, but it wasn't to say I couldn't take him down if I had to. The thing was, I didn't want to. That was the last thing I needed. Dixie would hate me if I roughed up her ranch manager.

"What is your intention with Dixie?" he asked before I could leave the stable.

Hell, I didn't even know myself what my intention was. All I knew was I had never felt the way I had with any other woman I had been with before. Then again, I really never gave it a chance either.

I spun around on my heels and met his gaze before walking toward him. I made sure I was looking him straight in the eye. "I can promise you one thing. My intention is not to hurt her if she'll have me."

I tipped my hat again and turned and walked away. I waited for a response, but never got one. I guess my answer must have satisfied him. I could tell by the way he looked at Dixie he cared about her too. Not like a man in love, but like a man who cared about family. A family was something I never really had. Sure, I had uncles and aunts—who were strangers—but I never had a sister or brother. I no longer had a mom and dad. It would be nice to be part of a family again.

~

Gail was unable to find Colton Stetson staying at any of the hotels, which meant he was staying somewhere else. I thought for sure he would be staying at a hotel in Deadwood. After taking a much-needed shower, I changed into a clean uniform and left my hotel room at the Super Eight. Ever since I got to Deadwood, I hadn't had the time to find a place of my own. The realtor I had been working with had shown me a couple of places she thought I might be interested in, but none of them appealed to me.

I holstered my gun and left the room. Hopping inside my truck, I headed down Pioneer Way on my way back to Pegasus Ranch. Today just became my lucky day. Just by chance I caught Colton Stetson exiting the parking lot of Cadillac Jacks and he wasn't alone or in the sedan that was parked in front of Dixie's house yesterday. This time, he was in an SUV and someone else was driving with two other passengers in the back seat. Even with the dark windows, the light from the sun provided the perfect view of the two men.

I stayed behind him, but not close enough that the driver would suspect me following them. Thank God, I had my truck instead of the sheriff's truck. The driver of the SUV drove past the road toward Pegasus Ranch. Relief washed over me, knowing Dixie was out of harm's way.

I followed the SUV until it turned off on a dirt road. I had no idea where the road led, but I didn't want to take any chances that they would spot me behind them. There was enough brush around to take cover. My only obstacle was the daylight. For now, I knew where he was staying. Instead of risking getting caught, I drove up the road a little way until I found a place to turn around. I needed to wait until night and bring more men.

It was just after five and the sun had gone down. I had three of my deputies with me. I wasn't sure what I would be up against, but I didn't want to take any chances. I wasn't sure how to approach the cabin that I learned this morning Colton Stetson was renting.

I was the first to arrive at the cabin while the other deputies remain in their vehicles close behind. When I reached the door, I tapped on it with my flashlight and waited for someone to answer. Despite the drawn light-colored curtains, I could see the cabin lights were on, but nobody appeared to be inside.

"I'm going around the cabin to check it out," I informed my men through the transmitter clipped to my bulletproof vest.

With a determined push of the button on my transmitter, I called out to my team when I spotted a light on in a shed behind the cabin, "I'm headed to a shed in the back of the cabin. Be ready to act."

"We'll be close by," responded Deputy Stone, his voice barely above a whisper through the device.

Heart racing, I made my way towards the side of the shed, pausing to take a quick glance through the small window. My gut sank as I saw what I had feared —three men inside, one of them Troy Jones. They were loading tranquilizer guns while a radio blasted behind them. No wonder they didn't hear me knocking at the front door of the cabin.

Carefully stepping away from the window, I returned to my truck and waited for Deputy Stone and the other deputies to arrive. We finally had a way to get to Colton Stetson. With their statements he was going to rot in jail for all the chaos he caused.

"What's the plan, Sheriff?" asked Deputy Stone upon reaching my side, flanked by two other armed deputies.

After quickly assessing our surroundings, I whispered my instructions, "It looks like there are only three men in the shed and no one in the house. They don't seem to be armed other than their tranquilizer guns. Our best chance is to catch them off guard."

We shared a silent understanding before slowly making our way towards the shed. When we reached it, Deputy Stone and I positioned ourselves on one side while the other two deputies took up positions on the opposite side. With our guns raised and ready, I cautiously swung open the door. The element of surprise worked in our favor as we caught the men off guard, and they quickly surrendered without a fight with their hands held high. It was a smart move on their part.

Swiftly cuffing them and hauling them off, we finally had Colton Shelton men in custody. With these men in custody, I had a strong feeling that they would reveal valuable information during questioning.

7
SEVEN

Dixie

Last night when Bridger's lips left mine, leaving me with only a kiss and no explanation for his sudden overprotective behavior, I should have been angry. But the minute Briggs walked through the front door, I knew I could get the answers I was looking for. I just had to keep a straight and convincing face, so he would think I was serious.

"Briggs, you better tell me what's going on and you better tell me now or you and your men can get the hell off of my ranch." I tried to be as stern as possible, but he could see right through me. He knew I would never let any of them go. They were like family.

Briggs shook his head and laughed. "Dixie, you don't have to pretend to be tough when I know you love all of us, like family."

"Am I that obvious?" I huffed, falling to the chair, feeling defeated. *Why did I think this was going to work?* "So, are you going to tell me?"

"Bridger is on his way here. He can tell you." Briggs filled his cup full of coffee and left the house with nothing more to say.

Men could be so frustrating. Even after all these years, I still couldn't quite understand them. Taking an exasperated breath, I just happened to look up and saw Bridger's sheriff's truck coming up the drive. Dust was bellowing behind him, signaling it was time to have Briggs spray chloride on the road.

Briggs was right about one thing; Bridger was on his way here. I was out the front door and across the yard before he even set foot on the ground. I stood on the edge of the lawn and waited for him to exit his truck, my arms crossed a my chest determined to get answers. When he walked toward me, his expression was much different from last night. He didn't seem as tense—more relaxed.

And then it happened. Without saying a word, he pulled me into his arms and pressed his lips against mine. The familiar scent of his cologne, a heady mix of woodsy and spicy notes, enveloped me like a warm embrace. In that moment, there was nowhere else I'd rather be than in Bridger's arms, feeling the steady beat of his heart against mine. His touch ignited a fire within me, and with each passing second, I knew there was no resisting this man any longer—my determination for answers falling away.

"Wow," I said, barely able to catch my breath as I stared up at this gorgeous man. "You can greet me like that any time you want to."

"Let's go inside. I've got some good news for you," he replied, with his arms still around my waist.

We walked inside the house and settled on the couch. My excitement was about to burst out of my mouth when Bridger turned to face me. I focused on his features, really focused. As I looked at him, I saw a man with a tender heart. His eyes spoke it. And the way he took hold of my hand only confirmed it.

"You don't have to worry about losing you ranch any more, Dixie. We caught the men who poisoned you cattle. They turned against Colton Stetson and told us everything about his business and his intention for wanting Pegasus Ranch. The Sheriff's Department in Texas, along with other law enforcement agencies, caught up with him in Fort Worth. He is going away for a long time. "

"So, it's over?" I asked, unable to believe that it was actually over.

"Yes, they will likely dissolve his business, and they will compensate the ranch owners he swindled. Some will be able to take their ranches back. Those that can't will be able to find suitable land to start over. His lawyers are already working on a plea deals to keep Colton Stetson safe from other prisoners."

"Can they do that?" It was the most absurd thing I had ever heard, but I supposed people with money could do anything.

"Not really." Bridger laughed. "They just want him to know what it feels like to be helpless."

There was an empty feeling in the pit of my stomach, like I wasn't going to see Bridger again. He had found the men responsible for poisoning my cattle, and there really wasn't any reason for him to come to the ranch. He never said how he felt about me, which led me to believe that he was only trying to help me. But way he kissed me, I thought there was something between us. I just didn't know if he felt it, too.

We locked eyes for a brief moment before he stood up, his movements graceful and fluid. I could see the tinge of regret in his gaze, as if he didn't want to leave.

"I need to head back to the office," he said, his voice tinged with longing. "I'm meeting a realtor there. She is going to show me some more properties."

My heart sank at the thought of him leaving so soon. I had never been this forward with a man before, but I couldn't bear the idea of never seeing him again. "Bridger... there is a small apartment above the equipment barn," I blurted out impulsively. "You are welcome to stay there until you find a place."

He looked surprised by my offer, but then his face softened into a grateful smile. "I don't want to put you out, although it would be better than staying in a hotel room. I'll pay you for letting me use it," he insisted.

I shrugged, trying to hide my eagerness. Deep down, I just wanted him to stay here on the ranch so I could see him every day. "It's no trouble, really. I'll get it ready for you."

Standing next to Bridger, I tilted my head up to look at him and smiled warmly. "Thank you for letting me do this for you."

He reached out and placed his hand on my cheek, his touch sending shivers down my spine. He leaned in closer, brushing his lips against mine tenderly. "It's me who should be thanking you," he whispered. "I'll see you later."

As he walked away, my heart swelled with warmth and anticipation. But more than that, the words he left me with confirmed that I would see him again —and that was all that mattered in that moment.

One Year Later

Bridger

"Ethan, can you hand me the wire cutters?" I asked as I held the barbed wire in place.

As I secured the wire to the wood post, my handy work impressed even me. Ethan and I had become close, and I was going to miss him this fall when he went off to college.

"When are you going to ask my mom to marry you?"

His question just about knocked me off of my feet. It was one I hadn't expected. From the moment I saw Dixie, I fell in love with her. When Leroy had told me about the tragic death of her husband, I wanted to take things slow with her and allow her to take the led on how fast she wanted our relationship to go. If she hadn't asked me a year ago to move into the apartment above the equipment barn, I wasn't sure how things would have gone between us.

"So are you hinting that if I ask you mom to marry me, I would have your blessing," I replied.

"It's been two years since my dad died and soon, I'll be going to college. She is going to need someone to take care of her and you are the only one I trust to make sure she keeps on smiling the same way she has been for the last year," Ethan walked toward me lifting up his right leg and placing it on the lower fence rail while resting his hands over the top railing. "So, yeah. Besides, you've kind of grown on me."

"Yeah," I laughed. "Then I'm sure you won't mind being my best man."

Ethan stepped away from the fence and held out his hand. "I would be honored to."

Gripping his hand in mine, I pulled him into a half hug. "Thanks. "I promise, I won't let you down."

It was close to five, and by now, Dixie is preparing supper. Ethan and I mounted our horses and rode back to the ranch. When we got there, Briggs and the other guys once again beat us in. They had been working in the south pasture, guiding the herd closer to the ranch. Tomorrow, the guys would weigh all the cattle and get the heaviest steers ready to be transported to the auction next week.

When we got to the stable, we quickly removed the saddles and gave our horses a good brushing before putting them back in their stalls. As we headed to the house, I looked over to the equipment barn and memories of the apartment and what took place there caused me to smile. The best one was the day Dixie told me it was time for me to move into the house.

The minute I pulled opened the screen door, the smell of Dixie's cooking filled my senses. I headed straight for the kitchen to give my girl a kiss, since I hadn't seen her all day. Ethan and I had gotten up early this morning to get a jump on the fence and I didn't want to wake her.

Dixie's smile radiated through the kitchen as she turned her head and faced me. It warmed my heart to see her so happy. Maybe Ethan was right. Maybe I was the only one who could make her smile. Walking over to where she stood, I wrapped my arms around her from behind and kissed the top of her head.

"I'm going to take a quick shower," I whispered in her ear.

"Okay. Dinner will be ready in half an hour," she smiled.

As I took the steps two at a time. I thought about Ethan's question. *"When are you going to ask my mom to marry you?"* Truth was, from the moment she came into the sheriff's office, I knew I would marry her. As I walked over to my side of the bed, I pulled open the drawer to the nightside. Hidden in the back was a box that had been there for far too long. As I held it in my hand and popped it open, the diamond ring and its matching band inside reminded me of the love my dad had for my mother. I still remember the day my mom slipped them off her finger and gave them to me the day before she died. It was like she knew it was her time. The doctors said it was her heart. Personally, I thought it was because it broke the day my dad died. My mom was never the same after that.

After getting cleaned up, I slipped my mom's ring inside the front pocket of my jeans and headed downstairs. When I reached the bottom of the stairs, Ethan was helping Dixie set the table. I wanted to pull him aside and let him know that I was going to propose to his mom tonight, but based on the expression on his face, I had a feeling he already knew.

We all gathered around the table like we had every other night. I never thought in a million years that I would be sitting here a year later having dinner with the woman I loved and a family who would do anything for one another including me. If I ever had any brothers, they would be just like the five men sitting around the table—Briggs, Vincent, Reggie, Walen and Josh, in that order. They all knew how much I loved Dixie and also wondered when I was going to pop the question. Tonight was a good a time as any especially since they were all here. I wasn't sure how special this moment was. It definitely wasn't over a candlelit dinner with just the two of us. Dixie was the kind of woman who didn't care about all that fluff.

The lively chatter at the table fell into a hushed silence as all eyes turned towards me, except for Dixie's. Her gaze was fixed on Ethan, beaming with pride for her son. This was my cue. Slowly pushing my chair back, I stood up next to Dixie and took her hand in mine and lifted her from her chair. We were the only two standing, and it felt like the perfect moment.

Reaching into my front pocket, I retrieved the ring that had once belonged to my mother. A single diamond sparkled in the center, surrounded by delicate diamonds along the band. It was a perfect match to the wedding band that I kept safely tucked away in a drawer upstairs. As I held the ring up for Dixie to see, her eyes followed my movements before locking onto mine again. Tears of love welled up in her eyes.

"Until I met you, I never thought I could give myself completely to any woman," I spoke from the depths of my heart, offering a part of myself that no one else had ever seen. "But the minute I saw you, everything changed. You opened up something inside of me that I thought was locked away forever."

I paused, taking a deep breath before continuing, "When my father passed away, it broke my mother's heart. Their love was pure and unconditional. Before she passed away, she gave me this ring and told me to give it to the woman who I loved as much as my dad loved her." My voice trembled with emotion as I recalled the memory.

"She said that my heart would know when I found the right woman," I added softly, looking into Dixie's eyes with complete honesty.

With shaking hands, I held out the ring towards her. "Dixie Coleman, will you marry me?"

A radiant smile spread across her face as she exclaimed, "What took you so long?" She leaned in and pressed her lips against mine as cheers and clapping erupted around us.

When our kiss finally broke, I gazed into her tear-filled eyes, feeling more content and in love than ever before. "I guess that's a yes."

The End

ABOUT THE AUTHOR

Award-winning Author of the Independent Press Award and NYC Big Book Award, A.L. Long is also the National Indie Excellence Award recipient.

Some would call me a little naughty, but I see myself writing spicy thoughts. Being a romance writer is something that I never imagined I would be doing. There is nothing more rewarding than to put your thoughts down in words and share them. I began writing in 2013 and have enjoyed every minute. When I first started writing, I wasn't sure what I would write. It didn't take me long to realize that romance would be my niche. I believe that every life deserves a little bit of romance; a little spice doesn't hurt either. When I am not writing, I enjoy the company of good friends and relaxing with a delicious glass of red wine.

Visit me at www.allongbooks.com for all of my new releases and book signing events.

Keep up with all A.L. Long's latest releases:

FURIOUS PROTECTOR

VIA MARI

BLURB

Bodyguard Protector Romance
Touch Her and Die
Mafia Romance, Morally Gray Anti-Hero
Mafia Connected Billionaire
Spicy, Small-Town Feels

BECKETT

When trouble comes to Deadwood, and a certain skill set is needed, I'm the one they call.

I have one thing on my mind when I get to town, and it's certainly not a relationship of any kind.

Until the blue-eyed blonde catches my eye.

She is a force to be reckoned with on a good day, and the job isn't as easy as I thought it would be.

When Jules gets caught in the crossfire, she's going to learn the only protection she will ever need is me.

Furious Protector is the explosive fourth book in the Ruthless Guardians series by International Best-Selling Author, Via Mari. You will love these spicy, instalove bodyguard novels set in Deadwood, South Dakota, where the passion is fiery, the loyalty is fierce, and the stakes are high. Each book is a standalone featuring different couples. All have a guaranteed happily ever after.

1

BECKETT

I slide into one of the wooden seats at Wild Deuces, scanning the crowd as some clap for a dancer coming out onto the stage, while a few keep their eyes and minds focused on the game of poker they're playing on a machine, and still others remain engrossed in conversation over dinner and a beer.

The patrons of this fine establishment don't have a clue in the world that two competing mafia families both want this town for their own, and neither of them like to lose.

A woman with kind, gentle eyes and slightly graying hair taps me on the shoulder, holding her pen and pad at the ready. "What'll you have tonight?" she asks.

The laminated menu glares from the overhead light as I pick it up and point to the illustrated image. "That burger right there, it looks good. A friend of mine and a couple of guys from town said it was the best they've ever eaten. I'll order one of those, well-done with all the toppings with a big order of fries."

She smiles widely. "Any chance I know these guys?" she asks, writing down my burger choice.

I give her a grin, because I've already been warned about the grandmotherly Lettie with a heart of gold and life's goal of finding everyone in town their perfect match, and by their description this has to be her. "I'm sure you know the guys. Cole, Garrett, and Mason. I'm Beckett. I came to help them with Kenny's expansion next week here at Wild Deuces. You're Lettie?"

Lettie's eyes light up. "I sure am. And, good lord, if you are anything like those boys, then we're happy to have you in Deadwood. I know why you're really here. And consider your burger on the house. Any friend of those three is a friend to Kenny and his Wild Deuces."

She leans down and whispers in my ear. "And soon to be casino, hotel, restaurant and expanded dance hall with room for more live bands and danc-ing." She straightens, bubbling with excitement. "It's going to be the best expansion yet. Wait and see."

It's hard not to share in her enthusiasm, even with my limited knowledge of the entire plan. "How about if I have a cold beer to go with that burger while I wait for the guys? When they get here would you put a round of beers for them on my tab? Pretty sure they'll fill me in on all the work going on at Wild Deuces."

She beams. "I sure will. Don't forget to enjoy the late show tonight. Marla is doing a special number. People come from miles around to see that." She gives me a wink. "You know, Marla's single, and very, very pretty, and so nice. She works all day long as a florist and then dances here at night a couple times a week for the extra money."

I smile, but the last thing I'm looking for is a relationship. I've tried the settling down thing, and right before she said I do, she said I don't. That's not something any self-respecting man wants to hear again.

These days, it's no strings, just a few good laughs, maybe a drink and dinner before sex, but never, ever, let them get close enough to stay the night or invite them to breakfast. That's how you keep that shit from happening again.

Lettie returns balancing a humongous tray full of plates laden with burgers and fries. I grin up at her. "Do I look hungry?"

She laughs. "I have it on good authority that a crew of young men who've been working all day long are about ready to walk through that door. We treat our help well, Beckett."

I glance toward the front and true to her word, Cole, and two guys who must be Garrett and Mason stride through the entrance, quickly scan the tables, and make a beeline toward me.

Lettie doesn't miss a thing. "You pass out those plates and keep your fingers out of everyone else's fries. I'll be back shortly with some drinks." She starts to leave, but then turns. "Oh, that extra plate, that's for Kenny. His wife Eileen called and said he was on his way, but was still probably about five minutes out."

"You know a lot, Lettie."

She grins and gives me a wink before making her way back to the bar, stop-ping to chat with the guys before they finish making their way to me. I stand, shaking hands with each of them as Cole introduces us all. "This is an old and close friend of mine, Beckett," he says to the others. "He's worked with me on some jobs around the country after he got out of the service and before I came back to town."

Cole turns to me. "This is Garrett and Mason. The three of us work together keeping Deadwood safe, but let's sit, have something to eat and a cold beer while we talk shop. It's been a hell of a day all the way round. Kenny should be here in a minute. He wanted to meet you too. Everyone is a little on edge right now with the expansion so close."

We've barely been seated a couple minutes when a hefty man strides in through the front door. He gives a nod to Lettie who's back behind the bar, and she bustles out with a pitcher of beer and hands it to him. He gets a big grin on his face and brings it over to us. He pulls up a seat, folds himself into it, and turns his attention to me. "You must be Beckett. Cole's told us all a lot of good things about you. Thanks for coming."

"You're more than welcome. Any problem of Cole's is a problem of mine."

Cole pours each of us a glass of beer from the pitcher on the table, but I cover my half empty glass with a hand. "One's good tonight. Lots of recon and catching up to do later tonight."

Kenny swallows half his beer in one long continuous gulp before jumping right into the business side of our meet. "We had some bad news today. We're really glad you're here because we need more manpower than we originally thought." Cole looks to Kenny while the others dive into the burgers. "You want to bring him up to speed?"

"No, you and Beckett go back a ways. You tell him what's going on, we'll jump in if you miss something."

Cole nods and takes a drink of his beer first. "The last few years we've had trouble with the Chicago Crime Family trying to get a stronghold into the town, threatening and extorting money from local shopkeepers, and even shooting Kenny as an example to the people of the town to do as they're told. The Larussio family, who Garrett, Mason and I work for, hired us to keep the town safe from the Chicago Crime Family while protecting their interests."

Aside from keeping this town safe, they obviously want to keep the territory for themselves with revenues from tourism being so lucrative. What people don't know is that the Chicago Crime Family are longtime rivals of the Larussios and are not done trying to stake their claim.

Kenny and the Larussios, in a joint venture, are expanding Wild Deuces. Cole gestures to the large black tarp that just looks like a wall at the back of the stage with the dim lighting. "Behind that is the parking lot. They're expanding to almost double the size, putting in more slots, bars, sports area and a large stage."

Cole doesn't get any farther. Garrett leans over. "The ladies just arrived." We glance up to where he's looking and watch as a group of five sexy women walk through the door, scan the lounge before spotting us, and make their way to our table. Mason laughs. "Now that's a whole lot of trouble heading our way."

2

JULES

A night out on the town is exactly what me and my friends need. Cut up and let loose. It's been tense again the last couple weeks, knowing that Kenny's expansion, while it should be cause for celebration, is bringing danger back to town.

The minute we walk through the door of Wild Deuces, we spot the guys sitting at a table near the back. Lettie gives us a big smile from behind the bar as we pass her and head for the guys.

The minute we reach them, Lacy drapes an arm playfully around Garrett's neck, letting her long red hair fall over his shoulder. Cole grins as we all surround the men. He starts introducing us to the dirty-blond-haired guy with smoldering green eyes sitting next to him, the incredibly handsome as sin one who locks eyes with me.

Krissy goes to the other side of the table to stand next to Cole. He takes her hand and puts a protective arm around her. "This is my wife, Krissy,"—he gestures to Lacy— "and this is Garrett's wife Lacy, and PJ and Mason have been together since last year."

The stranger is still looking straight at me and my cheeks heat. I clear my throat, not usually flustered in the slightest. "I'm Jules and this is Patti, we've all been friends for, well, forever."

His lips turn up in a half smile. "I'm Beckett. Friends with Cole, and in town working with the guys for a while." I don't miss his eyes flitting over my tucked in tee but still, even though tonight is supposed to be fun, if they called in more of their kind, there's reason for worry. Trouble is brewing in Deadwood again, I just know it.

My chest tightens with the same angst that hits me every time I think about those no-good men coming back to this historic and peaceful town. "You're here to help with the trouble? The Eldridge crew?"

Beckett picks up the glass of amber colored beer in front of him. "Hopefully there is none, but if it comes knocking, I'll be here."

Those pipes he has for arms look like he could deal with a whole hell of a lot of trouble too. And damn that gravelly voice and those deep green eyes all to hell. Now I can't concentrate on anything else. Not even those bad guys who ten seconds ago I couldn't get out of my mind.

And that smirk of his does not help, not one little bit, at all.

I clear my throat, trying to come up with something witty to say. I am so not good at small talk. I gesture to the guys around the table. "This team right here, they've kept this town safe for the last few years. I seriously don't know what would have come of the little shops along this strip if they weren't here. Right Kenny?"

Kenny holds up his beer, his eyes sparkling with amusement, barely a help with the conversation at all. "Without a doubt."

Krissy gives me a Cheshire smile, takes pity on me and turns to Cole. "The ladies and I thought since you guys weren't going to be home early that we'd come out for a little fun while you men talk about everything going on."

She turns to Beckett. "It's so nice to meet you finally. Cole has told me so much about you. Our kids are with the babysitter, so if you'll excuse us, we're going to have a little fun." She kisses her husband soundly on the lips. "We're going to be at the bar harassing Lettie. Don't get home too late."

Lacy smooches Garrett's face and he grins. PJ just gives Mason a wink. She whispers to me as we walk toward the bar. "Beckett didn't take his eyes off you the entire time we were at the table. You better watch out for that one, Jules."

"Yeah, that one, he's pure trouble, with a capital T," I tell her, not mentioning that I can feel the heat of that stare penetrating right through to my skin every step that I take.

Lacy, Krissy and Patti slide into the high stools at the bar with me and PJ joins Lettie on the other side, helping her mix up our faves. I try to calm the racing anxiety from thinking about what it means if the guys are pulling in other bodyguards to help them watch over this town. My mind wanders, but the laughter of the ladies pulls me back to the moment at hand.

I watch as PJ and Lettie work together. PJ salts the rim of my big margarita glass, just like she does most Saturday nights. "Next week I'll help you out behind the bar. It's going to be packed. I hear people from the next county over are heading into town. The hotel is sold out for the weekend and the expanded rooms aren't even open yet."

The other ladies talk softly, and with the low roar of the crowd behind us, I don't catch it all, but all I have to hear is the name Eldridge Jr., and my skin begins to crawl.

No amount of breathing exercises or trying to think about something else is going to calm the nerves that name causes. These ladies don't have to tell me a thing. Trouble is coming back to Deadwood. The kind that Jake Eldridge Sr. brings when he wants something that doesn't belong to him. Land, property, gambling, and liquor licenses that are not his to take. Him, his son and their cronies are all too happy to take anything they can get their dirty hands on.

PJ sliding back onto the stool next to mine and the touch of her hand on my arm pulls my gaze to her, but my wandering mind has no clue what she just said. I don't need to tell PJ that though. My best friend in the world knows me far better than I know myself sometimes.

Her eyes fill with concern. "You've been off since we found out about the expansion for Wild Deuces, worse still since the scheduling of the grand opening. Nothing like last year is going to happen again, okay?" Her expressive eyes meet mine. "I promise."

I take a long deep drink of the refreshing liquid, hoping the top shelf tequila hits my veins and gives me a little of that liquid courage people are always talking about. I turn to her. "You don't know that. And I know you went through a lot too, but getting kidnapped, it didn't really happen to you. It's hard to get that helpless feeling to go away."

The look on her face almost immediately fills me with remorse. "I'm so sorry, PJ. I know you're just trying to help, and I'm trying just as hard not to need it, you know? Nothing too bad happened, but that sense of helplessness, like it happened once, it could happen again, and this time something bad could really, really happen. You know, those thoughts, they just mess with your head. I didn't mean to be such a jerk."

PJ puts an arm around me and pulls me to her. "We won't let it. We've all got your back, and you've got ours. All of us, besties forever. Besides, look at those guys over there, and the army of your tough-ass lady friends here. You and I both know the guys can kick some ass and are putting a plan together as we speak."

That makes me smile and even feel a little bit better. Krissy shuffles on her stool and leans her head around PJ. "I don't mean to butt in, but these guys are not going to let anything happen. This time, they know what we're up against in terms of Eldridge Jr. and his dad, and the lengths they will go to in order to get what they want."

She believes it, I know she does, but something deep down tells me that the Eldridge crew isn't going to back down that easy. "Yeah, you seem pretty sure."

Krissy takes another drink. "Cole is sure they're going to try something and since they didn't get what they wanted last time, they'll probably try harder in all honesty. But these guys know it. That's the advantage. Beckett has some extremely valuable special ops training. He and the guys can take care of any situation that arises. We have some highly skilled alpha bodyguards at our service," she brags, giving me a wink.

Patti giggles from her seat next to me. "And, that highly skilled bodyguard in those tight-fitting jeans is walking straight over to you."

3
BECKETT

My eyes don't leave the ass of the blonde until she slides onto that bar seat, and even then, I have a hard time getting my mind back to the business at hand. Mason nudges me. "If you're going to have a chance with Jules, you better have some pretty thick skin. That little lady says what's on her mind and means what she says."

I grin. "I'm pretty sure it won't be a problem." Garrett and Cole exchange a look that I don't miss nor have time to try to figure out right now. "Alright, you guys, let's jump out of my personal business and back into the reason you hired me two months post military assignment to jump into this gig. I had visions of dancing girls, bikinis, and the cool breeze of the ocean on my face for at least a few more months."

Cole clears his throat. "It was probably good the ladies stopped by. Now, you have a good idea why we want more men on the ground this time. Those ladies mean the world to us, and we're spread too thin next week if we're going to keep our eyes open at the expansion and our eyes on them."

Kenny nods. "I couldn't agree more. I don't want the expansion to turn into a bloodbath."

My eyebrows go up. "I may have misjudged the severity of the situation then when Cole called last week."

Cole knows exactly what I'm thinking. "Things escalated since we spoke. You were on the road, so I didn't want to bother you. Figured I'd bring you up to speed once you arrived. It sounds like the Eldridge crew, the ones who work for the Chicago Crime Family, have been quietly intimidating the townspeople again. We're just getting wind of it, and it's way more than one."

I don't like the sound of that. Cole's told me all about the rivalry between the Chicago and Larussio Crime Families and it's about ready to get pretty ugly from the way things sound. "The Chicago Crime Family just doesn't quit, do they?"

Garrett shakes his head. "They sure as hell don't. My wife, Lacy, and Eldridge Jr. have a rocky history. They were dating before I came into the picture. He and his father were trying to intimidate her into selling her family home so they could put in more casinos. She broke it off and the situation got worse."

Now I'm getting the picture. Same MO different town and different revenue stream. The Chicago Crime Family will try to take over anything for an easy buck and a cash flow they can control.

Mason's face is grim. "Last year, Jake Eldridge and his son had Jules kidnapped and tried to kidnap Lacy from her bachelorette party. We got damn lucky that neither of them were hurt, but Jules, she'll probably never get over the reality of that night."

My chest tightens at the thought of the petite little blonde at the mercy of anyone trying to do her harm. I glance over at the bar, and see her friend put a protective arm around her and coax a little smile.

"Let me guess. Everything's been quiet, but now plans for the expansion are announced, and they start the same stuff all over again, because the Chicago Crime Family doesn't like to hear the word no."

Cole points a finger at me. "Exactly. They stayed pretty low after Bobby Ray got locked up, but Sheriff Cates said people have been coming forward with minor complaints of intimidation, and this time, all of the impacted folks have businesses adjacent to Wild Deuces. They're trying to buy up the surrounding property again."

Kenny's face turns red. "They just don't stop. The neighbors have agreements with the Larussios but apparently, they were too scared to tell Cole, Garrett and Mason. They could have gotten word back to the Larussios and nipped this in the bud before it became a thing again. Now, the sheriff is involved, and it's more than a mess."

Cole turns to his friend Kenny. "There's always going to be a bully in every neighborhood who wants to take what's yours. And look what you've done to this place. It's the biggest and most sought-after place in town, the casino and restaurant is par none. Expand the hotel, add that dance hall and sound stage you've been envisioning and it's going to be even more spectacular than it already is. We're going to get this resolved."

"I'm just nervous about the grand opening, and my family being there, all the community members who will show up. I don't want anyone hurt and the Chicago Crime family is notorious for doing just that."

Cole puts his beer glass down. "The Larussios, they're not going to let them. That's one of the things we want to talk about; the men on the ground we bring in to help, where we locate the Eldridges and their men, and the strategic details of keeping everyone safe."

I glance toward the entrance as a flurry of chaos catches my eye. "I think they just found us. I'll take the right, the rest of you fan out and cover the middle and left." My feet start moving with the training that's been ingrained in them with eight years of active-duty service in combat situations far trickier than this. Those boys should do themselves a favor and get the hell out of town, but of course they don't.

Instead, one walks right up to the very blonde I've had my eye on all night and starts to pick a fight. Her blue eyes flare indignantly and the minute his hand comes up to grab her shoulder I intervene, grabbing his hand in mine, bending his arm all the way back to the point right before it snaps in two. "Tell the lady good night."

The asshole's mouth clenches and his eyes fill with hatred, but we don't put up with that behavior here and if he doesn't do what I say, he's gonna learn that lesson tonight. "Tell Jules good night," I growl.

He spits it out reluctantly because he wants to be able to use that hand and arm tomorrow. No doubt for more trouble that we'll have to deal with then, but for now, I march him to the door and make sure he leaves.

Garrett's got another guy well under control, and before too long, the others are marching their guys to the door and we're all watching them leave while the bar erupts in applause. We head back to the bar as the crowd simmers down.

Lettie sighs heavily, fawning over the ladies. "I was so scared my mouth wouldn't even open. I swear that never happens to me. Usually, I would have had something smart to say."

Cole turns to me. "They're getting braver. I'm going to call the Larussios. We're going to have to get Tommy and his boys, and maybe even some of the bike clubs they affiliate with in this area to help."

I nod. Not a bad idea. Not a bad idea at all.

The guys partner up with their women while Jules and Patti talk quietly with each other. I walk up to the two of them. "Lettie, how about another round for the ladies, and a Dr. Pepper for me."

Jules looks up at me with those blue eyes swirling with emotion. "So, it begins huh? Those thugs are never going to stop, they're just going to keep coming and coming until they drive us right out of town."

"Don't let it get to you. They're bullies and they'll back down when they know they can't be beat. You don't worry, because they can and will be beat."

Still, she doesn't look convinced. "I'm about sick of it already. Maybe that's what I should do, get out of town, quit dealing with their shit day after day, month after month. If it weren't for Cole, Garrett and Mason it wouldn't be safe at all. It was a great town until those thugs decided they wanted a piece of what Kenny has built. I can't believe they had the audacity to walk in here like that."

Lacy leans over the bar. "What do you want to make a bet that Eldridge Jr. had his hand in this, at least his daddy did, that's for damn sure."

Lettie puts a margarita in front of Jules, a fancy little drink in front of Patti, and hands me a glass of soda before handing out one after another to the others.

"Glad you boys were here," she says. "I don't know how good of a shot I am these days."

The blue-eyed blonde's eyes sparkle as she downs more of her drink. "Next time one of those thugs come near me, I'll put a shot in their ass they won't soon forget."

I smirk. This one here is pure trouble, and I sure do love a little trouble.

She turns her pretty little head and looks up at me with those eyes. "Did you hear me? Don't think that I won't."

I heard every single word, but yet it all went in one ear and right out the other because the moment I locked eyes with the hot little blue-eyed blonde with the sassy attitude and tight jeans, my mind was on one thing only, and it wasn't on keeping her safe, at least not from me.

"I have no doubt you would have put them in their place," I tell her. "But let's be sure this is behind us for the night. The guys filled me in on what's happened in the past with Eldridge and his crew. Finish your drinks ladies. I'm going to walk around outside and take a look-see. When we leave, I'm going to drive you both home."

Jules raises her eyebrows, but she doesn't say no. Not that I would listen if she did. No one's getting hurt on my watch, especially not the little sweetheart sitting next to me who's already more scared than she wants to let on.

She may want everyone to think she can handle herself, but the erratically racing pulse at the base of her neck, and the look in her eyes when his hand reached out, I saw them both.

Patti puts her cell down on the bar after pounding a message into its screen. I gesture to the phone. "You have someone waiting for you at home?" She shakes her head. "Nope, Jules and I have become the minority in town. Single, unattached and we like it that way. Well, except when things like this happen, right Jules?"

Jules lifts her head up from the fishbowl of margarita. "It's a tough job, but someone has to stay available and single these days. Give the single guys in this town someone to dance with."

A perfect in to take the little darling in my arms and make our own little space to dance right in front of the stage but keeping her and the others safe has to be priority one. At least for now.

I find Mason a little way down the bar sitting next to PJ. She's looking at me like she overheard the conversation from three seats down. Mason clearly did. He gives me a smirk. I grin at the look on his face. "Mind your business," I mouth.

He raises his hand as in surrender. "I feel your pain. I really do." He lowers his voice.

"That was me last year when I saw PJ for the very first time. Man, she was a beautiful mixture of fire and ice, all rolled up into one."

PJ turns and smirks. "I'm still fire. Bank on it," she tells him.

"I'm going to take a walk around. You want to help me check the perimeter?" I ask Mason.

"Copy that. You take the left, I'll take the right," he answers, giving PJ a kiss on the lips before we head to the door.

"Once we make sure things are okay here, and they're not still hanging around, I'll run Jules and Patti home."

Mason glances at his watch. "Copy that." Not one of us after the grueling training we've endured through the years, no matter which division we received it from, needs to be told to have each other's six.

It's ingrained in us, as if we were brothers, because whether we know each other well or not, we are. United in a mission, a plan to rid this beautiful town nestled below the green summer hills of the villains that want to claim and shed blood just like years ago.

The minute we're both outside, I unholster my Glock from the waistband of my pants. Something's not right. I can feel it without anyone saying a word. Mason feels it too, it's that sixth sense that gets real sharp when you're face to face with combat soldiers deep in battle, and you only have your senses and skills to keep you alive.

He presses himself up against the building, walking in one direction. I take the other way, getting our timing in sync with a single nod before we turn our respective corners, out of sight from the other with plans to meet around back.

I walk slow, careful not to make a sound, and when I get to the end of the building, voices let me know that right around that back corner, lurking in the dark, I'm far from alone. I strain to hear every word they say without making a move or uttering a sound.

"No, Cole and his boys were in the bar tonight. And their ladies just happened to be at the bar. We'll follow Jules home tonight after the guys have said good night."

My jaw hardens and my hand tightens around the Glock. When they get to Jules' place, they're going to have more than a little surprise waiting for them. Because no one, especially them, is messing with the little blonde.

Unless it's me.

4

JULES

The minute I finish my drink, Mason and Beckett return from outside. "Did you see anything?" Patti asks, having finished her drink some time ago.

"Enough to know that you two aren't going home alone tonight." Beckett looks to me. "You live in town, right?"

I nod, finding it hard not to get lost in those deep green eyes. "I do. I have a small A-frame just a few blocks away."

He's all business right now and looks at Patti. "And where do you live?"

Her eyes widen in surprise. "Umm, a little way out of town, but not that far, about a mile and a half."

"I'm going to take you both home. I'd like for you to stay with Jules tonight," he says.

Patti and I both give him narrowed eyes. "Ladies, it's for your own good, or I wouldn't ask. We'll make sure you're safe, but it's better if we keep you together. Especially if it's out of town, no matter that it's not that far."

The looks on the men's faces are grim. They keep their concerns to themselves. But I've seen those looks before. They don't need to tell me that if they're going to protect all the families, we'll have to double up to get enough resources to protect.

"Does that work for you ladies?" Beckett asks, no doubt wanting confirmation so he can finalize the plan with the rest of the guys.

"It does, and thank you." I turn to Lettie cleaning up behind the bar. "Why don't you come home with us? We'll bring a little of Kenny's booze and have a sleepover."

Lacy lays her face on the bar and looks at us from three seats away. "Am I invited?"

I stick out my tongue. "You're married!" It doesn't faze her a bit. "That doesn't mean I can't still have fun. Besides, Garrett and the guys aren't going to mind having us all in the same place. Probably easier to guard. We can all stay there."

She's not wrong and Patti gives me a little nod. "Sure, it sounds better than hanging out by ourselves." My mind races back to the way I left the kitchen, bathrooms, and bedrooms. Nothing too terribly out of place, just a little lived in. The arrangements will have to do. We'll make it work, just like in our younger days.

Krissy sighs. "The kids are already sleeping. I really don't want to scare them. Eileen and Kenny can come over to our house if you don't want us to be alone. Then you guys will only have two places to watch, and they can stay asleep in the comfort of their beds." She looks to Kenny who's joined in on the conversation.

He nods in agreement. "Sounds like a good plan. I'll call Eileen. I'm sure it won't be a problem for her to pack an overnight bag. I'll head that way and pick her up. I don't want her driving over alone."

Cole puts a protective arm around his wife. "Why don't we all go together, stop by your house Kenny, pick up your stuff, Eileen, and head for our house. Sound good, baby?" he asks, looking down into the eyes of a woman who clearly adores her man and has become a good friend to me.

Krissy gives him a reassuring smile. "It sounds really good." I don't blame her, not one little bit. If I had babies at home, I would be a nervous wreck, but she's doing a damn good job of keeping her cool under pressure. She's had to be with all that she's been through over the years.

The thought of her past puts things in perspective for me. Or maybe it's the alcohol of two margaritas streaming through my veins. Maybe it's both, but either way, I can deal with this. I can handle whatever those fuckers bring. There is strength in numbers, and we've got that.

The minute we hit the cooler air and the darkness, my bravado cools a bit. These men could literally be lurking anywhere. We're fortunate to have the protection that we do.

We walk out together and the men gesture to stay on the sidewalk as we walk around the building to get to the vehicles. Less than one more week until the new parking area is finished. It can't come soon enough for me, but at the same time, the whole expansion is what's drawing the Eldridge boys back into town.

"I'll give you a call when we get everyone safely at the house," Cole says as Beckett holds the door of a big F150 truck open and then opens the back passenger door too.

Patti grins. "You can ride shotgun, Jules. You know, since you two can't seem to keep your eyes off each other."

"Not true," I whisper hiss, my cheeks heating with embarrassment as I step up onto the running boards. Beckett holds my arm as I balance myself. I manage to pull myself into the high seat of the truck with some modicum of decorum, while he helps Patti gets into the back before closing the doors and heading to the driver's side.

I turn to Patti before he gets to the door. "What the hell was that? Some kind of friend you are! Zip it!"

She laughs, pulls out a compact, dabs a little powder on her face, and then playfully puffs the tip of the sponge on my nose. "There, takes the shine away. Gotta look good for Mr. Hunky Protector. I saw you giving him the eye."

"You have had way too much to drink. That's ridiculous. I was not looking at him like that, at all, thank you very much."

Beckett opens the door, gets in, and shuts the door and then buckles his seat belt. "Ladies, get your belts on."

I shouldn't have had that second drink on an empty stomach. I know better than that. Still, I don't need a boss, especially the smirking kind who I know damn well heard her little comment. "You're so bossy! And I was not giving you the eye, whatever that means."

I am not attracted to the attractive, out of town bodyguard, who will be here for a brief moment in life and then back to the city as soon as the enemies clear out. I am not attracted to those muscles, or that smile or those eyes, or that butt...

Beckett turns to Patti. "Jules gives off some pretty mixed signals. See, I thought she was giving me the eye, too."

My head hits the back of the seat, and I scrunch my eyes tight. Oh good lord. I'm gonna die of embarrassment.

Patti laughs softly in the back. One day, I swear. Paybacks are hell. The shoes will be reversed. I buckle my seat belt, still slightly mortified, my head swimming in a not so little buzz, woefully regretting not eating a thing today. "Alright you two. Enough fun and games," I tell them feeling the effects of alcohol flush my skin.

Beckett pulls out onto the main street. I glance over at him, and he's still wearing that sexy little smirk. But when I turn to Patti, she quickly puts her smile away and gives me a set of wide eyes, glassy with a couple drinks and a whole lot of mischief.

My head spins just from turning in my seat and my stomach slightly rolls as we hit a bump. "Take Main Street to the light, turn right, and then a quick left. It's not far," I tell him groggily, laying my head against the coolness of the window's glass to stop the waves of nausea that threaten to ensue.

5

BECKETT

The little chatterbox is out cold before we even reach her street. "How many drinks did she have?" I ask, looking into the rearview to make sure we're not being followed by anyone before we pull up to her house, because I plan to set a trap for them, not the other way around.

Patti glances up and her eyes meet mine in the rearview. "Just her normal two. She forgot to eat today, so that probably didn't help. Krissy's usually designated driver. Thanks for driving us."

"Yep, I figured as much. She's sound asleep."

"Ever since she heard that the Eldridges hired people to go harassing the townsfolk, she hasn't been able to sleep very well. You know what happened last year, right?"

The sideview and periphery look clear as I near her address. "I've gotten most of the story. She was taken by a guy from Eagle's Swallow, a bar on the outside of town the night of Lacy's bachelorette party and drugged?"

"Yeah, she said nothing too much happened, but they drugged her drink, and kidnapped her. PJ and Mason found her tied up."

My jaw tightens just thinking about it. "That's a far cry from nothing. I'm sure hearing about the intimidation going on in town and knowing what's happened and then those assholes showing up didn't help. Memories like that don't just go away."

"No, that feeling of being completely incapacitated has to stay with you. Don't you think?" Patti asks me.

"It doesn't go away quickly, at least that's what I've heard." I know for damn sure it's going to take more time than Jules probably thinks it should.

I pull into the driveway that Patti points to from the back. "Don't tell Jules I told you her story. She likes to keep it under her hat, says she's over it and that it's not going to get the best of her, but sometimes you just need to talk things out a little. Me and the girls are trying to get her to loosen up and let it out. Or go talk to someone. Instead, she just runs for hours and hours, punishing the pavement like it's to blame."

"Jules is a runner?"

Patti laughs. "You wouldn't think so with her height. Most of the fast runners have long legs but she's out there six days a week putting us all to shame. That's why she looks so damn good in those jeans."

That does explain just how good of shape she's in, and why when she walks, the lean muscles of her thighs can be seen rippling through her jeans. But I don't say that. It would imply that I've been looking pretty damn closely at the lovely little blonde who's now curled up onto the window of my truck.

I inch the truck up close to the door of the double car garage and put it in park. "Garret, Lacy, Mason, and PJ aren't too far behind. We heard something that makes us think the men who came into Wild Deuces are going to be coming here. You can bow out if you want, but the guys and I believe you are all safer if you stay here together."

"No way I'm leaving Jules. I'm in."

"I'm going to help you both inside before they arrive. I'm sure she'd rather not have everyone see her like this. I was just hoping to explain things to her before we got here."

Patti reaches over the front of the seat and places a comforting hand on Jules' shoulders. "The main thing is she'll be safe. I'm sure she'll appreciate you taking her in before everyone arrives. The rest of our friends would understand, but still, thank you. She's never done this before. I mean, she's seriously out cold."

The neighborhood is quiet as I get out of the truck and walk around to the passenger door. Jules' purse is tossed on the floor, and I hand it to Patti who's already hopped out. "You want to find her key and open the door so I can carry her in?"

She gives me a smile. "You gonna tuck her in? At least let me get a picture of you carrying her in? Something to hold over her head?"

I shake my head. "No, go unlock the door."

Patti laughs. "Fine, Mr. Killjoy."

She rummages through Jules' purse and holds up a set of keys. She strides out in front of me so she can unlock the door as I lift Jules into my arms. Her eyes don't even flutter, but she tilts her head, leans into my chest, and tightens her hold on my arm as the silkiness of her long blonde hair caresses my arms.

Patti holds the door open so I can walk in before closing it behind us and taking the lead. She quickly guides me to a back bedroom so I can lay Jules gently on her bed.

I cover Jules with the decorative blanket on the end of the bed, staring down at the blonde beauty before the sound of another vehicle pulling into the drive causes me to hurry back to the living room to make sure those bastards haven't followed us.

The curtains hang long and dark over the windows. I pull one back a little to take a look outside. Mason and PJ jump out of their truck and walk up the sidewalk just as Garrett and Lacy pull up behind them and quickly catch up with the others.

They give a quick knock on the door. As soon as they enter, the guys and I exchange a glance. We don't like having the women part of this, and there's no way any of us are leaving Jules on her own after what we heard. At least this way, letting them come to the house, we have the advantage.

Garrett clears his throat. "We brought the girls up to speed on the way over. They know we may have visitors and that we'll take care of them."

"Good." I glance around and not one of them seems nervous. These women are ready for whatever may come their way. Tired of the crap this crew has been giving them in their town. "Keep everything normal. Like you were continuing the party from the bar at home. Garrett, Mason, and I are going to leave. We'll be around though. We just want them to think we dropped you ladies off. Keep the lights on, laugh, and maybe turn some music on. You ladies have Garrett and Mason's numbers." I write down my cell for Patti. "Keep this for yourself and Jules. Just in case you need to get ahold of me."

Patti nods. She looks a little more nervous than the other two. "It'll be fine. Check on Jules for me, please? And see if you can get her to drink a little water, eat some food, and take an ibuprofen. She'll thank us in the morning after two rounds of tequilla on an empty stomach."

Lacy and PJ try to hide the smiles on their faces. I set the record straight as Garrett and Mason head out the door. "I'm just being nice, ladies. Now, if you'll excuse me, we have work to do. Try not to have too much fun."

The ladies are giggling as the door clicks behind me, and I double check that it locked securely before making my way to the truck. A quick, nonchalant glance around as I settle into the seat and pull out of the driveway tells me that so far, we're alone. But, if what the assholes back at the bar said is true, it won't be long before they arrive and all hell breaks loose.

Even mentioning coming to Jules' house has put the bastards on my kick their ass list. If they do anything more than show up, they're going to learn a thing or two about the skills that were taught to me courtesy of the good old U. S. of A.

The guys are up a short distance and I catch up to them quickly, following them as they make their way toward the highway. They know this area far better than me and when they must think we're far enough out, they slow, pulling off the road to park under some heavy branches that with a little finessing will provide the coverage we need to keep them hidden.

Garrett and Mason jump into the back seat of my truck, and give me directions around the roadways, navigating until we've parked ourselves around the block. Garrett points. "Right there, pull in. The Jones' are out of town. Pull in backward and back right up to the garage. No one will ever be the wiser. We can walk right through their back yard and come out at Jules' place."

It takes very few minutes to make our way across the well-manicured lawn and get into position. And we're just in time, as the fuckers from town roll down the street in a black, souped-up SUV and pull into Jules' driveway as if they didn't have a care in the world.

We wait, but my jaw is tight as we crouch in the brush, knowing we have to stay put until they actually engage that door, break a fucking law that will hold up in court. These guys are on a mission too. And it sure as hell doesn't take the fuckers long to smash the glass of the front door.

Or for us to spring into action...

6

JULES

The smashing sound of glass pulls me from a groggy sleep and into an utter state of confusion. The last thing I remember was being in the truck with the handsome bodyguard, Mr. Green Eyes. Another crashing sound at the door spurs me into action. I grab my phone and call 911, whispering to the operator while she asks me a ton of questions I don't yet have the answer for. "I don't know what's happening, but I think someone just crashed the glass at my front door and is breaking into my home. Get here fast, please?"

I hang up on the still talking operator, slipping the cell into the back pocket of my jeans, looking frantically around for anything that could be used for a weapon. I screw off the shade of an old-fashioned lamp to use the heavy steel column to crack a head or two if need be. I should be scared out of my mind but right now I'm just mad as hell.

The darkness makes it hard to see until my eyes begin to adjust, but even then, it's difficult to see more than a few feet in front of me as I make my way from the bedroom, padding down the hall toward the living area and angry voices.

I'll see what's happening and then go back to the bedroom if there's more than one of them. One of them, I can take. Two of them, I could try but would probably lose. With a plan, I step forward tentatively, peeking around the corner as pandemonium breaks the sound barrier of my usually quiet home.

More crashing glass and Lacy's scream makes my blood curdle. I know who's behind the door bursting of my home. Eldridge Jr. and his father's goons will stop at nothing. They didn't get what they wanted last year, so they're going to try different tactics this year. Well, getting to me is not going to make Lacy do what they say, no matter what, and they are definitely not getting to her.

Maybe earlier in the night I was ready to give up without a fight, tired and scared, but that was before I realized that I'm made of tougher stuff than that. And I may not have a gun, but those are my friends out there and before they get to them, they're going to have to go through me.

I step out just as three men from the bar stride toward Lacy and PJ. It's dark, and they don't have a clue what weapon I have or don't have. "You take one more move toward my friends and I will blow your mother loving heads clean off. Get out of my house and don't come back."

The taller one turns his deadbeat stare at me. My heart races with angst, because he's not buying my tough girl act. I don't know how I know it, but I know it. Then he confirms it, sneering as he takes a step toward me, calling my bluff. "Now, I'm going to show you what happens when people stand in the way of progress. All of you are coming with us. We'll see how fast Kenny sells then. That is, if he wants you back alive."

Three shadows move quickly. Garrett, Mason and Beckett fly through the door, attacking the men head on with fists flying, quickly overpowering them before pushing them to the floor. Mason pulls swaths of rope from his belt loop and tosses one to Garrett who ropes his man's hands behind him quicker than anything I've ever seen.

Beckett holds his guy tight, kneeling on his chest. He reaches for his piece of rope, wraps his hands and ties them into his belt loops so he can't use them to take a swing. The guy should just keep his mouth shut, but he doesn't have a self-preserving bone in his body. He glares up at Beckett. "You think you've won. They'll just send more meaner than us and those women, they're going to wish they had never stood in the way of progress. We're going to get what we want, one way or another."

Beckett grabs him by the jacket lapels. "Who sent you?"

The guy laughs and spits at Beckett. "That pretty blonde, when they come for them, she's going to be mine."

Beckett's fist clenches and he looks like he wants to send it smashing into that guy's face, but he keeps it under control. "You, my friend, will be in jail," he growls, just as the sound of sirens in the near distance begin to wail, and lights begin to flash through the curtains.

Beckett looks down at his foe who didn't anticipate them pulling in the law. "I'd suggest you make that one phone call count tonight. Tell them not to come, or they're going to have a war they won't soon forget."

Sheriff Cates and his two deputies rush in with guns drawn and the guys haul their men to their feet. Sheriff Cates personally slaps the cuffs on the one Beckett subdued, while his deputies take care of the other two, and then hands his guy off to another deputy who walks in the door. We got a 911 call. What happened?"

Garrett gestures to the men. "These men came to Wild Deuces earlier tonight looking to intimidate whoever was working. We sent them packing. The girls came here afterward for a drink and a little fun, and those men busted through the door."

Mason points to the man who threatened me. "This one says there'll be more. They aim to get what they didn't get before. They didn't give any names, but I'd put money on Eldridge being behind it."

Sheriff Cates' jaw tightens. "Read them their rights, boys, and get 'em loaded up. We'll have that conversation down at the station." They walk out the door and he turns back to us. "If they're with the Eldridge crew, they'll be lawyered up before we get 'em booked."

I try to hide the shaking of my hands, but Sheriff Cates turns to me, notices, and gestures to the lamp. "What were you going to do with that? Next time you call 911 you stay put. Stay wherever you were when you called. You and that lamp weren't going to get the best of three grown-ass men with a mission to overpower you."

I try to keep the emotion out of my voice, but after a couple drinks and the emotion of the day, my runaway mouth just has too much to say. "That's easy for you to say. I am not going to sit by idly while some creep bursts through the door of my house and threatens me and my friends. It's not going to happen. I did nothing wrong. Why don't you go chew their ass and leave me alone."

The older man's features soften. "Look, I know it's a hard pill to swallow, but we'll get them, okay? I'm just worried about you, that's all, Jules."

I know he knows what I went through, what we all went through, and he's just doing his job, but still, knowing that isn't helping this dam of emotion that threatens to burst one little bit.

My heart is beating so fast. I try to calm it but it feels like a runaway train. "They're coming back. Maybe not the guys you have in custody, but they'll send others, they said so themselves. And when they do, I swear, they better bring a whole fucking team because I will defend myself with any means I have. I will not become a victim again. Got that? If you don't do something, you'll have to lock me up eventually too."

Sheriff Cates blows out a breath. "We're going to fix this, Jules. Take a seat, ladies. I'm going to talk to the men outside." He gestures to Beckett Garrett, and Mason to follow him.

Lacy's eyebrow arches in challenge. "Whatever you say to them you can say to us. We're not fragile little dolls who are scared of our shadows. We just want to know what's headed our way so we know what to expect. That's more than reasonable. And the four of us have already talked about it. We're not running so that better not be the plan. This is our town, and we're not running and hiding while the people we love are in danger. Screw that."

Garrett puts his arm around Lacy and whispers something in her ear, and slowly her ire begins to calm. "Fine," she says grudgingly, coming to stand by me. "Let them go talk."

PJ walks over to us from Mason's side as the guys walk out the door. "Let him talk to the guys. They'll tell us what's going on once he's gone and we'll plan together," she says. "In the meantime, let's get this place cleaned up." She walks to the cupboard and opens the door she knows I keep the good stuff in. "I need a good whiskey, anyone with me?"

I shake my head. "I'm still feeling the effects from the two drinks at the bar."

Patti puts her arm around me. "Sit, I have strict orders from Mr. Green Eyes that I am to give you water, food and ibuprofen in that order."

The ladies pass an *I know what she's thinking* look between them. I point to the kitchen. "Don't you have somewhere to be?" I'm hardly in any mood for their matchmaking.

Patti throws her hands in the air in mock despair. "I'm going. I'll pop a few pizzas in the oven. Make myself useful. Besides I know you have some of those delicious pies from the high school fundraiser left. You bought enough."

Lacy nods. "Good idea. I'm hungry, too. Besides the guys can always eat, no matter that they ate those big-ass burgers at Wild Deuces. They must burn calories like crazy. I'll cut up some stuff to go with it," she remarks, heading to the fridge to rummage around before setting out cauliflower, broccoli, and carrots at the washboard by the sink.

Patti has barely had time to turn the oven on or pour a drink before all four guys walk back in with somber looks on their faces. Garrett gives us the news. "The Larussios are sending some of their men, Tommy and his boys. You met some of them last year. They're already in the air and will be landing at the strip in less than an hour."

Mason starts his spiel, but he doesn't get very far. "We want you to be safe, and..."

PJ narrows her eyes at Mason. "We're not hiding out somewhere. None of us want that. Please don't tell me that's your plan."

He puts his arm around her. "If I had my way it would be, but we can't take everyone in town with us and hide them. We need to be here to protect everyone, including all of you."

"So, what's the plan?" I ask.

Beckett grins at me. "Looks like you're stuck with me for a while. Consider me your shadow. Wherever you go, I go. You go to the bar, you drink with me, you want to dance, you dance with me, that clear?"

7
BECKETT

Jules looks up at me with those deep blue eyes, this time filled with something other than flirty invitation. There's a vulnerability but also a resolve that she doesn't want me to see. She turns to the sink, busying herself with helping Lacy wash vegetables while Patti grabs a few pizzas from the freezer.

She's been hurt, scared and fearful, but it's clear she's had enough of being on the receiving end of what these douchebags want to deal. I slide in next to her and Lacy takes the hint, drying her hands on the towel, nudging Patti towards the door, and giving me a conspiratorial wink.

I take the vegetables as Jules washes them and pat them dry before cutting them on the big white board next to me. I lean over while she's washing some broccoli and hold a piece of cauliflower that I've smothered with dip. "Open."

Her big expressive eyes meet mine with shyness that causes my cock to shift. "You need to eat, darling." She leans forward and takes the floret from my fingers, the warmth of her lips caressing my skin.

She chews and then swallows daintily. "So, I'm stuck with you?"

The little darling makes me grin because damn she's cute. I'm here to protect her as much as get to the bottom of this situation, and the only way to do that is to be with her 24-7. "Yes, you're stuck with me, like it or not."

Her eyes roll slightly upward, but there's a little tilt to her lips that lets me know she's not as immune to me as she'd like me to think.

Jules scoops some vegetables and dip onto a small plate and sets it between us. "This should hold us over until the pizza is done. My oven is old, it takes forever to heat but it was my gramma's. I hate the idea of replacing it," she states, taking the tray of vegetables out to the others.

Lacy and Garrett are moving furniture back into place. "Hold up, there's some glass shards way over here." I grab a broom and start sweeping up the glass while the others finish pushing the furniture that got tossed around in the scuffle back into place.

Lacy swipes her hands on her jeans when we're done and grabs a carrot from the tray on the table. "I was going to have a whiskey, but I better keep my wits about me if those fuckers are coming back. Water for me tonight."

Jules walks into the living room with Patti and overhears her. "I've got some bottled water out in the garage, I'll grab it."

"I've got it," I tell her, heading back toward the kitchen to go out to the garage. Not that I think anyone is hiding out, but still, she's not out of my sight until this trouble with the townspeople and the Chicago Crime Family ends. Even if it's in her own garage.

PJ laughs as I walk back into the living room, my arms full of bottled water. I missed the first part of the conversation, but it seems to have helped break the gloom. PJ pats Jules on the back. "Unlike Jules here, Lacy will fill them full of buckshot if they step a foot into her house. No lamp needed."

Lacy turns from what she's doing. "Damn straight I will. I've dealt with these fuckers before, and I'll show them just how good of a shot I am. They'll be running down the street with their asses on fire before I'm through."

Jules' face falls, and she quietly turns to head off to the kitchen alone. I follow her with two of the waters and set hers on the counter, waiting for her to turn around from the stove. I wait patiently, because she doesn't need to see me to feel me.

"Jules?"

Her shoulders shudder slightly, and my chest tightens knowing this night has been more emotional for her then she's letting on. I touch her on the shoulder lightly, turning her to face me. "What's the matter, darling?"

Her shiny eyes look up at me, and the realization hits me. I may have been captured by the way she looks in those tight-fitting jeans, but there's something far more than physical attraction zipping between the two of us, a chemistry that's different than anything I've felt before.

She averts her eyes as though suddenly embarrassed at our nearness or something else, and I don't know which.

I tilt her chin up, so she has no choice but to look into my eyes, and ask her again. "What's the matter, darling?"

She sniffs, fighting tears that threaten to flood her lovely eyes. "Lacy is right. She would have been prepared and been strong enough to fight them off on her own. She wouldn't have let some prick put something in her drink. She wouldn't have let her guard down, and allowed it to happen, and if it did, she would have done just what she said and taken care of him herself. She wouldn't have needed her friends to rescue her at the mercy of that fucking asshole."

My chest tightens with unprecedented anger, but that's not going to help Jules one little bit. She's still blaming herself for what happened last year.

I stroke a finger down the soft creamy skin of her cheek. "No one is going to hurt you. It is not your fault that Bobby Ray was able to slip something into your drink. They are trained and paid to do those things, and if he did it to you, he's probably done it to others. There's no way you could have known."

She turns away from me and fumbles with the pizza wrapping before popping two pepperoni with the works pies into the oven. When she turns around, she looks more resolved again. "I just can't help feeling stupid tonight. All I could think of to grab to protect us was a lamp, like that was going to help."

I stroke a finger down her soft cheek. "Those guys were never going to get near you tonight, but we had to let them get inside the house in order to get them locked up, and force Eldridge to send in the others. I gave Patti a heads up on the way home, but you fell asleep. I'm sorry I didn't clue you in a little sooner. If I had, you wouldn't have been in that position. I'm the one at fault here."

She sniffs. "Not your fault at all. I fell asleep. Not my finest night. Thanks for protecting us, and for staying. It means a lot. I'm just a little on pins and needles."

"Don't worry, Jules. We have the upper hand now. The Larussio boys will be here shortly, and they'll take care of the ones coming while we take care of you. Okay?"

Her baby blues are still glassy with emotion but also reveal a little bit of mischievousness that I'd like to get to know a whole lot more. Then her lips turn up into a sweet smile, all for me. "I feel like I should say sorry that you got stuck with me, but I don't really mean it."

I smirk. "Are you flirting with me, Jules?"

She flashes those blue eyes at me. "Maybe."

I snake my hand beneath her hair, fighting the desire to kiss her right here and now. Instead, I lean down and whisper in her ear. "Darling, you save that flirting for when you haven't had too much to drink."

She rubs a bare foot into the plush green kitchen rug. "I do need to eat. My head is sort of still spinning. It's the tequila too though. I swear that stuff messes with you, it's so much different than a light beer.

I push back a strand of her silky hair and tuck it behind her ear just as the oven light comes on. "That it does. Why don't you go shower up for the night. I'll get the pizzas done, and we can eat before everyone heads out for the night."

Her eyes widen. "Everyone is leaving?"

"Hey." I tilt her chin and meet her gaze. "They are, I'm not. I won't leave you. But go get ready now while everyone is still here."

She gives me a coy smile. "You don't trust yourself with a naked woman in the next room? Should I be worried about my virtue?" She pauses a moment as if deciding to say it. "Or maybe I'm just imagining the heat between the two of us?"

I smirk, grasping her hands and walking her back to the wall of the kitchen, caging her to the wall. She looks up at me with not a fear in the world, all aglow with those bedroom eyes that make me want to toss her over my shoulder and cart her to bed.

Business with pleasure is usually a no, a hard no, but with her it's just simply a hell yes. But not until she's a hundred percent on her game. I let my breath brush over the sensitive shell of her ear. "If you flirt with me tomorrow, I'm going to show you just how hot it can get, darling."

Her sharp little intake of breath and the rapidly beating pulse on the side of her neck tell me everything that I need to know. She is as affected by me as I am by her. No matter that I don't do relationships, that I don't usually mix business with pleasure, and definitely no matter that I am not on the market for anything other than a toss in the hay.

It's a physical attraction, that's all. A chemistry between two people that spark, it happens in life. That's what this is, nothing more.

I've almost convinced myself of that when her arms wrap around my neck, pulling my head down so close to her lips that I could easily touch them with my own. "I love that you're such a hardass and gentleman at the same time. Thank you, Beckett."

With that she unwraps herself and slips from the cage I've made from my arms, and walks out of the kitchen, leaving me to ponder the emotions clamoring in my chest.

This can't be happening. I don't do relationships, and that's a known fact. Yet, with her, maybe I could give it a try. If it weren't for the fact that she is a hometown girl, probably just looking for a way out and someone who will protect her from it all.

I would do well to remember everything that's happened, keep this runaway attraction in check because there's no way I'm going through heartbreak again, and the easiest way to avoid that is to stay detached.

Cool, aloof, and no strings attached.

But yet, keeping Jules protected from everyone but me is the only thing on my mind.

8

JULES

A hot shower dispels the grogginess, even though a cold shower is probably what I really needed after that sweet-talking man filled my ears with all those dirty thoughts. There is no denying he is the real deal, through and through. Any number of men would have taken full advantage of my flirty self tonight, without any thought or remorse.

I wrap in one of the body-sized cashmere towels that I received for Christmas from Krissy and Cole last year and comb out and blow dry my hair. The eyes staring back at me look a little glossy still. *No more drinking on an empty stomach.* Duly chastised, I put the finishing touches on my hair before heading to the bedroom to get changed.

Dressed in a fresh pair of jeans and tee, I pad barefoot into the dining room to find the gang sitting around the table with four pizzas, cut and in the center. Plates sit in front of them along with napkins. I glance at Beckett who gives me a smirk. "I told you I'd do just fine. Sit down and grab something to eat."

Lacy gives me wide eyes and chews the bite in her mouth. "You better do what the boss says, or he may just flip you over and tan your hide."

My mouth gapes. "Lacy!"

She grins and looks at Garrett who just shakes his head and tries rather unsuccessfully to keep the smirk off of his face. Lacy shrugs, wiping her mouth with a napkin. "It's not like anyone in the room can't feel the sparks flying off the wall between the two of you. Whew!" she says.

PJ averts her eyes, trying to stay out of the conversation, but Lacy's not one to keep her nose to herself and she doesn't want to be alone. She gently pushes PJ's shoulders. "Come on, can't you feel the vibes between these two? What do you want to bet that the minute we're out that door they're smooching away?"

Beckett gives me a smile and a wink from his seat across from me. He looks first to Lacy, then to PJ. "I have no doubt that if anything develops, you two will be the first to know."

My cheeks flame. "Sure, encourage them, Beckett. Now rumors will be floating all over town. Lacy and PJ will tell Lettie and then Lettie will tell every single person that walks through the doors of Wild Deuces bar."

"A good way to get a message to the Eldridge crew that you're locked up and protected. Right? Let them think what they want right now. We know the truth."

The butterflies in my stomach stop dancing and a lump forming in the back of my throat makes it difficult to swallow. *Beckett doesn't really want me...*

So, maybe I got ahead of myself, or maybe the green-eyed hunk has had second thoughts about a fling with me. Either way, it shouldn't hurt my feelings or my pride and I'm not going to let on for a moment that it did. "Right, let them think what they want. They don't need to know you're about as far from my type as you can get."

I grab a piece of pizza, place it on a napkin, and grab a water. "I'm heading to bed everyone. It has been such a long day. Stay as long as you like. You know your way out. Just lock up behind you."

I make my way toward the hallway, not needing to turn around to feel his eyes on my body, because they heat my skin right through. Lacy, what a big mouth. At least PJ could have stood up for me, but she just sits there quiet and smug. It wasn't so funny when they were attracted to their guys, was it?

I've gotten myself worked up into quite the tizzy by the time I reach my bedroom, and the door closes behind me harder than intended. *So, we're not a thing. I never thought we were a thing. Not really.*

But he did say tomorrow. Maybe I just read more into that little statement than he meant, maybe my traitorous body just wanted him to want me the same way I wanted him. Damn that second drink all to hell. I swear it's messing with my hormones and my senses. Especially where that green-eyed devil is concerned.

Either way... I guess now I know.

I finish my pizza and guzzle down the bottle of water before padding to the bathroom to brush my teeth. The minute I slide under the covers and close my eyes my mind wanders in a million directions. Sleep, I just need sleep and for this damnable day to come to a long and uneventful end.

Ten minutes later, I'm still awake. I plump my pillow and curl into it again, pulling the blanket over my shoulder, closing my eyes tight, and this time willing my mind to shut down and for sleep to come and let me drift away.

The smell of bacon permeates my senses as the succulent aroma wafts through the air. I slowly open my eyes and slip out of bed to get dressed and go investigate. Beckett is in the kitchen wearing a deep, dark blue pair of jeans and a black tee shirt this morning. "I didn't realize when you said you were going to hang out that you meant you were going to cook and all."

He grins. "The others stayed a while and then left. The night was uneventful, but I didn't expect anything to happen last night. I'm usually up early."

I slide into the bar stool across the counter. "Thanks for staying. I appreciate it." He plates the scrambled eggs and bacon and sets it in front of me.

I'm so hungry the aroma absolutely fills my senses and causes my stomach to growl. "It looks and smells delicious. I ate plenty of pizza last night, but I'm famished."

"Butter on your toast?" he asks as the toaster pops. I nod, caught with half a mouth full already. I swallow and smile, grabbing a napkin from the counter. "Yes, please. What a way to wake up."

Beckett turns and brings back a small plate with three pieces of toast and places it between us, sliding into the chair next to me. His leg brushes my thigh as his eyes lock with mine. "I could think of a better way."

My cheeks flame. Damn that man and his uncanny ability to knock me off my game. I meet his green gaze. "I don't know. This is pretty good. It would be hard to beat."

He takes a drink of his coffee. "I'd beat it."

I arch an eyebrow. "What happened to, 'Oh, it's a good way to get a message to the Eldridge crew that you're locked up and protected? Right? Let them think what they want right now. We know the truth.'"

Mr. Smug has the audacity to smirk. "Memorized that bit, did you?"

I narrow my eyes and chomp my toast louder than intended, averting my eyes. "Maybe."

Beckett puts his coffee down and pushes a piece of hair from my face. "Look at me," he coaxes.

Slowly, my eyes meet his again. "I wanted you to be able to drive the narrative, and not to have to deal with any pressure from your friends. Besides, what we do or don't do is our business alone. We don't need the whole friend crew to weigh in."

His finger traces down my cheek from where he's tucked my hair behind my ear and follows the gentle slope of my neck, causing desire to pool at my center as though he had touched me somewhere else. "Okay?"

I try to calm the racing of my heart, but it has a mind of its own. This man pushes every little button that I have. "Thank you. Sincerely, it was very thoughtful, and I took it the wrong way. My friends were just trying to get back at me for all the matchmaking Lettie and I have done with them over the years."

He grins that sexy little smile of his. "Finish your breakfast before it gets cold. We have a lot to do. I'll pop these dishes into the washer and then we need to get moving. We're meeting Sheriff Cates at Wild Deuces' back lot this morning to get a rundown of the event planning and the security plans for next week."

"We?"

His brow arches. "We. You're glued to my hip for the duration of the week. If my guess is right, Eldridge was the first one those boys called when they got to jail last night and more men are probably on the way. Tommy and his crew got settled in at Wild Deuces, but I'd like to be a few steps ahead of the Eldridge crew myself."

"A lot has been going on since I fell asleep."

He places his dishes in the washer and comes back for mine just as I pick the last bit of bacon from the plate.

I finish the last of my coffee and bring the cup to the sink and wash down the sink area and stove. "This really was delicious. Thanks for making me breakfast, and for staying to protect me. I try not to let what happened last year get to me, but clearly it does sometimes."

"The guys told me what happened. I'm really sorry I wasn't here then. You damn sure wouldn't have been dancing with that drug-giving cowboy."

It's hard not to blush because every nerve on the inside is quivering with every little flirt, but I try hard to conceal that bubbling desire. "When my mind starts thinking about it too much, I usually put on a pair of sneakers and go for a run to get my mind on something else."

Beckett's hand snakes under my hair, caressing my nape, drawing me closer, but not yet touching my lips. "Ask me to kiss you."

My cheeks heat instantly. The woman not usually at a loss for words is definitely at a loss now and drowning in his deep green eyes. He's so close I can feel his heart beating. That feeling alone gets me going like never before. It was going to happen since the first time I set eyes on this guy. "Kiss me," I whisper.

His lips caress mine, gently, coaxing me to part, exploring, sending shivers of desire right down my spine as the smooth-tongued devil takes my breath away. My hands find their way into his hair, stroking the back of his neck, pulling him as close as he can be, returning his kiss with a passion that I've never experienced before.

One hand stays under my hair while his finger explores the contour of my face. "I knew you were going to be trouble from the very first moment I saw you, darling."

The butterflies in my stomach dance with the desire of it all. It's hard to keep the smile from my face. "I guess you're not immune to my charms, after all."

He smirks and taps my nose. "I'm not immune at all. I just think there's a time and a place. You needed sleep last night, Jules."

I pull his head down to me. "You just scored even more points in my book. Thank you for being a gentleman." I kiss his lips lightly. "I'll go freshen up, grab some shoes and my purse and I'll be ready to go."

I spin to walk out of the kitchen, but he turns me around and draws me into his big strong arms. "One more for the road, darling."

9
BECKETT

The minute I allow her to come up for air this time, she looks right into my eyes, those baby blues lit on fire with desire. The same look I plan to put on her face tonight, because just kissing Jules is never going to be enough. I want her in the worst of ways and consuming her with my desire is going to be hard to get off my mind today.

But keeping her and this town safe is priority one, at least right now. I stroke a hand down her luxurious silky hair. "We'll finish this later. Go get your things, Jules."

I grab my duffle from the living room and tuck it behind the couch while she's gone, fold the blanket I used last night and toss it back over the couch before checking for messages on my phone.

Things are coming together nicely; we'll have the boots on the ground we need and a good plan in place to keep everyone safe and end the intimidation of this town.

The barrel of my Glock is pointed to the floor, and I'm making sure all is intact when Jules walks into the living room.

Her blue eyes widen at the sight of it, and she inhales a deep breath. "All this playing house let me temporarily forget that you're here for some pretty serious business. I don't know how much Cole told you about Eldridge and his crew, but they are about as mean as they come. They work for the Chicago Crime Family. They want to turn our gold-hearted town into another Vegas. Buy up all the real estate, the bars and shops. They want to run all the shop-keepers out of town and take over."

Her eyes track my movements as I move the Glock, until it disappears from her sight and is safely holstered in the waistband of my pants. The worry she's feeling rolls from her like waves. I close the distance between us, put an arm around her, and guide her to the door. "It's just in case. The hope is always that I won't need it, but I won't hesitate to defend the members of this town. It's what I'm paid to do."

Jules nods, but there's a part of me that wonders if she'll look at me differently now. It's one thing to talk about security and protection, it's another thing to see exactly how it's handled if it comes right down to using that gun. She wouldn't be the first woman who's shied away from a relationship with a man like me and probably won't be the last.

My jaw tightens. I'm not looking for a relationship, yet I've never had to remind myself of that fact before. Damn the little blue-eyed darling all to hell.

She's looking up at me and I get the feeling she's expecting an answer to a question I didn't hear. "Sorry, what did you say?"

Her lip purses in the cutest of ways. "I asked if you know the history of the town. You know, with everything going on between the Eldridge crew and the shopkeepers?"

"Cole's been keeping me apprised of the situation over the last few years, but I don't pretend to have a handle on it all yet. The Larussios have been dealing with the Chicago Crime Family for quite some time."

She nods and steps around a crack in the sidewalk. "That's what I heard."

"They've given them every chance possible to settle things in an amiable way, forbid them from stepping foot back in this town, and instead of keeping the peace, they send men to intimidate."

"It's going to get messy, isn't it?"

"There's nothing for you to worry about. I won't let anyone hurt you, but you can bet there's going to be retribution."

"A mafia war?" she asks.

We reach my truck. "Call it what you will, but we're right in the middle of it and we're not on the side that's going to lose. I don't plan on you or any of the townspeople becoming a casualty of a turf battle either. The Larussios have eyes and ears all over the place. We'll know before they get here when the Eldridge crew sets foot in town."

"Tommy's guy? The ones you were talking about last night?"

I may want to give Jules as much information as I can, and some is public knowledge, but information about the Larussio's inside people is not and I don't plan for it to be. Better to just avoid the question all together. "We usually stay on the perimeter of the Larussio work. We guard the family and for those of us in Deadwood, this town."

"Cole, Garrett and Mason needed more bodies after learning about the intimidation and already dealing with security for the grand opening. They didn't want to take a chance and the Larussios are done sending quiet messages to the family in Chicago who seems to have deaf ears when it suits them the best. So now they're going to be up against us and Tommy and his men." I leave out reference to anyone else.

I open the passenger door of my truck. Jules hops in and puts her seat belt on before I close the door. The neighborhood looks clear as I scan the area around us before heading around the back of the truck.

The minute I'm in the front seat, a black sedan that sure as hell doesn't belong sitting on the side of the road in this neighborhood, catches my eye down the street.

I pull out my cell and connect with Cole, putting it on speaker so I don't have to repeat everything for Jules. "Jules and I are just heading out from her house. I've got you on speaker. I'm gonna have a tail on my ass in about five minutes heading out to the highway. Can you send Tommy and his boys to pick them up?"

"Copy that. Jay, Matt and Damian just touched down too. They flew in to help. I'll have Tommy let them know to head that way. Hell, they may even all be together by now. I'm at Wild Deuces with Garrett, Mason, Lacy, PJ, and Patti."

I can feel Jules let out a sigh of relief just knowing that her friends are safe in the protection of the guys she trusts. I reach for her hand and give it a squeeze.

"Okay, I'm going to keep the speaker on overhead, and be driving right by them in about two minutes," I tell Cole, backing down the driveway and heading right toward the sitting car and Main Street that will merge with the ramp right out to the highway.

"Don't look at the car, no matter how curious you are, don't do it. Eyes straight ahead," I tell Jules.

She exhales a deep breath. "Okay, got it. Eyes on the road. Looking straight ahead." We pass them and they flip a U-turn in the middle of the road to get on our ass.

Jules turns to me oblivious of the tail. "Do you think it's Eldridge Jr.? I swear we were all so scared for Lacy for months. It's not just the land you know. He and Lacy were a thing for a while, and when she broke it off, he did not take it well at all."

The four-way stop causes me to grimace, but I give the brake a tap, check all lanes and then roll right through. I do not want that sedan any closer than it is. "I did hear that from Garrett."

"His father owned half this town until the Larussios set them straight and took over the shopkeepers' debts from those bastards. Now everyone is making a good living again, and things are going great. They're just jealous of how well Kenny is doing. When he first opened, that place was just a little bar with a few areas for some slot gambling. He has really turned it into somewhere everyone wants to be."

My eyes scan the road ahead of me and then check the rearview again. "They're not so much jealous, darling. They're ruthless and greedy. They saw what a gold mine this town could be and wanted it for themselves, and now that it's doing so well, they want it even more. Territory, money and power, that's what they want, and it comes in that order."

She sighs as I accelerate onto the open highway. "I just feel sorry for Kenny. Even the two biggest rival bars want to see him do well, because he doesn't try to keep all the entertainment and customers for himself. He's worked with the two other establishments in town and created a rotation for holiday fun."

"Is that so?"

"Yep, he says there is enough business for all three, so now they're all supporting each other. It's been pretty fantastic to see. And now, Eldridge Jr. and Sr. and their Chicago Crime Family want to just ruin it all."

It's not that I'm not listening, I hear every word Jules is saying, it's just that I'm more focused on the sedan gaining speed, and the fact that I don't yet see Tommy or any of the guys anywhere in sight as that sedan gets closer to our ass.

But then I hear it ... and so does she. A loud whirring noise overhead that's hard not to hear.

"Beckett?" Jules asks from her seat, glancing up and out the back window. I would hit the sunroof window and slide it open, letting her see exactly what's in the sky, but she's far more protected from debris with it closed.

"Eyes straight ahead, brace yourself and the airbag will do its job. The guys are here," I tell Jules, still keeping both hands on the wheel in case we get some of the heat from what I know my buddies are about to do.

The speed of the helicopter's rapid descent almost on top of the sedan behind us sends the sedan into a spin. It veers off the road, sliding onto the sand and gravel shoulder, screeching to a stop before landing sideways, the front end almost hanging off of the road.

My foot presses down on the pedal, keeping the truck accelerating, speeding to get out of the way because when the Larussios send a message, absolutely nothing is left to claim.

The men chasing us know it just as well as I do. They race out of the vehicle, scrambling down the ravine and into the tumbleweeded terrain. They'd rather get caught than to have their remnants scraped from the inside of that car.

They and I both know that helicopter overhead will be sending a very strong message back to their boss. Don't fuck with the Larussios. And when that grenade is tossed, the entire car explodes in the rearview mirror, lighting the sky with a streak of orange fire as the helicopter veers away from it and on to a mission to round up the escaping men.

Jules' breathing is coming fast and furious. I don't need a medical degree to tell me exactly what's going on. I pull off the road now that we're out of the radius of the blast and release her from the seat belt and pull her into my arms. "Come here, darling."

I coax her head onto my shoulder while shifting her light frame over the center divider and into my lap. "This thing is going to be far from pretty, but it's a necessary evil in order to get them to stop."

"They were after us? Me?"

"Afraid so." I stroke a finger down her face. "What I don't understand is why you? Out of all of Lacy's friends, why do they keep coming for you? They haven't come after any of the others."

She lets out a little sob. "I think they thought last year that I could get Lacy to change her mind about marrying Garrett or talk her into selling her grandma's house. But they clearly don't know Lacy. No one talks Lacy into doing anything that she doesn't want to, not that I'd even try. Eldridge Jr. probably just knows me better than most of her friends. That's just a guess though."

"Well, the men who followed us won't be bothering you again. Tommy and his boys will take care of that."

"Now I feel like a helpless little female, wiping her tears away while the big hunky bodyguard protects me in his lap. It's like a dirty little twist."

I kiss her lips softly. "You're not helpless, and I happen to like being the one to protect you. I'm all about dirty little twists."

"Ahh ... one of those me man and you woman types?" she jokes, wiping a tear.

I shake my head. "No, but I protect and take care of what's mine. I know you can do certain things, but I'm going to be taking care of you, at least while I'm in town."

Her sweet smile dims. She kisses me softly and slips out of my arms and back into her seat, solemn again, just as the helicopter lifts up into the sky filled with a plume of grey smoke. I don't have time to find out what's wrong with Jules before Tommy's voice comes over the line. "We've got all four of the fuckers. Heading back to town."

Cole jumps onto the line. "Sheriff Cates is going to want to be involved. I'll call him and get him updated. Better it comes from us in case someone saw us out here."

"Can't happen yet, Cole." I grin, not realizing Jay was up in the chopper. I'd recognize his voice anywhere. "We're going to drop these guys off along with Tommy and his crew. They'll get them to talk, and then you can bring Sheriff Cates into the fold."

My jaw tightens knowing what a predicament that will put Cole, Garrett, and Mason right in the middle of with the sheriff. Nothing is ever as straightforward as it should be, that's for damn sure. "Jules and I are going to head to Wild Deuces and we'll catch up with you and the guys there, Cole. Thanks for the assist, everyone."

"Roger that."

Jules' eyebrows raise. "You think they'll talk to those guys?"

"They'll talk." They won't be given a choice, but that's nothing that Jules needs to deal with or know anything about. "As soon as they do, the sheriff can lock them up."

"Then your job is done, you'll join your group, and life will go on. You'll leave this town and I'll be a memory of a good time."

And now I know exactly what's bothering the blue-eyed little doll.

10

JULES

I should have never kissed him, or asked him to kiss me, or kissed him again. Damn it all to hell. I knew there was more to this than physical attraction, no matter how much I wanted to deny it.

I'm not sure at all how I feel about knowingly jumping into bed with someone who's going to be piling into his truck and then saying goodbye just a short time later. But that's exactly what I want to do, damn the consequences. What if I don't and always regret never feeling his touch?

Patti's message distracts me momentarily. I glance toward Beckett who seems deep in thought. "Patti sent me a text to let me know her and the others are in the back lot, going over the stage details with the contractors."

I point to the side road right before the block that Wild Deuces is on. "Take a right here, and then the second left. There's a little out of the way place to park, and we can walk in from there. The secondary lot we used last night will be full of trucks for the job."

Beckett follows my directions and we've no sooner parked and reached the construction area than Patti, Lacy, and PJ walk out. "Where's Krissy?" I ask, scanning the group, seeing the men and Sheriff Cates by the other side of the parking lot. "And Lettie?"

Patti gives me a wry look. "Lettie's serving lunch today. She absolutely insisted, and Krissy is with the kids at home. Cole has a perimeter of Tommy's men making sure no one gets to either of them."

Lacy shakes her head. "I think if the guys had their way, they would like all of us ladies in one place, but they knew none of us except Krissy would go for it. If I had kids, maybe. But I don't and they're not bullying me out of my home or off the streets of my hometown. Not while I have a breath left in this body."

Cole, Garrett, Mason, Sheriff Cates and Kenny stop talking as we approach. Cole glances directly at Beckett, then me, and winks. "Sounds like there was an explosion just outside of town. Sheriff Cates sent a few highway patrolmen out to investigate but it doesn't sound like there's much left. And no witnesses at all, at least that we know of yet."

Cole opens the flap on the black tented area. We all follow him in, thankful for the reprieve from the heat of the sun that's already beating down with an intensity that's not likely to let up until at least six o'clock tonight.

I don't say a word, but the truth is bound to come out, right? What if someone saw Beckett's truck and Sheriff Cates questions him and he becomes a suspect.

My mind races with all the possibilities, until Beckett's hand folds mine in his as we trail behind the others. He leans down, puts his arm around my shoulder, and whispers in my ear. "Stop worrying, darling."

Not worrying is easier said than done. I've never seen anything like what just happened out on the highway in my life. And those men who ran, somewhere they're being questioned. Beckett doesn't have to paint me a picture. I know exactly how the mafia makes people talk. I've watched a movie a time or two.

Tommy, his men, and Beckett's friends are on our side though. That should make me feel better but still, the threat is hardly over yet.

I may not know Beckett very well, but he's kept me safe. I know he will protect me and I can trust him to do exactly what he says. Kenny and Sheriff Cates stop walking and Kenny points out different points of access to the stage, areas that will be important to keep safeguarded Saturday when it will be open to the public.

Sheriff Cates fills us in on his department's plans to secure the area, and we let him, but everyone besides him knows there's a lot more to this little planning session needed in order to keep everyone in this town safe.

And the Larussios are going to come in heavy handed. This could be so bad. A real-life mafia war in the lovely town of Deadwood.

Cole clears his throat. "I want to make sure no one feels obligated to do anything but stay safe. Krissy is going to stay at our home with the kids. We have plenty of rooms and anyone here is welcome. We have guards there to protect those who stay."

Staying at the stunning mansion he built just outside of town with a horse ranch to boot, knowing it is heavily guarded is not a bad idea, but I'm sticking with my original vote. "No, I'm going to work with Lettie at the bar on Saturday and then go home just like any other night. If she's not scared and cowering in her home, I'm not going to be either."

Beckett's jaw locks tight. "How about Jules and I talk, then round back with the group about her plans."

All eyes look to him and then to me, causing my cheeks to heat. His stare draws me toward it in challenge. I know things are a little different now that they've come after me again, and he's only trying to protect me, but I also have to stand up for myself.

I'm not about to put him on the spot in front of the other men, but I'm sure as hell not backing down.

I'll still be here when he rides out of town in that fancy truck of his, and I'm not hiding year after year. No, this ends now. They can come and get me right out in the open, because everyone knows I tend bar with Lettie and PJ on Saturdays now that it's gotten so busy.

If I don't show up, they'll know I'm hiding, and that won't stop them anyway, so why hide? No, I am going to face these demons and get them right out of my mind.

I turn and head back toward the truck, still mulling over the options that I had, not seeing one other one I could have taken. At least that doesn't make me feel like a two-bit heel, a coward hiding behind a man who's not going be here after a week.

I've barely reached the passenger side of Beckett's truck when he opens it for me and grabs me by the waist, lifting me right into the front seat. "Seat belt on, darling. Then we talk," he says, shutting the door of the cab.

I pull the strap around me, watching as he walks around the front of the truck and hops in, closing his door. He doesn't say a word but once he's buckled and we're back on the road, the silence starts to get to me. "I have to do what I need to do."

"And I'm trying to be understanding of that, while still doing my job. Right now, my job is protecting you and I can't do that if you're going to hang out in the very bar that is at the top of the list for these men to hit."

"I'll be fine."

His jaw tightens. "And you recall that is exactly what Kenny thought before someone walked into his bar and shot him point blank. Surgeries and ICU, and still he barely pulled through. Is that how you want this thing to end for you?"

I start to say something, but he's clearly far from through.

"That's not going to happen. Not on my watch. Not today, not tomorrow, and not next week at the grand opening. I'm going to keep you safe until all of this is blown over."

The emotion cracks my voice. "Yeah, until you leave, and then what? Then they come for me again, just like last year, and this year, and then again after you leave? No, I've had enough. I am not going to hide behind your pants when I know you're not going to be here to protect me in the future."

He starts to say something but now I'm the one to cut him off. "I'm sorry, Beckett. I'm not changing my mind. I'm going to work Saturday night with Lettie and if they walk in the door, I'll have to deal with whatever happens. But make no mistake, I am done being scared and being intimidated by those bastards."

11

BECKETT

I've always prided myself on patience, but this cold shoulder treatment all week has gone on long enough. Walking through the house on eggshells, craving the touch of each other but her always looking away because she knows I'll be leaving after the grand opening. We'll take care of business, and then just like any other mission, I'll be expected to be on my way.

It's all I've been able to think about. Her, this town, what I want from life. Right now though, I need to focus on keeping her safe through one more night, the toughest night.

"I know we've been through it a hundred times this week, but I don't want you to be at the bar tomorrow tonight."

Her eyes meet mine, and I already know what her answer is going to be. Time and time again it's the same. "My decision isn't changing, Beckett."

My jaw locks tight, knowing this is one of those arguments I'm not going to win. I'm going to have to find another way to make sure she can do the things she loves, feel safe doing them, and get rid of those bastards for good at the very same time.

The rest of the drive out to her house is awkwardly silent, battle lines have been drawn, and neither one of us is backing down, but I'm not leaving her unprotected, no matter that stubborn little streak.

I jump down from the truck and walk around to open her door, but she's already opened it and is half down. I scoop her by the waist and put her on the ground, tilting her chin so she has no choice but to look at me. "You can go to work, but you're not going alone. You can argue with me until you're blue in the face, but when you show up tomorrow, I will be there."

Her blue eyes flash with defiance. "That doesn't send the same message. They'll just wait until you're gone and try it again. I'm going for a run."

"No, it's too dangerous."

She gives me a glare. "I'm going for a run. I am not hiding. That is final."

I close the truck door and take her hand. "Come on. It's been a long day. Get your running shoes. We're going to get the energy run right out of us then."

She looks up at me and her eyes settle before she nods. "I really could use a long run. Are you up for eight miles?" she asks, her eyes sparking to life a little.

"More than ready."

She eyes me with open suspicion. "How often do you run?"

"Every day in boot camp, every day we could on the battlefield and every day since I've been home."

Her eyes soften. "How long were you in the service?"

"About eight years. That was enough."

I tilt her chin to mine. "Get ready while I make a call." The minute we're inside she heads into her bedroom to get changed while I rummage in my duffle for clothes, change, and then call Jay.

"We're at Jules' house and heading out for a run. Any chance to get some cover? If we're going to draw them out, I want to be the one in control of the play, not them. They know Wild Deuces too damn well. Out in the open, we can see them coming and put them in their place. I want to get as many of these assholes as we can before the opening."

"Roger that. We're not far, we'll have you in our sights the minute you walk out the door."

I rearrange my holster, tucking it under my tee, and slide a small piece into my ankle holster and a bud in my ear before she returns with her hair pulled up in a ponytail, wearing leggings and a tee that show off that lovely silhouette. "A little wager?" I ask, hoping to bring some levity to the situation.

Her head tilts, interested but still wary and clearly dealing with the situation at hand. I know she's scared. "I win, and you stay home tomorrow night?"

She doesn't even crack a smile though. "Sorry, not going to happen, plus I'm going to smoke you."

It's hard not to grin. Jules is as fearless as she is beautiful. She has a spirit I've seldom seen, fighting a yearlong battle with a fear that this situation has brought to the forefront for her again. I may want to protect her from the bastards, but I can't help admiring her strength and desire to slay these demons all by herself.

But still, she doesn't know these ruthless bastards like I do, and I'm not about to let her get caught in the crosshairs of a mafia war. The minute we hit the pavement outside, Jules starts fast, but not too fast, pacing herself, but sure as hell not slow. If she can withstand this pace the duration of the run, she'll impress the hell out of me.

I monitor my stride so that we're side by side, and I don't get ahead of or behind her. No matter what I said about competition, I want to be as close as possible, just in case leaving the house draws any of the assholes out. Because if I know them at all, they're either already watching us or will be soon.

The shadow of an SUV passes my periphery a little way into our run. My chest lightens knowing that Jay and the boys have got eyes on us, as well as the others. A few blocks up she veers toward a park and along it's green-treed perimeter making her way to the outskirts of town.

I can see why as soon as the path in front of us appears. It may not be anything but hard dirt, but it's clean and debris free, unlike the ground around it, as though it's been packed in with a four-wheeler or some other vehicle making the perfect trail.

I hate like hell that Jules is in the sights of the Eldridge boys, but better here when we know they're coming, have backup, and can do something about it than a surprise we don't see coming. Still, I don't like it one little bit. But I won't force her to stay put against her will.

I see two shadows dip behind trees up ahead. I'm not worried in the slightest, because they're on my side of the lane, and they'll have to get through me to get to her.

She picks this very moment to get competitive, pulling out in front of me with a burst of speed that takes me by surprise. It takes only seconds to adjust my stride and get in step with her, but it gives our attackers just the moment they need to jump out from the bush.

I've been ready for them since we left her house. I hear and feel them closing in, and my elbow goes back, smashing one bastard in the face before spinning while grabbing my piece to put the other in his place. "On the ground!"

Jules watches it play out, wide eyed and shocked. "What the hell are you doing back in town?" she asks the man still standing with a hand against his jaw.

She marches right up to him. "What do you want from me? I don't know why you think getting to me will get you any closer to Lacy. Lacy is married, very happily married I might add, and she is not about to sell her grandmother's house to you, not two years ago, not last year and sure as hell not today."

He sneers, but his beady eyes haven't left the butt of my gun. "Eldridge?" I ask Jules.

"Eldridge Jr., the one and only. Couldn't intimidate Lacy so he sent Bobby Ray after me last year. He didn't get what he wanted and neither will you," she says as she glares at him.

He glares back at her with sullen eyes.

She gets way too close to his face for comfort. "Why me? That's what I want to know. Why are you harassing me? I own nothing in town, I have no pull with anyone, no matter what you think," she tells him.

He shrugs. "Easier."

Jules' blue eyes go wide and her jaw tightens. "Than Lacy? Why, because she fights back?"

He shrugs again and smirks. I'd like to slug that smirk right off his face, but I don't even get the chance. Her foot comes out and kicks him square in the crotch, doubling him over with a hand to his groin before she sends her fist right into his face.

But it's not her hand I'm watching...

12

JULES

The minute Eldridge Jr. doubles over and I slam my fist into his face, I feel better. Not just a little better, but somehow vindicated like I got a little justice. No matter that Bobby Ray got a little stint up the river, it was this guy who was behind it all. And look who came right back to town to cause havoc in my life again.

Maybe this time he'll stay out and stay out for good, but if not, at least now he knows I'm not scared of him, I'm able to fend for myself. But I got way too close. His left hand comes out of nowhere, and almost snakes around my neck, except Beckett throws a punch to his face that lands him on the ground instead.

Beckett puts an arm around me. "Great job, Jules. He'll probably think long and hard before messing with you again," he whispers, causing me to smile a little through it all.

An SUV pulls up next to us and four men get out. Their tall muscular frames close the distance. The blonde man takes in the scene and glances directly at Beckett. "Looked like you had it handled. We didn't want to give our position right away, just in case there were others."

Beckett grins. "I'd like to say I took care of business all by myself, but Jules is the reason this guy is hanging on to his junk and will wake up with a black eye tomorrow."

The blonde bodyguard turns my way. "Nice to see you again. I remember you from last year at the wedding. I'm Jay." He points to the others with him. "This is Matt, Damian and Dereck. We had to leave Nick, Sheldon, Trent, Liam and Kade back to help guard the family."

I smile at the guys. "I remember you all. It's hard to forget the men who save you from what would have surely turned out to be a wedding crash by the

Eldridge crew. Nice to see everyone again. We appreciate you coming to town to help.

Matt has a pair of cuffs and places Eldridge's hands behind his back, cinching them securely as he hauls him to the SUV. Jay turns to Beckett. "We're going to get him turned into Sheriff Cates and then head down to Wild Deuces and see Kenny. Meet us there?" he asks.

"Maybe," Beckett says. "We need to run by Jules' house, get a few things straightened out, and then we may stop down. We'll take a nice easy jog back to the house. Want to follow us until we're safe inside?"

"Roger that," Jay replies, as the guys start to load up, surrounding the hand-cuffed man who glares at me as though it's my fault he's found himself in this position and the other one who hasn't dared make a move after being put to the ground at the point of the gun. *Only partly my friend. You should have stayed out of this town and away from me and my friends.*

My eyebrows raise. I have no idea what he thinks we're going to get straightened out. If anything, my resolve about Saturday night is stronger than before. And he's still leaving. But I swear if he kisses me, it will be over. I'll cave right in and another notch of one-night stands in that broad leather belt of his will need to be made.

And that's not what I want, or do I?

It's a question that sits heavy the entire way home as we jog back in perfect sync, and then stop a little way from my driveway, to walk the rest of the way and cool down.

The minute we are in the door I expect him to give me the third degree about not working tomorrow, or try to give me a little kiss, or at least something. But he does nothing like that. "Do you mind if I use the shower down the hall while you're showering in yours?"

"Sure." I try not to show my disappointment. I'm the one who doesn't want his advances. Liar liar. I want that man so bad my blood is on fire. But that means being okay with a one-night stand—okay—maybe a few nights' fling before he leaves. And he's giving me the distance and chance to make the decision myself. Damn his gentlemanly behind.

I reach the bedroom and kick off my tennis shoes, then pull off my socks, making my way to the bathroom, but taking a shower alone is far from what I want to do right now.

I want Beckett. His closeness, his protection, and everything that he has to give.

I know it, he knows it, and the whole damn town probably knows it by now.

Even if it's just for a short time. I want to know that man in the most intimate of ways. With my mind made up, I pad down the hall toward the sound of running water and give a little knock on the door.

There's no response and I gingerly open the door, my heart pounding in my throat. I'm really going to do this, to take the first step, come out of my timid shell and fight for what I want.

Beckett.

I draw back the shower curtain a little and his eyes meet mine, holding them captive in that abyss of green that just draws me in and keeps me mesmerized. "Room for me?"

His eyes heat as water drips from his hair. "Always, darling. I was just thinking about you all wet and soapy just a few steps down the hall and now here you are, like a dream come true."

My apprehension eases, and my inner rebel slowly comes out of her shell, peeling my running clothes, one piece at a time, watching the desire in his eyes until I'm bared before the man who takes my breath away.

Beckett holds my hand as I step over the tub ledge. He doesn't make this awkward or embarrassing at all. Instead, he draws me to him, his hand snaking beneath my hair as he kisses me hard, taking every breath I have and making it his own.

I shamelessly explore his skin while every stroke of his hands, his fingers, and lips make me melt and crave even more. When he lifts me, my legs wrap around him, securing him to me as we become one, lost in each other in a dance as old as time, until we both explode, riding the delicious waves of passion together, holding each other tight until every wave has passed.

No one has ever made me feel like this, and when our breathing calms, he doesn't put me down. Instead, he holds me tighter, kissing me through every emotion that swirls in my mind. I lean my head on his shoulder as he carries me out of the shower and gently holds me until my feet touch the floor.

He grabs a towel, partially drying me before I take it from his hand, wrap my body with it, then take another to stroke the water from his skin, working from top to bottom, right down to his feet.

When I rise, he picks me up and places me on the vanity counter. "Now, we talk. I have never been the relationship man, the one looking for someone to settle down and have babies with. I've been more of a ship passing in the night, a little fun and keep moving type of guy. We were never in one place more than a short while when in the service, so it made that lifestyle seem normal."

The tears burn behind my eyes, but I swear on everything holy, I will not cry. Not one little drop. I wanted this no matter what, and at least he's being honest and not stringing me along. He's been nothing but decent and kind. And it's not his fault that he's just not the relationship type. Hell, before I met him, I didn't think I was either. But somehow, that all changed while being protected by this guy.

His finger to the tip of my chin draws my face to meet his eyes. "Darling, you didn't let me finish before misreading the signals."

13

BECKETT

Her emotions cause my chest to expand with a feeling I'm not accustomed to. I've taken care of a lot of ladies in sticky situations, protected them from many things, but not one of them has gotten under my skin like the little blue-eyed blonde.

I kiss her lips, and towel dry the rest of her body, totally unaccustomed to being taken care of like that. I do the taking care of, yet I can't deny the intimacy of the gesture of her drying me has sealed itself into my heart, just like the little darling herself. But just the thought of what happened years ago causes my chest to tighten with angst.

"Just because I haven't done relationships doesn't mean I'm not interested. It's just new." That's the truth, but I can't bring myself to tell her about what happened before or to commit to anything more. At least not yet. But she's the only woman that's ever made the thought cross my mind.

"Get dressed, darling. We'll head to Wild Deuces and grab something to eat there while we catch up. Hopefully they've been able to get some information from Eldridge. Then we can come back and talk some more."

Her eyes tell me everything she doesn't. She regrets letting herself go, regrets the moments in my arms, and is looking for far more than I can give. A man who moves around from place to place, going wherever there is a need has nothing to offer a woman like Jules. Because for her, I would want to give her everything. For her, I'd build a white picket fence. But I get the sense she just wants me to take her far away from all of this. And to what? Moving from town to town, wherever trouble goes?

She walks out of the bathroom, and I let her go. Jules needs space and time to process everything that's happened recently. Her emotions have to be all over the place and for one second, I let myself regret taking her at all. But that feeling is short lived. Even if just a short memory in the future, it will be the best one I've ever had.

The minute we reach Wild Deuces, Kenny and the guys wave to me from the back, and she catches sight of her friends talking with Lettie at the bar. "I'm going to join the ladies. Is that okay?" She's not being sarcastic in the slightest. Jules has seen first-hand just how dangerous these men can be and is trusting me to take care of her.

"It's fine. I'll be watching," I tell her, giving a nod to Jay, Matt, Damian and Dereck who are sitting at different tables not too far away. "We're in good hands, and my eyes won't be off you."

Leaving her at the bar, knowing how she feels, still reeling from the silent treatment of the ten-minute drive is hard to do. I should have said more, but hindsight is twenty-twenty and right now, there's work to be done.

I make my way through the throng of tables scattered throughout the establishment to a seat at the back table next to Garrett. "How is the intel going?"

He shrugs and takes a sip of soda. "Lots going on. Jay and Matt said Tommy and his men got some information from Eldridge. It corroborates what we learned before about the Chicago Crime Family sending others, but we don't yet know how many for sure. But you were right, our inside man confirmed that after you sent the first one to jail, the Chicago boys sent more guys and they're on their way."

"How are we in terms of manpower if they send an army?"

"Well, my friend, if they send an army, we're screwed, and if they don't, we're going to shut them down before they make it through the front door."

Lettie arrives with a huge laden platter of nachos piled high with beef, onions, olives, cheese, sour cream and guacamole. "Now that looks delicious," I tell her, taking all the little plates from the tray for her and passing them around.

She puts the platter in the center of the table, fills our water glasses, and gets her pen and pad of paper out. "What else will you have to drink, Beckett?"

We all know these men are either already here or will be soon and not one of us including me wants to be off our game. "Dr. Pepper, please."

"I thought maybe you might want a glass of milk to cry over."

My eyes meet the kindly older lady's, who looks a little harder at me now. "Come again?"

"Jules is one of the nicest women I know. You leave her behind and you're going to be crying in your milk for the longest of times. The chemistry between the two of you can be felt by everyone around."

Clearly, she talks to her friends but doesn't say a word to me. I probably deserve that in all fairness. I'm not accustomed to airing my laundry in public, especially intimate stuff, but I also don't want my friends or hers to think I treated her like a piece because that's simply not the case.

"Jules is special. Too special to be following me around the countryside, chasing every bad guy that comes out of the woodwork. She deserves someone who can give her a house, that white picket fence, and babies if that's what she wants. Security, maybe it's old fashioned these days, but it's important to me. I don't want her to miss out on that."

Her eyes narrow, and she places a hand on my shoulder. "Honey, Jules isn't looking to follow you out of town. She wants you to stay, to put roots down here." She gestures to the rest of the guys. "You'd have some pretty good company if I do say so myself."

I smirk at the matchmaker who's been in my business since the moment I stepped into this club. "Oh, yeah. You think the Larussios are just going to add yet another guard to the town. And what about Marla? I thought you had the two of us pegged for a couple?"

She laughs. "That thought went out the window the minute Jules walked in the door and your eyes were like glue on her behind. No, that type of chemistry comes once in a lifetime." She looks at Cole. "You fix this now, hear?"

He grins as she bustles away back to the bar. "Good lord, you've gone and gotten Lettie all stirred up. She is not going to rest until I offer you a job."

The glass of water in my hand stops midway in the air. "Come again?"

The whole crew laughs. Cole piles some nachos on his plate. Don't you dare tell Lettie that's exactly what we were going to ask you about tonight with or without her interference. She likes to think she has the ultimate influence, and we let her think just that."

Now it's my time to smile, looking from one to the other. "You're serious? You need another man out here in Deadwood?"

Garrett puts his drink down with a thud. "Damn straight. These assholes just don't back down. Year after year it's something new, some new angle. I wouldn't put anything past them. Until the Larussios and the Chicago Crime Family have it out. For good."

Cole clears his throat. "We need more men if they want us to protect this territory. We've all talked about it and agree. We'd love to have you. The Larussios won't bat an eyelash Beckett, so if you want the full-time job, just say so. And Lettie's right. Some things are obvious. You and Jules? When it's right, it's right."

I point to all of the smiling faces around the table. So all of you are under Lettie's matchmaking spell? She's forced you to ask me to join you in protecting the town."

They laugh. "Seriously, it's a good fit for everyone," Garrett says. We'll get you to town and then work on Mason to pop the big question to PJ. Then we'll see if we can get Patti and someone paired up."

Mason grins and looks at me. "It'll be good to have someone else they can bug the hell out of instead of me. I'm working on plans for PJ. I want it to be perfect."

Across the room, Jay stands up and looks out the window, and all conversation stops. His hand slides to his cell and I answer the call before it's had time to ring. "Trouble times three just rolled into town. Three black SUVs with about four men in each."

My blood pumps hard knowing we'll have to keep vigilant every second now. These men don't mess around. "Where are Tommy and the guys?"

"A couple of them are still getting information from Eldridge, but I think we have our answer now. Tommy and most of his boys are protecting Cole's house and are positioned around Main Street. They've got their eyes and ears open."

"Where's Kenny? The minute he finds out those guys are here, he may try to take things into his own hands. A lot of people could have seen them drive by," Cole says from across the table.

"Do you know where Kenny is?" I repeat into the phone for Jay.

I nod, listening to him for a minute before relaying the info back to the group. "Roger that," I say into the phone before turning to Cole. "He and Eileen haven't left your house and your kids. Don't worry. We've got them covered."

Jay stands a minute longer and then takes a seat. "Doesn't look like they're coming this way. They're heading out of town, probably to the outskirts. Probably Eldridge Sr.'s old place if I had to guess. Tommy will keep an eye out. In the meantime, let's finish the plan and go hang out with the ladies. Tomorrow is going to be a long-ass day."

14

JULES

Beckett and the guys join us at the bar. Cole puts his arms around Krissy and reaches around her to snag a french fry. She turns to look up at him and smacks his hand playfully. But that look between them, there's no denying they were meant to be.

It makes my chest tighten. It's only been days since Beckett came to town but deep down inside, I know it's the same. This invisible draw between two people that pulls you together like it was always meant to be.

He slides in beside me and his thigh brushes mine as he settles onto the stool. He looks down at my almost empty plate with only one chicken tender and a couple fries left. I smile feeling shy all of a sudden. "I was hungry."

Those green eyes shine bright, and he turns to whisper in my ear. "I'd love to make you hungry every night, darling."

My cheeks heat, and I swallow through the embarrassment of it all. "Now who's giving off some mixed messages?"

The overhead music begins to play, and it's a song that I like by the talented Chris Stapleton. He gives me a smile and then takes my hand. "Lettie, save our seats," he tells her, half dragging me off of my stool.

"Wait, there's no dance floor," I start, but he's already guiding me out to the front of the stage and onto his makeshift floor. "There's always a place for a couple falling in love to dance, darling," he says taking me into his arms.

The butterflies in my stomach dance and the blood in my veins begins to race. "Say that again, Beckett ..."

"I said, there's always a place for a couple falling in love to dance, darling."

He swings me around gently and tilts my face to his. "And I am definitely falling head over heels in love with you."

My arms snake around his neck, and I draw him down so I can whisper in his ear. "I have news for you, cowboy. I'm already head over heels in love with you."

His wide grin melts my heart. He holds me close and swirls me as Stapleton croons out that heart-jerking love song. I hold him tight, never wanting to let him go. "Take me home, cowboy."

His arm stays protectively around me as we walk back to the others. "Alright, back to your regularly scheduled show and gossip. We could hear you talking about us all the way out on that dance floor," Jules says.

Lacy laughs. "It wasn't us. It was Lettie. All Lettie." PJ nods. "Definitely all her. Patti grins at me and gives me a wink but throws a nod toward Lettie too.

I narrow my eyes at the little matchmaker we all know and love. "Well, you got your wish. Now, if you will excuse us, we're going to head out. Don't you all have some place to be other than in our business? Isn't there bodyguard work to be done or something?"

Beckett leans down and whispers in my ear. "Let's go home, darling."

15

BECKETT

The guys skillfully contain their smiles, and I have no doubt the ladies will be texting her the minute we walk out. I wrap my arms around Jules and walk protectively toward the door with her by my side, already knowing that Jay and at least two others will not be far behind. For whatever reason, Jules is the target. She has been the focus of their efforts since day one, and I'm not about to let my guard down for a minute. No matter what.

Not one soul follows us home. I'm sure they're out at the old Eldridge estate planning an attack on Wild Deuces tomorrow, and no matter how many times I bring it up, Jules is still insistent on tending bar with her friends.

It takes effort to hold my tongue and not argue the point. It's clearly something she needs to do, and hopefully doing it will help her clear all of the emotion away. Show herself and everyone else that she's not afraid and she's going to fight back with all her might. No matter that I don't want her anywhere near that fight and want to take it on myself and keep her out of the light.

But I have to remember it's what she needs to do, and as much as I'm here to protect her as a bodyguard, as her lover, I'm here to protect her emotionally too. And that comes before all else. But letting her walk into harm's way is not going to be easy to do.

The minute we're back at her house she tosses her purse on the couch and heads to the refrigerator for a couple bottles of water. "I'd offer you a beer, or a wine, but I overheard the ladies say you were all drinking soda and water.."

Small talk... The little chatterbox is nervous. I don't plan to let that stop me in any way. I walk over to her and set the waters down. "Let's save those for later. Right now, I want to leave off where we were on the dance floor. With you in my arms, telling me you've fallen head over heels in love with me, while I carry you to your bed and have my evil way with you."

"A devil with a smooth tongue."

"You're about to find out just how smooth, darling."

"Oh, my lord, I think I'm going to combust right here," she says as I scoop her up, sliding my hands over her tight-fitting jeans. She clenches her legs around my waist and settles against my groin, nuzzling her lips into the sensitive area of my neck while I walk her to her room.

This time, we're going slow, no matter the fires that ignite. I plan to draw out every single tremor and moan that I can, bringing her over the edge, time and time again.

When I lay her down and peel her clothes, she looks into my eyes, completely bared, a treasure worth more gold than I've ever seen. "Mine," I growl, starting with her toes, caressing her calves, and then her thighs before lowering my head.

Her moans send shock waves through my core, urging me on as we ride our passion, one touch, lick and thrust at a time. And when she grabs the bedsheets and screams my name, I know that sound, this memory, will be with me for a lifetime. And so will she.

Jules dozes off after I've cleaned her up, lying in my arms for hours as I listen to the gentle pattern of her breathing as it caresses my skin. I'm not sure how I ever thought I could fight this. From the minute I saw her, she was always going to be the one. Maybe I didn't know it but everyone else did.

Mine ... in every sense of the word. That's what I want for us.

I never thought it would happen to me, made every effort to avoid it, yet Jules' sweetness snuck right through my defenses and tore every wall I have to shreds.

Jules is strong. She battled the emotional challenge of dealing with last year's attack and came out fighting stronger than ever. Eldridge Jr.'s balls can attest to that. What's most amazing of all is her willingness to trust. To put her trust and faith in me. Maybe that's what really gave me the courage to put myself out there. Seeing her fight through her own demons and win. She doesn't see herself as strong, but she is so very wrong.

She curls against my chest, and I caress her soft cheek. "Mine," I say into the night. I challenge anyone to even think about coming near my golden-haired darling, because I protect what's mine and she is going to be mine for an eternity.

And tomorrow night, I'm going to make damn sure everyone and their brother knows it.

16

JULES

The eyes looking back at me in the reflection are happier than they've ever been. If someone had told me a week ago that I'd be in love and floating on a cloud I would have laughed. Maybe that's what getting shot by Cupids' arrow really means. I mean it seriously just came out of nowhere and shot me in the heart.

Beckett is in the living room when I come out. He gives me an appreciative glance as his eyes scan down the length of my tucked in tee and well-fitting blue jeans. "It's a good thing my job is keeping an eye on you tonight."

I grin. "Funny." I glance at the clock on the wall. "We really should get going. I'd like to help Lettie arrange all the new glassware Kenny had brought in for the occasion. PJ usually doesn't get done with the horses until late and then comes in to help after that."

Beckett's eyebrows raise. "What does she do with horses?"

I grab my purse as we head to the door. "She works for Cole. I didn't realize you didn't know. She loves animals and they have a pretty large and growing horse farm. She used to work at Kenny's until she moved over to the ranch. Now, she just works on Saturdays to give Lettie a hand. PJ is a fantastic bartender. She can make drinks I've never even heard of but her real passion is horses."

Beckett places his shoulder around me as we head for the truck and opens the passenger side door before helping me up. "Can't change your mind about tonight, huh?"

I smile. "Nope, but you can keep your eyes on my ass all night long. I won't be offended at all."

He grins before shutting my door, walking around and pulling himself into the driver's seat. "I hope for Kenny's sake this night goes well, and we've covered all the access points to the event. I'd hate for Kenny's grand opening to be trashed just because we missed something."

"Or for someone to be killed?" I ask, buckling my seat belt as he backs up the drive.

"I didn't say that."

"I know, it's just that it's happened before, and Kenny almost died. That's why the Larussio family hired Cole to stay out here in Deadwood. I just don't want to see something like that happen again. You know?"

"We'll do our best to make sure nothing happens to your friends, Jules. I promise you that."

I turn to him. "Just make sure you protect yourself, please? It's taken me a very long time to trust someone enough to love them. I don't want you to go and get yourself killed now that I've decided you're the one."

He stops the vehicle before turning out onto the street and kisses my lips. "Nothing's going to happen to me. I can't tell you how many battles I've been in, in the fields and on the streets. Different locations but not so different when it comes right down to it."

Beckett heads down Main Street toward the grand opening and everything is lit up and blinking. The new vertical Wild Deuces sign that can be seen from a long way back is more than impressive.

"Hang tight, Jules," Beckett yells, pressing his foot to the pedal on the floor and swerving out of the way as an SUV almost rams us from behind. "Where the fuck did you come from?" Beckett yells. "Hold tight and keep yourself braced," Beckett instructs as another SUV comes barreling down the road right toward us.

Beckett veers off the road and swerves into the bike lane as the SUV skids and then screeches to a halt right in front of the club. Men jump out with large guns, but that's all I can see before Beckett shoves my head between my knees. "Stay there, do not move."

I can't help but peek though. He grabs the gun from his waistband, slowly opening the door. "Do exactly what I say and do not move. Not even if you hear shots."

I hold my knees tight to stop the trembling but soon my jeans are soaked from the tears running uncontrollably down my face. Please Lord, let him be okay. Let this be over with fast but still, shot after shot rings out, shattering glass and screams fill the air of the street, until finally the only thing I hear is the unnerving quiet of an unknown fear.

My body is shaking so hard but there's no way I'm staying here trembling like a coward when Beckett and my friends could be out there hurt. I open the passenger door as quietly as I can, stepping down from the running boards trying not to make a noise or move that will draw attention to myself.

I've barely made it around the back of the truck when a solid band of arms wraps around me from behind, closing off my airway with a terrible squeeze.

"Now we'll see if Lacy is a good friend or not, won't we? Will she trade herself for you? I guess we'll soon find out," the man growls.

My breathing is erratic, and I know it has to be slowed. My mind drifts to my self-defense classes without even realizing it. And when I've finally got my breathing patterns under control, my right knee comes up, and I drive the heel of my foot backward, right into the bastard's groin.

He yells, letting loose of my neck for just a brief moment, but it's long enough to get an elbow into his face, and one strong kick to his gut. The momentum pushes him back, just long enough for me to run. My speed is my friend, but I listen closely for sounds behind me. I round the corner and only then peek back to see how far behind the guy is. But Beckett has a gun pointed at my assailant's head.

I can't hear what they say, but the man drops to his knees, and a few minutes later Sheriff Cates screeches onto the scene with lights blazing. I walk toward him and Beckett and look my assailant in the face. I've seen that face before, but I don't remember where. Some time ago, as though he has been following me for a while.

"Where's Lacy?" I ask Beckett, scared to death that they may have taken my friend.

"She's safe and with Garrett. We had the back completely sealed off and our snipers saw these guys coming but we were in their line of fire."

Sheriff Cates looks from Beckett to me and to the perp on the ground. "Someone want to fill me in?"

Beckett shakes his head. "This man attacked Jules. He was sent by the Eldridge crew. You'll have to ask them why. Jules protected herself and I kept him at gunpoint until you arrived. I don't know anything else," Beckett tells him.

Sheriff Cates nods, taking notes and talking into his walkie talkie, issuing orders to his deputies to come and help him clean up the mess. "It seems like every time one of you city boys comes to town we have a mess on our hands.

"I'm getting mighty tired of it, myself, but Kenny says if it weren't for you boys, we'd have a whole heap of trouble from the Chicago Crime Family, and they're well known around these parts. Let's do whatever we have to do in order to keep them at bay," he remarks, pushing the assailant into the back seat of his car.

Beckett looks at me. "You and I are going to have a little conversation about what it means when I say stay in the truck, no matter what."

My eyebrows arch in challenge and I may roll my eyes just a tad. "You were in danger, Beckett. I had to try and find you."

"Don't you roll those baby blues at me little darling. You are in trouble with a capital T."

17

BECKETT

I don't think I've ever been so scared in my life. The moment I looked toward the truck and saw Jules running for her life and a gun in that man's hand my heart almost stopped. If I didn't already know that Jules is the one for me, I damn well know it now. The prick is lucky Sheriff Cates arrived when he did, or I would have broken every bone in his worthless body.

It's clear Jules has gotten her power back, whether I wanted her in danger or not. She would rather put herself in danger to help me than to hide in that truck where I told her to be. We walk across the street, avoiding some of the shattered glass from car windows.

I hold her close, still processing just how close she was to that man and just how lucky I am.

The entire lounge is clearly in the know having bore witness to the shootout in the street. We're met with rounds of applause, cheers, and whistles as we walk through the door. Kenny and Eileen smile ear to ear as they hold hands by the bar. I can only imagine her relief after going through Kenny being shot a few years back. Kenny bangs a large glass on the bar. "Drinks are on the house!"

Jay, Matt, Damian and Dereck gather around as Kenny and Eileen watch on until the cheers from the community begin to die down. Jules gives me a shy kiss and joins PJ behind the bar while Lacy and Patti keep them company.

The gesture sure as hell didn't go unnoticed by the guys. I raise my hand in surrender. Better to come clean rather than to be badgered all dang night. "It's a thing. You know when you said when you find the one, you know it? Well, it's happened to me. Jules is the one. Now, can we skip the razzing?"

Damian laughs. "Oh, there's no skipping that. I'm going to have to get on the phone and call everyone and let them know. Pretty soon you'll be getting it in the form of texts, calls, social media and us to boot."

"Great," I say ruefully. "But on a serious note. Thanks for all the cover out there.

If the offer is still open, I'd love to take you up on moving out here and taking the job working alongside you guys. It's a great place to live, put down some roots and raise a family. I've never had any of it before, moving from place to place like the wind. It's time to settle down."

Cole slaps me on the back. "Hell yes, it's still open. We're happy to have another skilled person on deck. I threw it out to the Larussios and they were all in. I'll let them know and one of their people will get ahold of you with a comp package. You won't be sorry. You'll be surprised at just how good it is."

"That's great. I have a pretty nice nest egg saved up. Money's not much good in some of the places I've been. It's just been piling up over the years. Jules tells me you have a horse ranch outside of town. I'd love to come by and see it. I'll keep my eyes and ears open for anyone interested in selling property. I'd love to have some horses of my own."

Cole, Garrett and Mason all laugh at the same time. Mason gestures to Cole. "Cole and I were just having the same conversation. He and the Larussios own more land than Cole knows what to do with. He bought up a ton just to keep the Chicago Crime Family from running a new casino strip right through the town. He's going to sell me some acreage and I'm going to build a house." He looks around. "It's a surprise though so keep it under your hat."

Garret taps Mason on the shoulder. "We're still waiting for the wedding bells. Mason's a little slow on the draw with the wedding ring for PJ."

Mason laughs. "Not slow, just methodical. I want everything to be perfect. She loves the land and horses. She loves working at your ranch, but I want her to be able to have some of her own, too. Not that she doesn't love working for you, Cole, but it's not the same as having them yourself."

Cole nods. "I don't take one bit of offense. I've got enough land for both of you. You go out and take a look around at the parcels we discussed, decide what you're looking for and we'll sit down with some pen and paper. As long as it's clear the stipulation is that if it's ever sold, I get first rights to purchase it back. I'm not ever letting anything happen to this town."

When Mason glances over at PJ tending bar, their eyes meet and the look that passes between them tells me that the wedding proposal may be in the near future.

Maybe next summer we'll have ourselves a double wedding.

Thank you for reading this story, and for supporting the Deadwood anthology. We appreciate you so much! I'm most known for my novel-length steamy romances, but love writing these shorter romances too. You can find them all on my website.

Xoxo, Via

ABOUT THE AUTHOR

International Best-Selling author, Via Mari likes to keep her readers on the edge every step of the way, fanning themselves as the action unfolds and the heat rises. Her books, no matter the genre or subgenre, exemplify extreme romance and feature the most handsome, intense, powerful men who will stop at nothing to protect the women they love.

KILLIAN
LORDS OF KHAOS: DEADWOOD

K.O. NEWMAN

PROLOGUE
KILLIAN

The din around me was thick as pea soup, everyone had an opinion, afterall. The news played in the corner, volume too low for the humans that filled the majority of the space, but my eyes are on the two men in the corner looking more conspicuous than they thought.

On the television, a news anchor was reading absolute bullshit off a prompter. "What do you bet she ain't human," Knox grumbled, taking a long pull from the beer that had been sitting in front of him for over an hour. Not like we had any place to be. "Can you see that twitch every time she says something about shifters being put in their place?"

"Mafia, ten o'clock," I growl back, shifting myself to face where the rabbits in the corner are huddled together, black shades and suits done up too tight. "We got more problems if they're settling here too."

"Just as stuck as we are, if I had to guess." Ranger's signature drawl was even deeper now that we were drinking. Not that his cat could get drunk, his tolerance was higher than the average shifter. "What's the plan, boss man."

"Settling," I lifted one shoulder in a shrug before tipping my own bottle of beer to my lips and killing the last of it. "Nothing else we can do."

"Registration?" Maddox hissed, cracking his knuckles and gnashing his teeth. Badger felt trapped, and I couldn't blame him.

Coming up to South Dakota was my idea. A fucking stupid one in the wake of the Lords being outed as shifters thanks to a little grizzly getting tangle up with some government assholes with more ambition then sense. The borders slammed shut behind us just days after we rode out from the Denver clubhouse. Four fucking shifters didn't a full club make, but it wasn't like we would be able to head home, not in the foreseeable future.

"States have been tasked with making their own laws when it comes to shifters moving around. Some saying that they want none inside their borders, others calling for reservations for the animals, restricting their movement even further."

"Deadwood's gonna burn if the Dakota's choose to round us up." Ranger leaned back in his chair, hands lacing behind his head. "Ain't no one know how large the supe population is here."

"More magic in this town than human," Knox agreed, killing his own bottle, and dropping it on the table hard enough that I can see cracks up the side. "Humies ain't half the stiffs walking around."

"Doesn't mean anything," I mumbled, running a hand through my hair. "Especially if the bunnies are invading," I hissed as the two from the corner sidled up their way up to the table. "Don't want no part of your business, rabbit."

"Not looking to recruit you," one said, leaning against the table with both hands. He towered over the waitress who was scuffling around trying to clear bottles from between us. "We have no beef with Lords," he sighed. "Look, I'm Rupert. We just want to clear the air."

"Ain't nothing to clear," Maddox rasped. "Your kind stole from us."

"Not part of a burrow," the other rabbit sighed. "What the Vermont burrow did wasn't right."

"Oh, really?" I stood, my chest pushing against Rupert's, knocking him back a full step. "Cause what I know about your lot is that what went down with Holly was par for the course." I raised a brow and waited for a response, what I got, shocked even me.

"Ain't what you think." The bunny's eye ticked as he looked around the bar, like anyone could hear what we were saying under the conversation that filled the room to capacity.

"Looks to me like the mafia is trying to take Deadwood," I growled, bumping up against the man again. He didn't even resist, just let me push him around, and that made something in my brain twitch. "Not happening."

"Ex-mafia," he whispered just loud enough that I could hear him. He looks around again and leans in close. "We left," the bunny confides, "Shit that went down in Vermont wasn't kosher, not even with bunnies. Dude was way out of line. With all these new laws, we're just trying to start over. Far as we know, we're the only rabbits in the Dakotas. We slipped by while the word of border closures was happening."

"Feels like we all need to start over," Knox grumbled, hiking his finger over his shoulder to where the news lady was looking a little pale as she continued to read from her prompter. "Ain't none of us getting back to Colorado, not soon."

Nodding, I drop back into my seat and sigh. "Need roots here," I muttered, running a hand down my face. "At least for now."

Another round of drinks was left on the table, the waitress giving us all side eye. The scent of discomfort and fear wafted off of her as she made her exit without her tray. Didn't take eyes off of me until she was behind the bar again.

"Too many lies circulating." I tipped back my beer, letting the liquid flow down my throat. "Drink up boys, we got a ranch to invade."

∼

The sun was setting as I tossed my saddle bags down on the ancient twin sized bed, it was still made with the old Lightning McQueen sheets that mom had bought me for my tenth birthday. The comforter puffed out a lungful of dust as the leather bags settled in place. The entire room looked like a fucking shrine to my childhood. Nothing had changed. Shelf filled with trophies from little league, the battleship that I spent a summer piecing together, even still had the unfinished paint job, and so many stuffed animals that it looked like a fucking zoo.

My butt hit the mattress with a groan, sinking down until I was practically sitting on the boxsprings below. Plugging in my cell, I dropped it on the bedside table, and took in what I was stuck with.

"From clubhouse, to farmhouse," I muttered, pulling my hands down over my face. My beast was antsy under my skin, animal needing shit I couldn't give him. "Fuck."

The knock on the door was just an empty courtesy as Ranger opened the door and came in without my answer. He took one look around, I could see the humor in his eyes as he folded his arms over his chest. "What did the boss say?" he asked, sitting down hard on the bed opposite mine. "Have a bit of a Disney obsession?"

"Mom did," I grumbled. Everything needed to be stripped from my childhood room. Fuck me. "Prez said we might as well set up shop," I grunted, trying to not curse, not with the little ears that were still downstairs with my sister, making dinner. "Way the policies are being written, means that no shifter will be leaving the state any time soon. No supe movement from one territory to another. Not yet, anyway."

"Always meant to set up my own workshop," Ranger locked his hands behind his head and leaned back against a framed Toy Story poster. "You're most senior here, means you're Prez. Congratulations on the newest expansion chapter of Lords of Khaos. Lords: Deadwood. Has a ring to it."

"Need a vote," I murmured, picking up an old bear stuffy and pressing my face into the soft down of the creature. Deep down, almost unreachable was the sweet jasmine scent of mom. Tucked down in the depths of the stuffie's fibers, she still existed, and that alone started to settle my animal.

Knox breaks the moment, by pushing my door all the way open, until the knob bounces off the wall. "Voted," he practically shouted. "You're Prez." He siddled into the room, dumping a bunch of pillows off the end of the bed, and dropped down next to Ranger. "Fuck, it looks like the cartoon network exploded in here."

"Probably did," Maddox stood there, legs crossed as he leaned against the doorframe, picking his nails with a switchblade. Fucking psycho.

"Can't stay in this house," I nodded, pressing my face into the palms of my hands, trying to block out the riot of colors that filled the small room, along with the press of dominance from my brothers. "Too many innocences under this roof."

"Especially not with the bunnies sitting at the gate, looking for refuge." Maddox flipped his knife closed and stashed it somewhere. Man had more weapons stashed on his body than anyone I had ever met. Not to mention the claws and teeth his human skin hid.

"If I'm Prez, your ass is Sgt at Arms," I growled as I stood up, cracking my back as I stretched.

"Naturally," Maddox called from halfway down the hall. That asshole was going to get us in trouble. "Bunnies at the gates," he reminded me from the third floor landing. "We're going to need more than a few bedrolls in the attic."

"No shit," I grumbled, taking the front stairs two at a time, and strolling out the front door. "Shit."

Rupert and his friend waved from down the drive. I just shook my head and pressed the clicker to open the gates to the men and their bright yellow jeep. We were so fucked.

1

BIRDIE

Soft music played through my single earbud, but it was doing nothing for my pounding heart. Every noise around me made me jump, every unlit corner, any shadow out of place. My brain felt it was on guard twenty four seven, even in my sleep–if you could call what I happened when I closed my eyes sleep. I have never been so happy to see the end of the school year, than I was this year. Boxes filled the floor behind my desk as I moved things from the classroom into storage for the summer.

"So much for summer fun," I sighed, leaning back on one of the beanbag chairs that made up the silent reading area of my classroom. The ceiling above was painted a white that had gone yellow with age, darker places still showed though where there had been water damage a few years before when a particularly nasty storm came through and damaged the old roof. "Can't even be alone in my classroom without jumping at fucking shadows."

I pulled a handful of books off the shelf and sorted through them. Fanning the pages to see if any were torn or missing. By kindergarten, most kids had been taught book etiquette. But not all. Setting aside copies of Peter Rabbit and the Velveteen Rabbit, I took a long deep breath, pressing the open pages to my nose, and taking in the scent of nostalgia. I loved the smell of books, so much that my mother had been flabbergasted when I told her I wanted to teach kids. In high school I was voted most likely to be a librarian. My best friend Madison had been voted most likely to be stalked by a jilted lover. Oh how the hands of fate come down to completely screw with us. She was the elementary school librarian, and I was jumping at shadows.

Pulling down the sleeves of my shirt to cover the thick ring of bruises that circled my arms, I shivered. Vince wasn't there. He wasn't watching through the first floor windows of my room, or hiding behind the trees that circled the playground outside. He couldn't be. But still I looked between the shadows, trying to capture any shapes that were out of place. Magic could hide him practically in plain sight. I had learned the tells though. After all, I wasn't safe if I couldn't sense his particular brand of sorcery in the air, if I hadn't been taught to look at the places in between.

Madison made as much noise as she could, entering my room. Her little ballet flats stomped on the laminate flooring with little smacks. My five foot nothing best friend did all she could to put me at ease, even imitate an elephant when entering any room. She would do anything for me, but couldn't keep the impish smile off her face while she did it.

Dropping down onto the beanbag next to me, she stretched her arms up high, pushing her tits up as she arched her back. Lashes fluttering at me. "You hear the latest?" she asked, thumbs moving over her phone at lightning speed.

"With shifter affairs, or from the cops?" I asked, tipping my head to try and see her screen. Cops hadn't said shit, and the bruises on my wrists were just the beginning. Tylenol was barely touching the pain that radiated from my back where he had seared a poker into my skin, lines of burns that radiated from the nape of my neck down over my shoulders like macabre wings, or the pull of the stitches from just inside my hairline. Split heads bleed like a fucking bitch. I knew from insider experience. Fifteen stitches from my temple to my ear. The wound didn't hurt as much as it itched anymore. But the pull of the stitches burned when I smiled.

"I was talking about the shifter shit, but now that you mention it," Madison sat up and dropped her phone down on the carpet and leaned into me. "Vince's shop has been dark all week."

"Fucking supes," I sigh and drop my head back. "I need to get my stuff," I groaned. Two years of stuff. Clothes and furniture, and so much more.

"No you don't. You are going to stay away from that place until the police have finalized their investigation." She made eye contact with me until I could almost feel her searing her will into my soul. "Then you're going to get a judge to grant you a restraining order. Things can be replaced, you can't be."

Investigation wasn't even about the abuse he had been inflicting on me. No, that he just washed away from the cops minds as soon as I reported anything. Did the same with Madison, and my mother. The list goes on. Two years. Two lost years where I was scared and trapped and alone. Ironically, magic had gotten me out, the same way it had kept me caged. A quick protection pouch from the local pagan bookshop had released every memory that Vince had ever blocked, flooded my friend's brain. Guilt had been the side effect I hadn't anticipated. Too bad mom hadn't lived long enough.

"Earth to Birdie," Madison whispered, poking me gently in the shoulder. "You went somewhere."

"Just thinking," I shook my head. "Your pants are too tight, and short, I need my own things." I lifted my leg up to demonstrate. "Like five inches too short."

"But they're safe," she said, tugging at my foot until it dropped back to the ground, her legging still hiked halfway up my calf. "And capris are in. Plus, they aren't at the psycho's house, yeah? Nice safe, magic free pants."

"I'm getting a draft."

"Did Serenity say anything about withdrawals?" my best friend looked at me with worry crinkling up her forehead. "Cause, she said magic can be addictive."

"She's got me on a full regiment. Everything from sage infused water to crystals in my pockets." I shook my head. "I just..." Sighing, I roll off the bean bag and grab another handful of books, sitting down on top of the shelf. "How did this happen?"

"Some people are sick," Madison whispers, pulling me into a soft hug. "And Vince was a special kind of crazy."

"Fucking magic," I grumble against her shoulder. "Fuck assholes who want more power then they have. Fuck all the supernaturals who pray on humans. We have no way to protect ourselves."

"Small men want power they can't have," she mumbled. "And Vince was very small. You have to know that not all supes are like him, yeah?"

"Yeah," I whispered. "Very small. They hide in plain sight, Mads. If they weren't a threat, they wouldn't need to hide, right?"

My friend didn't have an answer for me, she just shrugged and grabbed a book off the shelf, sifting through it like I was doing. The little pile of books needing replacing grew as we worked in silence.

Tapping up the last of the boxes, I snuck a look out over the playground. Dusk hasn't quite landed, but the light had started to get a little hazy over the Black Hills. Deadwood used to feel safe. I used to love the fact that it was tucked up between the hills, nestled in the cradle of mother earth, holding us gently in her protection. Vince had changed all of that, and night in particular was the hardest time for me. When the shadows grew until they engulfed the entire valley, I could feel him. He used the night like a mistress, a lover who he plotted and cast into.

I didn't know enough about magic to really judge where he fell into the spectrum of things, but everything he did felt like black tar sliding down my spine. Darkness and anger suffused his spells, those that I was an unwitting witness to. I would be forever grateful to Serenity, who noticed me wandering the streets, and taking me into her home. A cup of tea, and a bag of herbs changed everything. I needed to go for our weekly tea date tomorrow. I needed the scent of her shop to surround me. It was safe. Tea was safe. Especially the teas that she pushed on me every week, filling up the cupboard in Madison's little house. I'd never been much of a tea drinker until a few months ago, but I had completely abandoned coffee since learning all of the horrors my lover had inflicted on me.

We walked the long way around the parking lot towards Madison's old truck, the sound of motorcycles ripped through the tranquil sounds of the wind through the trees. I nearly dropped my box when my eyes caught those of a man across the street. Black jeans, black leather, and black hair spelled bad boy as much as the Harley he was dismounting, but something inside of me locked on to him, pulling me in. My stomach dipped and soared all at once, making me dizzy. The rollercoaster of need and attraction had me spinning. A flash of Vince, his long hair hanging in my face as he grunted over me, made my stomach upend.

The crash of books hitting the pavement pulled me out of my stupor. "Looks like the Sturges crowd got lost, yeah?" I looked over at Madison–who was also in her own daze–swallowing down the bile that threatened to creep up my throat. "Maddie."

"Not Sturges." She shook her head. "Shifters," my friend whispered. "The Lords of Khaos are in town."

"Fuck my life." I grabbed the box off the ground and shoved it into the bed of the truck. Everyone in the country knew about the Lords. They had been plastered across the news for months. But how had they turned up in Deadwood, the borders were all closed. The man was still standing there, watching me. I could see the tip of a cigarette burning as he blew smoke rings, hand carding through his hair. The smirk he gave me made my heart do flips, and my stomach erupted into butterflies. "No more supes. None. I've had my fill."

2

KILLIAN

The little blonde pulled me in. From across the street I could feel the tether that urged me forwards, the need to scent her was almost too much for me to handle. She was perfect. Long tresses pulled back into a tight ponytail, with wisps framing her face. Legs went on for miles under those cut off shorts. Shapely, supple hips, thighs a man could suffocate between, and little ankles with some kind of tat that wrapped around. Dainty and beautiful, just like it's owner.

Our eyes met for a flash of a moment, the brown so light that when the sun hit them they almost looked like molten gold. The box she was carrying tumbled to the ground, and the startled look she gave me shot though me like a fucking arrow to the heart.

Rejection.

Not a word had been spoken, but I could feel it in my gut like a sinking ship. Anger and fear came to me on the wind like a tease of what she would really smell like. Burnt and sour, her scent was a jumbled mess, but magic, that was fully clear. Like honey dripping down the back of your throat, it coated my mouth with the power of it.

"Witch?" I guessed, tapping out a cigarette and placing it between my lips. "Don't look it."

"What the fuck do you think witches look like, man?" Knox growled, throwing a leg back over his bike. "Ain't like human movies. They don't have green skin or warts on their long pointed noses."

"You fucking know what I mean," I grumbled, lighting my smoke and taking in a lung full of the nicotine that my body couldn't care less about. "No floaty skirts, or like rings and charms and shit."

"Whatever," my friend said, running his hands over his handlebars and rolling his neck. "She certainly smells like magic. Magic and rotten anger."

"Shut your mouth," I hissed, blowing the rest of the smoke from my lungs and destroying my smoke rings. "You don't fucking say a word about her." Anger flooded me, but even through the thick red haze, I knew I was being a fucking prick for no gods damned reason. Swiping my hand down my face, I sat down on my bike. "Didn't mean that."

"Yeah, you did," Maddox cackled. "You thought about ripping his spine out through his chest and hitting him with it."

"Graphic," my old friend coughed. "I'm not touching your girl, Prez."

"Ain't Prez," I shook my head and kicked my bike to life, grinding the cigarette butt out under my heel. "We got shit to do."

"There was a vote," Knox reminded me, slipping his hand into his pocket and pulling out his shades. "And it's called grocery shopping. We ain't doing a pass on Longshot, we're buying eggs cause your chickens don't lay enough for six shifters and your sister's rugrats."

"Not my chickens," I huffed. "Not my ranch, not my cows, and not my horses. I walked away."

"Mandy says different."

"Mandy is fucking wrong." I pulled out into traffic, heading my nose towards the Grocery Mart.

∼

The old barn still smelled like manore and rotting hay. At least the roof didn't leak anymore, and the concrete floor had been sealed and smoothed down when my mom had wanted to host weddings at the ranch. Stalls were all removed and while it looked rustic and old, the inside was clean and pretty well isolated. The horse smell would probably never leave, even with four bikes propped up on their stands on one end and our temporary living quarters set up on the other.

"Could be worse," Rupert said, cleaning his pocket watch for what felt like the millionth time since we sat down. Six assholes around an old plastic folding table, staring at each other. "Could do without having a roommate." His eyes ticked over to Knox who just shrugged.

"We drew straws," I muttered, pinching my nose and trying to get my thoughts to circle back to why we were all sitting here. Six supes who were stuck in the Dakotas, and needed something to fucking do before we all started strangling each other.

"We drew straws," Ruper's friend, Casper said with an exaggerated roll of his eyes. "You got a de facto single."

"He's Prez," Maddox reminded everyone, again.

It was my turn to roll my eyes. "Can we not?" I asked, wishing I could just bang my head on the table until they would fucking stop. Table wouldn't last that long. Not by far. "Mandy is more than happy for us to work the ranch. With supes not being able to travel between states, she's lost nearly half her workforce to border patrol."

More regulations were coming out every day. I was just waiting for a curfew or door to door screenings.

"Can't work unless we're registered," Ranger sat with his feet up on a chair and flicked through his phone. "And once we register, we ain't free if they tighten this fucking noose any tighter." His eyes flashed the yellow of his panther, then back to a startling green that looked more otherworldly than his animal. "And don't ask if she can pay us under the table." He shook his head. "I did that, and man I din't know if you know this, but your sister is fucking scary."

"Yeah, ranch can't pay us cash." I pinched the bridge of my nose again, determined to get rid of this headache that had been forming for hours. "Gotta be on the up and up. And we need to be on the up and up. Any fucking person in this town who ain't a supe can report us. Too many people already know we're Lords, and that means we are instantly targeted."

"Could stop wearing those stupid vests," Rupert mumbled, the soft cloth making whispers as he slowly rubbed it into the metal of the watch. I wanted to rip it out of his hand and chuck it out the nearest window, but I pushed that urge down with a swallow.

"Cuts," Knox reminded him before I could get the words out. "Not vests."

"Don't really care what you call them," the rabbit hummed, slipping the watch back into his pocket along with the little cleaning cloth. "Just saying, you're literally advertising the fact that you aren't human."

"And you aren't?" I asked, looking him up and down. Pressed suit pants, long sleeve work shirt buttoned all the way up, dark grey tie, and a vest, sorry a waistcoat, with a fucking pocket watch chain hanging out of the pocket. "You look like you stepped off a movie set for the latest gangster movie."

"No one has outed the bunnies," his friend whispered, eyes so light the iris nearly disappeared into the sclera. "I do agree that we stick out, though. All things considered."

"None of this is helping." I stood and paced the room, looking back and forth like an answer was just going to appear. "Isn't any reason we shouldn't register," I said as I reached for my bottle of water and drank it down. "We can work then, do ranch shit, get paid, and put down fucking roots. Shifters aren't going to be able to move for a while."

"You ain't kidding," Ranger tipped his phone and showed the latest news scroll. "South Dakota just voted to keep all supes in. Still legislation bounding about for us to be rounded up, too."

"This is assuming that I'd even higher your asses," my sister stood leaning just inside the door of the barn, arms heavy with a tray of drinks in her hand. Lemonade. Tall glasses, condensation dripping down the sides, and for a moment, she looked just like mom. Mom ran the ranch. Dad wasn't much of a sticking around type, and popped in and out of our lives for longer than I can remember. But mom? She was a fucking Wonder Woman. Raising the two of us and our little brother, running the ranch and holding a job in town, cause ends never seemed to actually meet. "Though I can't say I hate having you around." Mandy put the tray down on the table and sank into an empty chair. "Aiden is starting to become a handful, and Chloe is just so small."

"Coulda called if shit was hard." I took the offered drink and set it down on the table, watching drops of water pool below it.

"You made your priorities known, Kill." She shook her head and picked up the tray again, tucking it under her arm. "Men in this family just can't stick around," she said with a far off sound to her voice. "Not their fault all the time."

"What happened to Max wasn't your fault," I told her without thinking. "It was a freak accident." A freak accident that took her husband from her, months before Chloe was born. Took mom from us too. "Mom left the ranch in the right hands."

"She left it to you, asshole," my sister growled, the flash of her bear knocking me back. "She thought that if she put your name on the title, then you would have to come back. But you didn't."

"I'm here now," I mumbled, looking down at my folded hands between my knees. "I came back."

"For what?" Mandy shouted, gesturing around the room. "Cause you got stuck! You came up to to South Dakota to do what? Run drugs? Magic? What are the Lords doing these days, anyhow?"

"To look into a human trafficking ring further north." Ranger stood, clapping his folding chair closed and dropping it on the rack with the others. "Lords are all working on closing down a ring that is trafficking humans and shifters into labs and experimenting on them." The door to his room closed with a soft click, and stunned silence followed.

Only reason we could hear it. A bang came from the road, loud enough to rattle the windows and pull my bear from where he had been relaxing, completely unbothered by the fight with Mandy. But the sound that came from outside the barn made my blood run cold. Insulated walls or not, I could feel the bang in my gut like I'd been shot.

"What the fuck?" Maddox was already out the barn door and down the gravel driveway before I could think. Hot on his heels, I slowed when I realized what had caused that thunderous noise. More specifically, who.

Mine.

She ain't, I told my bear, where he was on his hind legs watching her. "Little car trouble?" I asked as I broke into a slow jog. The moment our eyes met, the burning scent of fear flooded the wind. Her eyes were like saucers in her head, but all I could see was the cord that connected us. "You alright, ma'am?"

"No," she said quietly, but I had no trouble hearing her, or the tremble in her voice. "Just stubborn sometimes."

"The car or you?" I slowed to a walk, watching as she rounded back the other way and put the body of the car between us. "Ain't going to hurt you."

"That's what they all say." She opened her door and grabbed something from inside, holding it to her chest. The spicy scent of magic bloomed between us, and I couldn't catch my breath for a moment.

"So you aren't a witch," I grunted, tipping my head to one side to get a good look at her. Those same shorts that disappeared into the crease of her thigh with every step, enough meat on those hips for a man to sink his fingers in, hold on tight to. "No, you're human."

"Something wrong with that?" she threw back at me, nose turned up. "Don't like humans, shifter?"

"Hey," I held my hand up and took a step back, realizing I had been stalking her around her car like a fucking psycho. "Nothing wrong with being human, just filing that away. Doesn't happen often. And there ain't nothing wrong with being a shifter, either. Just saying."

She stopped in her tracks and put her hands on her hips, squinting at me. "What doesn't happen often?"

"A connection," I shrugged, not interested in going into the details on shifter culture while standing on opposite sides of her car, fear saturating the air around us. "Need help?"

"No," she clutched her bag tighter to her body and looked up and down the road. "I'm fine."

The lie stuck in my fucking craw. Even if I couldn't hear the waver in her voice as she said it, I would have known a bold faced lie when I heard one. "Try again, sweetheart."

"Don't call me that."

"What would you like me to call you, then?" I asked, hands flat on the hood of her little car, the heat from the engine soaking into my palms. I could smell the stink of smoke from where I leaned, but I wasn't going to force the issue, not with the pinched look on her face.

"Nothing," she said, taking a step back and looking over my shoulder. "I don't need any help, my friend should be here any minute."

"No service until you hit the treeline over there," I said, nodding my head back towards the house. "Wont get anyone coming this way. So, I say again, do you need help?"

"Not from supes," she growled, eyes flashing with anger. "Not ever again."

"Sweetheart," I started.

"No," her command pierced the air, and stopped me in my tracks. That single word, that once had just been a barrier I could push aside, was now a full dismissal. "You don't get to call me that. I said I don't need your help, and I don't." She straightened her spine and let her purse fall to where it hung over her shoulder. "I am more than capable of helping myself, thank you."

"Stubborn," I growled, my feet moving before I could stop them, circling the car as she skittered away again, shoulders hunching and fear filling the air again. "I'm not going to hurt you."

"Really?" she hissed, hand on the still open door of her car. "Cause that seems to be what everyone who hurts you says. Please leave me alone."

The plea caught me off guard. My bear practically grabbed me by the haunches and ground me to a standstill. "I don't like you alone out on this road," I muttered, looking over my shoulders at the club behind me. At my sister, still holding her tray just inside the gate. "People don't pay attention, they just come whipping down the road. You could get hit."

"I'm pretty sure that Birdie knows this road better than you do these days, Kill." Mandy patted my shoulder and pushed me behind her. "I can take it from here, boys. You all head back up to the house and call a tow, I can get her home."

"But," I looked at Birdie. Name fit her. Curvy and blonde and sassy. I wanted to pull her to me and get lost in those peach colored lips. I wanted whatever glossy girly shit that she'd smeared all over them to coat my tongue and paint my beard. But the sour look on her face said that wasn't going to happen, least not soon.

"Poor Bird's been through it, if town gossip has anything to say," Mandy muttered quietly enough that I was mostly sure that the woman in question hadn't heard. "Serenity has taken her in. Deadwood isn't just shifters and witches now, big brother. We got all kinds here, and some of them don't play by the rules." She patted my chest and took a step away. "I'll get this sorted, you call Serenity from the house, yeah?"

With a nod I turned and strode back up the drive, the boys falling in line behind me. The low murmur of voices filled my head, mixing with bird song and wind through the trees. Serenity wasn't just any witch. If Birdie had needed her, something had happened to her, something bad. And from her refusal of help, I bet that trouble had come with a dick attached, and probably more ambition than sense. I definitely needed to make a phone call. And I needed to get to know the neighbors, cause clearly my little bird was one of them.

Mine, my beast growled from my chest.

"Yeah, buddy," I sighed. "She doesn't seem to get that, though."

3

BIRDIE

Coffee was one of my few vices. Well, other than being tragically incapable of meeting a man who might actually be good for me. Vince was only one of a depressingly short line of shitty suitors who left me worse than when they found me. Granted, Vince was by far the worst. Even living in Maddie's house, I was always on high alert. Triple for when she dragged me out to what used to be my favorite coffee shop. Used to be. Before magic, before the supernatural existed, and before my boyfriend was using me to power his dark magic.

"Earth to Birdie," Madison sang, waving her hand in front of my face. "You okay in there?"

"I am a fucking mess in there, thank you," I replied, taking a sip of m coffee and trying to enjoy it. It was deep and aromatic, warm and nutty, a beautiful blend. But to me it was like drinking air. I couldn't feel it or taste it, the enjoyment of existing outside of my bedroom, where I only felt marginally safe, was gone. "I just..."

"I know," my friend said, putting her hand over mine on the metal table. Sitting out in the sun should have been relaxing and lovely. "But he can't hurt you now."

"The police don't know what to do with magic, Mads," I sighed, putting my cup on the table and looking around. The shop faced a nice park, pretty trees, grassy areas, and flowers that were bright and happy. But I could see the shadows that fluttered with the wind. I watched every single one, looking for anything out of the ordinary. "He's locked up, but that doesn't mean he can't reach me." Another sip of coffee and a bite out of the tasteless scone. "As long as he can cast, he can watch me."

Madison squeezed my hand and leaned back, looking over at the park with me. Watching shadows, checking the trees, waiting for one of his familiars to swoop down and catch me. "Serenity said you were safe, at least for now."

"Yeah, new herb bags, another round of casting wards, more salt. Do you know how much salt it takes to surround your entire house? Cause it was not an easy ask." Warding only worked when I was home. It only worked when we didn't invite anyone in. If you could come into Madison's old farm house, then you had the right intentions, or at least that's what Serenity had said. We hadn't really tested it as far as I can tell. "I smell like potpourri all the time."

"You smell fine." Madison raised a brow at me, and picked up her iced caramel macchiato and sipped. "I saw the salt, and the bill."

"Yeah," I was spending a small fortune to be safe. It felt like insanity. Buying herbs and crystals like some new age hippy. And even with all the things that Serenity had taught me, all the things she had shown me, I still only half believed any of this shit was actually working for me. "And yet here I am, jumping at shadows, having to rely on you to put burn cream on my fucking back where it's still not healing, wearing long sleeves in the fucking summer just to hide the bruises that seem to be stuck in time. I want out. I want it to all go away."

The buzz of my phone had us both jumping. Coffee sloshed on the table as I grabbed it and opened the notification.

303-555-6769: Your car is gonna need a new fuel pump most likely. I got a guy on it.

Birdie: Who is this?

My heart was up in my throat beating a thousand miles an hour. I watched the three little dots at the bottom of my screen, waiting for an answer.

303-555-6769: Killian, your car died in front of my place yesterday. Though you should know it was being taken care of.

Birdie: How did you get this number?

Killian: Its a small town.

Birdie: That's not an answer.

Killian: I have connections.

Birdie: That isn't suspicious in any way.

I put the phone face down on the table and wanted to scream. Looking around the small square, looking for anyone in the shadows. My hands trembled as I reached for my coffee and took a sip of the tepid mixture. "Who would give out my number to a perfect stranger?" I asked quietly, continuing to scan the surroundings. Cars drove by at a leisurely pace, kids played on the distant playset, birds sang in the trees, and my heart felt like it was ready to explode.

"Who's texting you?" Madison reached for my phone and picked it up, opening it with ease. "Killian? That who helped with your car?"

"Helped would be a strong word for it. Your neighbor is harboring criminals, by the way," I told her, dropping my head to the table and resisting the urge to bang it repeatedly on the metal surface. "Amanda has the Khaos boys living with her, the ones from the other day."

"Oooo, sexy bikers." Madison wiggled in her seat, rubbing her hands together. "Tell me all about the big bad biker helping the sweet little kindergarten teacher. Oh that sounds like a steamy romance." She gave me her biggest grin and waited.

"It's not a romance," I grumbled into my coffee cup, seaking the last dregs of the brew that swirled around the bottom. THey dripped onto my tongue, and still tasted like nothing. "He's a criminal biker and shifter, and I've sworn off supes." Putting the cup back down, mourning the lack of enjoyment I had gotten from my favorite pastime, I shook my head. "My car died outside of the Bear Foot Ranch gates. A bunch of guys came out, and Killian practically stalked me around the fucking car, trying to get me to let him help. In the end, even after I had told both him and Amanda that I didn't want or need help, they called a tow truck anyway, and Amanda drove me home. The rest you know."

"He texted you to tell you it was all good," Mads told me with a cock of her head. "He wanted to help, why not let him?"

"Because I don't need help. I can do the things on my own." My head hit the table again, the urge to scream filling my chest. "I don't need a man, I don't need a supe specifically. I want to stay the fuck away from that entire world."

"Might be hard," came a voice beside me. The warmth of a body blocking the wind, and radiating heat, soothed something in me, and that in itself put me on high alert. "Supes practically run this town."

Lifting my head up, I was caught in the crystal blue eyes of the man we had just been discussing. He slid a card in front of me, and gave me a smile that probably would have melted my fucking panties, if I wasn't so hopped up on adrinalin and anxiety.

"Here's the shop's card. Greg should be giving you a call as soon as you can pick up the car," Killian went to stand up, but paused. "It's all taken care of, if you need anything else, you have my number."

"Still didn't tell me who gave it to you," I growled, pulling the card to me and reading it. Elite Auto Body. "I'm not paying for the highest end mechanic shop in the fucking city."

"You aren't," was all he said before he turned on his heels and walked down the street, the other bikers falling in line behind him, and two secret service looking dudes.

"You can't just pay for my car to be fixed," I shouted after him.

"Turns out, I can," came the reply with a shrug of his shoulders. "Dude owed me a favor, and I gotta take care of my girl."

"I'm not..."

"Not up for discussion," Killian said with a wink, before he turned the corner and was gone. The rip of motorcycle engines filled my ears.

"What the fuck just happened?" I look over to Mads, who is furiously typing something on her phone, a wicked grin on her face. "What?"

"I think the big bad shifter just claimed you," my friend giggled, turning her phone around and handing it to me.

"While there is only a little bit known about the supernatural world, there are a few things that are well documented. The first one is that, unlike in movies, a shifter can't turn a human with a bite. The second is fated mates. Every supernatural has a different kind of mating bond, but they all have a concept of mates, fated or destined to be with that one creature for life. The bond with shifters is especially strong, as they share their animals with each other. In the cases that shifters find their mate in something other than another shifter, the ritual is the same, a claiming bite, and the ability to feel your mate in your head. Some shifters mate for life, meaning once you have found your mate, you cannot be with anyone else. Your body chemistry changes to reflect the bond, giving even a human access to shifter-like traits, even if they can never shift themselves."

I handed her the phone back and just stared off into nothing. There was no mating bond. There couldn't be. No more supes. None. Certainly not one who barged into my life and started taking over. I've done that. A man coming in and being the boss wasn't going to fly.

"I'm not his mate," I said after a long moment of silence. "I refuse."

"From what I've read, it's not really a choice." Madison kept scrolling through her phone. "If his animal has picked you, he's just as stuck as you are."

"I'm not doing it," I growled, grabbing my own phone and pulling stuff up. Namely the Lords of Khaos. "Started in Vermont, Grizzly shifters, their main house is in somewhere called Ironwood Heights, and it's an old mental institution." I skimmed the rest of the page, it gave me some stats on the current members and their lives. Namely their mates. "Grizzlies mate for life."

"We don't know what animal Killian is, this could be just him picking you for now?" My friend gave me a hopeful look, but I knew better.

"I'm not that lucky."

"Upside, he's fucking hot," she shrugged.

"He's a supe," I reminded her. Pulling up the sleeves of my shirt, I pointed at the bruises that refused to fade. "I'm not dating a supe, not now, not ever. I'm certainly not mating one."

My phone dinged and the wind blew out of my sails as my heart kicked in my chest. Every time. Every single time that my phone buzzed or dinged I went straight back into anxiety mode. I had to keep reminding myself that it wasn't Vince. It couldn't be. He was in jail, and I had changed my number. So I looked.

Killian: Who gave you those?

Birdie: Excuse me?

Killian: The bruises. Who did that? I need a name.

Birdie: Isn't your business.

Killian: Yes, it is.

I looked down at the last message, and turned the phone to Madison. "Now tell me how this is different."

"He's gone all 'Touch her and die,' I love that." She beamed at me, doing a little dance in her seat. "Congratulations, you are now claimed by a shifter. And he's going to annihilate Vince. Your new shifter bad boy is going to kill your ex."

My head hit the table. "I quit."

"You could try giving him a chance. You know, tell him what you don't want, but also what you do." Madison stood up and grabbed my cup along with hers. "The Lords are super protective of their women. Keep reading the wiki page on them. They've changed their MO from drug and gun running, to taking down a trafficking ring. And their women are not only badasses themselves, but also very well protected."

"I don't want a man for protection," I muttered into the metal of the table, not wanting to come back up for any reason. There were going to be wicked marks on my face when I did actually gather the energy to get up and go to my car. "I quit. All the things. I'm done."

My phone dinged again.

Killian: Vince who?

Birdie: Here's the thing, shifter boy. I have done the stalker boyfriend. I'm not impressed that you can hear my conversation. In fact, its giving off all kinds of creeper vibes, and I'm so fucking done with that shit that I don't even have words to describe it. So this is how things are going to go. I'm going to get up and head back to my house, you are going to stay where ever the hell you are, and once I have my car back, you leave me the entire fuck alone.

Killian: Vince who?

"I'm done." I shoved my phone into my purse and stood. "Just talk to me like a real person, and not a crazy stalker."

"You have to make up your mind, little bird," his voice came from behind me, thick as molasses and twice as strong. "Cause the moment I touch you, I'm not letting go. My bear won't let me."

"That's not creepy or anything." I whorled around, and there he was, leaning against the side of a building, shoulders as wide as a fucking school bus, taller than any man I had ever been with. Arguably, he was fucking delectable, and I had been without proper dessert for far too long. But the bright shine in his eyes told me too easily that he wasn't human. The way he moved would have been a hint even before the supes were outed.

"You're staring, is there something you like?" he asked, shoving himself off the wall and pocketing his phone. He tugged at the vest he was wearing, pulling it away from the moulded on t-shirt underneath. His jeans clung to his thighs for dear life.

"What are you doing to me?" I swallowed around the lump in my throat, the thick need that surged through my veins. "Stop it."

"So you can feel it?" he asked, crowding me against the brick wall of the coffee shop, the scent of Irish Spring and musk surrounded me. He wasn't touching, wasn't pressing, just leaning on the wall with one hand, looking down at me like I was the last piece of tiramisu and he was fucking starving. "The heat that rolls through your veins, the tug at your middle pulling you closer. Tell me you can feel it."

"I can't," I hissed as he pushed closer, his scent growing stronger, thicker until my head was spinning with it.

I don't know who moved first, but suddenly my hands were under his vest, pressing against the rock hard abs I found there, and his were in my hair, tugging me back until his lips pressed down on mine. They moved gracefully as they coaxed mine to play. The slide of his tongue past my lips, rolling against mine as the scent of jasmine swirled with the heady musk of this man, who was pulling feelings from me I thought I would never feel again, until I was drunk on them. Hands under his shirt, around his hips, nails scratching at his skin as he devoured me. I couldn't get enough, couldn't get close enough. I needed more.

A keening sound brought me back to the world, back pressed to the bricks, his hands holding my face with a reference I had never experienced before, and then the kiss ended. Killian tipped his forehead against mine, our noses just touching as we shared air.

"I can hear a lie, little bird," he whispered, pressing a chaste kiss to my swollen lips. "You feel it all."

"It's not a choice," I told him, eyes too close to focus, but I could still see the downward tilt of his lips. "This is a bond, yes?"

"Yes, you are my mate. My bear has chosen you, and I always listen to him. He's grumpy, but very wise." Killian rubbed his nose back and forth over mine, soothing me. "But there is always a choice, at least for you."

"What does that mean?" I asked, leaning back against the bricks so that I could see his face. "I get to choose, but you don't?"

"Fated bonds are complicated," he told me, sighing as he eased back. The moment that his hands left my skin I felt a chill. Cold and lonely. I wanted to step back into him, to feel that connection again, to feel like I wasn't alone. Cause I had been so alone for so long. "Grizzlies mate for life. The moment they scent their mate, that's it. You will be the last woman I will ever want, and can ever have."

"I need to go," I whispered, pulling away. "Cause that's a lot."

4

KILLIAN

I could hear my phone buzzing from way up in the rafters. Another fucking fuze had blown, and shorted one of the lights. But the happy little dance my cellular did on the table twenty feet below made my heart leap. Never thought I would be the type of guy to get twitter patted or whatever shit, at the thought of a girl, but fuck me, if my mate didn't get my entire body singing anytime she dained to send me a text.

Wouldn't talk to me, but texting she would occasionally throw my way.

"Hey boss," Ranger cocked a hip on the table, bumping my phone until it nearly slid off the table. "Well shit, looks like we got a job." He snatched the thing up, moments before it tipped off onto one of the chairs and opened it. "Says there's a club outside of some town east of here, need to have looked at. Says there's talk of girls going missing round there."

"How," I asked, leaning into the beam that spanned the entire barn, trying to see where the light connected. "Ain't no one going in and out of nothing," I grumbled, finally finding the junction. "Whole countries locked down cause the hummies are scared we're gonna eat them or some shit."

"You also got a text from your mate," he teased, wiggling the phone at me. "Want me to read it?"

"Fuck off man." I checked the connection for any current, and then went about unscrewing the box. "Who wired this shit?"

"What's wrong?" Ranger dropped my phone and went to lean on the bottom rung of the ladder, looking up.

"It's like spaghetti thrown up in here," I pulled a mass of wires out, searching for the one I actually needed. "We're gonna have to pull this shit out and start again."

"Like we did with the plumbing?" he asked, hiking a thumb over his shoulder and pointing towards the destruction that used to be the main bath-room. "Cause we can't have no water and no lights."

"Get the boys, get them up to speed," I grumbled, as I finally pulled the fixture free, and draped it over my shoulder. "Tell the bunnies that the suits stay home, but the steel can ride."

"You trust them on bikes?"

"Ha." I wouldn't trust them on trikes. "Not a fucking chance. They can take the truck." I jumped down the last few rungs and dropped the light on the table, snatching my phone from Ranger's hand. "Don't fucking read the personal shit, asshole."

"It's about as personal as my messages to my little brother dude." He shrugged, walking away. "She might just not be that into you. Humans are weird. Can't feel the shit we do, don't know about the bond. Right now it's just myth and legend to them."

"Birdie knows about mating bonds," I muttered, fingering through the texts.

"She tell you about her last beau?" Mandy asked, from where she was sitting in the little kitchenette. Her fingers were working quickly over her laptop keyboard doing god knows what with business shit for the ranch. "I've only heard what they've been saying down at the grocer, but from what I've heard, he was using some magic shit on her. He's been in jail for a minute, but there ain't any laws."

"Not yet," I growled, my bear surging to the front at the mention of the dickhead who had hurt her.

"I also heard that those bruises aren't fading." She shut the top of her computer and folded her arms over it. "Says dark work to me."

"Do you know this dude?" I asked, trying to be casual, but I knew I was failing fucking hard.

"Vince? Everyone in town does. He used to run haunted tours and shit. Big tourist draw during festivals and events." She leaned back in her chair and pulled out a brochure. "His were dead set the best. Rave reviews." She slid it across to me. "Shut down not long after he was arrested."

"Charges?" I asked, fingering through the slick pamflet. "Feel the spirits come to life as you travel through the old tavern, listen to the ghostly whispers in the cemetery, and don't forget to leave an offering before you go, lest you get followed home by a lost soul."

"Seems there were real thrills and chills. All fucking trumped up magic shit, but the hummies can't tell the difference." Mandy stood and took her computer with her. "Ain't gonna rewire the barn, bro," she said as she slipped the laptop. "He's in for attempted rape. That what you want to hear?" She looked at me dead in the eye. "Leave the mage alone, Kill. He's gonna get his. You need to focus on the girl." She pointed to where my phone was buzzing again in my hand. "Earn her trust. Make her safe. And fucking mate her so he can't get to her anymore. That's your fucking job."

My ass hit the chair so fast, I didn't know what happened.

Birdie: You would think a teacher would love summer break. But I can't look at these same four walls another second, I'm going to explode.

Birdie: Took one of Madison's horses out through the hills. Sometimes I forget how beautiful it is here. Can't see the forest through the trees, yeah?

Birdie: Can we chat? Like, real talk? Cause I have questions.

Killian: Of course. Any topic in particular?

Birdie: Serenity said something at tea today. Something about shifters and their mates.

Killian: That covers a lot of ground, little bird. Care to be more specific?

The phone rang in my hand, and I just looked at it for a moment. The picture was of Birdie, her blonde hair haloed in the sun, a smile on her face. I felt a little bad that I had taken it without her knowing. But her face became too serious when she looked at me. Guarded. I got it, but it still tore at something deep in my gut when she closed down.

"That was fast," I drawled, holding the phone up to my ear, and feeling a smile flicker across my face. "You eager to feel that bond?"

"I feel like I've jumped out of the frying pan into the fire, actually," Birdie whispered on the other end of the phone. I could hear her heart beating like a kick drum. "But Serenity seemed to think it was something we should consider, since..."

"Since what?" My back went straight as a shiver went up my spine. "You're not asking cause you like the idea."

"I'm scared shitless, Killian," she growled. "I have no idea what I'm doing."

"How about we do this differently," I said, standing up and grabbing my cut off the back of the chair. "Before you ask any questions, let me take you to dinner." I was halfway to my bike when I heard the boys revving their engines. "Shit."

"What?" I could hear the fluttering of her breath. Not sure if she was anticipating the idea of dinner with me, which I was going to have to cancel the moment I fucking said shit, or if she was that scared that she couldn't catch her breath. "What's wrong?"

"I'm an asshole," I grumbled, pulling my hand down my face and looking over at the boys. Even Rupert and Casper were in the truck, locked and loaded. "I have a job I gotta get moving. Can't drop it tonight."

"Oh," she almost sounded disappointed. "It's okay."

"Tomorrow," I said quickly, pulling my keys from my pocket and straddling my bike. "Here at the ranch. We're having a cookout. You can bring your friend. Meet the boys officially."

"That's a lot of people for a simple question," Birdie whispered. "I just..."

"Just come for dinner. Meet some supes that aren't stupidly toxic." I pulled a smoke from my pocket and put it between my lips. "We ain't so different."

"Except that cigarette won't kill you," she told me. "Dad smoked like a chimney, I can hear it through the phone."

"And I can hear the pitter patter of your heartbeat, I scare you."

"More than just about anything in the world."

"I would never, ever hurt you, you need to know that." Easing the stand up, I balanced the bike between my thighs. "My animal is yours to command. I am on this earth to keep you safe."

"And one day, I may even believe it." The call ended with a little click.

I sat there with her words spinning around in my head until the text came.

Birdie: What time?

Killian: Six sharp. Us beasts need to be fed on the regular.

Birdie: See you then.

~

You could see the blaze from nearly a mile away. Smoke filled the valley, making it nearly impossible to see the road ahead of us. Fire engines and flashing lights were all over Smoking Jack's parking lot by the time we pulled in and set our bikes on their stands.

"Looks like someone got here before us," Maddox growled under his breath as he pulled out a smoke and sat on his bike, looking through the haze towards where people were huddled under blankets. "You hear what those jokers are saying?" He nodded his head toward a group of cops off to one side, heads all together.

"Blaming shifters?" I hazarded a guess, my bear sitting up and pressing at my skin to be let out. "Not only that, but they're keeping people here, instead of sending them to get looked at." A girl off to one side looked like she had a nasty burn all up her arm. She was shaking under a coarse looking wool blanket, and huddled in on herself.

"No bikes," Ranger pointed out. "Not a single one in the lot. They cleared out before the fire started."

"You think that they might have been tipped off?" Rupert looked completely out of place in his loafers and iron creased jeans. Even his sunglasses looked like they had fallen out of some designer magazine. Bunny GQ and shit. "Only girls I see in the parking lot."

"Most of them human," Casper mumbled, hands folded behind his back like a good little enforcer. You could take the suits off the mob rabbits, but you couldn't take the mafia attitude from them. "Smell scared."

"Ain't prey shifters supposed to have dull senses or something?" Knox grunted as he flicked his own cigarette into the bushes.

"Should you be doing that right next to a fire?" Ranger asked. "Like, there's a million dudes in flame retardant shit twenty feet away."

"You see how none of the trees are burning, Rang?" Knox said real low. He pointed out towards the foliage around the nearly extinct Smoking Jack's–ironic name, since it was actually smoking. "Been raining a lot this past month, yeah?"

"So?"

"Fire season is when it's dry," Casper rolled his eyes and adjusted his stance. "We wanna be here when the cops notice us? Or we wanna split?"

"Ditch the cuts, we're here as normies, yeah?" My leather disappeared into my saddle bag, hands through my hair, and I locked eyes with the shivering girl. The flash that greeted me confirmed my suspicions, even though my nose was absolute shit with all the smoke. "Shifter girl over there." I nodded with my chin, and started walking. "Little sister," I growled as we got closer, holding my hands out to show her they were empty. "Got yourself in some trouble again I see."

"Couldn't help it," she whispered, her head lowered, tipped to the side, showing me her neck. Inside my blood boiled.

"Who the hell marked you up like that," I growled, my animal clawing at my skin to be let out. The gouge of flesh, shiny and new. Her throat looked like someone had used it as a damned chew toy. "Ain't no one learned you can't force bond marks?" I hisses as I grab her by the back of the neck. "Head to the truck."

"Cops said to stay here," she whispered.

"Lords say you head to the truck," I told her, my bear nearly filling my entire chest. "Any other girls here you know?"

"Cindy and Anna," she told me, pointing at the other two girls huddled in blankets. "They came with me. Was supposed to be an arranged mating," she said, looking up at me through her fringe. "Foxes do that sort of thing."

"All three of you from the same den?" I asked her more quietly, seeing the eyes we were drawing our way.

"Yes. We came up from Rapid City. Foxes aren't common around here anymore. Not as many dens as there used to be." She pulled her blanket up over her shoulders again and shivered. "We've had to be less choosy."

"Get your friends and get in the truck," I told her, squeezing the shoulder that wasn't torn to shreds. "I'll deal with Barnie Fife over there."

"What's the angle?" Rupert muttered as he locked steps with me.

"What was your job before this?" I asked, shoving my hands in my pockets and hunching my shoulders a bit as we got closer to the cops. Trying to make myself look less threatening wasn't going to happen, but I could do aw shucks country boy if I dug in a bit.

"Both Casper and I worked as fixers," he told me without missing a beat.

"You have got to be fucking kidding me," I stopped and turned to look at him. "You mean like the 'sleep with the fishies' guys or the clean up messes other people made and helped folks forget."

"Little of this, little of that," Rupert told me with a shrug, eyes still flitting from one person to another, I could practically feel the cogs turning. "Female cop, not the brunette, the red head. She's who you wanna chat with."

"Chat with?" I asked, raising my eyebrow. "Do you mean tell her I'm taking my traumatized sister and her friends home, and getting her card, or like," wiggling my brows. "Chat with."

"Get her card," Rupert growled with a very exaggerated eye roll. "This isn't the fucking movies. Those three girls are naked and scared. Your sweet sister, whose name is Violet, by the way, needs to go home and have her family around her right now."

"Got it." I tucked a tooth pick between my teeth and rolled my neck. "Violet, Cindy and Anna. Need to go home. We'll make sure they call with a statement." I looked over at the red head, who was looking super lost. "This chick is going to lose her job." Pinching my nose I let out a deep breath.

Walking up to her, she almost looked spooked. Her eyes traveled from my chest all the way up to the top of my head and out over my shoulders. I was a big man. I got that. But the widening of her eyes when she actually locked with mine was comical. After a moment, I scented it. Witch. Perfect.

"Violet, Cindy and Anna are with us," I said, holding my hand out to shake, fully aware of the fact that she would use it to read me. "I'll have them arrange to give their statements."

"You're a bear," was all she said, still tilting her head up to look at me, hand around mine. "Newly mated, not to any of them."

"Nope," I told her, popping the p hard enough to make her take a startled step back. "But they're ours. I know you casters like to keep tabs, but with the shit going down."

"Protect your own." She slid her hand out of mine and pulled a card out of her pocket. "Make sure they call. A statement needs to be made."

"You know if they're registered?" I asked, slipping the card into my back pocket.

"Been hard getting shifters to register up here. Lords coming in might not be the best move for them. Bring attention."

I just shrugged. "Borders got closed. Need to keep doing our jobs, same as you."

"Not about turf wars?"

"The whole thing? Starting with Ironwood, it's been about trafficking." I pulled the tooth pick from between my lips and flicked it towards the building. Smoke was starting to thin as the last of the ruins were covered in dirty water. "Then it became about the experiments. And now it's about rooting this shit out wherever we can. We don't got Lords in all fifty states, but we're damn fucking close."

"So you're taking advantage."

"Wouldn't you?" I threw over my shoulder as I fished my keys out of my pocket. "Nothing else here for us boys," I grunted as I passed, snagging my cut from my bike, and putting it back on. "Trail will get cold from here. Humans can help the human girls, we'll take these three back to the ranch and get things sorted from there."

5
BIRDIE

No texts. Not a single one since he said goodnight. Looking down at my phone, I couldn't help but feel my stomach drop. It was stupid really, I had known him for less than a month, and was still reeling from my last–very much failed–relationship. By all accounts, I should still be held up in my room riddled with anxiety over the man who had stalked, used and violated me. Instead I'm having daydreams about a biker, who I've only seen a handful of times in person.

Dropping my phone onto my nightstand, I flopped down, covers fluffing as I settled into the nest of blankets that I had acquired since moving in with Madison. Thick, heavy and soft. All the things that helped my little heart feel secure, while my brain was a complete mess.

"He's just not that into you," I muttered, taking another look at my phone. "That's all there is to it. You've been guarded and angry, and haven't given him any kind of chance."

"So," Madison drawled, setting her shoulder to my door. "According to what I've been reading, that's not how this works."

"Isn't how what works?"

"He called you his mate, Bird." Madison swung into the room and dropped down on the bed next to me. "That's like the real deal shit, you know?" She looked over at me, her face blank for just a second before a smile filled her lips, eyes sparkling. "I'm talking real happily ever after."

"Yeah, I read that too," I sighed, grabbing one of my pillows and screaming into it until my chest loosened. "But those are words. And I also read that it's not a choice. They're stuck with whoever is their mate, no matter what."

"So what?" Madison asked, snatching the pillow back from me. "Who cares if they're stuck, they'll be loyal forever."

"Think about that for a moment," I said, propping myself up on one elbow, cupping my cheek as I looked at her. "Really think about the implications of that. It's like the worst kind of arranged marriage. Like, here's your mate, you can never want anyone else ever again, even if you two don't work out. You're stuck. There's no walking away, and deciding that fate fucked up."

"When did you become so cynical?" my friend asked, eyebrows furrowing. "Cause I'm used to the sunny happy Birdie. Like crazy ex notwithstanding, you're not this jaded."

"I'm just quiet about it," I muttered, grabbing for my pillow again. Madison just dumped it off the side of the bed.

"You don't need pillow screaming, just talk," she told me, smile gone, face serious and open. "Tell me what's going on."

"Nothing," I grunted, sitting up and rubbing my hands down my face. "I'm just spiraling. I went from never wanting another man in my life ever, to knowing that if I do pursue a man in the future it would most definitely not be a supe, to now lusting after this man who is so far out of my type that it's laughable. I wait for his texts. I counted the minutes until he said he would call. I spend my entire mornings thinking about him, and I can't sleep until he's said goodnight." I threw myself back down with a grunt. "I even wore out my fucking favorite BOB, because of him."

"Sounds about right," Mads said thoughtfully, worrying her lip with her fingers. "Maybe do a little more research, because maybe not to the same extent, but humans feel the mate bond too."

"I didn't want a relationship, babe," I whispered, feeling the overwhelm prickle at the corners of my eyes. "I wanted time to heal, time to deal with all of these complex emotions and the trauma that Vince left me with."

"Sometimes you're thrown in at the deep end," my friend told me, eyes as glassy as mine. "Sometimes you just need to let fate take this one. Cause you need someone who loves you entirely. And just maybe being mated to a shifter won't be that bad. If nothing else, he can keep you safe from magic boy."

"But who will keep me safe from him?" I asked, finally getting the pillow from her, and shoving it over my face.

Then my phone cherped with a new text.

"That's him, isn't it?" Came Madison's muffled voice. "He likes you."

Killian: Bring Madison tonight, we are having a bit of a party.

Birdie: I'm not a big partier.

Killian: Small party, friends and family, nothing rowdy.

Birdie: So, I read some stuff...

Killian: Ain't that type of party, little bird.

Birdie: No like, don't ask any questions, cause women don't ask questions.

Killian: Ain't that type of club, either. Ask.

Birdie: What did you have to do last night?

I waited while the little dots kept going at the bottom of the screen. Long minutes of them cycling over and over again. And then they stopped. My heart beat like wild, so much that I had to press my hand to my chest to keep it from flying away.

"Just say it!" I growled at the phone, shaking it. "Just tell me its not me, its you. Tell me that me keeping everything at a distance has ruined it. I can't keep doing this." Dropping the phone on the bed, I turned over and burst into tears.

"Oh babe," my friend sighed, rubbing my back over and over again. "I think you need to see him. I'm betting this is the bond messing with you."

"It's not." I sobbed, hiccupping between breaths. "It's me and my messed up brain. Who doesn't notice that they're boyfriend isn't really interested in them? Who ignores the burns and cuts all up and down their arms? Who doesn't run the first time?"

"Birdie," Madison took a long breath and pulled me against her, cuddling us both against the headboard. "I'm not going to say that Vince didn't fucking you up royally. He did. He used tricks and magic, gaslighting and bullying. You might have chosen the wrong guy, but we've all done that."

"Mine just came with incantations and forgetting spells," I suck in a long breath and feel it shuddering in my chest. "I pulled you into it, and mom."

"Your mom never knew you were in trouble, and that's a blessing." Madison hugged me tight and leaned her head back against the wall. "She never knew that you were hurting, or that she was missing any signs. She never has had to worry that the reason you aren't home when you usually are, is that Vince has gotten out of jail and has taken you."

"He's still in jail, Maddie," I whisper, letting myself be rocked by her arms around me. "He's not supposed to get out until his court date."

"What I'm saying is that we both are scared, but if Killian is like the other Lords, then you're a lucky bitch, cause you will be protected, cared for and coveted." Her voice was wistful in a way I admired. My brain on the other hand was a mess.

The chirp caught me off guard, and I jumped, looking at the phone like it was a snake.

"Isn't going to read itself." She handed me the phone. "What's it say?"

I looked down at the phone, the little text icon blinking up at the top. Deep breaths, I thought to myself, closing my eyes and trying to find that calm center that my mother used to talk me to whenever I got anxious as a kid. Listen to the sound of your own breathing. Slowly in and hold, then out again.

"You look." I handed the phone to Madison without even opening my eyes. "If it's bad just close the phone, and I'll forget about him."

"It's not going to be bad," she said, typing in my password then tapping at the screen. "Have you seen any of the interviews that the bears up in Vermont have been giving?" she asked. It wasn't the first time she had asked. She had been dropping articles into our chat for days. "Okay, so you gotta read this, cause it's long. But the long and short of it is, the club sent them up to go check out a club that had some suspicious shit going on. They got there and the whole place was on fire, and Killian and the guys brought some shifters who were in trouble back to the ranch. They're celebrating the fact that they got three shifters out of a very bad situation, and they want us to come and celebrate with them."

"Oh," I said, looking up from where I had been hiding my face. "Um, okay."

Skimming the text, my heart slowly calmed. It was a massive text. Lots of language that didn't make a ton of sense to me, but the gist was all there. They were working to stop bad people from taking both humans and shifters and hurting them. That the Lords in general had been working towards moving from a one percenter club, to a fully legit organization. That their founding club was spearheaded by a man named Malachai and his wife, Bella, who was a bookstore owner. With the influence of the main club, many of the others had followed suit, including Lords Denver, which Killian and his friends had been a part of, until the laws messed that all up. There was more, but that was enough for me.

Birdie: So, we just lay it all out there? What if I'm working for whatever people are doing the kidnapping?

Killian: You aren't. You're a kindergarten teacher at Deadwood Elementary, your mother has just recently passed away. You are currently embroiled in a legal battle with a Mage who was abusing you. Which is good timing, cause a year ago, nothing could have been done.

Birdie: You investigated me?

Killian: My job is to help people get out of situations that they can't get out of on their own. I don't mean a little jam, I mean life altering. Of course I looked into my mate, I had to make sure I wasn't going to endanger anyone, including you. I looked Madison up, too. I'm not hiding it.

I sat in stunned silence, and just stared at the words. My rational brain was all on board. Of course he would make sure that things were safe. Of course he would be cautious. But the angry part of my mind, the one that had been broken apart by Vince, wasn't so forgiving.

Birdie: You should have told me.

Killian: You're right.

Growling down at my phone, I went to turn it off, and let myself be pissed. Living in the angry emotions, letting them settle in and darken my world just a little more.

Killian: But I didn't, honestly before meeting you, I wouldn't have cared that I upset someone because of a little investigation. But, with you, disappointing you hurts.

My jaw hit the floor.

"Oh, Birds, this guy," Madison made a hot sign with her hands, fanning herself and practically dancing around the room. "You don't find real men like this."

"That's what makes me cautious." I set the phone down on the nightstand

and stood up, stretching out my back and kicking my slippers off under the bed. "If we're going to a party, however low key it is, we need to shower."

"He texted again, don't you want to see what it is?"

"I'll see him at six. He can tell me all of this to my face, without a screen separating us," I told her, grabbing a towel. "It's easy to text the hard things. It's different saying it face to face."

6

KILLIAN

I was never one to watch the clock. Anticipation came in the form of grabbing my keys and heading out on the road. But the prospect of leaving the ranch, even for a moment while I waited for Birdie to come up the drive was a weight in my chest. In my middle, my beast was a mess. Not having our mate in our space for weeks had been driving him up the wall, to the point that he was becoming hard to handle. I understood her reluctance. Shifters and magic hadn't been out in the public eye for very long. We were new, and she had been introduced into our world the worst way possible. My bear didn't care. He wanted out mate and needed her. Anytime he took our skin, he would pace the property line between the ranch and her friend Madison's land, scenting, waiting, watching for any reason for us to cross that invisible, arbitrary line, and go to her. Now, she was coming to us.

"You don't watch that fire, those fucking stakes are gonna burn, my man," Knox drawled from where he was lounging in an old camp chair, beer in his hand, and eyes on the three vixens we had rescued. All three of them had settled in just fine up at the house and were more than happy to help out in exchange for the Lords' protection. Seems our reputations had preceded us more than we actually knew. But Knox watched them with an interest that wasn't purely about club business, and that was bugging the shit out of me.

"Could get off your ass and actually help," I growled, pushing my bear back down from where he wanted to jump out and fight the fucking lion shifter who was pissing us off. "Or you know, stop fucking creeping on the girls. Ain't here for you. This isn't a fucking club party with hangarounds, this is a respectable one. Kids here and shit, man."

"Not creeping," he grumbled, taking a long pull off his beer and turning fully towards me. "You wonder why a bunch of fox chicks wound up mixed in

406

with some humies? With the borders closed, you would think that Longshot was cooling off on their skin trade, but that place had been full of marked girls. And they were all girls. Not a one bust that Lords have made on their fucking operations was all female."

I looked over at where the girls were chatting, happily cutting up veggies and making sides for dinner. They had all been shaken up after the fire, but since they had been with us, their scents had become more anticipatory than scared. Not even a little sour since we had hit the ranch.

"What are you tossing around in there?" I asked. Knox and I had been friends since we both prospected for the Lords nearly a decade ago. It wasn't often that shifters with different animals settled together, and he had been the first lion to join, and one of the few that was a member at all. But we had become fast friends, I trusted his intuition, which was why him staring at these three bothered me. "You got some thoughts?"

"Did it feel too easy?" he asked, tipping back his bottle again. "You went up to this girl, just been through a fire, and not a normal one that got put out, but one that consumed an entire building, full on burned that shit down. And she just calmed and went with us. Brought her friends too."

"Lords are getting the word around," I shrugged, flipping the stakes and watching them sizzle on the grill for a moment. "It's the fire that bothers me. Did they know we were coming? Where's the leak if they did?" I glanced back towards where the bunnies were sitting. Both back in their black suits and sunglasses, looking like two conspicuous motherfuckers. So cliche mob that I wanted to punch something. "Ain't the rabbits."

"Not even my second thought," Knox agreed, dropping the empty beer in the can by him. Fucker was going to have enough empties to start his own recycling plant soon. Not that lions could get any more drunk than grizzlies. Just an expensive waste of time. "They might be fucking bunnies, but they pledged to us, and haven't wavered one bit. Consented to having one of us follow their shit for the past month, and just rolled with it."

"Then who?" I looked around the yard behind the old barn. It had once been a practice ring for horses, when the ranch was still in the riding business, and had been turned into a patio for weddings and shit. Pulling up the old rotten boards and replacing them had been easy enough. "Cause it isn't one of ours either."

Knox just sat there, watching and waiting. Lions were fucking patioent hunters. "Still working on that," he said after a long moment. The crack of a new beer bottle and hum of his beast rattled the air. "Might not even be here. But those three, we gotta watch them, yeah?"

I nodded, looking at my crew. Four Lords and two mafia shifters. Not the club I had ever anticipated having under me. "You watch," I said, hearing the crunch of gravel from down the road. "I have a mate to court."

"You gonna court her proper?" he asked, brow raised. Lions and grizzlies were very different in their binding practices. "Presents and food, showing off your skills so she wants you?"

"Bears mate for life." I pulled the stakes off the grill one at a time and wiped my hands off on the towel over my shoulder. "Not like lions. I don't want a pride under me, I want just her."

"We have fated mates," Knox countered, tipping back his bottle and sighing. "But lions don't breed near as well as bears. Prides ensure our genetics continue."

"Well lucky fucking you. I have Birdie. And will ever only have Birdie." I slid the tongs into their spot on the side of the old Weber, and ran my hands through my hair. "Fated mates didn't used to happen this frequently. Never thought I would have mine. Feels different than I thought. The way it was described, once you know, it all clicks into place."

"Good things need to be worked for," my friend told me sagely while practically shotgunning the last of his twenty four pack. "And animals didn't used to mix, or mix with humans. You notice how many of us have been fated to a mate that doesn't match our animals?"

"Harder convincing a human that we are predestined," I sighed. "Harder to convince a very traumatized woman that you mean her no harm, and only want to take care of her."

"You talk to Tweek about this mage?" he asked, watching the little car crawl up the drive. I could feel Birdie getting closer, but couldn't smell her yet. I needed to smell her. Not the faint afterimage of her perfume that my bear would pick up when he hunted, but the full blast of her musk in my nose.

"He's looking, but some of these dark wizards are hard to pin down." I shrugged, tracking Vince had turned out to be a huge cluster. We could find him, sure, he was being held in a prison not far from town. But getting any kind of information on him, that was the tricky bit. Magic fuckers were like shadows, slipping through the world in plain sight, until a light was shown on them, they they were fucking smoke, gone in a puff. "Serenity knew shit, but not enough. Mage, dark, uses women to enhance his spells. But she says he's only been around town for a few years. No saying where he was from, what coven had brought him up, and where were his people. She doesn't even know what he was casting, other than he used Birdie to power it. Motherfucker could be two fucking centuries old, and no one would know it."

The slam of a car door stopped any more conversation. My bear froze in my middle, waiting to smell her. The moment her honeyed notes hit my nose, my beast was pressed up against my front, pushing to burst out of my skin.

"So, we brought brownies," Birdie said, lifting a tray that she was holding. "And wine."

"Finally someone with taste," Mandy called from where she had been working with the vixens for dinner. "Can't get anything round here except Natty Light."

"Hey," Knox grumbled, holding up the box he had completely emptied. "I drink Miller, don't you disrespect."

"Oh, I'm so sorry your royal highness," Mandy dipped low in an exaggerated bow, practically dusting the patio with her hair flopping over her head. "No disrespect meant. Correction, all we can get here is an empty box of Miller, cause the lion fucking drinks all the beer." She wiped her hands off on a towel and took the brownie tray from Birdie. "Come take a load off, I'll grab us some glasses."

7

BIRDIE

Glass of wine spinning between my fingers I took stock of the group around the firepit. Killian and his friends were huddled together talking low. But his eyes never left mine, which was fortunate, because the three girls that were helping Mandy get dinner out were all looking at him like they wanted to eat him alive.

"You gonna take a seat, little bird?" Killian asked, nodding over to where the guys were seated. Each one with a beer in their hands, and not a single empty chair between them. "Come on, gotta introduce you nice and proper."

I pressed the cool glass against my lips, breathing in the fruity scent of the Vinho Verde, peering at him over the edge. I took a slow sip, swirling it around in my mouth, before nodding and taking a step towards where they were all watching. The crisp taste exploded on my tongue, shoring up my courage. My heart thudded in my chest, anticipation waring with worry and fear. I used to be good at this. Talking to men, cozying up to them and feeling like I ruled my own choices. My confidence had taken a serious hit with Vince.

"You smell anxious," Killian told me as he wrapped an arm around my hips from where he sat. "No one here will hurt you."

"Been told that before," I all but whispered. He stood behind me and pressed me back against his chest, taking my hand and weaving our fingers together. "Don't want to think about it."

"You don't have to, tonight," he said, voice rumbling in his chest and warmth spread through me. I leaned back and just let the feeling of safety fill me. It could all be a lie, he could be bewitching me, just like Vince. But everything felt different. I felt coveted, not just desired. "But we're gonna have to at some point." He tipped my chin up until I was looking at him over my shoulder. He towered over me, but for some reason, that didn't feel intimidating at all.

"I know," I sighed, turning in his arms until my face was pressed into his chest. Breathing in, he smelled like woods and male. Warm and musky. "But can we pretend tonight?"

"No pretending needed," Killian gave me a lopsided smile and tucked hair behind my ear. "Tonight, you are safe, safe as houses." Sitting back down in his camp chair, he took me with him, folding my legs over his lap, and tucking me against his chest. "Tonight, you're the alpha's lady, and my boys? They will all treat you that way."

"And you?" I asked, hiding a smile behind my wine glass as I took another sip. "Are you going to treat me like a lady?"

"Is that what you want, little bird?" he whispered against my ear, the reverberations sending shivers down my spine, my body lighting up and the feel of his lips across my earlobe. "Or do you want me raw and open to you?" he asked, his tongue tracing the shell of my ear. "Do you want me to worship at your altar, or do you crave the beast?"

My face heated, knowing that everyone around the circle could hear everything he said to me. Looking down at my glass, I swirled the wine around, watching as it held to the sides before melting back into down. "I don't know," I told him, peeking up at his eyes, then blinking back down. "Would you understand if I told you that all of it scares me, and I'm not sure what I want anymore, or who I am?"

"Birdie," Killian hummed, cupping my cheeks and lifting my gaze. "You set the pace, always. If you aren't ready, then neither am I." He settled us back into the chair, leaning back and holding me gently as I mulled over his words. Sips of wine disappeared as the boys started talking around me. I couldn't listen to what they were saying, I didn't hear a word, because the entire time, Killian's fingers were running through my hair, curling it around his fingers, rubbing up and down my arms, making me shiver in a way I hadn't ever understood. My body was in complete tune with each touch, every movement heating my center, until I could barely keep myself from squirming in his lap, searching for the thing that would settle this feeling.

"Dinner's ready," Mandy called from where she was standing with the other three women, one of whom was glaring at me like I had peed in her oats. "Come serve yourselves."

Killian helped me up out of the chair, then followed me, his hand always on my back, on my hip, my elbow. "Chicken's good, but I recommend the steak," he told me, whispering against my hair. "The green beans though, those are a must."

"And the mashed potatoes," one of the guys sang as he loaded his plate high with the fluffy white mash on his plate.

"Only if Knox doesn't fucking eat it all," Mandy smacked the man in question on the back of the hand with a wooden spoon. "We have guests," she growled.

"Birdie ain't a guest, she's clan," Knox grumbled, and pushed about half a spoonful of the potatoes back into the bowl. "Aren't you, princess?" He turned those golden eyes, shining bright with other at me. I waited for my heart to studer, for my body to go on alert. Instead I felt welcomed. They weren't pretending around me. "See, she's clan." He dug a heaping spoonful of the mash and dumped it on my plate. "Gonna need extra calories." Knox winked and forked a steak the size of my head onto his plate before dropping one slightly smaller onto mine.

"I cannot eat all of this," I gapped at the overfilled plate, holding it with both hands. "You know I'm not like you, right?"

"Course you aren't," one of the other men said. He stood apart from the rest, dark slacks and a light blue button down under a vest, with an honest to god pocket watch chain sticking out of it. "Even I can smell the human on you."

"I don't know what that means," I whispered to Killian, who just leaned down and pressed his lips to my forehead.

"Prey shifters don't have the same sense of smell that preds do," he told me. "Rupert and Casper," he pointed to the other man who was like a wrath, all dark clothing, with shocking white hair, eyes so light they almost looked like there was no iris at all. "Are rabbit shifters."

"Really," I looked at him up and down, and then laughed a little to myself. "You do dress a bit like the white rabbit," I told him before looking up at Killian again. He towered over me, enough that he could lean over and I could clearly see him by looking up. "You look like a bear, too."

"Gonna guess the rest of us, princess," Knox dropped down into his chair, kicking his feet up on the edge of the firepit and digging into his potatoes with gusto. "Fuck these are good. Mandy, were you unmated, I would have you in the family way like yesterday."

"Gross," Mandy scoffed, rolling her eyes. "Bears mate for life, and no, you wouldn't, cause absolutely not." She waved him away and went back to the girls who were all still standing apart from everyone else. "I told you before, Violet, we don't stand on invitation here. You're part of this clan as long as you want to be."

"Foxes don't mate for life," the tallest of the women said, her startlingly purple gaze washing over me, before looking at Killian. "If you're wondering."

"I'm pretty sure we weren't," Madison spoke up from where she was coming back from the house with a pitcher of tea. "And Killian is fucking taken. You heard the sow, bears mate for life, and this," she waved around over my head, and then less over Killian's cause she couldn't actually reach. "Is what mated looks like, in case you missed that."

Violet looked me over again, her gaze lingering far too long for my liking. She gave me vibes, not exactly creepy ones, but mean girl ones. The kind of looks I used to get in high school. "Doesn't have bond marks. Neither of them."

"First," Casper said from right behind me, making me jump and nearly lose my dinner into the gravel. Killian one handed saved my plate. "Not all shifters need bond marks for a fated situation." He pulled down the collar of his shirt to show a neat little circle of scars just over his heart. "And second, not all bonds hold, even with marks."

"Bunnies don't do bond marks," she told him, rolling her eyes so hard I thought that they would topple out of her head.

"So you do know how this all works," he growled, backing her up until she hit the buffet table, making it wobble. "Cause you need to understand, that in this clan, we don't fuck around with the mated shifters." He leaned all the way forward, until she was practically falling into the food. He snapped his teeth at her, then reached around her shoulder and grabbed a steak. "Also, you have more scars than any of us. Which one is your mate?"

"I didn't get these from a mate, and you know it," she whispered, her face draining of color.

"Then maybe remember that, before harassing Birdie." He took a huge bite out of the steak, then dropped the rest on her plate. "She doesn't deserve it, and you're making an idiot of yourself." He stepped back and strode away, the door to the old barn slamming behind him."

"Sharing food is how foxes choose their mates," Killian told me. "Bunnie, as far as I know, don't take fated mates."

"But..." I looked at where Casper had disappeared, and then over at Violet, who hadn't moved an inch from where he had put her. "Why is she looking at you then?"

"I'm pretty sure she's just as confused about that as you are." He shrugged and wrapped his arm around my shoulder, leading me back to his chair. "Sit, eat. I need your tummy full, my bear demands our mate is satiated in every possible way."

His lips descended on mine as we stumbled through the dark hall. Dinner had gone on for hours until it was just Killian, Knox and I sitting around the table. The latter had disappeared into the shadows not long after Madison had called it a night, but Killian kept me seated across his lap, feeding me bits of fresh strawberries and cream that his sister had brought out.

"Little mate," he growled against my lips, sending zips of excitement down to my toes. "Look how sweet you look, hair mussed, shirt untucked." His hands roamed down my body, tugging at the hem of my shirt before going back up. He pressed me against the door, cupping my breats as he took my lips with his again. "Open the door, Birdie."

"If we go in there, there isn't any going back," I whispered , my hand searching for the handle as I arched my back into his hands. Rough fingers pulling at my nipples though my shirt. The pinch was exquisite, shooting sparks of pleasure through me as his mouth devoured mine. "You ready for all my mess?" I asked, trying to guard myself from his answer. I was a fucking train wreck on a good day. What Vince had left of me wasn't even starting to fully heal.

"Birdie," Killian cupped my face in his hands and pressed his forehead to mine, letting us just share air for a moment before he licked his lips and stepped back. Cold water dumped through my veins. I could smell a rejection. "Your mess has always been my mess," he said quietly. "That's what fated means. I am literally born to fit you, and you me." My back hit a door, his hands holding my hips as he pulled me closer, pressing his thick cock against my belly, and making the butterflies inside turn into dragons, breathing fire into my core. "You feel this?" he asked. "This is me every moment I'm in your presence. We will figure out everything else as it comes, but between us, I want nothing, got me?"

"Yes please," I whispered, circling my legs around his waist as he lifted me, pressing me hard into the door as he felt for the knob I hadn't turned.

"Good," he hummed, the door coming open under his hand, and we both jolted through. The thud of the door closing hit me in the chest. My heart beat in time with the pulses of heat that were hitting my sex. "You smell so fucking good." Killian pressed his nose into the side of my neck, humming his pleasure into my skin. "Like sunlight and rain," he nipped at my throat, leaving little licks behind to soothe the sting of his teeth. Not enough to break skin, but enough to leave a mark. "Fuck Bird."

Abruptly he dropped me on the bed, my butt bouncing as he pulled his shirt off over the back of his head. The solid plains of his chest and stomach had me transfixed, running my hand in the valleys between the thick muscles. "You're not so bad yourself." The chuckle that came from him was purely masculan.

"You ready for all of this, mate?" he asked, leaning forward to cage me under him, crawling up my body and trapping me under his impressive mass. "I want to eat you up, you smell so good," he purred, tugging at the hem of my shirt and pulling it up to expose my belly. Curling down he pressed his lips to each inch he revealed until he got to where the shirt was trapped under my shoulders. "Won't do," he muttered, lifting me enough to try to tug it off. The rip of fabric caught us both off guard, making me freeze. "Sorry," he muttered, sitting back on his heels. "I'll replace it." The shirt clung to my shoulders, a deep tear down the center from bottom up.

I couldn't help but laugh, dropping back onto the bed with my hand over my mouth, shaking with the force of my mirth. Big strong bear shifter sitting between my legs, one hand on his thigh the other on a small bit of t-shirt material that had come away entirely. "Not a big deal, Kill," I told him, taking the bit out of his hand and dropping it on the ground. I crooked my finger at him. "You gonna finish what you started?" I asked, raising my hips and unbuttoning my jean shorts. "Or you just gonna watch?"

"Can I do both?" he asked, lifting my legs to free me from my shorts, taking my underwear along with them. "Need more," he grumbled, hands on my butt nearly lifting me off the bed before pressing his face directly between my thighs.

The eep that left my lips was quickly drowned out by a low moan. His tongue swept through my folds, swirling around my clit. His fingers tightened around the globes of my ass as he feasted. Pleasure and pain mixed together as he worked a finger inside of me, crooking it forward until he hit just the right spot.

"Killian," I hummed, locking my thighs around his head, doing my best to push him where I wanted him. Another finger joined the first, stretching me just a little. The tiny burn gave way to a flood of endorphins, making my head spin until I couldn't hold myself together anymore. Screaming my pleasure to the sky, I pressed myself harder against his mouth, stars exploding behind my eyes as he stroked me through every pulse of my body, every contraction, until I was set back down on the bed, body shaking and loose.

"So good," he muttered, leaning over me and pressing his lips to mine. He fumbled with his pants. Using my still trembling legs, I helped push them past his hips until the girth of him sprang free. I've never been one to want to just grab a cock and stroke it. Mostly I thought they looked weird and wrinkly. Oral wasn't something I was usually excited to give, but I wanted to feel him between my lips, filling my mouth as I gave him the pleasure that he had just given me, back. I had my hands on his the moment I saw it. Thick, veined and red with need. The dribble of precum that clung to the tip called to me. "Go ahead little bird," Killian hummed, hands on his hips, knees spread wide, and looking at me with absolute fire. "Taste it."

I sat up, leaning forward until I could take the tip into my mouth. I hummed as the musky taste hit my tongue. Holding his cock tight in my hands I explored him, flicking my tongue under the head, hollowing out my cheeks to pull more of his taste from him.

"Enough," he growled, hips stuttering as I tightened my hands, trying to pull him deeper. "Not today, baby," Killian said, putting his hands around my neck to gently push me back, not tight, just a little pressure until I let him go with a pop. "Tonight, I claim this pussy as mine. You can choke on my cock later." The words were followed by a soft slow kiss, completely at odds with the words. His body followed me back down to the bed, lips taking mine as he notched himself against my core. "Did that get you wet, baby?" he asked. I could feel a smile on his lips. "You gonna swallow me like a good girl later."

"Yes," I hissed as he pressed his cock into me, filling me, stretching me until I stuffed full of him, our hips kissing. "More," I told him, rolling my eyes up to meet him. "I'm not glass."

The grin that he gave me was wicked, sinister and beautiful. He drew back, fingers biting into my hips as he held me still and slammed back into me. Each stroke punched the air from my lungs and made me whine for more. The only sound in the room was his flesh smacking against mine.

"You like it rough?" he asked, grabbing my face and pressing his lips to me, teeth clashing together. Without warning he pulled out, flipping me on my stomach and smacked my ass hard, once on each cheek. "I can give you that." Lifting my hips he pressed back into me, slowly, giving me an inch at a time before ramming me full. "Look at those pretty pink cheeks." He spanked me again. "You good for this?" Killian asked, slowing for a moment until I looked at him over my shoulder, I lazy grin on my face. My insides felt like jelly, warm and ready to melt completely. "I need words, baby."

"I'm so good," I hummed, wiggling my ass back and forth with him deep inside. The stretch making me clench around him. Full. I was full and never wanted to be empty again.

"Good girl," he purred, leaning his body back and pulling me more into his lap. His hands clapped over them again, sting heating my skin. "If I'm not gonna bite your throat tonight, I want your ass bearing my mark."

"Yes, please," I moaned, pressing my hips back into him, taking him over and over as deep as he would go. I grabbed the headboard, using it to work us harder. The bed hit the wall with a thud. "Better," I hissed, rattle the head-board again. "More."

Killian grabbed my hips in he hands, nails digging into my skin. "Fuck you feel good." He slammed into me, rocking me hard enough that I had to lock my elbows. My belly tightened, heat spilling from between my thighs as the world exploded, my scream punctuated by the clang of metal and shattering glass.

"Well," Killian panted as he rolled us to the side, still deep as he could go. "I was meaning to replace that lamps. Guess I have to, now."

I couldn't help but burst into laughter, making both of us groan.

Curled together, Killian took his time sweeping his hand up and down my thigh, petting my skin like it was the softest fur coat. "You feel good," he said, puntuating his words with kisses peppering my shoulders. "Warm, soft, beautiful."

I sighed, leaning back until I could look up at him, my head pillowed on one of his arms. "You feel good too," I told him, pulling his hand down and pressing my own kiss to his palm. "Hot, hard and stupidly sexy."

"Yeah?" he asked with a wry grin. "Do tell."

"Always had a thing for the bad boy." Pulling him until his arm was around my hips, tickling my belly, and wandering back up to my breasts. "The tattoos, the broody expressions, but I also like to have fun."

"Having fun in bed is the best," he agreed, nipping at my shoulder. "I always thought that finding my fated mate would feel like a noose around my neck, tying me down and keeping me from the things I loved most."

"Which are," I asked, one brow raised.

"My bike, my clan and the open road." He gave me a shrug like it was a given. "Instead I feel like I'm free. Same feeling as I get when I'm on the back of my bike, doing eighty on a straightaway, wind pulling at my hair and clothes. Or when I shift. Shedding the human skin for something baser, closer to nature."

"I won't ever get to shift," I said, turning to face him and throwing my leg over his hip. Touching him felt like the most normal thing in the world, almost as if we had been tangled like that forever. "But I can ride on the back of your bike."

"You wont shift, no," he sighed, tucking a bit of hair behind my ear and cupping my face in one hand, stroking my cheek with his thumb. "But once we've claimed each other, you'll feel my bear inside of you. The warm press of his fur on the inside of your body. You'll get his emotions, and in time learn to speak his language. You may never wear a bear's skin, but my beast is already all yours."

~

The morning dawned cool and calm. Curled up in Killian's arms felt safe, his body soft and relaxed in sleep, I borrowed deeper into the covers, surrounding myself in his scent until I was lulled in this haze of comfort and quiet, only the distant birdsong as a bright soundtrack to my daydreams.

This was what it was supposed to be like. The quiet contentment that came with the feeling of absolute trust. My body was still buzzing from the night before, I was sore in the best possible way. Slowly I uncurled myself, feet touching the cool wood flooring, padding as softly as I could to the bathroom. The shower filled the small space with steam as I waited for it to come to temperature.

"You forget something, baby?" I heard from behind me, his voice languid with sleep. He was rumpled and grumbly, rubbing his eyes with one hand as he held out a towel for me. "Might need to borrow something to get home." The lazy smile that crossed his lips was pure masculine pride. "Your shirt is toast."

"And who's fault is that?" I asked him, putting my hand under the flow of the shower, testing the temperature. "You coming in, or are you just here to tease me."

"But teasing you is the best part." Killian tucked the towel over the rack and grabbed a second, securing it next to mine. "Best get cleaned up, so I can get you home," he rumbled, leaning down and pressing a kiss to my bare shoulder. "You weren't going to sneak out on me, were you?"

"Thought never crossed my mind." I turned in the circle of his arms and lifted my chin, silently asking for a kiss. There was no hesitation before his lips were on mine, a dance that we had indulged in so many times since the night before. Had it only been just the night before? It felt like Killian was the only man to ever touch me, that we had always been. "I do need to get moving, Jasper understands a few minutes of tardiness, but I can't be too late."

"This what all teachers do in the summer?" He helped me over the lip of the shower, directing me under the spray. Water pressure beat the fuck out of the pressure at Madison's. Water pounded into my skin, punching at sore muscles and loosening every fiber of my being.

Killian turned me around until my back was against his front. Warm hands skated over my skin, covering me in the scent of Irish Spring, and relaxing me until I was limp in his arms. Finger carded through my wet hair, scratching at my scalp, detangling the nest at the back of my head as he worked the shampoo through all the way to the ends.

"You're spoiling me," I hummed, pressing my ass back against his thick length. The groan that escaped his lips was as rich as honey. I wanted nothing more than to bend forward, and let him slip between my folds, and take me right in the shower. Give me a little extra morning boost before he sent me off for the day. The disappointment that I felt when he stepped back was immediate and sharp. "You don't want..."

A growl filled the shower, and I was spun and pressed against the cold tile so fast my heart tried to escape my chest. "Never ask that," Killian murmured against my cheek, his body flush with mine, erection pressed between us like a brand. "I want you every moment, I would freely show you how much you have taken over my soul. But you made me promise to get you to work on time, and I don't take oaths to my mate lightly. My self-control is paper thin right now. I take you again, I don't know if I can keep from marking you, claiming you for all to see."

"Would that be so bad?" I whispered, my body warming for his, ready to be sated once again. I could still feel the stretch of him, the way he had made room for himself inside me. Careful fingers and questing tongue, before he would even let me touch his skin. "I want you."

"Oh my little bird," he sighed against my lips, keeping me trapped against the wall, his hands still in my hair, but now curling it into his ever tightening grip. "I want it so badly," his lips traveled from my face, down the side of my neck. "Right here," he placed a kiss against my skin, before teasing it with his teeth. "My claim goes here. But not today."

He pulled himself away, tugging me back under the stinging spray of the shower, and rinsed my hair. "Soon?"

"Of course my love," Killian whispered. "Very soon."

~

Something was wrong. I knew it the moment I put my key in the lock. My heart leapt into my chest, as I turned the knob, Madison's car was missing from the driveway, but that wasn't unusual. Not enough that adrenalyn should surge through my body, making me shake as I pushed the door open. Curing Killian's sweatshirt over my hands and hugging the warmth of it around me, I stepped into the house. It was dead silent. Not quiet or lifeless, but like time had frozen inside. The usually warm welcome of the softly painted yellow hallway, felt sickly and sinister.

I dropped my keys into the bowl, listening to them ring and clatter as they settled. Still the house felt wrong, hot and cold at the same time. My fingers trailed under the carefully hung artwork that filled the walls. Pictures of family mixed with scenes by local and foreign artists. Madison loved photography, still life, renaissance. Her home was a mishmash of styles and aesthetics. Instead of enjoying the cacophony of colors and textures that I passed, I was focused on the door at the farthest end of the hall.

Mine. The door was just slightly cracked, light spilling from inside.

Blood rushed through my ears as I slowly made my way towards it. I swore I hadn't left it open. I closed it tight, because Maddie's cat liked to make my bed her own, and the long hairs of the beautiful Maine Coon would cover my pillow, making me sneeze.

"Took you long enough." Chills blasted down my body. I fumbled with my purse, trying to get my phone out. My fingers simply wouldn't cooperate as my body filled with panic, locking itself up, in place. "I can smell that animal on your skin, my beautiful finch," Vince smeared as he stood up from where he had been lounging on my bed, Gracian, Madison's cat, limp in his arms. "Did Jasper keep you after work? Can he smell the beast on you as well?"

"What are you doing here," I asked, my voice trembling until I had to clench my teeth to keep them from rattling against each other.

"I'm here to reclaim my muse," Vince told me, dropping the cat to the floor with a thud. My eyes followed Gracian's body as it slumped, unmoving against the hardwood. My breath hitched in my lungs as her head flopped down at an unnatural angle. "The rascal wouldn't stop scratching at the door. She screamed to be let in, demanded to be pet and soothed." He shrugged and wiped his hands on his jeans, like he had felt something sticky. "Wouldn't stop whining. And anyway, I needed a little boost before I took what I really came for."

My fingers finally closed around the phone, ready to pull it out. "You need to go," I hissed, trying to open the phone and hit the emergency button on my lock screen.

"Not a fucking chance." Power hit me like a brick, knocking me to the floor, phone spinning out and under the bed. "You think I'm going to let you get away this time?" Vince stood over me, leaning down until I could smell his feted breath, bathing my face in rotting air. "Oh, Birdie. You sent me away, and all I did while I was gone was gather power." Hand around my throat, he lifted me off the floor, toes dangling for purchase as he squeezed. "I'm going to teach both you, and that mutt a lesson."

My lungs burned as he pushed me down on the bed, my blankets surrounding me. Black dots filled my vision as Vince chanted. Magic pulsed around us, nearly a physical thing, as I gasped for air that I couldn't reach.

8

KILLIAN

A bottle of beer sweats between my fingers as I watch the front drive. Birdie should have been finished with work, showered and sitting in my lap with a plate of food between us. Instead I'm on my third beer and my animal is becoming unmanageable.

"Are you seriously pining?" Knox asked, rolling his eyes and drowning his own beer.

"She should be here," I shrug my shoulders and roll to my feet. "You don't understand."

"You are correct on that," he tells me, clinking his bottle with Ranger. "Ain't never gonna get tied down like that."

"You know what I miss?" Maddox drops down on his own chair, tossing a pack of cigarettes between us and digging into his plate, piled high with steak and potatoes. "Hangarounds," he says around a half chewed bite of meat. "We've been here for a stupid amount of time not to have house pussy scratching at the door."

"You realise that we live on a ranch half an hour from town, and that shifters are fucking persona non grata with more than half the fucking country right now?" I ask, twirling my empty bottle in my hands and searching the breeze for any trace of my mate's scent. There's nothing, just like there has been nothing for the last hour. The sun is rapidly setting, and my phone hasn't so much as dinged once. "Ain't gonna be hangarounds here, man."

"Sucks," he grumbled, still stuffing his face with food. "Just miss it."

"You miss getting your cock stroked, man, you don't miss the fucking hangarounds in Denver," Ranger called, laying back as far as he could in the seat, looking up at the sky. "You complained all the fucking time about there never being enough new blood," he muttered, trying to ballance his beer bottle on his forehead. "And you fucking hated half of them. Too needy, too pushy, too clingy."

"I liked Rachel," Maddox growled at him, knocking the bottle clear off his head letting it shatter in the dirt. "Drop your bottle, clumsy."

"Being bored isn't an excuse for being an asshole," I drawled, pulling myself to my feet and tossing my empty plate into the trash bin. I glanced down at my phone, checking the time for what had to be the millionth time since dinner had started over an hour before. "Something isn't right," I said, pinching the bridge of my nose and pressing my bear back where he belonged. The more agitated I got, the more worried, the harder he fought me for control, and the harder it was to resist. Looking out at the setting sun, I made a decision. "Suit up boys," I growled, my fist clenched tight as I fought the bear for control. "Something ain't right, and we're going to see what it is."

"What are you going to do if we go barging up there and nothing's wrong?" Rupert asked, already on his feet and dropping his plate in the trash.

"You got an opinion, keep it to yourself," I hissed, double timing it back to the barn to get my gear. "Don't know how you mafia assholes do it, but here, when the Pres speaks, the club listens."

"Not an opinion," the rabbit said. "Just playing devil's advocate. You and I both know that if she's just at home and we go in there like bats out of hell, she's going to spook. You're already treading lightly."

"Not anymore," I told him, rounding. "She needs to know exactly what kind of beast she has entranced. Birdie is stronger than she thinks. More than capable of handling my bear, and a fuck ton more. Now suit the fuck up, and get in your truck." I slammed the door and leaned back against it. Rupert wasn't wrong. If we went in there and nothing was wrong, I was going to have fucking hell to pay, and I knew it. I was this close to having my teeth in my mate's neck, and messing shit up now, meant delaying our bond. And the fucking sooner we were tied together, the sooner I would actually be able to feel if she was in danger.

She's in danger now, my bear growled from where I had locked him up tight. And you ain't moving fast enough.

Fair. I slipped off my cut and pulled my shoulder holster from where it hung in the closet. Shrugging that on, I slid the loops through my belt, and put my cut back on. Firepower probably wasn't a need, my bear could take on almost anything, but being prepared was always better than running in blind.

Maybe I was the fucking boy scout that Birdie had accused me of being.

Gravel roads weren't the most favorable for motorcycles, but hearing the growl of my engine in harmony with those of my club brothers settled my bear enough that he wasn't going to be problematic. Shifting while on the bike would mean a whole shitstorm of problems that I wasn't interested in seeing play out.

It wasn't far up the road to where Madison's ranch was. It had long ago shut down most of the actual business side of things. I knew her parents, or knew of them, since I was a kid. They had fallen on hard times, and hadn't been able to employ enough people to keep the business going. But they hadn't been willing to sell either.

Coming over the hill, I could see the sign that was still up over the front drive. Deer Hollow Ranch. That's when it hit me.

Magic smells like different things depending on the practitioner and the type of magic they employ. But it always had a spicy edge. The scent that hit my nose was so powerful it ground me to a halt. The scent of intensely thick cloves and burned cinnamon smacked me in the face, clinging to my throat and filling my lungs with tar.

"Fucking hell," Maddox hissed, leaning over the tank of his bike, pressing his nose into a bandana that usually hung around his neck. "What the entire fuck is that," he coughed.

"Magic," Casper said, leaning out of the window of the truck, looking completely unbothered as the four of us on bikes choked on the air. "Black magic if I had to take a guess." Scratching his chin he looked around at the entrance to the ranch. "No doubt now that something isn't right."

Shaking myself free of the cloying scent, I revved my engine. "Then we need to fix it," I coughed, squaring my shoulders and heading off. I could hear the gravel spinning out from under my tires, but my only thought was of my mate.

The smell just got stronger the closer we got to the house. Right by the back door, Birdie's car was parked, but I didn't see any other vehicle. Barn doors were closed, and so was the old garage behind the house. Nothing looked amiss, but the nearly physical presence of magic was heavy in the air.

"Back door," I choked out, pulling my own bandana around my nose and mouth. It didn't help at all. The magic slipped through the fabric like it wasn't even there. "Key under the mat."

I reached for the door handle, and it turned easily. The scent of blood hit me instantly. Knocking out any scent of magic in the air. It tasted like warm copper pennies on the back of my tongue, coating my throat, and pulling my bear right to the surface. Heart thumping in my chest, I pushed the door open all the way, until it hit one of the old kitchen chairs, wood screaming.

The entire house was still as death. Air thick and humid. My boots made almost no sound on the floors as I crept through the kitchen, my gun naked in my hand, senses alert for anything that might be around the corner.

What was around the corner wasn't anything I could have prepared myself for. Laid out in a circle of candles was my Birdie. A pool of blood staining her skin and seeping into the floor as the last notes of smoke were just dissipating from the candles. Thirteen in total, starting from just above her head to where her toes barely reached.

She lay there almost peacefully, eyes closed, hands up near her chin, and feet tucked up close to her butt. Her clothing had been completely removed. Not a trace of it was left in the room.

"Don't come in here," I grunted over my shoulder, picking my way closer to the circle that had been carved into the wooden living room floor. "Someone grab towels."

Shallow cuts littered her skin, not nearly enough to produce the sheer volume that was under her, congealed and sticking to where she had clearly moved. Smeared over her arms and chest. The closer I got to her, the thicker the smell of fear was. Acrid and sickening, hiding her natural smell. Bruises were already forming on her face and wrists. Her ankles were chaffed, rubbed raw from rope that was gone.

My ass hit the floor just on the outside of the circle, hands pulling down my bandana as I took in my beautiful mate. Rage like I had never felt filled me to the bursting, as my bear roared at the sky. "Someone search the fucking area," I grunted, red filling my vision as I pressed my hand passed the candles. When there was no resistance, I surged forward, pulling Birdie into my lap and holding her tight. Her breath was warm on my chest through my shirt, while the cold blood penetrated deep, chilling me to the very depths of my soul. "Should have fucking insisted on you staying with me," I muttered against her hair, not caring one bit about the red staining my face and neck. "Should have bitten you the moment we met." I rocked her back and forth, listening to her steady breath. "Fuck, little bird."

"No one's in the house," Knox said from behind me. I knew the second he took in the room, the sound of his knees hitting the floor reverberated, floorboards rattling at the impact. "Holy shit, boss."

"She's alive," I told him, not moving an inch from where I was holding her. "Need to call Serenity."

"Already on it." His boots scraped the wood as he sat down, phone alive in his hand, ringing the call through. "Magic is heavy shit."

"Yeah it is." Slowly I pulled myself to my feet and moved towards the stairs. The movement hadn't made my mate stir at all. Neither did me turning on the shower and putting us both in.

Leaving Birdie with Serenity was one of the hardest things I have ever done. Closing the door of the house, with my mate still unconscious, with a woman I hadn't known well in years was torture. Seeing her laying on her bed, eyes closed with dark hollows underneath, and face so pale that her lips were nearly blue, hurt my beast so badly that he was braying in my chest. Lamenting the broken creature that we were sworn to protect and had failed.

My bear was miserable, but me? I was seeing fucking red. No one should ever be treated the way Birdie was, left bloody and broken on the floor. Serenity had only been able to piece together the spell enough to narrow down the possibilities. And not one of them was good.

"Black magic, man," Knox grumbled, rubbing his hands up and down his arms like he was trying to push it off his skin. "Fucking clings worse that a newbie hangaround. Looking for old lady banner first fucking day."

"I'm going to be sick," Rupert leaned against the side panel of the truck and dry heaved into the dirt. "What the fuck was that?"

"The witch said seriously bad juju," Maddox pulled out a smoke and placed it between his lips. "Something about summoning."

"Serenity said that he was using Birdie to try and summon some nether-world creature or conjure some kind of next level power." I tapped my own smoke out of the pack inside my cut, and lit it. Pulling the smoke into my lungs, I searched for a place to start. "Whatever it was, it didn't manifest in the house, cause there was no residue."

"Sound like a magic slinger, Prez." Casper appeared out of nowhere, prob-ably where he got his name, cause his license definitely says Theadore. "Where are we headed?"

"Into town," I grumbled, kicking my leg over my bike and taking another long drag from my smoke before flicking it away. "Couple of places the magi-cally inclined like to gather, and I'm betting Vince is an Underground kind of guy, over the Dancing Fae." Kicking the bike to life, I reveled in the feeling of it between my thighs, centering me, clearing my head of the deep dark red that was threatening to steal my senses. "Let's move out."

More than anything, I needed to keep a level head. Walking into a crowded bar and shooting this motherfucker on sight wasn't a good idea. Also, I wasn't all that clear on what the bastard looked like. Wasn't a local when I was grow-ing up.

Underground was packed to the gills when we rode up, the rumble of bikes reverberating off the cinderblock and concrete building. An anomaly amongst magic users. Usually they tended towards wood, and surrounded it with wild nature. The Dancing Fae was at the far end of town, nearly outside of the downtown area entirely. It was a double lot, one of which was filled with flowers and herbs of all kinds. You could smell it before you saw it. But the Underground was born of a need for quick and dirty space. It looked like a fucking prison from the outside, nestled near the industrial areas, and away from the touristy shit.

"Feels like death," Ranger hissed as he set his bike down on the stand. "Like decay and rot."

"No surprise there," I muttered, pushing the thick iron door open. "Every-thing in this fucking place is against the natural order." Magic pulsed through the room like a thick bass beat. Thumping and purring until you almost wanted to surrender to its siren's song. There was always a risk of addiction when it came to the dark arts. The darker the art, the higher the risk. "What do you bet he's in there?" I pointed to the back room, the door was closed, but had a black aura around it. I could almost feel the fingers of magic leaching out into the room, a fog slowly filling the floor around our feet.

"I did not fucking sign up for death by mysterious fog," Maddox grumbled, the sharp cock of his gun filling the room. And for the first time I noticed that not one fucking person around us was moving, not even blinking.

"Suit up boys," I whispered, pulling my own gun from the back of my jeans. "We're apparently bringing guns to a magic fight."

Walking past vacant eyes, staring off into nothing. Not a single chest was moving, not a twitch. It was like they had all been frozen in time. An entire bar full of magic folk. A shiver ran down my spine as I touched the door to the back room. My skin felt like there were spiders under it, and I wanted to do nothing but turn tail and run in the opposite fucking direction.

The thick heavy door pulled open slowly, even under my strength. My shoulders burned as Maddox and Ranger both helped my pry the thing open enough to walk in. Nothing I expected was behind the door. A single man stood in the center of the room, arms crossed, waiting.

"Thought you would be here sooner," he drawled, picking at his fingernails. "Do you have any idea what kind of power it takes to keep up this level of control?"

"Golly gee," I growled, pointing into the center of his chest with my weapon, fully ready to take the shot. "Didn't know I was keeping you waiting, would have gotten here an hour ago, but your a fucking douch bag." The crack of my gun filled the room, heavy concrete walls making the sound multiply around us. "But my fucking mate comes first."

The bullet dissolved before it got anywhere close to Vince, just a wave of his hand and it was gone from existence. "You'll have to do better than that, bear." The lash of power that he volleyed ripped me off my feet, crashing into the far wall. My head rang with impact. Stars danced in my vision as I pulled myself to my feet. The crack and bang of weapons slowly filled my ears, while I shook my head, trying to get my bearings. "Seems your little club is out classed," Vince commented conversationally as the bodies of my friends ricocheted off the walls by me. "You can't win this, shifter. Magic is just superior to your puny weapons."

He leaned back against the wall behind him, framing himself between windows, ethereal light glowing. Nothing of the human world was back there. Not to mention that the Underground was, in fact, mostly underground. "You have no idea who you're up against."

"The newest chapter of the Lords of Khaos?" Vince shrugged, waving his hands wide. "You aren't a secret, boy," he said. "You are cut off from your brethren. A lonely group that isn't even enough to form a full clan. Mismatched shifters, huddling together in wake of the human government's oversight."

"Not impressive," Knox growled, pulling out his knife and flipping it in his hand. "You can read, and clearly watch the fucking news." He caught the blade between his thumb and forefinger, spinning it before flipping it again and catching the handle and doing it again. "But we don't go anywhere without backup."

The rush of displaced air came through the door, followed by the sound of life on the other side. Talking and music filtered through to us past the heavy door. The clank of dishes and gurgling of the beer taps working once again. I waited patiently and watched as Vince's face fell. With a woosh, the door opened, and smoke filled the ground. This time warm and filled with life. The woman who followed looked less like a green witch and more like a club girl, but the glow of her presence spoke to her power.

"If I get caught out of my little city," Cordelia growled, pointing a long red painted fingernail at me. "You will have fucking hell to pay."

"I will take that risk," I said, turning back to Vince. His face was chalk white as he watched the people milling about in the main bar. "What did you think would happen?" I asked him as his hand fluttered over the wall behind him, searching for the window sill. "Did you think you were going to continue to use my mate to power your spells? Did you not realize that this day would come one way or another?" I aimed directly between his eyes, and pulled the trigger. Bullet passed right through the bastard's head, and sank into the wall behind it as the body dissolved.

"Oh, sorry," Vince said from somewhere else. "Did you think I would just stand there and let you shoot me?" He sounded like he was coming through a staticky radio. "My sweet little bird already helped me open the gateway I needed," he said, voice fading with every word. "Such a good girl, I really will miss her. Suppose you'll bite her now. Pity. She won't be of use to me after that."

"Damned fucking right," I growled, shoving my gun back into the back of my jeans. "I'm going to bite her so good, even your grandchildren will fucking feel its power."

"Such a pity," he said again, voice watery and nearly too quiet for even me to hear. "I'll be back, though. Just you wait." With a pop, he was gone.

"Fucking anticlimactic as shit," Knox grumbled, dusting off his hands as he stretched. "I need a beer."

"Not here you don't," Cordelia told him, grabbing the knob and pulling the door open. "I expect a full ass dinner and a good place to fucking sleep after you wasted my fucking time."

"Boons a boon, witchy bitchy," Maddox hissed, grinning at her with a mouth full of sharp teeth. "We should be the ones put out, you did fucking nothing but walk in."

"Fair," she shrugged and strode towards the door. "I still want a nice steak."

9
BIRDIE

Voices woke me from sleep, a low drone that pulled me from the depths of dreams. My body felt heavy, sore, but warm. A golden glow filled the room and snuck past my eyelids before I could convince them to even open. For the first time in ages, I just let myself lay in the inbetween place. The soft lull of my dreams, and the bright waking world.

"We aren't prepared for a magic standoff," Killian said, his voice full of the bear I had yet to meet. "Shifters deal with shifter business, witches deal with magic."

"I'm not saying you're wrong," came a feminine voice I didn't know. It was deep and smoky, almost transfixing. "But you already stepped in this hornet's nest, its now your problem too."

"Can we circle back to the part where the fucker wasn't even in the room, but managed to freeze an entire bar full of spell casters?" Maddox grumbled, I could hear his feet tapping on the wood floor of my room. "How is he getting that kind of fucking power, cause it ain't from one little human, no offence Kill, but your mate can't fuel that shit."

"What?" I asked, finally choosing the real world. My eyes felt like they were stuck together with silly putty, and my bones felt old as I turned over and tried to sit up. "I'm gonna throw up," I muttered, and was immediately lifted in strong arms, a bowl between me and the floor and the soothing rumble of my mate's beast vibrating against my back.

The world spun, was too bright, too everything. My stomach lurched hard, rolling and reeling, until I was heaving up nothing. My belly cramped up, muscles locking as I tried to expel whatever it was in my stomach. Nothing but thin bile and tears landed in the bowl.

"Try not to make any sudden moves," the woman who was sitting across from the bed said. "You've been through the magic equivalent of the gauntlet." She pulled a crystal from her pocket and held it in her palm until it glowed a muddy grey. She handed it to Killian, who pressed it into my hand. "Smokey quartz will help with some of the withdrawal symptoms. But I'm going to have to mix something up stronger for long term." She sat back down in her seat, and crossed her legs. "I'm Cordelia, by the way, so nice of your boys to bother to introduce me."

"A name is nice," I whispered, my body feeling like it had literally been through the wringer and was laid out too thin. "But who are you?"

"I am a witch," she said simply. "I've been working with the Lords for several years, but most recently with some troubles that are more personal. Killian called me in when he went to look for your ex. Charming man by the way. Totally insane. Deep in the black magic."

"Yeah, I got that part." I leaned back in Killian's arms, letting him hold me together. "I thought this was all over," I moaned. "I thought he would go to jail, and get a sentence and I'd never see him again."

"The human justice system isn't equipped to handle mage's like Vince. They aren't prepared to handle the most mild of kitchen witches." Cordelia leaned back and looked around the room. "He's going to be back, you know that, right?" she asked, looking at me. "He's found a source for his power to grow, and he's going to keep trying to get at it."

"Not if we're bonded," Killian told her. "Not if I close off that potential."

"Vince will come anyway," Cordelia shook her head, picking at her long crimson fingernails. "If he can't have the power, he'll make sure no one can. Serenity has been doing her best, building wards around the house, reinforcing them, helping Birdie with her magic withdrawals, helping her protect herself out in the world. I can't even imagine the time it took to ward the whole elementary school. But here's the straight skinny. Birdie will be vulnerable until Vince is in the ground."

I looked up at Killian, who squeezed me against his chest. I could feel the panic rising inside of me, the trapped feeling that I got whenever I thought about finally being free of this cage i had been living in for so long. "Why me?" I asked in a small voice. Killian just shook his head and pulled me up into his lap, cradling me to him. "Why did Vince choose me?"

"I don't really know," Cordelia told me, her face clear of any emotions, but her eyes hard as diamonds. "But we're going to find out." She slapped her hand on her knees and stood up. "Talk to your mate, bear."

The door closed quietly behind her, and I looked around the room at the men standing and lounging around the small space. Killian's arms around me, holding me to his chest as he swayed back and forth for a long moment.

"Talk to me about what?" I asked when it was clear that no one was going to start.

"At the moment," Knox started, hands folded together, elbow on his knees as he sat on my trunk at the end of the bed. "Vince can still get to you. The house is as tight as Serenity and Cordelia can make it, but he's branded himself under your skin."

"Because of the intimate relationship that you two shared, he's got a lock on you right now. The wards keep out those with ill intentions, but he's far more powerful than either of our witches." Killian pulled me with him until he was leaning back against the headboard. "Black magic is tempting and seductive because it can give you power that you can't even begin to imagine. The downside is that it invades your blood, corrupts your body, and twists your soul until there's nothing left of the person you were."

"This is all my fault," I mutter, putting my hands over my face. Killian pryse them off and turns me to look at him. "It is, he wouldn't be here if it wasn't for me. He followed me back to Deadwood. We met in college." I scooted down the bed, but Killian wrapped his arms around me and pulled me back into his lap.

"Nope, you aren't getting away, I like this." He leaned down and nipped at my earlobe. "This guy would have found someone else then," he whispered into my ear. "And she might not have had anyone to pull her out of it."

"There's no saying he hasn't done this before, or there aren't other people he's drawing from," Knox said. It was so strange, looking at him without his usual goofy grin. The man bled humor, and now he was looking at me as if he was trying to tell me that my cat had died. "Birdie, the point is, he can get to you. But there's a solution to that."

"Why do I feel like this isn't a good solution?"

"It's a solution that's really inevitable," Killian hedged, still holding me tight, his breath fanning my shoulder as he rested his chin there. "He won't be able to touch you or draw from you once we've bonded. When my bite is on your throat, declaring to the supernatural world that you are spoken for, the magic doors slam closed."

"But he can still get to me physically," I guessed.

"Yes." He rubbed his beard over my shoulder, back and forth in a way that was loosening all the tension that had crept up since the conversation had started. "And he's already threatened to do just that."

"So neither way is safe." I leaned my head back on his chest and sighed. "Can I think about it?"

"Of course you can," Killian sat up and pressed a kiss to my hair. "It's completely your call. I won't take."

"But you want to," I told him, getting up on my knees and turning to look at him, his arms falling away from my sides. "If I said yes, you would be on me."

"Bears mate for life, Birdie," he said, framing my face with his hands, rubbing his thumbs up and down my skin. "The moment I saw you, my bond formed. I'm yours. There's not questions there, but if you don't want my bite, or don't want it yet, that's entirely your choice."

"It's a lot," I whispered, peeking up at him through my lashes. "I mean our whole relationship has been a lot. I was so sure I wouldn't fall for another supe.

I was going to steer as clear as I could away." I took a deep breath and swallowed around the lump in my throat. "Now look at everything. I'm in my bedroom at my best friend's house with a motorcycle club filled with shifters. I have two witches downstairs trying to tighten wards that surround my house, because my ex, who is the reason I never wanted to tangle with supes again, is back and wants me to make him more powerful."

"No bite then," Killian concluded, pulling me back into his lap, wrapping his arms and legs around me until I was surrounded by him. Held fast, tight and safe. "I still expect cuddles, cause I have discovered that I am definitely a cuddler, if only because of you."

"I will accept that blame," I muttered into his chest. The rest of the club got to their feet and left, likely setting themselves up downstairs with Serenity and Cordelia. "Probably not the right time, but where is Madison?"

"Trying to dodge Knox," Killian snorted. "Those two are gonna be complete idiots by sheer willpower, it seems."

"What do you mean?" I asked, tipping my chin up to look at him. "Why would Madison dodge Knox? She's not shy or anything."

"I think Knox will have to tell you about the way lions are. They're different from bears." He leaned us over until my head hit the pillow right next to his. "For now, the doctor has ordered rest." He pressed a kiss to the back of my head and then leaned up to pull the blankets down over us. "We can talk more in the morning."

EPILOGUE

MADISON

There was absolutely no reason that I should be stressing this much over dinner with the Lords. None, zero. But that didn't stop my hands from practically trembling as I pulled my famous extra chocolatey, super fudgy brownies. It was just dinner with the neighbors. Dinner with my bestie, who I loved and adored, not to mention missed. Helping Birdie move out of my house had been both one of the best days ever, and one of the worst. I loved her. I loved having her under my roof, but getting to watch her soar with her new man, that was the best part.

"You're stalling," Birdie told me over the phone as I put the brownies on top of the oven to start to cool. "Tell me about this guy you've been hinting about, cause I'm on pins and needles."

"I told you, he doesn't even notice I exist." I dropped my oven mitts on the counter and pulled my hair up into a high pony. Summer was nearly at its end, but it was going out with a bang, and having the oven on had made the kitchen sweltering. "I don't even really know him, but fuck does he get me going, just by being in the room." I fanned my face, trying to get the bright red to leave my cheeks. "I had to go out and get a new BOB, and can I tell you, it's not just a hop skip and a jump to get to a good toy store."

"I have also had this issue," my friend said sagely. I could almost see her nodding her head and folding her lips between her teeth. "Killian and I have just taken to ordering them."

"I do not need to know what you and your bear do," I hummed, trying to not picture anything to do with my best friend getting railed by her beau. I had heard enough. Which was what precipitated them moving to the ranch. "Anyway," I said, waving away the slightly disturbing image. "I just called to say I would be a little late, not that I wasn't coming."

"You skipped last week," Birdie reminded me. "Get in your car and come over, I can send one of the boys to get your brownies later."

"Awww," I coo. "You miss me."

"Of course I fucking do. Only woman over the age of seven is Mandy, and she's busy being a badass mama and business woman."

"True enough." I grab my keys off the counter and throw my purse over my shoulder. "Okay, I'm leaving the brownies." My keys jingle merrily as I jogged out to my car. And standing there, next to my car with a bouquet of deep purple tulips was the very man my entire body and mind had become attuned to. The one I thought didn't even know I was there.

"Not letting you avoid me anymore, Madison." Knox took the steps of the porch two at a time before he was right in front of me. "You, my little lioness, are mine."

LORDS OF KHAOS: IRONWOOD

Malachai has given up on finding his fated mate, even if his bear never stopped looking. As VP of the Lords of Khaos, he's been living the high life but a business trip to Las Vegas is set to turn his world upside down. When Kai crashes into his fated mate, he and his bear can agree on one thing. They're never letting her go.

Belladonna is happy with her life. She owns a bookshop with her mom, her best friend is her favorite person, and she's only a cat away from being a bridesmaid and never a bride for life. While running into a bad boy biker in Vegas was not on her to do list, waking up with a wedding ring on her finger is worse.

But when Kai brings a tentative Bella home to introduce her to MC life, they uncover a sordid plot which puts both of their lives at risk. Can this pair find their way to an HEA or was their love destined to crash and burn in Vegas?

Malachai is a paranormal MC romance. It's a full on steamfest with growly bear shifters and a heroine who loves adult language. If you have read K.O. Newman before you know her books are full of sexually explicit content, a little bit of blood and violence, and fated mates who are ready to throw down to keep their loved ones safe.

The Bears of the Lords of Khaos MC are on the prowl. There is nothing they want more than their fated mates, but its not always as simple as it sounds. Are you ready for some growly bears, feisty women, and a little bit of blood, guns and violence? Enter Ironwood Heights, a former psychiatric hospital that now houses the LOKI MC, and fall in love with all the chaos mates can bring.

Grab Malachai Today

ABOUT THE AUTHOR

K.O. Newman is a neurospicy author of steamy, panty-melting paranormal romance. She is a lifelong reader who has overcome dyslexia to bring sass and sizzle to your shelves. Her queer-inclusive books include motorcycle clubs of mythical monsters, aliens, and all the bearded bad-boys.

Outside her life as an author, K.O. is a mom of two brilliant children, and two precocious cats. Her little family lives in the gorgeous Midwestern U.S., but Kat's heart truly lies in a little town in Vermont, the home of her Lords of Khaos: Ironwood series.

If you're looking to keep up with all her releases and what's going on with K.O. and her authoring world, come check her out on Substack!

LOVE'S BEGINNING

AMANDA SPEIGHTS

1

I know I'm in trouble the moment Jack Bristow walks through the door of my establishment. The sight of those striking blue eyes up close nearly undoes me. For the first time, as the madam of this house, I feel a twinge of jealousy at the thought of a patron sharing intimacy with one of my girls.

This will be Mister Bristow's first visit to 'Open Flowers' since he arrived in town. Surprising. I believe I heard he's been here a month now. Normally, we're one of the first establishments sought out by the businessmen.

He hangs his hat on the rack beside the door. "Ma'am." His smile is youthful and almost innocent. *Almost.* His beard is well cared for, as I expect it to be for a man of his standing.

Squaring my shoulders, I look him in the eye, sure to exude professionalism and strength lest he see me as weak. "How can I help you today, sir?"

He clears his throat. "What are your rates?"

"It depends on what you're looking for, but they begin at $10 an hour."

"Three hours?" He cocks a brow, laying out thirty dollars on the desk.

"Kitty has time available." I try my hardest not to look up at him as I stuff the money into the bosom of my dress.

"I'm here for you, Miss Miller," he says in a gravelly tone.

My breath hitches and a flutter fills my middle. *He wants me? That can't be.*

"I'm a businesswoman, Mister..." I pretend not to know his name as I begin writing it in my ledger.

"Bristow," he rasps.

"Mister Bristow. I'm a madam, not a hooker." I find the origin of the term 'hooker'—referring to the working girls who followed General Hooker's troops during the war—oddly charming.

When my younger sister, Amelia, and I arrived two years ago at seventeen and fifteen years of age, our only possessions were what was in our wagon. That is, what we hadn't sold or traded. The remnants of a life, after the fever took our parents during our pilgrimage West. Together, we've managed to grow one of the most lucrative brothels in Deadwood.

The gentleman leans against the paper-covered wall and crosses his arms. Those eyes of his almost appear to glow beneath his dark lashes which causes a tingling sensation to run through me right down to my toes. He smirks and I can't help but wonder what it must be like to kiss those lips. I suppose Kitty will find out soon enough. I shutter at the thought of it.

"That's quite all right," he says. "We can find something else to do." His gaze darts about the room, as though searching for the next thing to say. "Do you know how to play cards, Miss Miller?"

His posture is relaxed against the wall, and I can't help but wonder what he's up to. *Cards?* I'm not falling for that.

I walk around the desk. "If you'll follow me. I believe you'll find Kitty to your liking."

He moves in front of me and places a hand on the other side of the wall, halting my steps.

The scent of leather caresses my senses and I momentarily close my eyes taking it in. But then reality smacks my awareness back to the life I've created for myself.

"I'm a very busy woman, Mister Bristow." I dare to peer into those eyes.

"Call me Jack," he whispers.

I can almost feel his breath on me he's so close, still not budging.

"I will do no such thing," I murmur, longing desperately for the feel of his strong arms around me in a tight embrace. Heavens, it's been so long since I've known the comfort of such a hug.

Pull yourself together, Laura.

Instead, I step aside, but he blocks me once more.

He takes my chin gently, lifting my face to his, "I wish for time with you, Miss Miller, not to bed you, but to learn about you."

I clear my throat and move my gaze to a button on his suit vest. "I'm afraid that's not possible." Reaching into my bosom I pull his money out and offer it to him. "It's Kitty or no one." I remain stern. Many in this town do not take me seriously. I will give him no reason to follow their lead.

"Keep the money, Miss Miller." He reaches for his hat and places it on his head. Once at the door he turns back with a smile playing on his lips. "But you should know, I don't give up easily." He tips his head and leaves.

My chest rises and falls as I draw steadying breaths once more. Feeling faint, I make my way to the desk chair as swiftly as I can. Yes, I knew I was in trouble when that man stepped foot in this room. I just didn't realize how much trouble.

I've heard his name in certain circles, Jack Bristow, Land Agent. And I've seen him around town, but I never believed he knew who I was or that he's ever noticed me. My dirty blonde locks and fair eyes don't compare to the beauty of my younger sister. Perhaps he has yet to see her.

~

It's been a week since Jack Bristow came into my establishment. As I carry my pails to the spring, my thoughts linger on him. Truth be told, he's on my mind more than I care to admit. I hadn't given much thought to the building I pass each morning with the sign that reads 'Bristow & Sons,' until last week. I wonder if he's Bristow or one of the sons. Surely, he must be a son, as he's much too young for children older than the toddler age.

I glance away trying desperately to not think further of the man.

I know not if he's married, although I wouldn't be surprised if he is. Many of the men who frequent my establishment are. And, although I know nothing of being intimate with a man, I know my girls have knowledge of things the wives do not. Perhaps the men are too bashful to ask their wives. Or, perhaps the wives are too prudish to oblige.

It's been exceptionally hot as of late, so I do my best to fill my buckets while the sun is still low in the mornings. Also, I prefer to avoid the town folk as much as possible.

"Don't you have someone to fetch your water for you?" I'm surprised when Jack Bristow takes a pail from my hand. He reaches for the other, but I hold it away.

My breath hitches at the sight and sound of him. *Keep your wits about you, Laura.*

"I can fetch my own water just fine, Mister Bristow, thank you for your concern."

He's not as dressed up today as he was the last I saw him. Simple suspenders and sleeves rolled up, showing his muscular forearms.

For heaven's sake. I inhale sharply and my cheeks warm.

"Well, today I'll help you," he insists, picking up his pace to meet mine, which has quickened, I realize.

"I don't need your help." I continue walking, faster. If I move any quicker, I may just be running. *I'm being entirely ridiculous.*

"I know you don't, but I want to help."

A dog barks in the distance.

I force a smile through my pride. "Just this once."

If I'm honest with myself, I welcome his help, although I'll never admit it out loud. The buckets are quite heavy once full, and I must stop often to gain relief from their weight.

"Have supper with me, Miss Miller." I'm taken aback by Jack's statement.

"I told you; I'm not for sale."

He halts. I stop and peer back at him, shading my eyes from the rising morning sun.

"I don't want to purchase you, Miss Miller, I wish to take you out for a lovely meal. One that you don't have to cook." He cocks a brow and points to the bucket in my hand. "I only assume you do the cooking since you're fetching your own water."

I turn back towards the direction of the spring, then glance back at the man who stands unmoving, still holding my other pail. He's relentless...exasperating.

"If I have supper with you, Mister Bristow, will you leave me be?"

"Perhaps." He shrugs. "Perhaps I'll find I don't care for you at all, and you shall not hear from me again."

"All right." *Good.*

"But perhaps I shall fall in love with you and wish to make you my wife." His lip curves into a grin.

This makes me laugh. *Darn him.* "That will never happen."

"Well?" he asks, eyebrows raised, waiting for my reply.

"One meal and that's all."

He moves his feet again and we make our way to the spring side by side. "But, I cannot guarantee you won't fall in love with *me.*"

I chuckle and repeat. "That will never happen."

When Jack and I enter Claretha's Fine Dining, the place is practically empty. It smells of my mother's home cooking—a scent I hadn't realized I missed so much—wrapping around me, stirring both an ache of hunger, and a longing for the woman I had to bury on the trail to the Dakotas.

An older woman with gray streaks running through her dark hair smiles at him. "Jack, please, have a seat wherever you like."

Jack removes his hat and gestures towards a nearby table. He pulls a chair out for me, and it's then the woman appears to recall who I am, because her smile fades. She straightens, moving closer, and lowers her voice. "I'm afraid I have no table available after all."

"Pardon?" He leans in.

"You, Jack, are welcome to stay, but *she* is not."

Jack looks me over. Since I was joining him for supper this evening, I made sure to wear one of my most conservative dresses. Turning back to the woman, he states, "I don't see the problem."

Claretha Parson leans in closer and spits out, "I will not have a *soiled dove* eating in my establishment."

Now, Jack straightens. "I see." He places his hat back on his head. "That's a shame." Holding out his arm for me to take his elbow, he turns back to the woman. "Missus Parson," he states. "If this young lady isn't welcome here, then you have lost my business. And I'll be sure to spread the word." He gives me a wink of reassurance.

～

"I'm sorry you're forced to eat cold sandwiches for supper." Jack says as we sit at his kitchen table enjoying roast beef on buttered bread with canned apples and tins of milk.

I chuckle. "I quite like them."

I find it sweet that he offered to prepare a meal for me...somewhere we wouldn't be turned out.

In the course of our meal, I've learned that he is, in fact, one of the sons of Bristow & Sons. His father remains in Pennsylvania until his mother gives birth, as she's due to have a child soon.

"Levi's the oldest of soon to be ten children. I'm the second oldest, less than a year younger than Levi."

"Is he married?" I sip my milk.

"No. We live here together. He's gone into the hills for a few days surveying some parcels." Jack bites into his sandwich.

I watch as he chews his food. His suit coat long shed, and his sleeves rolled to his elbows. "Why aren't you with him?"

He wipes his mouth with his napkin. "Someone has to take care of paper-work, and the town folk requests...and complaints."

Sitting his sandwich down he leans back in his chair. "Tell me about you. What brought you to Deadwood?"

"My sister, Amelia, and I came west with our parents. My older brother..." I inhale sharply not wanting to speak of Charlie, "left them practically penni-less. My father believed the West held opportunity." I peer at my plate. "Unfor-tunately, we lost both of our parents on the journey."

"I'm sorry to hear that."

"Yes, well, we made it, and here we are." I blink back tears and smile.

"Did you work at a brothel before you came here?"

"No. Rosie, one of my girls, I met her shortly after arriving. She was in a bad situation working at Ida Shulz's *den of iniquity*." I wag my head. "Anyway, Amelia and I sold what we could for food and slept in our wagon. One day the idea came to me of starting my own bordello. I set up a tent in the beginning with Rosie being my first girl, but it didn't take long until I had Kitty as well, then enough to pay for our current home." I lift my chin. "Business is thriving."

"Hmmm." Jack nods.

I tilt my head and look him in the eye. "I strictly run the business and see to it my girls are safe and cared for." Heat rises in my face as I imagine judgment from him.

"I have no doubt about that." His gaze holds mine.

He crosses his arms causing his biceps to pull his shirt taut. "And your brother?"

I shake my head and shrug. "I haven't seen him since I was a child."

He grabs his sandwich. "Probably just as well." Taking a large bite, he smiles, clearly understanding I'd prefer to change the subject.

"So, tell me, Jack Bristow, have you yet decided you don't like me and never want to see me again?"

He stills, his facial expression serious as he reaches across the table and his thumb gently glides over the corner of my mouth. "No." His gaze moves to my lips. "I'd right like to kiss you, Miss Miller."

I fear he thinks this evening is going somewhere that it can't. Lowering my eyes I sit back and fidget with my napkin. "Jack, I—"

His chair scrapes across the wood of the floor as he moves from his seat on the other side of the table to the one beside me. Taking my chin, he gently moves my face to his and softly lays a kiss on my lips.

My heart and my breath race. *He kissed me.*

Jack studies my face, still holding my chin. "I've wanted to do that since the moment I laid eyes on you."

I nibble my bottom lip. *He kissed me.* Warmth washes over me.

Placing his arm over the back of my chair, he leans in and presses his mouth to mine again. When I feel the wetness of his tongue, I jolt back.

"Laura?" His eyes are questioning.

I lower my gaze as self-consciousness wells within me. I'm a fierce business-woman, a madam of a brothel for heaven's sake, but I've never so much as kissed a man. And for all my fierceness, he's causing me to melt right here, like butter in a hot pan.

"Jack, I've never."

Will he even believe me?

There's no pity or judgment on his face or in his tone. "We'll take all the time you need." He takes my hand and places a soft kiss on the back. When he smiles at me, his eyes glimmer. "Would you like a piece of cake? I made it myself."

A deep sense of relief envelops me. "That would be delightful."

I flick the fan, with lace accents and hand-painted floral motif that shimmer, open and wave it delicately to my face. It was gifted to me by a gentleman patron who bragged that he brought it from France, "for such a time as this." He even paid triple my fee to spend the entire weekend with my most requested girl, Melody. We call her that because she leaves the men walking out of here with a lively tune on their lips.

The ringlets that frame my face are damp with perspiration, and I sorely wish I could get out of this blasted bustle. It must be a hundred degrees.

"We desperately need rain," Amelia huffs.

I glance at my younger sister, who plops onto the crushed velvet sofa.

"You must be more proper, Amelia. What if a client were to see you?" The long sleeves of my blouse itch and I fan more feverishly, feeling as my sister does.

The dear girl taps her fingers on the wooden arm of the settee. Her long chestnut colored hair is swept up in a stylish bun, and her mossy eyes glance around the room. She is a young woman of rare beauty. Often, I must remind the men who come through our door that she is not available for their entertainment, no matter the price they're willing to pay.

I worried that Jack would prefer her over me once he saw her, but she's like a younger sibling to him.

The women of this town who look down their noses at me for running a brothel would never imagine it's strictly business. Jack respects my wishes that I shall wait until marriage, which is something I'm unwilling to entertain at this time in my life.

Amelia picks up the medical book she left sitting on the end table. I sigh. My sister always has her nose in one of those. We call her our house nurse. Although not formally trained, she is forever reading about how to cure sickness and heal wounds. She even helps a local midwife at times when the woman is in need of more than her own two hands.

I exhale, thinking of her insistence to apply to medical school to become a doctor. A part of me wants this for her as well, as I believe a woman can and should do anything a man can do. But another part of me is fearful of losing her. I feel a responsibility to care for her in our parents' unfortunate absence.

"It's stifling in here," Amelia groans. "I'm opening the window. Look, the trees are swaying, maybe we'll catch a breeze."

"Probably a hot one," I grumble.

Amelia peers through the glass. "Perhaps a storm is coming. The sky is a spectacular orange hue." As soon as she opens it a strong scent of smoke wafts into the room.

"What on earth?" I leap from the chair to look out the window. "There's a fire, Amelia. Quick, let's go see." I close the fan and toss it on the table. Taking my sister by the hand, we head for the door.

Searching the sky, we make our way across the street. I gasp at the sight of black smoke billowing from behind our house.

"Laura, we must get everyone out, now." Amelia pleads while pulling at me, but I'm transfixed on the scene before us. Surely this cannot be real.

"Laura!" Amelia shouts and I realize folks are rushing about. Children crying as they're either carried or dragged by their mothers. Men yell orders as people scramble seeming unsure what exactly to do.

Thick black clouds roll in the sky. It's as dark as the darkest storm weather. Only no storm is coming. The town is burning to the ground. Amelia and I watch in horror as fire jumps from one structure to the next.

Her voice quivers. "No one will help us, Laura, we must take the girls and leave, at once," she urges.

We stand paralyzed at the sight of the building before us—once stately, with red velvet drapes and an elegant sign above the door that reads "Open Flowers" — now dejected against the raven plumes that surround it. This business is all we have, or...all we had. Now, with one lick of the approaching flames, it'll all be gone.

My girls stand close, their faces pale, their bosoms flowing from their dresses. Some wear little more than a robe; all are draped in the quilts they grabbed in haste. Arms filled with the few items they were able to retrieve before we had to flee the house. Amelia, of course, clutches a trunk filled with books.

The autumn wind is torrid, the air suffocating, and a bead of sweat trickles down my back.

"Laura?" A nudge from my sister pulls me from my rumination.

I wipe sweat from my brow and nod toward higher ground. "We must head into the hills with the others."

Amelia cries, "The house."

"The house is gone." I slide my arm through hers and urge the ladies to follow me in the direction of the other townsfolk.

This isn't the first time we've lost everything.

There was a time not long ago when power and wealth were all I wanted. Until the striking and influential young businessman Jack Bristow came into my life. His pursuit of me despite my profession drew me to him like a hummingbird to nectar. Now I wonder, is he all I need?

As our group approaches the crowd gathered in the hills, I search the dejected faces for Jack. Some families had the wherewithal to grab tents and other supplies for shelter. I want to be strong but everything I've worked for is being reduced to ashes. I have no idea what tomorrow holds and no idea where Jack is. It's been two hours and still no sign of him. Tears stream down my face and I swipe my nose with the arm of my sleeve.

Please, let him be all right. I need him.

"Jack! Jack!"

My voice is hoarse. Surely, he's got to be looking for me as well.

"Are you missing a child, ma'am?" The woman holds an infant in her arms. The child's dirty face is streaked with tears and his nose runs.

Unable to answer, I shake my head.

"They've set up a tent for injured patients over yonder." She points in the direction of the medical tent. "Perhaps you should check there."

At the shelter, I find some folks sprawled on strips of canvas on the ground. Calling Jack's name, I move from man to man attempting to get a good look at their faces.

"Laura." Jack's brother stands outside the erected shelter wiping his face with a rag.

"Levi!" A knowing tells me Jack's in there. "Can I see him?"

"He's been asking for you, so you'd better let him see for himself that you're safe." He pulls back the flap of the entrance and I hesitate before stepping inside not knowing what awaits me. "Far right corner," Levi murmurs from behind me. I can only hope my eyes show my gratitude as I look back at him.

The tent's dark, save for a few oil lamps and some candles, as the scent of smoke lingers.

I find Jack with his legs, an arm, and part of his face bandaged. Swallowing back tears, I lay a gentle hand on his shoulder. "Jack," I whisper.

His eyes open and a breath escapes him. "Have I died and gone to heaven?" he rasps.

His cheek is covered in soot. "I thought I lost you," I say with a trembling voice swiping my knuckles down his face and neck.

He struggles to reach for me, and I take his uninjured hand. Beautiful cobalt eyes stare up at me. Elation fills my being as the realization hits me. *He's alive.*

"I tried to help those around me. I'm sorry I wasn't there for you." He closes his eyes and his throat bobs. I'm certain he's swallowing past the pain. "I was making my way to you, I swear. A roof—"

"As you can see, I'm fine." I give his hand a gentle squeeze.

"The fire started in a stable behind the Gem Theatre. It took out *Claretha's Fine Dining*." He emphasizes the name of the restaurant. My mind goes back to the evening just months ago, when we ate cold sandwiches because Claretha Parson wouldn't have a *"soiled dove"* seen in her establishment. Of course, even though a man has never bedded me, the woman who mounts her religious high horse every morning before her feet hit the floor would still believe I'm partaking in sin—just by encouraging fornication. But that is of no significance. Right now, I must tend to Jack. He's all that matters at this moment.

"I'm just thankful you're here with me." I lay a tender kiss on his head.

"The fire got me pretty good. Scars don't go away." He says it as if I'll no longer find him to be a fit man, which of course is nonsense.

"That doesn't bother me none. You're still the same here." I tap his chest. "And here," I say, laying a peck on his brow.

"I'm smitten with you, Laura Miller. I've been smitten with you since the first moment I laid eyes on you from my desk window as you passed by to fetch water from the spring."

I smile and bow my head. After our supper date he confessed that he'd been watching me for a couple of weeks but was too shy to approach me.

He slowly reaches for my chin, forcing me to look at him. His eyes were the first thing I noticed the day he came into my business thinking he could pay for time with me. They're mesmerizing.

"I'm serious," he says, bringing my attention back to where we are today, in a dark tent with other injured from the fire. "You do things to my head that should be unlawful. Perhaps one day, I might persuade you to be my wife."

I must admit, I'm enamored with him. I hadn't anticipated he'd truly want to marry me. *Wife.* I let that word settle for a fleeting moment. *Is that possible? Can I marry him? What will happen to my sister? And the girls? Oh, Laura, you foolish woman, he hasn't even officially proposed.*

"Let's revisit this conversation later. Right now, I just need you to get well." I press his knuckles against my lips so very grateful he's still alive. A tear slips from my eye and runs down my cheek.

❁

With my industrious determination, I had my establishment back up and fully running within a few months. Our first house was a small stick-built home. It was so small, in fact, that I was forced to construct partitions to divide one of the bedrooms into two smaller rooms. Rosie and Kitty each had their own chamber, while Amelia and I shared the third. When I eventually hired Melody, the room Amelia and I shared was further divided, reducing our quarters even more.

The new house, built upon the same lot, is constructed of stone to guard against any future fires. Each girl has a spacious room, along with a parlor, while my sister and I now have our own separate quarters from the girls, no longer needing to share a space.

I used to get after Amelia about turning the lamp out so I could sleep. Now she can read all night long if she likes, and I can rest peacefully.

"Let me take a look at your arm." Amelia begins unwrapping Jack's bandages as he sits on our new sofa in our new sitting room.

He glances at me and gives me that smile that always makes me soft like dough. He no longer has a beard, as the scars from the burn won't allow him to grow a full one. But he's still my Jack, and as handsome as ever.

"Your sister is like a mother hen." He says with eyes still on me.

"You should be so lucky to have me to nurse you back to health, Jack Bristow," Amelia chides.

Folding fresh linens at the table, I hold his gaze and chuckle. I can't help but think of how easily he fits into our little family. Those two truly are like siblings sometimes.

"I never said I wasn't thankful, Lia."

My heart warms with the nickname he's given to my sister.

"Well, you should be, because you're healing up wonderfully, thanks to *me*." She secures the clean cloth on his arm and takes the sheets I've just folded. "I'm going to my room to read."

"What a surprise," Jack states in a raised voice so she can hear him from the other room.

I laugh and sit beside him. "How are you feeling overall?" He rests his hand in my lap, and I softly trace his bicep, savoring the closeness between us.

"Wonderful with you by my side."

I kiss his cheek and lay my head on his shoulder.

I know he's not truly happy that I built this business back up. It's even better than it was before, and because of that I've been able to raise my rates. It's amazing what men are willing to pay for time with a woman who will bend to all their desires. I refuse to be dependent on any man, even Jack, which means despite his protests, I've been full steam ahead on this project.

"Laura."

I sigh, knowing that tone in his voice all too well.

"Jack, please. Can't we just have a lovely moment?"

There's a knock at the door and Jack exhales loudly.

I pat his arm. "I need to get that."

Leaning forward, he places his elbows on his knees and runs a hand over his face. Sometimes I wonder if I'll drive him away with my own stubbornness.

The pudgy man at the door fidgets, his buttons about to burst at the middle.

"Why, Judge McArthur, do come in." I motion towards the parlor while offering him my sweetest smile. "It's such a delight to see you this evening. Can I get you a drink? I just received a crate of the finest scotch Scotland produces."

I don't entirely know if it's Scotland's finest, but I did spend a great deal on it. And knowing Judge McArthur will spend a great deal on Rosie, I'll happily provide him with as much of the whisky as he wishes.

In the parlor room, I find Rosie and Melody are in the middle of a card game, while Kitty plays softly at the piano. Our newest additions, Pearl, sit in the lap of the town banker, and Kate is gone to her room entertaining the banker's business associate.

"Look who's here to see you, Ro." I sing song, rolling my eyes at the girl knowing she dreads seeing Jasper McAuthur. He makes it quite clear to her how he hates the thought of any other man touching her. The portly judge has shown no mercy on any man who's gone before him in his courtroom knowing they've been with *his* Rosie.

She downs the shot of liquor that sits on the table beside her and moves to the man.

"Well, hello there, Jasper." Her voice is sultry as she runs her hand over his chest. She's a wonderful performer.

"Here you are, sir." I hand him the glass of whisky. "Please, enjoy yourself."

Sweat beads on his head and his collar clings to his neck. "I'm certain I will."

This business isn't glorious by any means, and I count myself fortunate that I can go back to my sitting room to Jack.

Reclining on the sofa, he pats the spot beside him. "Come sit with me, my sweetheart."

I snuggle into his arm. "I ordered wallpaper today," I say, wanting to change the subject I know he's intending to bring up. Business certainly has been good. Sometimes I can't believe this is my life. "From France." I add.

Jack furrows his brow. "Are you telling me there's no wallpaper in America?"

I chuckle knowing he wouldn't understand. "The person who is to hang it is coming with it."

He rears his head. "You ordered wallpaper *and* the hanger from France?" He shakes his head. "That's the most ridiculous thing I've ever heard, Laura."

Men know nothing of decorating. "It's a very detailed scene that must be placed on the wall just so."

He scoots to the edge of the sofa. "Sometimes I'm afraid wealth means more to you than I do."

"Oh, Jack, for heaven's sake, you know that isn't true in the least." *But is it? After all, my actions would seem to say otherwise, wouldn't they?*

"Then sell this place, Laura."

I straighten. "I grew up a poor farmer's daughter. When Amelia and I came to this town, we had nothing. You know that. We hardly knew where our next meal was coming from, and now I can hire a wallpaper hanger from France and a case of scotch from Scotland."

How dare he give me such a fuss about this.

"You knew what I did when you met me, Jack Bristow. Don't try to change me."

"I'm not trying to change you, Laura. And I know you can take care of yourself, but it's not a safe profession, and I don't like the way the townsfolk talk about you."

I get to my feet and place my hands on my hips. "You mean the common folk, the women, because I can guarantee you I am *highly* favored with the authority and businessmen of this town. So, Jack, the *townsfolk* can all go to hell. And if you continue to insist on me giving up my livelihood— you can go right with them."

Jack nods, rises from the sofa, and walks out the door.

Tears stream down my face and I flop back onto the couch the way I often see Amelia do. That blasted man, why can't he just accept the way things are.

"He's right, you know." My sister pulls a chair from the table and takes a seat.

All I can do is stare at her.

"I haven't known how to tell you this," she says, "but I've been accepted into the University of Michigan's Medical School."

I inhale sharply. I've always known this is something she wanted to do, I just didn't think it would truly happen. How foolish of me. I've paid for the best tutors I could so that she'd have the grades needed to get into medical school. Latin, arithmetic, chemistry, she has more education than I ever will. It's not easy for a woman in the world and I've done my best to prepare her in every way I know. We Miller sisters will not depend on any man.

"I'm to begin my studies in the fall."

Although I wonder how long she's known, whether a letter came, and how she can leave me...so many questions, I choose to swallow them down. Rather, I stretch my arms to her.

"Oh Amelia, I'm so happy for you."

"Thank you." Her eyes glisten when she pulls back. "But we must talk about Jack."

She joins me on the settee. "Laura, he loves you."

"He's never said that."

"He doesn't have to."

"I'm not giving up my independence, Amelia, my livelihood. I've worked too hard for it."

"I don't think Jack would do that to you. I don't believe he expects you to bear children and cook meals while he supports your family monetarily."

"You're talking nonsense. We haven't even spoken of marriage." I lean back and play with a bow on my blouse, recalling Jack mentioning making me his wife. Surely it was the laudanum speaking. "I believe he wishes me to sell this business and take up work under another's employ. Take care of his books or waitress at the hotel."

Amelia places a hand on my knee. "Has he said that?"

"Well, no. But what other choice do I have? There's no way I could earn what I do now in any other way. How else would I put you through school?"

"Perhaps I can help by finding a job when I get to Michigan. And perhaps you should ask Jack what he expects of you if you're to sell this place."

My sister is so wise. Although only two years younger than me, sometimes I feel she's years more knowledgeable than I'll ever be.

I watch as Amelia announces to Jack that he no longer needs the last of his bandages.

No matter how angry the man grows with me, he can't seem to keep himself away.

There's a wave in his hair where his hat usually sits. His eyes are the brightest blue, and scars cover a portion of the left side of his cheek and chin from the burns. As I watch him, it suddenly strikes me. I can no longer deny it, although I've tried so hard. I love this man. I love him with everything that is in me, and I swipe a tear that spills over onto my cheek.

His smile causes those all too familiar flutters in my belly.

"You hear that, sweetheart? Doctor Miller here says no more bandages."

Amelia blushes. "I'm not a doctor yet."

"To me you are. And I thank you, Lia, for helping me heal. You've done a better job than that specimen this town calls a doctor."

Jack wraps an arm around my waste. "Lia, can you manage things here while I whisk your sister away for an hour or so?"

"Of course I can," she replies with a grin. "Please, take her. Go on."

~

Jack pulls the team up to an empty lot on the other side of town. Trees line the back, and it's flanked by a livery and a barber. A for-sale sign posted into the ground has the words SOLD painted across it.

"What is this? What are we doing here?"

Jack helps me from the wagon then stretches his arm out towards the sign. "I bought it."

Well, obviously he's excited about this purchase. "Congratulations. What do you plan to put here?"

"I was thinking a saloon." He grins with enthusiasm.

"A saloon?"

"Unless you'd prefer something else."

"Me? I hardly believe my thoughts on the matter hold any consequence."

He pulls me into his arms and slides his thumb over my cheek. "Laura, I can't imagine my life without you. And I must admit, I want more of you than courting and kisses. I want you by my side every day and every night. I love you, Laura Miller, and I want you to be my wife. Will you marry me?"

Did he just formally propose?

I can't believe my ears. I open my mouth and close it.

Jack pulls away. "Now, before you respond, I want to be perfectly clear."

Here we go. I sigh.

"I would ask that you sell the brothel. But I know if you'll have me, that I wouldn't be marrying just *any* woman. I'd be marrying THE Laura Miller, an intelligent and independent woman who won't depend on no man."

I chuckle. He's heard my speech many times over.

"That's why I want to build you a *respectable* business."

He emphasizes the word respectable in a tone I'm certain he's heard from the women of this town.

"It would be all yours," he continues.

"Even on paper?"

I know a saloon isn't entirely considered respectable but is more tolerated than a brothel.

He pulls me in again, his mouth so close to mine his breath warms my lips. "Especially on paper." Playfully, he rubs his nose against mine. "Say yes, sweetheart. I give my word to make you the happiest woman this side of the Mississippi."

I wrap my arms around his neck, our lips still touching. "How can I say no to that?" He parts his mouth for my tongue and our kiss grows more passionate than it ever has. He picks me up and spins me around.

"I love you, Laura Miller."

"I love you too, Jack Bristow." The thought of marrying this man, selling my establishment, and taking up a saloon is both scary and exhilarating. "We're truly doing this?"

He sits my feet back to the ground. "We sure are."

I'm giddy with excitement as Jack and I enter the house. Amelia is going to be thrilled. But, my smile fades when I see the man that sits at our kitchen table. Amelia stands, offering me a sad look before leaving the room.

"Charlie."

"Hello, Laura." He doesn't rise. Just leans back and places a hand on his thigh. "You've got a real nice place here." His gaze roams the room.

Jack's hand presses against my lower back. "Charlie?"

I take a deep breath. "Charlie is our much *older* brother."

The last time I saw Charlie was a decade ago, when Father was forced to turn him out after whispers spread throughout the town that my brother had assaulted a young lady. By then he was already a grown man, always in trouble —a drunkard and a thief, stealing from Father, only to gamble away whatever possessions he had taken.

Something tells me he's not here to play the role of loving older brother and the hair on my neck bristles with unease. "How did you find us?"

"It was fate really—providential." He smiles and I see he's missing a couple of teeth. Disgust rolls in my stomach that we share the same parents.

He taps the table. "I saw this beautiful building and just knew I'd get myself a clean woman here. And to my surprise, my sweet little sister came to the desk to welcome me. Oh, I didn't realize at first that it was her, although I thought I was seeing a ghost because she looks just like our mother, and then I saw the sign that reads, "Laura Miller, Proprietor.""

Jack has told me many times that I should go by a made-up name like the girls do, but I've been too prideful.

I force a smile. "It was good to see you." Then I swallow back fear of why he's here. "But, I'm sure you're a busy man and need to get along now."

"On the contrary. I've decided to stay."

"Oh? Are you staying at the hotel, or have you rented an apartment?"

He laughs and shakes his head. "No, little sister. I'm staying here." He taps the table again.

"Pardon?"

Surely, I misunderstood.

"Now that Father is dead. This place is mine." He opens his arms, as if to claim it all for himself.

I move swiftly with venom on my tongue. "He was dead before Amelia and I ever made it to this town. *I* built this house and establishment. It is *mine*."

He leans forward, his gaze locking with mine. "I'm the only son. I'm entitled to our father's inheritance."

"He had no inheritance," I grit through clenched teeth. "Thanks to you, he died a poor man."

Jack steps between us. "Charlie, it's nice to meet you." He holds his hand out and Charlie looks at it as if he'd just as soon spit on it than shake it. "I'm Jack Bristow, land agent."

I peer at Jack. *What is he doing?*

Charlie glances between me and Jack.

Jack pulls his hand back. "Please excuse us, Charlie, while I speak with my fiancé."

"Fiancé?" His eyes grow wide.

Without a word, Jack takes my hand and leads me out into the yard.

~

"Just what in heaven's name do you think you're doing, Jack?" I seethe.

He pulls me into his arms. "Laura, who is your most loyal patron?"

My head spins. "What?" I search for answers in his face. What does that have to do with anything?

I wave towards the house. "My scoundrel of a brother is about to take everything I've worked for and you're concerned about my patrons?" Tears sting my eyes and it feels as though something is lodged in my throat.

Jack takes hold of my face, forcing me to look up into those eyes that so often make me weak in the knees. Except now when I study them, I question everything.

"Who is your most loyal patron?" he repeats slowly.

Jack's horses swish their tails and shift their feet.

My most loyal patron..."Jasper McArthur?" I peer back to Jack who's grinning. It hits me then, I have an ally in the judge. My eyes grow wide at the realization. "*Judge* Jasper McArthur."

Jack chuckles and nods.

"But what can he do?" Yes, the judge would be on my side, but what *could* he do?

"You have said your parents were poor. That means there was no inheritance or money. Am I correct? You built this establishment from the business itself."

"Yes?" I continue to study his smiling face.

"Sweetheart, he has no proof. Hell, he probably doesn't even have proof that he's your kin. Judge McArthur is going to see that. Even if he didn't, you own his favorite establishment in this town, and he's not about to lose Rosie."

I rise onto my toes to meet his lips. "This is one of the many reasons I love you. How long must I wait to be your wife?"

He pulls me in so my body is pressed to his. "We don't have to wait a moment longer if you don't wish." He whispers against my mouth before kissing me tenderly.

～

I've closed the door to 'Open Flowers' for the evening for the first time ever. This house is celebrating. With our friends, Amelia, and Jack's brother Levi by our side, Jack and I became husband and wife today. And, just as my clever husband said, Judge McArthur was on my side with the Charlie case. Charlie had no paperwork to prove he'd been given an inheritance by our father. It was his word against mine, and the judge ruled on my side. Not only did the judge rule in my favor, but he advised my brother it would be wise to leave town entirely.

Laughter fills the room as we raise our glasses to my and Jack's nuptials.

Jack slams his drink back then grabs me by the waist. "Next weekend I'm taking my bride away some place quiet. But tonight, I'm taking her to our room."

Our room. In all the day's activities and everything unfolding so quickly, I hadn't thought about where we'd live.

At the thought of finally sharing more than kisses with this man, my heart quickens, and I begin to clear the table.

Amelia gently takes the plates from my hands. "You two go on. The girls and I will clean up." She looks to Levi. "You don't mind helping, do you?"

"Not at all," Levi states, pouring another glass of the Irish whisky.

Melody nudges Jack. "Get on out of here."

～

Once in our bedroom I light the oil lamp and turn to Jack. My stomach flutters and I glance about the room, afraid to look him in the eye.

He pulls me in, tucking a curl behind my ear. "My bride." His lips claim mine. "I still can't believe you said yes." Warm breaths caress my mouth.

His fingers work to unbutton the top of my blouse as he kisses my neck. Heat builds in me and my head feels dizzy.

Laughter makes its way up the stairs and into our room. It feels strange doing this knowing there's a house full of people down there. For the first time, I think of how the girls do it.

Jack takes my hand and walks me to the bed. "We can take this slow," he says, guiding me to sit.

I watch as he begins unbuttoning his suit vest. "Would you feel better if the lamp were out?"

"No."

He leans in and kisses me as if he's starved. Heat washes over my body and I wrap my arms around his neck. His mouth moves to my cheek, then to my ear. *Oh, my.*

The sudden sound of glass shattering and a scream pulls us apart and to our feet. Jack grabs his pistol from the dresser, and I follow him down the stairs, rebuttoning the few buttons he'd unfastened on my blouse.

Once at the bottom of the stairs, I see Charlie has Kitty by the waist with a gun to her head. Levi and the other girls stare in shock, but Amelia speaks in a calm voice while holding a knife behind her back.

"Please, Charlie, Mama and Papa wouldn't want you doing this."

"Do not speak to me about them. This has nothing to do with them."

Kitty's eyes are squeezed closed and silent tears run down her face.

"You." Charlie's eyes shift to me. "If I can't have this place, then neither will you."

His eyes flash to Jack. "Put that gun down or I'll shoot her." He digs the barrel of the pistol into Kitty's temple, and she lets out a painful moan.

Jack sets the gun on the table and puts his hands up. "Let's talk about this, Charlie. Maybe we can work out some sort of deal."

"The time for working out deals is over. The only deal we're making is this lady's life for my little sister's."

My eyes grow wide and I shoot a glance to Amelia.

Charlie laughs. "Oh no. I want you." He points the gun at me.

Just as he does, Jack grabs his pistol from the table and shoots Charlie in the leg. Charlie folds in pain, releasing Kitty, which gives Jack a clear shot at Charlie's exposed torso.

Amelia drops the knife and runs to our brother, holding her hands to his stomach wound. "Go get the doctor," she screams.

Jack hands the scissors to me. "Missus Bristow, you get to do the honors." I'm in disbelief that this day has come. Eighteen months ago, I was the youngest madam in all the area, when the town was reduced to rubble, left in shambles, and Jack had burns on a quarter of his body. And now, he's recuperated, we're married, and celebrating the grand opening of our new business. *My* business.

I sure wish Amelia were here to celebrate with us, but she's studying to become one of the few female doctors in this country. I am so proud of her. She couldn't save Charlie, but I just know she'll save others.

"Why, thank you, Mister Bristow." I cut the ribbon as claps and hoots resound. "Let's go on in and have a toast," I shout to the crowd as Jack and I pass under the sign that reads, 'Bristow's Saloon.'

Inside, I take in the room. A long, polished pine bar stands proudly, its gleaming surface reflecting the soft light. Mirrors line the wall behind, showcasing rows of whisky bottles, while advertisements for liquor and cigars decorate the space. Card tables are scattered throughout, and a small stage stands in one corner. Tin tiles adorn the ceiling above. This, truly, is mine.

From behind the bar, Jack runs his thumb over my cheek. "I have a surprise for you."

I tip back the shot of whisky from my glass and run my tongue over my bottom lip. "I bet you do."

He grins and takes my hand. "Let's go."

"But Jack, we can't leave our guests," I say, as he pulls me out the door.

I glance back at Rory, the bartender I hired, and call, "We'll be right back, I assure you."

He tips his head while pouring shots. "I have this under control, Missus Bristow."

❀

It appears Jack's taking me away from town. "Where are we going?"

"You'll see." His face beams.

When we reach the edge of town, he turns the buggy around and brings the team to a halt.

"What am I looking at, Jack? It's just trees."

"It's not just trees, sweetheart, it's where I'm going to build you a proper house."

I study the large pines. "Build me a house?"

"I know it can't be your dream to live in the cabin with my brother as our roommate forever."

I can feel Jack's eyes on me. "Do you like it?"

My hand holds my chest. "Like it? Jack, I love it." My gaze turns to him. And he pulls me close.

Living with Levi since selling the brothel to Rosie hasn't been without its comforts. But the thought of us having our very own home, and one I can design and decorate, brings excitement to my heart.

"You deserve this, Laura. I'm so proud to call you my wife."

"Oh, Jack!" I wrap my arms around him, and the tears break free.

Had anyone told me, when I met this man, that I'd fall in love with him and become his wife, I'd have laughed in their face. All I cared for then was the wealth that flowed in daily from the men willing to pay the steep prices I placed on the girls who worked for me.

Taking Jack's face in my hands, I brush my lips against his. Our familiar tongues glide together, wet and on fire for one another. Heat consumes me from within as his mouth trails my neck.

"I want you, Jack."

"You'll always have me," he groans, returning his mouth to mine.

2

Deadwood, South Dakota 1883—Amelia

It feels as though I've been gone for an eternity. So much has changed, and this town no longer bears the warmth of home.

Staring at the sign that reads, 'Bristow's Saloon' I take a deep breath, preparing to grab my trunk and head inside. I've missed Laura sorely.

"Are you lost?" A man's voice pulls me from my thoughts.

I chuckle, still peering at the building before me. "No, sir. I—"

"Lia?"

I glance at the man. "Levi."

He pulls me into a hug. "I didn't know you were coming home. I thought you were still in Michigan?" Pushing his hat back, he scratches his head. "You certainly aren't the little girl who left here."

A flush rises to my cheeks. "I suppose leaving the nest and proving one's worth amongst men is enough to strip away the last of the traces of girlhood."

Levi nods. "I'll say."

He's gazing at me in a way he never has before. To be honest, I never thought much about Jack's brother, who, if memory serves, is only a year older than my brother-in-law. He places his hands on his hips, and my eyes are drawn to the gun at his side. I had forgotten that this is the way things are here. After studying for so long alongside clean, well-groomed young men in the latest fashions, I almost forgot what a true man looks like.

Levi's eyes are as blue as the sky. Why hadn't I noticed that before? Probably because I was a child with no thoughts of grown men. I straighten and inhale deeply. Yes, I'm a woman now, but still—I remind myself—my thoughts are of my doctoring career only.

"It was so lovely to see you, Levi." I motion towards the doors of the saloon. "But I really must go on in and see my sister."

"You won't find her in there. Jack came into the land office this morning and said Laura's home with the little one today—apparently, he's not feeling well." Levi inclines his head. "Shall I give you a ride?"

"If it's no trouble."

He grins and for the first time, I notice dimples that let a flurry of butterflies loose in my belly.

"No trouble at all."

I point to the heavy leather case behind me and grimace. "I was dropped here. Would you mind carrying this for me?"

"Not at all."

When we pull up to Jack and Laura's house, I can't help but smile. It resembles a true home, with lace curtains rather than the heavy red velvet drapes I've grown accustomed to. Instead of standing against other businesses, it's nestled among the towering Ponderosa pines and Black Hills spruce, a quiet retreat.

Levi helps me down from the wagon then carries my trunk to the door. I glance at him, and we grin at one another before I knock. I know I should have written to let Laura know I was arriving, but I wanted to surprise her.

The door opens slightly and my sister peeks out. Gasping, she swings the door open and pulls me into her arms.

"Amelia," she cries, pulling me into a tight embrace. She pulls away to study my face, tears streaking down her cheeks. "It's really you." She draws me close once more. "And you," she adds, stepping back and looking at Levi. "You knew she was coming?"

He chuckles softly, "No, I went to the saloon for the midday meal and found her standing by the front doors, staring."

Laura laughs, "Oh, goodness."

I shrug, "I suppose I thought that's where you'd be."

Levi lifts my trunk from the ground where he'd sat it. "I reckon the good doctor would like to go in and meet our nephew."

My sister gasps for the second time and excitement fills me at the thought of seeing this little one.

"Yes, yes. Please, come in."

The precious baby sits in a wooden nursery enclosure chewing on a stuffed bunny. His nose is wet, and his eyes are watery.

"Jack made this pen for him. It's ingenious, isn't it?" Laura states scooping the child up. "Jack, this is your Aunt Lia."

The child scowls at me.

"Well, hello, Jack." I hold out my hands to him. "Do you mind if I hold you?"

He looks to Laura then to me. She leans him towards me. "It's okay, Jack."

460

Without removing the bunny from his mouth, he reaches for me.

It feels so wonderful to finally hold him in my arms. I press his head to mine and place a firm kiss to his chubby cheek.

"I don't know what's wrong with him, Amelia. He's been so fussy. His nose is constantly runny. I told Jack if he wasn't better by tomorrow, I was taking him to see Doctor Ramble."

"Do you mind if I take a look at him?" I ask, studying his sweet little face. I'm just in awe that he's my nephew and that my sister is truly a mother.

"Of course not."

"I have my suspicions, but I'd like to wash my hands first." I hand the child back to my sister.

"Certainly, the kitchen is just around the corner."

When I return, with clean hands, I sit on the edge of the sofa with baby Jack in my lap. Pushing a finger into his mouth my suspicions are confirmed immediately by the feel of a sharp tooth against my finger. I giggle.

"Why, Mister Jack, you have a tooth coming in."

"A tooth?" Levi drops his hat on a table and kneels down by my side. "Jack, you're a big boy now."

Jack holds an arm out, the soaked bunny in this mouth, and feels Levi's beard.

I study the man's eyes, how they crease at the corners with his smile. His closeness warms me in ways I don't quite understand. Realizing my sister stands nearby I glance up at her to see she's studying us with a grin on her face.

I clear my throat. "Would you like to hold him?" I ask Levi.

The man's eyes don't leave our nephew and his smile doesn't fade. "No, I best get going." He takes Jack's head and pulls him in, placing a rough kiss on his brow. "My brother's probably wondering where his dinner is."

"Thank you, Levi, for the ride."

He winks, placing his hat back on his head. "No problem at all."

"Levi," Laura calls. "Won't you come back for supper?"

She peers at me with a sheepish grin.

Levi looks to me and flicks the brim of his hat. "I look forward to it."

"Why did you do that?" I hiss to my sister when the door closes behind the man.

"What?" She feigns innocence. "He's Jack's brother."

"You invited him because of me." I shake my head and squeeze the baby to my chest for the tenth time.

How am I going to leave this child?

"Doctor Miller, it's so good to have you home." Jack states, with a wide grin on his face.

"It's just wonderful to be here."

I look around the table at the smiles shining back at me and my heart aches.

"We'll have our own personal physician," Laura states while cutting into her meat.

"Yes," Jack raises his glass. "I hear you discovered Little Jack has a tooth coming in. I can't believe that's been what's caused all his fussing. It makes sense though, the way he chews on that bunny he refuses to let go of."

"Yes, well." I push the food around on my plate.

Cries from the child make their way into the dining room.

"Oh, dear," Laura murmurs, her eyes weary. "He's only content when he has his bunny or is being pushed in the carriage."

My chair scrapes across the floor as I rise. "Oh, I'd be happy to take him for a ride."

"I'll accompany you, if you don't mind." Levi says, rising to his feet. "I know where the carriage is."

I glance at Laura, who offers her brightest smile.

"Certainly." I push my chair in and follow Levi.

I walk beside him as he pushes a now contented Jack in the buggy, and we stroll down the dirt road, flanked by the tall pines.

"You're not staying in Deadwood. Are you?"

"I know that I'm wanted here, but I'm needed in Colorado." I shrug. "At least I won't be as far away as I was in Michigan."

"I suppose."

I peek down at my nephew, who has the blondest hair I've ever seen. "I've only known Jack a few hours and I already know I'll miss him sorely."

"I understand entirely."

I sigh. "I don't know how I'm going to tell Laura." My hands rest on my heart. "I'm truly thrilled for this opportunity, though, to help those who need me. I've dreamt of this my whole life."

"I can't say I won't be sorry to see you leave."

"That's kind of you."

"You've changed, Amelia. I can see it. Not just in the way you dress and carry yourself, but in the way you speak—your entire demeanor."

He tilts his head, a smirk playing on his lips. "You're a beautiful woman. And clever, which makes you even more striking. The way you took charge of Jack today was truly impressive."

Embarrassment at his words tugs at me, and I nudge him playfully. "Are you becoming soft, Levi Bristow?"

He laughs. "Don't tell anyone."

Before we reach the house with a sleeping child, Levi stops the carriage and turns to me. "There's a show at the theatre on Saturday. Would you mind accompanying me?"

His youthfulness shines through as he smiles, and those dimples appear again, sending a rush of warmth through me. "I'd be delighted to go with you."

~

Two months ago, I returned home, believing this day would be as simple as it was when I left three years ago for medical school. But since then, I've fallen in love, and my heart feels as though it may shatter into a thousand pieces.

"Oh, Jack Jack. Aunt Lia is going to miss you so much." Tears stream down my face as he presses his soft cheek to mine. He has no idea I'm leaving. No idea I won't be here to tell him stories, or push him in the carriage, or play with him at bathtime. I'll miss the hearty laugh he gives when I blow on his chubby neck, creating a comical sound and, no doubt, a tickle.

"Ma'am, we're leaving in five minutes," the stagecoach driver calls to me.

Jack stands with his arm around Laura, who wipes away silent tears.

I squeeze my nephew for what seems like the hundredth time, yet still not enough. "I'll write you letters and draw you pictures, all right, Jack Jack?"

He swipes his wet bunny over my already wet cheek, and I chuckle. I kiss his head and pass him back to my sister.

"Oh, Amelia." She pulls me in with her free arm. "Write as soon as you arrive so I know you made it safely."

"We're right proud of you, Lia." Jack draws us close, wrapping the three of us in a warm embrace.

I turn to Levi. He stands in a relaxed posture watching us, his legs apart, hands resting on his belt buckle. *How could I possibly leave this man?*

"Levi," I whisper, stepping close to him.

He lifts his head to the sky, as though afraid to look at my face, and pulls me close. I bury my head against his chest, allowing the tears to fall.

"I'm sorry," I say, feverishly wiping my face with my hands.

Levi takes my chin and lifts my face. "Don't be sorry, sunshine."

I look away and nod.

"Look at me," he says, softly. "Don't apologize. Write as soon as you've settled in, Doctor Miller."

I force a smile and nod in response.

He presses a gentle kiss to my lips. "I meant what I said. As soon as I get business squared away here with my father and Jack, I'll come to you."

I wrap my arms around his neck, not wanting to let him go.

The stagecoach driver clears his throat. "Ma'am, it's time."

"Don't make me wait too long," I whisper against his lips.

~

Laura

We wave to Amelia as she blows kisses to us from the window of the stage-coach. It's almost unbelievable that my baby sister is now an honest-to-goodness doctor. Our parents would be so proud of her. Life has changed so much in such a short time.

Who could have known that, despite what I once thought I wanted, I would receive the very thing I needed—love. And for us Miller sisters, this is just the beginning.

ABOUT THE AUTHOR

Historical Western Romance author Amanda Speights weaves spicy tales of resilient women and bold adventures from her home at the foot of America's Mountain, where she lives with her husband and daughter. Though her grown son, daughter-in-law, and three sweet-and-sour grandsons live 1,300 miles away, they are always close in her heart. Her passion for storytelling shines through her work, celebrating the Old West's timeless spirit. Amanda invites her readers to saddle up and journey through love stories that are as enduring as the Rocky Mountains themselves.

Her debut novel, *Love's Arrival*, is the first book in the Laurel Springs series, set in the Colorado Territory during the late 1800s. Amanda loves engaging with her readers and offers a newsletter, which can be found at www.AmandaSpeights.com, to keep fans informed about her latest releases and book news. Followers can also connect with her on Instagram, TikTok, and BlueSky.

Amanda divides her time between crafting her latest historical romance, homeschooling her daughter, and immersing herself in period fiction that spotlights formidable women.

THE LIBRARIAN

TINA SUSEDIK

1

April 1880
Dakota Territory

"Next stop, Sioux Falls." The conductor walked down the aisle of the train as it slowed, steam hissing and blowing cinders through the open windows. "End of the line. All passengers must depart."

Victoria Forry stood and brushed dust from her skirt. Never one to care much about fashion and, knowing what it was like traveling for days on end, she'd chosen a plain, black dress with a jacket to match to hide dirt and dust. To remain comfortable during the two-week trek from Pittsburgh, she wore the most comfortable shoes she could find, which were men's boots, and left her corsets and bustles in her trunks.

Once the excitement of traveling away from Philadelphia to points west wore off, she'd spent her time going over and over the notes she and her father had created for her traveling library. She poured over maps of the mining towns and camps until she had the trails between them memorized. It hadn't been easy figuring out the easiest routes to make the best use of her time, how long to let the books out before returning for pick-up, and how to make sure the people she lent books kept them in good shape.

As the only child of a steel magnate, she didn't need the money, but she and her father had decided anyone wanting to read a book would pay a penny. The penny would be refunded if the book was kept in good shape and the person didn't want to take another. It would make a lot of record keeping on her part, but what else would she have to do in the evenings?

The train eased to a stop. Ignoring her fellow passengers, she removed her carpet bag from beneath her seat, made sure her rounded brim, black hat was in place, and stood briefly at the exit, breathing in air devoid of sweaty bodies, odiferous cigar smoke, and babies' diapers in need of changing. Gripping her bag in one hand and the information on where to pick up her belongings in the other, she stepped onto the wooden platform.

As always, no matter where she went, stares and whispers followed her. As a woman, she was a bit of a freak of nature, as if God graced her with part woman and part man. At nearly six feet, she was way too tall for a woman, towering over all females and the majority of males. Without a corset to emphasize her bosom, it was nearly non-descript. Thin to a fault, she didn't need one of those whalebone and steel contraptions so confining, it was hard to breathe and make her waist seem tinier. Her feet were described as two-by-fours, her hands as saucers, and was called four-eyes because of the spectacles she wore over her green eyes.

And then there was her hair. Pa said it was like a gorgeous, blazing sunset. Ma called it bright as a brand-new copper penny. Her cousin was the closest when he called her carrot-top as it was the only way to describe her mass of curly, frizzy red hair – a carrot. The one thing missing was a crop of greenery sprouting from the top of her head. Add a face covered in freckles, and it was no wonder people stared. Of course, she didn't have a few cute freckles sprinkled across her nose like the five-year-old daughter of her best friend, but those blasted brown spots covered nearly every inch of her body. If a man were ever crazy enough to marry her, he'd be shocked where those freckles were hidden. It would ever happen, anyway, so she needn't worry.

On top of everything, she was smart and a bookworm. A love of reading was something she shared with her father and mother, but most men believed women in the upper class where her family resided, should excel at stitching, playing piano, how to run household, and catch herself a rich husband, all things she had no use for. With that in mind she, along with her parents, concocted the idea of creating a traveling library and heading west.

Most parents would worry about their daughter taking such a venture on her own. Would insist on her having a male chaperone. But at the age of twenty-five, combined with her looks and size, her training in firearms and self-defense, they knew she'd be fine.

Following the crowd, she located the dock where her boxes and bags were being unloaded onto a cart. According to a telegram from her father, a supply wagon and stagecoach would be waiting for her at the end of the train station. After giving the information to the porter handling her things, she followed him to the waiting vehicles.

A man, even taller than she with shoulders and arms the size of a bison, stood beside the wagon. "Miss Forry?" He tipped his battered hat. "I'm Boone. I'll load your things into my wagon and follow the stagecoach to Rapid City." He pulled a pocket watch from his bib overalls and checked the time. "We aren't leaving for another two hours, so if you want to freshen up and get something to eat, now would be the time. There is a nice restaurant at the hotel up the street."

Thank goodness. The latrines in the trains she'd traveled left much to be desired, plus her empty stomach was kissing her backbone. After she ate, hopefully she could get some food to take with her. It would be at least another week before she reached Rapid City, pick up the wagon her father had made to his specifications, a horse, and other supplies, and begin her travels. As much as the train trip thus far had been uncomfortable, a week crammed in a stagecoach with strangers was bound to be worse.

Boone lifted a box from the boxcar and grunted. "What do you have in this? Rocks?"

Victoria grinned. "No. Books."

2

One month later

On the road between Sturgis and Deadwood, Dakota Territory

"C'mon, Rascal." Victoria snapped the reins against the rump of the stubborn mule. "Get moving. I'd like to get to Deadwood sometime today." The only response was the munch of sweet summer grass in Rascal's mouth. Of course, his partner, Rosie, did everything Rascal did. So here she sat alongside the rutted road, hoping they'd get their fill soon.

But if there was anything she'd learned about these two, it was they never did what she wanted. Victoria sighed and rested the leather straps across her lap. At this rate, she'd be lucky if she got there by the end of the week. Beside her, Salty barked, his deep, loud woof doing nothing to move the mules along.

When she'd arrived in Rapid City three weeks ago, there was supposed to have been a sturdy horse and a covered wagon waiting for her. It's what her father had said anyway. Instead, she was shown these ornery mules hitched to a large, wooden, box-like contraption. At first, she was appalled by everything, including the ceiling being made of wood, but once she had the wagon covered in a white canvas for added protection from the elements and had everything situated the way she wanted, she didn't mind the vehicle.

From the outside, it resembled an ordinary covered wagon but inside was a haven with the front part used for her living quarters. Separated by a wall with a door she could close and lock, was the library. On both sides of the wagon, shelves went from the floor to the roof and were filled with the hundred or so books she'd brought with her. Her small desk containing her records was pushed up against the bookcase while she traveled.

Rascal brayed and jerked the wagon forward a few steps, nearly toppling Victoria from her seat. She grabbed her wide-brimmed, floppy hat before it fell into the road, and breathed a sigh of relief. "Dammit, Rascal." The first time he'd done this, her hat had flown off her head. Believing his only concern was about eating, she'd thought it was safe to wrap the reins around the brake and jump down to retrieve it. She'd picked up the hat, slapped the dust against her skirt, and turned to return to her perch, only to find the damn asses trotting down the road at a speed she'd only dreamed of. Their braying had sounded way too much like laughter as she'd raced after them.

Evidently, she needed to keep the reins tight against the harness, or Rascal thought he was free to take off. So, each time she wanted to leave her seat, she had to make sure to hold tight to the reins and tie him to something. It wasn't an issue if she were in a town with hitching posts or near woods where there were plentiful trees, but there were too many places where neither were available.

She'd also learned to secure everything inside the wagon. It only took one time of reshelving all the books, for her to nail narrow strips of wood across the shelves, find crates to hold her supplies, and raise her bed off the floor to make a storage place beneath. Her father had always told her she was resourceful, and with unlimited funds, she been able to make her new "home" comfortable and cozy. Both the back and front entrances were wooden and lockable, giving her another layer of protection. Along with the dog, her secure wagon, and Cindy, her trusty rifle, she felt secure.

There was even room inside for the large mastiff to sleep. Having a dog for protection hadn't been on her list of necessary supplies, but she had to admit he made her feel safe. She'd be forever grateful to the tall blacksmith who was traveling to Deadwood from Rapid City with his wife and had helped catch the runaway mules. Afterward, when she took them to eat as a thank you, she learned not only Bull was a blacksmith, but so was Serenity. In fact . . . she grinned to herself . . . not a story to go over now, as she somehow needed to get Rascal and Rosie moving, but she'd gladly accepted the huge mastiff from the couple as a gift, along with their invitation to visit when, and if, she ever made it to Deadwood.

The sound of hooves came up from behind her. A low rumble came from Salty's throat. She picked Cindy up and lay it across her lap. One thing she planned on adding to her wagon was mirrors attached to each side so she could see who may be sneaking up from the rear. This was Serenity's idea and said she could attach them when Victoria got to their blacksmith shop. So far in her travels, Salty's presence had kept men who thought she was fair game at bay.

Since she was as far off on the side of the dirt road as she could, whomever was riding up, had to approach from her left. She switched places with Salty.

"Hail the wagon," a man's booming voice called out.

Salty rumbled deep in his throat. "Shhh. Let's see who it is." All she had to do was say, 'twinkle' and Salty would attack. She'd thought Bull had been kidding, but evidently, whoever had trained the dog had a strange sense of humor. Besides, Bull had explained, who would associate the word with not only the large dog, but as a word of attack?

The man, sitting on a tall, bay roan pulled up beside her and tipped the brim of his dusty, black Stetson. He briefly took his eyes off Salty, glanced at her blasted mules then raised an eyebrow at her. "Ma'am, are you in trouble?"

What? He wasn't going to ask why she had a small pony sitting beside her? It was usually the first thing people said when they first saw Salty. The man's bright-blue eyes seemed to hold something like mirth. Irritation swept through her. Was he laughing at her? "No, sir. We're fine. Just fine."

Salty emitted something sounding a bit like a purr when the man moved his horse closer and reached his hand out to the dog. Why wasn't Salty growling? Usually when a stranger made a move toward him, the dog went on protection mode. She tightened her grip on her shotgun.

"Let me guess," he patted the mastiff on the head and grinned. "Your mules won't move."

The man's smile sent shivers down her spine. Not bad shivers like she got from some of the men who thought she needed a man, but something interesting, delicious, like her first taste of chocolate ice cream. She ignored the feeling.

"How did you guess?" She tried to keep sarcasm from her voice but didn't succeed. "Could it be I'm sitting here while those blasted animals eat their way into oblivion?" She raised the shotgun when he swung a leg over his saddle. "Don't be trying anything funny, mister. Besides this gun, my dog is trained to attack."

He chuckled as he strolled to the mules. "I highly doubt Salty will attack me."

What? "How do you know my dog's name?"

"The same way I know these mules are Rascal and Rosie." He tugged on Rascal's halter. "And Rascal is most cussed, ornery, stubborn mule this side of the Mississippi."

Normally able to speak her mind, the man had rendered her speechless and a bit nervous. Who was he?

∼

It had taken Zebulon Greer a moment to keep from staring at the woman gripping a shotgun, the barrel pointed at him. While stopping for a few days in Sturgis on his way to Deadwood, he'd heard about the traveling librarian. Had also heard how the unscrupulous livery owner in Rapid City had switched out two fine plow horses for these old Army mules and pocketed the extra money.

Zeb had let the man know in no uncertain terms what he thought of men who cheated people and especially women. Probably served the woman right for traveling alone, but it didn't mean she should be taken advantage of.

"I know Rascal and Rosie from the Army." He gave Rascal's halter another yank. "He was a problem then, and whatever he did, Rosie followed."

The woman jerked her chin toward the dog. "What about Salty?"

"He belonged to an Army buddy of mine."

"Oh, yeah? What's his name?"

The woman was wise not to believe him. "Titus Galloway, but because of his size, he's called Bull." With a final tug, he managed to move the mules back to the center of the road. "He loved Salty. How do you come to have him?"

The woman lowered her gun a fraction. "I met him and his wife in Rapid City when he helped catch those da . . . I mean blasted animals when they took take off. I took them to lunch as a thank you."

Bull was married? Zeb shook his head. He must have found a bear of a woman to handle a man his size. "That doesn't answer my question about Salty."

"For some reason the dog took a shine to me. Bull, along with Serenity, thought I needed protection while I travel around the country, so they gave him to me, and I must say he does make me feel safe."

Zeb pulled the reins tight until he reached the mule's rumps and handed the loose leather to her. "Here. Don't give them any slack, or they'll wander off."

She stared down at him and didn't move. What was her problem? She raised her shotgun. Oh. It had to be awful for women to be frightened of strange men. He kept hold of the reins in one hand, reached into the breast pocket of his coat, removed a card, and set it beside Salty. Would she take it or continue to aim the gun at him? With her face obscured by the wide brim of her hat, he couldn't see her expression.

Even though his card said he was a physician, which he had been during the war and still did some doctoring, he actually was currently working under-cover as a Secret Service agent. Right now, he was on the trail of counterfeiters. Someone had produced fake plates and was printing bogus money. It was his job to find the perpetrators and destroy the plates. His most recent, coded telegram from headquarters said the plates and counterfeit money might be hidden in a caravan.

Zeb pointed at the card. "What's the matter? Can't you read?"

Her voice was deep for a woman and sent a signal, one he'd been ignoring for the past few months, straight to his crotch. Thankfully, his long duster covered his body and hid his reaction. Maybe it was time to see what this woman looked like. He'd heard rumors, but he was never one to trust the gossips.

She raised her chin, giving him a slight glance of what looked like freckled skin. "I most certainly can read, sir. I have a wagon full of books to prove it."

So, as he'd thought, she was the librarian. "Doesn't mean you can read them."

With a sigh, and keeping the gun and her eyes on him, she reached around Salty and picked up the card.

He didn't wait for her to read it. "Zebulon Greer, Doctor of Medicine. People call me Zeb."

She slid her hat to the back of her head and eyed his black bag attached to his saddle, giving him his first look at her. His heart skipped a beat. She was . . . she wasn't . . . Well, maybe he had paid attention to the gossips. Her hair was certainly the color of carrots and her face splattered with freckles, but beneath those spectacles . . . He swallowed around the lump in his throat and managed to suck in a breath. Her green eyes were simply stunning. Had an arrow pierced his heart?

"You're staring, Dr. Greer. I know I'm rather strange looking, but didn't your mother tell you it's rude to stare?"

Her words finally broke through the trance her vision had put him in. Headquarters had to be wrong. This beautiful woman glaring at him could not be part of the counterfeit ring. "I'm sorry, you're . . ."

She sighed. "I know perfectly well what I am." She jutted her chin to his horse. "If you'll show me what's in your bags, maybe I'll believe this card of yours."

As if he's had too much to drink, Zeb staggered to his horse, untied his black medical bag, and placed it beside Salty. He opened it and pulled out his stethoscope, a glass thermometer wrapped in cotton, a pair of scissors, a roll of gauze, and a bar of soap. She stopped him when he produced the first bottle of medicine.

"All right, I believe you." She didn't place her gun in its scabbard as she climbed down. "Salty, guard." She disappeared around the side of the wagon.

Didn't the woman notice the smile Salty gave him? He'd more than likely knock him over with slobbery kisses than attack him. At least she was smart enough to climb off the wagon on the side away from him. It seemed he was dealing with a smart woman. But smart enough to head a ring of thieves? He was well aware looks could be deceiving. But a librarian counterfeiter? Ridiculous.

She came around the back of the wagon, holding the shotgun at her side, and stopping a few feet from him rendering him once again speechless. She was tall. The tallest woman he'd ever seen. At two inches over six feet himself, he'd barely have to lean down to kiss her. Wait. Why the hell was he thinking about kissing her? He didn't even know her name yet.

"You're staring, again."

"I apologize—again." He needed to regain his equilibrium. But how could he with this vision before him? "Um . . ." To distract himself from her slim, female form, he returned his things to the black bag. Idiot. Think of something to say. "Um . . ." He snapped the bag shut. He nearly snapped his fingers when a brilliant question jumped into his brain. "What's your name?" And he even asked without stuttering. He was on a roll.

"Victoria Rose Forry."

"Lovely name." What an idiotic thing to say. He chanced a look at her. Was she smirking at him?

"Thank you. My parents gave it to me." She tipped her head to the side as if contemplating his stupidity. "And to answer the many questions people always

476

ask, I'm from Pennsylvania, am a traveling librarian, my dog is not a small horse, I'm not married, am completely aware I'm tall for a woman, am covered in freckles, and . . ." She held up the shotgun. "Am fully capable of using this." She grinned. "Did I miss anything?"

He couldn't help chuckling. "I guess that about covers it, Miss Forry. Do people always ask those questions?"

"Over and over and over."

Thankfully, Rascal jerked forward distracting him and giving him an opportunity to gather his wits about what to do next.

3

Victoria's stomach muscles danced around as if they were doing a jig. When she'd been sitting on her perch on the wagon seat, it was obvious the doctor was handsome. But close up? Heavens to Betsy. Bright blue eyes which usually went with blond hair, not dark brown, almost black like his. She'd always wondered what made one person better looking than another, so describing why he made her heart race was difficult.

One thing was for sure, he was tall. It didn't matter to her, but if she came closer, she'd have to look up to see his face. His mustache was neatly trimmed, not thick and bushy as some men wore theirs. Not that she'd ever had, or would have a chance, but it seemed the bushy ones would tickle when kissing.

Those blue eyes reminded her of her father. Honest. Kind. Intelligent. Maybe she was crazy from spending so much time alone with only the mastiff and the stupid mules for company as she traveled the country, but an inner instinct told her she could trust this man. She rested the shotgun against the wagon wheel and folded her arms over her chest.

"Sorry for holding the gun on you, but a person can't be too careful around here."

His eyes twinkled when he smiled. "Especially a woman traveling alone."

She nodded. "I can honestly say I've met my fair share of male characters along the way.

He removed his hat and eyed her from the top of her head to the bottom of her heavy boots as if he were checking out a horse he was intending to buy. "Want to check my teeth, too?" She didn't bother to keep the sarcasm from her voice this time. "I assure you they are strong and healthy."

"What?"

"I've mentioned before it's rude to stare. Yet here you are again. Checking me out like a piece of horseflesh." She knew what he was thinking. Too tall? Too thin? Too ugly? How dare he? A flicker of anger flared. As she was taught when her temper flashed, she took a deep breath and counted to ten. She couldn't possibly know what the man was thinking.

His frown deepened as he shook his head. "What? No. I was simply trying to figure why you said, 'considering your looks.' I see nothing wrong with your looks. I find you quite fetching."

So maybe she shouldn't have set down the shotgun. Doctor or not, the man was clearly crazy. She retrieved her gun. "I'd best be getting along if I want to make some headway to Deadwood before sundown. From what I've heard of the town, I don't want to arrive after dark."

Zeb tipped his head up at sky. "Mind if I travel with you? Looks like we might hit some bad weather."

She glanced over his shoulder at the darkening western sky. A distant roll of thunder made her shiver. "It seems you're right, and yes, I'd appreciate your company. I understand Rosie tends to get skittish when it thunders. So far, I haven't had to experience it, and I don't want to start now." She picked up the shotgun, walked around the wagon, and climbed onto her seat. "She's always been inside a livery during a storm where I've seen her flinch and buck at thunder. I can't imagine what she'd do outside."

Zeb handed her the reins and mounted his horse. "I'd say keep a firm hand, then." He clicked his tongue to Solomon. Let's go, boy."

～

The first hour went smoothly. Was it because Zeb was riding alongside the mules, or did they sense the approaching storm and wanted to seek shelter? So far only the darkening clouds and a drop in the temperature were proof of what was coming. "Do you think the storm will go around us?"

"I certainly hope so." Zeb twisted in the saddle to get a look behind him. "We're still a way from Deadwood, and I don't relish the idea of getting wet."

No sooner had he uttered the words than a gust of wind hit the side of the wagon. A flash of lightning nearly blinded her, followed by a crack of thunder. Before she could react, Rosie reared, jerked the reins from her hands, and took off down the road. Rascal, with no other recourse, charged beside her.

"Rosie, Rascal. Whoa." Another rumble of thunder rolled across the sky, covering her screams. Salty leapt from his perch and nipped at the blasted mules' heels. "Salty, stop." She didn't need the dog to get trampled by their hooves.

Zeb raced his horse alongside the mules, reaching over to try picking up the reins flapping in the air. With each grab, her heart caught in her throat. Would he fall off and land under the mules? As if Salty understood what Zeb was trying to do, he ran to the other side of the bolting animals and seized the right rein in his teeth, slowing them down enough for Zeb to grasp the other one and for Victoria to jump down.

Keeping hold of the strap, Zeb leapt from his horse to Rosie's back, pulling back on the rein. Victoria ran to Salty, took the strap from his mouth, and tossed it to Zeb, who continued to struggle with Rosie.

"Get some rope," he yelled over another rumble. "We need to get them unhitched and tied to a tree." Victoria grabbed two ropes hanging from the side of the wagon. While tying the rope to Rascal's halter was easy as he'd settled down, Rosie tossed her head each time Victoria tried to attach it. A drop of rain hit her hand. Darn. Looked as if they weren't going to get inside the wagon before the rain started.

Zeb took the rope from her. When had he dismounted?

"Here, let me do this. You unhitch the wagon, and I'll tie them to a tree. Hurry!"

She ignored the irritation threatening to make her snipe back at him. What did he think she was going to do, move like she was going on a picnic? In short order, the mules were released and tied to a tree at the side of the road. Rosie continued to toss her head and roll her eyes, but there was nothing she could do about it.

As the drops of rain became persistent, she grabbed her shotgun and ran to the back of the wagon, Salty on her heels. She yanked open the wooden door, let the dog jump inside, and followed. Where was Zeb? If he didn't hurry up, he'd be soaked. The wind was becoming furious, nearly whipping the door from her hand. Zeb appeared in the opening. She stepped back to let him toss in his saddle and saddle bags and climb inside. As a torrent of rain came from the skies, he pulled the door shut.

A gust of wind rocked the wagon. The inside was dim but dry and cozy. His presence along with his saddle and saddle bags taking up so much room, made the space seem to shrink in size.

Zeb removed his damp Stetson and raked his fingers through his blond hair. "Whew, that was close." He set his hat on the saddle and glanced around the interior.

What was he thinking? "So, what do you think of my home away from home?"

4

What should he say? He couldn't very well tell her he was eying places she could hide the counterfeiting plates—if she was the person they were looking for. Were they hidden among the many books on the shelves covering three walls? In the small desk at the right of the door? "Not what I was expecting."

"And what were you expecting?"

He shrugged and grabbed a shelf to steady himself when the wagon shook again. Was the wind going to blow them over? If it did, they'd be buried and likely killed by books flying off the shelves. The strip of wood in the middle of each shelf likely to keep the books in place while she was traveling wouldn't help if they tipped.

"For one thing, it's more spacious than I thought. I was behind you for a few miles, and it seemed small from the rear." He took in the ceiling. Could the plates be hidden between the wooden and cloth roof? "I also didn't expect the interior to be wooden. From the outside, it looks like a regular covered wagon." Wait. Something was missing. "Where do you eat and sleep?"

Her grin made his heart flip, a reaction he hadn't had from a woman in a long time —if ever. His job had him traveling all the time and could be dangerous, both things making reacting to a woman's smile impossible, especially one he could end up arresting.

Victoria pulled out a center shelf in the front of the wagon to reveal an opening and smiled. "Ta, da."

Zeb stepped around her and peered inside a small room containing a narrow, raised bed, its length stretching from side to side. A bouquet of wildflowers tied with a yellow ribbon matching the top blanket, lay across her pillow. In a flash, a vision of her bright red hair spread like a halo across the pillow, made his insides quiver. Would her gorgeous hair smell like wildflowers? He banished the thoughts from his mind. Maybe it had been too long since he'd had the company of a woman, and here he was, confined to a small space with one who made his mind conjure up ideas of what he would do with her—if she wasn't the counterfeiter.

Several wooden crates were beneath the bed. A table on the left side of the wagon was devoid of any objects, but two shelves above it held an Alexis Soyer's Magic Stove, along with a few dishes, spices, and other cooking utensils. He recognized the camping stove from his days traveling with other agents. He wished he had one with him now. It would save time getting a fire started. The dishes rattled when another blast of wind hit the wagon.

On the opposite side was a small bureau with a mirror attached. "What's keeping this from falling over?"

"Like the table, it's nailed the wall." She folded her hands in front of her. "What do you think?"

He couldn't very well tell her it seemed like a lot of stuff to search through. "Impressive. Cozy." If a man could use such a word. Unlike the library section, which was bare wood, a colorful braided rug covered the floor. "I like it. I imagine you don't spend much time inside."

Victoria picked up the bouquet, closed her eyes, put the flowers to her nose, and sniffed. "Only as much as I have to."

Zeb's heart flipped like when one of his brothers spun him around and around by his arms and suddenly let go. Was he getting sick? He sucked in a deep breath, eased it from his lungs, and turned away from her. He needed to get his head back into what he was here for and away from how pretty and feminine she looked—even in worn work boots.

He left her "bedroom," walked through the "library," and opened the back door. "Looks like the worst of the storm has passed."

She followed him and glanced up at the ceiling. "Doesn't sound like it's stopped raining, though."

He stuck his head outside, glad for the overhang at the back keeping his head dry. The sky was gray as far as he could see. "I have a feeling this is going to last a while."

"Oh, dear. I was hoping to get to Deadwood tonight."

He popped his head back inside but left the door open to let in some fresh air. The air inside smelled a bit like wet dog. A wet, muddy dog. "I'm afraid we're going to have to stay put for a bit. The rain has made the road a boggy mess."

Victoria peered over his shoulder. "Oh, dear. I believe you're right." She pulled out her desk chair, sat down, rested her elbows on her knees, and propped her chin in her hand. "Now what? I've never been stuck in a storm like this. I guess I've been lucky enough to have been in towns where I could lay up for a bit. What about the mules?"

Zeb chuckled. "Those old things will be fine in the rain. Might even make them behave better, but I doubt it. If we were to leave now, you'd only get stuck in the mud, and I doubt those two would be able to pull you out. We're better off staying in place for the night." He pulled out his pocket watch. "Besides, if we leave now, we'd soon be traveling in the dark."

His problem now was whether or not she'd let him sleep in the wagon or if he would have to bunk beneath it and drown. With the storm and as much rain as they were getting, he'd be sleeping in muck or a puddle of water. He shivered. Not an idea he could warm up to.

"So, we're stuck here?"

"Or get mired in the mud. The choice is yours."

5

Victoria sighed and patted Salty on the head. The dog huffed a breath and rested his head on her forepaws. Heavens, he stunk. The dog, not the man. Zeb's scent was fresh, like when a person comes into a house after being outside in the winter. Like diamonds, raindrops glittered on his blond hair. He ran his fingers through it, sending the droplets to the floor, then went back to staring out the door.

A gust of wind rocked the wagon. When a gusher of rain splashed inside, he pulled the door shut, closing out some of the storm's noise.

But what did she do now? In all good conscience, she couldn't make him go back into the storm. Where would he sleep? With the way the rain was coming down, he'd either drown beneath the wagon or catch a chill and die from pneumonia. Neither idea was pleasant.

"I don't think this is going to end any time soon." Zeb toed his saddle.

Maybe she would regret this, but she simply couldn't send him back out into the storm. She mentally sighed. He seemed safe enough. Helped her with those blasted mules. Salty liked him, which alone said a lot. As she traveled, there were men who'd approached her and made her nervous. Whether the dog sensed her nervousness or knew the men were up to no good, Salty growled deep in his throat, making the men back off.

"I guess you'll have to stay in here."

"Are you sure?"

"No, but I won't have your death from pneumonia or drowning on my conscience. You can sleep out here on the floor."

"You trust me not to haul off with your books in the dark of night?"

She had to smile. "And where would you put all the books? In your back pocket?"

"Good point." He glanced around the small room. "Seriously. You don't mind if I bunk in here?"

"No." She narrowed her eyes at him and tipped her head to the dog. "Salty will take care of you if you try anything."

"But Salty and I are old friends. He wouldn't hurt me."

Victoria bit her bottom lip. "Wanna try? Take a step toward me and grab my arm and see what he does."

"Um. I'll take your word for it. I have seen what he can do to someone he doesn't like."

"And remember it, too." She had trouble keeping her eyes from him but it was improper for a woman to stare at a man. As if Salty knew he was being talked about, he lifted his head from his paws, opened one eye, huffed a breath, and went back to sleep.

With her hands clasped in her lap, she rolled her thumbs around each other as if the action would help her know what to do next. Offer him a book to read? Make some coffee or tea? Either would help warm them up. She had a deck of cards in a box beneath her bed. See if he played poker, which in itself was unladylike.

It was still pouring outside, but way too early to retire for the evening. Did she have enough food for another person for supper? She'd been planning on restocking in Deadwood today. Her stomach rumbled.

Zeb chuckled. "Are you as hungry as I am? Wrangling those mules and fighting the storm takes a lot out of a person."

"I can make some coffee, but I don't have a lot of food to offer. I was going to stock up in Deadwood."

"I have a few things in my saddlebag. Some beef jerky and hardtack."

Victoria licked her lips. "Mmm. Hardtack. My favorite."

"Beggars can't be choosers, my dear."

My dear? He called her 'my dear?' Those words certainly didn't mean anything. He probably used them on all females, which he surely had many adoring women dogging his heels. Even so, those simple two words made her heart skip a beat. *Hold it down, you foolish organ. Don't be a stupid twit over two silly words.*

"Are you all right?"

She brought her attention back to him. "Yes. Of course, I am. Why wouldn't I be?"

Zeb shrugged. "I don't know. Your face went all red like you were about to have a fit of apoplexy."

Darn blushing. Many women who blushed, did so prettily; their cheeks turning a soft rosy color. With her freckles and red hair, she ended up resembling something belonging in a circus.

"I'm fine. With the doors closed, it's getting stuffy in here." It was the best lie she could come up with quickly. There was no way he could read her mind. Would he believe her?

He opened the door a crack again and pulled it shut. "It's still raining cats and dogs out there." He opened his saddle bag and removed a two small packages. "Here are my contributions to supper."

"I do have a few eggs I can fry up. Maybe we can add the jerky to the eggs to soften them up. I'll see what I can do."

Without permission, he planted himself on the edge of her bed. Even without looking, she sensed his eyes following her every move. She tried to ignore his presence as she gathered her cast-iron skillet, a bowl to mix the eggs, and her four remaining eggs from its container filled with sawdust sitting alongside the stove. She'd become adept at starting a fire in her stove, so ignored his offer to help. There wasn't enough room to maneuver in her living space anyway. Besides, having him sitting on her bed while he watched was unnerving. She needed him to move.

"Wouldn't you like to look over my books and see if there are any you would like to read?"

"Trying to get rid of me?"

His smirk set her nerves on edge. "There isn't enough room in here for both of us. I'll bring out the food when it's ready."

"All right." He slapped his knees, sighed, and stood. "Let me see what stories I can bury myself in."

Victoria let out a breath when he brushed past her and left the room. She tossed butter in the skillet, and while it melted chopped up some onion and added it to the pan. Then she whipped up the eggs, cut up the jerky into small pieces, added salt and pepper to the mix, and when the onions were soft poured the mixture into the pan.

After cutting two pieces of bread from her remaining loaf, she set them on the edge of the stove to toast them. Her mouth watered at the aroma of the cooking eggs and the thought of spreading butter and strawberry jam on the bread. She was hungrier than she thought.

Luckily, she had two plates. After preparing them, she took them to the other room and halted in mid-stride. What was going on? Instead of checking out the books on the shelves, he was on his hands and knees looking beneath one of the bottom shelves.

"What are you doing?"

6

Damn. Caught in the act. He jerked his head up, smacking the back on a bottom shelf. He stood and rubbed his head. How had he not heard her come into the library? Sometimes he figured he wasn't a very good agent. A good one would have paid attention to the noise coming from the other room. A good one would have had a plan in place for such a situation. Now what? Think quick.

"Um. I thought I heard a book fall on the floor. I was checking to make sure none did."

Did her frown mean she didn't believe him? As it was, in the short time it took her to make their meal, he hardly had a chance to look for hiding places. Time to cover his tracks. Without looking, he removed a book from the shelf and held it out to her.

"I thought this one looked interesting."

She raised an eyebrow at him then smirked. "Really? That's the book you want to read?"

What was her problem? "Sure. Why not?" Her giggle made him wish he had paid attention. Now he was afraid to look at the book in his hand.

Victoria set their plates on her desk. "All right. If you really want it." She picked up a ledger and a pen and tapped her bottom lip with the pen. "Let's see. Your name? Oh, yeah. *Dr. Zebulon Greer*. Address?"

"Um. I don't really have one. I travel from camp to camp."

"So, how will I know where to reach you to get the book back?"

Did she have to ask so many questions? "I could probably find you." Especially since he needed to keep track of her. "I'm sure there aren't very many traveling libraries out here."

"I suppose. You do look like you can be trusted."

There was a twinkle in her eyes, that, even though he didn't know her, made him nervous. What was she finding so humorous?

"All right then. Title of book?" She held out her hand.

The second he passed it over, the title flashed before his eyes. Good heavens. Had he chosen...

"*Little Women* by Louisa May Alcott. Good choice, but I thought you'd go more for something by Jules Verne." She handed to book back to him. "That'll be a penny, which you will get back when you return the book."

Zeb bit back a groan. What an idiot. "Well. You know. I enjoy books of all kinds. It's always a good idea to expand one's horizons."

"I agree. So when you're done with this one, you may want to read *Wuthering Heights* or maybe *Pride and Prejudice*."

Maybe it was time to hide beneath the wagon. "I... Um..."

"I'm teasing Dr. Greer. You can exchange it for another one after we eat, which we should do before our food gets cold."

So, the not-so-little Miss Forry had a sense of humor. Smart, pretty, and funny. All the things enjoyed in women. Those simpering, empty-headed, only looking for a husband types weren't for him. He set the book on the edge of a shelf and took in the small space. There was only one chair, and after the book fiasco and being the gentleman he was, he wasn't about to take it from her.

"I'll sit on the floor. If you'll hand me my plate."

"Just be careful Salty doesn't go after your food."

Zeb eyed the massive dog. "I think I'll stand."

"Even though he recently ate, probably a good idea." Victoria gave him his plate and sat in her chair. "The guy has an enormous appetite."

"For his size, he'd have to." He took a bite of the egg mixture. "This is delicious. What did you do to the eggs?"

Victoria shrugged. "Just fried some onions and put some jerky and salt and pepper into the eggs. No big deal."

"I've been on the road for a while. This is the best I've had in a long time." He bit into the toast. "Wow. Did you make this jam?"

"Are you kidding? I took the train all the way from Pittsburgh to Sioux Falls. I didn't want to pack anything that would possibly break. I can't imagine the mess a broken jar of jam would have made. I bought the jam in Rapid City."

"You drove this thing all the way from Sioux Falls by yourself?"

Her giggle made his heart trip.

"Oh, heavens, no. My things were loaded on a wagon and followed the stagecoach I was in. I picked up this wagon in Rapid City."

"But, still, it's a long way for a woman to travel alone, isn't it?"

She frowned and gave him a glare. "I'm doing all right."

Oops. Guess he shouldn't have worded it the way he did. "I didn't mean anything by implying you shouldn't be traveling alone because you're a woman.

I can tell you're perfectly capable. I know women who homestead by themselves and do better than most men. I apologize if I offended you."

"Thank you. You didn't offend me." She took a drink of water. "I'm used to men, and women, staring at me. And at men thinking I need their help. Except for those darn mules, I'm doing fine."

Zeb pointed a fork at Salty. "I imagine one look at him and people tend to back off."

"Yeah. I'm glad to have him. I do feel safer with him along." She took another bite of eggs. "So, you want to tell me why you really were on the floor?"

Damn. She would have to bring it back up. He shoveled a large forkful of eggs into his mouth hoping to give himself time to come up with an answer. Best to keep with his original response.

"I really thought I heard something fall." He glanced at the outside wall. "Maybe the wind blew a branch into the side of the wagon." Would she accept his lie?

"Probably. It is still pretty windy out there."

Whew. He dodged a bullet. He swiped the last bit of toast over his plate to not waste a bit of the delicious food. He patted his stomach. "Thank you, Tory, for the meal. I'm much obliged."

7

Tory? He called her Tory? No one ever called her anything but Victoria. Should she reprimand him? First of all, she hadn't given him permission to use her first name. And second, how dare he shorten it? She stood, ready to give him a what for.

"I'm sorry Miss Forry. I shouldn't have presumed to use your first name without permission. Out west, we sometimes forget proper etiquette. Things are a bit more relaxed out here. Maybe because civilization as we know it out east hasn't come this far." He picked up her plate and placed it on top of hers. "Since we are traveling in the same direction, may I travel with you? May I call you by your first name? I give you permission to call me Zeb.

Well, what should she do now? He apologized and asked for permission to use her first name. No sense in getting upset now. "I accept your apologies. I have noticed people are less strict out here. And, yes, you may call me by my first name." For some reason, and even though she didn't quite believe his comment about hearing something fall on the floor, she trusted him. Having someone to talk to besides Salty would be nice, too.

"May I call you Tory? Victoria seems to easterny."

"Is easterny even a word?"

Zeb shrugged. "I doubt it, but it makes my point, doesn't it?"

Being called Tory did make her feel as if she was starting a new life. Like she had shed her staid, stuffy, and perfect ways. She wasn't ready to drop all etiquette, but some of it was all right. "You may call me Tory."

"Good. Since you did the cooking, let me take care of the dishes."

"I'm afraid it'll have to wait until it stops raining. I don't have much water in here."

A gust of wind slammed against the wagon, nearly knocking her over.

Without dropping the plates, Zeb grabbed her arm. Tingles from his touch ran through her body.

"Are you all right? Sounds like the storm is kicking up again."

Victoria shook her head. "I'm fine. There is a box under my bed where I keep my dirty dishes until I have time to clean them. Why don't you put them in there?"

"What are you going to do?"

"Do you play cards?"

"Does the sun rise in the East?"

"I'll take that as a yes." She opened a drawer in her desk. "I have a deck of cards. We can pass the time playing." Through the open door to her living quarters, she watched Zeb pull out a couple of boxes then return them until he found the correct one for the dirty dishes. Was it her imagination, or had he taken more than a quick glance in each box? But why? Was he searching for something? She would have to keep an eye on him.

He came back into the room. "So, what do you want to play and where should we sit?"

Oh, my. She hadn't thought of the seating situation. She only had the one chair and didn't relish the idea of sitting on the floor. It would be totally improper for them to both sit on the bed, wouldn't it? But she was a spinster with no hopes of ever marrying. He seemed like a true gentleman, and if she had Salty by her side and they sat on opposite ends of the bed, she should be safe. Plus, she had her gun in her pocket and no one need know.

"Um. We can sit on my bed. Opposite ends. I'll have Salty come in and chaperone."

8

Sit on her bed? Oh, the temptations. At his name, Salty raised his head, stared at him, and lumbered to his feet. Does he understand his job? Even though he knew the dog, he wouldn't want to take any chances on him getting the wrong idea and attack.

"I guess that would work." And maybe give him a better chance of checking out her space while they were playing cards. He didn't want to take too much time when he put the dishes away.

He swept out a hand. "Ladies first." Her subtle scent of some kind of flower wafted past his nose. His libido kicked up a notch. This was not going to be easy. "What are we going to play?"

Tory sat at one end of the bed and had Salty sit on the floor at her feet. "Poker?"

Huh. He didn't know too many women who knew how to play the game. "We aren't playing for money, are we?"

She shuffled the deck like an expert and gave him a sideways look. "Why? Are you afraid you'll lose?"

"No. I don't like to take advantage of women, is all."

She giggled. We'll see. We'll see."

~

It was a good thing he wasn't drinking or playing for money, or he'd be drunker than a skunk and as destitute as a preacher. So far, she had won nearly all the hands. He tried watching as she dealt the cards to see if she was dealing from the bottom, but even when he dealt, she won. There was no mirror behind him where she could see his cards. He'd checked.

"Are you cheating?"

Tory bit her bottom lip and giggled. "Me? Do I look like the type of person who would cheat?"

"So where did you learn to play poker? From Poker Alice?"

"Who is Poker Alice?"

"She's a widow who plays poker in gambling halls. She smokes cigars and makes a good living by gambling. She has other vices, too, but I don't want to go into them with you."

"Do I look like I smoke cigars?"

He chuckled. "No. And you are much better looking than her." Her blush made her even cuter. "So, where did you learn to play?"

"In my youth, I would sneak out of the house and go to the stables where a couple of the hands taught me to play. We used pieces of straw instead of money. If my parents had found out, the men would have all been fired, so I had to be very devious."

"In your youth? I know it's not polite to ask, but how old are you? You can't be more than eighteen."

"Oh, my. You're a sweet man. I'm practically in my dotage."

"If you're in your dotage, then I should be ten feet in the ground." The rain had stopped, so he cracked open the door to the front and let in the fresh, cool air.

"If you must know," Tory sighed. "I'm twenty-five and perfectly aware I'm on the shelf."

"I've always thought the idea that a woman is on the shelf after a certain age is ridiculous. They never say it about men."

Tory's eyes widened. "Why, what a wonderful and intriguing thing for a man to say. I always thought men wanted women who were young and dumb."

"Well, it's the truth. The stupid things society comes up with!" He shook his head. "And for men wanting women who are young and dumb, well, another misconception. Myself, I prefer a woman who can carry on a conversation. And I mean an intelligent conversation, not just about the weather and what dress or gewgaws they recently purchased. I've spent more time at balls and social events where I was bored to tears."

"I certainly have to agree with you. And a woman like me, well, men tend to overlook me because I'm tall," she flipped a loose curl at her shoulder. "love to read, discuss current events, and hate dancing."

Zeb frowned as he shuffled the cards. "You said it again."

"What?"

"A woman like me."

"Oh, c'mon. Look at me. Tall. Thin. This awful curly, red hair. Smart. Smarter than most men."

"Not all men are alike. And, in my opinion, those men were pretty stupid to overlook you." He dealt a card to her. "Personally, I find you quite fetching. And smart, too. Besides, your height is an advantage."

"How so?" She picked up her cards and tugged on her bottom lip with her teeth as she sorted them in her hand.

"Kissing a short woman hurts a man's back and neck. With me being only a few inches taller than you, I won't have to bend too far to kiss you." Her face, nearly as red as her hair made him grin. "Yes, I want to kiss you."

～

The cad. And here she thought he was a gentleman. She tossed her cards on the bed. "I think it's time to stop playing cards."

Zeb raised an eyebrow. "And do what, my dear?"

She scooped up the cards and stacked them in her hands. "Do I need to sic Salty on you? Do I need to ban you from my abode?"

"Tory, I'm joking." He ran a hand down his face. "I mean, I'm teasing. I would never have a problem kissing you, but only with your permission."

Victoria stood. "I won't kick you outside, but I think it's time you retire to the other room. I need to check on those darn mules, too. Make sure they didn't get loose in the storm." And she needed to attend to her needs. But how would it be possible with Zeb around? After dark, she generally used the chamber pot.

Zeb went into the library and opened the back door. "Um. I think you should stay inside."

She leaned over his shoulder. Even in the dim evening light, it was evident the rain had turned the road into a quagmire. "But I have to take care of the animals, plus Salty needs to go before he settles in."

"I tell you what. I'll take Salty out and check on the animals." His sharp whistle pierced the air. "C'mon Salty. Time for a walk."

Ignoring the steps, Salty leapt outside, splashing mud and water at Zeb.

"You don't by any chance have some old towels or blankets I can use to wipe him down before I let him in. I'll probably need one myself." A drop of mud ran down his chin.

Victoria bit back a laugh. "I do. Hold on a minute." She came back with two buckets. "If you want, fill these up and bring them in. You can use them to clean up."

While his murmured words and Salty's barking came through the open door, she raced into her room, pulled out the chamber pot, did her business, slapped the lid back on, and placed in in a wooden box beneath her bed. She'd have to find a time and place to dump it out without Zeb knowing. Things like this were easier when she was on her own, but she had to admit, it was nice not having to go outside after the storm.

After fifteen minutes and they hadn't returned, she was ready to go outside and make sure they weren't stuck in the mud somewhere. She removed her regular boots and was putting on her rubber galoshes when Zeb stuck his head inside the wagon.

"We may have a problem."

"Oh, no. What?"

"It's going to take more than two buckets of water to get Salty cleaned up. He's so muddy, it's hard to tell which end of him was which. What do you want to do?"

She stomped across the floor and peered outside. "Good heavens. What did you let him do?"

Zeb raised an eyebrow speckled with mud. "Let him do? Does anyone *let* him do anything? He took off like he was after something. I didn't see anything, but he was on the hunt." He glanced back outside. "Salty! Sit! Stay!"

"Do you think he'll be all right if he stayed outside tonight? I have some sturdy rope we can tied him to the wagon with."

"I'd hate to see him sleeping in the mud." He returned his attention back to the dog". Salty! I said sit. Maybe if we tie him up on the floorboard up front. You could keep an eye on him through the door."

"How would we keep him from jumping down? I wouldn't want him to hang himself."

"Good point. Give me the rope. I'll see what I can figure out."

She took a sturdy, thick rope from a hook by the back door. "I'll help you."

"No. Stay in there. No sense in both of us getting muddy." He took the rope from her. "Why don't you open the front door and hold a lantern so I can see what I'm doing. It's getting darker out here."

With a lantern in one hand, and Salty's blanket in the other, Victoria knelt on her bed and pushed the front door open with her elbow. Zeb was already at the front seat, holding Salty by the rope.

"C'mon, boy, get up here."

Even in the dim light it was obvious how filthy Salty was. How were they going to get him clean? Thankfully, it didn't take much time for him to settle down. Playing in the mud must have been exhausting.

"I think he'll be good for the night."

While Zeb disappeared into the dark, she retreated back into the wagon and pulled the door closed. She needn't worry about Salty waking up without her knowing. One bark from him and anyone withing a half mile would hear him.

"Tory?"

She carried the lamp into the library. "Yes?"

"I need your help."

Whatever could he need her help with?" She stuck her head out the door. "What do want?"

"With as dirty as I am, I don't want to come inside. Take one of these buckets of water and pour it over me."

"What?"

"You heard me. It's the only way I'm going to get relatively clean. Then I need you to give me a towel, take a set of clean clothes from my saddle bags. I'm going to change out here."

Was he serious? An image of him stripping off his clothes right outside the door sent shivers down her spine. She'd never seen a naked man in person before, but in her readings had seen pictures of statues, like Michelangelo's David. Plus, she had an active imagination.

Digging through his saddle bags was way too personal. A small bag held his shaving cup and brush, his straight razor, and a sliver of soap. She closed the bag and rummaged for a clean shirt and pants. When her hand touched a pair of drawers, she drew it back. Dare she give it to him or was it too embarrassing?

"Hey, Tory. Don't forget a pair of drawers, undershirt, and stockings, too."

Well, evidently he wasn't worried about being embarrassed.

After setting his garments and towel by the back door, Zeb handed her a bucket. Maybe it shouldn't give her pleasure, and maybe she had an evil side she wasn't aware of, but pouring the cold water over her and listening to his shouts was rather fun. She went slower with the second bucket, giving him a chance to wipe the water and mud from his clothing.

"Is that enough or do you need more water?"

He grinned over his shoulder at her. "I have a feeling you enjoyed yourself."

She shrugged. "Maybe. And maybe I don't want you to get my floors dirty."

"I just bet." He held out his hand for the clothes. "You may want to close the door."

And go to bed while he's still outside. She may have a good imagination, but imagination and the real thing were different. Not knowing how long he'd take to change, she scurried to her room, locked the door, got into her nightgown, washed her face, and brushed her teeth in record time. Tonight, instead of reading like usual, she turn off the lamp and snuggled down beneath the blankets. For the first time in memory, she ignored braiding her hair. It would be a tangled mess in the morning, but it would be tomorrow's problem.

The wagon wobbled. Zeb must be coming inside. Even though she couldn't see him, she pulled the blanket over her head. Too bad she couldn't do the same with her imagination. And what was he muttering about? Or was he humming? Whatever he was doing, the low timbre of his voice sent her system into overdrive.

When the wagon finally stopped jostling, she turned on her side, slammed her fist into her pillow, and tried to concentrate on Salty's deep breathing coming through the crack in the door. In what seemed like an eternity, snoring came from the library. Knowing he was asleep, she finally relaxed and let sleep overtake her.

❧

Resting his head on his saddle, Zeb shivered beneath the thin blanket covering him. Even though he was in dry clothing, the coldness of the water Tory poured over him wouldn't go away. It seemed to be seeping into his bones. A nice fire right about now would be welcoming, but, unfortunately, the stove was in the other room and he wasn't about to go back outside.

Stretched out on the floor, his long legs nearly touched the outer wall. He'd slept on hard ground before, but the wooden floor was twice as hard as anything he'd spent the night on. He scratched his chin. Even with the two buckets of water poured over him, it still felt as if he had mud covering him.

He rolled to his side and tucked the blanket beneath his chin. He needed to get some sleep. Since he hadn't had a chance to check out her wagon, he wanted to wake early and search this room, plus check the outside of it for any hidden places where those plates could be hidden. How to investigate her room would be a problem. His intention to look for anything suspicious had gone out the window since he had to pay attention to playing cards.

Jeb chuckled to himself. Who knew she would be such a card shark. Certainly not him. If she didn't make a go of the traveling library, and the way she was handling it, she probably wouldn't, she could make a living playing poker.

As his eyes grew heavy, his last thoughts were about spending another day with her. Hopefully, her wagon won't be stuck in the mud and her mules won't be so – well, mulish.

9

Victoria walked down the three steps at the back of the wagon and lifted her skirts. It had dried out a bit overnight, but getting the hem of her skirt dirty wasn't on her list of things to do this morning.

Even though she woke as the horizon was turning pink, Zeb was already outside. His horse was saddled and her blasted mules hitched to the wagon. Salty was chasing a leaf. If she wasn't so worried about why Zeb was leaning his arms on the saddle and scowling, she would have laughed at the gigantic dog trying to catch something so small.

"Is something wrong?"

Zeb jumped. "I didn't hear you come outside."

"The wet ground silenced my steps. And I believe it's because you were busy frowning. Is something wrong?"

He patted his horse on the rump, walked to the driver's box of the wagon, and picked up something wrapped in a dirty, white fabric. "Who are you?"

What a stupid question. "I already told you who I am."

"I don't believe you."

Her heart skipped a beat and goosebumps speckled her skin. "I don't have any reason to lie."

"Don't you?" He unwrapped the package. "Then tell me what these are."

Four metal plates rested in his hand. "What are those?"

"Oh, c'mon, Victoria, or whoever you are. You know darn well what these are."

Her stomach sank. Was she in trouble? By the way he was glowering at her, probably. "I'm telling you, I don't know what those are. Where did you find them?"

Zeb shook his head and sighed. "I'll play along. Follow me." He went to the side of the wagon and squatted by the water barrel. He pushed on a board which popped open revealing an opening in the bottom of the wagon.

"What? How? I don't understand. I had no idea there was an opening there. When I picked up this wagon in Rapid City, it was as it is now. Well, except for the books, my belongings, and the supplies I needed. I made sure the wagon was made the way I wanted it, but how was I to know to look for hidden compartments?"

She folded her arms over her chest and tapped her foot in the mud. "And why were you searching my wagon?" She snapped her fingers. "You were following me, weren't you? This was no coincidence. And last night when I caught you on the floor you were looking for something." She pointed at his hand. "Those things?"

"Yes, these things."

"But what are they and who are you? Now, I don't believe for a minute you are a doctor." Darn. She'd felt safe enough with him, she left her gun and rifle in the wagon. Stupid. Stupid, Stupid. Salty was still playing cat and mouse with the leaf. Would he come over and attack Zeb if she called? Probably not. He knows Zeb and likes him.

"I really am a doctor, but also an undercover agent for the government. We're trying to catch people making counterfeit money. I was told the plates were in a wagon heading to Deadwood." He held them out to her. "And surprise. Here they are."

"I really and truly don't know anything about counterfeit money and those plates. I *am* Victoria Forry from Pennsylvania. I have no need to make fake money. My family is rich. That's why I charge so little for people to check out books."

"Huh."

"It's the truth." Tears pooled in her eyes. Why wouldn't he believe her? "How about if I show you some of my money. If you are an agent like you say you are, you'll be able to tell if my money is counterfeit."

Zeb raked his fingers through his hair. "All right." He tapped the gun in his holster at his side. "I'll be right behind you, so don't try anything funny. I'll be taking your guns, too."

Taking her guns? Well, there went her protection, but what choice "All right."

Once inside the wagon, she dropped down her desk and pulled out a box hidden in the wall.

"I thought you said there were no hidden places in here."

"I said I didn't know about the hidden one outside. I actually made this one myself. In fact, I have several of them throughout the inside of the wagon. It doesn't make a lot of sense to keep all my money in one place."

"Then you'll have to show me all of them."

"How do I know you won't steal my money from me? How do I know you really are an undercover agent and not a thief?"

Zeb slipped his hand inside his coat and pulled something out. "Here's my badge and credentials."

After examining them, she handed them back. "All right. *I* believe *you*. Now all you have to do is believe me. And can we hurry this up? I want to get to Deadwood."

"Why. Are you meeting someone there?"

"No. I'm not meeting someone there. I need to get more supplies. Other than coffee, I don't have any more food."

∾

For the next fifteen minutes, she revealed six hiding places. He had to admit she'd been clever. Besides the one by her desk, there was the one behind a mirror, a slot in her mattress, a hole in the front door, a pocket behind several boring-looking books on ancient Greek history, and surprising of all a secret compartment in the driver's seat.

Each time, he examined the money. And each time, he had to admit there was nothing suspicious about it.

"Satisfied?"

"Just because you don't have any of the counterfeit money on you, doesn't mean you're not part of the ring." His gut feeling was she wasn't lying. Then why had he found the plates in her possession? She had seemed genuinely surprised when he showed them to her. And there was the real money she had hidden all over the place.

Not to mention how attractive he found her. He was an idiot and needed to get his feelings under control. There are plenty of beautiful women who, on the surface were mild-mannered, acted coy and stupid, but in reality were cunning and devious. Many men who fell for their charms, later found themselves broken both in spirit and financially.

"Oh, for Pete's sake." She held out her arms. "So, cuff and arrest me."

Zeb chuckled. "I am arresting you, but I won't cuff you. With those mules out there, I don't think you'll be running away from me anytime soon. As it is, we'll be lucky to make Deadwood before the stores close. Now give me your rifle and pistol and let's get going."

While she handed over her weapons, her stomach growled. "I hate to ask, but do you have any more hardtack and jerky left?"

"Desperate?"

"Desperately desperate."

His stomach answered the call to food. So was he.

∾

"Do you have any idea how much farther?" They had stopped only twice since leaving to feed and water the mules and horse and to take nature breaks. Her back ached and arms were tired. Not to mention the hardtack and jerky hadn't done much to fill up her stomach.

"Probably half an hour." He paused and glanced over his shoulder. "I think someone has been following us. Is one of your buddies waiting for the plates?"

"For the hundredth time, I'm not meeting anyone. I don't know anything about the plates. I'm simply a librarian trying to help people get books to read. Other than you, Bull, Serenity, and the few people I lent books to, I don't know anyone out here."

Zeb stared at her. "I don't like this. Whoever is following us has kept the same distance between us and them, like he doesn't want to catch up. And now there are two of them." He squinted his eyes. "Are you telling me the truth?"

"I have since the beginning. I don't lie. Never have. Never will." She slapped the reins against the mules' rumps. "C'mon Rascal, Rosie. Let's keep going. Rest is around the corner." In fact as they crested a hill, roofs of several buildings came into sight.

"I may regret this, but..." He guided his horse closer to the wagon. "I'm going to give you your guns back in case those men behind us are up to no good. Just don't shoot me."

"Don't worry, I won't. I've never shot a person before."

"Then why carry guns?"

She smirked at him. "There's always a first time for everything."

It was mid-afternoon as they came down the hill and approached Deadwood. They passed a Chinese laundry and restaurant. Zeb rode alongside her as they went through a part of town live with music, laughter, scantily dressed women calling from balconies, and men loitering outside buildings, staring at them as they passed.

"Don't look at anyone. It will only encourage these men to engage with you. This part of town is called The Badlands and aptly named. It's the seedier side of town. In a block or so, we'll be in the better part. I'm taking you to the sheriff's office."

As they drove down Main Street, Victoria took in the wooden and brick buildings. There were a few empty spaces where buildings must have once stood. She recalled reading an article in a Philadelphia paper about a fire last fall wiping out most of the town.

A lantern in a bakery had fallen over and started the fire. Because all the buildings in town were made of wood, and with high winds the fire quickly spread, sending residents scrambling up the hill where they watched their town being reduced to ashes. To make matters worse, when the fire reached a hardware store, it ignited barrels of gun powder. It was the explosion waking the residents and sending them racing to safety.

Over three hundred buildings had been destroyed and two thousand citizens left homeless. Amazingly enough, only one person perished. A deaf man who hadn't heard the screams and ruckus. Evidently, they were still rebuilding.

After two more blocks, when noise subsided, a gunshot rang out piercing the quiet. The mules balked and side stepped. Victoria tightened her grip on the reins. "Easy."

"Hold tight, Tory."

"I'm trying to." Her hands ached and arms burned trying to control them. The reins slipped from her hands. Another shot filled the air. Like a bullet from a gun, Rascal took off, pulling Rosie along with him. How were they able to run through all the mud and sludge in the street?

With the bouncing and swaying of the wagon, all she could do was grip the seat and hang on for dear life. Thank goodness Salty was inside the wagon, but his barking and yipping made her nervous. Was he injured?

Behind her, Zeb's swearing became increasingly more distant as the mules turned a corner. Something from her right jumped out at her. A person leaped onto the seat and shoved her over.

"It's about time you got here."

What was he talking about? Unable to grab her rifle from beneath the seat, she searched for her pistol she had sitting beside her. Unless the man was sitting on it, it probably fell and was buried in the mud.

"Who are you? What are you doing?"

"Shut up. You'll find out soon enough."

Like she hadn't been able to, the man, dressed and smelling like he hadn't taken a bath in a month of Sundays, retrieved the reins and got the mules under control. Gradually, the buildings, which seemed to be mostly houses, became more spread out until, at the end of the street, there was nothing but empty land. The man turned right onto a well-traveled road.

"Where are we going?"

"I told you to shut up."

She be darned if she'd take orders from this man. "What do you want?"

"Lady, if you don't shut your trap, I'll shut it for you. And get your dog to shut up, too."

Salty's barking and yipping had switched to growling and snarling. He charged and scratched the door behind her. Could she get the door open and let him out? Keeping an eye on the man, she eased her arm behind her.

"Don't move." A gun appeared in the man's hand and was pressed against her side.

Maybe now was a good time to do what he said. "Salty, be quiet. I'm all right."

The dog quit charging and scratching at the door, but his low growls continued.

"That's good, lady." The man removed the gun from her side, but not before digging it a bit deeper against her. "You keep him quiet."

Where was Zeb? Was he still following them? Had he been shot? Gone for the sheriff? Would he be able to follow their trail? If he waited too long, would their tracks be covered by other conveyances and animals?

Without warning, the man had the mules take a sharp right. Why were they following his instructions but fought her almost every step?

"C'mon Rascal, Rosie. We're almost there."

He knew the mules' names? What was going on? "How come you know my mules' names?"

"Because they belong to me. Now—"

"I know. Shut up."

"Good girl."

The single lane, rough path gradually went up hill through towering pines on either side. The scent of burning wood grew as they approached a clearing. A campsite?

"About time you got here, Jake. What took you so long?" A tall man, wearing a long duster and cowboy hat approached the wagon.

Jake pulled the mules to a stop. "With the rain and mud, I had trouble following her."

The other man pulled on her arm. "Get down, lady."

She hesitated. What were they going to do to her?

He pulled out his gun and waved it at her. "I said get down."

Victoria jumped down from the wagon. After being seated for so long, her tired legs shook.

"Get over by the fire."

"Give me a minute. My legs are wobbly."

"Too bad."

He pushed her forward making her legs give out and toppling her to the ground. Now was her chance. She kicked out her leg and hit Jake square in the knee. His howl set Salty barking. The tall man in the duster stomped over to her and yanked her over to a tree near the fire.

"Jake, get me some rope."

"My knee. I can't walk." Holding his knee, Jake rolled on the ground.

"Then crawl. When you're done, unhitch the mules."

It didn't take long for Jake to tie her to the tree all the while swearing at her. "Do you have to tie the rope so tight?"

"Shut up. You deserve it for hurting me."

The tall man stood over her. When he tipped back his hat, she got a good look at his face.

"You? You're the guy who sold me this wagon in Rapid City."

"You remember me?"

"How can I forget. You also sold me those awful mules."

The man chuckled. "Did it on purpose. I never thought you'd make it to Deadwood with those two. Nothing but a couple of stubborn..." He scratched his scraggly beard.

"Mules?" She struggled against the ropes at her wrists tied behind her. "What's your name?"

"Not sure why you want to know."

"Call it curiosity. I'd like to know the name of the man who kidnapped me."

"If you must." He puffed out his chest as if he was the most important person in the world. "Newell. Newell Potts. I'm sure you've heard of me."

"No."

Newall raised an eyebrow. "You haven't?"

"I'm glad to say I haven't."

"Oh. Well, you will."

Victoria shook her head. "I doubt it."

"Jake. Get the plates. Then we'll head to Deadwood and deliver them."

She bit her bottom lip. Nerves skittered down her back. What will happen to her when they don't find them? Will they kill her?

Jake limped to the wagon, groaned when he knelt on the ground, and reached beneath the water barrel. He scooted a foot to the left, then the right, pushing at boards along the way. "There's nothing here."

"What do you mean there's nothing there? The plates have to be there. I hid them there myself. Look again."

After a few minutes, Newell pushed Jake to the side to search for himself. When he came up empty-handed, he stormed to Victoria. "Where are they?"

"Where are what?"

"Don't act coy with me. You know darn well what."

"No, I don't. Tell me."

Newell leaned down until his nose practically touched hers. "The plates."

"I don't know what you're talking about. Why would you want my dinner plates?"

Before she said another word, he slapped her across the face.

"What did you do that for?" Blood trickled from the corner of her lip. "I truly don't know what you're talking about."

"Jake. Search the inside of the wagon. She must have hidden them there."

Jake shook his head. "I ain't gonna go in there where that dog is. We saw him in Rapid City. Remember how big he is? He'd probably kill me."

As if to prove a point, Salty growled and charged at the back door. The wagon jerked from side to side.

"See what I mean? He's a killer."

Victoria smiled. "He's very protective. He knows you hit me. Give him a few more minutes and he'll have the door broken down. He'll eat you both alive."

Jake widened his eyes. "I ain't gonna be here for that. I'm outta here."

Before Newell could stop him, Jake jumped on the back of a horse grazing on the other side of the fire and took off down the trail.

"Idiot."

"Now what are you going to do?" She chuckled. "Salty almost has the door broken down."

"Damn. You sure you don't have those plates?"

"I'm positive. And..."

"And what?"

She shrugged. "Once he's out ... Well, I haven't had him long, but he's a pretty big dog, so I'm not sure what he'll do."

Newell headed to the other horse, then stopped and turned around. "You were traveling with a man. Any chance he has those plates?"

"I have no idea." When had she become such a good liar? Oh yeah, when her life was threatened. "Any chance you can untie me before you leave? After-all, there may be wild animals around here."

"Too bad." He mounted his horse. "It shouldn't take long to find that guy. I won't be gone long." As if he were a proper gentleman, he tipped his hat at her and left.

Now what? As soon as Newell left, Salty must have thought the danger was gone. He no longer barked and charged the door. She had to get him riled up again.

"Salty. Help. Help me."

Immediately, he growled. The wagon shook as he attacked the door.

"C'mon, Salty. Help me." She kept calling to him as she worked on trying to loosen the ropes at her wrists enough to get free.

Finally, after what seemed like an eternity, Salty broke through the door, leapt to the ground, and ran around the site as if he was searching for the danger.

"They're gone, Salty. Come here." Could she get him to chew through the ropes? His teeth were sharp enough, but would he understand what she wanted?

He ran to her and licked her face. "Stop. Listen to me."

Surprisingly, he stopped and looked her in the eyes.

"I want you to chew through the ropes." She clicked her teeth together. "You know. Chew. Eat. Eat the ropes."

Salty tipped his head to the side and licked her face again.

"No. No kisses. Chew. Eat." She turned her back on him and raised her arms. "Rope." She gnashed her teeth together again. "Eat." She closed her eyes, sighed, and looked over her shoulder. "C'mon, Salty. Help me."

At first, the tug on the rope was barely discernable. "That's a good boy. Keep going." The tug became stronger. *C'mon. C'mon.* Was he chewing on the rope or pulling the knot loose? Either way, it was getting easier to move her hands.

"Just a bit more, Salty." While not completely untied, the knot was finally slack enough for her to get her hands free. She hugged him around his neck. "Good boy, Salty. Good boy." But now what? She had no idea where she was. Going into the woods was a crazy idea. If she took the path the two men had, would she bump into them? Hitching those darn mules up to the wagon would waste a lot of time—even if they listened to her.

Her shotgun. Maybe it was still beneath the driver's seat. She ran to the front of the wagon and swiped her hand under the seat. Yes! There it was. Next, with Salty dogging her heels, she went inside the wagon and stood in the library. Her brain didn't seem to want to function. What should she do?

A sound outside caught her attention, like someone walking on dried leaves. An animal? Newell? Maybe Jake? But Salty didn't react. No growling. No hair rising on his back. Footsteps sounded on the stairs. She swung around and aimed her rifle at the door.

"Psst. Tory. Are you in there?"

She relaxed her finger on the rifle's trigger and lowered the gun. "Zeb?"

"Yeah." His head poked through the door. "Are you all right?"

"I am. What are you doing here?"

Zeb motioned for her to come outside. "I saw the guy who jumped onto your wagon charge down the road. So, I waited a bit then the guy who sold you the mules came along. I took a chance and followed their tracks here."

He shook his head. "I'm sorry I lost you. My horse was pretty much done in, so I went to the sheriff's office to tell him the story and turn in the plates. He's going to keep his eyes out for anyone asking about the plates." He looked around the area. "Tell me what happened."

He stopped and stared. "You have a cut on your lip and the side of your face is red. What did they do to you?"

"Newell slapped me when I said I didn't know anything about the plates."

Zeb pulled her into his arms then leaned back and touched her face so gently, it was all she could do not to cry.

"Wait here." He went inside the wagon.

Where did he expect her to go? She patted Salty who sat beside her. What was he doing? She was tired, hungry, her face hurt, and was worried those men would come back.

Zeb finally came outside holding a clean towel in his hand. He opened the water barrel, dipped a corner of the towel inside, then returned to her. "Let me clean your cut."

Again his gentleness nearly brought tears to her eyes. Even though he was careful, she flinched at the first touch of the cloth.

"I'm sorry."

She couldn't resist teasing him. "Does this mean you won't kiss me now?"

He set the towel on the steps and cupped her cheeks. "If I knew I wouldn't hurt you more, I certainly would kiss you."

He would? Her heart skipped a beat and butterflies fluttered in her stomach. Dare she be bold? What did she have to lose? The chances of another man ever kissing her were slim. "The other side of my lip doesn't hurt." She grinned at his raised eyebrow before his mouth descended on hers.

Oh, my. His lips were soft. Warm. Gentle, yet powerful at the same time.

Everything but Zeb seemed to disappear. No woods. No Salty. No birds. No men hurting her. Much too soon he stepped away. To her surprise, he was breathing as rapidly as she.

"I've been wanting to kiss you since I first saw you."

"You have?"

Zeb tipped his head and grinned. "Did you think I was kidding when I mentioned it yesterday?"

"Well. Yes. No man has ever kissed me before."

"Fools. All of them." He took a step back. "We need to head back to town. The sheriff had overheard men at one of the saloons talking about using fake money in towns before moving on to others."

"Why didn't he do something about it?"

"He said he wouldn't know a fake bill from a hole in the ground. Which is why it's been so easy for these people to spread counterfeit money."

"What do I do, leave my wagon here? I don't care to hitch the mules up again. They probably wouldn't let me anyway."

"They would only slow us down. I doubt anyone would come up here and steal your things, anyway. The trail is pretty well hidden. We can come back later after we catch these guys." He went to the fire and kicked dirt onto it to extinguish the flames. "I'm sure we can both ride on my horse. You can tell me everything else on our way into town."

"What about Salty? I can't leave him here by himself."

"If you put a rope around him, he can run alongside us."

10

Even though she was nervous about what would happen in town, with her arms around his waist, and her head resting on Zeb's warm, broad back, she struggled to keep her eyes open. When she nearly dropped her rifle, she jerked upright.

It didn't take them long to reach the edge of town.

"Where are we going to go?"

"The sheriff's office."

"I don't want to complain, but do you think we could get something to eat first. I'm starving." Zeb's deep chuckle rumbled against her chest.

"Hungry?"

"Starving. Since they want those plates, Jake and Newell probably aren't heading out of town."

"Sounds like a good idea. We'll go to King's Restaurant. In the past, I've had some good meals there."

Had it been only a few hours ago when she'd first ridden past these houses? It seemed like days.

"There's the sheriff's department. We'll come back after we eat."

The rode another block when a shot rang out. Zeb's horse shied. Victoria lost her hold on Zeb, slid sideways, and landed on the muddy ground.

"There she is. How did she get loose?" Ignoring Zeb, Jake stomped over to her and yanked on her arm. "Get up. We know you have those plates."

Since he was too close to shoot, she held the barrel with those hands and swung as hard as she could, catching Jake in the side. The sound of breaking bone mixed with his high-pitched screams. Holding his ribs, Jake fell to the ground. Salty immediately sat on him.

"Get him off me. Don't let him eat me."

If the situation wasn't so serious, Victoria would have laughed. Did he really think the dog would eat him?

From her place on the ground, all she was able to see were men's legs moving around like they were dancing, then a voice yelling.

"Sheriff. Arrest these two. They're in possession of stolen goods."

She couldn't mistake Newell's voice. If she were able, and had the energy, she'd stand up and shoot the man in the leg.

"If you're referring to plates to make counterfeit money, I have them, and you two are under arrest for kidnapping."

"But we didn't kidnap her, she came with us willingly."

Victoria rolled to her knees and pushed herself to her feet. "I most certainly did not." She pointed at Jake. "He's the one who jumped on my wagon and took me to Newell. Newell is the one who had me tied up while they searched for some kind of plates. When I insisted I didn't have them, Newell hit me."

"Sounds like I need to add assault to the charges." The sheriff waved his gun at Newell and Jake. "Now, get moving. You're under arrest."

~

"Are we really done? Can we *please* get something to eat? Those sandwiches the sheriff had someone bring from a restaurant didn't do much for my stomach."

Victoria followed Zeb from the sheriff's office. "Oh, my goodness. How did my wagon get here?" Instead of Rascal and Rosie, two large draft horses were hitched to the front. Victoria ran to them and ran her hands down their dark brown coats. "They are beautiful. What happened to the darn mules?"

Zeb shook his head. "While you were telling your story over and over, the sheriff had one of his deputies retrieve your wagon. He even fixed the back door." He joined Victoria. "As for the mules? I don't know and don't care."

She held out her dirt-encrusted skirt. "Maybe I should clean up and change before we get something to eat."

"Might be a good idea." Zeb tied his horse to the back of Victoria's wagon. "I'll wait for you out here."

In a surprisingly short amount of time, Victoria emerged. Zeb's breath caught. How had she gone from a muddy, dirty, bedraggled woman, to this beautiful one walking toward him wearing a long-sleeved, high-collared, yellow blouse and blue skirt? A matching bonnet covered her bright curls. Even the bruise forming on her cheek didn't distract from her attractiveness. Good thing the sheriff kept him from punching Newell in the face, or he'd be in a cell.

Thank goodness she wasn't part of the counterfeiting ring. Thank goodness they'd caught Newell and Jake. They'd finally given up the name of the man they were supposed to deliver the plates to. The owner of one of the saloons and brothels in town was now behind bars with the other two. The sheriff swore he'd close down the establishment and not let it reopen, at least not as its current business.

As the gentleman he was, he gave Tory a hand up onto the driver's seat, climbed beside her, and took the reins. "C'mon you, two, let's get going."

"So, where did these horses come from?"

"The owner of King's restaurant, King Winson, had them brought over from his ranch."

"How much did they cost? I'll reimburse him."

Zeb glanced over at her and smiled. Not only was she comely, but generous, too. "You don't have too. It turns out the owner of the brothel has cheated King many times and is happy the man was arrested. They are a gift from King. You'll probably meet him at the restaurant."

"Well, I have to do something as a thanks."

"No. If you try, you'll only hurt his feelings. He's a proud man. Besides, his wife, Suzanna, the local school teacher who is a force to be reckoned with, wouldn't let you, either. Just accept for the gift and be happy."

Victoria sighed. "All right."

As he guided the horses around wagons, horses, and a few other animals wandering the street, something occurred to him.

"You know what, Tori?"

"Hmm?"

"I don't want to be an agent for the secret service anymore. I want to settle down somewhere. Get back to my doctoring."

"Really? Will they let you quit?"

"I think so. I have another idea." He pulled the wagon to the side of the street. "Whoa."

"And what would that be?"

"I know we have only known each other for what? A day? But I'm a man who makes up his mind easily." He angled his body so he could face her. He took one of her hands in his.

"You are?"

"Yes. And one of the things I've made up my mind about is how I want to spend more time with you. When I kissed you a vision of our life together came to me of us settling in Deadwood while we travel to nearby camps with your books and my doctor's kit. Maybe I could even set up an office here in town and you could find a more permanent place to lend out your books. What do you think?"

Her smile warmed him from his hair follicles to his toes and every place in between.

"I think you should kiss me again and see what else you vision."

And he did, his mind going into the future with kids, love, and happiness.

The End

ABOUT THE AUTHOR

Tina Susedik is a multi-award-winning, multi-published, best-selling author who has been researching and writing books since 1997. She is published in non-fiction with military and local history books. She has also published children's books and romantic mysteries. She loves to add humor to her books, putting her characters in situations, and finding humorous ways to get them out of them. With forty-four books and short stories under her belt, she loves to use her knowledge of the writing craft to help other authors.

She lives in northwestern Wisconsin with her husband of fifty-one years and adores her five grandchildren. In the spare time she has, Tina loves to camp, hike, bike, garden, scrapbook, do jigsaw puzzles, and, of course, read, read, read.

Web: www.tina-susedik.com

Blog: tinasusedik.wordpress.com

Facebook: Tina Susedik, Author

AFTERWORD

Are you ready for more? Be sure to read the rest in Wild in Deadwood, Wild Deadwood Reads Anthology Volume 2, featuring nine more stories set in Deadwood.

www.ingramcontent.com/pod-product-compliance
Lightning Source LLC
Chambersburg PA
CBHW032259020726
47495CB00001B/176